Black Sheep
The Grand Sophy

Georgette Heyer

arrow books

This edition published by Arrow Books in 2004

Copyright © Georgette Heyer, 2004

Georgette Heyer has asserted her right under the Copyright, Designs
and Patents Act, 1988 to be identified as the author of this work

Black Sheep copyright © Georgette Heyer, 1966
The Grand Sophy copyright © Georgette Heyer, 1950

Black Sheep first published in the United Kingdom in 1966 by Bodley Head Ltd
The Grand Sophy first published in the United Kingdom in 1950
by William Heinemann

Arrow Books
The Random House Group Limited
20 Vauxhall Bridge Road, London SW1V 2SA

Random House Australia (Pty) Limited
20 Alfred Street, Milsons Point, Sydney, New South Wales 2061, Australia

Random House New Zealand Limited
18 Poland Road, Glenfield, Auckland 10, New Zealand

Random House (Pty) Limited
Endulini, 5a Jubilee Road, Parktown 2193, South Africa

The Random House Group Limited Reg. No. 954009

randomhouse.co.uk

A CIP catalogue record for this book is available from the British Library

Initial lettering copyright © Stephen Raw, 2004

Papers used by Random House are natural, recyclable products made from
wood grown in sustainable forests. The manufacturing processes conform to
the environmental regulations of the country of origin

ISBN 0 09 190418 8

Typeset by SX Composing DTP, Rayleigh, Essex
Printed and bound in Great Britain by
Cox & Wyman Ltd, Reading, Berkshire

Black Sheep

Georgette Heyer

arrow books

One

A little before eight o'clock, at the close of a damp autumn day, a post-chaise entered Bath, on the London Road, and presently drew up outside a house in Sydney Place. It was a hired vehicle, but it was drawn by four horses, and there was nothing in the appearance of the lady who occupied it to suggest that a private chaise, with her own postilions, would have been rather beyond her touch. She was accompanied by a middle-aged maid; and she was attired in an olive-green redingote of twilled silk which so exactly fitted her admirable figure that any female, beholding it, would have recognised at a glance that it had been made for her by a modiste of the first stare. It combined the simplicity of a garment designed for travel with an elegance only rivalled by the hat which becomingly framed Miss Abigail Wendover's face. No curled plumes or bunches of flowers adorned this confection: it was made of *gros de Naples*, bound with a satin ribbon; its poke was moderate, and its crown shallow; but it was as fashionable as the redingote.

The face beneath it was neither that of a girl in her first bloom, nor that of an accredited beauty, but it held an elusive charm which was centred in the lady's eyes, and the shy laughter which lurked in them. They were gray, and they held a great deal of intelligence; but her other features were not remarkable, her mouth being too large for beauty, her nose too far removed from the classical, and her chin rather too resolute. Her hair was neither fashionably dark nor angelically fair, but of a soft brown.

I

It was not cropped, after the prevailing mode; she wore it braided round her head, or in a knot from which curls fell about her ears. Occasionally, and in defiance of her niece's vehemently expressed disapproval, she tied a lace cap over it. Fanny said that it made her look like an old maid, and cried out indignantly when she answered, in her pretty, musical voice: 'Well, I am an old maid!'

It seemed as if her approval had been eagerly awaited, for hardly had the chaise drawn up than the door of the house which was her home was flung open, and a footman came hurrying out to let down the steps of the chaise. He was followed by an elderly butler, who handed his mistress down, beaming a welcome, and saying: 'Good-evening, Miss Abby! Well, and it *is* a good evening which brings you home again! I am very happy to see you, ma'am!'

'Oh, and so happy as *I* am, Mitton!' she responded. 'I don't think I was ever away for so many weeks before! Is my sister well?'

'Pretty stout, ma'am – barring a touch of rheumatism. She was a trifle down pin when you first went away, and took the notion into her head that she was of a consumptive habit –'

'Oh, no!' exclaimed Abby, in comical dismay.

'No, ma'am,' agreed Mitton. 'It was no more than an epidemic cold, which left her with a little cough – as the *new* doctor was able to convince her.' His tone was one of bland respect, but there was a twinkle in his eye, which drew an involuntary chuckle from her. The twinkle deepened, but all he said was: 'Very glad she will be to see you, Miss Abby. Quite on the fidgets she has been for hours past, fearing that there might be another put-off.'

'Then I must go up to her immediately,' Abby said, and went with a light step into the house, leaving Mitton to extend a gracious welcome to her attendant.

Since the struggle for position between the butler grown old in the service of the family, and the one-time nurse to its three younger daughters, was unremitting, Mrs Grimston took this in bad part, detecting a note of patronage, and merely adjured him never to mind how she did, but to take care of Miss Abby's jewel-box.

Meanwhile, Abby, running up the stairs, found her sister awaiting her at the top of the first flight. Miss Wendover, enfolding her in a fond embrace, shed tears of joy, and begged her, in one tumbled speech, to retire instantly to bed after the fatigue of her journey; to come into the drawing-room; not to put herself to the trouble of uttering a word until she should be perfectly rested; and to tell her at once all about dear Jane, and dear Mary, and dear Jane's sweet new baby.

Sixteen years separated the sisters, for they were the eldest and the youngest members of a numerous family, three of whom had died in infancy, and one, the first-born son, when his only child was hardly out of leading-strings. Between Selina, on the shady side of forty, and Abigail, with a mere eight-and-twenty years in her dish, there now intervened only James, Mary, and Jane. It was with Jane, married to a man of considerable property in Huntingdonshire, that Abigail had been sojourning for the better part of the past six weeks, having been summoned to support her sister through the disasters which had befallen her. Measles had attacked her youthful family, and at the very moment when Nurse, falling down the backstairs, had broken her leg, and while she herself was in hourly expectation of presenting Sir Francis with a fourth *petit paquet*. In a letter heavy with underscorings, Lady Chesham had implored her dearest Abby to come to her at once, and to bring Grimston with her, since nothing could prevail upon her to abandon her beloved children to a strange nurse's care.

So Abigail had posted away to Huntingdonshire, where she had remained for five weeks, under trying conditions, all three children having succumbed to the measles before her arrival, her sister being brought to bed within two days of it, and her brother-in-law, at no time remarkable for amiability, apparently labouring under the conviction that this unfortunate con-catenation of circumstances had been designed for the express

3

purpose of causing him to suffer the maximum amount of undeserved hardship.

'You must be worn to a thread!' Selina said, leading her into the drawing-room. 'And then to be obliged to go to London, in all that racket and bustle! I don't think Mary should have asked it of you!'

'She didn't: I invited myself, as a reward for *not* having got into a quarrel with Sir Francis. Never have I known a more glumpish, disagreeable man! I sincerely pity Jane, and forgive her all her peevishness. You can't conceive how glad I was to see George's good-humoured countenance when I reached Brook Street, and to be made so welcome by him and Mary! I enjoyed myself very much, and did a vast deal of shopping. Only wait until you see the bonnet I've brought for you: you will look charmingly in it! Then I bought ells of the prettiest muslins for Fanny, besides a quantity of fripperies for myself, and – But where is Fanny?'

'She will be so vexed not to have been here to welcome you!'

'Fiddle! why should she be? It's Thursday, isn't it? Then I collect she is at the cotillion-ball?'

'I thought there could be no objection,' Selina said, a little defensively. 'Lady Weaverham invited her to dine, and to go to the Upper Rooms afterwards, in her party, and I consented to it, having then no apprehension that you would be with us again today.'

'Why, of course!' said Abby. 'Very uncivil of Fanny it would have been to have cried off!'

'Exactly so!' said Selina eagerly. 'With Lady Weaverham, too – such an amiable woman, as I know you must agree! Besides having two daughters, which makes it so particularly kind in her to have invited Fanny! Because it can't be denied that our dearest is the prettiest girl in Bath!'

'Oh, out of cry! As for Lady Weaverham, no one could be more amiable – or more shatterbrained! I wish – No, never mind! I'm glad she *has* taken Fanny to the ball on this occasion, for I must talk to you about Fanny.'

4

'Yes, my love, of course! But you are tired, and must be longing to go to bed! A bowl of broth –'

'No, no, just a little thin gruel!' said Abby, laughing at her. 'You goose, I stopped to dine in Chippenham, and I'm not in the least tired. We'll drink tea together, as soon as I've put off my hat, and enjoy a comfortable prose.' She added mischievously: 'You look the picture of guilt – as though you were in dread of a scold! But how should I dare to scold my eldest sister? I'm not so brassy!'

She went away, leaving Selina to ring for the tea-tray, and mounted the stairs to her bedroom, where she found Mrs Grimston unpacking her trunk. A look of disapproval had settled on this formidable dame's countenance, and she greeted Miss Wendover with the information that she had known at the outset how it would be if Miss Fanny were left with only Miss Selina, and Betty Conner (who had more hair than wit, and was flighty into the bargain) to take care of her. 'Jauntering about all over!' she said darkly. 'Concerts, and balls, and theatres, and picnics, and I don't know what more besides!'

Abby had her own reasons for suspecting that her niece had been enjoying far more licence than had previously been granted to her; but as she had no intention of discussing the matter with Mrs Grimston she merely replied: 'Well, how should you?' which effectually reduced her old nurse to offended silence.

The Misses Wendover had virtually had charge of their orphaned niece since she was two years old, when her mama had died in giving birth to a still-born son, and her papa had confided her to the care of her grandmama. His own death, three years later, in no way affected this arrangement; and when, in Fanny's twelfth year, her grandpapa had met with a fatal accident on the hunting-field, and his widow had chosen to retire to Bath, instead of continuing to endure, in her Dower House, a climate which had never agreed with her frail constitution, his surviving son, James, who was Fanny's guardian, had been only too glad to leave Fanny in her care. He was himself the father of a hopeful family, but his wife, a lady of forceful character, had no wish to assume the charge of his niece. When Mrs Wendover died, three years later, Fanny was bidding fair to become an uncommonly beautiful girl, and Mrs James Wendover had even less desire to include her in her household, where she would not only outshine her cousins, but might even teach them to be as light at hand as she was herself. So James, steward and tenant of the estate of which Fanny was the owner, graciously informed his sisters that they might, for the present, continue to act as the dear child's guardians. It would be a pity (as his Cornelia pointed out to him) to interrupt her education at one of Bath's exclusive seminaries. James, adhering to the custom of his family, was determined to arrange an advantageous marriage for Fanny; but he thought there was time enough before it would become Cornelia's duty to launch her into society, not foreseeing that when Fanny was ripe for presentation Cornelia would be more than ever determined to leave her with her aunts. Cornelia confessed that she could not like Fanny, in whom she detected a sad resemblance to her poor mama. It was to be hoped that she would not grow into one of these modern hurly-burly females; but for her part Cornelia considered that her vivacity led her to be far too coming. But what could one expect of a girl reared by a couple of doting old maids?

The younger of the doting old maids went downstairs again to the drawing-room, where her sister was already seated behind the tea-table. Miss Wendover, after one glance at her carriage-dress, with its rucked sleeves and its little winged ruff of starched muslin, greeted her with instant approval, exclaiming: 'I never saw you look so becoming! London, of course?'

'Yes: Mary was so obliging as to take me to her very own Thérèse, which I thought excessively goodnatured of her.'

'Thérèse! I daresay it was shockingly dear, then, because Cornelia once said to me – so spiteful of her! – that it was to be hoped George might not be ruined by Mary's extravagance, and that *she* couldn't afford to have her dresses made by Thérèse.'

'Could, but won't,' said Abby, sipping her tea. 'How happy James must be to have a wife who is as big a nip-farthing as he is himself!'

'Oh, Abby, how can you? Remember, he is your brother!'

'I do, and never cease to regret it!' retorted Abby. 'Now, don't, I beg of you, recite me a catalogue of his virtues, for they don't render him any more lovable – less, in fact! Besides, he's an incorrigible busyhead, and I'm quite out of charity with him.'

Selina had been uttering soft clucking sounds of protest, but they ceased at this, and she demanded quite sharply: 'Has James written to you too?'

'Written to me! He actually came up to London to read me one of his pompous lectures! My dear, what *have* you been doing here? Who is this ramshackle youth who has been making up to Fanny?'

'No such thing!' declared Selina, her colour much heightened. 'It was a case of love at first sight – and a very pretty-behaved young man! Only think of his running out of the Pump Room, with no umbrella, to procure a chair for me, and becoming drenched, because you know what it is in Bath when it suddenly comes on to rain, there is never a chair or a hackney to be had, and I was persuaded he would take a chill, which would settle on his lungs, but he made nothing of it – so very obliging! And he had not then exchanged one word with Fanny, because she wasn't with me, and although *I* remembered that I had seen him in the Upper Rooms two – no, *three* – days before, *he* did not, and Fanny *was* with me on that occasion, so if you are thinking that he got the chair for me because he wished to become acquainted with her you are quite mistaken, Abby! If that had been his object he would have desired Mr King to have introduced him to us, at the Upper Rooms. *And*,' she concluded, with the air of one delivering a clincher: 'he is not a *youth*! I daresay he is as old as you are, and very likely older!'

Abby could not help laughing at this tangled speech, but she shook her head as well, and sighed: 'Oh, Selina, you goosecap!'

'I collect you mean to reproach me,' said Selina, sitting very straight in her chair, 'but why you should do so I haven't the least guess, for Fanny had a great many admirers before you went away, and when *I* said she was too young to be going to balls, *you* said I was *Gothic*, and also that she would enjoy her London come-out much more if she had previously been into society a little, which is *perfectly* true, because there is nothing so – so *agonising* as to be fired off from the schoolroom, no matter how many dancing and deportment lessons one has had! Particularly if one is a trifle shy – not that I mean to say that Fanny is shy – indeed, I sometimes wonder if she is not a little *too* – though never unbecomingly! And if James has been tattling to you, depend upon it that odious woman who is Cornelia's bosom-piece – which is just what one would expect of Cornelia, to make a crony of a backbiting creature like Mrs Ruscombe! – well, you may depend upon it that it was she who set him on, because Mr Calverleigh never greets that tallow-faced daughter of hers with more than common civility, in spite of having been regularly introduced, and receiving every encouragement to dangle after the girl!'

'Yes, very likely,' agreed Abby.

'There, then!' said Selina triumphantly.

There was no immediate response to this, but, after a few moments, Abigail said: 'If that were all – but it isn't, Selina! George isn't a backbiter, and he spoke of Calverleigh with the greatest contempt, because he thought it right to warn me that the young man is not at all the thing. Besides being a gamester, it seems that he is what they call a gazetted fortune-hunter. In fact, the on-dit is that Fanny is not the first heiress he has made up to: there was some silly girl who was ready to elope with him, if you please, only last year! Fortunately, the plot was discovered, and the whole affair hushed up.'

'I don't believe it!' declared Selina, trembling with indignation. 'No, and I wonder that George should repeat such – such steward's room gossip! *Not the thing*, indeed! I consider him most truly the gentleman, and of the *first* respectability, and so does everyone else in Bath!'

'Oh, Selina, what a bouncer! You know very well that Lady Trevisian didn't hold him in high esteem. Indeed, she told Mary that she had warned you, just before she left Bath, that you would be wise to hint Calverleigh away. That was how George came to know about the business.'

Much flushed, Selina said: 'I wonder that she could think of nothing better to do than to go tattlemongering all over London! Making a mountain out of a molehill, too, as I very soon discovered – not that I mean to say that it was not very wrong of Fanny, and I assure you I told her so – and all because she saw Fanny walking with him in the Sydney Gardens, quite by accident – meeting him, I mean, and Betty with her, of course – at least, she was *then* – so I gave Fanny a *severe* scold, and told her how shocking it would be if people thought she was *fast*. Yes, and I said that I was surprised at Mr Calverleigh, which I collect she must have told him, because he paid me a morning visit the very next day, to beg pardon, and to explain to me that this was the first time he had ever been to Bath, which accounted for his not knowing that it was quite improper for a young female of breeding to wander round the gardens – to say nothing of the labyrinth! – without the vestige of a chaperon, not even her maid, because Fanny had sent Betty home, which was very naughty of her – most thoughtless, only she is such a child still that I'm persuaded she had no notion – and *he*, I promise you, felt it just as he ought!'

'Did he?' said the younger Miss Wendover rather dryly. 'Well, you can't suppose that I mean to make a mountain out of a molehill! But the thing is, Selina, that however engaging Calverleigh may be he will not do for Fanny. If George, who is far too good-natured to abuse people merely because he doesn't like them, calls him a *loose fish*, which I fancy means a libertine –'

'Abby! Oh, *no!*' exclaimed Selina, outraged.

'Well, there must be something very undesirable about him to bring James posting up to London in the greatest fuss imaginable!'

'Yes, because he wants poor Fanny to make a brilliant match! I hope I know how to value my brother as I ought, but I must say that I think he has a maggot in his head on *that* subject!'

'It was more than that,' Abby said slowly, a frown creasing her

9

brow. 'He seemed to me to be almost overpowered! Indeed, he couldn't utter the name without shuddering! I could have laughed, if he hadn't put me so much out of temper. For what must he do, when I asked him *why* he held Calverleigh in such violent dislike, but prim up his mouth, and say that it was not a matter fit for my ears! I must be content to abide by his judgment, and if I did not nip the affair in the bud there would be nothing for it but to remove Fanny from our care.'

'*What*?' Selina gasped.

'Don't fall into despair, my love!' said Abby, smiling at her. 'He may *talk* of removing Fanny to his – or, rather, *her* – own home, but I fancy he would meet with some sturdy opposition from Cornelia! If he overbore it I'm sure it would be for the first time in his life!'

'It would be the cruellest thing! She would be miserable!' uttered Selina, in palpitating accents.

'Oh, she would run away!' replied Abby cheerfully. 'I told him so, which gave him the chance to deplore her upbringing. However, before we got to actual dagger-drawing –'

'You should not! Oh, dear, oh, dear, how often has dear Mama begged you not to be so – so *impetuous*?'

'No, of course I should not, but there was no harm done, because Mary was there, and I defy anyone to brangle in the teeth of her placid good sense! She said, in her sweetly comfortable way, – *you* know, Selina! – what a to-do was being made over a flirtation, which would never grow to serious proportions if James would but refrain from turning it into a grand tragedy, and so putting it into Fanny's head that she was a modern Juliet. James was a good deal struck by this, and so was I, too!' She broke off, perceiving that her sister did not share her sentiments. 'You don't agree?'

Her mild eyes filling with sentimental tears, Selina said, in a trembling voice: 'How can you be so unfeeling? When you have said I don't know how many times that our darling should never be sacrificed as *you* were! When I recall your sufferings – when I think of your – of your blighted life –'

'Selina, have you run mad?' interrupted Abby, regarding her in astonishment. 'What sufferings?'

'You may try to hoax me, but you won't make me believe that you have forgotten your anguish when Papa forbade poor Mr Thornaby ever to approach you again! *I* shall never do so!' declared Selina.

'Good gracious!' The anxious look in Abby's eyes was put to rout by one of irrepressible merriment. 'My dearest goose, do *try* to forget it! I have, I promise you! Indeed, I haven't any very clear recollection of what he even looked like, though I do remember that I believed myself to be brokenhearted at the time. At seventeen, one does, only to discover that one has quite mistaken the matter.'

This sad want of sensibility daunted Selina for a moment, but she made a recover, saying, with an air of boundless understanding: 'You were always so brave, my dear one! But if you had forgotten Mr Thornaby why did you refuse Lord Broxbourne's offer? So very flattering, and such an excellent man, with a most superior mind, and *every* quality to render him acceptable!'

'Except one! He was a dead bore!' Abby's eyes began to dance again. 'Have you been picturing me nursing a broken heart all these years? My dear, I do beg your pardon, but it is quite useless to make me the heroine of a tragic romance: I must always disappoint you.'

'Next you will tell me that you too are determined to arrange a splendid match for poor little Fanny! I hope I know you rather too well to believe that!'

'I hope you do. I may own that Papa chanced to be right when he sent Thornaby packing, but I still hold to it that this resolve he had – and my grandfather before him, and James after him! – to arrange only the most advantageous marriages for every one of his children was nothing short of an obsession! And you may be sure I won't allow Fanny to be sacrificed as you and Jane were! Mary was so compliant as to fall in love with George, but only think of Jane, positively *forced* into marriage with that odious creature who had nothing but his wealth and his title to recommend him!'

Selina, who had derived consolation all her life from the inculcated belief that Papa must know best, said feebly: 'No, no! How can you say such things, Abby? One would think – not but what – perhaps sometimes he may have been a *trifle* – But I am sure he did only what he believed to be *right*!'

'But for Papa,' said Abby inexorably, 'you would have married that curate – I forget his name, but I daresay you would have been very happy, with a quiverful of children, and – Oh, dearest, forgive me! I didn't mean to make you cry!'

Selina had indeed dissolved into tears, but she wiped them away, saying: 'No, no! It was only *remembering*, and even dear Mama, who entered into all my feelings, couldn't conceal from me her apprehension that he would become bald before he was forty! It is *you* who should be pitied!'

'Not a bit of it! I don't regret Thornaby, and I was *not* sacrificed, as Jane was! No, and I won't let James make a burnt offering of Fanny either: that you may depend on! But, on the other hand, my dear, I won't – if I can prevent it – let her throw herself away on the first fortune-hunter who makes up to her!'

'But I am persuaded he is no such thing!' expostulated Selina. 'He is possessed of *considerable* estates in Berkshire, and he comes of a most *distinguished* family. I believe he can trace his lineage back for *hundreds* of years!'

'Well, I know nothing about his ancestors, but from all I have been able to discover the present family is distinguished for profligacy, and nothing else! *This* man's reputation is bad; and, according to James, his father was far from respectable; while as for his uncle, *he*, after having been expelled from Eton, seems to have gone his length in every extravagant folly until he was packed off to India, under orders never to show his face to his family again! As for the estates, George says they are grossly encumbered. And if you think all these circumstances make Stacy Calverleigh an eligible suitor –'

'Oh, no, no, no!' Selina cried distressfully. 'Only I *can't* believe that poor Mr Calverleigh – and it always seems to me *most* unjust to visit the sins of the fathers upon the children, and when it comes to an *uncle* positively wicked! Such engaging manners, and feels just as he ought, besides showing delicacy of mind, and – oh, I don't believe it!'

'Well, it was what George said, and you must allow that he is not at all prudish, as James is.' She paused, her brow wrinkled in thought. 'And I should suppose, wouldn't you, that a libertine *must* be engaging?'

'Abby!' gasped Selina. 'I must *beg* of you to guard your tongue! If anyone were to hear you – !'

'Well, no one but you can hear me,' Abby pointed out. 'And all I said was –'

'I know nothing about *that* class of person!' interrupted Selina hastily.

'No, nor do I,' said Abby, on a note of regret. 'Except what I've read, of course, and that diverting man who came to a ball the Ashendens gave – oh, years ago! Papa said he would not permit a daughter of his to stand up for as much as one dance with *such a fellow as that,* only I had already done so, and very agreeable it was! I don't know that he was a libertine, but I do know that he was a shocking flirt – and *not* because Rowland told me so! In that consequential way of his, which made him look just like Papa – *you* know!'

It was evident that whatever Miss Wendover might have known she was determined to forget. Summoning to her aid all the authority of her years, she said, in a voice of the gravest reproof: 'Must I remind you, Abigail, that dear Rowland is dead?'

'No, and you need not remind me that he was our eldest brother either. Or call me by that detestable name! Whatever else I might forgive Papa, *that* I never could! *Abigail*! Mashams and maidservants!'

'*Some* people think it a charming name!' said Selina, casting an arch look at her. '*One* of them is Canon Pinfold, who thinks *you* are charming too! He says that it is from the Hebrew, and means *father rejoiced*.'

After a stunned moment, her unregenerate sister went into a

peal of laughter. It was several minutes before she could do more than wail: 'Papa c-can't have kn-known that! He w-wanted another son!' and when she did manage to stop laughing Selina's look of pained reproach very nearly set her off again. She bit her lip, and said, a little shakily: 'Don't mind me! You know what I am! And what in the world has all this to do with Fanny? Selina, I realise that you have a decided tendre for Calverleigh, but if he were the biggest prize on the matrimonial mart I still should not like it! Good God, do you wish her to plunge into marriage with the first man she has met who is neither middle aged nor a youth she has known since he was a schoolboy? At seventeen!'

'I told her she was too young to be talking of having formed a lasting attachment,' answered Selina, thrown upon the defensive again. 'Yes, and I said that her uncle would never countenance it, and that she must put it out of her mind!'

This effectively banished any lingering desire in Abby to giggle. She exclaimed: 'You didn't! Oh, Selina, I wish you had not!'

'You wish I had not?' echoed Selina, her voice as much as her countenance betraying her bewilderment. 'But you have just said –'

'Yes, yes, but don't you *see* –' Abby interrupted, only to break off her sentence abruptly, as she realised the folly of expecting Selina to perceive what was so obvious to her own intelligence. She continued, in a gentler voice: 'I am afraid that it may have put up her back – roused the independence of spirit which you have so often deplored. Yes, I know that you think she ought to submit meekly to the decrees of her guardian, but recollect that she hasn't been reared as we were, to regard the lightest pronouncement of a parent – or an aunt! – as something it would be sacrilege to question, and *unthinkable* to disobey!'

Roused to indignation, Selina retorted: 'Well, I *must* say, Abby! For you to talk in such a way, when you never showed the least respect for Papa's judgment –! And when I recall how often you came to cuffs with him, casting dear Mama and me into agonies of apprehension – *Well*! Not, dearest,' she added hastily, 'that I mean to say that you ever actually disobeyed Papa, for that I know you didn't!'

'No,' agreed Abby, in a flattened tone. 'A very poor honey, wasn't I?'

The mournful note startled Miss Wendover, but in a very few seconds she realised that it had its origin in fatigue, aggravated by anxiety. It was incumbent upon her to divert poor Abby's mind, and with this amiable intention she first told her, with an indulgent laugh, that she was a naughty puss; and then launched into a recital of the various events which had lately occurred in Bath. Her rambling discourse embraced such topics as what her new doctor said about Russian Vapour Baths; how eagerly dear Mrs Grayshott was awaiting the return of her son from India – if the poor young man survived the voyage, so ill as he had been in that horrid country; how much she was obliged to poor Laura Butterbank, who had spared no pains to cheer and support her during Abby's absence, coming every day to sit with her, and always so chatty and companionable, besides being charmed to execute any little commission in the town. But at this point she broke off, to accuse her sister of not listening to a word she said.

Abby had indeed been allowing the gentle stream of inanities to flow past her, but at this reproach she recalled her thoughts, and said: 'Yes, I am! Mrs Grayshott – Miss Butterbank! I'm glad she bore you company while I was away – since Fanny seems not to have done so!'

'Good gracious, Abby, how you do take one up! No one could have been more attentive, the sweet child that she is! But with so much of her time occupied by her music-lessons, and the Italian class, besides having so many of her friends living here, who are for ever inviting her to join them for a country walk, or some picnic-party – *perfectly* unexceptionable! – I'm sure it is not to be wondered at – I mean, when Laura gave me the pleasure of her company every day there was no reason why Fanny should have stayed at home, and very selfish it would have been in me to have asked it of her! Yes, and most unnatural it would be if she didn't wish to be with girls of her own age!'

'True! Or even with the fascinating Calverleigh!'

'Now, Abby – !'

'Well, it would be,' said Abby candidly. 'Any girl would prefer the company of a taking young man to that of her aunt! But it won't do, Selina.'

'I am persuaded that when you have made his acquaintance – not that I would for a *moment* encourage her – oh, dear how very affecting it is! *You* will have to tell her, for I know I could never bring myself to do so!'

'Dearest, it isn't so dreadful that you need fall into affliction! It's certainly unfortunate, and I wish with all my heart that she might have been spared such a painful disappointment, but she'll recover from it. As for forbidding her to see Calverleigh, or telling her the things that are said of him, I'm not such a widgeon! She would fly to his defence! But if *he* were to draw off? Not compelled to do so, but because he discovered her to be not such a rich plum as he had supposed? She might suffer a little unhappiness, but not for long. She's not the girl to wear the willow for a mere flirt!' She added thoughtfully: 'And she couldn't, under those circumstances, fancy herself to be a star-crossed lover, could she? I do feel that that should be avoided at all costs, for although I've never been star-crossed myself I can readily perceive how romantic it would be. Selina, I never knew Fanny's mother at all well, but you must have done so. Was she high-spirited, like Fanny? Rather too dashing, perhaps, to suit the Wendover notions of propriety?'

'Celia? Good gracious, no!' replied Selina. 'She was very pretty – quite lovely, when she was a girl, but she went off sadly, which I do hope and pray Fanny won't, because she is very like her in *countenance*, and Mama always was used to say that *fair* beauties seldom wear well. But Fanny isn't in the least like her in disposition! She has so much liveliness, and poor Celia was a very quiet, shy girl, and *most* persuadable! What makes you ask me about her?'

'Something James said. I wasn't paying much heed, but it was something about Fanny's too close resemblance to her mother.

And then he stopped short, and when I asked him what he meant he fobbed me off, saying that Fanny was as foolish as her mother. But I didn't think he did mean that, and nor did Mary. She remembers more than I do, of course, and she tells me that you elder ones always thought that *something* had happened – some indiscretion, perhaps –'

'I never thought any such thing!' intervened Selina firmly. 'And if I had I should have considered it most improper to have pried into it! If Mama had wished me to know anything about it, she would have told me!'

'So there *was* something!' said Abby. 'A skeleton in our respectable cupboard! I wish I could know what it was! But I daresay it would prove to be no more than the skeleton of a mouse.'

Two

Not long after eleven o'clock that evening, a gentle tap on the door of Abby's bedchamber was followed immediately by the entrance of Miss Fanny Wendover, who first peeped cautiously into the room, and then, when she saw her aunt seated at the dressing-table, uttered a joyful squeak, and ran to fling herself into the arms held out to her, exclaiming: 'You aren't in bed and asleep! I told Grimston you wouldn't be! Oh, how glad I am to see you again! how much I've missed you, dear, dear Abby!'

It would not have surprised Abby if she had been greeted with reserve, even with the wary, half-defiant manner of one expectant of censure and ready to defend herself; but there was no trace of consciousness in the welcome accorded her, and nothing but affection in the beautiful eyes which, as Fanny sank down at her feet, clasping her hands, were raised so innocently to hers.

'It's horrid without you!' Fanny said, giving her hands a squeeze. 'You can't think!'

Abby bent to drop a kiss on her cheek, but said with mock sympathy: 'My poor darling! So strict and unkind as Aunt Selina has been! I feared it would be so.'

'*That's* what I've missed so much!' Fanny said, with a ripple of mirth. 'I am most sincerely attached to Aunt Selina, but – but she is not a great jokesmith, is she? And not a bit corky!'

'I shouldn't *think* so,' responded Abby cautiously. 'Not that I know what *corky* means, but it sounds very unlike Selina – and, I

18

may add, sadly unlike the language to be expected of a girl of genteel upbringing!'

That made Fanny's eyes dance. 'Yes – slang! It means – oh, bright, and lively! Like you!'

'Does it indeed? I collect you mean to pay me a handsome compliment, but if ever you dare to attach such an epithet to me again, Fanny, I shall – I shall – well, I don't yet know what I shall do, but you may depend upon it that it will be something terrible! *Corky*! Good God!'

'I won't,' Fanny promised. 'Now, do, do be serious, beloved! I have so much to tell you. Something of – of the first importance.'

Abby knew a craven impulse to fob her off, but subdued it, saying in what she hoped was not a hollow voice: 'No, have you? Then I will engage to be perfectly serious. What is it?'

Fanny directed a searching look at her. 'Didn't Aunt Selina – or Uncle James, perhaps – tell you about – about Mr Calverleigh?'

'About Mr – ? Oh! Is he the London smart you've slain with one dart from your eyes? To be sure they did, and very diverting I thought them! That is to say,' she corrected herself, in a ludicrously severe tone, 'that of course they are very right in thinking you to be far too young to be setting up a flirt! Most forward of you, my love – quite improper!'

She won no answering gleam. 'It isn't like that,' Fanny said. 'From the very first moment that we met –' She paused, and drew a long breath. 'We loved one another!' she blurted out.

Abby had not expected such an open avowal, and could think of nothing to say but that it sounded like a fairy-tale, which was not at all what she ought to have said, as she realised an instant later.

Raising glowing eyes to her face, Fanny said simply: 'Yes, it is just like that! Oh, I knew you would understand, dearest! Even though you haven't yet met him! And when you do meet him – oh, you will dote on him! I only wish you may not cut me out!'

Abby accorded this sally the tribute of a smile, but recommended her ecstatic niece not to be a pea-goose.

'Oh, I was only funning!' Fanny assured her. 'The thing is that he isn't a silly boy, like Jack Weaverham, or Charlie Ruscombe, or – or Peter Trevisian, but a man of the world, and *much* older than I am, which makes it so particularly gratifying – no, I don't mean that! – *so wonderful* that in spite of having been on the town, as they say, for years and years he never met anyone with whom he wished to form a *lasting* connection until he came to Bath, and met *me!*' Overcome by this reflection, she buried her face in Abby's lap, saying, in muffled accents: 'And he must have met much prettier girls than I am – don't you think?'

Miss Wendover, aware that her besetting sin was a tendency to give utterance to the first thought which sprang to her mind, swallowed an impulse to retort: 'But few so well-endowed!' and replied instead: 'Well, as I'm not acquainted with any of the latest beauties I can't say! But to have made a London beau your first victim is certainly a triumph. Of course I know I shouldn't say that to you – your Aunt Cornelia would call it *administering to your vanity!* – so pray don't expose me to her censure by growing puffed-up, my darling!'

Fanny looked up. 'Ah, you *don't* understand! Abby, this is a – a lasting attachment! You must believe that! Has my uncle told you that he is a desperate flirt? *Such* a sad reputation as he has! He told me so himself! But I don't care a rush, because, although he has frequently fancied himself to be in love, he never wished to *marry* anyone until he met *me!* And if my uncle said that he is a trifle rackety he might have spared his breath, for Stacy told me that too. He said – oh, Abby, he said he wasn't fit to touch my hand, and no one could blame my uncle if he refused to give his consent to our marriage!'

She once more hid her face in Abby's lap, raising it again to add: 'So you *see* – !'

Abby thought that she did, but she only said, stroking the golden head on her knee: 'But what is there in all this to cast you into agitation? Anyone would suppose that your uncle had already refused his consent, and had threatened you both with dire penalties into the bargain!'

'Oh!' breathed Fanny, looking eagerly up at her. 'Do you mean that you think he won't refuse it?'

'Oh, no!' said Abby. 'I am very sure that he will! And although I have no very high opinion of his judgment I give him credit for not being such a niddicock as to accept the first offer made to him for your hand! A pretty guardian he would be if he allowed you to become riveted before your first season! Yes, I know that sets up all your bristles, my darling, and makes you ready to pull caps with me, but I beg you won't! Your uncle may dream of a splendid alliance for you, but you know that I don't! I only dream of a happy one.'

'I know – oh, I know!' Fanny declared. 'And so you will support me! Best of my aunts, say that you will!'

'Why, yes, if you can convince me that your first love will also be your last love!'

'But I have told you!' Fanny said, sitting back on her heels, and staring at her in rising indignation. 'I could never love anyone as I love Stacy! Good God, how can you – *you*! – talk like that to me? I know – my aunt told me! – how my grandfather repulsed the man *you* loved! And you've never loved another, and – and your life was ruined!'

'Well, I thought so at the time,' Abby admitted. A smile quivered at the corners of her mouth. 'I must own, however, that whenever that first suitor of mine is recalled to my mind I can only be thankful that your grandfather did repulse him! You know, Fanny, the melancholy truth is that one's first love very rarely bears the least resemblance to one's last, and most enduring love! *He* is the man one marries, and with whom one lives happily ever after!'

'But you have not married!' muttered Fanny rebelliously.

'Very true, but not because I carried a broken heart in my bosom! I have fallen in and out of love a dozen times, I daresay. And as for your Aunt Mary – ! She, you know, was always accounted the Beauty of the family, and you might have reckoned her suitors by the score! The first of them was as unlike your Uncle George as any man could be.'

'I thought that my grandfather had arranged that marriage?' interpolated Fanny.

'Oh, no!' replied Abby. 'He certainly approved of it, but George was only one of three eligible suitors! He was neither the most handsome nor the most dashing of them, and he bore not the smallest resemblance to any of your aunt's first loves, but theirs is a very happy marriage, I promise you.'

'Yes, but I am not like my aunt,' returned Fanny. 'I daresay she would have been as happy with any other amiable man, because she has a happy disposition, besides being very – very conformable!' She twinkled naughtily up at Abby. 'Which I am *not!* My aunt is like a – oh, a deliciously soft cushion, which may be pushed and pummelled into any shape you choose! – but I – I *know* what I want, and have a great deal of resolution into the bargain!'

'More like a bolster, in fact,' agreed Abby, with an affability she was far from feeling.

Fanny laughed. 'Yes, if you like – *worst* of my aunts! In any event, I mean to marry Stacy Calverleigh, whatever my uncle may say or do!'

Well aware that few things were more invigorating to high spirited adolescents than opposition, Abby replied instantly: 'Oh, certainly! But your father, you know, was an excellent dragsman, and he was used to say that you should always get over heavy ground as light as possible. I am strongly of the opinion that you – and Mr Calverleigh – should refrain from declaring your intentions to your uncle until you can also present him with proof of the durability of your attachment.'

'He wouldn't care: you must know he wouldn't! And if you mean to say that I must wait until I come of age – oh, no, you couldn't be so heartless! Four whole years – ! When you have met Stacy, you will understand!'

'I shall be delighted to meet him, and wish it may be soon.'

'Oh, and so do I!' Fanny said eagerly. 'You can't think how much I miss him! You see, he was obliged to go to London, but he said it would only be for a few days, so he may be in Bath again by the end of the week. Or, at any rate, next week: that you may depend on!'

This was said with a radiant look, and was followed by a shyly ecstatic account of Fanny's first meeting with Mr Calverleigh, and a description of his manifold charms. Abby listened and commented suitably, but seized the first opportunity that offered of turning Fanny's thoughts into another channel. She directed her attention to the pile of dress-lengths she had procured in London, and bade her say if she liked them. This answered very well; and in going into raptures over a spidergauze, wondering whether to have a celestial-blue crape trimmed with ribbon or puff-muslin, and arguing with Abby over the respective merits of Circassian or Cottage sleeves for a morning-dress, Fanny temporarily forgot Mr Calverleigh, and went off to bed presently, to dream (Abby hoped) of fashions.

It seemed, on the following morning, as though she had done so, for she visited her aunt before Abby was out of bed, eager to show her several fashion-plates from the latest issue of the *Ladies' Home Journal*, and hopeful of coaxing her to sally forth before breakfast on a visit to the dressmaker on South Parade. In this she failed, Abby pointing out to her that her Aunt Selina, no early riser, would be very much hurt if excluded from the expedition. She added a reminder that in all matters of taste and fashion Selina was infallible.

Fanny pouted, but submitted, knowing the truth of this dictum. She might stigmatise many of Selina's notions as fusty, but no one had ever cast a slur on Selina's eye for the elegant and the becoming. In her youth she had been the least good-looking but the most modish of the Wendover girls; in her middle age, and endowed with an easy competence, she enjoyed the reputation of being the best-dressed woman in Bath. If Fanny did not, like Abby, seek her advice, she was shrewd enough to respect her judgment; so that when, presently, she showed Selina the sketch of a grossly overtrimmed walking-dress her secret longing to be seen abroad in this confection was nipped in the bud by Selina's devastating criticism. 'Oh, dear!' said Selina, wrinkling her nose in distaste. 'All those frills, and tucks, and ribbons – ! So – so *deedy*!'

So nothing more was seen of that fashion-plate, and in due course all three ladies set out in Miss Wendover's new barouche for South Parade, where Madame Lisette's elegant showrooms were situated.

Madame Lisette, who was born Eliza Mudford, enjoyed Royal Patronage, but although she was the particular protégée of the Princess Elizabeth, in whose service she had started her career, and rarely failed to receive orders from Bath's noblest and most fashionable visitors, the Misses Wendover ranked high amongst her favourite clients: they were rich, they were resident, and they set off to the greatest advantage the fruits of her genius. By no means all her customers were honoured by her personal attention, but no sooner had her head saleswoman caught sight of the barouche drawing up outside the door than she sent an apprentice scurrying upstairs to Madame's office with the news that the Misses Wendover – *all* the Misses Wendover! – were about to enter the shop. So, by the time the Misses Wendover had enquired kindly after Miss Snisby's health, and their footman had delivered into the care of an underling the package containing the silks, and the gauzes, and the muslins purchased in London by Miss Abigail, Miss Mudford had arrived on the scene, suitably but exquisitely gowned in a robe of rich silk but sober hue, and combining with the ease of an expert the deference due to ladies of quality with the chartered familiarities of an old and trusted retainer. No less skill did she show in convincing the youngest Miss Wendover that the style of dress, proper for a young matron, for which that damsel yearned, would not make her look dashing, but on the contrary, positively dowdy. Such was her tact that Fanny emerged from the salon an hour later with the comfortable persuasion that so far from having been treated like a schoolroom miss her taste had been approved, and that the resultant creations would set her in the highest kick of fashion.

This satisfactory session being at an end, the ladies betook themselves to the Pump Room, where it was Selina's custom (unless the weather were inclement, or some more agreeable diversion offered itself) to imbibe, in small, distasteful sips, a glass of the celebrated waters. Here they encountered a number of friends and acquaintances, prominent amongst whom were General Exford, one of Abby's more elderly admirers, and Mrs Grayshott, with her daughter, Lavinia, who was Fanny's chief crony. The two girls soon had their heads together; and while Abby gracefully countered the General's gallantries Selina, who was sometimes felt to take more interest in the affairs of strangers than in those of her family, engaged Mrs Grayshott in earnest conversation, the object of her sympathetic enquiries being to discover whether Mrs Grayshott had received any news of her only son, last heard of in Calcutta, but living in daily expectation of embarking on the long journey home to England. The look of anxiety on Mrs Grayshott's rather care-worn face deepened as she shook her head, and replied, with a resolute smile: 'Not yet. But my brother has assured me that he has made every imaginable arrangement for his comfort, and I'm persuaded it can't be long now before he will be with me again. My brother has been so good! Had it been possible, I really believe he would have sent his own doctor out to Oliver! He blames himself for that dreadful sickness, you know, but that is nonsensical. Oliver was very willing to go to India, and how, I ask him, could *he* have foreseen that the poor boy's constitution was so ill-suited to the climate? *I* did not, for he has always enjoyed excellent health.'

'Ah!' said Selina mournfully. 'If only it may not have been ruined by this sad misfortune!'

Her tone held out no hope for the future; and as she went on to recount the dismal story of the sufferings endured by just such another case – not *personally* known to her, but he was a cousin of one of her acquaintances, or, if not a cousin, a great *friend,* not that it signified – Mrs Grayshott could only be thankful that the arrival of Miss Butterbank on the scene interrupted the disheartening recital before it had reached its death-bed climax. She was able to escape, and lost no time in doing so. Perceiving that the younger Miss Wendover had just shaken off her elderly admirer, she went to join her, forestalling a gentleman in a blue coat and Angola pantaloons, who was bearing purposefully down upon her. Aware of this, she laughingly begged Abigail's pardon, adding: 'I only wish you cared, Abby!'

'I do, and would liefer by far talk to you, ma'am, than to Mr Dunston! How do you do? Not in very good point, I'm afraid – but don't doubt you will assure me that you're in high force! This is an anxious time for you.'

'Yes, but I know that if – if anything had happened – anything bad – I must have had news of it, so I won't let myself fall into dejection, or post up to London, until my brother sends me word. When *that* happens, I shall cast Lavinia on your hands, and be off. I was so very much obliged to Miss Wendover for offering to take charge of her! But it is you who will do that: you don't object?'

'My dear ma'am, how can you ask? I am naturally cast into the greatest agitation by the very thought of having so onerous a burden thrust upon me! It is only civility that prompts me to say that I shall be charmed to take care of Lavinia.'

Mrs Grayshott smiled, and pressed her hand. 'I knew I might depend on you. I don't think she will be a trouble to you. What I do think – Abby, may I speak frankly to you?'

'If you please! Though I fancy I know what it is that you do think. Fanny?'

Mrs Grayshott nodded. 'You know, then? I'm glad you've come home: I have been feeling a little anxious. Your sister is a dear kind creature, but –'

She hesitated, and Abby said coolly: 'Very true! A dear kind nodcock! She seems to have fallen quite under the spell of this Calverleigh.'

'Well, he – he *is* very engaging,' said Mrs Grayshott reluctantly. 'Only there is something about him which I can't quite like! It is difficult to explain, because I haven't any cause to take him in dislike. Except –' Again she hesitated, but upon being urged to continue, said: 'Abby, no man could be blamed for falling in love with Fanny, but I don't think that a man of principle, so much older than she is, would wish her – far less *urge* her! – to do what might easily set people in a bustle. His attentions are too particular to suit my old-fashioned notions. That makes me into a Bath quiz, I dare say, but you know, my dear, when a man of fashion and address makes a child of Fanny's age the object of his attentions it is not to be wondered at that she should be dazzled into losing her head, or be easily brought to believe that the rules of conduct, in which she has been reared, are outmoded – quite provincial, in fact!'

Abby nodded. 'Such as the impropriety of strolling about the Sydney Gardens with him? Give me a round tale, ma'am! – Have there been other – oh, clandestine meetings?'

'I am afraid so. Oh, nothing of a serious nature, or that is generally known, or – or that you will not speedily put an end to! I might not have spoken to you, if that had been all, for it's no bread-and-butter of mine, and I don't relish the office of being your intelligencer, but I have some reason to think that it is not quite all, and am a great deal too fond of Fanny *not* to tell you that certain things I have learned from what Lavinia –in all innocence! – has let fall, I apprehend that this unfortunate affair may be rather more serious than I had at first supposed. To what extent Lavinia is in Fanny's confidence I don't know, and – I must confess – shrink from enquiring, because perhaps, if she thought I was trying to discover a secret reposed in her, she would fob me off, even prevaricate, and certainly, in the future, guard her tongue when she talked to me. That may seem foolish to you: the thing is she has been so close a companion to me, so open and trusting in her affection –' Her voice became suspended. She shook her head, saying, after a moment's struggle: 'I can't explain it to you!'

'There is not the least need,' Abby responded. 'I understand you perfectly, ma'am. Don't fear me! I promise you I shan't let Fanny so much as suspect that Lavinia betrayed her confidence. Let me be frank with you! I've every reason to suppose that Calverleigh is a fortune-hunter, and it has been made abundantly clear to me that Fanny believes herself to have formed a lasting passion for him. I don't know if Calverleigh hopes to win my brother's consent to the match, but I should very much doubt it. So in what sort is the wind? Does he hope to enlist my support? Is he indulging himself with a flirtation? Or has he the intention of eloping with Fanny?' Her eyes widened, as she saw the quick look turned towards her, and a laugh trembled in her throat. 'My dear ma'am – ! I was only funning!'

'Yes, I know, but – Abby, sometimes I wonder if our parents were right when they forbade us to read novels! It is all the fault of the Circulating Libraries!'

'Putting romantical notions into girls' heads?' said Abby, smiling a little. 'I don't think so: I had a great many myself, and was never permitted to read any but the most improving works. I might be wrong, but I fancy that however much a girl may admire, or envy, the heroine of some romance, who finds herself in the most *extraordinary* situations; and however much she may picture herself in those situations, she knows it is nothing more than a child's game of make-believe, and that she would not, in fact, behave at all like her heroine. Like my sister's children, when they capture me in the shrubbery, and inform me that they are brigands, and mean to hold me to ransom!'

Her smile was reflected in Mrs Grayshott's eyes, but she sighed, and said: 'It may be so – I don't know! But when a girl falls in love, and with – oh, with what they call a man of the town! – who is practised in the art of seduction – ?'

'Well, I don't know either,' said Abby, 'but it occurs to me, ma'am, that your man of the town, assuming him to be in search of a fortune, would scarcely choose a girl four years short of her majority! Indeed, eight years short of it, because Fanny will not come into full possession of her inheritance until she is five-and-twenty. I'm not very well-informed in such matters, but would not that be rather too long to – to live on the expectation?'

'Is he aware of this?' Mrs Grayshott asked. 'Does Fanny know it?'

Abby's eyes, swiftly raised, held an arrested expression. She

28

said, after a moment's pause: 'No. That is, the question has never arisen. I don't know, but I should suppose she doesn't. I see that it must be my business to enlighten Calverleigh – if it should be necessary to do so. Meanwhile, –'

'Meanwhile,' said Mrs Grayshott, with a significant smile, 'Mr Dunston is advancing towards us, determined to wrest you from me, and so I shall take my leave of you! Don't think me impertinent if I say how much I wish I could see *you* happily established, Abby!'

She moved away as she spoke, leaving the road open to the gentleman in the blue coat and Angola pantaloons, who came up, saying simply: 'You have come back at last! Bath has been a desert without you.'

She turned this off with a laughing rejoinder; and, after enquiring politely how his mother did, and exchanging a little trivial conversation with him, said mendaciously that she saw her sister beckoning to her, and left him.

Miss Wendover, who had observed with satisfaction the presence of Mr Dunston in the Pump Room, sighed. Like Mrs Grayshott, she wished very much to see Abby happily established, and could think of no one who would make her a better husband than Peter Dunston. He was a very respectable man, the owner of a comfortable property situated not many miles from Bath; his manners were easy and agreeable; and Miss Wendover had it on the authority of his widowed mother, who resided with him, that his amiability was only rivalled by the elegance of his mind, and the superiority of his understanding. Such was the excellence of his character that he had never caused his mother to suffer a moment's anxiety. One might have supposed that Abby, in imminent danger of dwindling into an old maid, would have welcomed the addresses of so eligible a suitor, instead of declaring she had never been able to feel the least tendre for men of uniform virtues.

She certainly felt none for Peter Dunston, but Miss Wendover was mistaken when she suspected, in moods of depression, that her dear but perverse sister had set her face against marriage.

29

Abby was fully alive to the disadvantages of her situation, and she had more than once considered the possibility of accepting an offer from Mr Dunston. He would be a kind, if unexciting husband; he enjoyed all the comfort and consequence of a large house and an easy fortune; and in marrying him she would remain within reach of Selina. On the other hand, no romance would attend such a marriage, and Abby, who, in her salad days had declined the flattering offer made her by Lord Broxbourne, still believed that somewhere there existed the man for whom she would feel much more than mere friendly liking. She had once believed, too, that she was bound, sooner or later, to encounter him. She had never done so, and it had begun to seem unlikely that she ever would; but without indulging morbid repinings she was disinclined to accept a substitute who could only be second-best in her eyes.

At the moment, however, her mind was not exercised by this question, being fully occupied by the more important problem of how best, and most painlessly, to detach Fanny from the undesirable Mr Calverleigh. Mrs Grayshott was no tattlemonger; and since she had a great deal of reserve Abby knew that only a stringent sense of duty could have forced her to overcome her distaste of talebearing. What she knew, either from her own observation, or from the innocent disclosures of her daughter, she plainly thought to be too serious to be withheld from Fanny's aunt. At the same time, thought Abigail, dispassionately considering her, the well-bred calm of her manners concealed an over-anxious disposition, which led her to magnify possible dangers. The tragic circumstances of her life, coupled as they were with a sickly constitution, had not encouraged her in optimism. Married to an officer of the Line, and the mother of three hopeful children, she had endured years of separation, always looking forward to a blissful reunion, until her dreams were shattered by the news of Captain Grayshott's death, during the Siege of Burgos. This blow was followed, less than a year later, by the illness, and lingering death of her younger son, and the break-down of her own health, so that it was hardly surprising that she should be readier to foresee disaster than a happy outcome.

Not that she ever betrayed her lowness of spirit. If she could be brought to speak of her trials, which was seldom, and only to a few trusted friends, she said that she was by far more fortunate than many soldiers' widows, because she had been supported throughout by her brother, of whose affection and generosity she could not speak without emotion. He was an East India merchant – but, as the highest and most antiquated sticklers in Bath acknowledged, a most gentlemanly person – and a bachelor, commonly said to be rolling in riches. Not only had he coaxed and bullied his sister into accepting an allowance from him which enabled her to establish herself with modest elegance in Edgar Buildings, but he had claimed the right to maintain his surviving nephew at Rugby, and his only niece at Miss Trimble's select seminary in Bath. It was generally supposed that Oliver Grayshott was destined to be his heir, and although there were those who thought it rather too bad of Mr Balking to have sent his poor sister's sole remaining son to India, it was almost universally agreed that she would have been culpably in the wrong had she refused to be parted from him.

She had not done so, and now, as several persons had foreseen from the outset, he was returning to her, if not at death's door, at the best in a state of total collapse.

Abby, blessed with a cheerful mind, took a more optimistic view of Oliver's case, but she did realise the anxiety which Mrs Grayshott must be feeling, and was inclined to think that the consequent agitation of her nerves might well have led her to exaggerate the strength of Fanny's infatuation.

The following three days did nothing to promote such a comfortable notion. There could be no doubt that Fanny, dazzled by the attentions of a London beau, had plunged headlong into her first love-affair, and was ripe for any outrageous folly. Wholly unpractised in the art of dissimulation, her spasmodic attempts to appear unconcerned betrayed her youth, and might, under different circumstances, have amused

Abby. But it was not long before Abby found much more to dismay than to amuse her. She was herself impulsive, often impatient of convention, and, in her girlhood, rebellious, but she had been reared far more strictly than Fanny, and it came as a disagreeable shock to her when she discovered that Fanny watched for the postman every day, and, at the first glimpse of his scarlet coat and cockaded hat, slipped out of the room to intercept the delivery of letters to the house. Never, at her most rebellious, had Abby dreamed of engaging in clandestine correspondence! Such conduct, if it were known, must sink Fanny below reproach. Every feeling was offended; and had she not been tolerably certain, from Fanny's downcast looks, that no letter from Mr Calverleigh had reached her she thought she must have abandoned caution, and taken the girl roundly to task. At first inclined to give Mr Calverleigh credit for propriety, a little quiet reflection made her realise that if marriage was indeed his object he would scarcely commit an act of such folly as to write letters to Fanny which would be more than likely to fall into the hands of her aunts. His aim must be to propitiate Fanny's guardians; and in his dealings with Selina he had shown that he knew it. Abby thought that he had succeeded all too well. Selina had been very much shocked by the disclosures made to her, but she hoped, in a nebulous way, that perhaps, after all, they would be found to be untrue; and she was moved to what Abby considered an excess of sensibility by the spectacle of her niece running to look eagerly out of the window every time a vehicle drew up outside the house. 'Poor, poor child!' she mourned. 'It is so very affecting! I do not know how you can remain unmoved! I had not thought you so – so *unfeeling*, Abby!'

'I'm not unmoved,' responded Abby crossly. 'I am most deeply moved – with a strong desire to give Fanny the finest trimming of her life! I'd do it, too, if I didn't fear that it would encourage her in the belief that she is a persecuted heroine!'

In this noble resolve to abstain from gratifying her desire she was strengthened by Fanny's reception of the only piece of advice she permitted herself to give that lovelorn damsel: that she should not wear her heart on her sleeve. Chin up, eyes flashing, flying her colours in her cheeks, Fanny said: 'I am not ashamed of loving Stacy! Why should I dissemble?'

Quite a number of pungent retorts rose to Abby's tongue, and it said much for her self-control that she uttered none of them. Intuition had made Fanny suspect already that her favourite aunt was ranged on the side of Stacy Calverleigh's enemies; she was slightly on the defensive, not yet hostile, but ready to show hackle. No useful purpose would be served by coming to cuffs with her, Abby thought, and therefore held her peace.

Three

Mr Calverleigh did not reappear in Bath that week, nor did he write to Fanny. Abby began to entertain the hope that a mountain had indeed been made out of a molehill, and that he had merely been amusing himself with a flirtation; and could have borne with tolerable equanimity Fanny's wilting demeanour had it not been disclosed to her by the amiable Lady Weaverham that her ladyship had received a very proper letter from him, excusing himself from dining with her on the following Wednesday, but stating that he would certainly be in Bath again by the end of the next week, when he would call in Lower Camden Place to proffer his apologies in person.

This piece of news applied a damper to Abby's optimism. Her spirits were further depressed by the announcement by Selina, in the thread of a voice, that she had contracted a putrid sore throat, accompanied by fever, a severe headache, and a colicky disorder. She had not closed her eyes all night, and could only hope that these distressing symptoms did not presage an illness which, if not immediately fatal, would leave her to drag out the rest of her life between her bed and a sofa. Abby did not share these gloomy apprehensions, but she lost no time in sending for the latest practitioner to enjoy Selina's favour. She begged him not to encourage the sufferer to think herself hovering on the brink of the grave. He promised to reassure Selina, and very nearly lost his most lucrative patient by telling her, in hearty accents, that nothing worse had befallen her than what he was

34

tactless enough to term a *touch of influenza*. Before he had time to prophesy a speedy recovery he realised that he had fallen into error, and, with a dexterity which (in spite of herself) Abby was obliged to acknowledge, retrieved his position by saying that, although he would ordinarily consider the illness trifling, when it attacked persons of such frail constitution as Miss Wendover the greatest care must be exercised to ensure that no serious consequences should attend it. He recommended her to remain in bed; promised to send her within the hour a saline draught; approved of such remedies as extract of malt for a possible cough; goat's whey, to guard against consumption; laudanum drops in case of insomnia; and a diet of mutton-broth, tapioca-jelly, and barley-water, all of which she had herself suggested; and left the sickroom tolerably certain that he had restored her wavering faith in his skill. He told Abby, apologetically, that neither these remedies nor the depressing diet would do any harm, and with this she had to be content, resigning herself to the inevitable, and deriving what consolation she could from the reflection that for some days at least there was no danger that while she danced attendance on her sister Mr Calverleigh would be strengthening his hold on Fanny's youthful affections.

The eldest Miss Wendover showed every sign of enjoying a protracted illness, for although the fever soon abated she maintained a ticklish cough, and, after an attack of heart-burn, threw out so many dark hints to her entourage about cardiac nerves that Fanny became quite alarmed, and asked Abby if poor Aunt Selina's heart had indeed been affected.

'No, dear: not at all!' responded Abby cheerfully.

'But – Abby, I have sometimes wondered if – Abby, does my aunt *like* to be ill?'

'Yes, certainly she does. Why not? She has very little to divert her, after all! It makes her the centre of attention, too, and how unkind it would be to grudge it to her! The melancholy truth is, my love, that single females of her age are almost compelled to adopt dangerous diseases, if they wish to be objects of interest. Not only spinsters, either! You must surely have observed how

35

many matrons, whose children are all married, and who are so comfortably situated that they have really nothing very much to do, develop the most *interesting* disorders!'

Her eyes as round as saucers, Fanny asked: 'Do you mean that my aunt will lie on a sofa for the rest of her life?'

'No, no!' said Abby. 'Sooner or later something will happen to give her thoughts a new direction, and you will be surprised to see how quickly she will recover!'

In the event, this happened rather sooner than could have been expected. Shortly after noon one day, Abby entered her room to find her seated bolt upright on the day-bed, to which, supported by her maid, she had tottered an hour before, eagerly perusing the crossed sheet of a letter just delivered by the post.

'Oh, dearest, *whatever* do you think?' she exclaimed, in accents startlingly unlike those with which she had greeted her sister earlier in the day. 'The Leavenings are coming to spend the winter in Bath! Good God, they may have arrived already! Mrs Leavening writes that they mean to put up at the York House while they look about them for lodgings, and depend upon us to advise them, for they were never in Bath before, you know! I wonder if the lodgings the Thursleys hired in Westgate Building – but they are in the *lower* part of the town, of course, and though it is a broad street – and anything *here,* or in Pulteney Street, or Laura Place, *might* be above their price – not that Mrs Leavening tells what is the figure they have in mind, but I shouldn't suppose Mr Leavening's fortune to be more than *genteel,* would you?'

'My dear, since I haven't the least guess who the Leavenings may be, I can't answer you!' replied Abby, her eyes alight with laughter.

Miss Wendover was shocked. 'Abby! How *can* you have forgotten? From Bedfordshire – our *own* county! Almost our neighbours! *He* had a wart on his left cheek – such a pity! – but in all other respects *quite* unexceptionable! Or am I thinking of Mr Tarvin? Yes, I fancy it was he who had the wart, which makes it even more delightful, for there is something *about* warts, isn't there? Dearest, I wish you will go to York House this afternoon! So unfriendly not to welcome them immediately, and I wouldn't for the world have Mrs Leavening suspect that we had forgotten her! You will tell her how happy I am to hear of her arrival, and explain how it comes about that I am unable to visit her myself – not but what I am a great deal stronger today, and I daresay I may be able to come downstairs tomorrow. And if you were to walk up Milsom Street, Abby, you could pop into Godwin's, to discover if they haven't yet received that book Mrs Grayshott told me I should enjoy. It is called the Knight of something or other – not, of course, that I am an *advocate* for novel-reading. Perhaps Mrs. Leavening would come and sit with me for a little while tomorrow. What a lot she will have to tell us about our old friends, which James and Cornelia *never* do! I declare, it has put me in spirits only to think of it! We must hold one of our evening-parties, dearest! I shall occupy myself in making out a list of the people to be invited while you are in the town.' She added kindly: 'Such a fine afternoon as it is! It will do you good to take a walk, dearest. You have been cooped up with me for too long.'

Abby was too glad to promote these cheerful plans to raise any objection to Miss Wendover's disposal of her afternoon, which she had meant to have spent in quite another manner. Fanny had been persuaded to join a party of her friends on an expedition to Claverton Down, so Abby presently set forth alone on her two errands. Neither was successful: Godwin's Circulating Library was still unable to supply Miss Wendover with a copy of Mrs Porter's latest novel; and although Mr and Mrs Leavening were expected to arrive that day at York House they had not yet done so, and were scarcely looked for until dinner-time. Abby declined a civil invitation to await their coming in one of the hotel's lounges, began to deliver a verbal message for them, and then thought that Selina would say that she ought to have written a note. She went into the lounge on one side of the hall, and sat down at one of its two writing-tables to perform this duty. There was no one in the room, but just as she was about to seal her brief letter with a wafer found in one of the table's drawers she heard the sounds betokening an arrival, and paused, wondering if it could be the Leavenings. But only one person entered the hotel, a man, as she perceived, catching a glimpse of him through the open doorway. She fixed the wafer, and was writing the direction on the note when she saw, out of the corner of her eye, that he had strolled into the room. She paid no heed, but was startled, the next instant, by hearing someone in the hall command the boots to carry Mr Calverleigh's portmanteaux up to No. 12.

Taken thus by surprise, it was several moments before she was able to decide whether to make herself known to him, or to await a formal introduction. The strict propriety in which she had been reared urged her to adopt the latter course; then she remembered that she was not a young girl any longer, but a guardian-aunt, and one sufficiently advanced in years to be able to accost a strange gentleman without running the risk of being thought shockingly forward. She had wondered how she could contrive, without Fanny's knowledge, to talk privately to Mr Calverleigh, and here, by a veritable stroke of providence, was her opportunity. To flinch before what would certainly be an extremely disagreeable interview would be the act, she told herself, of a pudding-heart. Bracing herself resolutely, she got up from the writing-table, and turned, saying, in a cool, pleasant tone: 'Mr Calverleigh?'

He had picked up a newspaper from the table in the centre of the room, and was glancing through it, but he lowered it, and looked enquiringly across at her. His eyes, which were deep-set and of a light grey made the more striking by the swarthiness of his complexion, held an expression of faint surprise; he said: 'Yes?'

If he was surprised, Abby was wholly taken aback. She had formed no very precise mental picture of him, but nothing she had been told had led her to expect to be confronted with a tall, loose-limbed man, considerably older than she was herself, with harsh features in a deeply lined face, a deplorably sallow skin, and not the smallest air of fashion. He was wearing a coat which fitted too easily across his very broad shoulders for modishness, with buckskins and topboots; his neck-tie was almost negligently arranged; no fobs or seals dangled at his waist; and his shirt-points were not only extremely moderate, but even a little limp.

She was so much astonished that for a full minute she could only stare at him, her brain in a whirl. He had been described to her as a young, handsome town-beau, and he was nothing of the sort. He had also been described, by her brother-in-law, as a loose fish, and that she could far more readily believe: there was a suggestion of devil-may-care about him, and these deeply carven lines in his lean countenance might well (she supposed) betray dissipation. But what there was in him to have captivated Fanny – and Selina too! – she found herself quite unable to imagine. Then, as she continued to stare at him, she saw that a look of amusement had crept into his face, and that a smile was quivering at the corners of his mouth, and she perceived very clearly why Fanny had allowed herself to be fascinated by him. But, even as an answering smile was irresistibly drawn from her, it occurred to her that Selina, even in her sillier moments, would scarcely refer to a man of her own age as *a very pretty-behaved young man,* and she exclaimed, with that impetuosity so frequently deplored by the elder members of her family: 'Oh, I beg your pardon! I mistook – I mean, – I mean – *Are* you Mr Calverleigh?'

'Well, I've never been given any reason to suppose that I'm not!' he replied.

'You *are?* But *surely* – ?' Recollecting herself, Abby broke off, and said, with all the composure at her command: 'I must tell you, sir, that I am Miss Wendover!'

She observed, with satisfaction, that this disclosure exercised a powerful effect upon him. That disturbing smile vanished, and his black brows suddenly snapped together. He ejaculated: 'Miss *who?*'

'Miss Wendover,' she repeated, adding, for his further enlightenment: 'Miss *Abigail* Wendover!'

'Good God!' For a moment, he appeared to be startled, and

then, as his curiously light eyes scanned her, he disconcerted her by saying: 'I like that! It becomes you, too.'

Roused to indignation, Abby, losing sight of the main issue, allowed herself to be lured into retorting: 'Thank you! I am excessively obliged to you! It is an outdated name, commonly used to signify a maidservant! *You* may like it, but I do not!' She added hastily: 'Nor, sir, did I make myself known to you for the purpose of discussing my name!'

'Of course not!' he said, so soothingly that she longed to hit him. 'Do tell me what it is you *do* wish to discuss! I'll oblige you to the best of my power, even though I don't immediately understand why you should wish to discuss anything with me. Forgive me! – I've no social graces! – but have I ever met you before?'

'No,' replied Abby, her lips curling in a contemptuous smile. 'You have not, sir – as well you know! But you will scarcely deny that you are acquainted with another member of my family!'

'Oh, no! I won't deny that!' he assured her. 'Won't you sit down?'

'I, sir,' said Abby, ignoring this invitation, 'am Fanny's aunt!'

'No, are you indeed? You don't look old enough to be anyone's aunt,' he remarked.

This piece of audacity was uttered in the most casual way, as though it had been a commonplace instead of an impertinence. He did not seem to have any idea that he had said anything improper, nor, from his general air of indifference, could she suppose him to have intended a compliment. She began to think that he was a very strange man, and one with whom it was going to be more difficult to deal than she had foreseen. He was obviously fencing with her, and the sooner he was made to realise that such tactics would not answer the better it would be. So she said coldly: 'You must know very well that I am Fanny's aunt.'

'Yes, you've just told me so,' he agreed.

'You knew it as soon as I made made myself known to you!' She checked herself, determined not to lose her temper, and said, as pleasantly as she could: 'Come, Mr Calverleigh! let us be frank! I imagine you also know why I did make myself known to you. You certainly contrived to ingratiate yourself with my sister, but you can hardly have supposed that you would find *all* Fanny's relations so complaisant!'

He was watching her rather intently, but with an expression of enjoyment which she found infuriating. He said: 'No, I couldn't, could I? Still, if your *sister* likes me — !'

'My sister, Mr Calverleigh, was not aware, until I enlightened her, that you are not, as she had supposed, a man of character, but one of — of an unsavoury reputation!' she snapped.

'Well, what an unhandsome thing to have done!' he said reproachfully. 'Doesn't she like me any more?'

Abby now made the discovery that it was possible, at one and the same time, to be furiously angry, and to have the greatest difficulty in suppressing an almost irresistible desire to burst out laughing. After a severe struggle, she managed to say: 'This — this is useless, sir! Let me assure you that you have no hope whatever of gaining the consent of Fanny's guardian to your proposal; and let me also tell you that she will not come into possession of her inheritance until she is five-and-twenty! That, I collect, is something you were not aware of!'

'No,' he admitted. 'I wasn't!'

'Until that date,' Abby continued, 'her fortune is under the sole control of her guardian, and he, I must tell you, will not, under any circumstances, relinquish that control into the hands of her husband one moment before her twenty-fifth birthday, if she marries without his consent and approval. I think it doubtful, even, that he would continue to allow her to receive any part of the income accruing from her fortune. Not a very good bargain, sir, do you think?'

'It seems to be a very bad one. Who, by the way, *is* Fanny's guardian?'

'Her uncle, of course! Surely she must have told you so?' replied Abby impatiently.

'Well, no!' he said, still more apologetically. 'She really had no opportunity to do so!'

'Had no – Mr Calverleigh, are you asking me to believe that you – you embarked on this attempt to recover your own fortune without first discovering what were the exact terms of her father's will? That is coming it very much too strong!'

'Who *was* her father?' he interrupted, regarding her from under suddenly frowning brows. 'You talk of her inheritance – You don't mean to tell me she's *Rowland* Wendover's daughter?'

'Yes – if it should be necessary for me to do so – which I strongly doubt!' said Abby, eyeing him with hostility. 'She is an orphan, and the ward of my brother James.'

'Poor girl!' He studied her appraisingly. 'So you are a sister of Rowland Wendover! You know, I find that very hard to believe.'

'Indeed! It is nevertheless true – though in what way it concerns the point at issue –'

'Oh, it doesn't!' he said, smiling disarmingly at her. 'Now I come to think of it, he had several sisters, hadn't he? I expect you must be the youngest of them. He was older than I was, and you are a mere child. By the by, when did he die?'

This question, put to her in a tone of casual interest, seemed to her to be so inapposite that the suspicion that he was drunk occurred to her. He showed none of the recognisable signs of inebriation, but she knew that her experience was limited. If he was not drunk, the only other explanation of his quite fantastic behaviour must be that he was slightly deranged. Unless he was trying, in some obscure fashion, to set her at a disadvantage? She found it impossible to understand what he hoped to gain by his extraordinary tactics, but the look of amusement on his face made her feel, uneasily, that he had an end in view: probably an unscrupulous end. Watching him closely, she said: 'My brother died twelve years ago. I *am* his youngest sister, but you are mistaken in thinking me *a mere child*. I daresay you wish I were!'

'No, I don't. Why should I?' he asked, mildly surprised.

'Because you might find it easier to flummery me!'

'But I don't want to flummery you!'

'Just as well!' she retorted. 'You wouldn't succeed! I am more than eight-and-twenty, Mr Calverleigh!'

'Well, that seems like a child to me. How much more?'

She was by now extremely angry, but for the second time she was obliged to choke back an involuntary giggle. She said unsteadily: 'Talking to you is like – like talking to an eel!'

'No, is it? I've never tried to talk to an eel. Isn't it a waste of time?'

She choked. 'Not such a waste of time as talking to you!'

'You're surely not going to tell me that eels find you more entertaining than I do?' he said incredulously.

That was rather too much for her: she did giggle, and was furious with herself for having done so.

'That's better!' he said approvingly.

She recovered herself. 'Let me ask you one question, sir! If *I* seem like a child to you, in what light do you regard a girl of seventeen?'

'Oh, as a member of the infantry!'

This careless reply made her gasp. Her eyes flashed; she demanded: 'How old do you think my niece is, pray?'

'Never having met your niece, I haven't a notion!'

'Never having – But – Good God, then you cannot be Mr Calverleigh! But when I asked you, you said you *were*!'

'Of course I did! Tell me, is there a nephew of mine at large in Bath?'

'*Nephew?* A – a Mr Stacy Calverleigh!'

'Yes, that's it. I'm his Uncle Miles.'

'*Oh!*' she uttered, staring at him in the liveliest astonishment. 'You can't mean that you are the one who – ' She broke off in some confusion, and added hurriedly: 'The one who went to India!'

He laughed. 'Yes, I'm the black sheep of the family!'

She blushed, but said: 'I wasn't going to say that!'

'Weren't you? Why not? You won't hurt my feelings!'

'I wouldn't be so uncivil! And if it comes to *black sheep* – !'

'Once you become entangled with Calverleighs, it's bound to,' he said. 'We came to England with the Conqueror, you know. It's my belief that our ancestor was one of the thatchgallows

43

he brought with him. There were any number of 'em in his train.'

A delicious gurgle of laughter broke from her. 'Oh, no, were there? I didn't know – but I never heard anyone claim a *thatch-gallows* for his ancestor!'

'No, I don't suppose you did. *I* never met any of us *came over-with-the-Conquest* fellows who wouldn't hold to it, buckle and thong, that his ancestor was a Norman baron. Just as likely to have been one of the scaff and raff of Europe. I wish you will sit down!'

At this point, Abby knew that it behoved her to take polite leave of Mr Miles Calverleigh. She sat down, offering her conscience a sop in the form of a hope that Mr Miles Calverleigh might be of assistance to her in circumventing the designs of his nephew. She chose one of the straight-backed chairs ranged round the table, and watched him dispose his long limbs in another, at right-angles to her. His attitude was as negligent as his conversation, for he crossed his legs, dug one hand into his pocket, and laid his other arm along the table. He seemed to have very little regard for the conventions governing polite conduct, and Abby, in whom the conventions were deeply inculcated, was far less shocked than amused. Her expressive eyes twinkled engagingly as she said: 'May I speak frankly to you, sir? About your nephew? I do not wish to offend you, but I fancy he is more the black sheep of your family than you are!'

'Oh, I shouldn't think so at all!' he responded. 'He sounds more like a cawker to me, if he's making up to a girl who won't come into her inheritance for eight years!'

'I have every reason to think,' said Abby frostily, 'that my niece is not the first heiress he has – as you phrase it! – *made up to*!'

'Well, if he's hanging out for a rich wife I don't suppose she is.'

Her fingers tightened round the handle of her parasol. 'Mr Calverleigh, I have not yet met your nephew. He came to Bath while I was away, visiting my sisters, and was called to London, on matters of business, I am told, before I returned. My hope is

44

that he has realised that his – his suit is hopeless, and won't come back, but *your* presence in Bath quite dashes that hope, since I collect you must have come here in the expectation of seeing him.'

'Oh, no!' he assured her. 'Whatever put that notion into your head?'

She blinked. 'I assumed – well, *naturally* I assumed that you had come in search of him! I mean, – so close a relative, and, I understand, the only member of your immediate family still living – ?'

'What of it? You know, fiddle-faddle about families and close relatives is so much humbug! I haven't seen that nephew of mine since he was a grubby brat – if I saw him then, which very likely I didn't, for I never went near my brother if I could avoid it – so why the devil should I want to see him now?'

She could think of no answer to this, but it seemed to her so ruthless that she wondered, remembering that he had been packed off to India in disgrace, whether it arose from feelings of rancour. However, his next words, which were uttered in a thoughtful tone, and quite dispassionately, lent no colour to her suspicion. He said: 'You know, there's a great deal of balderdash talked about family affection. How much affection have you for *your* family?'

Such a question had never before been put to her; and, since it was one of the accepted tenets that one loved and respected one's parents, and (at the least) loved one's brothers and sisters, she had not previously considered the matter. But just as she was about to assure this outrageous person that she was devoted to every member of her family the unendearing images rose before her mind's eye of her father, of her two brothers, and even of her sister Jane. She said, a little ruefully: 'For my mother, and for two of my sisters, a great deal.'

'Ah, I never had any sisters, and my mother died when I was a schoolboy.'

'You are much to be pitied,' she said.

'Oh, no, I don't think so!' he replied. 'I don't like obligations.'

45

The disarming smile crept back into his eyes, as they rested on her face. 'My family disowned me more than twenty years ago, you know!'

'Yes, I did know. That is – I have been told that they did,' she said. She added, with the flicker of a shy smile: 'I think it was a *dreadful* thing to have done, and – and perhaps is the reason why you don't wish to meet your nephew?'

That made him laugh. 'Good God, no! What concern was it of his?'

'I only thought – wondered – since it was his father –'

'No, no, that's fustian!' he expostulated. 'You can't turn me into an object for compassion! I didn't like my brother Humphrey, and I didn't like my father either, but I don't bear them any grudge for shipping me off to India. In fact, it was the best thing they could do, and it suited me very well.'

'Compassion certainly seems to be wasted on you, sir!' she said tartly.

'Yes, of course it is. Besides, I like you, and I shan't if you pity me.'

She was goaded into swift retort. 'Well, that wouldn't trouble me!'

'That's the barber!' he said appreciatively. 'Tell me more about this niece of yours! I collect her mother's dead too?'

'Her mother died when she was two years old, sir.'

There was an inscrutable expression in his face, and although he kept his eyes on hers the fancy struck her that he was looking at something a long way beyond her. Then, with a sudden, wry smile, he seemed to bring her into focus again, and asked abruptly: 'Rowland did marry her, didn't he? – Celia Morval?'

'Why, yes! Were you acquainted with her?'

He did not answer this, but said: 'And my nephew is dangling after her daughter?'

'I am afraid it is more serious than that. I haven't met him, but he seems to be a young man of considerable address. He has succeeded in – in fixing his interest with her – well, to speak

46

roundly, sir, she imagines herself to be violently in love with him. You may think that no great matter, as young as she is, but the thing is that she is a high-spirited girl, and her character is – is determined. She has been virtually in my charge – and that of my eldest sister – from her childhood. Perhaps she has been too much indulged – granted too much independence. I was never used to think so – you see, I was myself – we all were! – brought up in such subjection that I vowed I wouldn't allow Fanny to be crushed as we were. I even thought – knowing how much I was used to long for the courage to rebel, and how bitterly I resented my father's tyranny – that if I encouraged her to be independent, to look on me as a friend rather than as an aunt, she wouldn't *feel* rebellious – would allow herself to be guided by me.'

'And she doesn't?' he asked sympathetically.

'Not in this instance. But until your nephew bewitched her she did! She's the dearest girl, but I own that she can be headstrong, and too impetuous.' She paused, and then said ruefully: 'Once she makes up her mind it is very hard to turn her from it. She – she isn't a *lukewarm* girl! It is one of the things I particularly like in her, but it is quite disastrous in this instance!'

'Infatuated, is she? I daresay she'll recover,' he said, a suggestion of boredom in his voice.

'Undoubtedly! My fear is that she may do so too late! Mr Calverleigh, if your nephew were the most eligible bachelor in the country I should be opposed to the match! She is by far too young to be thinking of marriage. As it is, I need not, I fancy, scruple to tell you that he is *not* eligible! He bears a most shocking reputation, and, apart from all else, I believe him to be a fortune hunter!'

'Very likely, I should think,' he nodded.

This cool rejoinder made it necessary for her to keep a firm hand on the rein of her temper. She said, in a dry voice: '*You* may regard that with complaisance, sir, but I do not!'

'No, I don't suppose you do,' he agreed amiably.

She flushed. 'And – which is of even more importance! – nor does my brother!'

This seemed to revive his interest. A gleam came into his eyes. 'What, does he know of this?'

'Yes, sir, he does know of it, and nothing, I assure you, could exceed his dislike of such a connection! It was he who told me what had been happening here, in Bath, during my absence, having himself learnt of it through someone who chances to be a close friend of his wife. He posted up to London from Bedfordshire to apprise me of it. Pray do not think I exaggerate when I say that I have seldom seen him more profoundly shocked, or – or heard him express himself with so much violence! Believe me, sir, *nothing* could prevail upon him to give his consent to your nephew's proposal!'

'I do – implicitly!' he replied, the light of unholy amusement in his eyes. 'What's more, I'd give a monkey to have seen him! Lord, how funny!'

'It was not in the least funny! And –'

'Yes, it was, but never mind that! Why should you fall into a fuss? If the virtuous James forbids the banns, and if my nephew is a fortune-hunter, depend upon it he will cry off!' He saw the doubt in her face, and said: 'You don't think so?'

She hesitated. 'I don't know. It may be that he hopes to win James over –'

'Well, he won't do that!'

'No. Unless – Mr Calverleigh, I have reason – some reason – to fear that he might persuade her into an *elopement*! Thinking that once the knot was tied my brother would be obliged – ' She stopped as he broke into a shout of laughter, and said indignantly: 'It may seem *funny* to you, but I promise you –'

'It does! What a subject for a roaring farce! History repeats itself – with a vengeance!'

Wholly bewildered, she demanded: 'What do you mean? What can you *possibly* mean?'

'My pretty innocent,' he said, in a voice of kindess spiced with mockery, 'did no one ever tell you that *I* am the man who ran off with your Fanny's mother?'

48

Four

*I*t was a full minute before Abby could collect her startled wits enough to enable her to speak, and when she did speak it was not entirely felicitously. She exclaimed: 'Then I was right! And *you* are it!'

With every appearance of enjoyment, he instantly replied: 'Until I know what *it* signifies, I reserve my defence.'

'The skeleton in the cupboard! Only I told Selina it would prove to be no more than the skeleton of a mouse!'

'You lied, then! The skeleton of a black sheep if you wish, but *not* that of a mouse – even a black mouse!'

Her voice quivered on the edge of laughter. 'No, indeed! How – how *very* dreadful! But how – when – Oh, do, pray, *tell* me!'

'You shock me Miss Abigail Wendover! – you know, I *do* like that name! – Who am I to divulge the secret which has been so carefully guarded?'

'The skeleton, of course!'

'But skeletons don't talk!' he pointed out.

Preoccupied with her own thoughts, she paid no heed to this, but said suddenly: '*That* was why James flew into such a stew! Now, isn't it *like* James not to have told me the truth?'

'Exactly like him!'

'But why didn't George – No, you may depend upon it that he didn't know either! Because Mary doesn't, though she has always suspected, as I did, that there was something about Celia which was being kept secret. I wonder if Selina knew? Not the whole, of course, for if she had she would never have encouraged your nephew, would she?'

'Oh, no! *She* wouldn't, and very likely *Mary* wouldn't either, but *George,* I feel, is another matter. Do enlighten me! Who *are* these people?'

She blinked. 'Who – ? Oh, I beg your pardon! I have been running on in the stupidest way! – talking to myself! Selina is my eldest sister: we live together, in Sydney Place; Mary is my *next* sister: next in age, I mean; and George Brede is her husband. Never mind that! *When* did you run off with Celia?'

'Oh, when she became engaged to be married to Rowland!' he answered, very much as if this were a matter of course.

'Good God! Do you mean that you *abducted* her?' she gasped.

'No, I don't recall that I ever abducted anyone,' he said, giving the matter his consideration. 'In fact, I'm sure of it. An unwilling bride would be the very devil, you know.'

'Well, that's precisely what I've always thought!' she exclaimed, pleased to find her opinion shared. 'Whenever I've read about it, in some trashy romance, I mean. Of course, if the heroine is a rich heiress the case is understandable, but – *Oh!*' Consternation sounded in her voice; painfully mortified, she stammered: 'I beg your pardon! I can't think what made me say –'

'Not at all!' he assured her kindly. 'A very natural observation!'

'Do you mean to tell me that that was why you – you ran off with Celia?' she asked incredulously.

'Well, no! But you must remember that I was very young in those days: halflings seldom have an eye to the main chance. It was All for Love, or the World Well Lost. We fell passionately in love – or, at any hand, we thought we did. You know, this is a damned sickly story! Let us talk of something else!'

'I think it is a sad story. But I don't perfectly understand how it was that Celia became engaged to my brother if she was in love with you?'

'Don't you? You should! Were you acquainted with Morval?'

She shook her head. 'I might perhaps have seen him, but I don't recall: I was only a child at that time. I know he was one of my father's closest friends.'

'Then you ought to be able to form a pretty accurate picture of him. They were as like as fourpence to a groat. The match was made between them. Celia was forbidden ever again to favour me with as much as a common bow in passing – mind you, I wasn't at all eligible – and ordered to accept Rowland's offer.'

'I understand her submission to the first order, but not to the second! I too submitted in a like case. It is not an easy matter to marry against the will of one's parents. But, with one's affections engaged, to accept another man's offer, merely because one's father wished it, is something I do *not* understand! If Celia was ready to elope with you she must have been a girl of spirit, too, and not in the least the meek, biddable creature we always thought her!'

'Oh, no, she hadn't an ounce of steel in her!' he said coolly. 'She was romantical, though, and certainly biddable: one of those pretty, clinging females who invariably yield to a stronger will! I hadn't the wit to perceive it, until the sticking point was reached, and she knuckled down in a flood of tears. And a very good thing she did,' he added. 'We might have carried it, if she had stood buff, and I should have been regularly in for it. I didn't think so at the time, of course, but I was never nearer to dishing myself. How did she deal with Rowland?'

He had stripped the affair of all its romantic pathos, but Abby could not help wondering whether his apparent unconcern hid a bruised heart. She answered his casual question reticently: 'I don't know. I wasn't of an age to know. She was always rather quiet, but she never appeared to be unhappy. I see now that she can't have *loved* Rowland, but I do know that she held him in the greatest respect. I mean, she depended wholly on his judgment, and was for ever saying *Rowland says,* as though that was a clincher to every argument!'

The slightly acid note on which she ended made him laugh. 'An opinion not shared by Abigail Wendover, I apprehend!'

'No!' she returned, her eyes kindling reminiscently. 'It was *not* shared by me! Rowland was a – ' She stopped, resolutely shutting her lips together.

'Rowland,' said Miles Calverleigh, stepping obligingly into the gap, 'was a pompous lobcock!'

'Yes!' said Abby, momentarily forgetting herself. 'That is exactly what he was! The most consequential, pot-sure –' Again she broke off short, adding hastily: 'Never mind that!'

'I don't – and it seems that Celia didn't either. No, she wouldn't, of course. You know, the more I think of it the more I feel that they must have been made for each other! Well, I'm glad to know she didn't fill into a green and yellow melancholy.'

Abby's brow was wrinkled. 'Yes, but – Did Rowland *know* of – of the elopement?'

'Oh, lord, yes!' He met her astonished look with a smile of pure derision. 'Come, come, ma'am! Where have your wits gone begging? Celia was an *heiress!* Consider, too, the scandal that would have attended a rupture of the engagement! People must have *talked*, and nothing could have been more obnoxious to a Wendover or a Morval! The affair had to be hushed up, and you must own that a very neat thing they made of it, between the four of them!'

'*Four* of them?'

'That's it: your father, Celia's father, my father, and Rowland,' he explained.

'Respectability!' she ejaculated bitterly. 'Oh, how much I have detested that – that god of my father's idolatry! Did *your* father worship at the same altar?'

'No, what he worshipped was good ton. I wasn't good ton at all, so he was glad of the chance to be rid of me, and I can't say I blame him. I was very expensive, you know.'

'From what I have heard, your brother was even more expensive!' she said. 'I wonder he didn't get rid of *him!*'

He smiled. 'Ah, but Humphrey was his heir! Besides, *his* debts were those of honour: quite unexceptionable, particularly when contracted in clubs of high fashion! He was used to move in the first circles, too, which I – er – didn't!'

'No doubt he would have taken no exception to *his* son's ruinous career!'

'Oh, that doesn't follow at all! Being badly under the hatches himself, he would probably have taken the most violent exception to it. However, he died before Stacy came of age, so we shall never know. Judging by my own experience, Stacy might have got himself into Dun territory at Oxford, but he could scarcely have gone to pigs-and-whistles – unless, of course, he was a regular out-and-outer, which, from what you've told me, he don't seem to be.'

'Were you up at Oxford?' she asked curiously.

'No, I was *down* from Oxford – *sent* down!' he replied affably.

She choked, but managed to say, after a brief struggle: 'What – whatever may have been your youthful f-follies, sir, I must believe that you have outgrown them, and – and I *cannot* think that you would wish your nephew – the head of your house! – to – to retrieve his fortunes by seducing a girl – oh, a *child*! – into a clandestine marriage!'

'But if the poor fellow is rolled-up what else can he do?' he asked.

She said through gritted teeth: 'For all I care, he may do anything he chooses, *except* marry my niece! *Surely – surely* you must perceive how – how *wrong* that would be!'.

'I must say, it seems mutton-headed to me,' he agreed. 'He'd do better to fix his interest with a girl who is already in possession of her fortune.'

'Good God, is that *all* you have to say?' she cried.

'Well, what do you expect me to say?' he asked.

'Say! I – I expect you to *do* something!'

'Do what?'

'Put an end to this affair!'

'How?'

'Speak to your nephew – tell him – oh, I don't know! You must be able to think of something!'

'Well, I'm not. Besides, why should I?'

'Because it is your duty! Because he is your nephew!'

'You'll have to think of some better reasons than those. I haven't any duty to Stacy, and I don't suppose I should do it if I had.'

'Mr Calverleigh, you *cannot* wish your nephew to sink himself so utterly below reproach!'

'Wish? I haven't any feelings in the matter at all. In fact, I don't care a straw what he does. So if you are looking to me to rake him down, don't!'

'Oh, you are impossible!' she cried, starting up.

'I daresay, but I'm damned if I'll preach morality to oblige you! A nice cake I should make of myself! I like the way your eyes sparkle when you're angry.'

They positively flashed at this. One fulminating glance she cast at him before turning sharply away, and walking out of the room.

The Leavenings were forgotten; it was not until she had reached Laura Place that she remembered that the note she had written had been left on the writing-table. She could only hope that it would be found, and delivered to Mrs Leavening. By this time her seething anger had abated a little, and she was able to review her encounter with Mr Miles Calverleigh in a more moderate spirit. Slackening her pace, she walked on, into Great Pulteney Street, so deeply preoccupied that she neither acknowledged, nor even saw, the salutation directed towards her from the other side of the street by her clerical admirer, Canon Pinfold: an aberration which caused the Very Reverend gentleman to subject his conscience to a severe search, in an effort to discover in what way he could have offended her.

It was not long before Miss Abigail Wendover, no self-deceiver, realised that she was strangely attracted to the abominable Mr Miles Calverleigh. Out of his own careless mouth he had convicted himself of being a person totally unworthy of respect, but when she recalled the things he had said to her a most reprehensible bubble of laughter rose within her. A very little reflection, however, was enough to bring a blush to her cheeks. It was no laughing matter, and strangely depraved she must be to have felt the smallest inclination to laugh at the cool recital of his misdeeds. She knew that he had been expelled from Eton; he had told her in the most unconcerned way, that he had been sent down from Oxford; and it now appeared that he had crowned his iniquities by attempting to elope with a girl out of the schoolroom. Curiously enough she was less shocked by this escapade than by the rest: he could hardly, she supposed, have been much older himself, and it did seem that he had been desperately in love. It was bad, of course, but what was worse was his unblushing avowal of his sins. He had not mentioned them in a boastful spirit, but as though they had been commonplaces, which he regarded with amusement – even with ribaldry, she thought, once more obliged to suppress a reminiscent smile. When she remembered his callous refusal to intervene to save Fanny from his nephew's designs, however, she had no desire to laugh: she felt it to be unpardonable. He disclaimed any affection for Stacy; and, although he was certainly not in love with the memory of Celia, it was surely reasonable to suppose that enough tenderness remained with him to make him not wholly indifferent to her daughter's fate.

Recalling, exactly, the closing stage of her interview with him, contempt and indignation rose in Abby's breast, and she reached Sydney Place in a very uncomfortable state of mind: uncertain whether she most loathed Mr Miles Calverleigh, for his detestable cynicism, or herself, for succumbing to his wicked charm. Quite carried away, she uttered, aloud: 'No better than a wet-goose!' a savage self-apostrophe which considerably discomposed Mitton, opening the door at that inopportune moment.

Learning from him that Miss Butterbank was with her sister, she retired to her own room; and by the time she emerged from it she had in some measure recovered her accustomed equanimity, and had decided (on undefined grounds) that it would be wisest not to yield to her first impulse, which had been to pour the story of the morning's encounter into Selina's ears. She said nothing about it, merely assuring Selina that she had left a note at York House, to be delivered to Mrs Leavening upon her arrival.

After all, one of the servants was bound to find it, and would no doubt give it to Mrs Leavening.

Fanny, returning from her expedition in time for dinner, seemed also to have recovered her equanimity: a circumstance which would have afforded Abby gratification had Fanny not artlessly disclosed that Miss Julia Weaverham, included in the equestrian party, had told her all about the very civil letter her mama had received from Mr Stacy Calverleigh, heralding his return to Bath at the end of the week. 'And when you meet him you will see for yourself – you'll understand why – *won't* she, Aunt Selina?'

Thrown into disorder by the glowing, appealing look cast towards her, Selina lost herself in a tangle of disjointed phrases, from which she was rescued by her sister, who said calmly that she would be happy to make Mr Calverleigh's acquaintance, and added that Selina must not forget to send him a card of invitation to her evening-party. This, while it made Fanny bestow on her a shy, grateful smile which made her feel that she was a traitress, had the desired effect of luring Selina into an exhaustive discussion of the persons to be invited to meet the Leavenings, and of the arrangements for their entertainment which it would be necessary to make. Nothing more was said about Stacy Calverleigh, but Abby went to bed, later, in a mood of unusual depression, and spent a large part of the night mulling over a problem which grew greater and more insoluble as the minutes ticked past.

She awoke not much refreshed, but, as she sat before her dressing-table, it occurred to her that there was one person who might be able to offer her valuable advice. Mrs Grayshott, a woman of superior sense, not only held Fanny in affection but was the mother of a pretty daughter, and might be supposed to know better than a mere spinster-aunt how best to handle a girl in the throes of her first love-affair. At all events, it could do no harm to consult her, for Abby guessed her to be a safe repository for confidences, and felt herself to be in need of such a repository.

So she presently told Fanny that she would escort her to Queen's Square, in Mrs Grimston's stead, that morning, and occupy herself, while Fanny wrestled with Italian grammar under the aegis of Miss Timble, with some necessary shopping. After which, she said, she would pay Mrs Grayshott a visit, and remain with her until Fanny and Miss Lavinia Grayshott were released from the Italian class, and could, with perfect propriety, escort each other to Edgar Buildings.

Fanny, greeting this suggestion with acclaim, said: 'Oh, famous! Then I can purchase a new pair of silk stockings, in Milsom Street! I wanted to do so when you were away, but my aunt was feeling too poorly to go shopping, and nothing will prevail upon me ever again to go with Nurse! Well, you know what she is, Abby! If she doesn't say that the very thing one wants isn't *suitable* – as though one were still in the schoolroom! – she *sinks* one with embarrassment by saying that it is by far too dear, and she knows where it can be bought at half the price!'

Edgar Buildings, in George Street, were situated just within the fashionable part of the town, which extended northward from the top of Milsom Street to the exclusive heights of Upper Camden Place. Failing to discover an eligible lodging for his sister in the equally exclusive district which lay across the bridge and included Laura Place, Great Pultney Street, and Sydney Place, Mr Leonard Balking would have chosen, had he consulted only his own pleasure, to have set Mrs Grayshott up in style there, even hiring an imposing house for her accommodation; but he had, besides his deep affection for her, a great deal of commonsense, and he realised that a large house would be a burden to her, and the long climb up to Camden Place not at all the thing for an invalid. So he had established her in Edgar Buildings, whence she could visit all the best shops, and even, without exhaustion, walk to the Pump Room, or to the Private Bath, in Stall Street. After condemning out of hand a set of apartments which he stigmatised as poky, he was fortunate enough to discover a first-floor suite which he thought tolerable, and everyone else described as handsome. Nearly all the lodgings in Bath were let in suites, and in the best part of the town these generally consisted of some four or five rooms, persons who wished for only two rooms being obliged either to look for them in an unfashionable quarter, or to endure all the disadvantages of one of Bath's numerous boarding-houses.

Mrs Grayshott's lodging was one of the most commodious sets of rooms to be had, providing her with bedrooms for herself, her daughter, her maid, and any chance visitor; and it had, besides a spacious drawing-room, a small dining-parlour. Mrs Grayshott, urgently assuring her brother that she and Lavinia could be perfectly comfortable in humbler lodgings, was silenced by his saying simply: 'You hurt me very much when you talk in that strain, my dear. You and your children are all the family I have, and surely I may be allowed to stand godfather to you?'

So Mrs Grayshott, whose circumstances were straitened, allowed herself to be installed in lodgings which were the envy of many of her acquaintances; and, since she made no secret of the fact that she owed her apparent affluence to the generosity of her brother, only such ill-natured persons as Mrs Ruscombe ever said that it seemed an odd thing that an impecunious widow should be able to live as high as a coach-horse.

Miss Abigail Wendover, admitted into the building by the very superior housekeeper, was informed that Mrs Grayshott was at home, and was about to mount the stairs when the housekeeper added, with an air of vicarious triumph: 'And Mr Oliver Grayshott, too, ma'am! Yesterday he arrived! I'm sure you could have knocked me down with a feather, and as for Madam it's a wonder she didn't suffer a spasm! But there! they say joy never kills!'

This news caused Abby to pause, feeling that her visit was ill-timed; but just as she was about to go away she heard her name

58

spoken, and looked up to see that Mrs Grayshott was standing on the half-landing, smiling a welcome.

'Come up, Abby!' she said. 'I saw you from the window, and guessed you wouldn't stay when you knew what had happened! Oh, my dear, such a wonderful, wonderful surprise as it was! I can still hardly believe that I have him with me again!'

'No indeed!' Abby responded warmly. 'I am so glad — so happy for you! But you can't want to receive tiresome morning-visitors!'

'You could never be that! I have one, in the person of Mrs Ancrum, but I hope she may soon take her leave of us, for I most particularly want you to meet Oliver. And also to tell you of a very surprising circumstance — But that must wait until we are rid of Mrs Ancrum!'

She held out a coaxing hand as she spoke but even as Abby set her foot on the stair two more morning-visitors arrived: Lady Weaverham, accompanied by Miss Sophia Weaverham.

Escape was impossible; Mrs Grayshott had nothing to do but to beg the new arrivals to come upstairs, which they did, Lady Weaverham, an immensely stout individual, beaming good-nature as she heaved herself up the half-flight, and assuring her hostess, rather breathlessly, that she would not stay above a minute, but that upon hearing the news of the safe return of Mrs Grayshott's son she had felt that the least she could do was to call on her, just to offer her felicitations. 'And here, I see, is Miss Wendover, come on the same errand, I make no doubt!' she said, pausing to recover her breath, and holding out a hand tightly enclosed in lavender kid. 'Well, my dear, how do you do? Not that I need ask, for I can see that you're in high bloom, and if you didn't buy that delicious hat in London you may call me a chucklehead! Which Sir Joshua tells me I am, but I am more than seven, I promise you, and I can recognise town-bronze when I see it!' She then surveyed Mrs Grayshott out of her little, twinkling eyes, and said: 'And quite in your best looks *you* are, ma'am, which is not to be wondered at! So should I be, if my Jack had been restored to me when I was on the very brink of ordering my mourning-clothes! Now, tell me – how *is* he?'

'Not in such good point as I could wish, ma'am,' Mrs Grayshott replied, helping her to mount the rest of the stairs, 'but you will see how quickly he will recover! You will think, however, that I am presenting a skeleton to you, I daresay!'

If Mr Oliver Grayshott was not exactly a skeleton, he was certainly a very thin young man; and as he pulled himself up from his chair to greet the visitors Abby saw that he was also very tall. The cast of his countenance was aquiline; he had a keen pair of eyes, a mobile mouth, and a look of humour underlying the natural gravity of his expression. She thought, as she presently shook hands with him, that he looked to be older than his two-and-twenty years, but perhaps his disastrous sojourn in India might account for his hollow cheeks, and the tiny lines at the corners of his eyes. His manners were assured, but held a little of the diffidence natural to a boy of strict upbringing. He responded to Lady Weaverham's flood of questions and exclamations with the courtesy of an experienced man of the world, but betrayed his youth in the quick flush, and stammered disclaimer, with which he repulsed her entreaty to him to lie down upon the sofa.

Thinking that one voluble matron was enough for an invalid, Abby made it her business to engage Mrs Ancrum, almost as overpowering a visitor as Lady Weaverham, in trifling conversation. She was listening, with an air of spurious interest, to an account of the complications which had attended the birth of Mrs Ancrum's first grandchild, confided to her in an earnest under-voice, when the door opened, and Mr Calverleigh was announced.

Startled, she looked quickly over her shoulder, thinking for an instant that she must have misheard the servant. But she had not: standing on the threshold was Mr Miles Calverleigh, as carelessly dressed as when he had arrived at York House on the previous day, and entirely at his ease. His eyes, glancing round the room, rested for a moment on her face, and she thought that they narrowed in the suspicion of a smile, but he gave no other sign of recognition. Mrs Grayshott and Oliver had both risen, Oliver ejaculating: 'Sir!' in a tone of gratification, and Mrs Grayshott moving forward with both hands held out in a gesture of impulsive welcome. 'Mr Calverleigh, how kind of you!' she exclaimed. 'You grant me the opportunity to repair yesterday's omission!'

'No, do I?' he said. 'What was that?'

She smiled. 'You must know very well that I was too much overpowered to be able to find words with which to express my gratitude!'

'What, for dumping that young spider-shanks on your doorstep? I didn't expect to be thanked for *that*!'

She laughed. 'Didn't you? Well, I won't embarrass you by telling you how *deeply* grateful I am! I'll make you known to my friends instead! Lady Weaverham, you must allow me to introduce Mr Calverleigh to you – Mr *Miles* Calverleigh!' She waited, while he bowed with casual grace to her ladyship, and her eyes met Abby's for a pregnant moment, before she continued her presentation. She ended it by saying: 'I must tell you that Mr Calverleigh is our good angel! But for his exceeding kindness I shouldn't have had my *young spider-shanks* restored to me yesterday – or even perhaps, at all!'

'Very true, Mama,' intervened her son, 'but you are putting him to the blush! Take care he doesn't cut his stick!'

'Not at all!' Mr Calverleigh responded. 'Never have I won more gratitude with less effort! Continue, ma'am!' As he spoke, he thrust Oliver back into his chair, effectually bringing Mrs Grayshott's encomiums to an end by sitting down beside Oliver, and asking him if he felt any the worse for yesterday's journey. Oliver had barely time to assure him that he felt as fresh as a nosegay before Lady Weaverham claimed his attention, telling him how delighted she was to make his acquaintance, and how much she liked his nephew. 'Such a very amiable young man, and of the *first* stare! I am sure he has won all our hearts!'

'No, has he indeed?' he replied, with a smile as bland as her own. '*All* of them, ma'am?'

To all outward appearances blind to the quizzical gleam in Mr Calverleigh's eyes as they fleetingly met her own, Abby seethed with indignation. Only the recollection that she had appointed Fanny to join her in Edgar Buildings prevented her from following the example set by Mrs Ancrum, who rose at this moment to take her leave. It was evident, from what Mrs Grayshott had said, that he must have accompanied Oliver home from Calcutta; and equally evident that he had thereby conquered the widow's grateful heart. Mrs Grayshott had called him a guardian angel, which would have made Abby laugh if it had not instead made her so cross. He might have been carelessly kind to Oliver, but he was far from being an angel; and it would have given Abby much pleasure to have told Mrs Grayshott how mistaken she was. But detestable though he was – and never more so than at this moment, when he was all too obviously enjoying her discomfiture – this thought was a mere wistful dream. There could be no divulging the disreputable nature of his past history without running into danger, for once it became known, or even suspected, that he was what Mr George Brede termed a loose fish there was no knowing how much the scandal mongers might discover. Besides, it would be a shabby thing to do: talebearers were odious; and one had to remember that he had paid for his youthful misdeeds by twenty years of exile. It might well be, Abby thought, rather doubtfully, that he had reformed his way of life.

Mrs Grayshott, coming back into the room from having escorted Mrs Ancrum to the head of the stairs, sat down beside Abby, saying softly: 'I had meant to have told you. I could see you were taken quite by surprise.'

'Yes, but it is of no consequence,' Abby assured her.

Mrs Grayshott looked as if she would have said more, but her attention was claimed by Lady Weaverham, and no further opportunity for private conversation offered itself, the arrival, a few minutes later, of the daughter of the house, accompanied by Miss Fanny Wendover, creating a lively diversion.

They came in, still sparkling with laughter at some

undisclosed joke, and a very charming picture they made: Lavinia, a pretty brunette, with innocent brown eyes, and a shy smile, providing Fanny with an excellent foil. Divinely fair, her beautiful features framed by a Villager straw hat with ribbons as blue as her eyes, Fanny made an instant hit with one at least of the assembled company: young Mr Grayshott, rising to his feet, stood gazing at her, apparently spellbound, until recalled from this trance by his mother, when he gave a little start, flushed darkly, and came forward to shake hands with Fanny.

Abby observed this without surprise: it was seldom that Fanny failed to rouse admiration, and she was looking particularly becoming today. Instinctively, Abby glanced at Mr Calverleigh, wondering how he was affected by the girl's resemblance to her mother, which was strong enough, she thought, to make him feel a reminiscent pang. If it did, he gave no sign of it. He was critically surveying Fanny; and when Mrs Grayshott made him known to her he caused Abby's heart to miss a beat by saying, as he took Fanny's hand: 'How do you do? So you are Celia Morval's daughter! I'm delighted to make your acquaintance: I was used to know your mother very well.'

Five

For one awful moment Abby felt sick with dread of what he might say next. Then, just as she caught his eyes, a desperate appeal in her own, she realised that he was merely amusing himself at her expense, and was mischievously enjoying her discomfiture. Fright was succeeded by wrath, but not wholehearted wrath: there was apology as well as mockery in the smile directed at her over Fanny's head, and a disarming suggestion of fellowship, as though Mr Miles Calverleigh believed that in Miss Abigail Wendover he had discovered a kindred spirit.

Fanny, looking up, in her unaffected way, into his face, exclaimed: 'Oh, did you know my mother, sir? I never did – that is to say, I can't remember that I did!' She hesitated, and then asked shyly: 'Are you Mr Stacy Calverleigh's uncle? He is a particular friend of mine!'

If anything, thought Abby, could convince Miles Calverleigh that Fanny was a lamb to be guarded from stray wolves, the artlessness of this remark must have done so. She hoped, but could not be sure. His expression was that of a man listening with slightly bored indulgence to a child's prattle. He said: 'Then you will be able to introduce him to me, won't you?'

It was evident, from the look of surprise in Fanny's eyes, that Mr Stacy Calverleigh had told her nothing about his reprobate uncle: an omission for which, decided Abby, submitting the matter to dispassionate consideration, he could scarcely be blamed. Fanny said, on the edge of laughter: 'Oh – ! You are joking me, aren't you? Did I say something gooseish? Of course you must know Stacy much better than I do!'

'On the contrary! I don't know him at all – shouldn't recognise him if he walked into the room at this moment! When I left England he must have been in leading-strings.'

'Oh, *I see!*' said Fanny, her puzzled brow clearing.

'Well, I'll venture to say that you won't be disappointed in him!' said Lady Weaverham. 'Though I won't say you may not mistake him for a Bond Street Spark, for I did so myself, until I found he was no such thing. He's not above being pleased, and, what is more, his head hasn't been turned, which it might well have been for the caps that have been set at him in Bath!' She added, as Fanny blushed scarlet, and moved away from Mr Calverleigh: 'No, no, my dear, I don't mean *you!* The boot is quite on the other leg! Not a bit of heed will he pay to the other girls, and I'm sure I'm not surprised!' A fat chuckle shook her massive bosom; she completed Fanny's discomfiture by saying: 'Many's the time Sir Joshua has said to me that you bear the palm, my dear – not that he had any need to, because well do I know it!'

At this point, Oliver won Abby's approval by withdrawing Fanny a little away from the group, under pretext of pointing something out to her in the street. They sat down together, and were soon joined by Lavinia and Miss Sophia Weaverham, all four chatting happily until the party was broken up by Lady Weaverham, who heaved herself up from her chair, saying that she and Sophy must be off, or Sir Joshua would be wondering what had become of them. Abby would have followed her example, but received such an unmistakable signal from Fanny that she obediently postponed her leave-taking. The reason for the signal was disclosed as soon as the Weaverhams had departed, Lavinia eagerly asking her mama if Fanny might not stay to dine with them. 'Do say she may, Mama! I want to show her the *ravishing* things Oliver bought for me in India, particularly the shawl – no, *not* a shawl: I don't mean the Cashmere shawls, though they are the finest I ever saw in my life! – but the *other* thing –'

'Sari,' supplied her brother, smiling.

'Oh, yes! Sari!' said Lavinia, committing it to memory. 'And the sketches you drew of all those strange places, and natives, and things! Mama – ?'

'Why, certainly, my love!' Mrs Grayshott responded. 'If Miss Wendover permits!'

'Miss Wendover thinks, as I am persuaded you do too, ma'am, that the invalid has had enough visitors for one day,' said Abby. 'Another time, Fanny!'

Fanny nodded, and got up. 'Yes, of course. I did think it might not be quite the thing to do!'

This instantly drew protests and assurances from Lavinia and Oliver, under cover of which Mrs. Grayshott said: 'I wish you will let her stay! She is doing Oliver so much good! He does his best to hide it from me, but he is in very low spirits, feeling, I think, that he has failed to justify his uncle's confidence – oh, absurd, of course, but one knows how it is with boys! But dear little Fanny has *three times* made him laugh, quite in his old way! Let her remain with us! You know we keep country-hours! Martha shall bring her home before it is dark, I promise you.'

'My dear ma'am, if you do indeed wish it – ! But as for putting your Martha to the trouble of escorting her, most certainly not! I'll send the carriage for her, and only hope she may not be very much in your way!'

She then took leave of her hostess. So did Mr Miles Calverleigh: a circumstance which she regarded with mixed feelings. He followed her down the stairs, and it occurred to her that his object might be to apologise for having alarmed her so much half-an-hour before. But as she had by this time formed a very fair estimate of his character she was not much surprised when his first words to her, as soon as the street-door was shut behind them, were: 'Do tell me! – Who, and what, is Sir Joshua?'

'Sir Joshua,' she replied primly, 'is Lady Weaverham's husband, sir.'

'Yes, my pretty pea-goose, and Sophy's father too!' he said

66

outrageously. 'My powerful intellect has enabled me to assimilate those barren facts! Don't act the dunce!'

'Let me tell you, sir, that if you wish to be accepted into Bath society you will do well to mend your manners!' retorted Abby.

'I've none to mend, and not the smallest wish to be accepted into Bath, or any other, society. And if Bath society is composed of Lady Weaverham and her like –'

'Of course it isn't!' she interrupted impulsively. 'I mean – Oh, what a detestable man you are!'

'Well, if that's what you meant to say you must have a very hubble-bubble mind!' he commented. 'I may be detestable – in fact, I know I am – but what has that to say to anything?' He added, as she resolutely bit her lip: 'Yes, do laugh! You have a pretty laugh, and I like the way your eyes dance.'

Guiltily aware that this very improper speech had pleased rather than offended her, she said, as coolly as she could: 'We were discussing the Weaverhams, I think. They are very kind, worthy people, and although they are not – not the pink of gentility, they are generally well-liked.'

'Full of juice, eh?' he said, showing at once his understanding and his disregard for polite ambiguities. 'Where did they pick up the title? In the City?'

'I don't know. Sir Joshua certainly was engaged in Trade, until he retired – they make no secret of that – but – but in a perfectly respectable way!'

'No need to defend him,' he said kindly. 'I've been engaged in trade myself, though I daresay you wouldn't say *respectably*.'

'I should be astonished if I discovered that you had done *anything* respectably!' declared Abby, goaded into retort. Shocked by her own lapse from propriety, she was thankful to see that they had reached York House, and added hastily: 'Our ways part here, sir, so I will say goodbye!'

'No, don't! it would be premature! I'm going to escort you to your home.'

'I am obliged to you, but it is quite unnecessary, I assure you!'

She had stopped by the entrance to the hotel, and held out her hand, repeating; 'Goodbye, Mr Calverleigh!'

'If you imagine that I am going to walk behind you, like a footman, all the way to Sydney Place, you are mightily mistaken, Miss Abigail Wendover!' he said, taking her hand, and drawing it within his arm. 'Is it now the established mode for young females to jaunter about the town unattended? It wasn't so when I lived in England!'

'I am not a young female, and I don't *jaunter*!' replied Abby hotly, pulling her hand away, but walking on beside him. 'Times have changed since *you* lived in England, sir!'

'Yes, alas, and not for the better!' he agreed, in a mournful tone. 'Bear with my foibles, ma'am! Being yourself stricken in years, that shouldn't be difficult!'

A chuckle escaped her. 'Don't be so absurd!' she admonished him. 'I may not be stricken in years, but I am no longer of an age when I need chaperonage. I don't care to let Fanny go out alone, though I know several mothers who see no objection to it *here*. Not in London, of course.' She paused, and said, after a moment: 'May I request you, sir, to take care what you say to Fanny? Since you have seen fit to inform her that you knew her mother *very well*, she may try to talk to you about Celia, and she is sufficiently needle-witted to add two and two together. I'm aware that you did it to put me in a quake, but, having succeeded, pray be satisfied!'

He laughed. 'No, no! just bantering you a little! You were looking such daggers at me that I couldn't resist!'

'Chivalrous!' she remarked.

'Not a bit! I warned you that there's no virtue in me.'

'Then why do you insist on escorting me home?'

'Because I want to escort you home, of course. What a birdwitted question!'

Her eyes began to dance, and her lips to quiver. 'You know, you are the most provoking creature I ever encountered!' she told him.

'Oh, come, now, that's doing it rather too brown!' he

expostulated. 'Remember, I was acquainted with your brother Rowland! I never saw much of James, but I shouldn't wonder at it if he's as bad. Or don't you find consequential bores provoking?'

'If I didn't believe you to be dead to all proper feeling,' said Abby, in a shaking voice, 'I should endeavour to point out to you that that is a – an *abominable* thing to say!'

'Well, thank God you do realise it!' he replied. 'Now we shall go on much more comfortably!'

'No we shan't. Not until you stop trying to hoax me into thinking you are uniformly odious! Pray, did you bring Oliver Grayshott home because you *wanted* to?'

'Yes, I like the boy. Don't you?'

'Yes, I daresay, but –'

'Now, don't run away with the notion that I came back to England on his account!' he admonished her. 'Nothing could be farther from the truth! All I did was to take charge of him on the voyage: no very arduous task!'

'And subsequently put yourself to the trouble of bringing him down to Bath,' said Abby pensively.

'Oh, that was because –' he checked himself, but continued blandly, after an infinitesimal pause: '– because his uncle is a man of vast interests, and one never knows when the favour of such a man might stand one in good stead.'

'How quickly you made a recover!' said Abby admiringly. 'You were within an ace of telling me that you came to Bath to see your nephew, too!'

'Ah, I *did* tell you that I didn't know he was here! I rather thought I did,' he said, quite unperturbed. 'I hope he means to return: according to Lady Weaverham, he is a perfect paragon, and I *should* like to meet a Calverleigh who fitted that description.'

'You won't meet him in the person of your nephew!'

'How do you know? You've never clapped eyes on him!'

'No, but –'

'Furthermore, Selina likes him,' he pursued. 'You told me that yourself, and I have the greatest respect for her judgment.'

'Oh, have you indeed?' she said wrathfully. 'When *you* have never clapped eyes on *her* – !'

'Not to my knowledge,' he admitted. 'However, I understand her to be your eldest sister, and there's no saying but what I may have met her – before I was excluded from polite circles, of course. If I didn't, I look forward to making her acquaintance.'

They had reached the corner of Bridge Street, and Abby came to an abrupt halt. '*No!*' she said forcefully. 'I don't wish you to make her acquaintance! She knows nothing of what you disclosed to me – she doesn't even know that I met you yesterday! And I have no intention – none whatsoever! – of introducing you to her!'

'Haven't you? But you'll be made to look no-how if you don't, won't you? If Mrs Grayshott doesn't perform that office, would you wager a groat on the chance that Lady Weaverham won't?'

'No – or on the chance that you wouldn't instantly tell my sister of our previous meetings!' said Abby, with considerable bitterness. 'Without a blush!'

'Very likely,' he agreed.

Unable to think of any suitable rejoinder, she walked on in silence.

'And I promise you I won't blush,' he added reassuringly.

She choked, but managed to retort with tolerable gravity: 'I shouldn't suppose that you know how to!'

'No, I don't think I do,' he said, subjecting the matter to consideration. 'At my age, it is rather too late to acquire the accomplishment, don't you think?'

'Mr Calverleigh!' she said, turning her head to look up at him, 'let us be a little serious! It is true that I haven't yet met your nephew, but you have met my niece! You don't want for sense; you are not a green youth, but a – a man of the world; and you loved Fanny's mother! I don't doubt that, or that seeing Fanny must have given you a – a pang – brought it all back to you!'

'You know, the odd thing is that it didn't,' he interrupted. '*Is* she so like Celia?'

Astonished, she gasped: 'Her image!'

'No, is she indeed? What tricks memory plays one! I had thought that Celia had brown eyes.

'Do you mean to say that you have *forgotten*?' demanded Abby, wholly taken aback.

'Well, it all happened more than twenty years ago,' he said apologetically.

'And no doubt your memory has confused her with some other lady!'

'Yes, that's very possible,' he acknowledged.

Miss Abigail Wendover decided, while she struggled with her emotions, that one of the worst features of Mr Miles Calverleigh's character was his obnoxious ability to throw her into giggles at quite the wrong moment. Being a woman of strong resolution, she mastered herself, and said: 'But you do remember that you once loved her, and I don't think you would wish her daughter to – to become the victim of a fortune-hunter – even if he is your nephew!'

'No. Not that I've considered the matter, but I don't wish anybody to become the victim of a fortune-hunter. Or, now I come to think of it, of any other predacious person. But I am of the opinion that you may be wronging my foolish nephew: he may well have tumbled into love with her, you know. Undoubtedly a piece of perfection!'

She looked up quickly, kindling to this praise of her darling. 'She *is* very pretty, isn't she?'

'Oh, past price! Which leads me to suspect that perhaps the poor fellow is in love with her!'

She frowned over this for a moment or two, before saying decidedly: 'It's of no consequence if he is: he is not a proper person for her! Besides, she's by far too young. Surely you must know that!'

'No, I don't. Her mother was about seventeen when she married Rowland.'

'Which *proves* she is too young!'

He grinned appreciatively, but said: 'You may be right, but

you can't expect me to agree with you. After all, I tried to marry Celia myself!'

'Yes, but you were only a boy then. You must be wiser now!'

'Much! Too wise to meddle in what doesn't concern me!'

'Mr Calverleigh, it should concern you!'

'Miss Wendover, it don't!'

'Then, if you've no interest in your nephew, why do you mean to linger in Bath? Why do you hope he means to return here?'

'I didn't say I had no interest in him. I own, I didn't think I had, but that was before I knew he was making up to your niece. You can't deny that that provides a very interesting situation!'

'Excessively diverting, too!'

'Yes, that's what I think.'

She said despairingly: 'I see that I might as well address myself to a gate-post!'

'What very odd things you seem to talk to!' he remarked. 'Do you find gate-posts less responsive than eels?'

She could not help smiling, but she said very earnestly: 'Promise me one thing at least, sir! Even though you won't intervene in this miserable affair, promise me that you won't *promote* it!'

'Oh, readily! I am a mere spectator.'

She was obliged to be satisfied, but said in somewhat minatory accents: 'I trust your word, sir.'

'You may safely do so. I shan't feel any temptation to break it,' he replied cheerfully.

Feeling that this remark showed him to be quite irreclaimable, Abby walked on in silence, trying to discover why she allowed herself to talk to him at all, far less to accept his escort. No satisfactory answer presented itself, for although he seemed to be impervious to snubs she knew that she could have snubbed his advances if she had made any real effort to do so. After a half-hearted attempt to convince herself that she endured his escort and his conversation with the sole object of winning his support in her crusade against his nephew she found herself to be under the shameful necessity of admitting that she enjoyed both, and – far worse! – would have suffered considerable disappointment had he announced his intention of leaving Bath within the immediate future. She could only suppose that it was his unlikeness to the other gentlemen of her acquaintance which appealed to her sense of humour, and made it possible for her to tolerate him, for there was really nothing else to render him acceptable: he was neither handsome nor elegant; his manners were careless; and his morals non-existent. He was, in fact, precisely the sort of ramshackle person to whom no lady of birth, breeding, and propriety would extend the smallest encouragement. He had nothing to recommend him but his smile, and she was surely too old, and had too much commonsense, to be beguiled by a smile however attractive it might be. But just as she reached this decision he spoke, and she glanced up at him, and realised that she had overestimated both her age and her commonsense. He was smiling down at her, and, try as she would, she was incapable of resisting the impulse to smile back at him. It was almost as if a bond existed between them, which was tightened by his smile. In repose his face was harsh, but the smile transformed it. His eyes lost their cold, rather cynical expression, warming to laughter, and holding, besides amusement, an indefinable look of understanding. He might mock, but not unkindly; and when he discomfited her his smiling eyes conveyed sympathy as well as amusement, and clearly invited her to share his amusement. And, thought Abby, the dreadful thing was that she did share it. He seemed to think that they were kindred spirits, and the shocking suspicion that he was right made her look resolutely ahead, saying: 'Yes, sir? What did you say?'

Quick to hear the repressive note in her voice, he replied meekly: 'Nothing, I assure you, to which you could take the least exception! In fact, no more than: *I wish you will tell me.* Upon which you turned your head, and looked up at me so charmingly that the rest went out of my mind! How the devil have you contrived to escape matrimony in all the unnumbered years of your life?'

An unruly dimple peeped, but she answered primly: 'I am very well content to remain single, sir.' It then occurred to her that this might lead him to suppose that her hand had never been sought in matrimony, which, for some reason unknown to herself, was an intolerable misapprehension, and she destroyed whatever quelling effect her dignified reply might have had upon him, by adding: 'Though you needn't suppose that I have not received *several* eligible offers!'

He chuckled. 'I don't!'

Blushing rosily, she said, trying to recover her lost dignity: 'And if that is what you wished me to tell you –'

'Oh, no!' he interrupted. 'Until you smiled so enchantingly I thought I knew. But you aren't old cattish – not in the least!'

'Oh!' gasped Abby. 'Old *cattish*? Oh, you – you – I am nothing of the sort!'

'That's what I said,' he pointed out.

'You didn't! You – you said –' Her sense of the ridiculous came to her rescue; she burst out laughing. 'Odious creature! Now, do, pray, stop roasting me! What do you really wish me to tell you?'

'Oh, I was merely seeking information! I don't recall that I ever visited Bath in the days of my youth, so I rely on you to tell me just what are its rules and etiquette – as they concern one desirous of entering society.'

'You?' she exclaimed, casting a surprised look up at him.

'But of course! How else could I hope to pursue my acquaintance with –' He paused, encountering a dangerous gleam in her eyes, and continued smoothly: 'Lady Weaverham, and her amiable daughter!'

She bit her lip. 'No, indeed! How shatterbrained I am! Lady Weaverham has several amiable daughters, too.'

'Good God! Are they all fubsy-faced?'

'A – a little!' she acknowledged. 'You will be able to judge for yourself, if you mean to attend the balls at the New Assembly Rooms. I am afraid there are no balls or concerts held at the Lower Rooms until November. You will find it an agreeable day promenade, however, and I expect there will be some public lectures given there. Concerts are given every Wednesday evening at the New Rooms. And there is also the Harmonic Society,' she said, warming to her task. 'They sing catches and glees, and meet at the White Hart. At least, they do during the season, but I am not perfectly sure –'

'I shall make it my business to discover the date of the first meeting. Meanwhile, my pretty rogue, that will do!'

Miss Wendover toyed for a moment with the idea of giving him a sharp set-down for addressing her so improperly, but decided that it would be wiser to ignore his impertinence. She said: 'Not fond of music, sir? Oh, well, perhaps you have a taste for cards! There are two card-rooms at the New Assembly Rooms: one of them is an octagon, and generally much admired – but I ought to warn you that hazard is not allowed, or *any* unlawful game. And you cannot play cards at all on Sundays.'

'You dismay me! What, by the way, are the unlawful games you speak of?'

'I don't know,' she said frankly, 'but that's what it says in the Rules. I expect it wouldn't do to start a faro bank, or anything of that nature.'

'I shouldn't wonder at it if you were right,' he agreed, with the utmost gravity. 'And how do I gain admittance to this establishment?'

'Oh, you write your name in Mr King's book, if you wish to become a subscriber! He is the M.C., and the book is kept at the Pump Room. Dress balls are on Monday, card assemblies on Tuesday, and Fancy balls on Thursday. The balls begin soon after seven o'clock, and end punctually at eleven. Only country dances are permitted at the Dress balls, but there are in general two cotillions danced at the Fancy balls. Oh, and you pay sixpence for Tea, on admission!'

'And they say Bath is a slow place! You appear to be gay to dissipation. What happens, by the way, if eleven o'clock strikes in the middle of one of your country dances?'

She laughed. 'The music stops! That's in the Rules too!'

They had reached Sydney Place by this time, and she stopped outside her house, and held out her hand. 'This is where I live, so I will say goodbye to you, Mr Calverleigh. I am much obliged to you for escorting me home, and trust you will enjoy your sojourn in Bath.'

'Yes, if only I am not knocked-up by all the frisks and jollifications you've described to me,' he said, taking her hand, and retaining it for a moment in a strong clasp. He smiled down at her. 'I won't say goodbye to you, but *au revoir,* Miss Wendover!'

She had been afraid that he would insist on entering the house with her to make Selina's acquaintance, and was relieved when he made no such attempt, merely waiting until Mitton opened the door, and then striding away, with no more than a wave of his hand.

She found, on going upstairs, that Selina had promoted herself to the sofa in the drawing-room, and had had the gratification of receiving a visit from Mrs Leavening. She was so full of Bedfordshire gossip that it was some time before Abby had the opportunity to tell her that Mrs Grayshott's son had at last been restored to her. She found it unaccountably difficult to disclose that Mr Miles Calverleigh had brought him to Bath, and when, after responding to her sister's exclamatory enquiries, she did disclose it, her voice was a trifle too airy.

Selina, fortunately, was too much surprised to notice it. She ejaculated: '*What?* Poor Mr Calverleigh's uncle? The one you told me about? The one that was sent away in disgrace? You don't mean it! But why did *he* bring the young man home? I should have thought Mr Balking would have done so!'

'I believe he took care of him on the voyage.'

'Good gracious! Well, he can't be so very bad after all! and very likely Mr Stacy Calverleigh isn't either! Unless, of course, he only came to find his nephew – not that there is anything bad about that: in fact, it shows he has very proper feeling!'

'Well, he hasn't!' said Abby. 'He didn't know his nephew was in Bath, and he hasn't any *family* feelings whatsoever!'

'Now, my love, how can you possibly – Don't tell me you've actually *met* him?'

'He came to call on Mrs Grayshott while I was there – and was so obliging as to escort me home. Quite Gothic!'

'I don't think it in the least Gothic,' asserted Selina. 'It gives me a very good opinion of him! *Just* like his nephew, whose manners are so particularly pleasing!'

'From all you have told me about his nephew, Mr Miles Calverleigh is nothing like him!' said Abby, with an involuntary choke of laughter. 'He is neither handsome nor fashionable, and his manners are deplorable!'

Selina, regarding her with real concern, said: 'Dearest, I am persuaded you must be yielding to prejudice, and indeed you should not, though, to be sure, dear Rowland was always used to say it was your besetting sin, but that was when you were a mere child, and *perfectly* understandable, as I told Rowland, because one cannot expect to find young heads – no, I mean *old* heads on *young* shoulders – not that I should expect to find heads on any shoulders at all, unless, of course, it was *a freak*! Which I know very little about, because you must remember, Abby, that dear Papa had the greatest dislike of *affairs*, and would never permit us to go to one. Now, what in the world have I said to cast you into whoops?'

'*Nothing* in the world, Selina!' Abby said, as well as she could for laughter. 'On – on the contrary! You've t-told me that in spite of all my f-faults I'm not a freak!'

'My dear, you allow your love of drollery to carry you too far,' said Selina reprovingly. 'There has never been anything like *that* in our family!'

Overcome by this comforting assurance, Abby fled, conscious of a wish that Mr Calverleigh could have been present to share her amusement.

Selina continued to speculate, in her rambling way, throughout dinner, on his probable character, what he had done to deserve being banished, and what had brought him back to England; but Fanny's arrival, just before the tea-tray was brought in, gave the conversation a welcome turn. Fanny was full of the quaint or the beautiful things Oliver Grayshott had brought home from India, and although Selina's interest in ivory carvings or Benares brass might be tepid, the first mention of Cashmere shawls, and lengths of the finest Indian muslin, aroused all her sartorial instincts; while a minute description of the sari caused her to wonder how long it would be before she dared venture out of doors, and to adjure Fanny to beg Lavinia not to have it made up until she had seen it. 'For you know, my dear, excellent creature though she is, dear Mrs Grayshott has *no* taste, and what a shocking thing it would be if such an exquisite thing were to be ruined!'

Fanny had spent a delightful day in Edgar Buildings, and she meant – if her aunts saw no objection – to repeat her visit. Lavinia, who was her dearest friend, had told her how low and oppressed poor Oliver was, and had asked her to come again, because funning with her, and making up charades, had quite got up his spirits. 'So I think I should, don't you?' Fanny said, frowning over her own thoughts. 'It isn't *me*, particularly, but being obliged to be polite and cheerful with a visitor, which does one a great deal of good when one has been ill, and feels dreadfully pulled.'

She had very little to say about Miles Calverleigh. It was plain that the only interest he had for her was his relationship to Stacy. She said that he was not at all like Stacy; and mentioned, as an afterthought, that he said he had known her mama well.

To Abby's relief, Selina accepted this without question, seeing in it an added reason for thinking he could not be as black as he had been painted. Having decided that it would be both unsafe and unkind to divulge to her the story of Miles Calverleigh and Celia Morval, Abby was thankful to be spared searching enquiries into the circumstances under which Miles Calverleigh had contrived to become intimately acquainted with a girl who had been married within two months of her come-out, and had lived thereafter in a Bedfordshire manor.

She retired to bed presently, devoutly hoping that Mr Calverleigh would have left Bath before Selina emerged from her self-imposed seclusion.

Six

*B*ut Mr Calverleigh called in Sydney Place on the following day. Mitton, recognising him as the gentleman who had escorted Miss Abby home on the previous afternoon, admitted him without hesitation, and took him up to the drawing-room, where Abby, under her sister's instruction, was engaged in directing cards of invitation to their projected rout-party. She was unprepared, and gave such a start that her pen spluttered. Turning quickly, and almost incredulously, she encountered the blandest of smiles, and the slightest of bows, before Mr Calverleigh advanced towards her sister. What excuse he meant to offer for his visit was a puzzle that was speedily solved: Mr Calverleigh, taking Selina's tremblingly outstretched hand in his, and smiling reassuringly down into her agitated countenance, told her that he had known her elder brother, and found himself unable to resist the impulse to extend his acquaintance with Rowland's family. 'Two of whom I had the pleasure of meeting yesterday,' he said, nodding with friendly informality at Abby. 'How do you do, Miss Abigail?'

She acknowledged this greeting in the frostiest manner, but so far from being abashed, he laughed, and said: 'Still out of charity with me? I must tell you, ma'am, that your sister was as cross as crabs with me for escorting her home. But in my day it was not at all the thing for girls of her quality to go out walking alone.'

Selina, already flustered by the style and manner of her unexpected visitor, lost herself in a tangle of words, for while on

79

the one hand, she shared his old-fashioned prejudice, on the other, she knew very well that to agree with him would be to incur Abby's wrath. So after floundering between a number of unfinished sentences, she begged him to be seated, and asked him where he had met her brother. Abby held her breath, but he returned a vague answer, and she let it go again.

'And you knew my sister-in-law too!' pursued Selina. 'It seems so odd that I never – not that I was acquainted with all their friends, of course, but I thought – that is to say – dear me, how stupid! I have forgot what I was going to say!'

He regarded her confusion with a twinkle. 'No, no, don't turn short about! You thought I had been sent packing to India before your brother was married, and you were perfectly right: I knew Celia when she was still Miss Morval.'

'A long time ago,' said Abby. 'Too long for me, I am afraid: you see, I didn't.'

The unmistakable boredom in her voice scandalised Selina into uttering a protesting: 'Abby *dear* – !'

Abby shrugged pettishly. 'Oh, well, it is so tedious to be obliged to discuss old times in which one played no part! Anecdotes, too! I have a surfeit of them from General Exford. I wish you will rather tell us of your Indian experiences, Mr Calverleigh.'

'But that would be merely to exchange one form of anecdote for another,' he pointed out. 'And *much* more boring, I assure you!'

'Oh, no! I am persuaded – so very interesting! All those Mahrattas, and things!' fluttered Selina, aghast at her sister's behaviour. 'Not that I should care to live there myself – and the climate *far* from salubrious – well, only think of poor young Mr Grayshott! But I daresay you had *many* exciting adventures!'

'Not nearly as many as I had in England!' He looked at Abby, wickedly quizzing her. 'No need to look so dismayed, Miss Abigail: I don't mean to recount them! Let us instead discuss the amenities of Bath! Do you mean to attend the concert this evening?'

For one sulphurous moment it was on the tip of her tongue to disclaim any intention of attending the concert, but the recollection that she was engaged to do so with a select party of friends checked her. She replied, with a glittering smile: 'Yes, indeed! The Signora Neroli is to sing, you know – a high treat for those of us who love music. You, I daresay, would find it a dead bore, for I believe you *don't* love music!'

'On the contrary: I find it wonderfully sopor – wonderfully soothing!'

A smile quivered at the corners of her mouth. 'I doubt if you will find the benches wonderfully sopor-soothing, sir!'

'That card takes the trick!' he said approvingly.

She chuckled, and then as she caught sight of her sister's face, blushed.

At that moment, Fanny came into the room, much to Abby's relief. She greeted Mr Calverleigh with unaffected pleasure: just as she would have greeted any other of her aunt's elderly admirers, Abby watched in some amusement, wondering how much Mr Calverleigh liked the touch of pretty deference which paid tribute to his advanced years. She was obliged to own that he took it with unshaken composure, responding in a manner that was positively avuncular. He did not stay long: a circumstance which caused Selina to say, when he had taken his leave, that although his manners were very odd, which was due, no doubt, to his having lived in India, he did know better than to remain for more than half-an-hour on a visit of ceremony.

'I warned you that his manners are deplorable!' said Abby. 'I shouldn't think he has the least notion of ceremony.'

'To be sure, it is not at all the thing to call on us in breeches and topboots – at least, gentlemen may do so in the country, of course, but not in Bath, without a horse, and it would have been more correct merely to have left his card – but I saw nothing in his manners to disgust me, precisely. He has a great deal of ease, but he is not at all vulgar. In fact, he has a well-bred air, and it would be very unjust to blame him for his complexion, poor man, because you may depend upon it *that* was India, and excessively unfeeling I think it of his father to have sent him there, no matter *what* he did!'

'Why, *did* he do something dreadful?' exclaimed Fanny, round-eyed with surprise.

'No, dear, certainly not!' said Selina hurriedly.

'But you said –'

'My love, I said nothing of the sort! How you do pick one up! It is not at all becoming! And that puts me in mind of something! Abby, *never* did I think to be put to the blush by a want of conduct in you! I declare, I was so mortified – so petulant and uncivil of you! And then, after placing yourself on *far* too high a form, besides snubbing him in the *rudest* way, you laughed in his face! As if you had known him for years!'

'Good God, why did no one ever tell me that I mustn't laugh at what a man says until I have known him for years?' countered Abby.

Before Selina could assemble her inchoate thoughts, Fanny said suddenly: 'Yes, but one has! I mean, one *feels* as if one has! For my part, I don't care a straw for his being shabbily dressed, and not having formal manners: I *like* him! I should have thought you would too, Abby, because he is just such a jokesmith as you are yourself! *Don't* you?'

'I must say,' interpolated Selina, 'that he was very diverting. And when he smiles –'

'Mr Calverleigh's smile must be reckoned as his greatest – if not his only – asset!' said Abby tartly. 'As to whether I like him or not, how can I possibly say? I am barely acquainted with him, Fanny!'

'That doesn't signify! He is barely acquainted with you, but anyone can see that he likes you very much!' retorted Fanny saucily. 'Do you think he will be at the concert this evening?'

'I haven't the least notion,' replied Abby. 'Certainly not, if riding-dress is his only wear!'

'Poor man!' said Selina, her compassion stirred. 'I daresay he may be sadly purse-pinched.'

However this might have been, Mr Calverleigh had either the means, or the credit, to have provided himself with the long-tailed-coat, the knee-breeches, and the silk stockings which constituted the correct evening-wear for gentlemen, for he appeared in the New Assembly Rooms, thus arrayed, a few minutes before the concert began, escorting Mrs Grayshott. But as he wore it as casually as his riding-dress, and appeared to set more store by comfort than elegance, no aspirant to fashion would have felt the smallest inclination to discover the name of his tailor.

Miss Abigail Wendover observed his arrival from under her lashes, and thereafter confined her attention to her own party. She was herself looking (as her niece very improperly told her) as fine as fivepence, in one of the new gowns made for her in London, of Imperial muslin, with short sleeves, worn low on her shoulders, a narrow skirt, and a bodice trimmed with a double pleating of ribbon. It became her slender figure to admiration, and it had not been her original intention to have wasted it on a mere out-of-season concert; but when she had looked more closely at her lilac crape she had realised that it was really too shabby to be worn again. This, at least, was the explanation that she offered to her surprised sister. As for her hair, which she had dressed in loose curls, with one shining ringlet disposed over her left shoulder, what did Selina think of it? It was all the kick in London, but perhaps it would not do in Bath?

'Oh, my dearest, I never saw you look so becoming!' said Selina, in a gush of sentimental tears. 'In such high bloom! I know you will be ready to eat me, but I must and I will say that no one would take you for Fanny's *aunt*!'

So far from showing a disposition to take umbrage, Abby laughed, cast an appraising look at her reflection in the mirror above the fireplace, and said candidly: 'Well, I never was a beauty, but I'm not a mean bit yet, am I?'

Certainly no one who was present at the concert that evening thought so. In the octagon room, where they waited for the rest of the party to assemble, Abby received quite as many compliments as Fanny; and on her way through the concert-room had the doubtful felicity of being ogled by a complete stranger.

During the interval, she did not immediately follow Mrs

Faversham into the adjoining room, where tea was being served, being waylaid by Mr Dunston, who came up with his mother on his arm. Civility obliged her to exchange commonplaces with Mrs Dunston, and when that amiable and platitudinous lady's attention was claimed by one of her acquaintances her son stepped instantly into the breach, saying simply: *'Fair as is the rose of May!* Do you know, that line has been running through my head ever since I set eyes on you this evening? You shine everyone else down, Miss Abby!'

'Flummery!' said an amused voice at Abby's elbow. 'You can't have seen her niece!'

'Sir!' uttered Mr Dunston, outraged. 'I believe I have not the pleasure of your acquaintance?'

'Let me make you known to one another!' said Abby hastily. 'Mr Dunston, Mr Calverleigh – Mr *Miles* Calverleigh!'

Mr Dunston executed a small, stiff bow, received in return a nod, and, for the first time in his stolid career, wished that the days of calling a man out on the slightest provocation did not belong to the past.

'I've come to carry you off to drink tea with Mrs Grayshott,' said Mr Calverleigh, taking Abby's hand, and drawing it within his arm. 'I left her guarding a chair for you, so come along!' He favoured Mr Dunston with another nod, and a brief smile, and led Abby inexorably away, saying: 'He did empty the butter-boat over you, didn't he? Who the devil is he?'

'He is a very respectable man, who lives with his mother a few miles distant from the town,' she replied severely. 'And even if he was talking flummery it was not at all handsome of you to say so!'

'I don't offer Spanish coin, if that's what you mean,' he retorted. 'Do you wish for it?'

'Surely, Mr Calverleigh, your wide experience of females must have taught you that compliments are always acceptable to us?' she said demurely.

'To nine out of ten females, yes! but not to you, Miss Abigail Wendover! You're more than seven! You know very well that in point of beauty you don't shine every other lady down: there are at least three real diamonds here tonight, leaving Fanny out of the reckoning.'

'My dear sir, only point them out to me, and I'll present you! I expect I'm acquainted with them – indeed, I've a shrewd notion I know who they are!'

He shook his head. 'No. I prefer to admire them from a distance. My wide experience warns me that they lack that certain sort of something which you have in abundance.'

'My – *sufficiently* wide experience of you, Mr Calverleigh, warns me that you are about to say something outrageous!'

'No, I assure you! Nothing derogatory! Charming girls, all of them! Only I don't want to kiss them!'

She gave a startled gasp. 'You don't want – Well, upon my word! And if you mean me to understand from that –'

'I do,' he said, smiling down at her. 'I should dearly love to kiss you – here and now!'

'W-well you can't!' said Abby, rocked off her balance.

'I know I can't – not here and now, at all events!'

'*Ever!*' she uttered, furiously aware of flaming cheeks.

'Oh, that is quite another matter! Do you care to wager a small sum on the chance?'

Making a desperate recovery, she said: 'No! I never bet on certainties!'

He laughed. 'You know, you are a darling!' he said, completing her confusion.

'Well, what *you* are is a – a –'

'Hedge-bird?' he suggested helpfully, as she stopped, at a loss for words opprobrious enough to describe him. 'Gullcatcher? Bermondsey boy? Rudesby? Queer Nabs?'

She broke into laughter, and threw at him over her shoulder, as she went before him into the tea-room: 'All of those – and worse! In a word, infamous! Mrs Grayshott! How do you do? And – which I know you will think more important! – How does your invalid do?'

She sat down beside Mrs Grayshott as she spoke, wholly withdrawing her attention from the infamous Mr Calverleigh, who lounged away to procure her a cup of tea. Mrs Grayshott said: 'My invalid is not as stout as I could wish, nor as docile! Dr Wilkinson has seen him, however, and assures me that I have no need to fear that any permanent damage has been done to his health. He recommends a course of hot baths, which, he tells me and, indeed, I know from my own experience – do much to restore a debilitated frame. Abby, my dear, you must let me compliment you on this new way you have of dressing your hair! You look delightfully – and have set a new fashion in Bath, if I am any judge of the matter! Yes, I know you only care for compliments on Fanny's appearance, so not another word will I say in your praise! I imagine you have had a surfeit of compliments already – if not from Mr Dunston, who appeared to me to be quite moonstruck, certainly from Mr Calverleigh!'

'Not at all!' replied Abby. 'Mr Calverleigh thinks me a candle in the sunshine of three veritable diamonds present tonight! Four, including Fanny!'

'Does he, indeed?' replied Mrs Grayshott, a good deal amused. 'I suspect he is what Oliver calls *a complete hand*! You know, my dear, I must own that I am glad to see you on such good terms with him, for it has been very much on my conscience that I almost *forced* him upon you, which, as I hope you know, I never meant to do!'

'Oh, I know you didn't, ma'am! I wish you won't give it another thought. Sooner or later I must have met him, you know.'

'And you like him? I was afraid that his free-and-easy manners might offend you.'

'On the contrary! They amuse me. He is certainly an original!'

Mrs Grayshott smiled, but said rather wistfully: 'Why, yes! But not only that! He is so very *kind*! He makes light of the services he rendered Oliver throughout that weary voyage, but I've heard the truth from Oliver himself. But for Mr Calverleigh's unremitting care I don't think that my poor boy would have survived, for he tells me that he suffered a recrudescence of that horrible fever within two days of having been carried aboard! It was Mr Calverleigh, rather than the ship's surgeon, who preserved his life, his long residence in India having made him far more familiar with the disorder than any ship's surgeon could be! I must be eternally obliged to him!' Her voice shook; she overcame the little surge of emotion, and said, with an effort at liveliness: 'And, as though he had not done enough for me, what must he do but procure tickets for this concert tonight, and positively *bully* me into accompanying him! Something I must have said gave him the notion that I should very much like to hear Neroli, and I think it particularly kind in him to have given me the opportunity to do so, because I am afraid he is not himself a music-lover.'

Having very good reason to suppose that Mr Calverleigh's kindness sprang from pure self-interest, Abby was hard put to it to hold her tongue. It was perhaps fortunate that he rejoined them at this moment, thus putting an end to any further discussion of his character. She accepted the tea he had brought, with a word of thanks and a charming smile, but could not resist the impulse to ask him if he was not ravished by Neroli's voice.

He replied promptly: 'Not entirely. A little too much *vibrato*, don't you agree?'

'Ah, I perceive that you are an expert!' said Abby, controlling a quivering lip. 'You must enlighten my ignorance, sir! What does that mean, if you please?'

'Well, my Latin is pretty rusty, but I should think it means to tremble,' he said coolly. 'She does, too, like a blancmanger. And much the same shape as one,' he added thoughtfully.

'Oh, you *dreadful* creature!' protested Mrs Grayshott, bubbling over. 'I didn't mean *that,* when I said I thought she had rather too much *vibrato*! You know I didn't!'

'I thought she had too much of everything,' he said frankly.

Mrs Grayshott cried shame upon him; but Abby, caught in the act of sipping her tea, choked.

When he presently restored her to her own party, she was spared the necessity of introducing him to Mrs Faversham by that lady's greeting him by name, and with a gracious smile:

Lady Weaverham had already performed that office, in the Pump Room that morning.

Mr Faversham said, taking his seat beside Abby: 'So that's young Calverleigh's uncle!' He looked critically after Mr Calverleigh's tall, retreating figure. 'Got the look of a care-for nobody, but I like him better than his nephew: too insinuating by half, that young man!'

'You don't like him, sir?'

'No, I can't say I do,' he replied bluntly. 'Fact of the matter is I set no store by these young sprigs of fashion! My wife calls me an old fogey: daresay you will too, for the ladies all seem to have run wild over him! Haven't met him yet, have you?'

'No, that pleasure hasn't been granted me,' she said, in a dry tone.

It was to be granted her on the following day. Mr Stacy Calverleigh, coming down from London on the mail-coach, arrived at the White Hart midway through the morning, and stayed only to change his travelling-dress for the corbeau-coloured coat of superfine, the pale pantaloons, and the gleaming Hessian boots of the Bond Street beau, before setting out in a hack for Sydney Place.

The ladies were all at home, Abby, who had just come in from a visit to Milsom Street, submitting to her sister's critical inspection some patterns of lace; Selina reclining on the sofa; and Fanny wrestling with the composition of an acrostic in the back drawing-room. She did not immediately look up when Mitton announced *Mr Calverleigh*, but as Stacy advanced into the room he spoke, saying in a rallying tone: 'Miss Wendover! What is this I hear about you? Mitton has been telling me that you have been quite out of frame since I saw you last! I am so very sorry!'

His voice brought Fanny's head up with a jerk. She sprang to her feet, and almost ran into the front room, exclaiming with unaffected joy: 'Stacy: Oh, I thought it was only your uncle!'

She was holding out her hands to him, and he caught them in his, carrying first one and then the other to his lips with what Abby, observing her niece's fervour with disapprobation, recognised as practised grace. 'You thought I was my uncle? Now, I begin to suspect that it is you rather than Miss Wendover who must be out of frame!' he said caressingly. 'Indeed I am not my uncle!' He gave her hands a slight squeeze before releasing them, and moving forward to drop on his knee beside the sofa. 'Dear Miss Wendover, what has been amiss? I can see that you are sadly pulled, and my suspicion is that you have been trotting too hard!'

The demure laughter in his voice robbed his words of offence. Selina all too obviously succumbed to the charm of a personable and audacious young man, scolding him for his impertinence, in the manner of an indulgent aunt, and favouring him with an account of her late indisposition.

Abby was thus afforded an opportunity to study him at her leisure. She thought that it was easy to see why he had made so swift a conquest of Fanny: he was handsome, and he was possessed of ease and address, his manners being distinguished by a nice mixture of deference and assurance. Only in the slightly aquiline cast of his features could she detect any resemblance to his uncle: in all other respects no two men could have been more dissimilar. His height was not above the average, but, in contrast to Miles Calverleigh's long, loosely-knit limbs, his figure was particularly good; he did not, like Miles, look as if he had shrugged himself into his coat: rather, the coat appeared to have been moulded to his form; the ears of his collars were as stiff as starch could make them; his neckcloths were never carelessly knotted, but always beautifully arranged, whether in the simple style of the Napoleon, or the more intricate folds of the Mathematical; and he showed exquisite taste in his choice of waistcoats. Such old fashioned persons as Mr Faversham might stigmatise him as a tippy, a dandy, a bandbox creature, but their instinctive dislike of the younger generation of dashing blades on the strut carried them too far: Stacy Calverleigh was a smart, but not quite a dandy, for he affected few of the extravagances of fashion. His shirt-points might be a little too high, his coats a trifle too much padded at the shoulder and nipped in at the waist, but he never overloaded his person with jewellery, or revolted plain men by helping himself to snuff with a silver shovel.

His profile, as he knelt beside the sofa, was turned towards Abby, and she was obliged to acknowledge that it was a singularly handsome profile. Then, when Fanny seized the opportunity offered by a pause in Selina's garrulity to present him to her other aunt, and he turned his head to look up at Abby, she thought him less handsome, but without quite knowing why.

He jumped up, exclaiming, with a boyishness which, to her critical ears, had a false ring: 'Oh! This is a moment to which I've been looking forward – and yet dreading! Your very humble servant, ma'am!'

'Dreading?' said Abby, lifting her brows. 'Were you led to suppose I was a gorgon?'

'Ah, no, far from it! A most beloved aunt!'

His ready smile curled his lips as he spoke, but Abby, looking in vain for a trace of the charm which awoke instant response in her when the elder Calverleigh smiled, realised that it did not reach his eyes. She thought they held a calculating look, and suspected him of watching her closely to discover whether he was making a good or a bad impression on her.

She said lightly: 'That doesn't seem to be a reason for your dread, sir.'

'No, and it's moonshine!' Fanny said. 'How can you talk such nonsense, Stacy?'

'It isn't nonsense. Miss Abigail loves you, and must think me unworthy of you – oh, an impudent jackstraw even to dream of aspiring to your hand!' He smiled again, and said simply: 'I think it too, ma'am. No one knows better than I how unworthy I am.'

A sentimental sigh and an inarticulate murmur from Selina showed that this frank avowal had moved her profoundly. Upon Abby it had a different effect. 'Trying to take the wind out of my eye, Mr Calverleigh?' she said.

If he was disconcerted he did not betray it, but answered

immediately: 'No, but, perhaps – the words out of your mouth?'

Privately, she gave him credit for considerable adroitness, but all she said was: 'You are mistaken: I am not so uncivil.'

'And it isn't true!' Fanny declared passionately. 'I won't permit anyone to say such a thing – not even you, Abby!'

'Well, I haven't said it, my dear, nor am I likely to, so there is really no need for you to fly up into the boughs! Tell me, Mr Calverleigh, have you made the acquaintance of your uncle yet?'

'My uncle?' he repeated. He glanced at Fanny, a question in his eyes. 'But what is this? *You* said, when I came in, that you thought I was my uncle! The only uncle I possess – if I do still possess him – lives at the other end of the world!'

'No, he doesn't,' replied Fanny. 'I mean, he doesn't do so now! He brought Lavinia Grayshott's brother home from Calcutta, and he is here, at the York House!'

'Good God!' he said blankly.

'He is not at all like you, but *very* agreeable, isn't he, Aunt Selina?'

'Yes, indeed,' agreed Selina. 'He is quite an oddity – so informal, but I daresay that comes of having lived for so long in India, which does not sound to me at all the sort of place anyone would *wish* to live in, but that, after all, was not his fault, poor man, and he is *perfectly* gentlemanly!'

'I'm glad to know that at least!' Stacy said ruefully. 'I never met him in my life, but I heartily wish him otherwise, for I fear he may destroy what little credit I may have with you! Alas, the round tale is that he is the black sheep in my family!'

'Oh, I fancy you have met him!' said Abby, showing hackle. 'He has no recollection of having done so, I own, but thinks he might have seen you when you were, as he phrased it, *a grubby brat*!'

He shot a quick look at her, but said, smiling again: 'Ah, very likely! I can't be blamed for having forgotten the circumstance, can I? I wonder what has brought him back to England?'

'But I told you!' Fanny reminded him. 'He brought poor Mr Oliver Grayshott home! And such good care did he take of him that Mrs Grayshott feels she cannot be sufficiently obliged to him! As for Oli – as for Mr Grayshott, he says he is a *trump*, and won't listen to a word in his disparagement!'

'Worse and worse!' he declared, with a comical grimace. 'A male attendant, in fact! A faint – a very faint – hope that he might have made his fortune in India withers at the outset!'

'Much might be forgiven in the prodigal son who returned to the fold with well-lined pockets, might it not?' said Abby, bestowing upon him a smile as false as she believed his own to be.

'Oh, everything!' he assured her gaily. 'That's the way of the world, ma'am!'

'Very wrong – most improper!' interpolated Selina, trying, not very successfully, to assemble her inchoate ideas into comprehensible words. 'I mean – I mean, money ought not, and *cannot* re-establish character! And to expect a man who had been cast off in a perfectly inhuman way (for so it seems to me, and I don't care what *anyone* says!) to come home to – to *shower* guineas on his *most* unnatural relations, is – is *monstrous*! Or, at any rate,' she temporised, 'absurd!'

'Bravo, Selina!' exclaimed Abby.

Faintly blushing under this applause, Selina said: 'Well, so it seems to me, though it had nothing to do with you, Mr Calverleigh, so you must not be thinking that I mean to censure *you*, and in any event poor Mr Miles Calverleigh hasn't made his fortune – at least, he doesn't look as if he had, because he wears the shabbiest clothes! On the other hand, he is putting up at York House, and that, you know, is by no means *dagger-cheap*, as some dear friends of ours, who are staying there, tell me.'

'The reverse!' he said. 'You terrify me, ma'am! He had always the reputation of being excessively expensive, and with never a feather to fly with! I only hope he doesn't tip them the double at York House, leaving me to stand the reckoning!' He saw that this speech had shocked Selina, and had made Fanny look gravely at him, and quickly and smoothly retrieved his position, saying:

'The truth is, you know, that he caused my grandfather, and my father too, a great deal of embarrassment, so that I never heard any good of him. I own, however, that I have often wondered if he could be quite as black as he was painted to me. Indeed, if *you* do not dislike him, Miss Wendover, he cannot be! I shall lose no time in making his acquaintance.' He turned towards Fanny, his smile a caress. 'Tell me all the latest Bath-news!' he begged. 'Has Lady Weaverham forgiven me for having been obliged to cry off from my engagement to dine with her? Has Miss Ancrum summoned up the courage to have that tooth drawn, or is she still wearing a swollen face? Did – oh, tell me everything! I feel as if I had been absent for a twelvemonth!'

Since the most interesting event which had lately occurred in Bath was the return of Oliver Grayshott to his mother's fond care it was not long before Fanny was telling him all about this, and denmanding his help with the acrostic she was composing for Oliver's amusement. 'You see, I am doing what I may to entertain him,' she explained. 'Poor boy, he is so dreadfully pulled that he can't join in any of our expeditions, or attend the assemblies, or *anything*, so when Lavinia asked me to lend her my aid in keeping up his spirits *of course* I said I would!' She added, to her younger aunt's suppressed indignation: 'I thought you could not object?'

He responded suitably, but Abby, who was rapidly taking him in strong dislike, received (and welcomed) the impression that he did not regard the intrusion on the Bath scene of Mr Oliver Grayshott with favour.

Seven

*M*r Stacy Calverleigh, having partaken of a light
nuncheon in Sydney Place, strolled back towards
the centre of the town, but instead of turning left
at the end of Bridge Street, into High Street, he hesitated at
the junction of the roads, and then, with a shrug of his
shoulders, walked on, along Borough Wall to Burton Street.
Turning northward up this he soon reached Milsom Street, at
the top of which, in George Street, the York House Hotel was
situated.

This hostelry was the most exclusive as well as the most
expensive to be found in Bath; and it vaguely irritated Stacy that
his ne'er-do-well uncle should be staying in it. Not that he had
any wish to stay there himself, for however much money he
might owe his tailor, and a great many other London tradesmen,
he had no intention of damaging his reputation in Bath by going
on tick there. In fact, the White Hart suited him very well,
situated as it was in Stall Street, with many of its rooms
overlooking the Pump Yard. The quiet of York House was not at
all to his taste: he liked to be at the hub of things, and had no
objection to the noise and bustle of a busy posting-house.

The weather had been uncertain all day, and by the time he
reached York House it had begun to rain again. There was a
damp chill in the air which made the sight of a small fire, burning
in Mr Miles Calverleigh's private parlour, not unwelcome. Mr
Calverleigh was seated on one side of it, his ankles crossed on a
stool, and a cheroot between his fingers. He was glancing

through a newspaper when the waiter announced Stacy, but after lowering it, and directing a critical look at his nephew, he threw it aside, saying, in a tone of tolerant amusement: 'Good God! Are you my nephew?'

'So I've been led to believe, sir,' replied Stacy, bowing slightly. '*If* you are indeed Miles Calverleigh?'

'I am, but you mustn't let it worry you,' said Miles kindly. 'You don't favour your father much: for one thing, he wasn't such a dapper-dog. Hadn't the figure for it. I collect that yellow calf-clingers are now all the crack?'

'Oh, decidedly!' said Stacy, whose primrose pantaloons were indeed of the first stare. He laid his hat, and his gloves, and his clouded cane down on the table. 'I have been absent from Bath or I should have visited you earlier, sir. You must forgive my seeming remissness.'

'Well, there's no difficulty about that: I hadn't the least expectation of seeing you.'

'One would not wish to be backward in any attention to so close a relative,' said Stacy, a trifle haughtily.

'What, not even to such a loose screw as I am? Come, come, nevvy! that's doing it rather too brown! You are wondering what the devil brings me here, and wishing that nothing had done so!' He laughed, seeing that he had taken Stacy aback, and said: 'Come down from your high ropes, and don't try to stand on points with me: I've no taste for punctilio. You don't owe me respect or observance, you know. Sit down, and empty your budget!'

'Well, sir – what *has* brought you home to England?' asked Stacy, with a forced smile.

'Inclination. Cheroot?'

'Thank you, no!'

'A snuff-taker, are you? You'll end with yellow stains all round your nose, but I daresay you may have caught your heiress before that happens, so it don't signify.'

Stacy said quickly, on the defensive: 'I don't know what you – who has told you –'

'Don't act the dunce! Miss Wendover told me – Miss Abigail Wendover – and I don't fancy your suit will prosper.'

'Not if she has anything to say in the matter!' Stacy said, his brow darkening. 'I believe her to be my enemy. I met her for the first time today, and it is very plain she'll knock me up if she can!'

'Not a doubt of it. I can tell you of another who is likely to bum squabble you, and that's James Wendover.'

'Oh, him!' Stacy said, shrugging. 'He may try to do so, but he won't succeed. Fanny doesn't care a rush for him. But this curst aunt is another matter. Fanny –' He broke off, realising suddenly that he had been betrayed into indiscretion, and summoned his boyish smile to his aid. 'The thing is that Fanny *is* an heiress. One can't blame her family for wishing her to make a great match, but when one is deep in love considerations of wealth or rank don't signify.'

'Well, at seventeen a girl may fancy herself to be deep in love, but in my experience it isn't a lasting passion,' commented Miles cynically. 'You aren't going to tell me that considerations of wealth don't signify to you, are you?'

The smile died under that ironic gaze; Stacy said angrily: 'Damn it, how could I marry a girl without fortune?'

'I shouldn't think you could. According to what I hear, your windmill has dwindled to a nutshell.'

'Who told you that?' Stacy demanded suspiciously. 'I wasn't aware that you had any acquaintance in England!'

'How should you be? I have, but it was Letty who told me you're monstrously in the wind.'

'Do you mean my great-aunt Kelham?' Stacy said incredulously. 'Are you asking me to believe that you have visited *her*?'

'Oh, no! I don't give a straw what you believe. Why should I?' said Miles, with unabated affability.

Flushing, Stacy stammered: 'Beg pardon! It was only that – well, she's such a devil of a high stickler that I shouldn't have thought – that is to say, –'

'*I* see!' said Miles encouragingly. 'What you would have thought is that she'd have shut the door in my face!'

Stacy burst out laughing. 'Well, yes!' he admitted. 'If I don't owe you respect, I need not wrap it up in clean linen, I collect!'

'Oh, no, not the least need to do that!' Miles assured him. 'The thing is that your great-aunt – lord, to think of Letty's being a great-aunt! She's no more than a dozen years older than I am! – well, the thing is that she was used to have a kindness for me. That might have been because she detested my father, of course. Come to think of it, *your* father wasn't first oars with her by any means. Or it might have been because most females are partial to rakes,' he added thoughtfully.

'Was *that* why you were sent abroad?' Stacy asked. 'I've never known precisely – you see, my father never spoke of you, except to say that you were *not* to be spoken of!'

'Oh, I was shockingly loose in the haft!' responded his uncle cordially. 'I started in the petticoat-line at Eton: that's why they expelled me.'

Stacy regarded him in some awe. 'And – and at Oxford?'

'I don't recall, but I should think very likely. The trouble then was that I was too ripe and ready by half: always raising some kind of a breeze. Nothing to the larks I kicked up in London, though. A peep-of-day boy, that was me – and a damned young fool! I crowned my career by trying to elope with an heiress. That was coming it rather too strong for the family, so they got rid of me, and I'm sure I don't blame them.' He smiled mockingly at his nephew. 'The luck didn't favour you either, did it?'

Stacy stiffened. 'Sir?'

'Tried to leap the book yourself, didn't you?'

'That, sir, is something I prefer not to discuss! It was an unfortunate episode! We were carried away by what we believed to be an unalterable passion! The circumstances – the whole truth – cannot be known to you, and – in short, I don't feel obliged to justify myself to you!'

'Good God, I trust you won't! It's no concern of mine. I may be your uncle, but I've really very little interest in you. You're too like me, and I find myself a dead bore. The only difference I can discover is that you're a gamester. That's the one vice I never had, and it don't awake a spark of interest in me, because I find gaming a dead bore too.'

'I suppose you're trying to gammon me – or know nothing of gaming, and that I don't believe!'

'Oh, no! I tried gaming, but it held no lure for me. Too slow!'

'Slow?' Stacy gasped.

'Why, yes! What have you to do but stake your blunt, and watch the turn of a card, or the fall of the dice? Same with horse-racing. Now, if I'd ever been offered a match, to ride my own horse against another man's, that would have been sport, if you like! But I ride too heavy, and always did.'

'But they said – I was given to understand – that you cost my grandfather a fortune!'

'I *was* expensive,' admitted Miles, 'though I shouldn't have put it as high as a fortune. But I got a deal of amusement out of my spendings. What the devil is there to amuse one in hazard or faro?'

It was evident that Stacy found this incomprehensible. He stared, and said, after a moment: 'I should envy you, I suppose! But I don't. It's in my blood, and surely in yours too! Father – my grandfather – great-uncle Charles – oh, all of them!'

'Yes, but you must remember that I was a sad disappointment to the family. My father even suspected me of being a changeling. A delightful theory, but without foundation, I fear.' He threw the butt of his cheroot into the fire, and got up, stretching his long limbs. His light eyes looked down at Stacy, their expression hard to interpret. 'Have you lost Danescourt yet?' he enquired.

Stacy laughed shortly. 'Good God, what would any man in his senses stake against that damned barrack? It's mortgaged to the hilt, and falling into ruin besides! It was encumbered when my father died, and *I* can't bring it about. I hate the place – wouldn't waste a groat on it!'

'Shades of our ancestors!' said Miles flippantly. 'They must all be turning in their graves. Perhaps *you* are a changeling! Or did you come to visit me in the hope that I might be able to restore your fallen fortunes?'

'Hardly!' Stacy said, flicking a glance at his uncle's person. 'I'm told you came home bear-leading Mrs Grayshott's son, which doesn't lead me to suppose you're swimming in lard! I hope to God that won't leak out!'

'Oh, I don't think so!' said Miles reassuringly. 'But you have it wrong: I wasn't bear-leading him. I was combining the duties of sick-nurse and valet.'

'Good God! If *that* should become known – ! I wish you will consider *my* position, sir!'

'But why should I?'

'Well, damme, I *am* your nephew!' Stacy said indignantly. 'And you are, after all, a Calverleigh!'

'Yes, but not at all high in the instep, I promise you. As for our relationship, no one can blame you for being my nephew – I don't myself – but if it irks you, don't acknowledge me!'

'It may seem to you to be a funning matter,' returned Stacy, reddening, 'but I shall beg leave to tell you, sir, that it is no very pleasant thing for me to have you here, looking like – oh, dash it, like a regular rough diamond!' He rose, and picked up his hat. 'I don't know how long you mean to remain in Bath, but I trust you are aware of what the charges are in this hotel!'

'Don't give them a thought!' said Miles. 'I won't chalk 'em up to you. if I find myself at a stand, I can always shoot the crow.'

'Vastly diverting, sir!' snapped Stacy, collecting his gloves and his cane, ''Servant!'

He executed a slight bow, and left the room. He was so much ruffled that he had reached the White Hart before his anger had cooled enough to allow him to consider whether he had acted wisely in letting his temper ride him. He was not naturally an even-tempered man, but he had cultivated an air of smiling good humour, knowing that it was as great an asset to anyone living precariously on the fringe of society as his handsome countenance. It was rarely that he betrayed irritability, or lost his poise, even under the severe provocation of receiving a set-down from some out-and-outer into whose circle he had tried to insinuate himself, or a high-nosed stare from a great lady whose favour he wanted to win. He began to be vexed with himself, and to wonder what quality it was in his uncle which had set up his bristles; but it was not for some time, and then with reluctance, that it dawned on him that he had been made to feel small. This had nothing to do with Miles's superior height, and even less with his manner, which had not been that of a man talking to his nephew, but that of a man talking to a contemporary whom he regarded with indifference. Recalling how Miles had lounged at his ease, looking as though he had dressed all by guess, in an outmoded coat, his neckcloth loosened, and an abominable cheroot between his long brown fingers, he felt resentment stir again. He, and not his disreputable uncle, should have been master of the situation, but in some mysterious way he had been made to feel awkward. He had expected to have been received, if not with gratification, at least with pleasure: it had been a piece of condescension on the part of the head of the family to have visited its reprobate, but the reprobate was apparently unaware of this. He had been neither pleased nor displeased, and certainly not gratified; and the only interest he had shown in his nephew was of the most casual order. Stacy found this so galling that he almost wished himself back at the York House, for the purpose of giving the impudent fellow a well-deserved set-down.

It soon occurred to him, however, that it behoved him to tread warily: even, if he could do it, to make a friend of Miles. Miles knew of his courtship of Fanny Wendover, and there could be small doubt that he had learnt of it from her aunts. He had shown no sign of disapproval: indeed, he had taken as little interest in that as in the disclosure that Danescourt was heavily encumbered, but if he was on terms with Miss Abigail Wendover it might be worth while to make a push to gain his support.

Marriage had few attractions for Mr Stacy Calverleigh, but it had been forcibly borne in upon him that only by a rich marriage could he escape from embarrassments which had become extremely pressing; and he was determined to marry Fanny, even if he were forced to persuade her to elope with him. But it would be infinitely preferable to marry her with the consent of her aunts and her uncle. Selina he could bring round his thumb, but he had guessed from the outset that Selina was of less importance than Abigail, and that it was Abigail's influence which was the more likely to weigh with Mr James Wendover.

He had no illusions about James. He had never known James's father, or his elder brother, far less his grandfather, but he knew that they had been bywords in their day, and that James was commonly held to be the epitome of a Wendover. He was ruled by two passions: a determination to advance the interests of the family, and an even stronger determination to avoid at all costs anything savouring remotely of the scandalous. He could be depended on to oppose Fanny's marriage to an impecunious young man of slightly damaged reputation, but once the knot was tied he could also be depended on to hush up the resultant scandal. And if he did not immediately make suitable provision for his wealthy ward he would very soon be obliged to do so, for fear of *what people would say*. This (according to the malicious) was the dread which governed his conduct. And if Stacy showed himself to be a reformed character people would certainly say very rude things indeed, unless James put Fanny in possession of at least the income from her large fortune, and of her ancestral home. Particularly, thought Stacy, if the clandestine marriage were blessed with an heir. For himself, he had every intention of behaving with the utmost propriety, even of resigning himself for quite some time to living for several months of the year at Amberfield. It would be boring, but once it was known that he was married to an heiress whose property would become his within a few years he would be able to exist comfortably on the expectation. It should be possible for him to settle with his most pressing creditors, and although he would still be in Dun territory there would be no longer any fear of finding himself locked up for debt. Not the most avaricious bluntmonger would proceed to extremes against a man who was heir (by marriage) to a handsome fortune.

It was not, of course, the ideal marriage. He would have preferred – and, indeed, had preferred – a bride who had attained her majority; but heiresses were few and far between, and since his abortive attempt at an elopement his chances of being allowed to come within speaking distance of one had lessened to vanishing point. On the other hand, Fanny was a little beauty, and he thought that if he must become leg-shackled he would as lief marry her as any other. But he wanted to do so with the approval of her aunts; and, having made a conquest of Selina, he had been hopeful of achieving a like success with Abigail. Five minutes in her company had been enough to shatter optimism: Abigail was made of sterner stuff than her sister, and had plainly set her face against him. Probably James Wendover was to blame for that; perhaps another man's influence could be brought to bear with advantage. She seemed to be on friendly terms with Miles, which made it desirable to lose no time in enlisting Miles's support.

So when he attended the ball at the Upper Rooms that evening, and found that his uncle was present, talking to Mrs Grayshott, he seized the first opportunity that offered of greeting him with every sign of pleasure. He was relieved to see that Miles did at least possess knee-smalls and a swallow-tailed coat, but his fingers itched to rearrange a necktie which he thought deplorable, and to brush into a more fashionable style his uncle's raven locks. His own were beautifully pomaded, and swept into a Brutus; his coat exactly fitted his trim figure; a fob dangled at his waist; a quizzing-glass hung round his neck; the subtle fragrance of Steek's lavender water clung to his person; and a diamond pin nestled in the folds of his Oriental tie. In fact, as Lady Weaverham observed to Mrs Slinfold, he had the unmistakable London touch. Mrs Slinfold, concurring, added that in her opinion he was the first in elegance of all the gentlemen present; but Mrs Ruscombe, overhearing, said with her shallow laugh: 'Oh, do you think so? Such a fribble! My husband – so naughty of him! – calls him a positive coxcomb!'

But since everyone knew not only that it was Mrs Ruscombe's custom to attribute her more damaging criticisms to her meek spouse, but also that she had made every effort to throw the eldest of her five daughters in Mr Stacy Calverleigh's way, this remark was received in stony silence. Mr Stacy Calverleigh might be too much of a bandbox creature for everyone's taste, but he was not a coxcomb, for he neither strutted, nor played off the airs of an exquisite. His manners were very agreeable, so that even the most censorious of his elders were obliged to admit that he was pretty-behaved enough.

When Miss Abigail Wendover arrived, chaperoning her lovely niece, it was seen that she was wearing another of her London gowns, and agreed amongst her friends that she was in quite her best looks, only Mrs Ruscombe advancing the opinion that it was easy to appear to advantage if one was prepared to squander a fortune on one's back.

This estimate was an exaggeration, but, being comfortably endowed, Abby was not obliged to study economy, and had had no hesitation in purchasing an extremely costly gown of figured lace, worn over a satin robe, which hung in soft folds to her feet, and ended in a demi-train. This, as much as the diamond aigrette in her hair, proclaimed to the knowledgeable that she had no intention of dancing; but Mr Miles Calverleigh was not of their number, and presently made his way to where she was sitting, and begged to have the honour of leading her into the set which was then forming.

She smiled, but shook her head, saying: 'Thank you, but I don't dance.'

'I'm glad of that,' he said. Then, as surprise and quick amusement leapt into her eyes, he laughed, and added: 'I'm a shocking bad hand at it, you see! May I sit down, and talk to you instead?'

'Pray do!' she responded. 'I have been wishing for the opportunity of talking to you, sir. Have you yet made the acquaintance of your nephew?'

'Yes, he was so obliging as to pay me a visit today.'

'What do you think of him?' she demanded.

'Why, nothing! Must I?'

'I wish you won't be so provoking!' said Abby.

'I wouldn't provoke you for the world. But what would you have me say? He was with me for less than an hour, and I can't recall that he said anything that interested me to the point of *thinking* about him.'

'You are a most unnatural uncle!' she told him, with a severity at variance with the dimple that peeped in her cheek.

'Am I?' He reflected for a moment. 'No, I don't think so. I'd three uncles, and none of 'em took the smallest interest in me. After all, why should they?'

'For no reason at all, I daresay! Are you trying to make me – oh, what is it the hunting men say? – fly from a scent? Yes, that's it. Well, you won't do it! I also made the acquaintance of your nephew today, and I don't scruple to tell you that I like him even less than I had expected I should!'

'No, did you? Your expectations must have been much higher than you led me to suppose!'

'No, but – oh, I suppose I did expect him to be a man of charm! I don't find him charming at all, and I can't conceive how Fanny came to fall in love with him! Now, tell me to my head, can you?'

'Oh, easily!' he replied. 'He is a very pretty fellow, you must allow! Turns out in excellent trim, too, and has both air and address.'

'Oh, yes!' she said bitterly. 'Playing off his cajolery! He tried to turn me up sweet, but it's my belief he is one who hides his teeth. And when he smiles there's no smile in his eyes: only – only a *measuring* look! Surely you must have seen it?'

'Well, no!' he confessed. 'But that might be because he didn't smile very often when he was with me. Or perhaps because he saw no need to – er – measure me!'

She said quickly: 'You didn't like him either, did you?'

'Oh, no! But how many people does one like?'

She frowned over this, momentarily diverted. 'Upon first

acquaintance? I don't know: not very many, perhaps. But one need not *dis*like them, and I *do* dislike Mr Stacy Calverleigh!'

'Yes, I thought you did,' he said gravely.

'And I don't believe, for all his protestations and caressing ways, that he *truly* loves Fanny, or would have made the least push to engage her affections had she not been possessed of a large fortune!'

'Oh, lord, no!'

She turned her head, looking up into his face with pleading eyes, and laying one of her expensively gloved hands on his arm. 'If you too think that, won't you – oh, Mr Calverleigh, *won't* you do *anything* to save my poor Fanny?'

He was regarding her with the smile which, unlike his nephew's, sprang to life in his eyes, but all he said was: 'My dear girl – No, no, don't poker up! It was a slip of the tongue! My dear Miss Wendover, what do you imagine I *could* do?'

Never having considered this, she was at a loss for an answer. She said lamely: 'Surely you must be able to do *something*!'

'What leads you to think so?'

'Well – well, you are his uncle, after all!'

'Oh, that's no reason! You've told me already that I am an unnatural uncle, and if that means one who don't meddle in the affairs of a nephew over whom he has no authority, and who might, for aught he cares, have been any other man's nephew, you are undoubtedly right!'

'Not authority, no! But whatever you may say the relationship exists, and you must have *influence,* if you would but exert it?'

He looked down at her in some amusement. 'You know, you have some remarkably hubble-bubble notions in that charming head of yours! How the devil should I have influence over a nephew who met me for the first time this afternoon?'

She perceived the force of this argument, but the conviction that he could drive off Stacy, if he chose to do it, remained with her. It was irrational, to be accounted for only by the strength she believed she had detected in his harsh-featured countenance, and by a certain ruthlessness which underlay his careless manners. She said, with a tiny sigh: 'I suppose you can have none. And yet – and yet – I think you *could,* if you but wanted to!'

'For my part,' he retorted, 'I think you are very well able to button it up yourself, without any assistance from me.

There did not seem to be anything more to be said, nor was she granted the opportunity to pursue the subject, her attention being claimed just then by Mr Dunston, who had been watching her jealously for some minutes, and now came up to beg for the privilege of taking her into the tea-room presently.

They met again, two days later, in Edgar Buildings; and however little pleased Abby may have been to find Mr Stacy Calverleigh in Mrs Grayshott's drawing-room, making himself agreeable to his hostess, and winning Fanny's favour by the engaging solicitude with which he treated Mr Oliver Grayshott, she was undoubtedly pleased to see his uncle, and betrayed it by the sudden smile which lit her eyes, and the readiness with which she put out her hand.

She discovered that her arrival had interrupted a lively discussion. Mr Grayshott's medical adviser, visiting him earlier in the day, had professed himself very well satisfied with his progress, and had endorsed a somewhat recalcitrant patient's belief that it would do him a great deal of good to abandon the sofa, and to get out for a little air and exercise. A drive up to Lansdown, and a gentle walk there, enjoying the view of the Bristol Channel, was what he recommended; but when Mr Grayshott took exception to this programme, saying, very improperly, that he would be damned if he allowed himself to be driven to Lansdown or anywhere else, as though he were dying of a deep decline, the doctor laughed, and said: 'Well, well, go for a ride, if you choose! It won't do you any harm, provided you don't go too far, or exhaust yourself.'

This was by no means what Mrs Grayshott wanted. She believed Oliver to be a long way from complete recovery, unable to forget how grey and worn he had looked after the journey from London; and she could not like his scheme of riding out of Bath with his sister as his only companion. Lavinia was a nervous horsewoman, requiring constant surveillance: not at all the sort of escort one would choose to send out with an invalid; and Fanny, instantly offering to accompany the Grayshotts, was no more acceptable to the widow. Fanny was not nervous. Mrs Grayshott, herself no horsewoman, had heard her described by one of her admirers as a clipping rider, a regular good 'un to go, which was an encomium to strike dread into a mother's anxious heart. And then, to make matters worse, Stacy Calverleigh, who had met the two girls in Queen's Square, and accompanied them to Edgar Buildings, proffered his services, laughingly assuring Mrs Grayshott that he would engage himself to bring the party back to her in good time, and none the worse for wear.

This question was instantly approved of by the girls, if not by Oliver, which made it difficult for Mrs Grayshott to decline it. She was floundering amongst some rather lame excuses when Abigail was announced.

'In a good hour! Come in, my dear, and lend me your support!' she exclaimed going forward to greet Abby. 'Here is my wilful son determined on riding up to Lansdown, and these other young people bent on making up a party to go with him! I am persuaded you cannot like the scheme any more than I do, for although Mr Stacy Calverleigh has very kindly offered to go with them I fear that he would find the task of preventing three such harum-scarum children from going much too far quite beyond his power!'

'No, indeed we wouldn't!' cried Fanny. 'We mean to take the greatest care of Oliver, and I promise you it wouldn't be at all hard for Stacy to prevent us from going too far, even if we wished to do so, ma'am!' She turned impulsively towards Abby. '*You* don't object to it, do you, Abby?'

Misliking the scheme, yet unable to think of any other reason for placing a veto on it but the inclusion of Stacy in the party, Abby hesitated. Rescue came from an unexpected quarter. 'Do you ride, Miss Wendover?' asked Mr Miles Calverleigh, smiling across the room at her with such complete understanding in his eyes that an answering smile was won from her.

'Why, yes!' she replied.

'In that case, you may be easy, ma'am,' said Miles, to Mrs Grayshott. 'Between us, Miss Wendover and I should be able to control the activities of the younger members of this hazardous expedition.'

The only objection raised to this unexpected augmentation of the party came from Oliver, who said, with feeling, that he had not yet received notice to quit, and was very well able to take care of himself. He added that if he had had the least apprehension that his wish to hack out of Bath would have caused such a commotion he would never have uttered it.

'Silence, halfling!' said Miles, in shocked accents. 'You are leading Miss Wendover to suppose that you don't want her to go with you!'

This intervention naturally cast Oliver into confusion, and he hastened to reassure Abby. She laughed at him, telling him that she had not the smallest intention of enacting the role of dry-nurse; and was herself much heartened by Fanny's instant approval of the revised scheme.

'Oh, capital!' Fanny exclaimed. 'You will come, won't you, *Best* of my aunts?'

Eight

ince Oliver showed no signs of exhaustion, and Stacy, behaving with great circumspection, made no attempt to monopolise Fanny's attention, nothing occurred to spoil Abby's enjoyment of this mild form of exhilaration. Miles Calverleigh rode beside her for most of the time, and made himself so agreeable that she forgot her anxieties in listening to what he had to tell her of India, and the customs of its people. He had to be coaxed to talk, saying at first that persons who gabbed about their foreign experiences were dead bores, but the questions she put to him were intelligent, and her interest in his replies so real that he soon dropped his reserve, painting a vivid picture for her, and even recounting some of his experiences. These ranged from the adventurous to the comical, but it was not long before he brought them to an end, saying: 'And that is enough about me! Now tell me of yourself!'

'Alas, there's nothing to tell! I've done nothing, and have been nowhere. You don't know how much I envy you – how often I have wished I were a man!'

'Have you, indeed? You must be alone in that wish!'

'Thank you! But you are wrong: my father wished it too! He wanted another son.'

'What, with Rowland and James as grim examples? Or because he hoped that a third son might be less of a slow-top?'

'Certainly not! And although I didn't like him I must in common justice say that Rowland, at least, was not a slow-top. He was hunting-mad, you know, and a very hard goer.'

'I wasn't talking about that. Intellectually a slow-top!'

'Oh, yes, but so was my father! Naturally he didn't count his stupidity a fault in Rowland. In fact, he had the greatest dislike of clever people.'

He chuckled appreciatively, which made her say, in a conscience-stricken voice: 'I ought not to have said that. My wretched tongue! I do *try* to mind it!'

'Then don't! I like the way you have of saying just what comes into your head.'

She smiled, but shook her head. 'No, it is my besetting sin, and I ought long since to have overcome it.'

'From what I recall of your father, I should suppose that he made every effort to help you to do so. Did he dislike you as much as you disliked him?'

'Yes, he – Oh, how dare you? You are quite abominable! You know very well that it would be the height of impropriety for me to say that I disliked my father! Every feeling must be offended!'

'Well, none of mine are,' he responded imperturbably. 'You did, didn't you?'

'Yes, but it is one of the things which must never be said. And if he disliked me I am bound to own that it was quite my own fault. I was a sad trial to him, I fear.'

'Yes, of course: too clever by half!'

'I'm not clever – or only if you compare me with the rest of my family,' she said reflectively. 'I love them dearly, but Selina and Mary are perfect widgeons, and although my sister Jane has a good deal of commonsense she never thinks of anything but her children, and the failings of her servants. My father merely thought I was bookish, which was the worst he could say of anyone! He ascribed all my undutiful conduct to it.'

'Now, I should have said that you had an all too lively sense of your duty,' he remarked.

'Not when I was a girl. I was for ever rebelling against the restrictions imposed upon me, and oh, how much I detested that hateful word, *propriety*! That's why I was used to wish I were a man: so that I could have escaped from it! Girls can't, you know. We are always shackled – hedged about –'

'*Cabin'd, cribb'd, confined,*' he supplied, adding grandiloquently: 'I'm bookish too.'

A ripple of laughter broke from her. 'So I perceive! And that is just how it was in my family.'

'Was? Still is!'

She turned her head, startled. 'No! Why, what can you mean?'

He nodded towards the four younger members of the party, riding ahead. 'Fanny, of course. Don't you cabin, crib, and confine her?'

'Indeed I don't!' she said warmly. 'She enjoys far, far more liberty than ever I did!' A quizzically raised eyebrow brought the blood rushing to her cheeks. She stammered: 'It's true! You – you are thinking that I don't permit her to go anywhere without me, but that is *not* true! I have never, until your odious nephew came to Bath, accompanied her on such expeditions as this and if *he* had not been in question, and young Grayshott had invited her to go with him, she might have done so with my goodwill!' She paused, and, after considering for a moment, said frankly: 'No. Not alone. *I* should have no qualms, but where she is concerned I must take care that she does nothing to provide all the Bath quizzes with food for gossip! You see, my brother entrusted her to my guardianship, and however nonsensical I may think many of the conventions which hedge us about I must, for her own sake, compel her to abide by them. Pray try to understand! What I, at my age, might choose to disregard, she, on the verge of her come-out, must not!'

'Poor girl!' he said lightly. 'How many nonsensical conventions are *you* ready to flout?'

'Oh, a great many, if I had only myself to consider!'

'We'll put that to the test. Will you go with me to the play on Saturday?'

She hesitated, in equal surprise and doubt. After a moment, she said: 'Are you inviting me to form one of your party, sir?'

'Good God, no! I haven't a party.'

'Oh!' She relapsed again into silence. 'I collect you mean to invite Fanny as well?' she hazarded at last.

'Oh, no, you don't!' he retorted. 'You know very well that Fanny is engaged to go with the Grayshotts to Mrs Faversham's waltzing-party! I wonder you will let her!'

'Do you, indeed? Well, if you think me so – so *stuffy*, *I* wonder that you should suppose I would go to the theatre with you alone! The waltz is not danced in the Rooms, but Bath is a very old-fashioned place, and, in London, waltzes, and quadrilles too, are extensively danced. I am very happy that Fanny should be given the opportunity of – of getting into the way of it, before her come-out in the spring! But when it comes to going to the theatre –' She paused, frowning over it.

He waited, regarding her profile with a derisive smile, until she said, struck by a sudden inspiration: 'If you were to invite my sister as well! That would make it perfectly unexceptionable!'

'No doubt!'

She could not help laughing. 'Yes, I know, but – Well, it is quite absurd, but there is a difference – or there is thought to be – between escorting a lady to – oh, to a concert, in the Assembly Rooms, and to the theatre! I think it is because the concerts, being held by subscription, are more private. Then, too, one doesn't sit apart, and one mingles with –'

'Oh, if that's all, we can sit in the pit!'

' – with one's friends!' finished Abby severely.

'And at the end of the first act, when your escort hopes to enjoy your company, some impudent fellow snabbles you from under his nose, and takes you off to tea – just as I did, when that mooncalf who paid you slip-slop compliments thought you were his own!'

'Well! At least you have the grace to own your impudence!' she retaliated. 'However gracelessly you may do so! But Mr Dunston is not a mooncalf, and the compliments he paid me were very pretty.'

'Any man who could tell you that you shone down every other

woman present, and said you were as fair as a rose in May can't help but be a mooncalf. Trying it on much too rare and thick!'

Piqued, she said: 'I am not a beauty, and I never was, but I am not an *antidote*, I hope!'

He smiled. 'No, you are neither the one nor the other. What that dunderheaded admirer of yours hasn't the wit to perceive is that you've something of more worth than mere beauty.'

Miss Wendover was well aware that it behoved her to give the audacious Mr Calverleigh a cold set-down, or, at the very least, to ignore this remark; but instead of doing either of these things she directed a look of shy enquiry at him. 'Have I? Pray tell me what it may be!'

He looked her over critically, the amusement lingering in his eyes. 'Well, you have a great deal of countenance, and an elegant figure. I like your eyes too, particularly when they laugh. But that's not it. What you have in abundance is charm!'

She blushed rosily, and stammered: 'I am afraid, sir, that it is now you who are offering me Spanish coin!'

'Oh, no! Your nose is indifferent, and your mouth a trifle too large, and your hair, though it grows prettily, is an unremarkable brown.'

She broke into laughter. 'I acquit you!'

'So I should hope! I might have added that you had also courage, but I doubt it.'

She fired up at that. 'Then you are mistaken! I collect that's a jibe, because I hesitated to accept your invitation! Very well, I will go to the play with you!'

'Good girl!' he said approvingly. 'Pluck to the backbone! But I won't take you if you really feel that it would damage your reputation.'

'No,' she said, in a resolute tone. 'Not at my age!'

'Just what I was thinking myself,' he agreed.

She looked sharply at him, but he was perfectly grave. 'Would it be proper for you to dine with me first, at York House?' he asked.

'Thank you, but I should prefer you to dine in Sydney Place,' she replied. 'My sister will be very happy to further her acquaintance with you.'

He bowed a meek acceptance, and, as they had by this time reached their goal, which was the monument erected to the memory of one Sir Basil Grenville, killed in the Civil Wars, their conversation came to an end.

Nor was it resumed; for after the remains of a Saxon fortification, situated near by, had been shown to the Calverleighs, one of whom affected a civil but artificial interest in it, and the other no interest at all, it was judged to be time to turn homeward; and upon the return journey the party split up into a different order, Mr Stacy Calverleigh contriving that Abby should ride with him instead of with his uncle.

'Do, pray, allow me to be your escort, ma'am!' he said. 'I have been seeking an opportunity to talk to you, and – I hope – to better my acquaintance with you.'

'By all means,' she answered, in a cool voice. 'What is it you wish to say to me, sir?'

He bestowed his flashing smile upon her. 'Ah, you know what I wish to say! And I, alas, know that I am addressing myself to an ear little inclined to listen to me!'

'If you mean to address yourself to me in rehearsed periods, you are perfectly right!' she told him. 'Without roundaboutation, you wish to obtain my consent to Fanny's becoming engaged to you. I am afraid you haven't understood the case: Fanny isn't my ward, but my brother's. You must apply to him, not to me. In fact,' she added thoughtfully, 'you should have done so before making Fanny an offer. To form a connection with a girl of seventeen without the knowledge of her guardian is really not at all the thing, you know.'

He looked a little discomposed. 'Had I known – I thought, at first, that she was Miss Wendover's ward! Naturally, if I had known –'

'Then what prevented you from asking my sister's permission before you declared yourself to Fanny?' asked Abby, in an interested voice.

He bit his lip. 'I should have done so, of course, but I had no reason to suppose – that is to say, I believed she was aware – did not look upon my suit with disfavour! Then, too, conscious as I am of my unworthiness I did not intend – Ah, Miss Abby, you don't understand! You make no allowance for the violence of my feelings, which, I confess, carried me beyond the bounds of propriety!'

'No, I don't think I do,' agreed Abby.

He shot a challenging look at her, which she met with a faint bland smile. 'From the moment I saw her I was lost!' he said dramatically. 'Oh, I have fancied myself in love before, many times – you see, I don't attempt to deceive you, ma'am! – but when I met Fanny I knew that it had never been more than fancy, and bitterly did I regret the past – all my follies and indiscretions! Yes, and determined to become worthy of that beautiful angel!'

'Well, you have plenty of time to achieve your ambition,' said Abby cordially. 'There is no saying but what, if you were to succeed, my brother might look more kindly upon you, when Fanny reaches her majority.'

'Four years! Miss Abby, neither she nor I could endure it! We hoped – Fanny was fully persuaded that you – her favourite aunt, as she calls you! – would stand our friend! *Your* support must weigh with Mr Wendover!'

'My dear sir, if I were to lend my support to such an unsuitable and improvident marriage, Mr Wendover would suppose me to have run mad, and would be more likely to have me placed under restraint. And I must say that I shouldn't blame him!'

'Improvident!' he exclaimed, catching at the word. 'Ay, that is the obstacle! Believe me, I feel it as keenly as you do! My inheritance was wasted before I came into it, and when I tell you that my father died before I was of age you may judge how unripe I was, how little able to restore what had been squandered! I hope I am wiser now.'

'I am sure,' said Abby politely, 'that all your friends must share that hope. I fear, however, that my brother will require some rather more solid proof.'

Nettled, he said: 'You misunderstand me, ma'am! When I spoke of my inheritance having been wasted, I did not mean that I am reduced to penury! Between my fortune and Fanny's I fear there may be disparity, but although my lands are not in such good heart as I could wish they are extensive, and I am, after all, the head of my family! There have been Calverleighs at Danescourt since I don't know when!'

'Since the Conquest,' she supplied, with a reminiscent chuckle. 'According to your uncle, the founder of your house was in all probability one of the – the *thatchgallows* in the Conqueror's train.'

'My uncle is fond of cutting jokes,' he replied, with a forced smile. 'Even Mr James Wendover can scarcely find fault with my lineage! As for fortune, I don't know what Fanny's may be, nor do I care – except that if it is to form an insuperable barrier between us I wish it at Jericho!'

'Well, for the next eight years it might as well be,' she said prosaically. 'It was left to my brother to be held in trust for Fanny until she reaches the age of five-and-twenty, you know.'

'Five-and-twenty!' he ejaculated, the smile wiped suddenly from his lips. He recovered himself in a flash, saying: 'I didn't know it, and am agreeably surprised. Under those circumstances I must surely escape the stigma of being thought a fortune-hunter.'

This seemed to her so disingenuous that she was too much disgusted to answer him. She rode on at a quickened pace, so that the rest of the party was soon overtaken, and Stacy was obliged to bring his confidences to an end.

Whatever discomfiture he might feel, no sign of it was to be detected, either in his face or in his manner. He seemed, rather, to be in spirits, full of liveliness and wit, keeping Lavinia in giggles, and causing Fanny to ask her aunt, when they rode down Great Pulteney Street together, if she did not find him as charming as he was handsome.

'Why, as to that – he has agreeable manners, but – do you think him *charming*, Fanny?' said Abby, on a note of surprise.

'Good gracious, Abby, *everyone* does so!' Fanny cried.

'Oh!'

Ruffled, Fanny said: 'This must be prejudice! Pray, what fault do you find in him?'

Abby smiled. 'If I were to tell you, love, you would be ready to pull caps with me!'

'Yes – if you said what I believe to be in your mind! You think him a fortune-hunter, don't you?' She waited for a moment, but as Abby said nothing, continued hotly: 'It is false, and – and unworthy of you, Abby! I beg your pardon, but I won't allow you to abuse him! He didn't know about my fortune when he fell in love with me, and later, when he learned of it from some odious tattle-box, he was utterly cast down – talked of his *presumption*, said his case was hopeless, and that he would never, never have approached me if he had known the truth! Such stuff! I verily believe he would have gone away if I hadn't been able to tell him that it will be four whole years before I have a penny more than the pin-money my uncle doles out to me!'

'I am afraid you misled him a little, dearest, and that the blame rests on my shoulders,' said Abby apologetically. 'I thought you knew – at least, that's what I should have supposed, had I thought about it all. I'm ashamed to say that I didn't. My excuse is that we have never discussed money-matters, have we? You won't come into possession of your fortune until you are five-and-twenty.'

Fanny looked very much taken aback, and exclaimed heatedly: 'You don't mean it! Well, of all the shabby things to do – ! Why, *already* I need more than my uncle gives me, and I shall need *much* more when I go to London for my come-out!'

'Of course you will!' agreed Abby, considerably heartened by this naïve speech. 'Your uncle knows that – indeed, we had some discussion about it when I was in London. You won't find him ungenerous, I promise you. He wishes you to present what he calls a creditable appearance!'

'Not ungenerous if I am meek and obedient! But if I don't submit to his tyranny – what then?'

'Really, Fanny!' Abby protested. 'What cause have you ever had to talk of his tyranny?'

'None – *yet*! But if he tries to part me from Stacy it *will* be tyranny! And I'll tell you this, Abby! – I don't care a rush for my hateful fortune, or even if my uncle cuts off my allowance, and Stacy won't care either! No, and I don't care if I don't go to London – not a bit!'

'I wish you will not talk in that skimble-skamble style!' said Abby, with asperity. 'Anyone would take you for a perfect zero! Do you, in all seriousness, expect your uncle to allow you to be married out of the schoolroom?'

'He would, if Stacy were wealthy, and were an Earl, or some such thing!' said Fanny, on an angry sob.

'Oh, no, he would not!' replied Abby. 'He would have me to reckon with! Do, for heaven's sake, try for a little commonsense, child! You have tumbled into love, and you believe it to be a lasting attachment – '

'I *know* it is!' Fanny declared passionately.

'Very well! It may be as you say, and if it should prove to be so you may rest assured of my support. Young Calverleigh has told me that he means to become worthy of you, and if he succeeds in reforming his way of life –'

'He has done so!'

'In that case, I see no reason at all for you to fall into affliction. Neither your uncle nor I are monsters of cruelty, and if, when you have seen a little of the world, you still prefer Calverleigh to all the other men you will meet, and he shows himself to be equally constant, we shall not oppose the marriage.'

'What, wait for nearly a whole year?' cried Fanny, aghast. 'Oh, no, no, no! If you had ever been in love you *could* not be so heartless!'

'I see nothing very heartless in wishing you to enjoy at least one London season before you embark on eight years of poverty,' said Abby dryly.

'That isn't what you wish!' Fanny said, her voice trembling. 'You wish to take me away from my beloved Stacy! I know just how it would be if I consented! You, and my Aunt Mary, would take good care n-never to let me so m-much as *see* him! I daresay you think I should soon forget him, but I shan't! Oh, Abby, Abby, I thought you loved me!'

'You know very well that I do.'

But Fanny, swallowing her tears, shook her head, and rode on in silence.

Meanwhile, Stacy, having begged for the honour of entertaining his uncle to dinner that evening, was taking great pains to order such dishes and wines as would be most likely to put Mr Miles Calverleigh in a mellow mood. Having scrutinised the bill of fare, and bored the waiter by changing his mind three times, he decided at last in favour of a soup, to be removed with a loin of veal, and followed by partridges, accompanied by broiled mushrooms and French beans, with a dressed crab, fat livers in cases, and some artichoke bottoms in sauce, as side-dishes. This elegant repast was served in his private parlour, and although Miles, a sparing eater, could not have been said to do full justice to it, toying with the veal, and refusing the crab and the livers, he ate two partridges, and raised no demur at having his glass constantly refilled.

Until the covers were removed, and a bottle of brandy set upon the table, Stacy confined his conversation to everyday chit-chat, which consisted largely of anecdotes of ton, and the latest titbits of London scandal, but when the waiter left the parlour Miles Calverleigh, pushing his chair back, and stretching his legs out before him, one ankle crossed over the other, yawned, and said: 'Cut line, nevvy! You didn't invite me here to regale me with on-dits. What do you want of me?'

'Good God, sir, nothing! Why, what should I want?'

'I've no idea. Or what you imagine I could – or would – do for you.'

This was not encouraging, but Stacy persevered. 'Don't you feel that we should get to know one another, sir?'

'No, why?'

Stacy blinked at him. 'Well – our relationship!'

'Don't give it a thought! Relations are a dead bore.'

'Not you, sir!' said Stacy, with his ready laugh. 'Indeed, far from it! I can't tell you how many times in the past week I've heard your praises sung!'

'Well, don't try. Are you hopeful of borrowing money from me?'

'Much good that would do me! I daresay your pockets are as much to let as mine!' Stacy said, tossing off the brandy in his glass, and stretching out his hand for the bottle.

Miles, who was warming his own glass in his cupped hands, said: 'As I don't know to what extent your pockets are to let –'

He was interrupted. 'Wholly!' Stacy said, with yet another laugh, this time one devoid of mirth. 'I'm all to pieces!' He waited for a moment, but as he won no other response than a polite look of enquiry from his unfeeling relative continued jerkily: 'The devil's been in the cards! Yes, and in the bones too! I've only to rattle them and they fall crabs! If I can't contrive to fly a kite, I shall be gutted!'

Mr Miles Calverleigh, having warmed his glass to his satisfaction, and savoured the aroma of the brandy, sipped it delicately. 'I daresay you'll come about,' he said.

Anger rose in Stacy, and, with it, his colour. 'Not if that curst aunt of Fanny's has anything to say to it! And now she tells me that Fanny don't come of full age until she's five-and-twenty!'

'You will have to look for another kite to fly, won't you?'

Stacy disposed of his second glass of brandy. 'Do you suppose I haven't done so? Damn it, I thought it was all hollow! But when a man's luck is out it's ames-ace with him, whatever he sets his hand to! I've been punting on tick for weeks past – hardly dare show my face in town!'

'I should go abroad, if I were you.'

'Pray, what should I subsist on?' snapped Stacy.

'Oh, on your wits!' said Miles cheerfully.

'I collect that's what you did!'

'Yes, of course.'

'They don't seem to have served you very well!'

Miles laughed. 'Better than an apron-string hold would have done, I promise you!'

There was just enough contempt in his voice to put Stacy, already embarking on a third glass, in a flame. He exclaimed: 'I don't know what right you have to hold up your nose, sir! It's what you did – or tried to do – yourself!'

'Is it?' said Miles. 'You seem to be remarkably well informed!'

'You as good as told me so,' Stacy muttered. 'In any event, I've always known that you ran off with some heiress or another.'

'So I did,' agreed Miles, without the smallest sign of discomposure. 'I shouldn't recommend you to follow my example: you would do better to regard me in the light of a grim warning.'

'I don't wish to run off with Fanny! It was never my intention, until that archwife returned to Bath to thrust a spoke in my wheel!'

'That *what*?'

The astonishment in his uncle's voice recalled to Stacy's mind his reason for having invited him to dinner, and, with an abrupt change of front, he said: 'I should not abuse her! No, or blame her either, I suppose. But when one's hopes are cut up – She has set her face against the marriage, sir!'

'Well, you certainly can't blame her for that.'

'I have said I don't! I've done my utmost to bring her about – assured her of my determination to be worthy of Fanny – all to no avail! She is unmoved! Nothing I could say had the least effect on her!'

'You can't tell that. The chances are you made her feel damned queasy.'

'But it's true!' Stacy declared, flushing hotly. 'I'll be a pattern-husband, I swear!'

'Hornswoggle!' said his uncle, not mincing matters.

'No, I tell you!'

'Well, don't! What the devil's the use of telling me that, or anything else? *I'm* not the girl's guardian!'

'You could help me, if you chose to do it!'

'I doubt it.'

'Yes, yes, I'm certain of it!' Stacy said eagerly, once more refilling his glass. 'Miss Abigail likes you – you're wondrous great with her! I heard how she was talking to you today, and laughing at the things you said to her! If you were to support me, plead my cause –'

'Yes, you're a trifle disguised!' interrupted Miles.

'No such thing! I'll have you know, sir –'

'Oh, not ape-drunk!' said Miles reassuringly. 'Just about half-sprung!'

'I'll engage to see *you* out, sir!'

Miles looked amused. 'You'd be obliged to knock under! However, I'd as lief you made the attempt rather than talk any more balderdash! *I* plead your cause? What the devil gave you the notion that I plead any causes but my own? Believe me, it's wide of the mark!'

'You *can't* be such a – such care-for-nobody as to refuse to lift as much as a finger to assist me!' said Stacy indignantly.

'Oh, you're quite mistaken! I am precisely such a care-for-nobody.'

'But I'm your nephew! You can't want me to be rolled-up!'

'It's a matter of indifference to me.'

'Well, upon my soul!' Stacy exploded.

'As it would be to you if that fate befell me,' said Miles, slightly smiling. 'Why should either of us care a straw for what becomes of the other?'

Stacy gave an uncertain laugh. 'Damme if ever I met such a queer-card as you are!'

'Don't let it distress you! Comfort yourself with the reflection that it would do you no good if I did choose to recommend you to Miss Abigail Wendover.'

'She would listen to you,' Stacy argued. 'And if *she* could be brought to consent to the marriage I don't doubt that

122

Wendover would do so too. He doesn't concern himself with Fanny – never has done so! – and his wife don't like her. *She* isn't going to bring her out next year! I'll lay you a guinea to a gooseberry she'd be glad to see Fanny safely buckled before she brings out her own daughter!'

'Then why waste your eloquence on me? Address yourself to Mrs James Wendover!'

'With Miss Abigail against me?' Stacy said scornfully. 'I'm not such a clunch!'

'My good boy, if you imagine that James Wendover could be persuaded by his sister, or by anyone else, to consent to Fanny's marriage to a basket-scrambler, you're a lunatic!' said Miles brutally.

Stacy drained his fourth glass. 'What'll you wager against the chance that he'll find himself forced to consent?' he demanded, his utterance a little slurred. 'Got to force him to – nothing else to be done to bring myself about!'

'What about Danescourt?'

Stacy stared at him rather owlishly. 'Danescourt?'

'Why don't you sell it?' asked Miles coolly.

'Sell it! I'm going to save it! Before they can foreclose!'

'As bad as that?'

'Yes, damn you! Besides – I don't want to sell it!'

'Why not? You told me you hated it!'

'Yes, but it means something. Gives one consequence. Place in the country, you know: Calverleigh of Danescourt! No substance without it – bellows to mend with me!'

'It appears to be bellows to mend with you already,' said his uncle caustically.

Nine

*M*r Stacy Calverleigh, having slept off the result of his potations, awoke, far into the following day, with only the haziest recollections of what might have passed between himself and his uncle. So much did he plume himself on his ability to drink all other men under the table that he ascribed the circumstance of his having been put to bed by the boots to the vile quality of the brandy supplied by the White Hart; and when he encountered Mr Miles Calverleigh in Milsom Street, two days later, he laughingly apologised for it, and for its effect upon himself, describing this as having been rendered a trifle above oar. He spoke gaily, but under his insouciance there lurked a fear that he might have been betrayed into indiscretion. He said that he hoped he had not talked a great deal of nonsense, and was reassured by his uncle's palpable lack of interest. He then ventured to express the hope that Miles would not betray him to the ladies in Sydney Place, saying: 'I should find myself in the briars if Miss Abigail even suspected that I do, now and then, have a cup too much!'

'What a good thing you've warned me not to do so!' responded Miles sardonically. 'Entertaining females with accounts of jug-bitten maunderings is one of my favourite pastimes.'

He left Stacy with one of his careless nods, and strode on down the street, bound for the Pump Room. Here he found all the Wendovers: Abby listening with an expression of courteous interest to one of General Exford's anecdotes; Fanny making one of a group of lively young persons; and Selina, with Miss

Butterbank in close attendance, receiving the congratulations of her friends on her emergence from seclusion. After an amused glance in Abby's direction, Miles made his way towards Selina, greeting her with the ease of long friendship, and saying, with his attractive smile: 'I shan't ask you how you do, ma'am: to enquire after a lady's health implies that she is not in her best looks. Besides, I can see that you are in high bloom.'

She had watched his approach rather doubtfully, but she was by no means impervious to flattery, or to his elusive charm, and she returned the smile, even though she deprecated his compliment, saying: 'Good gracious, sir, at my age one doesn't talk of being in high bloom! *That* is quite a thing of the past – not that I ever was – I mean, no more than *passable*!'

'Oh, my dear Miss Wendover, how can you say so?' exclaimed Miss Butterbank throwing up her hands, 'Such a farradiddle I declare I never heard! But you are always so modest! I must positively beg Mr Calverleigh to turn a deaf ear to you!'

Since he was at that moment asking Mrs Leavening how she had prospered that morning in her search for lodgings, he had no difficulty in obeying this behest. The only difficulty he experienced was how to extricate himself from a discussion of all the merits, and demerits, of the several sets of apartments Mrs Leavening had inspected. But having agreed with Selina that Axford Buildings were situated in a horrid part of the town, and with Mrs Leavening that Gay Street was too steep for elderly persons, he laughed, and disclosed with disarming candour that he knew nothing of either locality. 'But I believe people speak well of Marlborough Buildings,' he offered. 'Unless you would perhaps prefer the peace and quiet of Belmont?'

'Belmont?' said Selina incredulously. 'But that would never do! It is uphill all the way! You can't be serious!'

'Of course he isn't, my dear!' said Mrs Leavening, chuckling. 'He hasn't the least notion where it is. Now, have you, sir?'

'Not the least! I shall make it my business to find out, however, and I'll tell you this evening, ma'am,' he promised.

He then bowed slightly, and walked away. Selina, taking umbrage at the suggestion that there was any part of Bath with which she was not fully acquainted, exclaimed: 'Well, I must say I think him a very odd creature! One might have supposed – not that I know him at all well, and one shouldn't judge anyone on a single morning-visit, even in his riding-dress, which I cannot like – though Abby assures me he won't *dine* with us in it – but his manners are very strange and abrupt!'

'Oh, he is certainly an original, but so droll!' said Mrs Leavening. 'We like him very much, you know, and find nothing in his manners to disgust us.'

'Exactly what I have been saying to dear Miss Wendover!' interpolated Miss Butterbank. 'Anyone of whom Miss Abby approves cannot be other than gentlemanlike!'

'Yes, but it is not at all the thing for her to be going to the play in his company. At least, it doesn't suit *my* sense of propriety, though no doubt my notions are antiquated, and, of course, Abby is not a girl, precisely, but to talk as if she was on the shelf is a great piece of nonsense!'

Mrs Leavening agreed to this, but as her husband came up at that moment Selina did not tell her old friend that Abby, not content with accompanying Mr Calverleigh to the theatre, had actually invited him to dine in Sydney Place.

This bold stroke had quite overset Selina. The news that Mr Calverleigh had been so kind as to invite Abby to go to the play she had received placidly enough, if with a little surprise: it seemed very odd that a single gentleman should get up a party, but no doubt he wished to return the hospitality of such ladies as Mrs Grayshott, and Lady Weaverham. Were the Ancrums going as well?

Abby was tempted, for a craven moment, to return a non-committal answer, but she overcame the impulse, and replied in an airy tone: 'Oh, it is not a party! Do you think I ought not to have accepted? I did hesitate, but at my age it is surely not improper? Besides, the play is *The Venetian Outlaw*, which I particularly want to see! From some cause or another I never have seen it, you know: once I was ill, when it was put on here, and once I was away from home; but you went to see it twice, didn't you? And were in raptures!'

'Yes, but not with a *gentleman*!' Selina said, scandalised. *'Once,* I went with dear Mama, only you were too young then; and the second time Lady Trevisian invited me – or was that the *third* time? Yes, because the *second* time was when George and Mary were with us, and you had a putrid sore throat, and so could not go with us!'

'This time I am determined *not* to have a putrid sore throat!'

'No, indeed! I hope you will not! But Mr Calverleigh must invite some others as well! I wonder he shouldn't have done so. It argues a want of conduct in him, for it is not at all the thing, and India cannot be held to excuse it, because there are no theatres there – at least, I shouldn't think there would be, should you?'

'No, dear. So naturally Mr Calverleigh couldn't know that he was doing anything at all out of the way, poor man! As for telling him that he must invite others as well as me, I hope you don't expect *me* to do so! That would indeed be improper! And, really, Selina, what possible objection can there be to my going to the play under the escort of a middle-aged man? Here, too, where I am well known, and shall no doubt meet many of our friends in the theatre!'

'It will make you look so – so *particular,* dearest! You would never do so in London! Of course, Bath is a different matter, but worse! Only think how disagreeable it would be if people said you were encouraging Mr Calverleigh to dangle after you!'

This thought had already occurred to Abby, causing her to hover on the brink of excusing herself from the engagement; and had Selina said no more she might possibly have done so. But Selina's evil genius prompted her to utter fatal words. 'I am persuaded that James would tell you to cry off, Abby!'

'Are you indeed?' retorted Abby, instantly showing hackle. 'Well, that settles the matter! I shall do no such thing! Oh, Selina, pray don't fly into a great fuss! If you are afraid of what the quizzes may say, you have only to tell them that since you don't yet venture out in the evening Mr Calverleigh very kindly offered to act as your deputy. And once it becomes known that he dined with us here, before escorting me to the theatre –'

'Nothing – *nothing*! – would prevail upon me to do anything so unbecoming as to invite a single gentleman to dine with us!' declared Selina, with unwonted vigour.

'No, dear, but you are not obliged to do so,' said Abby mischievously. 'I've done it for you!'

'*Abby!*' gasped Selina, turning pale with dismay. 'Asked a *man* to dine with us *alone*? You can't be serious! *Never* have we done such a thing! Except, of course, James, which is a very different matter!'

'Very different!' agreed Abby. 'Mr Calverleigh may be an oddity, but he's not a dreadful bore!'

'I was never so mortified!' moaned Selina. 'So brass-faced of you, as though you knew no better, and *exactly* what dear Papa deplored, and what he would say to it, if he were alive, which I am *devoutly* thankful he is not, I shudder to think!'

It had taken time, patience, and much tact to reconcile Selina but in the end she consented to entertain Mr Miles Calverleigh, persuaded by the horrid suspicion that if she refused to do so her highty-tighty young sister was quite capable of setting the town in an uproar by dining with him at York House. She had then devoted the better part of the afternoon to the composition of a formal invitation, written in her beautiful copper-plate, and combining to a nicety condescension with gracious civility. Mr Miles Calverleigh responded to this missive with commendable promptness, in a brief but well-expressed note, which conveyed to Selina's mind the impression that he had invited her sister to go with him to the play in a spirit of avuncular philanthropy. She was thus able to meet him in the Pump Room with a modicum of complaisance; and although, when he left her side, he joined the group round Abby, she had no apprehension of danger. It was not at all remarkable that he should show a preference for her: a great many gentlemen did so; but if it had been suggested to Selina that Abby was quite as strongly attracted to him as he to her she would have thought it not so much remarkable as absurd. Abby enjoyed light flirtations, but Selina had almost ceased to hope that she would ever discover amongst her suitors one who was endowed with all the perfections she apparently demanded. They were certainly not to be found in Mr Miles Calverleigh, with his swarthy countenance, his casual manners, and his deplorable want of address.

Nor was Abby apprehensive that in pursuing her acquaintance with him she might be running into danger. She was by no means sure that she liked him. He was amusing, and she enjoyed his company; but he frequently put her quite out of temper, besides shocking her by his unconcerned repudiation of any of the virtues indispensable in a man of principle. He was undoubtedly what her brother-in-law succinctly described as a loose screw, and so hopelessly ineligible that it never so much as crossed her mind that in him she had met her fate. Nor did it occur to her that in encouraging his advances she was influenced by anything other than the hope that she might be able to persuade him to send his nephew to the rightabout. He had refused unequivocally to meddle, but the hope persisted, and, with it, the growing conviction that if he wished to bring Stacy's schemes to fiddlestick's end he would know just how it could be done. To inspire him with such a wish was clearly her duty; if it had been suggested to her that her duty, in this instance, had assumed an unusually agreeable aspect, she would have acknowledged readily that it was fortunate that she did not find Mr Calverleigh repellent; but she would have been much amused by a further suggestion that she was rapidly losing her heart to a black sheep.

So she was able to greet him, when he descended upon her in the Pump Room, with calm friendliness; and when he presently detached her from her circle, inviting her, with his customary lack of finesse, to take a stroll about the Room, in the accepted manner of those who made the Promenade their daily business, she was perfectly willing to walk off with him.

'I've received an invitation from your sister,' he told her. 'She hopes that I will give you both the pleasure of dining in Sydney Place on Saturday, but I'm not deceived: her hope is that I may break a leg, or be laid low of a severe colic, before I can expose you to the censure of all your acquaintance. Shall I be doing so?'

She laughed. 'Good God, no! I hope my credit is good enough to survive a visit to the theatre in your company! Much I should care if it proved otherwise! I've a great desire to see this particular play, and have never yet done so. It has always been popular in Bath, you know.' Her eyes danced. 'If only you had had the good sense to have been a *widower,* I daresay Selina wouldn't have raised the least objection! She saw no harm in my attending the races with General Exford: there is something very respectable about widowers! *Single* gentlemen, in her view, are surrounded by an aura of impropriety.'

'What, even the turnip-sucker who pays you extravagant compliments?'

'If,' said Abby, a trifle unsteadily, but with severity, 'you are speaking of Mr Dunston, Selina knows him to be a very worthy man who has far too much conduct to transgress the bounds of propriety by as much as an inch!'

'He *is* a slow-top, isn't he? Poor fellow!'

'He may be a slow-top, but that's better than being ramshackle!' retorted Abby, with spirit.

'No, do you think so indeed? Was that a cut at me, by the way, or at Stacy?'

'Well, it was at you,' said Abby frankly. 'I don't think Stacy *ramshackle*: I think him a shuffling rogue! Mr Calverleigh, if you had heard him trying to cut a wheedle, when we rode back from Lansdown, you must have been disgusted!'

'Very likely. The wonder is that Fanny seems to be not at all disgusted.'

'She is very young, and had never, until that wretch came here, known any men but those who reside here: Selina's and my friends, or the schoolboy brothers of her own friends! You must know that she has only lately begun to go out into society a little;

and although, during the winter, a number of London-visitors come to Bath, she has met none of them. I saw to that!'

'Why let yourself be blue-devilled?' he asked. 'She'll recover!'

'I don't doubt she would do so, if he were removed from her sight!'

'Or even if she were to be removed from his,' he suggested.

She frowned over that for a moment, and then said, with a sigh: 'I've thought of it, of course, but I believe it wouldn't answer. James talked of removing her to Amberfield, and that would be fatal: she would run away! And if my sister Brede were to invite her to stay with her in London she would know that it was at my instigation, and to separate her from your nephew. What is more, he would follow her, and you may depend upon it that it would be easier for them to meet in London than it is here, where everyone knows her. I think, too, that if it were possible to prevent this she *wouldn't* recover – or, at any hand, not for a long time. Towards me she would be bound to feel resentment: oh, she's resentful already!' She hesitated, before saying, with a faint smile: 'I was used to think, you know, that we stood upon such terms as would make it a simple matter for me to guide her – even to check her! That my influence was strong enough to – But I seem to have none at all. I suppose I've gone the wrong way to work with her: nothing I could urge would carry the least weight with her! I wish – oh, how much I wish – that her eyes might be opened to what I am persuaded is his true character! That would be the best thing that could happen! It would be painful for her, poor child, but she wouldn't wear the willow for long: she has too much pride! And above all she wouldn't fancy herself a martyr! That's *very* important, because if one thinks oneself the victim of tyranny there is every inducement to fall into a lethargy.'

'I should imagine that that would make life very uncomfortable for you. But hasn't it occurred to you that my nephew has a rival?'

'Oliver Grayshott?' She shook her head. 'I don't think it. She says he is like a brother to her! And although I fancy *he* has a strong tendre for *her* he has done nothing to attach her.'

'Well, if you think it nothing to send her laudatory verses masquerading as acrostics, and to ransack all the libraries for the works of her favourite poets, you must be as green as she is!' he said caustically.

She could not help laughing. 'Does he do so? I thought they were his favourites too: he is certainly very well read in them.'

'Pea-goose! So would you be, if you made it your business to study them!'

'Poor young man! But even if Fanny did prefer him to your nephew it wouldn't do, I'm afraid.'

'Why not?'

'Because – as you very well know! – James would consider him to be almost as ineligible as Stacy!'

'I know nothing of the sort. Your brother James whistle a fortune down the wind? Gammon!'

'But he has no fortune!' she protested. 'He is connected with trade, too, which James would very much dislike.'

'Oh, would he? My sweet simpleton, let James get but one whiff of an East India merchant's heir in Bath, and he won't lose a moment in setting snares to catch such a prize!'

She disregarded this, exclaiming: 'You must be mistaken! Oliver has no such expectations! Indeed, he feels that he has miserably disappointed his uncle.'

'Not he! Balking thinks the world of him, means to take him into partnership as soon as he's in good point again.'

'No, does he indeed? I am so glad! But as for thinking of his marrying Fanny, that's moonshine! I own, I should be thankful if she did fall in love with him – though she is much too young for marriage – but there's no likelihood of her doing so while she's besotted of your odious nephew.'

'You know, if you mean to talk of nothing but your totty-headed niece and my odious nephew I *shall* have a colic,' he informed her.

'Well, of all the detestably uncivil things to say – !' she gasped.

'If it comes to that, what a detestably boring thing to talk about!'

'I beg your pardon!' she said icily. 'To me, it is a subject of paramount importance!'

'Yes, but it isn't so to me.'

Since Miss Butterbank came up at that moment, to tell her that dear Miss Wendover was ready to go home, she was prevented from uttering the retort that rose to her lips; but when her graceless tormentor presented himself in Sydney Place on Saturday she received him with a good deal of chilly reserve. As far as she could discover, this had no effect on him whatsoever. He devoted himself largely to Selina, listening good-naturedly to her rambling discourse, until she embarked on a catalogue of the various illnesses suffered by herself and several of her friends when he retaliated by telling her of the terrible diseases rife in India. From there it was a small step to a description of such aspects of Indian life, climate, and scenery as were most calculated to hold spellbound a middle-aged lady of enquiring mind and credulous disposition. Selina mellowed perceptibly under this treatment, and told Abby, when they had withdrawn from the dining-room, leaving their guest to enjoy a glass of port in solitary state, that really Mr Calverleigh was a most interesting man. 'I declare I feel as if I had actually been to India myself!' she said. 'So vivid, and droll – all those strange customs! Tigers and elephants, too – not that I should care to live with tigers, and although I believe elephants are wonderfully docile I don't think I could ever feel myself at ease with them. But so *very* interesting – quite like a fairy story!'

Abby, who thought that some of Mr Calverleigh's tales were exactly like fairy stories, was able to agree to this with perfect sincerity. She had every intention of maintaining her punctilious civility, and might have done so had he not said, as he took his seat beside her in the carriage he had hired for the evening: 'I wish I had ordered a hot brick to be provided.'

'Thank you, but there was not the least need to do so: I don't feel at all cold.'

'I daresay icebergs don't feel cold either, but I do!'

She was betrayed into a smothered choke of laughter,

whereupon he added: 'From having lived so long in a hot climate, you understand.'

'I understand you perfectly, sir, and shall take leave to tell you that there's neither truth nor shame in you!'

'Well, not *much*, perhaps!' he owned.

Since this quite overset her gravity, she was obliged to relent towards him, and by the time Beaufort Square was reached their former good relationship had been so well restored that she was able to look forward to an evening of unalloyed enjoyment, which not even the surprised stares of several persons with whom she was acquainted seriously disturbed. Mr Calverleigh proved himself to be an excellent host: not only had he hired one of the handsomely appointed first-tier boxes, but he had also arranged for tea and cakes to be brought to it during one of the intervals. Abby said appreciatively: 'How comfortable it is not to be obliged to inch one's way through the press in the foyer! You are entertaining me in royal style, Mr Calverleigh!'

'What, with cat-lap and cakes? If I entertained you royally I should give you pink champagne!'

'Which I shouldn't have liked half as well!'

'No, that's why I didn't give it to you.'

'I expect,' said Abby, quizzing him, 'it is invariably drunk in India – even for breakfast! Another of the strange customs you described to my sister!'

He laughed. 'Just so, ma'am!'

'Well, if she recounts your Canterbury tales to young Grayshott you will have come by your deserts! *He* will refute them, and *you* will look no-how!'

'No, no, you wrong the boy! He's not such a clodpole!'

'Incorrigible! It was a great deal too bad of you to make a May-game of poor Selina.'

'Oh, I didn't! It was made plain to me that she has a very romantical disposition, and delights in the marvellous, so I did my best to gratify her. Turning her up sweet, you know.'

'Trying how many brummish stories you could persuade her to swallow is what you mean! How many did you tell me?'

He shook his head. 'None! You should know better than to ask me that. I told you once that I don't offer you Spanish coin, and I'll tell you now that I don't offer you Canterbury tales either.' He saw the startled look in her eyes, the almost imperceptible gesture of withdrawal, and added simply: 'You wouldn't believe 'em.'

This made her laugh again, but for a moment she had indeed been startled, perceiving in his light eyes a glow there could be no mistaking. She had felt suddenly breathless, and embarrassed, for she had hitherto suspected him of pursuing nothing more serious than an idle flirtation. But there had been a note of sincerity in his voice, and his smile was a caress. Then, just as she was thinking: *This will never do!* he had uttered one of his impishly disconcerting remarks, which left her wondering whether she had allowed her imagination to mislead her.

His subsequent behaviour was irreproachable, and there was so little of the lover in his manner that her embarrassment swiftly died. She reflected that he was really a very agreeable companion, with a mind so much akin to her own that she was never obliged to explain what she meant by some elliptical remark, or to guard her tongue for fear of shocking him. He was attentive to her comfort, too, but in an everyday style: putting her shawl round her shoulders without turning the office into an act of homage; and neither pressing nor retaining her hand when he assisted her to enter the carriage. This treatment made her feel so much at her ease that when he asked her casually if she would join an expedition to Wells, and show him the cathedral there, she had no hesitation in replying: 'Yes, willingly: going to Wells, to see the knights on horseback, has always been a high treat to me!'

'What the deuce are they?' he enquired.

'A mechanical device – but I shan't tell you any more! You shall see for yourself! Who else is to join your expedition?'

'I don't know. Yes, I do, though! We'll take Fanny and young Grayshott!'

She smiled, but said: 'You should invite Lavinia too.'

'Oliver wouldn't agree with you. Nor do I. There will be no room in the carriage for a fifth person.'

'She could take my place. Or even Mrs Grayshott. She would enjoy the drive.'

'She would find it too fatiguing. Can't you think of anyone else to take your place?'

'Yes, Lady Weaverham!' she said instantly, a gurgle of merriment in her throat.

'No, I think, if I must find a substitute for you, I shall invite your sister's bosom-bow – what's her name? Buttertub? Tallow-faced female, with rabbit's teeth.'

'Laura Butterbank!' said Abby, in a failing voice. 'Odious, *infamous* creature that you are!'

'Oh, I can be far more odious than that!' he told her. 'And if I have any more wit and liveliness from you, Miss Abigail Wendover, I'll give you proof of it!'

'*Quite* unnecessary!' she assured him. 'I haven't the least doubt of it!'

She could not see his face in the darkness of the carriage, but she knew that he was smiling. He said, however, in stern accents: 'Will you go with me to Wells, ma'am, or will you not?'

'Yes, sir,' said Abby meekly. 'If you are quite sure you wouldn't prefer Miss Butterbank's company to mine!'

The carriage had drawn up in front of her house. Mr Calverleigh, alighting from it, and turning to hand her down, said: 'I should, of course, but having already invited you I feel it would be uncivil to fob you off.'

'Piqued, repiqued, and capoted!' said Abby, acknowledging defeat.

Ten

The visit to the theatre produced its inevitable repercussions. Only such severe critics as Mrs Ruscombe saw anything to shock them in it, but it was surprising how quickly the word sped round Bath that Mr Miles Calverleigh was becoming extremely particular in his attentions to Miss Abigail Wendover. There was nothing in this to give rise to speculation, for Abby had never lacked admirers; but considerable interest was lent to the affair by what was generally considered to be her encouragement of the gentleman's pretensions.

'Only think of her going to the play with him all by herself! When Lady Templeton told me of it I could only stare at her! I'm sure she has never done such a thing before!' said Mrs Ancrum.

'Mark my words,' said Lady Weaverham, 'it's a Case! Well, I'm sure I wish them both very happy!'

'Quite a new come-out!' said Mrs Ruscombe, with her thin smile. 'It doesn't astonish me: I have always thought her a trifle bold.'

Abby was well aware that she had become overnight an object for curiosity; and so, within a couple of days, was Selina, who was thrown into what she called a taking by the arch efforts of one of her acquaintances to discover whether dear Miss Abigail was about to contract an engagement.

'I was never so much provoked in my life!' she declared. 'Such impertinence! I gave her a sharp set-down, as you may suppose! You and Mr Calverleigh – ! If I hadn't been vexed to death, I could have laughed in her face! Why, he isn't even well-favoured, besides being *quite* beneath your touch – not, of course, by *birth*, but a man of *most* unsavoury reputation, though *that* Mrs Swainswick knows nothing about, and you may depend upon it I didn't breathe a *syllable* to her. But how she could have the impudence to imagine – not but what I knew how it would be from the start, and I must *beg* you, dear Abby, to keep him at a proper distance!'

Abby was quite as much vexed as Selina, but her indignation took a different form. 'What a piece of work about nothing!' she said contemptuously. 'I should rather think you would give that vulgar busy head a sharp set-down! What *would* be quite beneath my touch would be to pay the smallest attention to anything she, or others like her, may choose to say of me!'

If more than the vulgar Mrs Swainswick's sly question had been needed to rouse the spirit of rebellion slumbering in her breast, it was provided by Mr Peter Dunston, who told her that he was afraid his mother had been quite shocked by the news of her escapade. 'She is old-fashioned, you know. I need hardly assure you that *I* do not share her sentiments! What *you* do could never be wrong, Miss Abigail. Indeed, if I had as little regard for your good name in Bath as Calverleigh I should have ventured to invite you to go to the play in *my* company!'

This put Abby in such a flame that if Mr Calverleigh had asked her to jaunter off to Wells with only himself as escort she would instantly have agreed to it. Not being informed of her state of mind, he did not do so; but as the two younger members of his party soon wandered off together, when they reached Wells, he did, in fact, become her only escort for a large part of the day, the only flaw to this agreeable arrangement being that none of the Bath quidnuncs knew anything about it. But this regret was soon forgotten in the pleasure of introducing, to a Cathedral she loved, one who was quick to appreciate its beauty, needing no prompting from her. She thought, in touching innocence, that in Miles Calverleigh she had found a friend, and a better one by far than any other, because his mind moved swiftly, because he could make her laugh even when she was out of charity with him, and because of a dozen other attributes which were quite frivolous – hardly attributes at all, in fact – but which added up to a charming total, outweighing the more important faults in his character. She was aware of these, but she could find excuses for his cynicism, and even for the coldness of heart which made him look upon the problems or the troubles besetting other people with a detachment so profound as to seem inhuman. It was no wonder that twenty years of exile had made him uncaring: the wonder was that he was not embittered. As for the life he had led during those years, she did not suppose that virtue had played a noticeable part in it, but she felt it to be no concern of hers. Nor did she wish to know how many mistresses he had had, or what excesses he might have committed: the past might keep its secrets, leaving her to the enjoyment of the present.

If she spared a thought for her niece, whom she had so reprehensibly allowed to escape from her chaperonage, it was merely to hope that Fanny was enjoying the day as much as she was. The child had not been in spirits at the start of the expedition. She had tried to hide it with rather more than her usual vivacity, but her gaiety had had a brittle quality. Abby dared not hope that she had quarrelled with Stacy; probably she was downcast because she had begun to despair of winning her family's consent to her projected engagement. Perhaps Oliver would succeed in coaxing her out of the dumps; perhaps, if Lavinia, who had not yet learnt to withhold confidences from those she loved, had told him the story of Fanny's infatuation, he might even venture to offer her a little advice. Abby had no doubt that it would be good advice, and very little that advice from a man with whom Fanny stood on friendly terms would be listened to far more readily than advice from an aunt.

Oliver did know the story, but the only advice he gave was addressed to his sister. He had listened to her sentimental out-pourings in silence, disappointing her by saying quietly, when she had done: 'Lavvy, you shouldn't repeat what Fanny tells you.'

'Oh, no! Only to you – and Mama, of course!'

'Well, to Mama, perhaps, but not to me. I let you do so only because I already knew, from Mama, that Fanny had formed an – an attachment which her aunt dislikes. And because I fancy you are much in sympathy with her.'

'Yes, indeed I am!' she said earnestly. 'It is the most affecting thing imaginable, for they fell in love the first time they met! He is so handsome, too, and has *such* an air! And merely because he hasn't the advantage of fortune – as though it signified, when Fanny is positively *rolling* in riches! –'

'It isn't that,' he interrupted, hesitating a little. 'Not wholly that.'

'Oh, you are thinking that he was used to be very wild, and expensive, but –'

'No, I'm not, Lavvy. I know nothing about him, except that –' Again he hesitated; and then, as she directed a look of puzzled enquiry at him, said, with a little difficulty: 'He isn't a halfling, you know, or a greenhorn. He must be a dozen years older than Fanny, and a man of the world into the bargain.'

'Yes!' said Lavinia enthusiastically. '*Anyone* can see he is of the first stare, which makes it so particularly romantic that he should have fallen in love with Fanny! I don't mean to say that she isn't ravishingly pretty, because she is, but I should think there must be *scores* of fashionable London-girls on the catch for him, wouldn't you?'

'Listen, Lavvy!' he said. 'The thing is that he hasn't behaved as he ought! A man of honour don't flummery a girl into meeting him upon the sly, and, he don't pop the question to her without asking leave of her guardian!'

'Oh, Oliver, you are repeating what Mama says! How can you be so stuffy? Next you will be saying that Fanny ought to wait meekly until her guardian bestows her on a man of *his* choice!'

'I shan't say anything of the sort. But I'll tell you this, Lavvy: if Calverleigh had made *you* the object of his havey-cavey attentions I'd knock his teeth down his throat!'

Startled, and rather impressed, she said: 'Good gracious! Would you? *Well!*'

'Try to, at all events,' he said, laughing. 'It's what any man would do.'

She did not look to be entirely convinced. He put his arm round her, and gave her a brotherly hug. 'It isn't for me to interfere: I haven't the right. But you'll be a poor friend to Fanny if you don't make a push to persuade her not to throw her cap over the windmill. That's the way to return by Weeping Cross.'

He had said no more, and how much of what he had said was repeated to Fanny he had no means of knowing, because he was wary of betraying to his sister that he took far more than a neutral interest in the affair, and so would not ask her. Between himself and Fanny it was never discussed, and much as he longed to beg her not to throw herself away on a court-card who, in his view, was an ugly customer if ever he saw one, it did not come within his province to meddle in the affairs of a girl who would never be more to him than an unattainable dream, or within his code of honour to cry rope upon a fellow behind his back. Given the flimsiest of excuses – if only he had been even remotely related to Fanny! – he would speedily have cut the fellow's comb for him; for although he was not yet in high force he had no doubt of his ability to draw the elegant Mr Stacy Calverleigh's cork, besides darkening both his daylights, before tipping him a settler. His hands clenched themselves instinctively into two bunches of purposeful fives as he allowed his fancy to dwell for a moment on the pleasing vision of a regular set-to with Stacy. He was innately chivalrous, but he would have no compunction whatsoever in milling down this sneaking rascal, who, if he had ever come to handy-blows in his life (which Mr Grayshott doubted) was certainly no match for one whose science, and punishing left, had won fame for him in the annals of his school and college. But only for a moment did the vision endure: even the excuse of rivalry was denied him. Mr Grayshott, setting out for India in high hope, and eager determination to prove himself worthy of his uncle's trust, had been defeated by his constitution, and saw himself as a failure. Mr Balking had told him not to tease himself about the future, and not to take it so much to heart that his health had broken down. 'For how could you help it? I wish I'd never sent you to Calcutta – except that the experience you've gained will stand you in good stead. I've a place for you in the London house, but time enough to talk of that when you're on your pins again.'

Mr Balking had been kindness itself, but Oliver, his spirits as much as his gaunt frame worn down by recurrent fever, foresaw that he was destined to become a clerk in the counting-house, from which lowly position he was unlikely to rise for many dreary years. He had set no store by Uncle Leonard's assurances that he was very well satisfied with his work in Calcutta: that was the sort of thing that an affectionate uncle might be expected to say. He had reached Bath in a state of deep depression, but as his health improved so did his spirits, and he began to think that it might not be so very long before he worked his way up to a position of trust. When he was able to look back dispassionately over the two years he had spent in India, he thought that perhaps his uncle really was satisfied with his progress there. He had found his work of absorbing interest, and knew that he had a talent for business. In fact, if he had been a windy-wallets, boasting of his every small success, he would have said that he had done pretty well in the Calcutta house. As he was a diffident, and rather reticent young man, he maintained a strict silence on the subject, and waited, in gradually increasing hopefulness, for the day when his doctor should pronounce him well enough to apply himself once more to business.

But his optimism did not lead him to the length of supposing that the Wendovers would ever consider him to be an eligible husband for Fanny. Older than his years, he recognised in Fanny's passionate attachment to Stacy a schoolgirl's brief, violent infatuation. He was reminded of the throes into which Lavinia, at the age of fifteen, had been cast when she fell suddenly, and inexplicably, in love with one of the visiting professors at Miss Timble's Seminary. It had made her remarkably tiresome for several weeks, but there had been no harm in it, her passion being unrequited, and the professor a respectable man, with a

142

wife, and five children, to all of whom he was devoted. Neither
Oliver nor Mrs Grayshott had set any store by the event; Oliver
thought that he would have set as little by Fanny's present
bewitchment had she but lost her foolish heart to a man of
character. As it was, he was pretty sure that she had walked into
a snare set for her by a handsome fortune-hunter, and he was
extremely uneasy. Something Lavinia had let slip from her
tongue, and hastily retracted, had given rise in his mind to the
incredible suspicion that a runaway marriage was in contemplation. He found that his mother shared this suspicion, and was
only partly reassured when he learned that she had warned Miss
Abigail Wendover of a possible danger. Miss Abigail was no fool,
but he felt that the situation demanded a man's hand. Failing her
brother, who did not seem to be one on whom Miss Abigail
placed any reliance, the obvious man to intervene was Mr Miles
Calverleigh. But Miles showed no disposition to do so, or even to
take any interest in his nephew's activities. That did not surprise
Oliver: he had not spent several weeks in Mr Calverleigh's
company without discovering that he never did take any interest
in persons he didn't like. It was inconceivable that a man of his cut
could like Stacy, and useless to suppose that regard for the good
name of his family would impel him to exert himself to preserve
it: he had no such regard. On the other hand, there could be no
doubt that he liked Miss Abigail Wendover very much indeed.
Oliver, naturally precluded from discussing Stacy with Stacy's
uncle, could only hope that his tendre for her would move him to
come to her assistance. He was a strange man, so cold, and yet so
kind; there was no understanding him, but one thing was sure: if
he did befriend one, there were no limits to the help he would, in
his unconcerned way, extend. It was possible, of course, that Miss
Abigail, like himself, would feel all the awkwardness of broaching
the matter to him. Oliver thought that perhaps his mother might
prevail upon her to overcome such scruples, and decided to
nudge her into making the attempt.

During the drive to Wells he realised, as quickly as her aunt,
that Fanny was doing her best to hide some inward care under a

mask of gaiety. His heart went out to her, the sweet, silly baby that she was. He felt almost sick with the longing to gather her into his arms; but that desire must be repressed: not only did his circumstances make it impossible for him to declare himself, but Fanny did not want his love, but only his friendship. She had said once, when his mother had reproved him for calling her by her name: 'Oh, but I begged him to do so, ma'am! Because Lavvy and I have always been like sisters, so Oliver must be my brother!'

Half a loaf was better than no bread: he didn't know who had been responsible for that silly proverb, only that he must have been a cod's head. It wasn't better; when the lovely, darling girl you would have given your soul to possess invited you to be her brother it was infinitely worse.

But if a brother was what Fanny wanted, a brother she should have; and perhaps, adopting that distasteful rôle, he might, at least, be admitted into her confidence, and be granted the opportunity to offer her wiser counsel than she would get from his foolish sister.

So when they had stayed for some time in the chapel in the north aisle of the Cathedral, where the famous clock had been placed, and had watched the little knights endlessly tilting at each other across the barrier which surmounted it, he detained Fanny, as she was preparing to follow her aunt and Mr Calverleigh to another part of the Cathedral, and suggested that they might go and sit down outside for a while. She agreed readily to this, causing his heart to melt by looking up at him in quick anxiety, and saying: 'Yes, to be sure we'll do that, if you wouldn't liefer go back to the Swan? There's nothing so fatiguing as Cathedrals! You are tired already, aren't you?'

'No, I promise you I'm not – or only a very little!' he answered. 'I think I might be, however, if I were obliged to go all over this place, because that would mean standing to gaze at tombs, and screens, and windows! I don't know why it should be so, but standing is a thing I can't yet do, though I am beginning to walk with the best of you.'

'Well, you shan't stand. If it is not too chilly for you, we'll go and sit by the moat round the Palace, and watch the swans. And if my aunt should ask you what you think of the figures on the West Front you may say that you've never seen anything so truly exquisite. That wouldn't be a fib, do you think?'

His eyes were full of tender amusement; he said gravely: 'No, just *suggestio falsi*! Ought I to see them?'

'Good gracious, no! There are tiers and tiers of them!'

'In that case, I'm ready to tell any number of fibs – even a real bouncer!'

She laughed, and then fell silent for a minute or two. He made no attempt to break into her abstraction, but presently she seemed to recall herself, and embarked on some light, everyday chit-chat, rather in the manner of a hostess trying to entertain a difficult guest. It was plainly an effort, and he stopped her, saying involuntarily: 'Ah, don't, Fanny!'

Startled, she looked quickly up at him, a question in her big eyes. 'Don't?'

'Don't think yourself obliged to make conversation! That's not treating me as though I were your brother!'

'Oh – !' She blushed, and turned her head away.

'Is something troubling you?' he asked gently.

'No – oh, no! Of course not! Look, there are two of the swans! If only we had brought some bread to throw to them! I do think swans are the most beautiful birds in the world, don't you? Or do you prefer peacocks?'

'No,' he replied baldly, leading her to a conveniently placed bench. Sitting down beside her, he said: 'What is it, Fanny? Don't say you're not blue-devilled! That *would* be a bouncer – almost a *plumper*!'

She gave a nervous little laugh. 'It's nothing. Well, nothing very much! Just that I'm at outs with Abby – at least, not precisely at outs with her, but –' She paused, and her eyes darkened. 'I thought – But people – grown-up people –' she said, betraying her youth, 'don't *understand*! They don't care for anything but consequence, and propriety, and respectability, and – and eligibility, and whenever you wish to do anything *they* don't wish you to do, they say you are far too young, and will soon forget about it!'

'Yes, and also that one day you will thank them for it!' he agreed sympathetically. 'And the worst of it is that, in general, they are right!'

'Not always!'

'No, but odiously often!'

'*When you are as old as I am* – !' said Fanny, in bitter mimicry.

'Don't tell me that Miss Abigail has ever uttered those abominable words!'

'No. No, she hasn't done that, but she doesn't enter into my feelings, and I thought she would! I never *dreamed* she would be just like my uncle! Worldly, and – and prejudiced, and not thinking it signifies if you are unhappy, as long as you don't do anything your horrid uncle doesn't approve of!' She added, with strong indignation: 'And she doesn't even *like* him!'

He said nothing for a few moments, but sat frowning ahead at the embattled wall beyond the moat. Fanny, pulling a handkerchief out of her reticule, defiantly blew her nose. Oliver drew a resolute breath, and said, picking his words with care: 'If someone who is very dear to you – as you are to Miss Abigail – seems to be set on taking what you believe to be a false step, you must try to prevent it, don't you agree?'

'Yes, but I am not taking a false step!' said Fanny. 'And I am not too young to know my own mind! I have always known it! And I won't let them ruin my life, even if I have to do something *desperate*!'

'Don't!' he said. 'How could you be happy if you did what must pretty well break Miss Abigail's heart? Forgive me, Fanny, but I fancy I know what the trouble is, and I wish there was something I could do to help you.' He paused. 'Have you ever met my uncle? Not, I'm thankful to say, at all like *your* uncle! He's very kind, and very wise, and he once told me never to make important decisions hastily – not to do what couldn't be *un*done until I was perfectly sure that I should never *wish* to undo it.'

'Of course not!' said Fanny simply. She got up. 'Are you rested? Would you care to stroll about the town for a little while? I don't think it *is* warm enough here, do you? We'll go through the Dean's Eye into Sadler Street: I expect you will like to see that.'

Her confidences were at an end; and since she had so unmistakably drawn to the blinds against prying eyes there was nothing for him to do but to acquiesce. He won a laugh from her by saying that while he placed himself unreservedly in her hands he could not help feeling that they ran a grave risk of being clapped into prison for such irreverence; and expressed great relief when she explained that the Dean's Eye was merely an old gateway. This mild joke did much to restore her to ease; he set himself thereafter to divert her, and succeeded well enough to make her say, when they joined their elders at the Swan, to partake of an early dinner there before driving back to Bath, that she had spent a charming afternoon. A little nervously, she added: 'And you won't regard anything I said, will you? It was all nonsense! I daresay you know how it is when one falls into a fit of the dismals: one says things one doesn't mean.'

He reassured her, but could not refrain from saying: 'Even though I'm only a pretence-brother, will you tell me if ever you are in any kind of a hobble, or – or are not quite sure what you should do?'

'Oh, thank you! You are very good!' she stammered. 'But there's no need – I mean, it was only being blue-devilled, as you said! Nothing is *really* amiss!'

He said no more, but this speech, far from allaying his anxiety, considerably increased it. He wished grimly that he could know what had occurred to agitate her, but it was perhaps as well that his suspicion received no confirmation, since he had neither the right nor, as yet, the physical strength to deal appropriately with Mr Stacy Calverleigh, and would have found it impossible to control his instinct. For Mr Calverleigh, living in imminent danger of foreclosure, and seeing the shadow of the King's Bench Prison creeping inexorably towards him, had abandoned the hope of winning his heiress by fair means, and had decided (with a strong sense of ill-usage) that there was nothing for it but to elope with her.

But Fanny, who had so enthusiastically pictured herself in such a romantic adventure, had suddenly been brought to realise that it was one thing to declare one's readiness to cast off the shackles of one's upbringing, and to divorce oneself from home and family, and quite another actually to do it.

Stacy had urged his desperate proposal on her in Bath Abbey, a circumstance which made her feel nervous and uncomfortable at the outset. When he had appointed this rendezvous, she had been almost shocked. It was surely not at all the thing! But he had laughed at her scruples, calling her his adorable little prude, and she had agreed to the assignation – if only to prove to him that she was no prude. It had been made hurriedly, in Meyler's Library, and it had entailed some difficult, and what she could not but feel horridly deceitful, planning. However, she had done it, and had been rewarded for her hardihood by having her hands passionately kissed, and her bravery extolled. But she was feeling far from brave, and looked round nervously in dread of seeing someone she knew. It was not, of course, very likely that any resident of Bath would be found in the Abbey at an hour when no service was being held, but there was no telling but what someone might be entertaining a guest who wished to visit it. She whispered: 'Oh, pray take care!' and pulled her hands away. 'If I were to be recognised – ! I am in such a quake! I don't *think* anyone saw me on the way, but how can one be sure? Grimston went with me to Miss Timble's, and she will call for me later at Mrs Grayshott's, but, oh, Stacy, I was obliged to pretend to Miss Timble that I had mistaken the day for my singing lesson, and it made me feel a *wretch*!'

'No wonder!' he agreed warmly. 'It is intolerable that we

should be obliged to stoop to subterfuge: I feel it as acutely as you do, beloved! But since your aunt returned to Bath I've been granted no opportunity to snatch as much as five minutes alone with you. How can I talk to you at a concert, or in a ballroom? And talk to you I must!'

'Yes – oh, yes! I have longed so much to be with you! If only I had a veil! Who are those people over there?'

'Only a parcel of trippers,' he replied soothingly. 'Don't be afraid, my sweet one! There is no one here who knows you. We will sit down over there, where it is dark, and there's nothing of interest to attract the trippers. That I should be forced into *stealing* a meeting with you! It is of all things the most repugnant to me, but what other course is open to me? Only one! – to renounce you wholly, and that I *cannot* bear to do!'

'Stacy, *no*!' she gasped, clutching his arm.

He laid his other hand over hers, clasping it firmly. 'I shall never win your aunt's support: she has made that abundantly plain to me! She will take care that we never see one another, except in company, or as we have done today. Dearest, how can we go on in such a way?' He took her hand and mumbled kisses into its palm. 'If you knew how much I long to take you in my arms, to call you my own!'

'I want that too,' she said shyly.

'Then come away with me, as we planned! Dare you snap your fingers in the face of the world? Tell me!'

'Yes, indeed I dare!' she said, with a sparkling look.

'How shall I ever be able to prove to you how much I adore you? Let us put a period to this hateful situation into which we have been driven, and let us do it as soon as may be contrived! Tomorrow!'

'*Tomorrow*?' Fanny echoed blankly. 'Oh, *no*, Stacy! I – I couldn't! I mean, it is too soon!'

'The next day, then!'

It was at this moment that Fanny began to perceive the difference between dreams and reality. She shook her head, saying pleadingly: 'I wish I could, but – you don't perfectly understand, Stacy! It would be too difficult. I have so many things to attend to!'

'It must be soon!' he urged. 'At any moment you may be swept from me! I suspect that your aunt is contemplating doing so already. If that were to happen, our tale would be told!'

'No, it wouldn't!' she objected. 'Besides, she isn't contemplating it! How could she, when we are holding a rout-party next week? And that's another reason why I couldn't possibly run away immediately. I daresay you may have forgotten about it, but – '

'What do I care for rout-parties?' he exclaimed. 'Our happiness is at stake!'

Fanny had no objection to Mr Calverleigh's dramatic utterances, for they bore a close resemblance to the impassioned speeches of her favourite heroes of romance, but a strong vein of commonsense underlay her imaginings, and she replied, in an alarmingly practical spirit: 'No, no! How should that be? It means only a little put-off!'

'Only – ! When every hour that I am apart from you seems a week, and every week a year!'

No arithmetician, she found no fault with this mathematical progression. The sentiment thus expressed made her blush rosily, and slide her hand into his again. 'I know. It's so with me too, but you haven't considered, my dearest one! How *could* I run away before Aunt Selina's party? It would be the most infamous thing to do, because she is looking forward to it so much, poor darling, and it would destroy all her pleasure in it if – Good God! she wouldn't be able to hold it at all! Only think what an uproar there will be!'

Exasperation seized him, and for an instant she caught a glimpse of it in his face. It was gone so quickly that she could not be sure that it had ever been there at all. He saw doubt in her widening eyes, and said ruefully: 'That I should be willing to consign Aunt Selina to perdition! Isn't it shocking? So kind as she is, and – as I believe – so much my friend! For how long must I wait before I can call you my own – to cherish and protect?'

Had she been privileged to hear these noble words, Miss Abigail Wendover would have informed Mr Calverleigh, in explicit terms, that Fanny needed to be protected only from himself. Their effect on Fanny was to make her blush still more vividly, and to whisper: 'Not long! I promise!'

He had seldom felt less amorous, for he considered that she was being irritatingly capricious, but he responded at once with one of his lover-like speeches. His fear was that she might, if she were given time for reflection, draw back from the proposed elopement. It had not escaped his notice that she had recoiled from his suggestion of an immediate flight. He set himself to the task of winning her back to her former mood of eager acceptance, employing all the arts at his command. He did not doubt his power over her, but he reckoned without the streak of obstinacy her aunts knew well: she responded deliciously to his love-making; she listened in soft-eyed rapture to the idyllic picture he drew of the life they would lead together; but she would not consent to elope with him before her aunts' party. He dared not persist, for there was a mulish look in her face, and his fear was that if he pressed her too hard she might cry off altogether. He assured her that he had no other wish than to please her, and hoped to God that she did not often fall into distempered freaks.

Eleven

The clandestine meeting in the Abbey was undetected; but although Fanny was relieved to find her aunts quite unsuspicious she was also made to feel guilty, and ashamed. Nor did she any longer feel quite so happy in her love. It was not that she did not most ardently desire to pass the rest of her life in Stacy's protective arms, but she could not help thinking how very much more pleasant it would be if she could be married to him with the blessing of her family. There was a flavour of high adventure about an elopement; she had been quite sincere when she had said that she neither shrank from taking so bold a step, nor cared a button for the inevitable censure of the world. It had not occurred to her, until she had recollected her aunts' rout-party, that her elopement would pitchfork them into a very disagreeable situation. Floating in a dream of love and heroism, she had scarcely considered any but the broader aspects of the case, and even those only as they concerned herself. The opinion of the world was of no consequence; she and Stacy would be blissfully indifferent if the world cast them off, for they needed only each other for perfect happiness. As for her aunts, they would be very much shocked at first, even angry, but when they saw how right she had been to marry Stacy they would come round, and end by doting as fondly upon him as upon her. Not until Stacy urged her to fly with him immediately did she begin to perceive some of the minor objections attached to an elopement. Such things as rout-parties were quite unimportant, of course: Stacy said so, and it was so. But they were not unimportant to two maiden ladies who had been numbered for years amongst Bath's most respected residents. Not one of the invitations sent out on Aunt Selina's gilt-edged cards had been declined, for an invitation to attend one of the Misses Wendover's select parties was considered to confer distinction on the recipient. It had flashed through Fanny's mind as soon as Stacy had made his proposal that to subject her aunts to the humiliation of being obliged to cancel their party would be conduct too base ever to be pardoned. It would be even worse if they decided to hold it, as though they had not been plunged into a scandal (and it was stupid to suppose that the news of the elopement would not spread through Bath like wildfire), for if they did that they would find their big double drawing-room woefully thin of company. Several other minor objections occurred to her, but she resolutely banished them. One could not be expected to sacrifice the happiness of one-self and one's beloved merely to save one's aunts from embarrassment.

There was yet another objection which she found oddly daunting. Never having formed any very clear picture of the actual ceremony, who was to perform it, and where it was to take place, it came as a shock to her when Stacy described in romantic detail a flight to the Border. Innocent as she was, she yet knew that nothing could be more improper. Even her closest friends would find it hard to excuse conduct so indelicate: she had as well tie her garter in public! 'You cannot mean *Gretna Green*?' she had exclaimed incredulously. 'No, no! I know people do so in novels, but not – *real* people, like us! It is not at all the thing, Stacy! Why, I daresay it would take us two or three days to reach the Border! You can't have considered! We must be married in London, or – Bristol, or somewhere much nearer to Bath!'

So Stacy had had to explain to her that there were certain difficulties attached to the clandestine marriages of minors. He had done it very well, so that by the time they had parted at the door of the Abbey she was convinced that there was no other way open to them, and that it was as repugnant to him as it was to her. He would be no more than her courier until the knot was tied. 'But I will not press you,' he had said. 'If your courage fails you – if you cannot trust me enough – tell me! I'll go away – try to forget you!' He had added with a melancholy smile: 'You will forget me more easily!'

She had cried out against this. She was not so fickle, or so hen-hearted, and as for her trust in him, it was infinite!

She had promised to fly with him as soon after the rout-party as could be contrived; and, in the heat of an impassioned moment, had done so with enthusiasm. It was only later that an unacknowledged doubt began to trouble her.

Then had come the expedition to Wells, and her conversation with Oliver. He had said that he wished he could help her, but the things he had said to her had not helped her at all: in fact, they had increased her discomfort.

Abby, recognising the signs of inward turmoil, tried in vain to win her confidence. She could not discover that there had been any falling-out between the lovers, and the fear that Stacy was trying to persuade Fanny to elope with him began to haunt her. She told Mr Miles Calverleigh, when he drove her to Stanton-Drew, to inspect the Druidical monument there, that she lived in dread of waking one morning to find Fanny gone.

'Oh, I shouldn't think that at all likely!' he replied. 'Speaking as one who is not without experience, it's not as easy to elope at dead of night as you might think.'

She could not suppress her responsive dimple, but she said austerely: 'You are perfectly shameless! Why isn't it easy? I should have supposed it to be much easier than to do it during the day.'

'That's because you haven't applied your mind to it.'

'Very true! It so happens that the need to do so has never come in my way.'

'Oh, I can see that! It wouldn't surprise me to learn that you imagine a rope-ladder to be employed in the business.'

'It would surprise *me* very much to learn that it was! You know, I have never been able to understand how anyone *could* escape by means of a rope-ladder, particularly a female. It's all very well to talk of throwing it up to the window, but the chances are one wouldn't be able to catch it, or would fall out of the window, trying to do so. And what would you attach it to, if you *did* catch it?'

'I can't think.'

'No, and even if it was attached I have a strong notion that it is not at all easy to come down a rope-ladder. Depend upon it, it requires a great deal of practice.'

'Hampered by your petticoats, too,' he said thoughtfully. 'I see that you *have* applied your mind to the problem: tell me all about it!'

She laughed. 'No, I won't allow you to divert me. This is not a funning matter. I know that you think it a great bore, but –'

'Well, don't you?'

'How could I? I think it *vexatious* – indeed, I could slap Fanny for being such a wet-goose! – but one cannot be *bored* by what nearly concerns anyone to whom one is very much attached, and for whom one is responsible, can one?'

'As I have never found myself in such a position, I can't say.'

She said, with quick sympathy: 'I know that, and I pity you! You told me once – you said that you were not an object for compassion, but you are, Mr Calverleigh!'

'Yes, I've come to that conclusion myself,' he said unexpectedly. 'I was used not to think so, but ever since I came to Bath I have been growing steadily more convinced that I was mistaken.'

Taken by surprise, feeling very much as if she had suffered an electric shock, Abby gave a gasp. After a brief, but perceptible, pause, she said with as much composure as she could summon to her aid: 'You might not have felt the want of family ties whilst you were abroad, I daresay. But we were speaking of Fanny, and you were about to explain to me why I need not be afraid that she will run away in the night, when we fell into an absurd digression on the subject of rope-ladders. I should be very glad to believe you, but – but why?'

'Oh, it would be much too dangerous! The poor girl would be obliged to get up and scramble on her clothes in the dark, in case some other member of the household should be wakeful, and see the light under her door. After which, she must grope her way down two pairs of stairs, and if their creakings didn't rouse you the approach of a chaise over the cobblestones at that hour of night would certainly do so. Then, too, she must draw back the bolts on the front-door, take off the chain, and lastly, most difficult task of all, shut the door behind her – all without a sound! Of course, she might choose to leave the house open to any chance marauder, but I feel sure that you will tell me she is not so lost to all sense of what is due to you as *that*!'

'Yes!' said Abby, perceiving the force of these objections. 'And her room is at the back of the house, so how could she know that your horrid nephew was punctual to his appointment? Something might have happened to detain him, and only think how awkward it would be for her! She would be bound to consider that possibility. Anyone would! Furthermore, Grimston – our old nurse – sleeps in a little room next to hers, and although *I* may believe that nothing less than a trumpet-blast in her ear would wake her, you may depend upon it that Fanny would be in a quake! Oh, I think you are undoubtedly right! She won't make the attempt at night, and I'll take good care she has no opportunity during the day, even if I must accompany her everywhere, like the dragon I vowed I never would be.'

'That might become a trifle tedious. Are you so sure that she is planning to elope with my horrid nephew?'

'No,' she replied at once. 'Sometimes I tell myself that I am suffering from a stupid irritation of nerves: that however much she might fancy herself in love she would never do anything so improper, so unprincipled! And then I think that he has taken such strong possession of her mind that she will do whatever he wishes. But she has been in low spirits lately, in a worry, I conjecture. It might be that she can't bring herself to do what she knows is very wrong. I *did* entertain the hope that she had quarrelled with Stacy, but she hasn't.' She sighed. 'He was at the concert last night, and she looked at him as if he were her whole dependence and delight.'

'No, did she? I envy him. Not, of course, that I've the smallest desire that *Fanny* should bestow such a look upon me, but I wish that you would.'

She was aware suddenly that her heart, in general a very reliable organ, was behaving in a most alarming way, first trying to jump into her throat, and then beginning to thump so violently that she felt breathless, and uncomfortably hot. It was an effort to speak, but she managed to do so, saying: 'Mr Calverleigh – I am in no mood – for flirting!'

'Now, when have I ever tried to flirt with you?' he protested.

She felt herself impelled to steal a look at him, which she instantly realised was a very imprudent thing to have done, because he was smiling at her, and in a way which made her heart beat still more violently.

'I love you, you know,' he said conversationally. 'Will you marry me?'

The manner in which he made this abrupt proposal struck her as being so typical of him that a shaky laugh was dragged from her. 'Of all the graceless ways of making me an offer – ! No, no, you are not serious! you cannot be!'

'Of course I'm serious! A pretty hobble I should be in if I weren't, and you accepted my offer! The thing is that it is such a devil of a time since I proposed marriage to a girl that I've forgotten how to set about it. If I ever knew, but I daresay I didn't, for I was always a poor hand at making flowery speeches.' He smiled at her again, a little ruefully. *'That I should love a bright particular star!'*

'Oh – !' she breathed. 'Oh, pray don't say such things!'

'I won't, if you dislike it,' he said obligingly.

'Dislike it! How could anyone dislike to have such a thing said to her? But it won't do! You mustn't say any more on this head! *Pray* do not!'

'No, that's quite unreasonable,' he said. 'I won't pay you any compliments, but you can't expect me not to say any more! I've asked you to marry me, Abigail!'

'You must know I can't – how impossible it would be!'

'No, I don't. Why should it be?'

'The – the circumstances!' she uttered, in a stifled voice.

He looked to be a good deal puzzled. 'What circumstances? Mine? Oh, I'm perfectly well able to support a wife! You must have been listening to my horrid nephew.'

'I've done no such thing!' she said, much incensed. 'And if I had I shouldn't believe a word he said! What's more, considerations of that nature wouldn't weigh with me, if – if I returned your regard!'

'Don't you? Not at all?'

'I – No! I mean – I mean, it isn't *that!*'

'Well, if it isn't that – Good God, you don't mean to tell me it's because I made a cake of myself over Celia Morval twenty years ago? No, really, my sweet life, that's doing it much too brown! What had it to do with you? You must have been in the nursery!'

'Yes, but – Oh, *surely* you can perceive how impossible it would be for me to marry you? She was my brother's wife!'

'No, she wasn't.'

'She was engaged to be married to him, at all events, and she *became* his wife! And, if it hadn't been hushed up, there would have been a shocking scandal – of your making!'

'But it *was* hushed up,' he pointed out.

She looked helplessly at him. 'How can I make you understand?'

'Oh, I do understand! You don't care a straw for all that ancient history, but you know that James would, and you're afraid he'd kick up the devil of a dust. He wouldn't, but I daresay he'd wear you to death, trying to heckle or cajole you into giving me up. However, you needn't let that worry you: I can deal with James.'

She said, in a low tone: 'I'm not afraid of James. If – if I knew that I was doing right. But it wouldn't be James only. My sisters – all my family – would be thrown into such an uproar! I only

158

wish I might not be wholly cast off!' She glanced up fleetingly, and tried to speak more lightly. 'I shouldn't like that, you know. They may not know about Celia – indeed, I am very sure they don't, though I suppose Cornelia might, being James's wife – but, alas, they *do* know that you are the prodigal son!'

'Alas? What if they didn't know it? Would my disreputable past weigh with *you*?'

Her head was down-bent; she shook it slightly. 'Not if I loved you enough.'

'That sounds to me remarkably like a leveller. Don't you?'

She said frankly: 'I don't know. That's to say, it is so easy to mistake one's feelings: that I *do* know, for I cut my eye-teeth years ago. I hadn't any thought of marriage, and I didn't think that you had either, so – so I've had no time to consider. I own that if the circumstances had been different I – I should have been sorely tempted! But to marry – and at my age, too! – to disoblige one's family ought *not* to be considered. Do you understand?'

'Well, I understand that you've the devil of a lot of scruples, but it's no use expecting me to enter into them,' he replied. 'Family ties don't mean anything to me: didn't I tell you so once? As for making a sacrifice of yourself to suit your family's notions of respectability, I call it addlebrained!'

She smiled reluctantly. 'You would, of course! But it isn't quite that. I don't think I can explain it, because it's all tangled in my head – making me addlebrained! Do I seem odiously missish?'

'Yes, but I wasn't going to say so,' he assured her.

The laughter sprang into her eyes. '*Obnoxious* creature! If only you didn't always make me laugh! Sometimes I wonder if you have any proper feelings at all!'

'Almost none, I fear. Would you marry me if I had?'

She ignored this. 'Or any sense of shame either! But you have a great deal of quickness, and I'm persuaded you must see how outrageous it would be if I were to do the very thing I am trying to prevent Fanny from doing!'

'O my God!' he ejaculated. 'These Calverleighs – !'

'Exactly so!'

'Do you think *exactly*?' he asked diffidently. 'Would you object to it if I were to point out to you certain differences between the Calverleighs?'

She put out her hand impulsively. 'Oh, I know, I know! There is no comparison between you!'

He took her hand, and held it lightly on his knee. 'Oh, there is *some* comparison! Shocking fellows, both of us! I was one of the roaring-boys when I was on the town: they used to say of me that I was a hell-born babe – too rackety by half! But what no one ever said of me, not even my loving family, was that I was a bounce, or a queer-nabs!'

'Do they say that of Stacy?' she asked anxiously.

'So I've been informed, and I don't find it at all difficult to believe. Well, to continue our respective histories, each of us eloped with an heiress – or, rather, attempted to do so.'

'But you were in love with Celia! You didn't care for her fortune!' she interpolated swiftly.

'No, nor was I nine-and-twenty. I'm in love with you, and I don't care for *your* fortune.'

'You need not tell me that! Besides, I haven't a fortune. Not like Fanny! I think you would call it an *independence*, perhaps, or an easy competence.'

'Well, that's one objection disposed of: no one would be able to say that I married you for your fortune.'

'You wouldn't care if they did!' she said shrewdly.

'No, but you would.' There was a good deal of amusement in his eyes as they rested on her face. 'Just what do you imagine I've been doing during the past twenty years, dear innocent?'

'I don't know. How should I? You have never told me!'

'I'll tell you now. I've been making *my* fortune, of course.'

She laughed. 'So now you are a nabob! How stupid of me not to have guessed it!'

An odd smile flickered at the corners of his mouth. 'Just so!' he said. 'You aren't even interested, are you?'

'Well, no!' she confessed. 'Except that I did think you were perhaps a trifle purse-pinched, and I collect that this isn't the case, which I'm glad of, for your sake.'

'Thank you,' he said meekly.

'You know, if you *were* a rich nabob, your nephew might look to you rather than to Fanny to rescue him from his embarrassments,' she said.

'Not unless he was touched in his upper works! That would be rainbow-chasing, my dear!'

She smiled, but her own words had recalled her overriding anxiety to her mind. She drew her hand away, which had been resting snugly in his clasp, and gave a sigh. 'Wouldn't you do it, if it lay within your power? No, I suppose you wouldn't. Isn't there *anything* you might do to save my poor Fanny?'

'I thought it wouldn't be long before we came back to your poor Fanny. You are determined to embroil me in her affairs, aren't you?'

'Don't be vexed with me!' she begged. 'It is so very important! Perhaps you couldn't do anything, but you *might* be able to – if not for Fanny's sake, for mine?'

'Yes, well, let us now emerge from this pretty fairy-story!' he said, with a touch of astringency. 'If you imagine that I have the smallest desire to receive your hand as a reward for having performed a difficult task to your satisfaction you're beside the bridge, my child! I've no fancy for a reluctant wife. I want your love, not your gratitude.'

'I didn't say that!' she faltered. 'Indeed, I didn't!'

'You came mighty near it, didn't you?' he said quizzically. He got up, and held out his hands to her.' Come! If we don't make our way back to that inn, and get the horses put-to again, we shall be devilish late, and Miss Wendover will be thinking that *you* have eloped, not Fanny!'

She allowed him to pull her to her feet. As she walked beside him, towards the inn where they had left the curricle, she said tentatively: 'I hope you are not offended?'

He glanced down at her, and she was relieved to see that he was smiling again, very tenderly. 'No, not a bit. I was trying to decide whether I love you most when you're awake upon every suit, or when you're a pea-goose.'

Her eyes sank, as her colour rose; she said, with an uncertain laugh: 'I must seem like a pea-goose, I know. It is your fault, for – for putting windmills into my head! It doesn't seem so to you, but you have set me a problem, which I must solve, I think, by myself – if you understand me?'

'Well enough, at all events, not to press you further today. When I *do* press you further, I'll take care I don't do so here! Or in any other place where there's a hoary legend to take possession of your mind!'

'Hoary legend?' she repeated, momentarily puzzled. Her brow cleared suddenly. 'Oh, the bride and her attendants being turned into those stones! I had forgotten it.'

This interlude did much to lessen her constraint. During the drive back to Bath he talked on indifferent topics, so that she was very soon at her ease. She was careful not to introduce Fanny's name into her conversation, and was considerably surprised when he did so, saying abruptly: 'Don't tease yourself too much over Fanny! Have you any reason for fearing that she means to run away with Stacy? I'm inclined to doubt it, you know.'

She replied calmly: 'I don't know. She doesn't mean to do so before Thursday, I believe. She was discussing which of her new gowns she should wear for the party only this morning, so I think myself reasonably safe for the present. Afterwards – well, if she does mean to elope, she will find it a more difficult adventure than she bargained for!'

'I should think you would be more than a match for her,' he said. 'But that puts me in mind of something! I must make my excuses to your sister: I shan't be in Bath next week.'

She was conscious of feeling a disproportionate degree of disappointment, and a little disquiet. She said: 'My sister will be sorry. Are you – do you expect to be away for long?'

'Not longer than I need. There's some business I must attend to, and it won't do to put it off.'

'No, of course not,' she replied sedately. Then, as a thought occurred to her, she uttered an exclamation of annoyance, and said: 'Now, if only I had known, we need not have sent a card to Stacy!'

'Did you do so? Why?'

'Oh, because Selina *would* have it that if you were to be invited, Stacy must be too!'

'No! Did she really wish to invite me so much that she was prepared to receive Stacy? I must have made a bigger hit with her than I knew!' he remarked, in gratified accents.

Abby bit her lip, and replied with great dignity: 'My sister – I regret to say! – doesn't hold him in dislike. She thinks him very pretty-behaved, so it isn't a hardship to her to be obliged to entertain *him*!'

Twelve

The news that Mr Calverleigh had left Bath was brought to Sydney Place by Miss Butterbank on the following morning. She was a little disappointed to find that Miss Wendover was already aware of it, having received a brief note from him excusing himself from attending her rout-party; but as he had not divulged his reason for leaving Bath, his destination, or the means by which he proposed to travel, she was quickly able to repair two of these omissions. She was known, behind her back, as the Bath Intelligencer, but although she could tell Miss Wendover that Mr Calverleigh had set out on the London Mail Coach, at five o'clock on the previous evening, she had not discovered the nature of his business, and could only advance a few conjectures.

Miss Wendover heard of the departure with relief, and indulged the hope that Mr Calverleigh did not mean to return to Bath. Foolish she might be, but it had not escaped her notice that he and Abby had become wondrous great, which was a circumstance which filled her with misgiving. He was an interesting man, and one who had been, in her opinion, hardly used, but no more ineligible husband for Abby could have been imagined. When the suggestion had first been slyly made to her that Abby was encouraging his advances she had been as incredulous as she was indignant, but when Abby, not content with accompanying him to the theatre, took to driving about the neighbouring countryside with him, she became very uneasy, and disclosed to the faithful Miss

Butterbank that she wished neither of the Calverleighs had ever come to Bath.

Their coming had certainly cut up her peace. First, there had been Stacy (poor young man!), whose very understandable attentions to Fanny had brought down James's wrath upon her head, and even, to some extent, Abby's; and who had turned out to be sadly unsteady, if James and George were to be believed, though it would not surprise her to find that they had grossly exaggerated Stacy's failings, for there was something so particularly winning about his graceful manners, and the deference he used towards his elders. He was the head of his family, too, and the owner of a considerable estate in Berkshire. She had never visited Danescourt, but she had looked for it in an old volume entitled *Seats of the Nobility and Gentry*, and there, sure enough, it was, with an illustration depicting a large, sprawling house of obvious antiquity, and a quantity of interesting information about its history, and that of the Calverleighs, who seemed to have owned it for an impressive number of centuries. If it was true, as George had told Abby it was, that it was so grossly encumbered that it was in imminent danger of passing out of Calverleigh hands, it could not be regarded as an asset, of course, for its loss must diminish Stacy's consequence to vanishing point, and transform him from a desirable *parti* into a scapegrace who had wasted his inheritance, and reduced himself to penury. But how could she have known this, when she had welcomed Stacy to Sydney Place? It was most unjust of James to have sent her such a scold; and for her part she would find it hard to believe that, whatever the poor young man's misfortunes might be, he had come to Bath in search of a rich wife. As for the shocking suspicion Abby had, that he meant to elope with Fanny, *that* she never would believe; and she wondered how Abby could suppose dear little Fanny to be so dead to all feelings of shame, or how she herself could be so regardless of her sister's precarious health as to put such ideas into her head as must give rise to the sort of agitating reflections calculated to throw her nerves into disorder.

And then, as though all this were not bad enough, Mr Miles Calverleigh had descended upon them, and lost no time at all in attaching himself particularly to Abby! There was no doubt about *his* reputation, for, however much one might pity him for the harsh treatment meted out to him by his father, the fact remained that not the most rigorous father would pack his son off to India without good reason. And if James thought he could lay the blame for this black sheep's intrusion into Abby's life at her door he was never more mistaken, and so she would tell him. Who, in the world, could have thought that Abby, rejecting the offer of the noble lord who addressed himself to her surrounded by the aura of dear Papa's approval, holding up her nose at such admirable suitors as Mr Peter Dunston, would succumb to the advances of a man who had nothing whatsoever to recommend him to one so notoriously picksome as she was? He was not at all handsome; he had none of his nephew's address; his manners were the reverse of graceful; and his raiment, so far from being elegant, showed neither neatness nor propriety. Not only did he pay morning-visits in riding-breeches and indifferently polished top-boots, but, more often than not, he looked as though he had dressed all by guess, tying his neckcloth in a careless knot, and shrugging himself into his coat. Anyone would have supposed that Abby, herself always precise to a pin, would have held such a shabrag in disgust – even if he had been unrelated to the Calverleigh she held in positive abhorrence! She had always been capricious, but to allow the uncle to make up to her while she refused to countenance the nephew's courtship of her niece carried caprice into the realm of distempered freakishness. And one had thought that she had outgrown what dear Rowland had called the odd kick in her gallop!

Abby, well aware that Selina was watching her with misgiving, betrayed none of her own misgivings. Away from Miles Calverleigh's disturbing presence, she could be mistress of herself; and she pursued her usual avocations without a sign that her cheerful calm concealed a heart and a mind suffering from a serious disorder. Mr Calverleigh's shortcomings were as obvious

166

to her as to Selina, and as little as Selina did she know why, after so many fancy-free years, she should have fallen in love with one so hopelessly ineligible and so totally unlike any of the gentlemen with whom she had enjoyed passing flirtations. She had been attracted by his smile, but no smile, however fascinating it might be, could cause a cool-headed female of more than eight-and-twenty so wholly to lose her poise and her judgment that she felt she had met, in its owner, the embodiment of an ideal. Fumbling for an explanation, she thought that it was not Miles Calverleigh's smile which had awakened an instant response in her, but the understanding behind the smile. She had been conscious, almost from the start of their acquaintance, of an intangible link between them, as though he had been her counterpart; and nothing he had said, no disclosure of cynical unconcern, or total disregard of morals, had weakened the link. He could infuriate her, he frequently shocked her, but still she felt herself akin to him.

She had told him that she was not sure that she loved him, but she had done so not in doubt of her love for him, but in dismay at the realization that she did love him, whatever he was, or whatever he had done. If she had been a besotted schoolgirl, like her niece, she would have melted into his embrace, and have thought the world well lost. But at eight-and-twenty one did not, on an impulse, cast aside all the canons of one's upbringing; and still less did one lightly ignore the duty owed to one's family. Miles Calverleigh did not recognise family claims, and what shocked her most in this was the discovery that she was not shocked, but had experienced instead a pang of envy.

She wondered whether it was the rebellious streak in her, so frequently deplored even by her mother, which had drawn her irresistibly to Miles Calverleigh; but when she considered this, as dispassionately as she could, she thought that it could hardly be so. It might lead her to throw her cap over the windmill, but it found no answering chord in Miles. He was not a rebel. Rebels fought against the trammels of convention, and burned to rectify what they saw to be evil in the shibboleths of an elder generation, but Miles Calverleigh was not of their number. No wish to reform the world inspired him, not the smallest desire to convert others to his own way of thinking. He accepted, out of a vast and perhaps idle tolerance, the rules laid down by a civilised society, and, when he transgressed these, accepted also, and with unshaken good-humour, society's revenge on him. Neither the zeal of a reformer, nor the rancour of one bitterly punished for the sins of his youth, awoke a spark of resentment in his breast. He did not defy convention: when it did not interfere with whatever line of conduct he meant to pursue he conformed to it; and when it did he ignored it, affably conceding to his critics their right to censure him, if they felt so inclined, and caring neither for their praise nor their blame.

Such a character should have been alien to a Wendover. Abby knew it, and tried to convince herself that she was suffering from much the same adolescent madness which had attacked her niece, and from which she would soon recover. She met with no success: she was not an adolescent, but she could remember the throes of her first, frustrated love-affair, and she knew that her present condition was quite unlike the joys and agonies experienced ten years earlier. Like Fanny, she had fallen in love with a handsome countenance, and had endowed its owner with every imaginable virtue. Looking back in amusement upon this episode, she thought how fortunate it was for the undesirable suitor that her father had sent him packing before he had had time to tumble off the pedestal she had built for him. But she had built no pedestal for Miles Calverleigh: the very thought of setting him upon one appealed irresistibly to her lively sense of humour, and made it necessary for her to explain to Selina that her sudden laugh, breaking a long silence, had been caused by the recollection of an old joke, too foolish to be repeated. The discovery that her first suitor had feet of clay would have shattered her infatuation; she had known from the beginning that Miles Calverleigh was no paladin, but his sins were of as little importance to her as his sallow, harsh-featured face. If she married him, it would be with her eyes open to his faults, and in the knowledge that, in consulting only her own ardent desire, she would be subjecting every member of her family to varying degrees of shock, dismay, and even, where Selina and Mary were concerned, to grave distress.

It was a hard problem to solve, and none of the arguments that dashed endlessly in her brain brought her any nearer to a decision, though they nagged at her all day, and kept her awake long into the night.

But no one, watching her as she moved amongst her guests on Thursday evening, would have suspected that anything had occurred to ruffle her serenity; and not the keenest eyes could detect in her face any sign that she was labouring under the pangs of love. So much in command of herself was she that she was even able, when Lady Weaverham enquired archly when they might expect to see Mr Miles Calverleigh in Bath again, to reply smilingly: 'I don't know, ma'am. We miss him, don't we? My sister thinks him much too free and easy, but for my part I find him most entertaining. One never knows what he will say next!'

'Which, to my mind,' Lady Weaverham told Mrs Ancrum, 'isn't the way a young woman talks about a gentleman she's nutty upon! And never a blush, or a conscious look either! Well, I did think it was a case between them, but I daresay it wouldn't have done, so it's as well that it ain't.'

Though nobody suspected that there was anything amiss with Abby, several people noticed that Fanny was not in her best looks. She was a little flushed, and decidedly heavy-eyed, but when Mrs Grayshott asked her kindly if she was feeling quite well she assured her that indeed she was, except for a slight headache. 'Don't say anything to Abby about it, ma'am!' she begged. 'It would spoil the party for her if she knew, and I promise you it is *very* slight!' She added, before flitting away to greet some fresh arrivals: 'You know how it is, when one holds a large party! However carefully you may plan it, there seem always to be such a number of things to do at the last moment that you can't help but be rather tired by the time the party begins!'

It was true that she had been busy for most of the day, but neither fatigue nor a slight headache would, under normal circumstances, have much impaired her enjoyment of the party. But she too was faced with a difficult problem; and although she had made up her mind that if the choice lay between eloping with Stacy to Scotland and losing him for ever, Scotland it must be, the decision had not put an end to her heart-searchings, and it had certainly not raised her spirits. When Selina chatted happily of winter plans, and discussed the numerous dresses she must have for her come-out in the spring, she felt an absurd desire to burst into tears; yet when she tried to imagine what it would be like to bid Stacy goodbye, her impulse was to fly to him immediately, just to assure him that she meant to keep her promise. The trouble was that she had been granted no opportunity since their stolen meeting in the Abbey to exchange more than a few words with him, and those only in public. It was no wonder that she should be feeling low. Once she was with him, and no longer lived in dread of being separated from him, everything would be right: it was only the actual severing of the ties which bound her to Sydney Place which made her feel wretched, and she must naturally be sad at wrenching herself from her home. After all, she had been miserable for days before she had gone, once, to spend a month with her Uncle James and her Aunt Cornelia. She had been extremely homesick, too, but she had recovered from this in a week. And if she could do so when staying with her uncle, who was so precise and prosy, and her aunt, who was detestable, how much more rapidly would she recover when she was in the arms of a husband whom she adored!

Her heart leaped up when she saw Stacy bowing over Selina's hand. How handsome he was! how elegant! how easy and polished were his manners, and how gracefully he made his bow! He made every other man in the room look dowdy and clumsy. He was top-of-the-trees – the Real Thing – and from amongst all the fashionable beauties who must surely have cast out lures to him he had chosen her – little Fanny Wendover, who hadn't even made her come-out! She felt a rush of pride in him, and wondered how she could have hesitated for a moment to go away with him.

Yet when, presently, he made his way to her side, and tried to draw her apart, she would not allow it, saying in an urgent undervoice: 'No, no, not here! not now!'

'But, my darling – !' he expostulated caressingly.

She was terribly nervous, fancying that at least a dozen pairs of eyes were on her; a stab of pain shot through her head; and suddenly she was shaken by a wave of irritation, and whispered quite fiercely: *'Don't!'*

He looked to be a good deal taken-aback. 'But, Fanny, I must talk to you!'

'Not now!' she repeated. 'I can't – All these people – ! Oh, pray don't tease me! I have *such* a headache!'

The smile faded from his lips. He said: 'I see what it is: your courage has failed you, or your love is not as strong as I believed it to be.'

'No, no, I *promise* it isn't so! Only we cannot talk here! Surely you must perceive the danger?'

'Then where?'

'Oh, I don't know!' She saw the frown gathering on his brow, and said hurriedly: 'Tomorrow – in the Gardens! At – at two o'clock! Aunt Selina will be resting on her bed, and Abby always visits old Mrs Nibley on Fridays. I'll contrive to join you there without Grimston's knowing. No more now: Abby is looking at us!'

She turned away on the words. The stabs of pain in her head were increasing, making her feel sick, and almost blinding her. A couple of uncertain steps brought her into collision with someone. She stammered: 'Oh, I beg your pardon! I didn't see!'

Her hand was caught, and held in a sustaining grasp; Oliver Grayshott's voice sounded above her head. 'Fanny, what it is? You are ill!'

'Oh, it's you!' she said, clinging gratefully to his hand. 'I'm not ill. It is only that my head aches so dreadfully! I shall be better directly.'

'Yes, but not in this squeeze,' he said. 'You must go to bed at once!'

'Oh, no, how can I? It would break up the party, and create a horrid fuss!'

'No, it won't,' he said calmly. 'No one will notice it, if you slip out of the room. I think you have a *migraine,* and I know, because I've had 'em myself, that there's only one thing for it, and that's to lie down on your bed. Shall I fetch Lavinia to go with you?'

'No, pray don't! It isn't as bad as *that*! Nurse will know what to do for me. Only don't say anything to frighten my aunts!'

'Of course not,' he replied.

'Thank you,' she sighed. 'I'm very much obliged to you!'

He watched her go unobtrusively out of the room, and then made his way to where his mother was seated, talking to Canon Pinfold. He soon found an opportunity to tell her that Fanny had retired with a headache, and was anxious that her aunts should not be alarmed. She said reassuringly that she would convey the news to Abby, who would be neither alarmed nor even surprised. 'She told me, when I said I thought Fanny not looking quite the thing, that she was pretty sure she had the headache, only the silly child wouldn't own to it.'

In point of fact, Abby had observed Fanny's departure. She said: 'Yes, I saw her go, and I was excessively grateful to Oliver for persuading her to do so. What a kind young man he is! I shall take a peep at her when I go upstairs to bed, but I need never be in a worry about her when Grimston has her in charge! I expect she will be quite restored by tomorrow.'

She was mistaken. While she was still sipping a cup of chocolate on the following morning, she received a visit from Mrs Grimston, who came to request her, ominously, to take a look at Miss Fanny as soon as might be convenient.

'It's no more than I expected, miss,' said Mrs Grimston, with the peculiar satisfaction of the devoted retainer who has detected incipient illness in one of her nurslings. "Yes," I said to myself, when she came up to me last night, "there's more to this than a headache. If I know anything about it," I said, "what you've got, poor lamb, is the influenza!" Which she has, Miss Abby.' She took the empty cup from Abby, and added: 'And, if I was you, ma'am, I would send the footboy to fetch the doctor to her, because she's in a high fever, and there's no saying but what she may throw out a rash presently, though the measles it *can't* be!'

'No, of course it can't!' said Abby, throwing back the bedclothes. 'I don't doubt it's nothing more than influenza, just as you say!'

'If it's not the scarlet fever,' said Mrs Grimston, depressing optimism. She held up Abby's dressing-gown for her. 'For I shouldn't be doing my duty, Miss Abby, if I didn't tell you that she's been complaining for the past hour and more that she has a sore throat!'

'Very likely,' Abby returned. 'So did I, when I was laid up for a sennight with the influenza, last year!'

Balked of her wish to allay anxiety by her superior knowledge and commonsense, Mrs Grimston threw in a doubler. 'Yes, Miss Abby, and if it *is* the influenza, it's to be hoped Miss Selina hasn't taken it from her!'

'Oh, Grimston, you – you *wretch*!' Abby exclaimed ruefully. 'If she has, we *shall* be in the suds! Well! all my dependence is upon you!'

Mollified by this tribute, Mrs Grimston relented, and said, as she accompanied Abby to the sickroom: 'And so I should hope, ma'am! They say that there's a lot of this influenza going about, so I daresay Miss Fanny hasn't taken anything worse. But you know what she is, Miss Abby, and if you'll take my advice, you'll send for the doctor!'

Abby did indeed know what Miss Fanny was, and she gave a ready consent to the footboy's being sent off immediately on this errand. Fanny, though rarely ill, was a bad patient. If any seasonal ailment, or epidemic disease, attacked her, it invariably did so with unprecedented violence. None of her school-friends had been as full of the measles as she had been; none had whooped more distressingly; or had been more tormented by the mumps; so it came as no surprise to Abby, upon entering a room redolent with the fumes of burning pastilles, to find her in a high fever, and complaining in a miserable wail that she was hot, uncomfortable, aching in every limb, and hardly able to lift her eyelids.

'Poor Fanny!' Abby said softly, lifting the folded handkerchief from her brow, and soaking it afresh with vinegar. 'There! is that better? Don't cry, my pet! Dr Rowton is coming to see you, and he will soon make you more comfortable.'

'I don't want him! I'm not ill! I'm not, I'm not! I want to get up! I *must* get up!'

'To be sure, and so you shall, just as soon as you feel more the thing,' Abby said soothingly.

'I *do* feel the thing! It's only that my head hurts me, and I can't hold my eyes open, and everything aches all over me!' wept the sufferer. 'Oh, Abby, *please* make me better *quickly*!'

'Yes, darling, of course I will.'

This assurance seemed to calm Fanny. She lay still for a while, dropping into an uneasy doze; but within a very few minutes she became restless again, insisting that she was better, trying to get up, and bursting into tears when Abby gently pressed her back on to her pillows.

Having had considerable experience of her mercurial temperament, and knowing that whenever she was condemned to lie in bed it took much to persuade her that her ills would not be instantly alleviated by her getting up, and going for a walk, Abby set no particular store by her agitation. Leaving Mrs Grimston to sit with her, she withdrew, to dress, and – when fortified by breakfast – to break the news to Selina.

She found that Fardle, Selina's maid, had been before her, carrying such an unpromising account of Fanny's condition that Selina's appetite had been destroyed. When Abby came into her room, she was sitting up in bed, eating pieces of toast dipped in weak tea: a melancholy diet to which it was her custom to resort in times of stress. She greeted her sister with a moan, and a demand to be told whether the doctor had been sent for.

'Yes, dear, an hour ago! I daresay he will be here directly,' replied Abby cheerfully. 'Not that I think there is much to be done for her, but I hope he may be able to make her more comfortable at least. Grimston gave her a fever powder at seven o'clock but it hasn't answered, so I have told her not to repeat it.'

'No, no, don't let Grimston quack her! Oh, Abby, if she should be beginning in the smallpox – !' uttered Selina, staring fearfully at her.

'Beginning in the *smallpox*?' echoed Abby, in astonishment. 'Good God, no! How can you be so absurd, Selina? Why, surely you haven't forgotten that Dr Rowton persuaded us all to be inoculated last year? Besides, where could she have contracted it? There are no cases of it in Bath that I've heard of!'

'No, dear, very likely not, but one never *knows*, and Fardle has been telling me –'

'Fardle!' exclaimed Abby. 'I might have guessed as much! I am perfectly sure that she has a sister, or an aunt, or a cousin, who nearly died in the smallpox, and that her symptoms precisely resembled Fanny's, for we've never yet had an illness in this household, but what one of Fardle's relations had had it too, only *far* worse! Pray don't fly into a fuss, dear! I shall own myself surprised if Dr Rowton finds Fanny to be suffering from anything more serious than influenza.'

'Oh, my love, why didn't you send for Dr Dent? I have no great opinion of Rowton, though an excellent man in his way, of course, but *not* clever! You know how well Dr Dent understood my case when *I* had influenza!'

'Yes, dear, but I was persuaded you would wish me to send for Rowton, because he is familiar with her constitution,' said Abby diplomatically. 'Do you mean to drive into town this morning? Will you buy a bottle of lavender-water, if you please?'

'Fardle must procure it,' said Selina, in a failing voice. 'I shall rest quietly in bed this morning, for I have already felt a spasm, and heaven forbid *I* should be ill at this moment! Such a dreadful shock to be roused with such news! Yes, and she must bring me some camphor, for I don't believe there is any in the house, and you know how susceptible I am to colds and influenza!'

Abby agreed to this, but ventured to suggest that not the most susceptible person would be very likely to contract influenza twice within the space of a month.

'No, dearest,' replied Selina, directing a look of patient reproach at her. 'I daresay an ordinary person might not, but, alas, I have never enjoyed high health, and as for not contracting influenza twice in a month, I had *three* epidemic colds last winter, one after another! And I recall that you said exactly the same when you came home from Lady Trevisian's card-party, sneezing and snuffling, and I begged you not to come *near* me, but to go up to your bed immediately! You said *I* could not catch it from you, because I had not been out of *my* bed above a sennight! But I did!'

Abby begged pardon, kissed her cheek, and left her to the enjoyment of her mild triumph.

In the sickroom, she found Fanny tossing restlessly, and alternately expressing her determination to get up, and complaining of the various aches and pains which assailed her. Her pulse was rapid, and her skin very hot and dry, and it was obvious that her fever was mounting.

Mrs Grimston, drawing Abby out of the room, said that if anyone were to ask her she would feel herself impelled to say that they were regularly in for it. 'As nasty an attack as any I've nursed her through!' she said. 'Well, I'm sure it's not to be wondered at, the way she's been gallivanting to parties all over, and her no more than a baby! Burnt to the socket, that's what she is, Miss Abby, and so full of crotchets and nonsense as is enough to put one quite out of patience! First she must get up, and the moment my back's turned so she did! Only that turned her so dizzy she was glad enough to be put back into bed. Then she began to cry, but I soon put a stop to that, ma'am, for we don't want her to get into one of her ways, for, as I told her, *that* won't make her feel better!

Then nothing will do for her but what she must speak to Betty about mending a frill on her blue muslin. "There'll be time enough for that, Miss Fanny," I said, "and no need to bring Betty into the room to take the influenza, for I'll speak to her about it myself."'

The arrival of Dr Rowton brought this monologue to a close. He was a sensible-looking man, with a latent twinkle in his eye, but it was not difficult to see why Selina thought poorly of him. He had cheerful, matter-of-fact manners, and had been known to tell ladies in failing health that their mysterious ailments arose from want of occupation, or from thinking too much about themselves. He said, as he shook hands with Abby: 'And how is Miss Wendover? I hear she has my old friend, Dent, attending her now. I thought it wouldn't be long before she gave poor Ockley the go-by: not her style at all!'

He did not take a very serious view of Fanny's case; but when he left her he told Abby that she would probably be laid up for some little time. 'Oh, yes, it's influenza right enough,' he said. 'It's running very much about, you know, and unusually virulent. A pity Fanny should have caught it. Now, had it been you, Miss Abby, I should have said you'd be as bobbish as ever in a week but we both know what Fanny is, don't we? Always the way with girls of her cut! You'll have to keep her quiet – as quiet as you can! I was used to call her Miss Quicksilver, when she was a child, and she hasn't altered much. I'll send my man round with some medicine for her to take, and we'll see how she goes on tomorrow.'

He was a favourite of Fanny's, ranking amongst her oldest friends, and Abby had hoped that his visit would do her good. She did indeed manage to conjure up a wan smile, when he walked up to the bedside, saying: 'Well, Miss Quicksilver, and pray what's all this?' but the voice in which she responded: 'Oh, *dear* Dr "Wowton", make me well again quickly!' was very lachrymose; and when he told her, in his blunt way that she would certainly not be able to get up that day, or for several days, she burst into tears.

When Abby returned to the sickroom, however, she seemed to be resigned to her fate, and to be inclined to sleep.

She did drop off into an uneasy doze from time to time, but her dreams were haunted by Stacy, either waiting for hour upon hour in Sydney Gardens, or accusing her of being false to him; and more than once she woke with tears on her cheeks, and a jumble of words on her feverish lips.

She retained no very clear memory of what had happened at the previous night's party, but she did remember that she had promised to meet Stacy, and that he had been angry with her for not talking to him. He had said that he could see she didn't love him, and now he would be sure of it. She had racked her brains to hit upon some way of conveying a message to him, but Abby and Nurse were in league against her; they would not even let her see Betty Conner, who could have done it for her. Perhaps he would think that she had stayed away on purpose, to show him that she didn't want to run off with him after all. Perhaps he would leave Bath, as he had threatened to do, and she would never see him again, never be able to tell him that it hadn't been her fault, or that she did love him, and wasn't afraid to elope with him to Scotland.

These agitating reflections did nothing to improve her condition; and as her fever mounted they became even more lurid, until they included visions of her own death-bed, and Stacy's remorse at having so misjudged her. But towards evening Dr Rowton's paregoric medicine began to take effect, and she grew calmer, emerging from the state of semi-delirium which had kept Abby hovering on the verge of sending a second, and far more urgent, summons to the doctor. She felt so ill, and so much exhausted, that she no longer wanted to get up, or even to exert herself sufficiently to try once more to think how she might send a message to Stacy. It must be too late by now, she thought apathetically. Her whole life was ruined, but it didn't seem to matter nearly as much as her aching body, and the stabbing pain in her temple, and her terrible thirstiness. When Abby raised her, she leaned her head gratefully on Abby's shoulder, murmuring her name.

'Yes, my darling, I'm here,' Abby said tenderly. 'Nurse is going to shake up your pillows while you have a cool drink of lemonade. There, is that better?'

'Oh, yes!' she sighed, her thirst for the moment assuaged. She opened her eyes, and they fell on a big bowl of flowers. 'Oh!' she breathed.

'Looking at your beautiful flowers?' Abby said, laying her gently down again. 'Oliver and Lavinia brought them, when they came to enquire how you did. They left their love to you, and were so sorry to hear that you're so poorly. Go to sleep again now, darling: I won't leave you.'

The spark of hope that had flickered in Fanny's breast died, but as she lay dreamily looking at the flowers it occurred to her that if the Grayshotts knew that she was ill they would be very likely to tell other people, and so, perhaps, the news would reach Stacy's ears, and he would know why she had broken her word to him. With a deep sigh of relief, she turned her head on the pillow, snuggling her cheek into it, and drifted back into sleep.

Thirteen

*I*t was not long before the news reached Stacy Calverleigh, but when it did it brought no relief to his anxieties, which were rapidly becoming acute. He had not supposed, when he kicked his heels in the Sydney Gardens, that Fanny had failed him from intention, nor did it occur to him that she might be ill. Not being endowed with the perception which distinguished Mr Oliver Grayshott, he had failed to notice her flushed cheeks and heavy eyes, and had ascribed the headache of which she had complained to a tiresome fit of missishness. The likeliest explanation that presented itself to him was that she had been prevented from keeping her assignation by the vigilance of her aunt. It had at first exasperated him; but, upon reflection, he had come to the conclusion that the frustration of her plan might well prove to be all that was needed to cause such a wilful, headstrong girl as Fanny to throw herself into his arms in a fury of indignation. Confident that she must be pantingly eager to tell him why she had been unable to meet him, and equally eager to escape from her shackles, he paraded the Pump Room on the following morning; and, when neither she nor Miss Wendover put in an appearance, wasted considerable time in taking a look-in at the libraries, strolling up such fashionable streets as Fanny would be most likely to visit on a shopping expedition, and loitering interminably in Queen's Square. No balls or concerts took place at the Assembly Rooms on Fridays, and as he had received no invitation to any private party it was not until Saturday that he learned of Fanny's indisposition.

It struck him with dismay. It must mean delay, even if she made a quick recovery, and delay was what he could not afford. It was not in his nature to envisage disaster. He had the true gamester's belief in his luck, and experience had encouraged him to think that when this failed him some unexpected stroke of Providence would rescue him from his predicaments. But several unpleasant communications, which not the most hardened of optimists could have failed to recognise as the precursors to writs, had reached him; and a most disquieting letter from his man of business had conveyed to him the intelligence that foreclosure on his estates was now imminent. For perhaps the first time in his life, he knew panic, and for a few wild moments entertained thoughts of a flight to the Continent. While these endured, his spirits rose: life abroad held out its attractions. A clever gamester, one who knew what time of day it was, could make a fortune if he set up a gaming establishment in any one of half a dozen cities which instantly leaped to his mind. Not Paris: no, not Paris. Now that Napoleon was marooned on St Helena Island, far too many Englishmen were to be found disporting themselves in Paris: he had as well – or as ill – set up such an establishment in London. But there were other promising cities, rather farther afield, where the chances of his being recognised by an English traveller were negligible.

This was important. Mr Stacy Calverleigh, eyed askance by the society into which he had been born, even being obliged, since his disastrous attempt to secure an heiress, to endure more than one cut direct, bent on seducing yet a second heiress to elope with him, was not so lost to a sense of his obligations that he did not recoil from the thought of transforming himself, openly, into the proprietor of a gaming-house. He had often thought what a capital hand he would have made of it, had it been possible for him to join the company of these gentry; he had never regarded his estates as anything other than a coffer into which he could dip his hand at will; but the inculcated precepts of his breeding remained with him. There were some things a Calverleigh of Danescourt must never do; and high on the list of these prohibitions ranked the only profession at which he felt he might have excelled.

But if one could enter it without the knowledge of those who would most contemptuously condemn him? As his fancy played with the possibilities of such a situation, his eyes brightened, and he began to picture a future rosier, and far more to his secret taste, than any that had yet presented itself to him.

Only for a few, fleeting moments, however. To embark on such a career, it was necessary that the dibs should be in tune, and the dibs were not in tune. There was no other solution to his difficulties than a rich marriage. Marriage to Fanny was not the ideal solution, but a notice (he had already drafted it) sent to the Gazette, and the Morning Post, of his marriage to the only daughter of the late Rowland Wendover Esquire, of Amberfield, in the County of Bedfordshire, would stave off his creditors, and might, at the least, make it very difficult for Mr James Wendover to repudiate the alliance.

A visit of enquiry and condolence to Sydney Place did not strengthen this more hopeful view. He was received by the elder Miss Wendover; and although she welcomed him with rather guilty kindness, her account of her niece's illness was not encouraging. Mr Miles Calverleigh, with his dispassionate yet shrewd ability to sum up his fellow-creatures, would have appreciated it at its true value; Mr Stacy Calverleigh, absorbed in his own entity, only noticed the peculiarities of the persons with whom he came in contact when their idiosyncrasies directly affected him, and so made no allowance for the exaggerations of an elderly lady whose paramount interest lay in the ailments of herself, or of anyone attached to her. He left Sydney Place with the impression that if Fanny were not lying at death's door she was so gravely ill that it must be many weeks before she could hope to be restored to health. Miss Wendover said that she had often feared that Fanny's constitution too closely resembled her own, and embroidered this statement with some instances which, had he been listening to her with as much attention as his solicitous expression indicated, might well have led him to conclude that Fanny, for all her looks and vitality, was a frail creature, supported by her nerves, which too frequently betrayed her.

He was not listening. The delicacy of Fanny's constitution was a matter of secondary importance. What was of the first importance was the apparent likelihood that her recovery from her present disorder would be too slow to admit of her being able, or even willing, to undertake the long journey to the Scottish Border for several weeks.

He maintained his smile, and his air of courteous concern, but when he took his leave of Miss Wendover, consigning to her care the tasteful bouquet he had ventured to bring with him for the invalid, he was as near to despair as it was possible for anyone of his temperament to be. He walked slowly back to the centre of the town, trying in vain to think of some other means of recruiting his fortunes than marriage. A run of luck might save him from immediate ruin, but a prolonged run of damnable ill-luck had made it impossible for him to continue punting on tick. If his vowels were still accepted in certain circles, it was with reluctance; and he had been refused admittance – in the politest way – to two of the exclusive hells which had for several years enjoyed his patronage. For the first time in his life he knew himself to be at a stand, and without any hope of deliverance.

But Providence, in whom he had for so long reposed his careless trust, had not forgotten him. Providence, in the guise of Mrs Clapham, was at that very moment entering the portals of the White Hart, preceded by her courier, accompanied by her female companion, and followed by her maid, and her footman.

He did not immediately realise that Providence had inter-vened on his behalf. By the time he had reached the White Hart, Mrs Clapham had been reverently escorted to the suite of rooms bespoken by her courier, and the only signs of her presence which were observable were the elegant travelling-chariot which had brought her to Bath, and was still standing in the yard, and the unusual state of bustle prevailing amongst the various servants employed at the hotel.

There were those who considered the situation of the White Hart to be too noisy for comfort, but it was patronised by so many persons of rank and consequence that the stir created by the arrival of Mrs Clapham was remarkable enough to arouse Stacy's interest. He enquired of the waiter who brought a bottle of brandy to his room who the devil was Mrs Clapham, and why were they all tumbling over themselves to administer to her comfort? The waiter replied, with strict civility, but repressively, that she was the lady who had engaged the largest and most luxurious set of apartments in the house. The boots was more informative, and from him Stacy gathered that Mrs Clapham was a widow-lady, full of juice, and flashing the rags all over. Everything of the best she had to have, and ready to pay through the nose for it. Very affable and pleasant-spoken, too, which was more than could be said of her companion. Top-lofty *she* was, giving her orders as if she was a duchess, and saying that first this and then that would not do for her mistress, and her own sheets and pillows must be put on her bed, and her own tea served to her, and dear knows what more besides!

Stacy's curiosity was only mildly tickled by this description. It was not until he encountered Mrs Clapham on the following morning that the thought that Providence might once more have come to his rescue darted through his brain. A widow, travelling with a large entourage, and bringing with her her own bedlinen, suggested to him a turbaned dowager, the relict of a bygone generation. Mrs Clapham might be a widow, but she was no dowager. She was quite a young woman: past her girlhood, but not a day older than thirty, if as old. She was remarkably pretty, too, with an inviting mouth, and a pair of brown eyes which were as innocent as they were enormous, until she dropped demure eyelids over them, and looked sidelong from under the screen of her curling lashes. Then they became unmistakably provocative. She was dressed with great elegance, but in a subdued shade of lavender, which seemed to indicate that, while she had cast off her weeds, her bereavement was of fairly recent date. When Stacy saw her first, she was tripping down the stairs, trying to button one of her gloves, without dropping the prayer-book she was holding. As Stacy looked up at her, it slipped from her imperfect grasp, and fell almost at his feet.

'Oh – !' she exclaimed distressfully. Then, as he picked it up, and straightened its crumpled leaves: 'Oh, how very obliging of you! Thank you! So stupid of me! It is all the fault of these tiresome gloves, which *will* come unbuttoned!'

Her companion, following her down the stairs, clicked her tongue, and said; 'Pray allow me, Mrs Clapham!'

Mrs Clapham held out her wrist helplessly, repeating, with a rueful smile cast at Stacy: 'So *stupid* of me! Oh, thank you, dear Mrs Winkworth! I don't know how I should go on without you!'

Stacy, presenting her prayer-book to her, bowed with his exquisite grace, and said: 'One or two of the pages a little crumpled, ma'am, but no irreparable damage, I fancy! May I beg leave to make myself known to you? – Stacy Calverleigh, wholly at your service!'

She gave him her tightly gloved hand. 'Oh, yes! And I am Mrs Clapham, sir. This is Mrs Winkworth, who takes such good care of me. We are on our way to Church, in the Abbey. The *feel* it gives me! I have never attended a service in an abbey before: isn't it absurd?'

'Your first visit to Bath, ma'am?' he enquired, bestowing a modified bow upon her companion.

'Oh, yes! I was never here before in my life, though I have been to Tunbridge Wells. But I have been living retired lately, in the country, only it was so *very* melancholy that I was quite moped. So the doctor advised me to come to Bath, and take the Hot Bath, and perhaps drink the waters.'

'They are very nasty!'

'Mrs Clapham, the bell has stopped ringing,' interposed Mrs Winkworth.

'So it has! We must make haste!'

She smiled, bowed, and hurried away. Mrs Winkworth also bowed, very slightly, but she did not smile.

His spirits much improved, Stacy retired to his own room to

consider the possibilities of this new and unexpected event. Mrs Clapham was obviously wealthy, but the presence of Mrs Winkworth argued that a careful watch was being kept over her. Mrs Winkworth was a middle aged woman, who must have been handsome in her youth, for she had good features, and fine, if rather hard, grey eyes. Stacy thought, from her forbidding mien and the somewhat authoritative manner she used towards Mrs Clapham, that she had been hired rather as a chaperon than as a companion, and this indicated that the widow's relations were jealously guarding her from gentlemen hanging out for rich wives. Neither lady, he was quick to realise, was of the first stare. Mrs Winkworth was plainly of Cockney origin: her refined accents were superimposed on that unmistakable twang; Mrs Clapham he wrote down as a provincial, whose husband had almost certainly made his fortune in trade.

If there was a fortune, which was not yet certain. It was not unknown for a pretty widow, desirous of contracting a second, and more genteel, marriage, to invest a modest competence as Mrs Clapham might be doing: rigging herself out in style, and visiting a fashionable watering-place in the hope of attracting, and ensnaring, an eligible suitor. Not that Bath was any longer a resort of high fashion, but very likely she did not know that its visitors nowadays were rarely smart bachelors, but for the most part elderly persons, who wintered there for the sake of its mild climate; or invalids who came to drink the waters, or to take a course of Vapour Baths. On the other hand, the employment of a courier and a footman, not to mention her insistence on having her bed furnished with her own linen, seemed excessive; and the presence of a dragon-like companion lent no colour to the suspicion that she might be an ambitious female on the catch. Nor did her dress, which was costly but unostentatious. He recalled that she had been wearing large pearl drops in her ears, and round her throat a necklace of pearls which, if they were indeed pearls, must have cost the late Mr Clapham a pretty penny. But in these days one never knew: the most convincing pearls could be made out of glass and fish-scales. He had purchased one of these sham necklaces himself once, to gratify the lightskirt at that time living in his keeping, and the sheen on those trumpery beads would have deceived anyone but a jeweller.

He decided, coldly considering Mrs Clapham, that he must make it his business to ingratiate himself with her companion, and did not doubt his ability to do so: elderly females – witness Miss Wendover! – could easily be bamboozled. It would do no harm to bring Mrs Winkworth round his thumb; and, if he could be satisfied that Mrs Clapham was as wealthy as she appeared to be, it would be of the first importance to do so.

Another possibility suggested itself to him: all too frequently the wealth inherited by widows was so tightly tied up that they might as well have been paupers. Not so long since, he had himself been as near as a toucher to being completely taken-in. Within ames-ace of offering for the hand of a widow in affluent circumstances, he had discovered that the better part of her very handsome independence would be lost to her if she embarked upon a second marriage. A very near-run thing that had been, and he meant to take good care he did not again court such a risk.

In these calculations Fanny was not forgotten. If Fanny had been of full age, he would not have considered for a moment Mrs Clapham's claims to his attention, for although (had it been possible for him to consult only his inclination) he would not have chosen such a high-spirited and self-willed bride as Fanny, she was a lovely little creature, and marriage to her would do much to rehabilitate him in the eyes of society. The Wendovers did not figure amongst the members of the *haut ton*, but they might have done so, had they so wished. The family, though not of such ancient lineage as the Calverleighs, was of undoubted gentility, and had been for long established in the county of Bedfordshire. It was also extremely well-connected. When Mr James Wendover, who had no taste for town-life, was constrained by his equally well-connected spouse to hire a house in London for his eldest daughter's come-out, it would require no effort on his part to introduce Miss Albinia into the first circles. Everyone knew the Wendovers, and a surprising number of distinguished persons acknowledged some sort of relationship with the family. Frivolous people might make game of Mr James Wendover's prejudices, but marriage to his niece, the heiress to Amberfield, could be depended on to restore the bridegroom to respectability.

But Fanny was not of full age; and while Stacy knew enough of her uncle to be tolerably sure that he would be obliged, by his dread of scandal, to condone her runaway marriage, and, at the least, put her in possession of the income derived from her estates, – if not immediately, certainly when she became seized with the effects of matrimony – it had been rudely borne in upon him that there was no time to be wasted in extricating himself from his embarrassments. He had hoped to have carried Fanny off within a day of her aunts' curst rout-party, but she had contracted influenza, and it might now be weeks before she was well enough even to contemplate an elopement. Nor could he be sure that he could bring her to the sticking-point when she was restored to health. It had taken much coaxing to overcome her unexpected recoil from a Gretna Green marriage – if he had overcome it, which was doubtful. He had thought that he had done so, but she had almost repulsed him at the rout-party. It seemed all too probable that still more precious time would be wasted in bringing her under his spell again.

But if Mrs Clapham was indeed in untrammelled possession of a handsome fortune; if she could be swept off her feet by the attentions of a personable man of birth and fashion – and one, moreover, who owned a seat which was mentioned, if not minutely described, in any Guide Book to Berkshire – Badbury, his man of business, would not find it impossible to persuade his mortgagees to grant him a few more weeks' grace before instituting forfeiture proceedings. There would be no question of an expensive elopement – and that, when the proprietors of the old-established house with whom one's family had banked since time out of mind were indicating, sorrowfully but implacably, that unless one's debt to them was substantially reduced they would be forced to dishonour any further drafts upon their resources, would be an advantage. Mrs Clapham was not a minor, and the notice of his engagement to her, coupled with a disclosure to Badbury of her circumstances, would be enough to fob off his creditors.

There was very little doubt in his mind that the conquest of Mrs Clapham would not be difficult. He had instantly recognised the invitation in her eyes, and the widening look which betrayed admiration; and what, in her ingenuous way, she had already divulged, informed him that she was heartily bored by the decorous conduct imposed upon her by her widowhood. She might be the daughter and the relict of respectable tradesmen, but experience made it easy for Mr Stacy Calverleigh to detect in her the signs of the Approachable.

It was possible that she had come to Bath merely in search of diversion, and that when she threw him that tantalising glance from under her sweeping lashes she had nothing more serious in mind than flirtation; but he thought it unlikely. She might have the instincts of a straw damsel, but he judged her to be sprung from middle-class parents, and to be too much imbued with the boring, shabby-genteel notions obtaining amongst the depressing and regrettably increasing members of this class to encourage the advances of any gentleman unable, or unwilling, to offer her the security of marriage.

He would have preferred, of course, to have become legshackled to a female of his own order, but the exigencies of his position made it impossible for him to be too nice in his choice. She seemed, at all events, to be a simple creature, who could be groomed into the semblance of a woman of quality. Her simplicity had led her to Bath, which was at once fortunate, and a trifle ticklish. Passing under review the numerous acquaintances he had made in Bath, he could discover no rival amongst them. But for weeks past the eyes of the residents had been interestedly watching his courtship of Fanny, and however little he might regard the censure of such as Mrs Ancrum, or Lady Weaverham, he would find himself in the suds if that determined pursuit came to the ears of Mrs Clapham. If he decided that it would be worth his while to transfer his attentions to her, he would be obliged to seek a way out of an obviously awkward situation. Well, it would be time enough to think how best to deal with trouble when he was brought face to face with it: that had always been his rule, and, on the whole, it had answered pretty well. Meanwhile, his first and most pressing need was to enquire more precisely into Mrs Clapham's circumstances.

From his window, he was able to observe her return to the White Hart; and thus it came about that just as she had begun to mount the stairs he rounded the turn in the first pair, and came running lightly down. At sight of her, he checked, and, with a startled apology, retreated to the half-landing.

'Oh, pray don't – why, if it isn't you, Mr Calverleigh!' she exclaimed. 'Don't tell me you're putting up here too!'

He laughed. 'Must I not? I'm afraid I am! I'm sorry if you should object to it, but I was here before you, you know! What is to be done?'

She went into a trill of mirth. 'As though I meant anything so uncivil! You're bantering me, sir! No, indeed, I'm sure I'm glad you are putting up here, for I've no other acquaintance in Bath. I was only saying to Mrs Winkworth, a couple of minutes past, how much I wished I knew someone here who could tell me how to find my way about, or where to go to purchase an umbrella, which I can see is what I shall be needing!'

'What, have you come to Bath without an umbrella, ma'am? Oh, that will never do! I will certainly direct you to the nearest shop which sells them! You will be wishing to write your name in Mr King's subscription book too, I daresay.'

'Ought I to do so? You'll think me a regular zany, but I don't perfectly understand. Who – who is Mr King?'

'He is the Master of Ceremonies at the New Assembly Rooms – the Upper Rooms, as they are often called. They hold balls and concerts there, and card-parties.'

'Balls! Oh, no, I don't think I ought! Not *yet*! You see, it is not *quite* a year since Mr Clapham died, and although I have put off my blacks, because he never liked me to wear black, I shouldn't care to show disrespect. I'm sure it wouldn't be seemly for me to go to balls. Not but what I will become a subscriber, if it is the thing, which is what Mr Clapham would have wished, for *never* did he behave scaly, even when there was no good to be got by paying down his dust! So you must tell me – oh, dear, there are so many things I want to know!' She paused, and then said shyly: 'I wonder – Would you care to drink tea with us in my private parlour? We should be very happy – shouldn't we, Mrs Winkworth?' A thought seemed to occur to her; she added: 'Unless, of course – no, I don't mean that! I mean – I mean, you might, perhaps be engaged with your own party? Or – if you should chance to be a *married* man, we should be honoured to receive Mrs Calverleigh too!'

'No, I'm not married,' he replied. 'I shall be delighted to drink tea with you, ma'am!'

Her face brightening, she said: 'Oh, then, pray come whenever you choose! This evening?'

Far too astute to jump at an invitation, he excused himself, but, after a little hesitation, allowed her to persuade him to accept one for the following evening. He fancied that he read a certain measure of approval in Mrs Winkworth's expression, and took his leave of both ladies, feeling that a promising start had been made in his new venture.

The tea-drinking was very successful. He found her seated on one side of a small fire, dressed all in grey, with no ornaments but her pearls, and one fine diamond ring, which he judged to have sentimental associations, since she gazed at it, from time to time, with wistful fondness.

It was not at all difficult to draw her out, for she was of a chatty and confiding disposition. Her tongue might run on wheels, but he was able to gather various important pieces of information from amongst the chaff of her conversation. He learned that she had lived almost her whole life in Birmingham, until Mr Clapham had bought a house a few miles outside the town, and had bestowed it upon her, just because he knew she had always hankered after a house in the country. Well, *house* – ! It was more of a Property.

'But that was Mr Clapham all over,' she said. 'He was quite elderly, you know, but I was excessively attached to him.'

'So you should have been,' dryly interpolated Mrs Winkworth. 'The way he doted on you!'

'Oh, you mean to say that he spoiled me!' Mrs Clapham pouted. She threw a laughing, rueful glance at Stacy. 'That's what she is for ever telling me, unkind thing! I'm afraid it's true; I've always been sadly spoilt. You see, I was Papa's only child, and my mama died when I was very young. And then, when he died, Mr Clapham was so *very* kind, settling everything for me, and looking after all my affairs, and trying to make me understand about horrid things like *Consols,* only I never did, and I don't think I ever shall, except that Papa had a great many of them. Business makes my head ache! So when Mr Clapham asked me to marry him I was truly thankful. Oh, he was so kind to me! He was used to say nothing was too good for me, and that after having nobody to care for so many years – for his sister, who kept house for him died, and so he was the only one left – he *liked* to give me things. If ever I took a fancy to something, he would buy it, not saying a word to me, and there it would be the very next day, for a Surprise! Oh, I do wish I could show you my rubies! They are my favourite jewels, but Mrs Winkworth *would* have me lock them up in the Bank before we came to Bath, because it isn't proper to wear coloured stones until one is out of black gloves, and she thinks they would be stolen if I kept them in a hotel.'

'My dear ma'am, how you do run on!' said Mrs Winkworth, frowning at her.

She was instantly penitent. 'I never *could* learn to bite the tongue! It is very bad! Papa was used to say it ran like a fiddlestick, but Mr Clapham liked my silly bibble-babble. But you are very right: I have been boring on for ever! I won't do so any more. Tell us about yourself, Mr Calverleigh! Do you live in London, or in the country?'

'Oh, in London – though I was bred up in the country.'

'I thought you did,' she said artlessly. 'I mean to live there myself, for I'm sure I couldn't bear to continue living at the

Towers without Mr Clapham. He took me there once, and I liked it excessively. We stayed at a very comfortable hotel – I can't remember what it was called, but Mr Clapham always stayed there when he was obliged to go to London, because he said they served the best dinners of all the hotels.'

'Then I collect it was the Clarendon.'

She clapped her hands together. 'Yes, that was it! How clever of you to guess! Only I shouldn't wish to *live* in a hotel. I mean to buy a house.'

'*Hire* a house, ma'am,' corrected Mrs Winkworth.

'Well, perhaps – if that's what they do in London,' said Mrs Clapham doubtfully. She looked at Stacy. 'Is it? Do you hire *your* house?'

He smiled, and said, with a great air of frankness: 'No, I have a lodging merely.'

'Oh!' She considered this for a moment. 'I daresay a lodging is less trouble to you – being a gentleman.'

'Much less trouble!' he said, with a comical grimace.

'Yes, but – but a house of one's own is more agreeable, I think. More homelike!'

'Not my house!' he said humorously.

'But you said you had only a lodging!'

'In London! I have a place in Berkshire: my family has owned it for generations. I daresay you know the style of thing: very historical, very inconvenient, and needs an army of servants to keep it in order. Quite beyond my touch! I'd sell it, if I could.'

'Can't you? If you don't wish to live in it?'

He threw up his hands in mock horror. 'Sell Danescourt? My dear ma'am, never let any member of my family hear you suggest such a thing! I promise you, they would think it little short of blasphemy!'

He judged that he had said quite enough (and rather neatly, too) to impress her, and soon took his leave. Mrs Winkworth bestowed quite an approving smile upon him, which showed him that his candid avowal of his straitened circumstances had had its calculated effect on her.

Fourteen

*T*he acquaintance, so promisingly begun, ripened quickly, but the difficulties foreseen by Mr Stacy Calverleigh soon began to loom large. Within the walls of the White Hart it was an easy matter to pursue his delicate courtship; outside this hostelry, it became perilous. He had known that it would be; and his forebodings were confirmed when (at her request) he escorted Mrs Clapham to the Pump Room, and instantly attracted unwelcome notice. It had been impossible to evade that public appearance. 'Oh, Mr Calverleigh!' had uttered the widow, in a flutter of shyness. '*Pray* go with me! For I don't know a soul, and that is so very uncomfortable!'

He had been obliged to accompany her, and even to introduce her to such ladies of his acquaintance as he could not avoid; but although he fancied he had carried it off pretty well ('Your la'ship must allow me to present Mrs – Mrs Clapham to you. She is a stranger to Bath – putting up at the White Hart!') he was well aware that he had become the subject for every kind of inquisitive conjecture. He realised, too late, what a gudgeon he had been to have devoted himself so exclusively to Miss Fanny Wendover, and did what he could to allay suspicion by replying to the demand of a matron, famed for her blunt manners, to be told who, pray, was this Mrs Clapham? with his engaging air of boyish candour: 'I haven't the least notion, ma'am, but *perfectly* respectable, I believe! Yes, I know what you are thinking, but I won't have her abused! Not, perhaps, quite up to the rig, but – but excessively amiable!'

The droll look that went with this conveyed volumes, but he could not be sure that these had been read with understanding. He was thankful that Mrs Clapham's scruples forbade her to attend any balls, and wished that these had included concerts. But Mrs Winkworth had said that concerts were unexceptionable, and he was obliged to accept, with every sign of pleasure, an invitation to accompany both ladies to one which held out, as an apparently irresistible lure, the promise of a performance, by four distinguished instrumentalists, of Mozart's Quartet in G Minor. Mr Stacy Calverleigh was not musical, and nor, judging by the infelicitous nature of her remarks, was Mrs Clapham; but when he entered the concert-room, with the widow leaning on his arm, it seemed, to his jaundiced eyes, that not one of the Bath residents with whom he was acquainted shared his indifference to classical music. The room was packed as full as it could hold. He felt, as he escorted his ladies past the benches, to the chairs provided for such well-inlaid persons as Mrs Clapham, that the entire genteel population of Bath was present. Amongst the company, were Mrs Grayshott, with her son and daughter, and when he glanced in their direction, Stacy encountered a long, unsmiling look from Oliver. It made him rage inwardly, for he read into it contempt and condemnation. He thought that it would not be long before the insufferable puppy found the means to communicate with Fanny; and wondered if there was any fear that when she next met him she would subject him to a painful scene. He spent the better part of the evening trying to hit upon some means of detaching Mrs Clapham from Bath. It was not until they emerged from the Rooms into a mizzle of rain that a possible solution occurred to him. Then, as Mrs Clapham asked despairingly if it was *always* raining in Bath, he expressed surprise that she should not have chosen to go to Leamington Priors rather than to Bath. No doubt she must know that it was a spa enjoying notoriously good weather, and offering visitors, besides beneficial waters, every amenity, from Pleasure Gardens to Assembly Rooms as elegant as any in the country. No, Mrs Clapham, strangely enough, had never been there, for all it was so close to Birmingham. She accused him archly of wishing to be rid of her. '*That*, ma'am, is an absurdity which neither merits, nor will obtain, notice!' he replied. 'To own the truth, I have a strong notion of going there myself!'

'I wonder,' said Mrs Clapham demurely, 'if drinking the waters there would do me good?'

It was as well that this question was merely rhetorical, for, never having visited the spa, he had no idea for what the Leamington Waters were held to be beneficial, and could scarcely have answered it. Nor, when he procured, on the following day, a guide book to the Principal Watering and Sea-bathing places, was he any better equipped to do so. The guide book was not reticent on the subject: it presented him with a list of the diseases for which the waters were known to be efficacious, but as these consisted of such distressing disorders as Obstinately Costive Habits, Scrofulous Tumours, White Swellings of the Knee, and Intestinal Worms, Mr Calverleigh could only hope that Mrs Clapham would not enquire more closely into the matter.

He told Mrs Winkworth that Bath was a hotbed of scandal, warning her, with his ready laugh, that it was enough for an unattached gentleman to offer his arm to a single lady for the length of a street to set all the quizzies tattling that he was dangling after her. That, he hoped, would drive a spoke in the wheel of any mischief-maker who might seek to convince her that he was a fickle and desperate flirt.

Mrs Winkworth had relented towards him, and no longer directed suspicious looks at him. She even apologised for having been, as she phrased it, a trifle starched-up when she had first made his acquaintance. 'You wouldn't wonder at it, if you knew how many burrs and downright fortune-hunters I've had to drive off, Mr Calverleigh,' she said. 'Sometimes I wish to goodness I hadn't agreed to live with Nancy, when Clapham died, but I've known her since she was a child, and I hadn't the heart to say no to her. No more than anyone ever has had, more's the pity! Not that she isn't a sweet little thing, but she'd let any scamp come over her, because she hasn't a particle of nous. And as for being fit to manage her affairs – well, there!'

'I expect her trustees will take care she doesn't fritter away her fortune,' Stacy said.

But Mrs Winkworth replied, with a snort: 'Yes, I daresay they might, if she had any!'

It appeared that Mr Clapham had died, leaving all he possessed to his beloved wife, in a Will written on an odd scrap of paper: an aberration which Mrs Winkworth ascribed partly to his having been carried off very suddenly, and partly to his besottedness. 'And a harder-headed man of business you'd be hard put to it to find!' she told Stacy. 'Well, they say there's no fool like an old fool, don't they?'

Inevitably, it was Miss Butterbank who bore the news of Mrs Clapham's arrival in Bath to Sydney Place. She was able to tell Miss Wendover how many times Mr Stacy Calverleigh had been seen in her company, how many trunks the lady had brought to Bath, and was even able to disclose, in a shocked whisper, that she had twice dined with him at the *table d'hôte*, and that it was *said* that he took tea with her, in her private parlour, every evening.

'Which I cannot bring myself to believe!' Selina told Abby. 'Not that I mean to say that poor Laura Butterbank is not a very truthful woman, but you may depend upon it she must have been misinformed.'

Abby had had little leisure for visiting, but she had chanced to meet Mrs Grayshott at the chemist's a few days earlier, and had received from her a less high-coloured account of the affair.

'A wealthy widow!' she had exclaimed. 'Nothing could be better! I wish he may run off with her tomorrow!'

She had not mentioned the matter to Selina, but she did so now, saying: 'I believe it to be quite true – that Calverleigh is now bent on fixing his interest with this Mrs Clapham; at least Mrs Grayshott told me of it a day or two ago, but she can't be as well-informed as Laura Butterbank, for she didn't mention the tea-drinking, or the *table-d'hôte*. My dear, why look so dismayed? You don't *still* want him to marry Fanny, surely!'

No, Selina did not want that, but it was so very shocking, so distressing to think that a young man with such agreeable manners should turn out to be a monster of duplicity! She had never been so much deceived in her life. 'And when I think of poor little Fanny – if it *is* true, not that I am at all convinced, because very likely it is nothing but a Banbury story, and I do implore you, not to breathe a *word* to her!'

'Certainly not! She will discover it soon enough, poor child! It may not come as quite such a shock to her as we fear. You must have noticed, Selina, that amongst all the bouquets, and the bunches of grapes, which are handed in by her admirers, only one bunch of flowers bore young Calverleigh's card, and he has only once called to enquire how she goes on. If you haven't noticed it, I am persuaded that she has. She says nothing, but it is painful to see how eagerly she looks for the card attached to each new posy that is carried up to her room, and how her face falls when she finds that it is *only* from Oliver – or Jack Weaverham – or Peter Trevisian!'

Miss Abigail Wendover was looking tired, as well she might. Fanny's attack had been severe; the fever had lasted for longer than even Dr Rowton had pessimistically foretold; and although she was now allowed to lie on the sofa in the drawing-room for a few hours each day, and even to receive visits from her particular friends, her temperature still showed a tendency to rise towards evening, and it was evident that she was sadly pulled by her illness. The bulk of the nursing had fallen to Abby's lot, for Fanny could scarcely endure Mrs Grimston's brisk ministrations. She complained that her hands were rough, that the floor shook every time she stumped across it, that she could not come near the bed without knocking against it, and that she never stopped scolding and fussing. These grievances, whether real or imaginary, made her cross, restless, and recalcitrant; she reverted to her childhood's cry of: 'I want *Abby*!' and Abby, just as she had always done, instantly responded to it.

She was reasonably docile with her aunt, but constant attendance on her, coupled as it was with a certain degree of anxiety, were beginning to take their toll. Selina, bemoaning the fragility of her own constitution, which prevented her from sharing the task of nursing Fanny, told Abby that she was looking positively hagged, and begged her, at all the most unseasonable moments, to lie down on the sofa, if only for an hour.

It might have been supposed that Abby would have had no time or thought to spare for her own troubles, but they seemed always to be at the back of her mind until she retired to bed, when they immediately leaped to the fore, and kept her awake, tossing and turning almost as restlessly as Fanny. She might tell herself that it was a very good thing that Miles Calverleigh had left Bath, but the melancholy truth was that she missed him so much that it was like a physical ache. No word had come from him; he had been absent for longer than she had anticipated; and the fear that perhaps he did not mean to return to Bath at all was a heavy weight on her spirits. She found herself continually wondering where he was, and what he was doing, and wishing that she could at least know that no accident had befallen him.

None had. He was in London, but while Abby would have considered a visit to his aunt, several to the City, and some prolonged conferences with his lawyer unexceptionable it was as well that one at least of his activities was unknown to her.

Lady Lenham greeted him with a tart demand to be told when he meant to furbish himself up.

'I don't know. Must I?' he replied, lightly kissing her cheek.

'It's no use expecting me to bring you back into fashion if you don't adonise yourself a trifle.'

'Then I won't expect it,' he said amiably. 'I never was one of your dapper-dogs, and it's too late to change my habits, and if you're thinking I should look well in a wasp-waisted coat, and with the points of my collars reaching half-way up my cheeks, you are letting your imagination run off with you, Letty – take my word for it!'

'There's reason in all things,' she retorted. 'Where have you been all these weeks? Don't tell me you've been getting into mischief again!'

'No, no, I've been behaving very decorously!' he assured her. 'You have to, in Bath. A devilish place!'

She stared at him. 'You've been in *Bath*?'

'That's it. I took Leonard Balking's nephew there, you know.'

'Yes, you told me you were going to do that, but what in the world kept you there?' she asked suspiciously.

'Just circumstances!'

'Oh! Philandering, I collect! Well, what do you mean to do now?'

'Become a tenant-for-life. You told me it was what I ought to do: remember?'

'What!' she exclaimed. 'Are you trying to play off your tricks on me? Who is she?'

'Abigail Wendover,' he replied coolly.

She gave a gasp. 'You're not serious? One of the *Wendovers*? Miles, she's never accepted an offer from you?'

'No, but she will.'

'Well, either you've windmills in the head, or she's very very different from the rest of her family!'

'Of course she is! You don't suppose I'd have fallen in love with her if she hadn't been, do you?'

'No, and I don't suppose her family would countenance it for an instant!'

'Lord, Letty, what's that got to say to anything?'

She laughed. 'You don't change much, Miles! You always were a care-for-nobody, and you always will be! I wish you may succeed with your Abigail. She's the youngest sister, isn't she? I never met her, but I'm acquainted with Mary Brede, and have been avoiding James Wendover and his odious wife for years.'

'Yes, that's what I mean to do,' he said.

His next visit was to a slightly portly gentleman, residing in Mount Street, who stared unbelievingly at him for a moment, before ejaculating: '*Calverleigh!*' and starting forward to wring his hand. 'Well, well, well. After all these years! I hardly recognised you, you old devil!'

'No, I had to look twice at you, too. You're as fat as a flawn, Naffy!'

'Well, at least no one would take me for a dashed blackamoor!' retorted Mr Nafferton.

After this exchange of compliments, the two middle-aged gentlemen settled down, with a bottle between them, to indulge in reminiscences which, had they been privileged to hear them, would have startled Mr Nafferton's wife, and considerably diminished his credit with his heir.

'Lord, how it takes me back, seeing you again!' said Mr Nafferton a trifle wistfully. 'Those were the days!'

'Nights, mostly,' said Mr Calverleigh. 'How many times did *you* end up in a lighthouse? *I* lost count! What became of the Dasher, by the way?'

'Dolly!' uttered Mr Nafferton. 'To think I should have forgotten she was used to be your peculiar!' He chuckled. 'You'd never recognise her! She set up a fancy-house a dozen or more years ago! Drives in the park in a smart barouche, with one or two of her prime articles, and looks like a duchess! Behaves like one, too! No Haymarket ware in *her* house: all regular Incognitas! Or so I'm told!' he added hastily.

Mr Calverleigh grinned, but merely said: 'Became an Abbess, did she? Yes, she always was as shrewd as she could hold together. Where's this fancy-house of hers?'

Armed with this information, his next visit was to a house in Bloomsbury, where he sent in his card. Miss Abigail Wendover would certainly not have approved of this excursion.

Mr Calverleigh, ushered into a saloon, was still inspecting the elegance of its furnishings with deep appreciation when the lady upon whom he had come to call entered the room, his card in her hand, and exclaimed: 'It *is* you! Good God! I couldn't believe it!'

Mr Calverleigh, laughter in his eyes, took two long strides

towards her, caught her in his arms, and heartily embraced her.

She returned the embrace, but said: 'Now, that's quite enough! I'll have you know I'm a respectable woman now!'

Mr Calverleigh, most reprehensibly, gave a shout of mirth.

'Well, you know what I mean!' said the lady, bridling a little.

'Yes, to be sure, I do. Who gave you the gingerbread, Dolly?'

'Oh, he was a regular rabshackle!' she disclosed. 'You wouldn't have known him, for he was long after your time. I never liked him above half, but he was full of juice, and I'm bound to say he bled very freely. What I mean is, he was very generous to me,' she amended, suddenly attacked by a fit of alarming primness.

Mr Calverleigh was unimpressed. 'No, is *that* what you mean? Come down from your high ropes! Do you remember the night a party of us went on a spree to Tothill Fields, and you broke a bottle of Stark Naked over the head of the fellow that was trying to gouge my eyes out?'

'No, I don't!' she said sharply. 'And if you hadn't got into a mill with a bruiser and a couple of draymen because you was as drunk as Davy's sow I wouldn't have had to demean myself! *If* I did do anything of the sort, which I don't at all remember!'

'I must be thinking of someone else,' said Mr Calverleigh meekly. 'What was the name of that towheaded bit of game Tom Plumley brought along with him?'

'*That* fussock!' she exclaimed, in a voice vibrant with scorn. 'Why, she hadn't enough spunk to hit a blackbeetle on the head! Now, give over, Miles, do! I don't say I'm not glad to see you again: well, it's like a breath of old times, but that's the trouble! Seeing you makes me forget myself, and start talking flash, which is a thing I haven't done in years! What's more, you didn't come here to crack about old revel-routs! And if, Mr Calverleigh,' she added, with another transition into gentility, but with a twinkle in her sharp eyes, 'you have come here in search of *a bit of game*, I must warn you that you will find no cheap molls in *this* establishment, but only young ladies of refinement.'

'That's very good, Dolly!' he approved. 'Did it take you long to learn to talk like that?'

'Out with it! What is it you want?' she demanded, ignoring this sally.

'Just what you said, of course,' he replied. 'A young lady of refinement!'

Fifteen

The Leavenings had hired lodgings in Orange Grove. Not an ideal situation, perhaps, admitted Mrs Leavening, when Selina pointed out to her its several disadvantages, but it was a fine, open place, and no need at all to summon up a chair every time she wanted to visit the Pump Room, or do a little shopping. As for the Abbey bells, she didn't doubt that they would soon grow to be so accustomed to them that they would scarcely notice them. 'Well, my dear,' she told Selina placidly, 'when you get to be of our age, you must have learnt that you won't find anything that's exactly what you want, so, if you've a particle of commonsense, you'll take the best that's offered you.' She then said, with a chuckle: 'Mr Calverleigh will laugh when he hears of it! He *would* have it, only because I like looking out of the window at what's passing in the street, that I should never be happy but in the centre of the Town!'

Abby had been taking no more than a polite interest in the Leavenings' plans, but these words affected her powerfully. She said: 'If he ever does hear of it! Does he mean to return to Bath, ma'am?'

She spoke with studied nonchalance, but Mrs Leavening was not deceived. The quizzical gleam in her eye brought the blood into Abby's cheeks, but all she said was: 'Well, my dear, as his rooms are being kept for him at the York House, it's to be supposed he does!'

That was the only ray of sunlight permitted for many days to break through the clouds surrounding Miss Abigail Wendover.

She was enduring a time of trial, for which not Miles Calverleigh alone was responsible, but also her dear sister, and her cherished niece.

Influenza had left Fanny irritable and depressed. It was quite unnecessary for Dr Rowton to say that this uncharacteristic mood was attributable to her illness, and only what was to be expected. Abby knew that, but neither her own good sense nor the doctor's reassurance made it easier for her to bear patiently the extremely wearing demands made upon her spirits by a convalescent who, when not sunk in gloom which affected everyone in her vicinity, peevishly found fault with everything, from the strength of the tea carried up to her room on her breakfast-tray, to the intolerable dullness of the books so hopefully chosen by Abby at Meyler's Library; or stared resentfully out of a rain-spotted window at a leaden sky, and sighed: 'If only it would stop raining! If only I could go out!'

Poor little Fanny, said Selina, was quite unlike her merry self: an understatement which kindled a spark of amusement in Abby's shadowed eyes. Dr Rowton told Abby, in his blunt way, that the sooner she stopped indulging Fanny the better it would be for herself, and Fanny too; but Dr Rowton did not know that there was another and deeper cause of Fanny's crotchets than influenza. Abby did know, and even when she most wanted to slap her tiresome darling her heart went out to her. She was herself suffering from much the same malady, and if she had been seventeen, instead of eight-and-twenty, no doubt she would have abandoned herself to despair, just as Fanny was doing.

Fanny's megrims might impose a severe strain upon Abby's nerves, but it was Selina who rasped them raw, and broke down her command over herself.

Selina had seen Mrs Clapham, and she knew that it was all Too True. She had seen her in the Pump Room, whither a twinge of rheumatism had sent her (braving the elements in her carriage, with the hood drawn up) that morning. She had not at first known who she was, for how should she? She had merely been thinking that the bonnet she was wearing was in excellent style (though she had realised rather later that it bore too many plumes, and was of a disagreeable shade of purple, besides being a most unsuitable hat for a widow), when dear Laura Butterbank had whispered that she was Mrs Clapham.

'Which was a most unpleasant shock, as you may suppose, and almost brought on one of my distressing spasms. Fortunately, I had my vinaigrette in my reticule, for just when I was thinking that I did not at all like the look of her (not that I saw her face, for she had her back turned to me, but one can always tell), whom should I see but young Calverleigh, making his way towards her, with that hoaxing smile on his face, all delight and cordiality, as though he hadn't been dangling after Fanny for weeks! *And*, Abby, he had the impudence to *cut* me! It's of no use to say that he didn't see me, because I am persuaded he did, for he took very good care not to look in my way again, besides going off with that vulgar creature almost immediately. When I recall the way he has been running tame in this house, inching himself in – at least, he did so until you came home and snubbed him, and although I thought it a little unkind in you at the time, you were perfectly right, which I *freely* own – well, dearest, I was almost overpowered, and I trembled so much that I don't know how I was able to reach the carriage, and if it hadn't been for Mr Ancrum, who gave me his arm, very likely I never should have done so.

She was obviously much upset. Abbey did what she could to soothe her agitation, but there was worse to come. That Woman (under which title Abby had no difficulty in recognising the odious Mrs Ruscombe) had had the effrontery to come up to her to commiserate her, with her false, honeyed smile, on poor little Fanny's humiliating disappointment. And not one word had she been able, in the desperation of the moment, to utter in crushing retort. Nothing had occurred to her!

Unfortunately, all too many retorts occurred to her during the succeeding days, and whenever she was alone with Abby she recalled exactly what Mrs Ruscombe had said, adding to the episode the various annihilating things she herself might have said, and reminding Abby of the numerous occasions when Mrs Ruscombe had behaved abominably. She could think of nothing else; and when, for the third time in one evening, she broke a brooding silence by saying, as though they had been in the middle of a discussion: 'And *another* thing . . . !' Abby's patience deserted her, and she exclaimed: 'For heaven's sake, Selina, don't start again! As though it wasn't bad enough to have Fanny saying: "If only it would stop raining!" a dozen times a day! If you don't wish to drive me into hysterics, *stop* talking about Mrs Ruscombe! What she said to you I have by heart, and as for what you *might* have said to her, you know very well you would never say any such things.'

She repented immediately, of course: indeed, she was horrified by her loss of temper. Begging Selina's pardon, she said that she thought she was perhaps overtired.

'Yes, dear, no doubt you must be,' said Selina. 'It is a pity you wouldn't rest, as I *repeatedly* recommended you to do.'

Selina was not offended, oh, dear me, no! Just a little hurt, but she did not intend to say any more about that. She was sure Abby had not meant to wound her: it was merely that she was a trifle lacking in sensibility, but she did not intend to say any more about that either.

Nor did she, but her silence on that and every other topic was eloquent enough, and soon provided Abby with all that was needed to make her long passionately for Miles Calverleigh to come back, and to snatch her out of the stricken household without any more ado.

But it was not Miles Calverleigh who made an unexpected appearance in Sydney Place shortly before noon one morning. It was Mr James Wendover, carrying a small cloak-bag, and wearing the resentful expression of one forced, by the inconsiderate behaviour of his relations, to endure the discomforts of a night-journey to Bath on the Mail Coach.

It was Fanny, seated disconsolately by the window in the drawing-room, who saw him first. When the hack drew up, the hope that it had brought Stacy Calverleigh to her at last soared in her breast for one ecstatic moment, before it sank like a plummet at the sight of Mr Wendover's spare, soberly clad figure. She exclaimed, startling Abby: 'It is my uncle! No, no, I won't – I can't! Don't let him come *near* me!'

With these distraught words, she rushed from the room, leaving Abby to make her excuses as best she might.

Forewarned, Abby betrayed neither perturbation nor astonishment when Mr Wendover presently entered the room, though she did say, as she got up from her chair: 'Well, this is a surprise, James! What brings you to Bath, I wonder?'

Bestowing a perfunctory salute upon her cheek, he replied, in acrid accents: 'I must suppose that you know very well what has brought me, Abby! I may add that it has been most inconvenient – *most* inconvenient! – but since you have apparently run mad I felt myself compelled to undertake the journey! Where is Selina?'

'Probably drinking the waters, in the Pump Room,' replied Abby calmly. 'She will be here directly, I daresay. Did you come by the Mail? What made it so late?'

'It was not late. I arrived in Bath punctually at ten o'clock and have already accomplished *part* of my mission. Why it should have been *necessary* for me to do so I shall leave it to your conscience to answer, Abby! If,' he added bitterly, 'you *have* a conscience, which sometimes I am compelled to doubt!'

'It certainly seems as though I can't have. However, I console myself with the reflection that at least I'm not as buffle-headed as the rest of my family!' said Abby brightly. 'I collect that you came to try whether you could put an end to Fanny's rather unfortunate flirtation with young Calverleigh. Now, if only you had warned me of your intention you would have been spared the journey! You have wasted your time, my dear James!'

His eyes snapped; he said, with a dry, triumphant laugh: 'Have I? Have I indeed? I have already seen the young coxcomb, and I made it very plain to him that if he attempted to persuade my foolish niece into a clandestine marriage he would find himself taken very much at fault – *very* much at fault! I informed him that I should have no hesitation – none whatsoever! – in taking steps to have such a marriage annulled, and that under *no* circumstances should I disburse one penny of her fortune if she contracted an alliance without my sanction! I further informed him that he would have eight years to wait before deriving any benefit from that fortune!'

'I said you had wasted your time,' observed Abby. 'I, too, informed him of these circumstances. I don't think he believed me, and I am very sure he didn't set much store by all this bluster of yours. I have no great opinion of his intelligence, but I fancy he is sufficiently shrewd to have taken your measure before ever he decided to make a push to captivate Fanny. Good God, if he *had* succeeded in eloping with Fanny you would have gone to any lengths to hush up the scandal, and so, depend upon it, he very well knows!'

An angry flush mounted into Mr Wendover's thin cheeks. 'Indeed? In-deed! You are very much mistaken, my dear sister! I am aware that you fancy yourself to be awake upon every suit, but in *my* humble opinion you are as big a wet-goose as Selina! I don't doubt for a moment that he paid little heed to anything you may have said to him: only a gudgeon could have failed to take *your* measure! When, however, he was confronted by *me*, the case was altered! I am happy to be able to inform you that this lamentable affair is now at an end!'

'Yes, it came to an end when Fanny took ill. You had really nothing to do with it, you know. According to all accounts, Stacy Calverleigh, for the past fortnight, has being laying determined siege to a rich widow – a far more desirable conquest than Fanny, I assure you! I have not myself had the felicity of meeting the lady, but I understand that she is much inclined to succumb to his attractions.'

He was so much surprised that his anger was instantly quenched. He exclaimed: 'You don't mean it! Is it indeed so? Well, upon my word! Nothing could be better! A widow, you say? Well! They say he is all to pieces, you know – quite gutted! And Danescourt falling to ruin! I was never more shocked in my life! Fanny is to be congratulated!'

'Very true, but I fear you won't be able to do so. She is still far from well. In fact, I think it would be wiser if she doesn't come downstairs today – in case she should still be infectious.'

Since James, as she knew well, shared Selina's dread of contracting any infectious complaint, he agreed hastily that it would be wisest for Fanny to remain in her room. He said that there was now no need for him to see her: a remark hardly calculated to endear him to his sister. He continued for several minutes to animadvert on Stacy Calverleigh's character; but suddenly he fell silent, and the pleased expression vanished from his face. He began to fidget about the room, twice began to say something, and apparently thought better of it, and finally came to a halt in front of Abby's chair, and said portentously; 'Abby! There is something I must say to you!'

She could guess what was coming, but she merely raised her brows enquiringly.

'Something of more importance than Fanny's frippery affair – of far graver importance! It has upset me very much. It made me bilious for two days. You must know that I have always been subject to stomach disorders, and nothing brings on one of my attacks more surely than shock! I suffered a severe shock, sister, when it came to my knowledge that not only was young Calverleigh in Bath, but also his uncle! I had not thought it to have been possible!'

'Why not?' asked Abby.

He seemed to find it difficult to answer this, for after glaring down at her for a moment, he ejaculated, somewhat lamely: 'Here! In Bath! I had supposed him to be in India!'

'Well, so he was, but he has now returned to England. I believe it is quite customary for people to do so.'

'Customary! Ay, for *some* people! And here – here of all unlucky places! That I might be obliged actually to meet the fellow – !'

'Don't let it distress you!' she said, in a deceptively kind voice. 'I don't wish to seem unfeeling, but you cannot be laid up with a bilious-attack in this house! I hope, since there is no likelihood of your meeting Miles Calverleigh, that *that* trial at least may be spared us. It so happens that he is *not* in Bath.'

'He is not?' he said eagerly. 'Then where is he?'

'I have no notion where he may be,' she responded coldly.

He regarded her out of narrowed, suspicious eyes. 'Does he mean to return?'

'Oh, I hope so!' she said, smiling in a way which should have warned him of danger.

'You hope so! Then it is true, is it? Not only has the fellow had the effrontery to make you the object of his *gallantry*, but you *have* encouraged him to do so! You have *not* outgrown that – unsteadiness of character, which my father was used to fear would one day lead you into serious imprudence. You still have what Cornelia has always believed to be a love of singularity. You still –'

'Do you know, James, I can't but believe that you would be happier if you paid rather less heed to the reports Mrs Ruscombe so regularly sends to Cornelia?' she interrupted. 'If you lived here, you would pay none at all!'

He reddened. 'If you tell me that there is no truth in the intelligence she thought it her duty to send Cornelia, I must naturally accept your word.'

'The only thing I have to tell you is what I have already told you: you are wasting your time! I am not a child, and what I do is my own concern! Now, if you please, let us discuss some other subject before we come to dagger-drawing!'

She spoke quite quietly, but she was by this time very angry. He seemed to realise it, for when he had taken another turn about the room he said, in a more moderate tone: 'I do not mean to set up your back. Recollect that although I have no authority over you I am your brother! What you do cannot but be of concern to me. I beg you will tell me – have you indeed a partiality for this man?'

She looked at him without speaking, but it was Miles Calverleigh's face she saw, not his. A smile crept into her eyes;

she turned them away from her brother, and sat looking into the fire. 'Oh, yes!' she said softly.

He groaned. 'And he? Has he had the imp – has he made you an offer?' She nodded, and again he groaned. 'My poor girl! I do most sincerely pity you! Rest assured that not one word of what you have divulged to me shall ever pass my lips! You cannot marry Calverleigh. Good God, one would have thought that at your age –' He broke off, and said, with what was meant for an indulgent smile: 'Well, well, you are not so old, after all, and one may fancy oneself in love at any age, eh? But you are old enough to reflect before you abandon yourself to folly – to an act of such madness as must ruin your life! You must allow me to speak plainly to you, little though I may relish the task. I own that I look upon it with repulsion: indeed, I never thought to be obliged to discuss such matters with any of my sisters! Calverleigh is a ne'er-do-well. His reputation –'

'Very bad, wasn't it?' she agreed.

'Yes, my dear sister, it was! I shall not sully your ears with the details of his career – Abigail! Do you find it a matter for *laughter*?'

'Oh, I beg your pardon!' she said, choking on a giggle. 'It is most uncivil to laugh in a person's face, but I couldn't help but do so! I suddenly thought how much Miles Calverleigh would enjoy hearing you talk such fustian, and wondered what he would say! Though I have a very good notion of that! It would certainly be outrageous, so perhaps it is as well that he isn't here, for he would shock you very much – quite enough to make you bilious, I daresay! Don't s-sully my ears any more, James! Remember that I came out of leading-strings a long time ago! I find that I don't care a straw for his reputation.'

'You are hysterical!' he exclaimed. 'You do not know what you are saying! He is a man without principles, without regard for any of the virtues *you* have been taught to revere!'

'Oh, quite without regard for *them*!' she said cordially. 'He hasn't any regard for family obligations either, and I am fast coming to the conclusion that he is perfectly right.'

He said repressively: 'I make all allowance for the freakish things you delight in saying, but such wild, unthinking talk as this is very unbecoming in you. When you say that you don't care a straw for Calverleigh's reputation, you don't understand what you are saying, for you know nothing about it. It would be shocking if you did.'

'Well, you don't know anything about it either, do you?' she said. 'You can't have known very much before he was sent to India, for you are younger than he is, and he was only twenty at that time; and you can know nothing at all about him from that date onward.'

He found himself obliged to take another turn about the room, his hands clasped behind his back, and his fingers working convulsively. Coming to a halt again, he drew an audible breath, and said: 'Abby! There are circumstances which render any alliance between a Wendover and a Calverleigh impossible – unthinkable! I cannot say more: you must believe me when I tell you that it *is* so!'

'There is no need for you to say more,' she replied, with composure. 'I know what happened – twenty years ago!'

'*What?*' He looked, for a moment, horrified, and then incredulous. 'You cannot know!'

'Oh, yes! He eloped with Celia, didn't he? But it was all hushed up, after the manner of her family and ours, and she married Rowland after all.'

'Who told you this?' he demanded, thunderstruck.

'Why, he did, of course – Miles Calverleigh!'

His jaw dropped. He seemed to find it difficult to speak, and stuttered: '*C-Calverleigh* t-told you? C-Calverleigh himself? Good God!' Words failed him. While she watched him in some amusement, he pulled out his handkerchief, and wiped his brow. Regaining a measure of control over his emotions, he said: 'It is worse than I had thought it possible it could be! He must be dead to shame! Lost to every vestige of propriety!'

'I shouldn't think he ever had a vestige of propriety to lose,' she said reflectively. 'As for shame, I don't know, but he is not ashamed of running off with Celia. I see little reason why he should be. It was imprudent – and, of course, improper – but he was very young, and when her father forced Celia to become engaged to Rowland, I daresay it seemed to him to be the only thing to be done. I don't blame him. Those whom I do blame, and from the bottom of my heart despise, are Papa, and Morval, and Rowland!'

He looked fixedly at her, and, lowering his voice, said, in apocalyptic accents: 'You do not know all! They were not overtaken *until the following day*!'

She tried not to laugh, but his awful aspect was too much for her. Quite appalled by such depravity, he said sharply: 'Upon my soul! I begin to think you are well matched, you and that scoundrel!'

'Yes, James: I begin to think so too!' she agreed, between irrepressible outbreaks of laughter.

It was perhaps fortunate that they were interrupted at this moment by Selina, who came into the room in a flutter of welcome. To Selina, family ties were all-important; her affections, though not deep, were sincere and enduring, and she was genuinely glad to see James, forgetting, as she fondly embraced him, that the last letter she had received from him had roused her to considerable indignation.

'James! *Well!* Such a surprise! I hadn't the least notion – and only a fricassee of rabbit and onions for dinner! Now, if only I had known! But Betty or Jane can go into town, and procure some partridges, or perhaps a haunch of venison, which Fletching dresses very well, and is something you were always partial to.'

But James was not staying to dine with his sisters. He was returning to London on the Mail Coach.

Dismayed, Selina faltered: 'Not staying? But, James – ! You brought your cloak-bag! Mitton has carried it up to your room, and means to unpack it as soon as the bed has been made up!'

'Desire him to bring it down again, if you please. It *was* my intention to have put up here for a night, but what I have learnt since I entered this room has shocked me so much – I may say, appalled me! – that I prefer to return to London!'

'Good God!' uttered Selina, casting a wildly enquiring look at Abby. 'You cannot mean – oh, but Abby has told you, *surely*, that we believe there is no danger to be apprehended now? There has been no continued observance: the *wretch* has only *once* called since dear Fanny took ill, and with my own eyes I have seen the Creature he is making up to!'

'I am not referring to young Calverleigh,' said James stiffly. 'I came to Bath in the hope of discovering that the very disturbing rumours which have reached me had little foundation in truth. Instead, I learn that your sister has become infatuated with a man who should never have been permitted to cross your threshold!'

'No, no! Oh, pray do not say such things, James!' begged Selina faintly. 'He is perfectly respectable, though I cannot like the way he dresses – so very careless, and coming to pay us a formal visit in top-boots! – and, of course, he must have been sadly rackety when he was young, to have been sent away to India – not that I think it was right to do such a cruel thing, for I don't, and I never shall, and I consider it to be most unjust to say that he ought not to have been allowed to cross the threshold after all these years of being condemned to live in India, which may be a very interesting place, but is *most* unhealthy, and has burnt him as brown as a nut! And Abby is as much your sister as mine!'

'If Abby is so lost to propriety, to all sense of the duty she owes her family, as to marry Calverleigh, she will no longer be a sister of mine!' he said terribly.

'That's no way to dissuade me!' said Abby.

'No, no, dearest!' implored Selina. 'Pray don't – ! James didn't mean it!'

'When you have heard what I have to say, Selina –'

'Yes, but not now!' said Selina, much agitated. 'Mitton is fetching up the sherry, and I must take off my hat and my pelisse, and then it will be time for luncheon, which we always have, you know – just a baked egg, or a morsel of cold meat – and afterwards, when you are *calmer*, and we shan't be interrupted, which is always so vexatious when one is enjoying a serious discussion. No, I don't mean that! Not *enjoying* it, because already I am beginning to feel a spasm!'

James eyed her a little uneasily, and said, in a milder voice: 'Very well, I will postpone what I have to say. I do not myself partake of luncheon, but I should be glad of a cup of tea.'

'Yes, dear, of course, though I am persuaded it would do you good to eat a mouthful of *something* after your journey!'

'Don't press him, Selina! he's bilious,' said Abby.

'Bilious! Oh, then, no *wonder* –!' cried Selina, her countenance lightening. 'I have the very thing for you, dear James! I will fetch it directly, but on no account sherry!'

She then fled from the room, paying no heed to his exasperated denial of biliousness.

'Take care, James!' said Abby maliciously. 'You will find yourself in the suds if you throw Selina into strong convulsions!'

He cast her a repulsive glance. 'Spare me any more of your levity, Abigail! I shall say no more until after luncheon.'

'You won't say any more to me at any time,' replied Abby. 'You have already said too much! You may not have noticed it, but the sun came out half an hour ago. What *I* am going to do after luncheon, dear James, is to take Fanny out for a drive!'

With these words, accompanied by a smile of great sweetness, she went away to inform Fanny of the treat in store for her.

Fanny was also suffering from agitation. She turned an apprehensive, suspicious face towards her aunt, and said: 'How long does my uncle mean to remain here? I don't want to see him!'

'Have no fear, my love!' said Abby cheerfully. 'Your uncle is equally reluctant to see you! I told him you were still infectious.'

Fanny gave a spontaneous laugh. 'Oh, *Abby*! What a fib!'

'Yes, it weighs heavily on my conscience, but I don't grudge a fib or two to save you from what I cannot myself endure. Grimston will bring a tray to you. I must send a message to the stables now.'

But in the end it was not Abby who took Fanny for her drive, but Lavinia Grayshott. Just as Abby was preparing to take her place in the barouche beside Fanny, Lavinia came running up, and exclaimed breathlessly: 'Oh famous! Going out at last! *Now* you will soon be better! Oh, Miss Abby, I beg your pardon! – how do you do? I was coming to see Fanny, just to bring her this book! Oh, and, Fanny, take care how you open it! There's an acrostic in it, from Oliver!'

Abby saw the brightening look in Fanny's face, and realised that Fanny would prefer Lavinia's company to hers. The knowledge caused her to feel a tiny heartache, but she did not hesitate. She said, smiling at Lavinia: 'Why don't you go with Fanny in my place? Would you like to?'

The answer was to be read in Lavinia's face. 'Oh – ! But you, ma'am? Don't *you* wish to go with her?'

'Not a bit!' Abby said. 'I have a thousand and one things to do, and shall be glad to be rid of her! The carriage shall take you home, so if Martha sees no objection I shall resign Fanny into your charge.'

Martha, following more slowly in Lavinia's wake, readily consented to the scheme; so Lavinia jumped into the carriage. Before it drew out of sight, Abby saw the two heads together, and guessed that confidences were already being exchanged. She stifled a sigh, as she turned back into the house. Between herself and Fanny there was constraint, for Fanny knew her to be hostile to Stacy Calverleigh. Well, perhaps she would unburden herself to Lavinia, and feel the better for it.

Sixteen

*B*elatedly following Selina's advice, Abby retired to her bedroom, to lie down. Contrary to her expectation, she fell asleep almost at once, and was still sleeping when James left the house. When she awoke it was almost five o'clock, and the house was very quiet. She encountered Mrs Grimston on the landing, and learned from her that Miss Fanny was in the drawing-room, and seemingly none the worse for her drive; and that Miss Selina had gone up to rest as soon as Mr James had taken himself off. These words had a sinister ring, but as they were not followed by any mention of spasms or palpitations, and no distressing sounds could be heard emanating from Selina's room, Abby hoped that they had been inspired merely by Mrs Grimston's dislike of James. She went on down the stairs, and found Fanny with her head bent over the novel Lavinia had bestowed on her. She glanced up when Abby came into the room, and it struck Abby immediately that she was looking pale, and that her perfunctory smile was forced.

'Not tired, my darling?' she asked.

'No, thank you. No, not at all! I am reading the book Lavvy brought me: it is the most exciting story! I can't put it down!'

But it did not seem to Abby, as she occupied herself with embroidery, and covertly observed her niece between the setting of her stitches, that the book was holding Fanny absorbed. She was using it as a shield. The suspicion that Lavinia's indiscreet tongue had been at work crossed Abby's mind. As she presently folded her work, she said: 'Going to sit up for dinner, Fanny?'

'Oh!' Fanny gave a little start. 'Oh, is it dinner-time already? Yes – I don't know – Oh, yes! I'm not ill now!'

Abby smiled at her. 'Of course you're not, but you have been out for the first time today, and it wouldn't surprise me to learn that Lavinia has chattered you into a headache! A dear girl, but *such* a little gabster!'

She was now sure that Lavinia had been tattling. Fanny's chin came up, and her eyes were at once challenging and defensive. 'Oh, I don't regard her!' she said, with a pathetically unconvincing laugh. 'She is always full of the marvellous, but – but very diverting, you know!'

Yes, thought Abby, Lavinia has poured the tale of Stacy's perfidy into her ears, and although she does not quite believe it, she is afraid it may be true.

Her impulse was to take Fanny in her arms, petting and comforting her as she had so often done in the past, but a new and deeper understanding made her hesitate.

'If you please, Miss Abby,' said Fardle ominously, from the doorway, 'I should wish to have a word with you, if convenient!'

'Why, certainly!' Abby said, with a lightness she was far from feeling. She followed Fardle out of the room, and asked: 'What is it?'

The eldest Miss Wendover's devoted handmaid fixed her with an eye of doom, and delivered herself of a surprising statement. 'I feel it to be my duty to tell you, Miss Abby, that I don't like the look of Miss Selina – not at all I don't!'

'Oh!' said Abby weakly. 'Is – is she feeling poorly? I will come up to her.'

'Yes, miss. I was never one to make a mountain out of a molehill, as the saying is,' stated Fardle inaccurately, 'but it gave me quite a turn when I went to dress Miss Selina not ten minutes ago. It is not for me to say what knocked her up, Miss Abby, and I hope I know my duty better than to tell you that it's my belief it was Mr James that burnt her to the socket. All I know is that no sooner had he left the house than she went up to her room, saying she was going to rest on her bed, which was only to be expected. But when I went up to her she wasn't on her bed, nor hadn't been, as you will see for yourself, miss. And hardly a word did she speak, except to say she wouldn't be going down to dinner, and didn't want a tray sent up to her. Which is not like her, Miss Abby, and can't but make one fear that she's going into a Decline.'

On this heartening suggestion, she ushered Abby into Selina's room.

Kindly but firmly shutting the door upon her, Abby looked across the room at her sister, who was seated motionless beside the fire, with a shawl huddled round her shoulders, and a look in her face which Abby had never seen there before.

'Selina! Dearest!' she said, going quickly forward, to drop on her knees, gathering Selina's hands into her own.

Selina's eyes turned towards her in a stunned gaze which alarmed Abby far more than a flood of tears would have done. 'I have been thinking,' she said. 'Thinking, and thinking . . . It was my fault. If I hadn't invited her to our party she wouldn't have written such things to Cornelia.'

'Nonsense, dearest!' Abby said, gently chafing her hands. 'Now, you know you promised me you wouldn't say another word about That Woman!'

She had hoped to have coaxed a smile out of Selina, but after staring at her uncomprehendingly Selina uttered: 'It was because I was cross! *That* was why you said you would marry him, wasn't it? But I didn't mean it, Abby, I didn't mean it!'

'Goosecap! I know you didn't!'

Selina's thin fingers closed round her own like claws. 'James said – But I told him it was no such thing! He put you all on end, didn't he? I guessed how it must have been. I told him. I said that there was no question of – I said you would never dream of marrying Mr Calverleigh. And you wouldn't, would you, Abby?'

Meeting Selina's strained, searching eyes, Abby hesitated, before saying: 'My dear, why put yourself into such a taking? I thought you *wished* me to marry?'

'Not Mr Calverleigh! I never *wished* it, except for your sake, but I thought, if you married Mr Dunston – so kind – in every way so suitable – and everyone would have been pleased, and you wouldn't have gone away from me, not *quite* away from me, because I might have seen you every day –'

'Selina, I shall never go quite away from you,' Abby said quietly. 'This is the merest agitation of nerves! You have let James talk you into high fidgets. In spite of his top-boots, and his careless ways, you don't dislike Mr Calverleigh. Why, it was you who first said how unjust it was to condemn him for the sins of his youth!'

'But I didn't know that you meant to marry him,' said Selina simply.

'Well, nor did I, at that time. Come, my dear, there is no occasion for this despair!'

But by the time Selina, still clutching her hand, had enumerated the ills which would result from such a marriage there seemed to be every reason for despair. The list was a long one, and it ranged over a wide ground, which included the mortification which would be suffered by the family at the marriage of one of its members to a black sheep; the sneers of Mrs Ruscombe; the impossibility of Selina's remaining in Bath, where she was so well known; the harm that would be done to Fanny, on the verge of her come-out; of Fanny's unhappiness at being separated from her dearest aunt; of her own misery at being estranged from James, and Jane, and perhaps even Mary.

At this point, Abby was moved to expostulate: 'But you wouldn't be, stoopid!'

'James warned me. He left me in such anger! Because I told him that I should never give you up, whatever you did, which I never, never would! And he said that if I supported you I should cut myself off from the family – so *dreadful*, Abby! – so that I should do well to consider carefully before I made my choice, only there *is* no choice, so what a silly thing to say, and how could he suppose I would choose anyone but you, if there were? And as for not looking to see his face again, I said that if he was unkind to you he need not look to see *my* face, which is true, only I can't bear to think of it, because we have always been so happy, and even if we don't very often see the others they are our *family*!'

Abby was so much touched by this unexpected championship that tears started to her eyes. 'Oh, my dearest! How brave of you – how *loyal*! Do you indeed love me so much?'

'But of course I do!' said Selina.

Abby kissed her. 'Best of my sisters!' she said, mistily smiling. 'But as for James – ! How *dared* he talk to you like that? I wish very much that *I had* been present!'

'Oh, no, Abby! It would have been much, much worse! And I couldn't blame him. Not when he told me!'

'Told you what?' asked Abby sharply.

Selina turned her face away, shuddering. 'Celia . . . !'

'So he told you that, did he? Of all the chuckleheaded *dummies*!' Abby exclaimed wrathfully.

'He felt himself obliged to tell me, and, of course, I quite see – because I thought it was just that Mr Calverleigh had been very wild when he was young, which is not what I could *like*, but still – ! So he had to tell me the truth, and it has sunk me utterly, and I can't help wishing that he hadn't, for it would have been so much more comfortable, only very wrong, but I shouldn't have known it was!'

'Put it out of your mind!' said Abby. 'If it doesn't concern me, it need not concern you! To be sure, it would be a little awkward if people knew of it, but they don't, and, in any event, Celia wasn't Rowland's *wife* when it happened!'

Selina stared at her in horror. 'Abby, you *could* not! A man who – Abby, *think*! No, no, *promise* me you won't do it!' Tears began to roll down her cheeks. 'Oh, Abby, don't leave me! How could I live without you?'

'Hush, Selina! Nothing is decided yet. Don't, I beg of you, fall into one of your – into a fuss! Come, let me put you into bed! You're tired out. Fardle shall bring up your dinner to you, and –'

'Rabbit and onions!' uttered Selina, breaking into sobs of despair. 'I couldn't, I couldn't!'

'Oh!' A wry smile twisted Abby's lips. 'No, I don't think I could either.'

This was perhaps fortunate, for no opportunity was offered her to partake of this or any other dish. Selina's sobs were the prelude to one of her dreaded fits of hysteria, and as this was accompanied by spasms and palpitations it was long before Abby could leave her. When Selina at last fell into an exhausted sleep, the only thing her equally exhausted sister wished for was her bed.

The morning brought confirmation of her suspicion that Lavinia had indeed been tattling. Mrs Grayshott came to Sydney Place to see Abby.

'For I could do no less than tell you, Abby, and beg your pardon! I have never been so vexed with Lavinia! And the worst of it is that she did it on purpose, and is not sorry for it! She told me what she had done the instant she came home yesterday, knowing, of course, that I should be extremely displeased, but saying that she was Fanny's friend, and that she knew she had been right to warn her.'

'Perhaps she was,' said Abby. 'I don't know. I don't think Fanny quite believes it.'

'No, that also Lavinia told me. But Oliver thinks that even if she does not the shock of discovering that it is true will have been lessened for the poor child. But it was not Lavinia's business to have meddled! My dear, how tired you look!'

'I *am* a little tired,' owned Abby. 'My sister is not quite well today, so . . .'

She left the sentence unfinished, but she had said enough to send Mrs Grayshott back to Edgar Buildings in a state of such seething and impotent indignation that she informed her son, with unusual venom, that the sooner Miss Wendover's numerous ailments carried her off the better it would be for Abby.

Hardly had she left Sydney Place than a sealed letter was delivered at the house. It was directed to Fanny, and brought to her in the drawing-room by Mitton. She took it with a shaking hand, made as if to tear it open, and then, with an inarticulate excuse, went out of the room.

She did not return. Abby, who had guessed that the missive must have been sent by Stacy Calverleigh, waited in growing disquiet for a full hour, and then went up to her room.

Fanny was seated by the window. She looked at Abby, but said nothing, and her face was so stony that Abby hesitated. Then she saw the helpless suffering in Fanny's eyes, and went to her, not speaking, but folding her in her arms, and holding her close. Fanny did not resist, but for perhaps a minute she was as rigid as a statue. Stroking the bright curls, Abby said huskily, as though to a much younger Fanny, who had tumbled down, and grazed her knees: 'Never mind, my darling, never mind!'

She could have cursed herself for the inadequacy of these foolish words; but a quiver ran through Fanny, a rending sob broke from her, she turned in Abby's arms, and clung to her, torn and shaken by the pent-up emotions of the past fortnight.

It was long before she could be calm again, but gradually the sobs dwindled into pathetic hiccups, and she lay limply in Abby's embrace, her head on Abby's shoulder, and her lashes wet on her cheeks. When Abby would have fetched some water for her to drink, she said brokenly: 'Oh, no! This is so comfortable!' Presently she said: 'You knew, didn't you?'

'I knew, but I haven't known how to tell you.'

'Lavinia told me. I wouldn't believe her. But it was true. It was just my fortune, wasn't it?'

'I am afraid so, darling.'

Another silence fell, before Fanny said: 'I've been very stupid. Wicked, too. I meant to elope with him.'

'I don't suppose you would have done so, however.'

Fanny sighed. 'I don't know. Sometimes I thought I couldn't, but when I was with him —' Her voice failed, and it was a moment or two before she could speak again. 'Then I was ill, and he didn't come, or — or write to me, even when other people came to visit me. I tried to believe it was because he was afraid you might not let him see me, but I think I knew. . . . Only I went on hoping, and when Lavinia told me about Mrs Clapham I felt at first that it *couldn't* be true, and then I wasn't quite sure, and then – and then the letter came.' A shudder ran through her. 'Abby, it made me feel *sick*! *Really* sick!'

'He told you that he had changed his mind?'

'No. I – I think I could have borne that. People *do* fall out of love, don't they? If he had told me that he had met someone he liked better than me – But he didn't. I was only a silly schoolgirl before I was ill, but I'm grown-up now, and I shall never be taken-in again.'

Abby was not tempted to smile. She said: 'I hope no one will ever try to take you in again, dearest.'

'No, for I don't feel that I shall ever fall in love again. My uncle saw him yesterday, didn't he? Abby, *you* didn't send for him, did you?'

'I not only didn't send for him, but I came to cuffs with him before he had been in the house above ten minutes.'

'I thought you could not have done so. Oh, Abby, I beg your pardon! I've been horridly cross and unkind, but I didn't mean it! I love you more than anyone in the world!'

'Then I shall try my *very* hardest to forgive you!'

A watery chuckle greeted this sally. 'I'm so glad I've got you still. For always, Abby!' She lifted Abby's hand to her cheek, and cuddled it there. 'I love Aunt Selina too, of course, but in a – dutiful way. I couldn't bear to go on living here, if there was *only* my Aunt Selina.'

Abby heard this with mixed feelings. Though it warmed her heart it also caused it to sink. Miles Calverleigh's image seemed to be drawing farther and farther away.

'I burned the letter,' Fanny said abruptly. 'And the lock of hair. Do you think I might write to tell him so?'

'Oh, I shouldn't do that! Far more dignified to pay no heed to him at all!'

'Y-yes, only –' Her breast heaved. 'He says he shall keep mine to the day of his death, in memory of the only girl he ever truly loved! *That* was what made me feel sick!'

'I'm not surprised. It is making me feel sick too.'

'And he pretends that he is giving me up for my own sake, because he realises, since he has talked to my uncle, that he has no hope of winning his consent, and it would be very wrong for us to be married without it, and he fears I should regret it, and – Abby, it was *false*, every word of it! I could not have believed that he could write me such stuff! And to think I was widgeon enough to be taken-in! Because he knew from the very start that my uncle wouldn't consent, and he knew you wouldn't either, and that was why he wanted me to elope with him!' She sat up, her eyes and cheeks aflame with indignation, and her hands clenched. 'I hate him! I can't *think* how I ever came to fall in love with him!'

Abby was happy to encourage her in this frame of mind. Fanny raged for several minutes, but the mood could not last. Suddenly she flung herself back into Abby's arms in a fresh passion of grief, wailing: 'What shall I *do*? Oh, Abby, I'm so unhappy! What shall I *do*?'

'Well, I think the best thing to do is to follow Dr Rowton's advice,' replied Abby.

'Go away? Oh, no! I don't want to go away! I can't! I won't!'

'To be sure, when he first told me that you ought to go to the sea-side, to set you up again, I own that I felt doubtful, for in my opinion there is nothing more melancholy than the sea-side in November. But when he suggested Exmouth I remembered how delighted the Trevisians were with the place – and they, you know, were there in December. They stayed at the Globe, and Lady Trevisian almost persuaded your aunt to go there, when she was so sadly out of frame last winter, for she said they had been as comfortable there as in their own home. The climate is excellent, too, and there are several charming walks, besides I know not how many interesting expeditions to be made. I have been wondering whether, if we decided to try how we liked it, Mrs Grayshott would spare Lavinia to us. Do you think she might?'

The bait failed. Fanny was vehement in her entreaties not to be taken away from Bath. 'Everyone would think it was because I have been *jilted*!'

'Well,' said Abby dryly, 'when I consider that poor Mitton is worn out with plodding to the front-door to take in flowers, and fruit, and books from your army of admirers, my love, I think it very much more likely that *you* will be held to have been the jilt!'

She did not press the matter; but derived a certain amount of comfort from the belief that Fanny's pride had received almost as severe a blow as her heart.

Fanny meant to be good, not to be cross, or to allow it to be seen that she was in great affliction, but although she tried very hard, every now and then, to appear cheerful, her spirits remained low and oppressed, and, like her eldest aunt, she could not forbear discussion of her trouble with Abby. Hoping that she might soon talk herself out of her despair, Abby listened patiently, diverting her mind whenever an opportunity presented itself but never withholding her sympathy.

Selina, on the other hand, made no attempt to appear cheerful, but as she kept her bed for three days after her brother's disastrous visit, and complained when she left it of a great many aches and ails, perhaps only Fardle and Mrs Grimston ascribed her rather lachrymose condition to anything other than one of the disorders which so frequently attacked her. She spent most of her time on the sofa, wincing at the slamming of a door in the distance, or the postman's horn in the street; infuriating her excellent cook by thinking, in the morning, that she could fancy a particular dish, and by laboriously eating three mouthfuls of it when it made its appearance on the dinner-table; and trying by every means known to her to keep Abby by her side. 'Let me enjoy your company while I still may!' she said, shedding tears.

Between her sister and her niece, Abby's lot was not enviable, and might well have driven her to distraction had it not been eased by Mr Oliver Grayshott, who came nearly every day with Lavinia to visit Fanny, to divert her with parlour-games, if the weather was inclement, or, on fine days, to accompany her on her drives, or to take her for gentle walks in the Sydney Gardens. It was noticeable that she was always more cheerful after these visits, and if Abby grew to dread the two words: *Oliver says,* she had the comfort of knowing that Oliver's sayings were distinguished by their good sense. It was a little galling to discover that Fanny would accept Oliver's advice rather than hers – particularly when his advice tallied exactly with hers – but she suppressed such ignoble feelings. She wondered what would be the outcome of this close friendship. Fanny was not in love with Oliver. She continued to regard him as a brother, and almost certainly confided in him, and sought his guidance; but Abby could not help feeling that he was too quiet a man to appeal to her. Still, one never knew: perhaps, in a year or two's time, her trust and liking would have grown into love. One knew of many cases of a lively woman's finding happiness with a husband who was cast in a more sober mould than her own. There was no doubt that Oliver loved Fanny, though he treated her just as he treated Lavinia. It was only when he looked at her that he unconsciously betrayed himself. One could always tell, Abby thought, and instantly tried to decide when it was that she had first seen in Miles Calverleigh's very different eyes just that inner glow.

Seventeen

Meanwhile, Mr Stacy Calverleigh's star had been in the ascendant, and this in spite of his uncomfortably diminishing resources. He had been obliged to hang up his shot at the White Hart for several weeks; and he knew that only his increasing intimacy with the wealthy Mrs Clapham was restraining the proprietor of this establishment from indicating that the settlement of his bill would be appreciated. His efforts to persuade the widow to remove to Leamington had failed, and he had been obliged to show himself in public with her more often than was prudent; but these were small evils when compared with Mrs Clapham's coquettish encouragement of his advances. He had not enjoyed his session with Mr James Wendover, but he had been swift to turn it to good account. He had taken great pains over the letter he had written to Fanny, and by the time he had polished its well-turned phrases, and copied the whole out fair, he really felt that in renouncing her he was behaving as nobly as he expected her to believe. He was a little afraid that she might address a passionate reply to him, or even accost him in public, and silently cursed the obstinacy of Mrs Clapham in refusing to withdraw from Bath; but when he received no letter from Fanny, and was accorded only a slight, distant bow from her when her carriage was held up by the usual press of traffic in Cheap Street, his mind was relieved of care, and he felt himself to be at liberty to pop the question to Mrs Clapham.

It had not occurred to him that he might meet with a refusal, nor did her response to his proposal alarm him.

'Marry you?' said Mrs Clapham, laughing. 'Me? Good gracious no!'

He took this for coyness, and was rather impatient of it, but he said, in his most caressing voice: 'I think it was your sportive playfulness which made me tumble headlong in love with you. And I had believed myself to be case-hardened!'

Her next words were disturbing. 'Well, by what I'm told, you weren't so case-hardened but what you were making up to that pretty little girl who bowed to you in Cheap Street, before I came to Bath!'

It was the manner in which she spoke which disturbed him more than her words. There had always been a danger that she might discover how particularly he had attached himself to Fanny, and he knew just how to deal with that. He was unprepared for the change in her voice, and in her demeanour, and it startled him. He had hitherto supposed her to be a silly, fluttering little *ingénue,* but she was not looking at all ingenuous, and her voice was not only decidedly tart, but it had lost some of its gentility. It disconcerted him, but only momentarily: he realised that she was suspicious of a rival, and jealous of her. He laughed, flinging up his hands. 'What, little Fanny Wendover? Oh, Nancy, Nancy, you absurd and adorable witch! My dear, do you know how old she is? Seventeen! Not out of school yet!'

'More shame to you!' she said.

'Yes, indeed, if I *had* made up to her. Oh, these Bath quizzies! I warned you how it would be! But I own I did not think that at my age I should be suspected of dangling after a mere child only because I took notice of her, and indulged her with a little very mild flirtation!'

He trod over to her chair, and dropped gracefully on to his knee, and possessed himself of her hands, smiling up into her face. 'I have had many flirts, but never a true love till now!' he said whimsically.

'Well, you haven't got one in me!' said Mrs Clapham. 'I've had many flirts too, but I've no wish for a husband, so you may as well stop making a cake of yourself! Going down on your knees, as if you was playing Romeo!'

'I know how unworthy of you I am, but I dared to hope you were not indifferent to me!' he persevered.

'Get up, do!' responded the lady unromantically, pulling her hands away.

He obeyed her, looking remarkably foolish, and shaken quite off his balance. He stammered: 'How is this? It cannot be that you have been trifling with me! I cannot believe you could be so heartless!'

'Oh, can't you?' she retorted, getting up, and shaking out her skirt. 'Now, you listen to me, Mr Flat-catching Calverleigh! It don't become you to talk of hearts, and it isn't a particle of use pitching me any more of your gammon; because I'm up to all the rigs! We've had an agreeable flirtation, and the best thing you can do now is to own yourself beaten at your own game, and take yourself off! Otherwise you might hear a few things you wouldn't relish. Taking notice of a school-girl! Cutting a sham with an heiress is what *you* were doing, and not for the first time, I'll be bound! Well, I don't want to say anything unladylike, *but*,' she ended, overcoming this reluctance, 'you're one as would marry a midden for muck, and that's the truth!'

He was white with mingled shock and rage. He opened his mouth to speak, but shut it again, for there was nothing he could say. He turned, and walked out of the room.

His was not a sensitive nature. He could shrug off a snub; he could listen with indifference to the strictures of Mr James Wendover. But Mr Wendover's contempt had been expressed with icy propriety. No one had ever torn his character to shreds with the crude vulgarity favoured by Mrs Clapham, and it was some time before he could in any way recover from his fury. It was not the truth of what she had said that provoked this fury: it was her incredible insolence in daring to address him – a Calverleigh! – in such terms.

When his rage abated, it was succeeded by fear, a more deadly fear than he had ever before experienced, for it was unattended by even a glimmer of optimism. There was no way left to him of staving off his creditors; he would be forced to pawn his few pieces of jewellery to enable him to pay his shot at the White Hart, and to buy himself a seat on the stage-coach to London. He tried to think of someone from whom he might be able to borrow a hundred pounds, or even fifty pounds, but there was no one – certainly no one in Bath.

He had reached the point of entertaining wild thoughts of abandoning his luggage, and escaping from the White Hart with his bill unpaid, when he was interrupted by the entrance of one of the waiters, who presented him with a letter, which had been brought, he said, by one of the servants employed at the York House Hotel.

Stacy did not recognise the careless scrawl, but when he spread open the single sheet he found that it was from his uncle, and briefly invited him to dine at York House that evening.

His first impulse was to send back a refusal. Then it occurred to him that he might be able to induce Miles to lend him some money, even if it was only a pony. He must be fairly flush in the pocket, he thought, for although he bore none of the signs of being well-inlaid he was again putting up at the most expensive hotel in Bath, which he could not have done had he left his shot unpaid when he went off to London so suddenly. He bade the waiter stay a moment while he wrote a reply to his uncle's letter, and was considerably provoked when he learned that the messenger had departed, having been told that no answer was expected. Coupled with the curt nature of the invitation, which might well have been mistaken for a command, this amounted to an affront, and set up Stacy's bristles. He decided to overlook it: his uncle's manners were deplorably casual, and probably he had had no intention of offending.

Upon arrival at York House, he was taken to Miles Calverleigh's sitting-room, where the table had already been laid for dinner. Determined to please, he exerted himself to be an affable, conversable, and even deferential guest. He praised the excellence of the dishes set before him; he said that it was not often that he was offered burgundy of such rare quality; he recounted such items of Bath-news as might be supposed to be of interest; he tried to draw Miles out on the subject of India. Miles regarded him with an amused eye, contributed little to the conversation, but outdid him in affability.

When the cloth had been removed, and the brandy placed on the table, Stacy said, with his air of rueful frankness: 'I must tell you, sir, that I was devilish glad to get your letter! I've been drawing the bustle a trifle too freely, and find myself on the rocks. Only temporarily, of course, but I've no banking accommodation in Bath, which puts me in a stupid fix. I don't like to ask it of you but I should be very grateful if you could lend me a trifle – just to keep me in pitch and pay over an awkward period, you know!'

His uncle removed the stopper from the decanter in his leisurely way, and poured brandy into the glasses. 'No, I won't lend you money,' he said.

He spoke with his usual amiability, but there was something in his voice which Stacy had never heard before. It was almost an implacable note, he thought. Surprised, and slightly nettled, he said: 'Good God, sir, I don't want any considerable sum!'

Miles shook his head. Without quite knowing why, Stacy felt a stir of alarm in his breast. He forced up a laugh. 'If you must have it, sir, it's damned low water with me – until I can bring myself about! I haven't sixpence to scratch with!'

'I know you haven't.'

The placidity with which this was uttered made Stacy flame into anger. He jumped up, his hands clenching and unclenching.

'Do you indeed? Well, let me tell you, my very dear uncle, that unless I can be given time to find some means of raising the recruits there will be a writ of forfeiture served on me!'

'Oh, it needn't come to that!'

'Needn't come to it? Are you *quite* blubber-headed? Don't you –'

Miles laughed. 'No, no, I'm not at all blubber-headed!'

'I beg pardon!' Stacy said, choking down his rage. 'I didn't mean to say that! The thing is –'

'No need to apologise,' said Miles kindly. 'No need to tell me what the thing is either.'

'I am afraid, sir,' said Stacy, trying to speak politely, 'that owing, no doubt, to your long residence abroad you are not familiar with the – the various conditions attached to mortgages. I must explain to you –'

'You are in arrears with the interest, and you have no possible means of paying up. Sit down!' He picked up his glass, and sipped some of the brandy in it. 'That's why I sent for you.'

'*Sent* for me?' interrupted Stacy.

'Did I say sent for you? It must have been a slip of the tongue. Begged for the honour of your company!'

'I cannot imagine why,' muttered Stacy resentfully.

'Just on a matter of business. I want two things from you: one is an equity of redemption; the other is Danescourt – by which is to be understood the house, and the small amount of unencumbered land on which it stands. For these I am prepared to forgo the interest owing on the existent mortgages, and to pay you fifteen thousand pounds.'

Stacy was so thunderstruck by these calmly spoken words that his brain whirled. He almost doubted whether he had heard his uncle aright, for what he had said was entirely fantastic. Feeling dazed and incredulous, he watched Miles stroll over to the fire, and take a spill from a jar on the mantelpiece. He found his voice, but only to stammer: 'B-but – equity of redemption – why, that means – Damn you, is this your notion of a joke?'

'No, no, I never cut jokes in business!' replied Miles. He came back to his chair, a lighted cheroot between his fingers, and sat down again, stretching his long legs out before him, with one ankle crossed over the other, after his usual fashion. He regarded his stunned nephew with mild amusement, and said: 'I'm a very rich man, you know.'

Since Stacy knew nothing of the sort, he felt more strongly than before that he had strayed into a world of fantasy. 'I don't believe it!' he blurted out.

'I am afraid,' said Miles, apologetically, 'that you have been misled into thinking that because I've no fancy for rigging myself out in the first style of elegance, cutting a dash, or saddling myself with a multitude of things I haven't the least wish to possess, I must be as cucumberish as you are yourself. You should never judge by appearances, nevvy!'

It seemed monstrous to Stacy that his uncle should not have informed him that he was in affluent circumstances. He exclaimed hotly: 'You have been deceiving me, then! Deliberately deceiving me!'

'Not at all. You deceived yourself. That isn't to say that I wouldn't have deceived you, had it been expedient to do so. But, to own the truth, it was of no consequence to me whether you thought me a Nabob or a Church rat. Except, of course,' he added reflectively, 'that if you had known I was full of juice I should have found you an intolerable nuisance. You see, I never lend money without security.'

Stacy reddened, but said: 'If you can indeed afford to buy up the mortgages – if you don't wish to see Danescourt pass out of our hands – if you are willing to help me to bring myself about – we could come to some agreement! We could –' He broke off, encountering his uncle's eyes, and seeing in them a look as implacable as the note he had detected in his voice. There was no smile in them, and no warmth; nor could he perceive in them anger, impatience, contempt, or any human emotion whatsoever. They were coldly dispassionate, and as hard as quartz.

'You know, you labour under too many misapprehensions,' said Miles pleasantly.

'But – Good God, you can't dispossess me!'

'What makes you think so?'

'You wouldn't! We are both Calverleighs! You are my *uncle*!'

'You have a remarkably false notion of my character if you think that that circumstance will prevail upon me to maintain Danescourt for your benefit. I can't think where you came by it.'

The brief, vague vision of being able once more to draw upon his estates for his needs faded. Miles had spoken amiably, but with finality. Stacy was conscious of an unreasoning resentment. He said: 'What is it to you? Much you care for being Calverleigh of Danescourt! Or *is* that it?'

'Oh, lord, no! I care for Danescourt, that's all.'

'That's what I said!'

'It's not what you meant, or what I mean. I want Danescourt because I'm fond of it, and for the same reason I won't see it fall into ruins. If I weren't, I wouldn't lift a finger to save it. All that fiddle-faddle you talk about being Calverleigh of Danescourt don't mean a thing to me.'

'Coming it too strong, uncle! And just as well if it *were* true, for *I* am the head of the family, and while I'm alive *I* am Calverleigh of Danescourt!'

'Yes, yes!' said Miles, on a soothing note. 'You can go on calling yourself Calverleigh of Danescourt, or anything else you like: I've no objection.'

'How the devil can I do so if I don't own even the house?' demanded Stacy hotly. 'I'll sell you an equity of redemption, but I'll not sell the house or the demesne!'

'Well, once I foreclose, you won't have any choice in the matter, will you? You'll be glad to sell it to me at any figure I name.'

Stacy stared at him, very white about the mouth. 'You'd do that? Foreclose on me – your own nephew! – force me out of my very birthplace? My God, is that what you've been doing all these years? Waiting for the chance of revenge?'

'No, I've been far too busy. I wish you would rid your mind of its apparent conviction that I think myself hardly used. I don't, and I never did. I didn't like your grandfather, or your father either, but I've often been grateful to them for the good turn they didn't know they'd done me. India suited me down to the ground. What's more, if they hadn't sent me there I might never have discovered that I had a turn for business. But I had, Stacy, and you'd do well to bear it in mind. When you prate to me about our relationship, you're wasting your time. Sentiment has no place in business, even if I had any, which I haven't. As for your talk about *revenge*, it's balderdash! I don't like you any more than I liked your father – in fact, less – but why the devil should I want to be revenged on you?'

'On him! Because I am his son!'

'Good God! You must have watched the deuce of a lot of melodramas in your time! Until I met you, I'd no feeling for you of any kind: why should I? If I had found Danescourt as I'd left it – or if I'd even found you making a push to restore it – I shouldn't have interfered. But I didn't. I had been warned of it, which was why I decided to come home, but I wasn't prepared –'

'It wasn't my fault!' Stacy said quickly, his colour surging into his face. 'It was my father who granted the first mortgage! He was in Dun territory when he died, and how the devil could I –'

'Don't excuse yourself! It makes no odds to me which of you let it fall into decay.'

'I should have been glad enough to set it in order, but I hadn't the means!'

'No, and as you wouldn't have spent a groat more than you were obliged to on it if you had had the means, and would sell it tomorrow, if you could find a fool willing to purchase a place which you described to me, on the occasion of our first meeting, as a damned barrack, mortgaged to the hilt, and falling into ruin besides, I am now going to relieve you of it.'

'You'd be better advised to leave it in my possession! What do you imagine will be said of you, if you – you usurp my place?'

'Well, according to Colonel Ongar, my arrival will be regarded in the light of a successful relieving force. You seem to have made yourself odious to the entire county.'

'Exactly as you did, in fact!'

'No, no, I was never *odious*! Merely a scapegrace! My youthful sins will be forgiven me the moment I remove the padlock from the main gate, and cut down that hayfield of yours. I must say, I don't at all care for it.'

'*Hayfield?* What the devil – ?'

'In my day it was the South Lawn.'

There was an uncomfortable silence. 'So you've been there, have you?' Stacy said sullenly.

'Yes, I've been there. I thought poor old Penn was going to burst into tears. Mrs Penn did. Fell on my neck, too, and went straight off to kill a fatted calf. The return of the Prodigal Son was nothing to it. No, I don't think I shall be shunned by the county, Stacy.'

Another silence fell, during which Stacy sat scowling down at the table. He said suddenly: 'Fifteen thousand? Paltry!'

'Perhaps,' suggested Miles, 'you are forgetting the little matter of the mortgages.'

Stacy bit his lip, but said: 'It's worth more – much more!'

'It is, in fact, worth much less. However, if you believe you can sell it for more, by all means make the attempt!'

'With you holding all the rest of the estate? Who the devil would buy a place like Danescourt with no more land attached to it than the gardens, and the park?'

'I shouldn't think anyone would.'

'Brought me to Point Non-Plus, haven't you?' said Stacy, with an ugly laugh.

'You're certainly there, but what I had to do with it I don't know.'

'You could help me to make a recover – give me time!'

'I could. I could also ruin you. I don't choose to do either – though when I saw Danescourt I was strongly tempted to let you take up residence in the King's Bench Prison, and leave you to rot there! Which is what you will do, if you refuse my offer.'

'Oh, damn you, I can't refuse it! How soon can I have the blunt?'

'As soon as the conveyance is completed. The necessary documents are being prepared, and you will find them with my lawyer. I'll furnish you with his direction. You had better take your own man with you, to see all's right, by the way.'

'I shall certainly do so! And I shall be very much obliged to you if you'll advance me a hundred, sir, at once!'

'I'll make you a present of it,' said Miles, drawing a roll of bills from his pocket.

'You're very good!' said Stacy stiffly. 'Then, if there's nothing more you wish to say, I'll bid you goodnight!'

'No, nothing,' replied Miles. 'Goodnight!'

Eighteen

ince Miss Butterbank, after a night and the better part of a day enduring the agonies of violent toothache, was closeted with the dentist when Mr Miles Calverleigh returned to Bath, the news of his arrival was not carried to Sydney Place until several hours after he had made an unexpected descent upon Miss Abigail Wendover.

He took her entirely by surprise. Not only did he present himself at an unusually early hour, but when Mitton admitted that he rather thought Miss Abigail was at home he said that there was no need to announce him, and ran up the stairs, leaving Mitton in possession of his hat and malacca cane, and torn between romantic speculation and disapproval of such informal behaviour.

Abby was alone, and engaged on the task of fashioning a collar out of a length of broad lace. The table in the drawing-room was covered with pins, patterns, and sheets of parchment, and Abby had just picked up a pair of shaping scissors when Mr Calverleigh walked into the room. She glanced up; something between a gasp and a shriek escaped her; the scissors fell with a clatter; and she started forward involuntarily, with her hands held out. 'You've come back! Oh, you *have* come back!' she cried.

The unwisdom, and, indeed, the impropriety of this unguarded betrayal of her sentiments occurred to her too late, and did not seem to occur to Mr Calverleigh at all. Before she could recover herself she was in his arms, being kissed with considerable violence. 'My bright, particular star!' uttered Mr Calverleigh, into her ear.

Mr Calverleigh had very strong arms, and a shoulder most conveniently placed for the use of a tall lady. Abby, gasping for breath, gratefully leaned her cheek against it, feeling, for a few brief moments, that she had come safely to harbour after a stormy passage. She said, clinging to him: 'Miles! Oh, my dear. I've missed you so dreadfully!' But hardly had she uttered these words than all the difficulties of her situation rushed in upon her, with the recollection of the decision she had so painfully reached, and she said, trying to wrench herself free: 'No! Oh, I can't think what made me – ! I can't, Miles, I can't!'

Mr Calverleigh, that successful man of affairs, was not one to be easily rocked off his balance. 'What can't you, my heart's dearest?' he enquired.

Abby quivered. 'Marry you! Oh, Miles, *don't*!'

She broke from him, and turned away, groping blindly for her handkerchief, and trying very hard not to let her emotion get the better of her.

'Well!' said Mr Calverleigh, in stunned accents. 'This is beyond everything! After what has just passed between us! I wonder you dare look me in the face!'

Abby, was not, in fact, daring to look him in the face: she was occupied in drying her wet cheeks.

'Has no one ever told you that it is the height of impropriety to kiss any gentleman, unless you have the intention of accompanying him immediately to the altar?' demanded the outraged Mr Calverleigh. 'It will not do, ma'am! Such conduct –' He broke off abruptly, as she looked up, between tears and laughter, and said, in quite another voice: 'Now, what's this? Let me look at you!'

As he took her face between his hands as he spoke, and turned it up, she was obliged to let him. She dared not meet his eyes, however, and very nearly broke down again when he said, after a moment's scrutiny: 'My loved one, I left you in a high state of preservation! What has been happening here?'

She moved away, saying: 'Do I look hagged? I am – I am rather tired. Fanny has been ill. And there have been other things.' She smiled, with an effort, and made a gesture towards a chair. 'Won't you sit down? I must tell you – explain to you – why I can't marry you.'

'Yes, I think you must do that,' he said, drawing her to the sofa. 'I can think of only one reason: that you find you don't love me enough.'

She allowed him, though reluctantly, to push her gently down on to the sofa, and sat there, primly upright, with her hands tightly folded in her lap. 'I meant to tell you that that was it,' she said, keeping her eyes lowered. 'I – thought it would be best to say just that. I never, never meant to –' She stopped, as a thought occurred to her, and looked up, a sparkle of indignation in her eyes. 'I should like to know what Mitton was about to let you walk in on me, without coming first to ask me if I was at home to visitors, and not even announcing you!' she said, with a strong suggestion of ill-usage in her voice.

He had taken his place at the other end of the sofa, seated sideways, with one arm lying along the back of it: a position which enabled him to keep his eyes on her profile. He seemed to be quite at his ease; and there was nothing in his demeanour to suggest that he was suffering from any of the chagrin natural to a gentleman whose suit had been rejected. He said: 'Oh, you mustn't blame the poor fellow! I told him I would announce myself.'

'You had no business to do so!' scolded Abby. 'If you hadn't startled me – if I had had a *moment's* warning – I shouldn't have – it wouldn't have happened!'

'Well, you might not have kissed me, but I had every intention of kissing you, so it's just as well he didn't announce me,' said Mr Calverleigh. 'Do you always kiss gentlemen who walk in unannounced? I'll take good care none is allowed to do so when we are married!'

A smile trembled on her lips, and she blushed faintly, but also she shook her head, saying: 'We are not going to be married.'

'I was forgetting that,' he apologised. 'Why are we not going to be married?'

'That is what I feel I must explain to you. I didn't mean to, but after behaving so very improperly it wouldn't be any use to tell you that I don't love you, would it?'

'No, none at all,' he agreed.

'No. Well – you must try to understand, Miles! I know you don't enter into my feelings on this subject, so it is very difficult to explain it to you. I have thought and thought – argued with myself until my head aches – but in the end I've realised that I cannot marry you – ought not to do so!'

'What brought you to this conclusion?' he asked conversationally.

She began carefully to pleat her damp handkerchief. 'I suppose you might say it was Mrs Ruscombe. She is Cornelia's bosom-bow – James's wife, you know – and she makes it her business to spy on us, and to send a record of all our doings to Cornelia.' She raised her eyes to his for an instant, smiling wryly. 'I am afraid we were not very discreet, Miles, for she told Cornelia that I was encouraging your advances, and that brought James down upon us, as you may imagine. Of course we came to points – we always do – but even though I was in the most shocking pelter I couldn't keep from laughing. You never heard such pompous fustian in your life! I found myself wishing you could have been there to enjoy it!'

'I rather wish that too,' acknowledged Mr Calverleigh. 'Did he forbid the banns?'

'Heavens, yes! He said that if I married you I should be cast out of the family, and he would have divulged the Awful Truth about you and Celia if I hadn't told him that I knew it already, and that shocked him so much that he said he began to think we – you and I – were well matched!'

'You know, he's not such a bad fellow after all!' remarked Miles.

'He is a toad. It wasn't anything he said which made me realise how impossible it is. Nothing he said to me. But he said it

242

all over again to Selina, and, I daresay, a great deal more.' She fell silent, deeply troubled. At last, she sighed, and said: 'I never knew how much Selina loved me. James told her she would have to choose between me and the family, and, oh, Miles, she said that she would never give me up, whatever I did! Selina! But she was dreadfully upset – she made herself ill, and she is still quite overpowered, and – and can scarcely bear to let me out of her sight. She says over and over again that she doesn't know what she will do when I'm gone, and that – has made me realise how wrong – how heartless – it would be if I were to marry you. If you had been the sort of dull, respectable man of whom the family would have approved I think she would have grown accustomed – though sometimes I feel I ought not to leave her, no matter who asked me to marry him. You see, we have been together all my life, and for years – ever since my mother died – I've managed everything for her, and taken care of her. But if you had been Peter Dunston, whom she has been trying to persuade me to marry these three years, she would have been pleased, and that would have helped her to bear the loneliness she dreads. She would have known I was near at hand, and she wouldn't have been estranged from the family, or – Oh, I can't explain it to you! So – so many evils would result from our marriage! If you think it wouldn't become known that I had married you against the wishes of my family, you cannot know Bath! They might seem insignificant to you; they seem so to me; but not to Selina. And then there is Fanny!'

'I wondered when we were going to come to Fanny,' remarked Miles chattily.

'We must come to her. I can't desert her, Miles. She is in great affliction poor child, for she has discovered what is your vile nephew's true character!'

'Just as you hoped she might,' he interpolated.

'Yes, indeed, and I am thankful for it! But it has quite overset her, and – and she too needs me. It would never do to leave her here with Selina – wholly separated from me! For she would be, you see. James wouldn't permit me even to write to her. When she knew about Stacy, she told me that she was glad she had me – for always. She won't want me always, of course, but perhaps for some years to come she will.'

'Would it be of any use for me to suggest that there are answers to all these problems?' he said.

She shook her head. 'No. You see, one can argue – one can persuade oneself that none of these things matter, but one knows, all the time, that they do matter. Miles, I *could* not, deliberately, and selfishly, for the sake of my own happiness, plunge my whole family into so much trouble, and the two I love most into misery as well! I beg of you, don't try to convince me! I'm worn out with thinking!'

Her voice cracked; she put up her hand to shield her eyes; and felt her other taken into a sustaining clasp. 'No, I won't try to convince you,' said Miles reassuringly.

Someone must have told Selina that her sister was closeted with Mr Calverleigh. Since James Wendover's visit she had not left her room until noon, yet here she was, entering the drawing-room with a nervous cough, and looking far less trim than usual, as if she had dressed in a hurry. 'Oh!' she exclaimed, in rehearsed surprise. 'Mr Calverleigh! Dear me, I had no notion you were in Bath! So civil of you to call! Such a wretched day too!'

Abby sprang up and walked over to the window; Mr Calverleigh, rising more leisurely, showed no sign of discomfiture, but shook hands with Selina, and in the calmest way enquired after her health. He remained only for a few minutes longer, and when he took his leave it was with unruffled composure.

Hardly was the door shut behind him than Selina said in an agitated voice: 'He was holding your hand! Oh, Abby, why did he come? Do not keep me in suspense! I can't bear it!'

'I imagine you must know why he came,' said Abby, in a level voice.

'I guessed it!' moaned Selina, pressing a hand to her heart. 'What was your answer? *Tell* me, Abby!'

'Don't distress yourself!' Abby said wearily. 'I have refused his offer.'

'Oh!' cried Selina, suddenly radiant. 'Oh, how glad I am! Dear, dear Abby, now we can be happy again!'

Feeling quite unable to respond to this, Abby left the room without a word, and sought the seclusion of her bedchamber. She remained there for some considerable time, and was thus spared the account of Mr Calverleigh's arrival in Bath, which Miss Butterbank, with a scarf still wrapped round her face, brought to Sydney Place. Selina said nothing about this when she later told Abby the rest of the news Miss Butterbank had poured into her ears. This was of a startling and an intriguing nature: Mrs Clapham, accompanied by her retinue, had left Bath on the previous evening; and Mr Stacy Calverleigh had undoubtedly followed her, for he had boarded one of the post coaches that very morning, and without, said Miss Butterbank, a word of warning to anyone.

Abby was relieved to know that he had removed himself from Bath, but although she made an effort to enter into Selina's speculations on the various possible causes of these separate departures, she felt no flicker of interest. The next piece of Bath news came from Mrs Leavening, and interested her too much.

Mrs Leavening, now established in Orange Grove, had called at York House for any letters which might have been sent there, and she had learnt of Mr Calverleigh's return. She had also learnt that he had remained for only one night before disappearing again, like a perfect will-o'-the-wisp. 'There's no knowing what freakish thing he'll do next!' chuckled Mrs Leavening. 'What in the world made him come all the way from London only for one night? It seems he's set up his own chaise, too, but where it has taken him off to goodness knows! He is quite in my black books, as I shall tell him, for he promised to give us a look-in when he came back to Bath, and never a glimpse of him did we get. However, they say he means to return, so I daresay I shall have an opportunity to give him a scold.'

Abby, knowing that it would be better for her not to see Mr Calverleigh again, tried to school herself into hoping that he would not call in Sydney Place, but failed. Their parting had been too abrupt; there had been so much left unsaid; and to have been obliged to say goodbye to him as to the merest acquaintance was too painful to be borne.

Nothing more was heard of him for three interminable days. Selina, miraculously restored to health and spirits, wrote a surreptitious letter to James, informing him, in the strictest confidence, that all was at an end between Abby and Mr Miles Calverleigh, and that she had known from the start that the affair had been grossly exaggerated by Mrs Ruscombe. She added that she hoped dear Cornelia would not, in future, allow herself to pay so much heed to That Woman's malicious gossip.

Her expression of dismay, when, upon the fourth day, Mitton announced the arrival of Mr Calverleigh was almost ludicrous. It caught Fanny's attention, and made her look quickly at Abby, a sudden suspicion entering her mind.

Mr Calverleigh, with his customary disregard for the conventions governing polite circles, had chosen a most unseasonable hour for his visit. The ladies had only ten minutes earlier left the breakfast-parlour. He seemed to be quite unaware that he was committing a social solecism, but entered the room as though sure that he must be welcome, and cheerfully greeted its occupants. He said that he was glad to have found them at home, congratulated Fanny on her recovery from her illness, and, turning to Abby, said, smiling at her: 'I've come to take you for a drive.'

Selina seethed with indignation. What Abby found to like in this abrupt, mannerless creature was a matter passing her comprehension! She hurried into speech. 'So obliging of you, sir, but it would be *most* unwise for my sister to venture out in an open carriage! The weather is so unsettled – it will come on to pour in another hour, I daresay, for at this season there is no depending on it! Besides, I wish her to go with me to the Pump Room!'

Forgetting her own troubles in the liveliest curiosity, Fanny said brightly: 'I'll go with you, Aunt Selina. A drive is just what will do Abby good, after being cooped up in the house for so long!'

Mr Calverleigh, smiling at her, said: 'Good girl!' which made her giggle, and told Abby to go and put on her bonnet. He added a recommendation to bring a tippet, or a shawl, with her. 'So that you may be easy!' he said, addressing himself to Selina. 'I don't think she will take cold, if she wraps herself up well, and if it should come on to rain we can always find shelter, you know.'

He then engaged Fanny in idle conversation, while Selina sought in vain for further reasons why Abby should not drive out with him.

When Abby came back into the room, suitably attired for the expedition, Selina made a last attempt to convince her that she was running the gravest risk of contracting a heavy cold, if not an inflammation of the lungs, but Fanny, giving Abby an impulsive kiss, interrupted her very rudely, saying: 'Fiddle! It is the finest day we have had for weeks! I'll come and tuck you up in *quantities* of shawls, Abby!'

'Thank you!' Abby said, laughing. 'I fancy one will be enough! Goodbye, Selina: there is no need for you to be in a fidget, I promise you.'

Mr Calverleigh watched her go out of the room, and turned to take leave of Selina. 'Don't worry!' he said. 'I shall take great care of her.'

Five minutes later, leaving Fanny waving farewell on the doorstep, he drove off at a smart trot, and said darkly: '*Indian* manners, my dear!'

Abby chuckled. '*Rag*-manners! Poor Selina!'

'I was afraid you might yield to her entreaties.'

'No. I hoped I might see you again. It was so uncomfortable – saying goodbye as we did. I never told you about Fanny, either. We – we won't discuss that other matter, for there is nothing to be said, and I know you won't distress me by trying to persuade me, will you?'

'No, no, I won't try to persuade you!' he promised.

This ready acquiescence was unexpected, and not altogether welcome; but after a few moments Abby said, with determined cheerfulness: 'Stacy *did* mean to elope with Fanny, you know.

247

She told me the whole. If she hadn't contracted influenza, heaven knows what might have happened! But she did, and while she was laid up we had the most amazing stroke of good fortune befall us!'

He laughed. 'No, did you?'

'Yes, for who should arrive in Bath but a rich widow! *Fabulously* rich, by all accounts! I never saw her myself, but I believe she is quite young, and very pretty. And she put up at the White Hart!'

'No!'

'Yes! With a companion, and a maid, and a footman – oh, and a courier as well! You wouldn't have believed it!'

'Oh, wouldn't I!' said Mr Calverleigh.

'And she hadn't been there for a day before Stacy was busy fixing his interest with her! Would you have thought it possible?'

'Not only possible, but certain.'

'Well, I must say I didn't, when I first heard of it. I never supposed him to be as – as shameless as that!'

'My odious nephew, I regret to say, is entirely shameless.'

'He must be. I can't help pitying the widow, for I think she must have found him out. She left Bath quite suddenly, and although I was excessively thankful that Stacy *did* attach himself to her, it must have been very painful for her.'

'Set your mind at rest, my love! It wasn't at all painful for her.'

'You can't know that!' objected Abby.

'Oh, yes, I can!' he retorted. 'I sent her here!'

'*You?*' she gasped.

'Yes, of course. Didn't you guess it? I rather thought you would.'

'Good God, no! But who was she? *How* did you contrive to send her to Bath? And what a *shocking* thing to do! Exposing her to – Miles, it was *monstrous*! How *can* you laugh?'

'You shouldn't make me laugh. My precious pea-goose, I hired her to bamboozle Stacy! As far as I can discover, her performance was most talented – though she seems to have broken down a trifle before she rang down the final curtain. As to who she is, I really don't know, except that she was at one time an actress.'

Miss Abigail Wendover, having digested this information, said, in accents of stern disapproval: 'I collect, sir, that she is not a – a respectable female?'

'Let us rather say, ma'am, that you are unlikely to meet her in the first circles.'

'*You* seem to have done so!'

'No, no, not in the first circles!'

Her dimple quivered, but she suppressed it. 'And are you very well acquainted with her?' she enquired politely.

'Oh, no! I only met her once – to rehearse her in her rôle, you know. Dolly found her for me. Dolly was Mrs Clapham's companion. I was extremely well acquainted with *her* – some twenty years ago,' he explained outrageously. 'She used to be known as the Dasher, and a very dashing little barque of frailty she was! She is now engaged in – er – a different branch of the profession, and has become alarmingly tonnish. However, she consented, at an extortionate price, to take part in my masquerade. In fact, she insisted on doing so. She never could resist a spree.'

'You,' said Abby, in a shaking voice, 'are the most disreputable person I have ever encountered!'

'Well, that's not saying much! Except for my odious nephew, I don't suppose you've encountered any disreputable persons at all.' He turned his head, and added: 'You never knew me in my disreputable days, Abigail. They are all in the past.'

Her eyes fell. After a minute, she said: 'It must have cost you a great deal, I fear. The masquerade, I mean. When I asked you to rescue Fanny, I never intended –'

'Oh, I had an axe of my own to grind as well!' he assured her.

'Oh!' she said doubtfully. 'Well, –' She stopped suddenly, recognising a landmark. 'Good gracious, we are on the London road! Where are we going?'

'Reading,' he replied.

'*Reading?*' she echoed blankly. 'Don't be so absurd! It must be sixty miles away!'

'Sixty-eight.'

She laughed. 'Just a gentle drive, to exercise the horses! Seriously, where are we going?'

'I am perfectly serious.'

'Oh, are you, indeed?' she retorted. 'And we shall be back in good time for dinner, no doubt!'

'No, my darling, we shall not,' he said. 'We are not going back at all.'

She stared incredulously at him. 'Not – Miles, stop bantering me! It is too ridiculous! You cannot suppose I'm such a ninny as to believe we could drive all the way to Reading in a curricle-and-pair!'

'Oh, no, of course I don't! We are only going as far as to Chippenham in the curricle. My post-chaise is waiting there, to carry us the rest of the way.'

She still felt that he must be trying to hoax her, but she began to be uneasy. 'And what do we do when we reach Reading?' she asked.

'We get married, my very dear.'

'Have you run mad?' she demanded.

'Well, I don't *think* so!'

'Miles – Miles, you *are* joking me, aren't you?'

'I promise you I was never more in earnest. I can't show it to you at the moment, but I have a special licence in my pocket.'

'Oh, how dare you?' she gasped. 'Stop *at once!* If you think I am going to elope with you –'

'No, no!' he said. 'This isn't an elopement! I'm abducting you!'

She tried to speak, but dared not trust her voice.

'I thought it would be the best thing to do,' he explained.

That was too much for her self-control; for the life of her she could not help bursting into laughter. But when she managed to stop laughing, she said: 'Oh, do, please, take me home! How *could* you think I would consent to such a shocking thing?'

'My dear girl, you don't consent to an abduction! You consent to an *elopement,* and I knew you wouldn't do that.'

'You told me once that you thought an unwilling bride would be the very devil!' she reminded him.

'If I had thought that you were unwilling you wouldn't be sitting beside me now,' he replied.

'But I am unwilling! Miles, I won't – I can't! Oh, I believed you understood!'

'I did. You said you wouldn't marry me for a great many reasons which were most of them quite idiotish, but you also said that you couldn't seek your own happiness at the cost of Selina's and Fanny's. Well, you have the right to make a sacrifice of yourself, but I'll be damned if I'll let you sacrifice me!'

After a moment's stricken silence, Abby said remorsefully: 'I never thought of that! Would it – would it be – ?'

'Yes,' he said. 'It would!'

'Oh, if only I knew what I ought to do!' she cried wretchedly.

'You don't, but I do. So don't argue with yourself any more! You haven't any choice in the matter, you know. That's why I've forcibly carried you off. It makes it much easier for you, don't you think?'

'Miles, you are the most impossible, disgraceful – Only think what a scandal there would be!'

'What, you don't imagine that any member of your family would breathe a word about it, do you? No, no! The marriage was private, of course! I expect James will think of some excellent reason for that.'

'James! He will utterly disown me!'

'No hope of that,' he said. 'I daresay he may hold off for a few months to save his dignity, but it won't be for long. You, my loved one, little though it interests you, are about to become an extremely wealthy woman. You are also going to become the mistress of Danescourt.'

'Danescourt? But doesn't that belong to Stacy?'

'No, it belongs to me: I've bought it from him. I am taking you there tonight. It's in a deplorable state, but I threw an army into it last week to put it into some kind of order, and told our old housekeeper to hire some servants, so I hope you won't find it too uncomfortable. We won't stay there above a day or two, but I want you to inspect it, and decide what you wish for in the way of curtains and things of that nature. Where would you like to go after that?'

She said helplessly: 'I don't know. Oh, this is too fantastic! For heaven's sake, take me home! Only think of poor Selina!'

'Nothing would prevail upon me to take you home. You may write a note to poor Selina from Chippenham: I'll send it by a post-boy: but you are not going to see her again until you are firmly riveted, my girl, and it is too late for her to cling round your neck!'

'But what will she *do*?' said Abby distractedly.

'She will in all probability find a substitute for you in Miss Butterbank,' he replied calmly. 'What's more, they will deal extremely together. Fanny, I daresay, will go to your sister in London. By the by, do you wish for a London house?'

'No, of course I don't! Miles, do you realise that I haven't even a *toothbrush*?'

'Do you know, I believe you're right?' he said. 'And I thought I had remembered everything! What a fortunate thing that you mentioned it! We must buy one in Reading.'

'Have you had the audacity to – Oh, you are too abominable! I won't marry you! I will *not*! Take me home!'

Mr Miles Calverleigh brought his horses to a halt at the side of the road, and turned, and smiled at her. 'Tell me that that is what, *in your heart*, you want me to do, and I will!'

She looked into his eyes, and what she saw in them made her pulses race.

'Tell me, Abby!'

'You may be able to abduct me,' said Abby, with dignity, 'but you can't force me to tell lies! . . . *Miles!* there's a coach coming, and a man staring at us over the hedge! For heaven's sake – !'

The
Grand Sophy

Georgette Heyer

arrow books

One

The butler, recognizing her ladyship's only surviving brother at a glance, as he afterwards informed his less percipient subordinates, favoured Sir Horace with a low bow, and took it upon himself to say that my lady, although not at home to less nearly-connected persons, would be happy to see him. Sir Horace, unimpressed by this condescension, handed his caped-greatcoat to one footman, his hat and cane to the other, tossed his gloves on to the marble-topped table, and said that he had no doubt of that, and how was Dassett keeping these days? The butler, torn between gratification at having his name remembered and disapproval of Sir Horace's free and easy ways, said that he was as well as could be expected, and happy (if he might venture to say so) to see Sir Horace looking not a day older than when he had last had the pleasure of announcing him to her ladyship. He then led the way, in a very stately manner, up the imposing stairway to the Blue Saloon, where Lady Ombersley was dozing gently on a sofa by the fire, a Paisley shawl spread over her feet, and her cap decidedly askew. Mr Dassett, observing these details, coughed, and made his announcement in commanding accents: 'Sir Horace Stanton-Lacy, my lady!'

Lady Ombersley awoke with a start, stared for an uncomprehending moment, made an ineffective clutch at her cap, and uttered a faint shriek. 'Horace!'

'Hallo, Lizzie, how are you?' said Sir Horace, walking across the room, and bestowing an invigorating buffet upon her shoulder.

'Good heavens, what a fright you gave me!' exclaimed her ladyship, uncorking the vinaigrette which was never out of her reach.

The butler, having tolerantly observed these transports, closed the door upon the reunited brother and sister, and went away to disclose to his underlings that Sir Horace was a gentleman as lived much abroad, being, as he was informed, employed by the Government on Diplomatic Business too delicate for their understanding.

The diplomatist, meanwhile, warming his coat-tails by the fire, refreshed himself with a pinch of snuff and told his sister that she was putting on weight. 'Not growing any younger, either of us,' he added handsomely. 'Not but what I can give you five years, Lizzie, unless my memory's at fault, which I don't think it is.'

There was a large gilded mirror on the wall opposite to the fireplace, and as he spoke Sir Horace allowed his gaze to rest upon his own image, not in a conceited spirit, but with critical approval. His forty-five years had treated him kindly. If his outline had thickened a little, his height, which was well above six foot, made a slight portliness negligible. He was a very fine figure of a man, and had, besides a large and well-proportioned frame, a handsome countenance, topped by luxuriant brown locks as yet unmarred by silver streaks. He was always dressed with elegance, but was by far too wise a man to adopt such extravagances of fashion as could only show up the imperfections of a middle-aged figure. 'Take a look at poor Prinny!' said Sir Horace to less discriminating cronies. 'He's a lesson to us all!'

His sister accepted the implied criticism unresentfully. Twenty-seven years of wedlock had left their mark upon her; and the dutiful presentation to her erratic and far from grateful spouse of eight pledges of her affection had long since destroyed any pretensions to beauty in her. Her health was indifferent, her disposition compliant, and she was fond of saying that when one was a grandmother it was time to be done with thinking of one's appearance.

2

'How's Ombersley?' asked Sir Horace, with more civility than interest.

'He feels his gout a little, but considering everything he is remarkably well,' she responded.

Sir Horace took a mere figure of speech in an undesirably literal spirit, saying with a nod: 'Always did drink too much. Still, he must be going on for sixty now, and I don't suppose you have so much of the other trouble, do you?'

'No, no!' said his sister hastily. Lord Ombersley's infidelities, though mortifying when conducted, as they too often were, in the full glare of publicity, had never greatly troubled her, but she had no desire to discuss them with her outspoken relative, and gave the conversation an abrupt turn by asking where he had come from.

'Lisbon,' he replied, taking another pinch of snuff.

Lady Ombersley was vaguely surprised. It was now two years since the close of the long Peninsular War, and she rather thought that, when last heard of, Sir Horace had been in Vienna, no doubt taking mysterious part in the Congress, which had been so rudely interrupted by the escape of that dreadful Monster from Elba. 'Oh!' she said, a little blankly. 'Of course, you have a house there! I was forgetting! And how is dear Sophia?'

'As a matter of fact,' said Sir Horace, shutting his snuff-box, and restoring it to his pocket, 'it's about Sophy that I've come to see you.'

Sir Horace had been a widower for fifteen years, during which period he had neither requested his sister's help in rearing his daughter nor paid the least heed to her unsolicited advice, but at these words an uneasy feeling stole over her. She said: 'Yes, Horace? Dear little Sophia! It must be four years or more since I saw her. How old is she now? I suppose she must be almost out?'

'Been out for years,' responded Sir Horace. 'Never anything else really. She's twenty.'

'Twenty!' exclaimed Lady Ombersley. She applied her mind to arithmetic, and said: 'Yes, she must be, for my own Cecilia is

3

just turned nineteen, and I remember that your Sophia was born almost a year before. Dear me, yes! Poor Marianne! What a lovely creatures she was, to be sure!'

With a slight effort Sir Horace conjured up the vision of his dead wife. 'Yes, so she was,' he agreed. 'One forgets, you know. Sophy's not much like her: favours me!'

'I know what a comfort she must have been to you,' sighed Lady Ombersley. 'And I'm sure, dear Horace, that nothing could be more affecting than your devotion to the child!'

'I wasn't in the least devoted,' interrupted Sir Horace. 'I shouldn't have kept her with me if she'd been troublesome. Never was: good little thing, Sophy!'

'Yes, my dear, no doubt, but to be dragging a little girl all over Spain and Portugal, when she would have been far better in a select school –'

'Not she! She'd have learnt to be missish,' said Sir Horace cynically. 'Besides, no use to prose to me now on that head: it's too late! The thing is, Lizzie, I'm in something of a fix. I want you to take care of Sophy while I'm in South America.'

'South America?' gasped Lady Ombersley.

'Brazil. I don't expect to be away very long, but I can't take my little Sophy, and I can't leave her with Tilly, because Tilly's dead. Died in Vienna, couple of years ago. A devilish inconvenient thing to do, but I daresay she didn't mean it.'

'Tilly?' said Lady Ombersley, all at sea.

'Lord, Elizabeth, don't keep on repeating everything I say! Shocking bad habit! Miss Tillingham, Sophy's governess!'

'Good heavens! Do you mean to tell me that the child has no governess now?'

'Of course she has not! She don't need a governess. I always found plenty of chaperons for her when we were in Paris, and in Lisbon it don't signify. But I can't leave her alone in England.'

'Indeed, I should think not! But, my dearest Horace, though I would do anything to oblige you, I am not quite sure –'

'Nonsense!' said Sir Horace bracingly. 'She'll be a nice

4

companion for your girl – what's her name? Cecilia? Dear little soul, you know: not an ounce of vice in her!'

This fatherly tribute made his sister blink, and utter a faint protest. Sir Horace paid no heed to it. 'What's more, she won't cause you any trouble,' he said. 'She has her head well on her shoulders, my Sophy. I never worry about her.'

An intimate knowledge of her brother's character made it perfectly possible for Lady Ombersley to believe this, but since she herself was blessed with much the same easy-going temperament, no acid comment even rose to her lips. 'I am sure she must be a dear girl,' she said. 'But, you see, Horace –'

'And another thing is that it's time we were thinking of a husband for her,' pursued Sir Horace, seating himself in a chair on the opposite side of the fireplace. 'I knew I could depend on you. Dash it, you're her aunt! My only sister, too.'

'I should be only too happy to bring her out,' said Lady Ombersley wistfully. 'But the thing is I don't think – I am rather afraid – You see, what with the really dreadful expense of presenting Cecilia last year, and dearest Maria's wedding only a little time before that, and Hubert's going up to Oxford, not to mention the fees at Eton for poor Theodore –'

'If it's expense that bothers you, Lizzie, you needn't give it a thought, for I'll stand the nonsense. You won't have to present her at Court: I'll attend to all that when I come home, and if you don't want to be put to the trouble of it then I can find some other lady to do it. What I want at this present is for her to go about with her cousins, meet the right set of people – you know the style of thing!'

'Of course I know, and as for *trouble* it would be no such thing! But I can't help feeling that perhaps – perhaps it would not do! We do not entertain very much.'

'Well, with a pack of girls on your hands you ought to,' said Sir Horace bluntly.

'But, Horace, I have not got a pack of girls on my hands!' protested Lady Ombersley. 'Selina is only sixteen, and Gertrude and Amabel are barely out of the nursery!'

5

'I see what it is,' said Sir Horace indulgently. 'You're afraid she may take the shine out of Cecilia. No, no, my dear! My little Sophy's no beauty. She's well enough – in fact, I daresay you'll think she's a very pretty girl – but Cecilia's something quite out of the common way. Remember thinking so when I saw her last year. I was surprised, for you were never above the average yourself, Lizzie, while I was always thought Ombersley a plain-looking fellow.'

His sister accepted these strictures meekly, but was quite distressed that he should suppose her capable of harbouring such unhandsome thoughts about her niece. 'And even if I was so odious, there is no longer the least need for such notions,' she added. 'Nothing has as yet been announced, Horace, but I don't scruple to tell you that Cecilia is about to contract a very eligible alliance.'

'That's good,' said Sir Horace. 'You'll have leisure to look about you for a husband for Sophy. You won't have any difficulty: she's a taking little thing, and she'll have a snug fortune one of these days, besides what her mother left her. No need to be afraid of her marrying to disoblige us, either: she's a sensible girl, and she's been about the world enough to be well up to snuff. Whom have you got for Cecilia?'

'Lord Charlbury has asked Ombersley's permission to address her,' said his sister, swelling a little with pride.

'Charlbury, eh,' said Sir Horace. 'Very well indeed, Elizabeth! I must say, I didn't think you'd catch much of a prize, because looks aren't everything, and from the way Ombersley was running through his fortune when I last saw him –'

'Lord Charlbury,' said Lady Ombersley a little stiffly, 'is an extremely wealthy man, and, I know, has no such vulgar consideration in mind. Indeed, he told me himself that it was a case of love at first sight with him!'

'Capital!' said Sir Horace. 'I should suppose him to have been hanging out for a wife for some time – thirty at least, ain't he? – but if he has a veritable *tendre* for the girl, so much the better! It should fix his interest with her.'

6

'Yes,' agreed Lady Ombersley. 'And I am persuaded they will suit very well. He is everything that is amiable and obliging, his manners most gentleman-like, his understanding decidedly superior, and his person such as must please.'

Sir Horace, who was not much interested in his niece's affairs, said: 'Well, well, he is plainly a paragon, and we must allow Cecilia to think herself fortunate to be forming such a connection! I hope you may manage as prettily for Sophy!'

'Indeed, I wish I might!' she responded, sighing. 'Only it is an awkward moment, because – The thing is, you see, that I am afraid Charles may not quite like it!'

Sir Horace frowned in an effort of memory. 'I thought his name was Bernard. Why shouldn't he like it?'

'I am not speaking of Ombersley, Horace. You must remember Charles!'

'If you're talking about the eldest boy of yours, of course I remember him! But why has he to say anything, and why the devil should he object to my Sophy!'

'Oh, no, not to her! I am sure he could not do so! But I fear he may not like it if we are to be plunged into gaiety just now! I daresay you may not have seen the announcement of his own approaching marriage, but I should tell you that he has contracted an engagement to Miss Wraxton.'

'What, not old Brinklow's daughter? Upon my word, Lizzie, you have been busy to some purpose! Never knew you had so much sense! Eligible, indeed! You are to be congratulated!'

'Yes,' said Lady Ombersley. 'Oh, yes! Miss Wraxton is a most superior girl. I am sure she has a thousand excellent qualities. A most well-informed mind, and principles such as must command respect.'

'She sounds to me like a dead bore,' said Sir Horace frankly.

'Charles,' said Lady Ombersley, staring mournfully into the fire, 'does not care for very lively girls, or – or for any extravagant folly. I own, I could wish Miss Wraxton had rather more *vivacity* – but you are not to regard that, Horace, for I had never the least inclination towards being a blue-stocking myself,

7

and in these days, when so many young females are wild to a fault, it is gratifying to find one who – Charles thinks Miss Wraxton's air of grave reflection very becoming!' she ended, in rather a hurry.

'You know, Lizzie, it's a queer thing that any son of yours and Ombersley's should have grown into such a dull stick,' remarked Sir Horace dispassionately. 'I suppose you didn't play Ombersley false, did you?'

'Horace!'

'No, I know you didn't! No need to fly into a pucker! Not with your eldest: you know better than that! Still, it *is* an odd circumstance: often thought so! He can marry his blue-stocking, and welcome, for anything I care, but none of this explains why you should be caring a fig for what he likes or don't like!'

Lady Ombersley transferred her gaze from the glowing coals to his face. 'You do not perfectly understand, Horace.'

'That's what I said!' he retorted.

'Yes, but – Horace, Matthew Rivenhall left his whole fortune to Charles!'

Sir Horace was generally accounted an astute man, but he appeared to find it difficult correctly to assimilate this information. He stared fixedly at his sister for a moment or two, and then said: 'You don't mean that old uncle of Ombersley's?'

'Yes, I do.'

'The Nabob?'

Lady Ombersley nodded, but her brother was still not satisfied. 'Fellow who made a fortune in India?'

'Yes, and we always thought – but he said Charles was the only Rivenhall other than himself who had the least grain of sense, and he left him everything, Horace! *Everything!*'

'Good God!'

This ejaculation seemed to appear to Lady Ombersley as fitting, for she nodded again, looking at her brother in a woebegone fashion, and twisting the fringe of her shawl between her fingers.

'So it is Charles who calls the tune!' said Sir Horace.

8

'No one could have been more generous,' said Lady Ombersley unhappily. 'We cannot but be sensible of it.'

'Damn his impudence!' said Sir Horace, himself a father. 'What's he done?'

'Well, Horace, you might not know it, because you are always abroad, but poor Ombersley had a great many debts.'

'Everyone knows that! Never knew him when he wasn't under a cloud! You're not going to tell me the boy was fool enough to settle 'em?'

'But, Horace, someone had to settle them!' she protested. 'You can have no notion how difficult things were becoming! And with the younger boys to establish creditably, and the dear girls – it is no wonder that Charles should be so anxious that Cecilia should make a good match!'

'Providing for the whole pack, is he? More fool he! What about the mortgages? If the greater part of Ombersley's inheritance had not been entailed he would have gambled the whole away long since!'

'I do not properly understand entails,' said his sister, 'but I am afraid that Charles did not behave just as he should over it. Ombersley was very much displeased – though I shall always say that to call one's first-born a serpent's tooth is to use quite unbecoming language! It seems that when Charles came of age he might have made everything quite easy for his poor papa, if only he had been in the least degree obliging! But nothing would prevail upon him to agree to break the entail, so all was at a standstill, and one cannot blame Ombersley for being vexed! And then that odious old man died –'

'When?' demanded Sir Horace. 'How comes it about that I never heard a word of this before today?'

'It was rather more than two years ago, and –'

'That accounts for it, then: I was devilish busy, dealing with Angoulême, and all that set. Must have happened at the time of Toulouse, I dare swear. But when I saw you last year you never spoke a word, Lizzie!'

She was stung by the injustice to this, and said indignantly: 'I

9

am sure I don't know how I should have been thinking of such paltry things, with that Monster at large, and the Champs de Mars, and the banks suspending payment, and heaven knows what beside! And you coming over from Brussels without a word of warning, and sitting with me a bare twenty minutes! My head was in a whirl, and if I answered you to the point it is more than I would have bargained for!'

Sir Horace, disregarding this irrelevancy, said, with what for him was strong feeling: 'Outrageous! I don't say Ombersley's not a shocking loose-screw, because there's no sense in wrapping plain facts up in clean linen, but to be cutting a man out of one's will and setting up his son to lord it over him – which I'll be bound he does!'

'No, no!' expostulated Lady Ombersley feebly. 'Charles is fully sensible of what is due to his father! It is not that he is ever lacking in respect, I do assure you! Only poor Ombersley cannot but feel it a little, now that Charles has taken everything into his own hands.'

'A pretty state of affairs!'

'Yes, but one comfort is that it is not generally known. And I cannot deny that in some ways it is by far more pleasant. You would scarcely credit it, Horace, but I do believe there is not an unpaid bill in the house!' A moment's reflection caused her to modify this statement. 'At least, I cannot answer for Ombersley, but all those dreadful household accounts, which Eckington – you remember our good Eckington, Ombersley's agent? – used to pull such a face over; and the fees at Eton and Oxford – *everything*, my dear brother, Charles takes care of!'

'You aren't going to tell me Charles is fool enough to fritter away old Matt Rivenhall's fortune paying all the expenses of this barrack of a house!' exclaimed Sir Horace.

'No. Oh, no! I have not the least head for business, so it is of no use to ask me to explain it to you, but I believe that Charles persuaded his father to – to allow him to administer the estate.'

'Blackmailed him into it, more like!' said Sir Horace grimly.

'Rare times we live in! Mind, I see the boy's point, Lizzie, but, by God, I'm sorry for you!'

'Oh, pray believe it's no such thing!' cried Lady Ombersley, distressed. 'I did not wish you to think – to give you cause to suppose that Charles is ever disagreeable, for indeed he is not, except when he is put out of temper, and one must own that he has a great deal to try his patience! Which is why I can't but feel, dear Horace, that if he does not like me to take charge of Sophia for you, I ought not to tease him!'

'Fiddlesticks!' said Sir Horace. 'And why shouldn't he like it?'

'We – we decided not to give any parties this season, beyond what must be thought necessary. It is a most unfortunate circumstance that Charles's wedding has had to be postponed, on account of a bereavement Miss Wraxton has suffered. One of Lady Brinklow's sisters, and they will not be out of black gloves for six months. You must know that the Brinklows are very particular in all matters of correct conduct. Eugenia goes only to very quiet parties, and – and naturally one must expect Charles to partake of her sentiments!'

'Lord, Elizabeth, a man don't have to wear black gloves for the aunt of a female he ain't even married to!'

'Of course not, but Charles seemed to feel – and then there is Charlbury!'

'What the devil ails him!'

'Mumps,' replied Lady Ombersley tragically.

'He?' Sir Horace burst out laughing. 'Well, what a fellow he must be to have mumps when he should be getting married to Cecilia!'

'Really, Horace, I must say that I think that most unjust of you, for how could he help it? It is so mortifying for him! And, what is more, excessively unfortunate, because I don't doubt that had he been able to attach Cecilia – which I am sure he must have done, for nothing could be more amiable than his disposition, while his manners and address are just what they ought to be! But girls are so foolish, and take romantical notions into their heads, besides all kinds of encroaching fancies – however, I am happy to think that Cecilia is not one of those dreadful modern misses, and of course she will be guided by her parents! But no one can deny that nothing could be more ill-timed than Charlbury's mumps!'

Sir Horace, once more opening his snuff-box, regarded her with an amused and a sapient eye. 'And what is Miss Cecilia's particular encroaching fancy?' he enquired.

Lady Ombersley knew that her eldest son would have counselled her to preserve a discreet silence; but the impulse to unburden herself to her brother was too strong to be denied. She said: 'Well, you will not repeat it, I know, Horace, but the fact is that the silly child thinks she is in love with Augustus Fawnhope!'

'One of Lutterworth's boys?' asked Sir Horace. 'I don't think much of that for a match, I must say!'

'Good heavens, don't mention such a thing! The youngest son, too, with not the least expectation in the world! But he is a poet.'

'Very dangerous,' agreed Sir Horace. 'Don't think I ever saw the boy: what's he like?'

'Quite beautiful!' said Lady Ombersley, in despairing accents.

'What, in the style of Lord Byron? That fellow has a great deal to answer for!'

'No-no. I mean, he is as fair as Cecilia is herself, and he doesn't limp, and though his poems are very pretty, bound up in white vellum, they don't seem to *take* very well. I mean, not at all like Lord Byron's. It seems sadly unjust, for I believe it cost a great deal of money to have them printed, and he had to bear the whole – or, rather, Lady Lutterworth did, according to what I have heard.'

'Now I come to think of it,' said Sir Horace, 'I do know the boy. He was with Stuart, in Brussels last year. If you take my advice, you'll marry Cecilia off to Charlbury as quickly as you can!'

'Well, and so I would, if only – that is to say, of course I would not, if I thought she held him in aversion! And you must see, Horace, that it is quite out of my power to do anything of the sort when he is in bed with the mumps!'

Sir Horace shook his head. 'She will marry the poet.'

'Do not say so! But Charles thinks that I should do wisely not to take her where she is bound to meet the young man, which is another reason why we are living in a quiet style for the present. It is of all things the most awkward! Indeed, sometimes I feel that it would be much easier if the wretched creature were quite ineligible – a fortune-hunter, or a merchant's son, or something of that nature! One could then forbid him the house, and forbid Cecilia to stand up with him at balls, only it would not be in the least necessary for we should never meet him in society. But naturally one meets the Fawnhopes everywhere! Nothing could be more provoking! And although I am sure Charles's manner towards him is most repellent, even he acknowledges the impropriety of being so repulsive to him as to offend his family. Almeria Lutterworth is one of my oldest friends!'

Sir Horace, who was already bored with the subject, yawned, and said lazily: 'I daresay there is no occasion for you to be on the fidgets. The Fawnhopes are all as poor as Church mice, and very likely Lady Lutterworth desires the match as little as you do.'

'Nothing of the sort!' she replied, quite crossly. 'She is foolish beyond permission, Horace! Whatever Augustus wants he must have! She has given me the most unmistakable hints, so that I scarcely knew where to look, much less what to say, except that Lord Charlbury had requested our leave to address Cecilia, and I believed her to be – well, not indifferent to him! It never entered my head that Augustus was so lost to all sense of propriety as to apply to Cecilia without first approaching Ombersley, yet that is precisely what he has done!'

'Oh, well!' said Sir Horace. 'If she has such a fancy for him, you had better let her take him. It's not as though she would be marrying beneath her, and if she chooses to be the wife of a penniless younger son it is quite her own affair.'

'You would not say so if it were Sophia!' said his sister.

'Sophy's not such a fool.'

'Cecilia is not a fool either,' declared Lady Ombersley,

affronted. 'If you have seen Augustus you can not wonder at her! No one could help feeling a decided partiality for him! I own, I did myself. But Charles is quite right, as I was soon brought to acknowledge: it would not answer!'

'Ah, well, when she has her cousin to keep her company it will divert her, and very likely give her thoughts another direction,' said Sir Horace consolingly.

Lady Ombersley appeared to be much struck by this suggestion. Her face brightened; she said: 'I wonder if it might be so? She is a little shy, you must know, and does not make friends easily, and since her dear friend, Miss Friston, was married, and has gone to live in the Midlands, there is really no young female with whom she is upon terms of intimacy. Now, if we had dear Sophia to stay with us . . .' She broke off, obviously turning plans over in her mind. She was still engaged on this exercise when the door opened, and her eldest son entered the saloon.

The Honourable Charles Rivenhall was twenty-six years old, but a rather harsh-featured countenance, coupled with a manner that combined assurance with a good deal of reserve, made him give the impression of being some years older. He was a tall, powerfully-built young man, who looked as though he would have been better pleased to have been striding over his father's acres than exchanging civilities in his mother's sitting-room. He nearly always wore riding-dress in preference to the more fashionable pantaloons and Hessians; tied his cravat in the plainest of styles; would permit only a modicum of starch to stiffen his very moderate shirt-points; wholly disdained such fopperies as seals, fobs, or quizzing-glasses; and offended his tailor by insisting on having his coats cut so that he could shrug himself into them without the assistance of his valet. He had been heard to express the hope that heaven would forbid he should ever be mistaken for one of the dandy-set; but, as his friend, Mr Cyprian Wychbold, kindly pointed out to him, there was not the least need for heavenly intervention in the matter. The dandies, said Mr Wychbold with some severity, were distinguished as much for their polished address as for their exquisite apparel, and were in general an amiable set of men, whose polite manners and winning graces made them acceptable in any drawing-room. As Mr Rivenhall's notion of making himself agreeable in company was to treat with cold civility anyone for whom he felt no particular liking; and his graces – far from winning – included a trick of staring out of countenance those whose pretensions he deprecated, and of uttering blighting comments, which put an abrupt end to social intercourse, he stood in far greater danger (Mr Wychbold said) of being mistaken for a Yahoo.

As he shut the door behind him, his mother looked up, started slightly, and said with a nervous inflection which annoyed her brother: 'Oh! Charles! Only fancy! Your Uncle Horace!'

'So Dassett informed me,' responded Mr Rivenhall. 'How do you do, sir?'

He shook hands with his uncle, drew up a chair, and sat down, civilly engaging Sir Horace in conversation. His mother, fidgeting first with the fringe of her shawl and then with her handkerchief, presently broke in on this interchange to say: 'Charles, you remember Sophia? Your little cousin?'

Mr Rivenhall did not present the appearance of one who remembered his little cousin, but he said in his cool way: 'Certainly. I hope she is well, sir?'

'Never had a day's illness in her life, barring the measles,' said Sir Horace. 'You'll see her for yourself soon; your mother is going to take charge of her while I'm in Brazil.'

It was plain that this way of breaking the news did not recommend itself to Lady Ombersley, who at once hurried into speech. 'Well, of course it is not quite decided yet, though I am sure there is nothing I should like better than to have my dear brother's daughter to stay with me. I was thinking, too, Charles, that it would be so pleasant for Cecilia: Sophia and she are nearly the same age, you know.'

'Brazil?' said Mr Rivenhall. 'That should be very interesting, I daresay. Do you make a long stay there, sir?'

'Oh, no!' replied Sir Horace vaguely. 'Probably not. It will depend upon circumstance. I have been telling your mother that

15

I shall be much in her debt if she can find an eligible husband for my Sophy. It's time she was married, and your mother seems, from what I hear, to be quite a dab in that line. I understand I have to offer you my felicitations, my boy?'

'Thank you: yes,' said Mr Rivenhall, with a slight bow.

'If you should not dislike it, Charles, I own I should be very happy to have Sophia,' said Lady Ombersley placatingly.

He cast her an impatient glance, and replied: 'I beg you will do precisely as you wish, ma'am. I cannot conceive what business it is of mine.'

'Of course I have explained to your uncle that we lead very quiet lives.'

'She won't give a fig for that,' said Sir Horace comfortably. 'She's a good little thing: never at a loss for something to occupy herself with. Just as happy in a Spanish village as in Vienna, or Brussels.'

At this, Lady Ombersley sat up with a jerk. 'Do not tell me you dragged the child to Brussels last year!'

'Of course she was in Brussels! Where the devil should she have been?' replied Sir Horace testily. 'You wouldn't have had me leave her in Vienna, would you? Besides, she enjoyed it. We met a great many old friends there.'

'The danger!'

'Oh, pooh! nonsense! Precious little of that with Wellington in command!'

'When, sir, may we have the pleasure of expecting my cousin?' interposed Mr Rivenhall. 'We must hope that she will not find life in London too humdrum after the superior excitement of the Continent.'

'Not she!' said Sir Horace. 'I never knew Sophy when she wasn't always busy with some ploy or another. Give her her head! I always do, and she never comes to any harm. Don't quite know when she'll be with you. She's bound to want to see the last of me, but she'll post up to London as soon as I've sailed.'

'Post up to London as soon as – Horace, surely you will bring her to me!' gasped his sister, quite scandalized. 'A girl of her age, travelling alone! I never heard of such a thing!'

'Won't be alone. She'll have her maid with her – dragon of a woman, she is: journeyed all over Europe with us! – and John Potton as well.' He caught sight of his nephew's raised brows, and felt himself impelled to add: 'Groom – courier – general factotum! Looked after Sophy since she was a baby.' He drew out his watch, and consulted it. 'Well, now that we've settled everything, I must be off, Lizzie. I shall rely upon you to take care of Sophy, and look about your for a match. It's important, because – but I've no time to explain that now! She'll tell you all about it, I expect.'

'But, Horace, we have not settled everything!' protested his sister. 'And Ombersley will be disappointed not to see you! I hoped you would dine with us!'

'No, I can't do that,' he replied. 'I'm dining at Carlton House. You may give my respects to Ombersley: daresay I shall see him again one of these days!'

He then kissed her in a perfunctory style, bestowed another of his hearty pats upon her shoulder, and took himself off, followed by his nephew. 'Just as if I had nothing more to wish for!' Lady Ombersley said indignantly, when Charles came back into the room. 'And I have not the least notion when that child is to come to me!'

'It doesn't signify,' said Charles, with an indifference she found exasperating. 'You will give orders for a room to be prepared for her, I suppose, and she may come when she pleases. It's to be hoped Cecilia likes her, since I imagine she will be obliged to see the most of her.'

'Poor little thing!' sighed Lady Ombersley. 'I declare I quite long to mother her, Charles! What a strange, lonely life she must lead!'

'Strange certainly; hardly lonely, if she has been acting hostess for my uncle. I must suppose that she has had some elder lady to live with her: a governess, or some such thing.'

'Indeed, one would think it must have been so, but your uncle distinctly told me that the governess died when they were in Vienna! I do not like to say such a thing of my only brother, but really it seems as though Horace is quite unfit to have the care of a daughter!'

'Extremely unfit,' he said dryly. 'I trust you will not have cause to regret your kindness, Mama.'

'Oh, no, I am sure I shall not!' she said. 'Your uncle spoke of her in such a way that gave me the greatest desire to welcome her! Poor child, I fear she has not been used to have her wishes or her comfort much considered! I could almost have been angry with Horace when he would keep on telling me that she is a good little thing, and had never been a worry to him! I daresay he has never allowed anyone to be a worry to him, for a more selfish man I believe you could hardly meet! Sophia must have her poor mother's sweet disposition: I have no doubt of her being a charming companion for Cecilia.'

'I hope so,' said Charles. 'And that reminds me, Mama! I have just intercepted another of that puppy's floral offerings to my sister. This billet was attached to it.'

Lady Ombersley took the proffered missive, and looked at it in dismay. 'What shall I do with it?' she asked.

'Put it on the fire,' he recommended.

'Oh, no, I could not, Charles! It might be quite unexceptionable! Besides – why, it might even contain a message from his mother for me!'

'Highly unlikely, but if you think that, you had better read it.'

'Of course, I know it is my duty to do so,' she agreed unhappily.

He looked rather contemptuous, but said nothing, and after a moment's indecision she broke the seal, and spread open the single sheet. 'Oh, dear, it is a poem!' she announced. 'I must say, it is very pretty! Listen, Charles! *Nymph, when thy mild cerulean gaze Upon my restless spirit casts it beam –*'

'I thank you, I have no taste for verse!' interrupted Mr Rivenhall harshly. 'Put it on the fire, ma'am, and tell Cecilia she is not to be receiving letters without your sanction!'

'Yes, but do you think I should burn it, Charles? Only think if this were the only copy of the poem! Perhaps he wants to have it printed!'

'He is not going to print such stuff about any sister of mine!' said Mr Rivenhall grimly, holding out an imperative hand.

Lady Ombersley, always overborne by a stronger will, was just about to give the paper to him when a trembling voice from the doorway arrested her: 'Mama! Do not!'

Two

Lady Ombersley's hand dropped; Mr Rivenhall turned sharply, a frown on his brow. His sister, casting him a look of burning reproach, ran across the room to her mother, and said: 'Give it to me, Mama! What right has Charles to burn my letters?'

Lady Ombersley looked helplessly at her son, but he said nothing. Cecilia twitched the open sheet of paper from her mother's fingers, and clasped it to her palpitating bosom. This did goad Mr Rivenhall into speech. 'For God's sake, Cecilia, let us have no play-acting!' he said.

'How dared you read my letter?' she retorted.

'I did not read your letter! I gave it to Mama, and you will scarcely say that she had no right to read it!'

Her soft blue eyes swam with tears; she said in a low voice: 'It is all your fault! Mama would never – I hate you, Charles! I hate you!'

He shrugged, and turned away. Lady Ombersley said feebly: 'You should not talk so, Cecilia! You know it is quite improper in you to be receiving letters without my knowledge! I do not know what your Papa would say if he heard of it.'

'Papa!' exclaimed Cecilia scornfully. 'No! It is Charles who delights in making me unhappy!'

He glanced over his shoulder at her. 'It would be useless, I collect, to say that my earnest wish is that you should *not* be made unhappy!'

She returned no answer, but folded the letter with shaking

20

hands, and bestowed it in her bosom, throwing a defiant look at him as she did so. It was met with one of contempt; Mr Rivenhall propped his shoulders against the mantelshelf, dug his hands into his breeches' pockets, and waited sardonically for what she might say next.

She dried her eyes instead, catching her breath on little sobs. She was a very lovely girl, with pale golden locks arranged in ringlets about an exquisitely shaped face, whose delicate complexion was at the moment heightened, not unbecomingly, by an angry flush. In general, her expression was one of sweet pensiveness, but the agitation of the moment had kindled a martial spark in her eyes, and she was gripping her underlip between her teeth in a way that made her look quite vicious. Her brother, cynically observing this, said that she should make a practice of losing her temper, since it improved her, lending animation to a countenance well enough in its way but a trifle insipid.

This unkind remark left Cecilia unmoved. She could hardly fail to know that she was much admired, but she was a very modest girl, quite unappreciative of her own beauty, and would much have preferred to have been fashionably dark. She sighed, released her lip, and sat down on a low chair beside her Mama's sofa, saying in a more moderate tone: 'You cannot deny, Charles, that it is your doing that Mama has taken this – this unaccountable dislike to Augustus!'

'Now, there,' said Lady Ombersley earnestly, 'you are at fault, dearest, for I do not dislike him at all! Only I cannot think him an eligible husband!'

'I don't care for that!' declared Cecilia. 'He is the only man for whom I could ever feel that degree of attachment which – in short, I beg you will abandon any notion you may have that I could ever entertain Lord Charlbury's extremely flattering proposal, for I never shall!'

Lady Ombersley uttered a distressful but incoherent protest; Mr Rivenhall said in his prosaic way: 'Yet you were not, I fancy, so much averse from Charlbury's proposal when it was first told you.'

Cecilia turned her lambent gaze upon him, and answered: 'I had not then met Augustus.'

Lady Ombersley appeared to be a good deal struck by the logic of this pronouncement, but her son was less impressionable. He said: 'Don't waste these high flights on me, I beg of you! You have been acquainted with young Fawnhope any time these nineteen years!'

'It was not the same,' said Cecilia simply.

'That,' said Lady Ombersley, in a judicial way, 'is perfectly true, Charles. I am sure he was the most ordinary little boy, and when he was up at Oxford he had the most dreadful spots, so that no one would have supposed he would have grown into such an excessively handsome young man! But the time he spent in Brussels with Sir Charles Stuart improved him out of all knowledge! I own, I never should have known him for the same man!'

'I have sometimes wondered,' retorted Mr Rivenhall, 'whether Sir Charles will ever be the same man again either! How Lady Lutterworth can have reconciled it with her conscience to have foisted upon a public man such a nincompoop to be his secretary I must leave it to herself to decide! All *we* are privileged to know is that your precious Augustus no longer fills that office! Or any other!' he added trenchantly.

'Augustus,' said Cecilia loftily, 'is a poet. He is quite unfitted for the – the humdrum business of an ambassador's secretary.'

'I do not deny it,' said Mr Rivenhall. 'He is equally unfitted to support a wife, my dear sister. Do not imagine that *I* will frank you in this folly, for I tell you now I will not! And do not delude yourself into believing that you will obtain my father's consent to this most imprudent match, for while I have anything to say you will not!'

'I know well that it is only you who have anything to say in this house!' cried Cecilia, large tear-drops welling over her eyelids. 'I hope that when you have driven me to desperation you may be satisfied!'

From the tightening of the muscles about his mouth it was to be seen that Mr Rivenhall was making a praise-worthy effort to keep his none too amiable temper in check. His mother glanced anxiously up at him, but the voice in which he answered Cecilia was almost alarmingly even. 'Will you, my dear sister, have the goodness to reserve these Cheltenham tragedies for some moment when I am not within hearing? And before you carry Mama away upon the tide of all this rodomontade, may I be permitted to remind you that so far from being forced into a unwelcome marriage you expressed your willingness to listen to what you have yourself described as Lord Charlbury's very flattering offer?'

Lady Ombersley leaned forward to take one of Cecilia's hands in hers, and to squeeze it compassionately. 'Well, you know, my dearest love, that is quite true!' she said. 'Indeed, I thought you liked him excessively! You must not imagine that Papa or I have the least notion of compelling you to marry anyone whom you hold in aversion, for I am sure that such a thing would be quite shocking! And Charles would not do so either, would you, dear Charles?'

'No, certainly not. But neither would I consent to her marriage with any such frippery fellow as Augustus Fawnhope!'

'Augustus,' announced Cecilia, putting up her chin, 'will be remembered long after you have sunk into oblivion!'

'By his creditors? I don't doubt it. Will that compensate you for a lifetime spent in dodging duns?'

Lady Ombersley could not repress a shudder. 'Alas, my love, it is too true! You cannot know the mortification – but we will not speak of that!'

'It was useless to speak to my sister of anything outside the covers of a novel from the lending-library!' said Charles. 'I might have supposed that she would be thankful, in the state to which this family has been reduced, to have been on the point of contracting even a respectable alliance! But no! She is offered not a respectable but a brilliant match, and she chooses to behave like any Bath Miss, swooning and languishing over a poet! A *poet!* Good God, Mama, if the specimen of his talent which you were so ill-advised as to read me – but I have no patience to argue further on that head! If you cannot prevail upon her to conduct herself in a manner worthy of her breeding she had better be sent down to Ombersley, to rusticate for a while, and see if that will bring her to her senses!'

With this terrible threat he strode out of the room, leaving his sister to dissolve into tears, and his mother to recruit her strength through the medium of the vinaigrette.

Between sobs Cecilia animadverted for some moments on the cruelty of fate, which had saddled her with a brother who was as heartless as he was tyrannical, and parents who were totally unable to enter into her feelings. Lady Ombersley, though sympathetic in the main, could not allow this to pass. Without taking it upon herself to answer for her husband's sensibilities, she assured Cecilia that her own were extremely nice, making it perfectly possible for her to appreciate the anguish of a forbidden love.

'When I was a girl, dearest, something of the same nature happened to me,' she said, sighing. 'He was not a poet, of course, but I fancied myself very much in love with him. But it would not do, and in the end I was married to your Papa, which was thought to be a splendid match, for in those days he had scarcely began to run through his fortune, and –' She broke off, realizing that these reminiscences were infelicitous. 'In short, Cecilia, – and I should not be obliged to say this to you – persons of our order do not marry only to please themselves.'

Cecilia was silenced, and could only hang down her head, dabbing at her eyes with an already damp handkerchief. She knew herself to have been a good deal indulged through the fondness of one parent and the cheerful indifference of the other, and was well aware that in discovering her inclination before permitting Lord Charlbury to address his suit to her Lady Ombersley had shown more consideration for her than would have been approved of by the greater part of her contemporaries. Cecilia might read novels, but she knew that the spirited behaviour of her favourite heroines was not for her to imitate. She foresaw that she was doomed to spinsterhood; and this reflection was so melancholy that she drooped more than ever, and once more applied her handkerchief to her eyes.

'Only think how happy your sister is!' said Lady Ombersley, in a heartening tone. 'I am sure nothing could be more gratifying than to see her in her own home, with her dear baby, and James so attentive and obliging, and – and everything just what one would wish! I declare I did not believe that any love-match could have turned out better – not that I mean to say that Maria is not sincerely attached to James! But she had not met him above half a dozen times when he asked Papa's leave to speak to her, and her affections were not engaged. Naturally, she felt a strong degree of liking, or I should never – but Maria was such a good, pretty-behaved girl! She told me herself that she felt it to be her duty to accept such a respectable offer, with Papa in such difficulties, and four more of you to be provided for!'

'Mama, I hope I am not an unnatural daughter, but I had rather be dead than married to James!' declared Cecilia, raising her head. 'He thinks of nothing but hunting, and when they do have company in the evening, he goes to sleep, and *snores!*'

Daunted by this disclosure, Lady Ombersley could find nothing to say for a minute to two. Cecilia blew her nose, and added: 'And Lord Charlbury is even older than James!'

'Yes, but we do not know that he snores, my love,' Lady Ombersley pointed out. 'Indeed, we may be almost certain that he does not, for his manners are so very gentleman-like!'

'A man who would contract the mumps,' declared Cecilia, 'would do anything!'

Lady Ombersley saw nothing unreasonable in this pronouncement, nor was she surprised that his lordship's unromantic behaviour had given Cecilia a distaste for him. She had herself been sadly disappointed, for she had thought him a man of sense, certainly not one to be succumbing to childish ailments at inopportune moments. She could think of nothing to say to palliate his offence, and as Cecilia had apparently no further observations to make, silence reigned uneasily for a time. Cecilia presently broke it, asking rather listlessly whether it was true that her uncle had been in the house that afternoon. Glad of an excuse to talk of more cheerful matters, Lady Ombersley at once told her of the treat in store for her, and had the satisfaction of seeing the cloud lift a little from her daughter's brow. It was not difficult to enlist Cecilia's sympathies on behalf of her cousin: she could scarcely envisage a more horrid fate than to be sent to stay for an indefinite period amongst relatives who were almost strangers, and warmly promised to do all that lay in her power to make Sophia feel herself at home in Berkeley Square. She could conjure up no very clear recollection of her cousin, for it had been some years since they had met; and although she had sometimes thought that to travel about Europe must be exciting, she had also suspected that it might also be extremely uncomfortable, and readily agreed with Lady Ombersley that such an unconventional existence was scarcely an ideal preparation for a London début. The reflection that Sophia's arrival in Berkeley Square must mean some relaxation of the almost conventual life imposed upon the family by Charles's determination to economize sent her away to change her dress for dinner, in a far happier frame of mind.

Four of the family sat down at the huge table in the dining-room that evening, his lordship having decided to gratify his wife with one of his rare appearances at his own board. He was the only unconstrained member of the party, for he had a happy disposition which made it possible for him to remain oblivious to the most blatant signs of discontent in his companions. In the same spirit he contrived with amazing ease to be cheerful under the humiliation of being little more than his son's pensioner. He had the greatest dread of being obliged to face unpleasantness, so he never allowed himself to think about unpleasant things, which answered very well, and could be supported in times of really inescapable stress by his genius for persuading himself that any disagreeable necessity forced upon him by his own folly, or his son's overriding will, was the outcome of his own choice and wise decision. While Charles continued to render him the observances of filial respect he was able to forget that the reins of government had been wrenched out of his hands; and when, as sometimes happened, filial respect wore a little thin, at least these regrettable lapses did not last for long, and were not difficult for a man of his sanguine temperament to forget. He bore his son no malice, though he thought him a dull dog; and provided that the luck was running his way, and he was not expected to bear any distasteful part in the management of his young family, he was very well satisfied with his lot.

He could hardly have been unaware of the dissension at present raging in his household, for a request from his wife that he should exercise parental authority over Cecilia had driven him post-haste to Newmarket not a fortnight before. But neither his son's heavy frown, nor his daughter's reddened eyelids, occasioned the slightest comment from him. He appeared to derive no small satisfaction from partaking of a lengthy meal in the company of an anxious wife, an injured daughter, and a glowering son. He said: 'Well, upon my soul, this is very pleasant, to be dining *en famille* in this cosy way! You may tell your cook, Lady Ombersley, that I like this way of serving a duck. I declare I don't get as good at White's!' After that he recounted the latest piece of society gossip, and enquired affably how his children had spent the day.

'If you mean me, Papa,' said Cecilia, 'I have spent the day just as I spend every day. I shopped with Mama; I walked in the Park with my sisters and Miss Adderbury; and I practised my music.'

Her tone did not suggest that she had found these amusements exhilarating, but Lord Ombersley said Capital! and turned his attention to his wife. She told him of her brother's visit, and of his proposal that she should assume the charge of Sophia; and Lord Ombersley gave his gracious consent to the scheme, saying that nothing could be better, and congratulating his daughter upon her good luck in so unexpectedly acquiring a charming companion. Charles, who was irritated enough by all this bland insensibility to sympathize with his sister, said dampingly that they had as yet no reason to suppose that Sophia

27

would be in the least charming. But Lord Ombersley said that he entertained no doubts on that head, and added that they must all do their best to make their cousin's stay agreeable. After that, he asked Charles whether he intended to go to the races next day. Charles, who knew that the races referred to were run under the patronage of the Duke of York, and would entail, for that jovial personage's cronies, several evenings spent at Oatlands, playing whist for pound points, looked more forbidding than ever, and said that he was going down to Ombersley Park for a few days.

'To be sure you are!' agreed his father cheerfully. 'I was forgetting that business about the South Hanger. Yes, yes, I wish you will attend to that, my boy!'

'I will, sir,' responded Mr Rivenhall politely. He then glanced across the table at his sister, and asked: 'Do you care to accompany me, Cecilia? I am very willing to take you, if you should like it.'

She hesitated. This might be an olive-branch; on the other hand it might be a singularly futile attempt to wean her mind from thoughts of Mr Fawnhope. The reflection that Charles's absence from town might, with a little contrivance, make it possible for her to meet Mr Fawnhope decided the matter. She shrugged, and said: 'No, I thank you. I do not know what I should do in the country at this season.'

'Ride with me,' suggested Charles.

'I prefer to ride in the Park. If you desire company, I wonder you to do not invite the children to go with you: I am sure they would be delighted to oblige you.'

'As you please,' he replied indifferently.

Dinner at an end, Lord Ombersley withdrew from the family circle. Charles, who had no evening engagement, accompanied his mother and sister to the drawing-room, and, while Cecilia strummed idly at the piano, sat talking to his mother about Sophia's visit. Much to her relief, he seemed to be resigned to the necessity of holding at least one moderate party in Sophia's honour, but he strongly advised her against charging herself with the office of finding a suitable husband for her niece.

'Why my uncle, having allowed her to reach the age of – twenty, is it? – without bestirring himself in the matter,' he said, 'must suddenly take it into his head to persuade you to undertake the business, is a matter beyond my comprehension.'

'It does seem odd,' agreed Lady Ombersley. 'I daresay he might not have realized how time flies, you know. Twenty! Why, she is almost upon the shelf! I must say, Horace has been most remiss! There could be no difficulty, I am sure, for she must be quite an heiress! Even if she were a very plain girl, which I do not for moment suppose she can be, for you will allow Horace to be a handsome man, while poor dear Marianne was excessively pretty, though I don't expect that you can remember her – well, even if she *were* plain, it should be the easiest thing in the world to arrange a respectable match for her!'

'Very easy, but you would do well to leave it to my uncle, ma'am,' was all he would say.

At this moment, the school-room party came into the room, escorted by Miss Adderbury, a little gray mouse of a woman, who had originally been hired to take charge of Lady Ombersley's numerous offspring when Charles and Maria had been adjudged old enough to leave Nurse's jealous care. It might have been supposed that a twenty-year's residence in the household, under the aegis of a kind-hearted mistress, and the encouragement of her pupils' affection, would long since have allayed Miss Adderbury's nervousness, but this had endured with the years. Not all her accomplishments – and these included, besides a sufficient knowledge of Latin to enable her to prepare little boys for school, the expert use of the globes, a thorough grounding in the Theory of Music, enough proficiency upon the pianoforte and the harp to satisfy all but the most exacting and considerable talent in the correct use of water-colours – made it possible for her to enter the drawing-room without an inward shrinking, or to converse with her employer on terms of equality. Those of her pupils who had outgrown her care found her shyness and her anxiety to please tiresome, but they could never forget her kindness to them in their

29

schoolroom days, and always treated her with something more than civility. So Cecilia smiled at her, and Charles said: 'Well, Addy, and how are you today?' which slight attentions made her grow pink with pleasure, and stammer a good deal in her replies.

Her charges now numbered three only, for Theodore, the youngest son of the house, had lately been sent to Eton. Selina, a sharp-looking damsel of sixteen, went to sit beside her sister on the pianoforte-stool; and Gertrude, bidding fair, at twelve, to rival Cecilia in beauty, and Amabel, a stout ten-year old, cast themselves upon their brother, with loud professions of delight at seeing him, and rather louder reminders to him of a promise he had made them to play at lottery-tickets the very next time he should spend an evening at home. Miss Adderbury, kindly invited by Lady Ombersley to take a seat by the fire, made faint clucking noises in deprecation of this exuberance. She had no hope of being attended to, but was relieved to observe that Lady Ombersley was regarding the group about Charles with a fond smile. Lady Ombersley, in fact, was wishing that Charles, who was so popular with the children, could bring himself to be equally kind to the brother and sister nearer to him in age. There had been a rather painful scene at Christmas, when poor Hubert's Oxford debts had been discovered. . . .

The card-table had been set up, and Amabel was already counting out the mother-of-pearl fishes on its green-baize cloth. Cecilia begged to be excused from joining in the game, and Selina, who would have liked to play but always made a point of following her sister's example, said that she found lottery-tickets a dead bore. Charles paid no heed to this, but as he passed behind the music-stool on his way to fetch the playing-cards from a tall marquetry chest, bent to say something in Cecilia's ear. Lady Ombersley, anxiously watching, could not hear what it was, but she saw, her heart sinking, that it had the effect of making Cecilia colour up to the roots of her hair. However, she rose from the stool, and went to the table, saying, Very well, she would play for a little while. So Selina relented too, and after a very few minutes both young ladies were making quite as much noise as their juniors, and laughing enough to make an impartial observer think that the one had forgotten her advanced years, and the other her lacerated sensibilities. Lady Ombersley was able to withdraw her attention from the table, and to settle down to a comfortable chat with Miss Adderbury.

Miss Adderbury had already heard form Cecilia of Sophia's proposed visit, and was all eagerness to discuss it with Lady Ombersley. She could enter into her ladyship's feelings upon the event, join her in the sighing over the melancholy situation of a girl left motherless at five years old, agree with her plans for Sophia's accommodation and amusement, and, while deploring the irregularity of Sophia's upbringing, feel sure that she would be found to be a very sweet girl.

'I always know I can rely upon you, Miss Adderbury,' said Lady Ombersley. 'Such a comfort to me!'

In what way she was to be relied on Miss Adderbury had no idea, but she did not ask enlightenment, which was just as well, since her ladyship had no idea either, and had merely uttered the gratifying phrase from a general desire to please. Miss Adderbury said: 'Oh, Lady Ombersley! So good – ! So very obliging – !' and was almost ready to burst into tears at the thought of so much confidence being placed in one so unworthy as herself. Most fervently did she hope that her ladyship would never discover that she had nursed a snake in her bosom; and dolefully did she regret the lack of resolution that made it impossible for her to withstand her dear Miss Rivenhall's coaxing. Only two days before she had permitted young Mr Fawnhope to join the walking-party in the Green Park, and – far worse – had made no objection to his falling behind with Cecilia. It was true that Lady Ombersley had not mentioned Cecilia's unhappy infatuation to her, much less laid commands upon her to repulse Mr Fawnhope, but Miss Adderbury was the daughter of a clergyman (mercifully deceased) of stern and rigid morals, and she knew that such quibbling merely aggravated her depravity.

These reflections were interrupted by a further observation

made by her ladyship, in a lowered tone, and with a glance cast towards the card-table at the other end of the room. 'I am persuaded that I have no need to tell you, Miss Adderbury, that we had been made a trifle uneasy lately by one of those fancies which young females are subject to. I shall say no more, but you will appreciate how glad I shall be to welcome my niece. Cecilia has been too much alone, and her sisters are not of an age to be the companions which her cousin must be. I am hopeful that in striving to make dear Sophia feel at home amongst us – for the poor little thing will be sadly lost in the middle of such a large family, I daresay – and in showing her how she should go on in London, she will have enough to occupy her to give her thoughts another direction.'

This view of the matter had not until now presented itself to Miss Adderbury, but she grasped it eagerly, and felt sure that all would happen precisely as Lady Ombersley anticipated. 'Oh, yes, indeed!' she declared. 'Nothing could be better! So condescending of your ladyship to – I had collected from dear Miss Rivenhall – but she is such a sweet girl I know she will devote herself to her less fortunate cousin! When do you expect Miss Stanton-Lacy, dear Lady Ombersley?'

'Sir Horace was able to give me no very precise information,' replied Lady Ombersley, 'but I understand that he expects to sail for South America almost immediately. No doubt my niece will be in London very shortly. Indeed, I shall speak to the house-keeper tomorrow about preparing a bedchamber for her.'

Three

*B*ut it was not until the Easter holidays were a week old that Sophia arrived in Berkeley Square. The only intelligence received by her aunt during the intervening ten days was a brief scrawl from Sir Horace, conveying the information that his mission was a trifle delayed, but that she would assuredly see her niece before very long. The flowers which Cecilia so prettily arranged in her cousin's room withered, and had to be thrown away; and Mrs Ludstock, a meticulously careful housekeeper, had twice aired the sheets before, in the middle of a bright spring afternoon, a post-chaise-and-four, generously splashed with mud, drew up at the door.

It so happened that Cecilia and Selina had been driving with their Mama in the Park, and had returned to the house not five minutes earlier. All three were just about to ascend the staircase when Mr Hubert Rivenhall came bounding down, uttering: 'It must be my cousin, for there is a mountain of baggage on the roof! Such a horse! By Jupiter, if ever I saw such a bang-up piece of flesh-and-blood!'

This extraordinary speech made the three ladies stare at him in bewilderment. The butler, who had only a minute before withdrawn from the hall, sailed back again, with his attendant satellites, and trod across the marble floor to the front door, announcing, with a bow to his mistress, that he apprehended Miss Stanton-Lacy had that instant arrived. The satellites then threw open the double doors, and the ladies had a clear view, not only of the equipage in the road, but of the awed and inquisitive faces of the younger members of the family, who had been playing at bat-and-ball in the garden of the Square, and were now crowded close to the railings, gazing, in spite of Miss Adderbury's remonstrances, at the animal which had brought Hubert in such pelting haste down the stairs.

Miss Stanton-Lacy's arrival was certainly impressive. Four steaming horses drew her chaise, two outriders accompanied it, and behind it rode a middle-aged groom, leading a splendid black horse. The steps of the chaise were let down, the door opened, and out leaped an Italian greyhound, to be followed a moment later by a gaunt-looking female, holding a dressing-bag, three parasols, and a birdcage. Lastly, Miss Stanton-Lacy herself descended, thanking the footman for his proffered help, but requesting him instead to hold her poor little Jacko. Her poor little Jacko was seen to be a monkey in a scarlet coat, and no sooner had this magnificent fact dawned on the school-room party than they brushed past their scandalized preceptress, tore open the garden-gate, and tumbled out into the road, shouting: 'A monkey! She has brought a monkey!'

Lady Ombersley, meanwhile, standing as though rooted to her own doorstep, was realizing, with strong indignation, that the light in which a gentleman of great height and large proportions regarded his daughter had been misleading. Sir Horace's little Sophy stood five feet nine inches in her stockinged feet, and was built on generous lines, a long-legged, deep-bosomed creature, with a merry face, and a quantity of glossy brown ringlets under one of the most dashing hats her cousins had ever seen. A pelisse was buttoned up to her throat, a very long sable stole was slipping from her shoulders, and she carried an enormous sable muff. This, however, she thrust into the second footman's hands so that she was better able to greet Amabel, who was the first to reach her. Her dazed aunt watched her stoop gracefully over the little girl, catching her hands, and saying laughingly: 'Yes, yes, indeed I am your cousin Sophia, but pray won't you call me Sophy? If any one calls me Sophia I think I am in disgrace, which is a very uncomfortable thing. Tell me your name!'

'It's Amabel, and oh, if you please, may I talk to the monkey?' stammered the youngest Miss Rivenhall.

'Of course you may, for I brought him for you. Only be a little gentle with him at first, because he is shy, you know.'

'Brought him for *me?*' gasped Amabel, quite pale with excitement.

'For you all,' said Sophy, embracing Gertrude and Theodore in her warm smile. 'And also the parrot. Do you like pets better than toys and books? I always did, so I thought very likely you would too.'

'Cousin!' said Hubert, breaking in on the fervent assurances of his juniors that their new relative had gauged their tastes with an accuracy utterly unequalled in all their experience of adults. 'Is that *your* horse?'

She turned, surveying him with a certain unselfconscious candour, the smile still lingering on her mouth. 'Yes, that is Salamanca. Do you like him?'

'By Jove, I should think I do! Is he Spanish? Did you bring him from Portugal?'

'Cousin Sophy, what is your dear little dog's name? What kind of a dog is it?'

'Cousin Sophy, can the parrot talk? Addy may we keep it in the schoolroom?'

'Mama, Mama, Cousin Sophy has brought us a monkey!'

This last shout, from Theodore, made Sophy look quickly round. Perceiving her aunt and her two other cousins in the doorway, she ran up the steps, exclaiming: 'Dear Aunt Elizabeth! I beg your pardon! I was making friends with the children! How do you do? I am so happy to be with you! Thank you for letting me come to you!'

Lady Ombersley was still dazed, still clutching feebly at the fast-vanishing picture of the shy little niece of her imaginings, but at these words that insipid damsel was cast into the limbo of things unregretted and unremembered. She clasped Sophy in her arms, raising her face to the glowing one above her, and saying tremulously: 'Dear, dear

Sophy! So happy! So like your father! Welcome, dear child, welcome!'

She was quite overcome, and it was several moments before she could recollect herself enough to introduce Sophy to Cecilia and Selina. Sophy stared at Cecilia, and exclaimed: 'Are you Cecilia? But you are so beautiful! Why don't I remember that?'

Cecilia, who had been feeling quite overpowered, began to laugh. You could not suspect Sophy of saying things like that only to please you, she said exactly what came into her head. 'Well, *I* did not remember either!' she retorted. 'I thought you were a little brown cousin, all legs and tangled hair!'

'Yes, but I am – oh, not tangled, perhaps, but all legs, I assure you, and dreadfully brown! *I* have not grown into a beauty! Sir Horace tells me I must abandon all pretensions – and *he* is a judge, you know!'

Sir Horace was right: Sophy would never be a beauty. She was by far too tall; nose and mouth were both too large, and a pair of expressive gray eyes could scarcely be held to atone entirely for these defects. Only you could not forget Sophy, even though you could not recall the shape of her face, or the colour of her eyes.

She turned again towards her aunt. 'Will your people direct John Potton where he may stable Salamanca, ma'am? Only for tonight! And a room for himself? I shall arrange everything just as soon as I have learnt my way about!'

Mr Hubert Rivenhall made haste to assure her that he would himself conduct John Potton to the stables. She smiled, and thanked him, and Lady Ombersley said that there was room and to spare for Salamanca in the stables, and she must not trouble her head about such matters. But it seemed that Sophy was determined to trouble her head, for she answered quickly: 'No, no, my horses are not to be a charge on you, dear aunt!' Sir Horace most particularly charged me to make my own arrangements, if I should be setting up my stable, and indeed I mean to do so! But for tonight it would be so kind in you!'

There was enough here to set her aunt's brain reeling. What

kind of a niece was this, who set up her stable, made her own arrangements, and called her father Sir Horace? Then Theodore created a diversion, coming up with the scared monkey clasped in his arms, demanding that she should tell Addy that he might take it to the schoolroom, since Cousin Sophy had given it to them. Lady Ombersley shrank from the monkey, and said feebly: 'My love, I don't think – oh, dear, whatever will Charles say?'

'Charles is not such a muff as to be afraid of a monkey!' declared Theodore. 'Oh, Mama, pray tell Addy we may keep it!'

'Indeed, Jacko will not bite anyone!' Sophy said. 'I have had him with me for close on a week, and he is the gentlest creature! You will not banish him, Miss – Miss Addy? No, I know that is wrong!'

'Miss Adderbury – but we always call her Addy!' Cecelia explained.

'How do you do?' Sophy said, holding out her hand. 'Forgive me! It was impertinent, but I did not know! Do you permit the children to keep poor Jacko!'

Between her dismay at having a monkey thrust upon her, and her desire to please this glowing girl, who smiled so kindly down at her, and extended her hand with such frank good-nature, Miss Adderbury lost herself in a morass of half-sentences. Lady Ombersley said that they must ask Charles, a remark which was at once interpreted as permission to take Jacko up to the schoolroom, none of the children thinking so poorly of their brother as to believe that he would raise the least objection to their new pet. Sophy was then led up to the blue Saloon, where she at once cast her sables on to a chair, unbuttoned her pelisse, and tossed off her modish hat. Her aunt, fondly drawing her down to sit beside her on the sofa, asked if she were tired from the long journey, and if she would like to take some refreshment.

'No, indeed! Thank you, but I am never tired, and although it was a trifle tedious I could not count it as a *journey!*' Sophy replied. 'I should have been with you this morning, only that I was obliged to go first to Merton.'

'Go first to Merton?' echoed Lady Ombersley. 'But why, my love? Have you acquaintances there?'

'No, no, but Sir Horace particularly desired it!'

'My dear, do you always call your Papa Sir Horace?' asked Lady Ombersley.

The gray eyes began to dance again. 'No, if he makes me very cross I call him Papa!' Sophy said. 'It is of all things what he most dislikes! Poor angel, it is a great deal too bad that he should be saddled with such a maypole for a daughter, and no one could expect him to bear it!' She perceived that her aunt was looking a little shocked, and added, with her disconcerting frankness: 'You don't like that. I am so sorry, but indeed he is a delightful parent, and I love him dearly! But it is one of his maxims, you know, that one should never allow one's partiality to blind one to a person's defects.'

The startling proposition that a daughter should be encouraged to take note of her father's faults so much horrified Lady Ombersley that she could think of nothing to say. Selina, who liked to get to the root of everything, asked why Sir Horace had particularly desired Sophy to go to Merton.

'Only to take Sancia to her new home,' Sophy explained. 'That was why you saw me with those absurd outriders. Nothing will convince poor Sancia that English roads are not infested with bandits and guerilleros!'

'But who is Sancia?' demanded Lady Ombersley, in some bewilderment.

'Oh, she is the Marquesa de Villacañas! Did Sir Horace not tell you her name? You will like her – indeed, you *must* like her! She is quite stupid, and dreadfully indolent, like all Spaniards, but so pretty and good-natured!' She saw that her aunt was now wholly perplexed, and her straight, rather thick brows drew together. 'You don't know? He did not tell you? Now, how infamous of him! Sir Horace is going to marry Sancia.'

'*What?*' gasped Lady Ombersley.

Sophy leaned forward to take her hand, and to press it coaxingly. 'Yes, indeed he is, and you must be glad, if you please, because she will suit him very well. She is a widow, and extremely wealthy.'

'A Spaniard!' said Lady Ombersley. 'He never breathed a word of this to me!'

'Sir Horace says that explanations are so tedious,' said Sophy excusingly. 'I daresay he might have felt that it would take too long. Or,' she added, a mischievous look in her eyes, 'that I would do it for him!'

'I never heard of such a thing!' said Lady Ombersley, almost roused to wrath. 'Just like Horace! And when, pray, my dear, does he mean to marry this Marquesa?'

'Well,' said Sophy seriously, 'that, I fancy, is why he did not care to explain it all to you. Sir Horace cannot marry Sancia until I am off his hands. It is so awkward for him, poor dear! I have promised to do my best, but I *cannot* engage to marry anyone I don't like! He understands my feelings perfectly: I will say this for Sir Horace, that he is *never* unreasonable!'

Lady Ombersley was strongly of the opinion that these remarks were quite unsuited to her daughters' ears, but she saw no way of stemming them. Selina, still delving to the roots, asked: 'Why cannot your Papa be married until you are, Sophy?'

'On account of Sancia,' replied Sophy readily. 'Sancia says she does not at all wish to be my stepmama.'

Lady Ombersley was smitten to the heart. 'My poor child!' she said, laying a hand on Sophy's knee. 'You are so brave, but you may confide in me! She is jealous of you: I believe all Spaniards have the most shockingly jealous natures! It is too bad of Horace! If I had known this – ! Is she unkind, Sophy? Does she dislike you?'

Sophy went off into a peal of laughter. 'Oh, no, no, no! I am sure she never disliked anyone in all her life! The thing is that if she marries Sir Horace while I am still on his hands everyone will expect her to behave to me like a mama, and she is much too lazy! Then, too, with the best will in the world, I might continue to manage Sir Horace, and his house, and everything that I have been accustomed to do. We have talked it over, and I can't but see that there is a great deal in what she says. But as for jealousy, no indeed! She is much too handsome to be jealous of me, and much too good-natured as well. She says that she has the greatest imaginable affection for me, but share a house with me she will not. I do not blame her: pray do not think I blame her!'

'She sounds a very odd sort of a woman,' said Lady Ombersley disapprovingly. 'And why does she live in Merton?'

'Oh, Sir Horace hired the prettiest villa for her there! She means to live retired until he comes back to England. That,' said Sophy with a gurgle of mirth, 'is because she is excessively idle. She will lie in bed until the morning is half gone, eat a great many sweetmeats, read a great many novels, and be perfectly pleased to see any of her friends who will give themselves the trouble of driving out to visit her. Sir Horace says she is the most restful female of his acquaintance.' She bent, to stroke her little dog, which had all the time been sitting at her feet. 'Except Tina here, of course! Dear ma'am, I hope you do not dislike dogs? She is very good, I promise you, and I could not part with her!'

Lady Ombersley assured her that she had no objection to dogs, but was by no means partial to monkeys. Sophy laughed, and said: 'Oh, dear! Was it wrong of me to bring him for the children? Only when I saw him, in Bristol, he seemed to me to be just the thing! And now that I have given him to them, I daresay it will be difficult to persuade them to give him up.'

Lady Ombersley rather thought that it would be impossible, and as there did not seem to be anything more to be said on that subject, and she was feeling quite bemused by her niece's various disclosures, she suggested that Cecilia should escort Sophy up to her room, where she would no doubt like to rest for a while before changing her dress for dinner.

Cecilia rose with alacrity, ready to add her persuasions to her mother's if it should be necessary. She did not suppose that Sophy wished to rest, for the little she had seen of her cousin had been enough to convince her that a creature so full of vitality rarely stood in need of rest. But she felt herself strongly drawn to Sophy, and was anxious to make a friend of her as soon as possible. So when it was discovered that Sophy's maid was unpacking her trunks in her bedchamber, she begged Sophy to come to her own room for a chat. Selina, finding that she was not to be admitted to this tête-à-tête, pouted, but went off, deriving consolation from the reflection that to her would fall the agreeable task of describing to Miss Adderbury every detail of Sophy's conversation in the Blue Saloon.

Cecilia's disposition was shy, and although her manners lacked the forbidding reserve which distinguished those of her elder brother they were never confiding. Yet within a very few minutes she found herself pouring into her cousin's ears some at least of the evils of her situation. Sophy listened to her with interest and sympathy, but the constant recurrence of Mr Rivenhall's name seemed to puzzle her, and she presently interrupted to say: 'I beg your pardon, but this Charles – is he not your brother?'

'My eldest brother,' said Cecilia.

'Well, that is what I collected. But what has he to say to anything?'

Cecilia sighed. 'You will soon discover, Sophy, that nothing may be done in this house without Charles's sanction. It is he who orders everything, arranges everything, and rules everything!'

'Now, let us understand this!' said Sophy. 'My uncle has not died, has he? I am sure Sir Horace never told me so!'

'Oh, no! But Papa – I should not be talking about him, and of course I don't know precisely – but I think poor Papa found himself in difficulties! In fact, I know it was so, for I found my mother in great distress once, and she told me a little, because she was so distracted she hardly knew what she was doing. In general, she would never say a word about Papa to any of us – except Charles, I suppose, and I daresay Maria, now that she is a married lady. Only then my great-uncle Matthew died, and he left all his fortune to Charles, and I don't understand exactly how it was, but I believe Charles did something with mortgages. Whatever it was, it seems to have placed poor Papa quite in his power. And I am very certain that it is Charles who pays for Hubert and Theodore, besides settling all the debts, for that Mama did tell me.'

'Dear me, how very uncomfortable it must be for your Papa!' remarked Sophy. 'My cousin Charles sounds a most disagreeable creature!'

'He is quite *odious!*' said Cecilia. 'I sometimes think he takes a delight in making everyone miserable, for I am sure he grudges us the least pleasure, and is only anxious to marry us to *respectable* men with large fortunes, who are quite middle-aged, and sober, and can do nothing but catch the mumps!'

Since Sophy was far too intelligent to suppose that this embittered speech was a mere generalization she at once pressed Cecilia to tell her more about the respectable man with mumps, and after a little hesitation, and a good deal of circumlocution, Cecilia not only divulged that a marriage between herself and Lord Charlbury had been arranged (though not as yet announced), but favoured her with a word-picture of the Honourable Augustus Fawnhope which must have seemed like the ravings of delirium to anyone who had not been privileged to behold that beautiful young man. But Sophy had already met Mr Fawnhope and instead of coaxing her cousin to lie down upon her bed with a cooling draught, she said in the most matter-of-fact way: 'Yes, very true. I have never seen Lord Byron, but they tell me that he is nothing to Mr Fawnhope. He is quite the most handsome man I think I ever saw.'

'You now Augustus!' Cecilia breathed, clasping her hands at her palpitating bosom.

'Yes – that is to say, I am acquainted with him. I fancy I danced with him once or twice at the balls in Brussels last year. Was he not attached to Sir Charles Stuart in some capacity or another?'

'One of his secretaries, but Augustus is a poet, and of course he has no head for business, or affairs, which is a circumstance that disgusts Charles more than all the rest, I believe! Oh, Sophy, when we met – it was at Almack's Assembly Rooms, and I was wearing a gown of palest blue satin, embroidered all over with silken rosebuds, and knots of silver twist! – we no sooner saw each other than – He has assured me that it was the same with him! How could I suppose that there would be the least objection? The Fawnhopes, you know! I daresay they have been here since the Conquest, or some such thing! If *I* do not care a button for such things as fortunes and titles, what concern is it of Charles's?'

'None at all,' said Sophy. 'Dear Cecilia, don't cry, I beg of you! Only tell me this! Does your Mama dislike the notion of your marrying Mr Fawnhope?'

'Dearest Mama has such sensibility that I know she must feel for me!' declared Cecilia, obediently drying her eyes. 'She has as good as told me so, but she dare not withstand Charles! That, Sophy, is what governs all in this house!'

'Sir Horace is *always* right!' declared Sophy, rising, and shaking out her skirts. 'I teased him to take me to Brazil, you know, because, to own the truth, I could not imagine how I should contrive to occupy myself in London, with nothing to do but amuse myself in my aunt's house! He assured me that I should find something to be busy with, and you see that he had gauged the matter exactly! I wonder if he knew of all this? My dear Cecilia – oh, may I call you Cecy instead? Cecilia! Such a mouthful! – only trust me! You have fallen into a fit of despondency, and there is not the least need! In fact, nothing could be more fatal, in any predicament! It encourages one to suppose that there is nothing to be done, when a little resolution is all that is wanted to bring matters to a happy conclusion. I must go to my room, and dress for dinner, or I shall be late, and there is nothing more odious than a guest who comes late to meals!'

'But, Sophy, what can you possibly mean?' gasped Cecilia. 'What can *you* do to help me?'

'I have not the least notion, but I daresay a hundred things. Everything you have told me shows me that you are fallen, all of you, into a shocking state of melancholy! Your brother! Good gracious, what were you about to let him grow into such a tyrant? Why, I would not permit even Sir Horace to become so dictatorial, which is a thing the best of men will do, if the females of their families are so foolish as to encourage them! It is not at all good for them, beside making them such dead bores! Is Charles a dead bore? I am sure he must be! Never mind! If he has a fancy for making eligible matches he shall look about him for a husband for me, and that will divert his mind. Cecy, do come with me to my bedroom! Sir Horace desired me to choose mantillas for you and my aunt, and I daresay Jane will have unpacked them by now. How clever it was of me to have selected a white one for you! I am by far too brown-complexioned to wear white, but you will look enchantingly in it!'

She then swept Cecilia off to her own room, where she found the mantillas, carefully wrapped in silver paper, one of which she instantly carried to Lady Ombersley's dressing-room, declaring that Sir Horace had charged her to present it, with his love, to his dear sister. Lady Ombersley was delighted with the mantilla, a particularly handsome black one; and much touched (as she afterwards told Cecilia) by the message that went with it, not one word of which did she believe, but which showed, she said, such thoughtful delicacy in her niece.

By the time Sophy had changed her travelling-dress for an evening-gown of pale green crape, festooned at the bottom with rich silk trimming, and confined at the waist with a cord and tassels, Cecilia had completed her own toilet, and was waiting to escort her downstairs to the drawing-room. Sophy was trying to clasp a necklace of pearls round her throat while the gaunt maid, adjuring her not to be so fidgety, was equally determined to button up the cuffs of her long, full sleeves. Cecilia, tastefully but not strikingly attired in sprigged muslin, with a blue sash, supposed enviously that Sophy had had her gown made in Paris. She was quite right; nearly all Sophy's dresses came from Paris.

'One consolation,' said Cecilia naïvely, 'is that Eugenia will dislike it excessively!'

'Good gracious, who is Eugenia?' exclaimed Sophy, wheeling

round upon her dressing-stool. 'Why should she dislike it? I don't think it ugly, do you?'

'Miss Sophy, drat you, *will* you sit still?' interpolated Jane Storridge, giving her a shake.

'No, of course I do not!' responded Cecilia. 'But Eugenia never wears modish gowns. She says there are more important things to think of than one's dresses.'

'What a stupid thing to say!' remarked Sophy. 'Naturally there are, but not, I hold, when one is dressing for dinner. Who is she?'

'Miss Wraxton: Charles is betrothed to her, and Mama sent to warn me a few minutes ago that she is dining here tonight. We had all of us forgotten it in the bustle of your arrival. I daresay she will be in the drawing-room already, for she is always very punctual. Are you ready? Shall we go down?'

'If only my dear Jane would bestir herself a little!' Sophy said, giving her other wrist to her maid, and casting a roguish look into Miss Storridge's disapproving face.

The maid smiled rather grimly, but said nothing. She did up the tiny buttons, draped a gold-embroidered scarf over her mistress's elbows, and gave a little nod of approval. Sophy bent, and kissed her cheek, saying: 'Thank you! Go to bed, and don't think I will let you undress me, for I assure you I will not! Good-night, Jane dear!'

Cecilia, a good deal astonished, said as they descended the stairs together: 'I suppose she has been with you a long time? I fear Mama would stare to see you kiss your maid!'

Sophy lifted her eyebrows at this. 'Indeed? Jane was my mother's maid, and my own kind nurse when my mother died. I hope I may do nothing worse to make my aunt stare.'

'Oh! Of course she would perfectly understand the circumstances!' Cecilia said hastily. 'Only it looked so odd, you know!'

A decided sparkle in her cousin's fine eyes seemed to indicate that she did not much relish this criticism of her conduct, but as they had by this time reached the drawing-room door she did not say anything, but allowed herself to be ushered into the room.

45

Lady Ombersley, her two elder sons, and Miss Wraxton were seated in a group about the fire. All looked round at the opening of the door, and the two gentlemen rose to their feet, Hubert gazing at his cousin in frank admiration, Charles looking her over critically.

'Come in, dear Sophy!' Lady Ombersley said, in a welcoming tone. 'You see that I am wearing the beautiful mantilla instead of a shawl! Such exquisite lace! Miss Wraxton has been much admiring it. You will let me introduce Miss Stanton-Lacy to you, my dear Eugenia. Cecilia will have told you, Sophy, that we are soon to have the joy of counting Miss Wraxton one of the family.'

'Yes, indeed!' said Sophy, smiling, and holding out her hand. 'I wish you very happy, Miss Wraxton, and my cousin also.' She turned, having briefly clasped Miss Wraxton's hand, and extended her own to Charles. 'How do you do?'

He shook hands, and discovered that he was being looked at in a manner quite as critical as his own. This surprised him, but it amused him too, and he smiled. 'How do you do? I shall not say that I remember you very well, cousin, for I am sure that neither of us has the least recollection of the other!'

She laughed. 'Very true! Not even Aunt Elizabeth could remember me! Cousin – Hubert, is it? – tell me, if you please, about Salamanca, and John Potton! Did you see both safely bestowed?'

She moved a little aside, to talk to Hubert. Lady Ombersley, who had been anxiously watching her son, was relieved to see that he was looking perfectly amiable, even rather appreciative. A half smile lingered on his lips, and he continued to observe Sophy until his attention was recalled by his betrothed.

The Honourable Eugenie Wraxton was a slender young woman, rather above the average height, who was accustomed to hearing herself described as a tall, elegant girl. Her features were aristocratic, and she was generally held to be a good-looking girl, if a trifle colourless. She was dressed with propriety but great modesty in a gown of dove-coloured crape, whose sober hue seemed to indicate her mourning estate. Her hair, which she wore in neat bands, was of a soft tint between brown and gold; she had long, narrow hands and feet; and rather a thin chest, which, however, was rarely seen, her Mama having the greatest objection to such low-cut bodices as (for instance) Miss Stanton-Lacy was wearing. She was the daughter of a Viscount, and, although she was always careful not to appear proud, perfectly aware of her worth. Her manners were gracious, and she took pains to put people at their ease. She had had every intention of being particularly gracious to Sophy, but when she rose to shake hands with her she had found herself looking up into Sophy's face, which made it very difficult to be gracious. She felt just a little ruffled for a moment, but overcame this, and said to Charles in a low voice, and with her calm smile: 'How very tall Miss Stanton-Lacy is! I am quite dwarfed.'

'Yes, too tall,' he replied.

She could not help being glad that he apparently did not admire his cousin, for although she perceived, on closer scrutiny, that Sophy was not as handsome as herself, her first impression had been of a very striking young woman. She now saw that she had been misled by the size and brilliance of Sophy's eyes: her other features were less remarkable. She said: 'Perhaps, a trifle, but she is very graceful.'

Sophy at this moment went to sit down beside her aunt, and Charles caught sight of the fairy-like little greyhound, which had been clinging close to her skirts, not liking so many strangers. His brows rose; he said: 'We seem to have two guests. What is her name, cousin?'

He was holding down his hand to the greyhound, but Sophy said: 'Tina. I am afraid she will not go to you: she is very shy.'

'Oh, yes, she will!' he replied, snapping his fingers.

Sophy found his air of cool certainty rather annoying, but when she saw that he was quite right, and watched her pet making coquettish overtures of friendship, she forgave him, and was inclined to think he could not be as black as he had been painted.

'What a pretty little creature!' remarked Miss Wraxton

amiably. 'I am not, in general, fond of pets in the house – my Mama, dear Lady Ombersley, will never have even a cat, you know – but I am sure this must be quite an exception.'

'Mama has a great liking for pet dogs,' said Cecilia. 'We are not usually without one, are we, ma'am?'

'Fat and overfed pugs,' said Charles, with a grimace at his mother. 'I prefer this elegant lady, I confess.'

'Oh, that is not the most famous of Cousin Sophy's pets!' declared Hubert. 'You wait, Charles, until you see what else she has brought from Portugal!'

Lady Ombersley stirred uneasily, for she had not yet broken the news to her eldest son that a monkey in a red coat was now King of the Schoolroom. But Charles only said: 'I understand, cousin, that you have brought your horse with you too. Hubert can talk of nothing else. Spanish?'

'Yes, and Mameluke-trained. He is very beautiful.'

'I'll go bail you're a famous horsewoman, cousin!' Hubert said.

'I don't know that. I have had to ride a great deal.'

The door opened just then, but not, as Lady Ombersley had expected, to admit her butler, with an announcement that dinner awaited her pleasure. Her husband walked in, announcing that he must just catch a glimpse of his little niece before going off to White's. Lady Ombersley felt that it was bad enough of him to have refused to dine at home in Miss Wraxton's honour without this added piece of casual behaviour, but she did not let her irritation appear, merely saying, 'She is not so very little, after all, my love, as you may see.'

'Good Gad!' exclaimed his lordship, as Sophy rose to greet him. Then he burst out laughing, embraced Sophy, and said: 'Well, well, well! You're almost as tall as your father, my dear! Devilish like him, too, now I come to look at you!'

'Miss Wraxton, Lord Ombersley,' said his wife reprovingly.

'Eh! Oh, yes, how-de-do?' said his lordship, bestowing a cheerful nod on Miss Wraxton. 'I count you as one of the family, and stand on no ceremony with you. Come and sit down beside me, Sophy, and tell me how your father does these days!'

He then drew Sophy to a sofa, and plunged into animated conversation, recalling incidents thirty years old, laughing heartily over them, and presenting all the appearance of one who had completely forgotten an engagement to dine at his club. He was always well-disposed towards pretty young women, and when they added liveliness to their charms, and guessed exactly how he liked to conduct a flirtation, he enjoyed himself very much in their company, and was in no hurry to leave them. Dassett, coming in a few minutes later to announce dinner, took in the situation immediately, and after exchanging a glance with his mistress withdrew again to superintend the laying of another place at the table. When he returned to make his announcement, Lord Ombersley exclaimed: 'What's that? Dinner-time already? I declare, I'll dine at home after all!'

He then took Sophy down on his arm, ignoring Miss Wraxton's superior claims to this honour, and as they took their places at the dining-table commanded her to tell him what maggot has got into her father's head to make him go off to Peru.

'Not Peru: Brazil, sir,' Sophy replied.

'Much the same, my dear, and just as outlandish! I never knew such a fellow for travelling all over the world! He'll be going off to China next!'

'No, Lord Amherst went to China,' said Sophy. 'In February, I think. Sir Horace was wanted for Brazil because he perfectly understands Portuguese affairs, and it is hoped he may be able to persuade the Regent to go back to Lisbon. Marshal Beresford has become so excessively unpopular, you know. No wonder! He does not know how to be conciliating, and has not a grain of tact.'

'Marshal Beresford,' Miss Wraxton informed Charles, in a well modulated voice, 'is a friend of my father's.'

'Then you must forgive me for saying that he has no tact,' said Sophy at once, and with her swift smile. 'It is perfectly true, but I believe no one ever doubted that he is a man of many excellent

49

qualities. It is a pity that he should be making such a cake of himself.'

This made Lord Ombersley and Hubert laugh, but Miss Wraxton stiffened a little, and Charles shot a frowning look across the table at his cousin, as though he were revising his first favourable impression of her. His betrothed, who always conducted herself with rigid propriety, could not, even at an informal family party, bring herself to talk across the table, and demonstrated her superior upbringing by ignoring Sophy's remark, and beginning to talk to Charles about Dante, with a particular reference to Mr Cary's translation. He listened to her with courtesy, but when Cecilia, following her cousin's unconventional example, joined in their conversation to express her own preference for the style of Lord Byron, he made no effort to snub her, but, on the contrary, seemed rather to welcome her entrance into the discussion. Sophy enthusiastically applauded Cecilia's taste, announcing that her copy of *The Corsair* was so well-worn as to be in danger of disintegrating. Miss Wraxton said that she was unable to give an opinion on the merits of this poem, as her Mama did not care to have any of his lordship's works in the house. Since Lord Byron's marital difficulties were amongst the most scandalous *on dits* of the town, it being widely rumoured that he was, at the earnest solicitations of his friends, on the point of leaving the country, this remark at once made the discussion seem undesirably raffish, and everyone was relieved when Hubert, disclaiming any liking for poetry, went into raptures over that capital novel, *Waverley*. Here again Miss Wraxton was unable to edify the company with any measured criticism, but she graciously said that she believed the work in question to be, for a novel, quite unexceptionable. Lord Ombersley then said that they were all very bookish, but Ruff's *Guide to the Turf* was good enough reading for him, and drew Sophy out of the conversation by asking her a great many questions about old friends of his own whom, since they now adorned various Embassies, she might be counted upon to know.

After dinner, Lord Ombersley put in no appearance in the

drawing-room, the claims of faro being too insistent to be ignored; and Miss Wraxton very prettily begged that the children might be permitted to come downstairs, adding, with a smile cast upwards at Charles, that she had not had the felicity of seeing her little friend Theodore since he had come home for the Easter holidays. However, when her little friend presently appeared he was carrying Jacko upon his shoulder, which made her shrink back in her chair, and utter an exclamation of protest.

The awful moment of disclosure had come, and, thanks (Lady Ombersley bitterly reflected) to Miss Adderbury's lamentable lack of control over her young charges, at quite the wrong moment. Charles, at first inclined to be amused, was speedily brought to his senses by Miss Wraxton's evident disapproval. He said that however desirable a denizen of a schoolroom a monkey might be – which was a question to be discussed later – it was no fit creature for his mother's drawing-room; and ordered Theodore, in a tone that invited no argument, to remove Jacko at once. A sullen scowl descended on to Theodore's brow, and for a horrid instant his mother feared that she trembled on the brink of an ugly scene. But Sophy stepped quickly into the breach, saying: 'Yes, take him upstairs, Theodore! I should have warned you that of all things he most dislikes being brought into company! And pray make haste, for I am going to show you a famous game of cards which I learned in Vienna!'

She thrust him out of the room as she spoke, and shut the door on him. Turning, she found Charles eyeing her frostily, and said: 'Am I in disgrace with you for having brought the children a pet you don't approve of? I assure you, he is perfectly gentle: you need not be afraid of him.'

'I am not in the least afraid of him!' snapped Charles. 'Extremely obliging of you to have bestowed him upon the children!'

'Charles! Charles!' said Amabel, tugging at his sleeve. 'She has brought us a parrot too, and it talks capitally! Only Addy would put her shawl over its cage, because she said horrid, rough sailors must have taught it to speak. Do tell her not to!'

'Oh, good God, I am quite undone!' Sophy exclaimed in comical dismay. 'And the man *promised* the wretched bird would say nothing to put anyone to the blush! Now, what is to be done?'

But Charles was laughing. He said: 'You must say your Collect to it every day, Amabel, to put it in a better frame of mind. Cousin, my uncle Horace informed us that you were a good little thing, who would give us no trouble. You have been with us for rather less than half a day: I shudder to think what havoc you will have wrought by the end of a week!'

Four

*I*t could not have been said that Lady Ombersley's family dinner-party had been entirely successful, but it gave rise to a good deal of speculation in the minds of most of those who had been present at it. Miss Wraxton, who had seized the opportunity afforded by the rest of the company's sitting down to a round game to draw near to her prospective mother-in-law, and to engage her in low-voiced conversation, returned to her own home quite convinced that however little harm there might be in Sophy she had been very badly brought-up, and stood in need of tactful guidance. She had told Lady Ombersley that she was sorry indeed that the bereavement in her family had postponed her wedding-day, for she felt, in all sincerity, that she could have been both a support and a comfort to her mother-in-law under her present affliction. When Lady Ombersley said, rather defiantly, that she did not feel the visit of her niece to be an affliction, Miss Wraxton smiled at her in a way that showed how well she understood the brave front she was determined to present to the world, pressed her hand, and said that she looked forward to the time when she would be able to relieve dear Lady Ombersley of so many of the duties which now fell to her lot. Since this could only refer to the young couple's scheme of occupying one floor of the family mansion, a profound depression descended upon Lady Ombersley. The arrangement would not be an unusual one, but Lady Ombersley was able to think of many examples where it had been proved a failure, notably in the Melbourne household. Miss Wraxton would certainly not render the Ombersley house hideous by hysterical spasms, or really dreadful scandals, but Lady Ombersley derived small comfort from this knowledge. Almost as insupportable as Lady Caroline Lamb's frenzied behaviour would be Miss Wraxton's determination to exert a beneficent influence over her young brothers and sisters-in-law; and her conviction that it was her duty to take upon her own shoulders many of the burdens which Lady Ombersley was not at all anxious to relinquish.

Charles, who had enjoyed a few minutes' grave talk with his betrothed before handing her into her carriage at the end of the evening, went to bed with mixed feelings. He could not but acknowledge the justice of his Eugenia's criticisms, but since he was himself of a forthright disposition he was inclined to like Sophy's frank, open manners, and obstinately refused to agree that she put herself forward unbecomingly. He did not think that she put herself forward at all, which made it difficult to see just how it was that she contrived to introduce quite a new atmosphere into the house. She had certainly done this: he was not sure that he approved of it.

As for Sophy herself, she retired to her bedchamber with even more to think about than her hosts. It seemed to her that she had taken up her residence in an unhappy household. Cecilia held Charles accountable for this, which no doubt he was. But Sophy was no schoolroom miss, and it had not taken her more than ten minutes to get Lord Ombersley's measure. Unquestionably Charles had had much to bear from that quarter; and since the rest of his family plainly held him in awe it was not marvellous that a naturally stern and autocratic temper, thus unchecked, should have turned him into a domestic tyrant. Sophy could not believe that he was past reclaim, for not only had Tina made friends with him, but when he laughed his whole personality underwent a change. The worst she yet knew of him was that he had selected for his bride a very tiresome girl. She felt it a pity that so promising a young man should be cast away on one who would make it her business to encourage all the more disagreeable features of his character.

54

There was no need to worry about the children, she decided, but her quick intelligence had informed her, during the course of the evening, that all was not well with Mr Hubert Rivenhall. She had a strong suspicion that some undisclosed trouble nagged at him. He might forget this in admiration of Salamanca, or in playing an absurd game with his juniors, but when nothing else occupied his mind the trouble crept back into it, and he grew silent, until somebody looked at him, when he instantly began to talk again, in a rattling, over-cheerful style which seemed to satisfy his relations. Sophy, guided by her experience of young officers, thought that he was probably in some foolish scrape which would turn out to be far less serious than he imagined. He ought, of course, to tell his elder brother about it, for no one could doubt, looking at Mr Rivenhall's countenance, that he was competent to deal with any scrape; but since Hubert was obviously afraid to do so it might be a good thing to persuade him to confide in his cousin.

Then there was Cecilia, so lovely, and so helpless! Her affairs might be much more difficult to arrange satisfactorily, for although Sophy, reared in quite a different school, thought it iniquitous to force any girl into a distasteful marriage, she was by no means determined to further the pretensions of Augustus Fawnhope. Sophy, strongly practical, could not feel that Mr Fawnhope would make a satisfactory husband, for he lacked visible means of support, and was apt, when under the influence of his Muse, to forget such mundane considerations as dinner-engagements, or the delivery of important messages. However, he would certainly be preferable to a middle-aged man with mumps, and if Cecilia's passion for him proved to be more than a mere infatuation her friends must busy themselves in finding for him some well-paid and genteel post in which his handsome person and charm of manner would outweigh his erratic habits. Sophy was still trying to think of such a post when she fell asleep.

Breakfast was served, at Ombersley House, in a parlour at the back of the house. Only the three ladies sat down to the table at nine o'clock, for Lord Ombersley, a man of nocturnal habits, never left his room until noon, and his two elder sons had breakfasted an hour earlier, and had gone off to ride in the Park.

Lady Ombersley, whose indifferent health made restful nights rarities in her life, had employed some part of her wakeful hours in planning entertainments for her niece, and as she dipped fingers of dry toast into her tea she propounded a scheme for an evening-party, with dancing. Cecilia's eyes brightened, but she said rather sceptically: 'If Charles will permit it!'

'My dear, you know your brother has no objection to any rational enjoyment. I do not mean that we should give a really large ball, of course.'

Sophy, who had been watching in some awe her aunt's languid consumption of tea-and-toast, said: 'Dear ma'am, I would infinitely prefer that you should not put yourself out for me!'

'I am quite determined to give a party for you,' replied Lady Ombersley firmly. 'I promised your father that I would do so. Besides, I am very fond of entertaining. I assure you, we are not in general so quiet as you find us at present. When I brought dear Maria out we gave a ball, two rout-parties, a Venetian breakfast, and a masquerade! But then,' she added, with a sigh, 'poor cousin Mathilda was still alive, and she sent out all the invitation-cards, and arranged everything with Gunter's. I miss her sadly: she was carried off by an inflammation of the lung, you know.'

'No, but if that is all that troubles you, ma'am, pray do not give it another thought!' said Sophy. 'Cecy and I will arrange everything, and you shall have nothing to do but choose what dress you will wear, and receive your guests.'

Lady Ombersley blinked at her. 'But, my love, you could not!'

'Indeed I could!' asserted Sophy, smiling warmly at her. 'Why, I have managed all Sir Horace's parties since I was seventeen years old! And that puts me in mind of something I must do at once! Where shall I find Hoare's Bank, Aunt Lizzie?'

'Find Hoare's Bank?' echoed Lady Ombersley blankly.

'What in the world can you want to know *that* for?' asked Cecilia.

Sophy looked a little surprised. 'Why, to present Sir Horace's letter of authorization, to be sure!' she answered. 'I must do so at once, or I may find myself quite at a loss.' She perceived that her aunt and cousin were looking, if anything, rather more bewildered than ever, and lifted her brows. 'But what have I said?' she asked, between amusement and dismay. 'Hoare's, you know! Sir Horace banks with them!'

'Yes, my dear, I daresay he may, but *you* do not have an account with a bank!' expostulated Lady Ombersley.

'No, alas! It is such a bore! However, we settled it that I should draw upon Sir Horace's funds for my needs. And for the expenses of the household, of course, but at this present we have no house,' said Sophy, lavishly spreading butter on her fourth slice of bread.

'My love! Young ladies *never* – ! Why, I myself have never entered your uncle's bank in my life!' said Lady Ombersley, deeply moved.

'No?' said Sophy. 'Perhaps he prefers to settle all the bills himself? Nothing teases Sir Horace more than to be for ever applied to for money! He taught me years ago to understand business, and so we go on very happily.' Her brow wrinkled. 'I hope that Sancia will learn to manage for him. Poor angel! He will very much dislike it if he must study the bills, and pay all the wages.'

'I never heard of such a thing!' said Lady Ombersley. 'Really, Horace – But never mind that! Dear child, you cannot possibly need to draw funds while you are with me!'

Sophy could not help laughing at her aunt's evident conviction that Hoare's Bank must be a haunt of vice, but she said: 'Indeed I shall need funds! You have no notion how expensive I am, ma'am! And Sir Horace warned me most particularly not to allow myself to be a charge on you.'

Cecilia, her eyes round with wonder, asked: 'Does your Papa set no limit to what you spend?'

'No, how could he do so, when he has gone quite out of reach, and can have no notion what I might suddenly need? He knows

I shall not outrun the carpenter. But I did not mean to tease you with my affairs! Only, in what part of the town is Hoare's situated, if you please?'

Fortunately, since neither of the other ladies had the smallest idea of the locality of any bank, Mr Rivenhall came into the room at this moment. He was dressed for riding, and had merely looked in to ask his mother if she had any commissions she might desire him to execute in the City, whither he was bound. She had none, but did not hesitate (in spite of his probable disapproval) to divulge to him Sophy's extraordinary wish to be directed to Hoare's Bank. He took this with equanimity, and even bore up wonderfully under the disclosure that she was at liberty to draw on her father's account. He said: 'Unusual!' but he seemed to be more amused than disapproving. 'Hoare's Bank is at Temple Bar,' he added. 'If your need is urgent, I am driving into the City myself this morning, and shall be happy to escort you.'

'Thank you! If my aunt has no objection I shall be glad to go with you. When do you wish to start?'

'I shall await your convenience, cousin,' he replied politely.

This civility augured well for the expedition, and made Lady Ombersley, always inclined to be optimistic, nourish the hope that Charles had taken one of his rare likings to his cousin. He was certainly predisposed in her favour when he found that she did not keep him waiting; and she, for her part, could not think very badly of a man who drove such a splendid pair of horses in his curricle. She took her place beside him in this vehicle; the groom swung himself up behind, as the horses plunged past him; and Sophy, herself no mean whip, preserved a critical but not unappreciative silence while Charles controlled the first ardour of his pair. Reserving her ultimate judgement until she should have seen him with a tandem, or a four-in-hand, she yet felt that she could safely repose confidence in his ability to aid her in the purchase of carriage-horses for her own use, and said presently: 'I must buy a carriage, and don't know whether to choose a curricle or a high-perch phaeton. Which do you recommend, cousin?'

'Neither,' he replied, steadying his horses round a bend in the street.

'Oh?' said Sophy, rather surprised. 'What, then?'

He glanced down at her. 'You are not serious, are you?'

'Not serious? Of course I am serious!'

'If you wish to drive, I will take you in the Park one day,' he said. 'I expect I can find a horse – or even a pair – in the stables quiet enough for a lady to drive.'

'Oh, I fear that would never do!' said Sophy, shaking her head.

'Indeed? Why not?'

'I might excite the horse,' said Sophy dulcetly.

He was momentarily taken aback. Then he laughed, and said: 'I beg your pardon: I had no intention of offending you! But you cannot need a carriage in London. You will no doubt drive out with my mother, and if you should wish to go on some particular errand you may always order one of the carriages to be sent round to the house for your use.'

'That,' said Sophy, 'is very obliging of you, but will not suit me quite so well. Where does one buy carriages in London?'

'You will scarcely drive yourself about the town in a curricle!' he said. 'Nor do I consider a high-perch phaeton at all a suitable vehicle for a lady. They are not easy to drive. I should not care to see any of my sisters making the attempt.'

'You must remember to tell them so,' said Sophy affably. 'Do they mind what you say to them? I never had a brother myself, so I can't know.'

There was a slight pause, while Mr Rivenhall, unaccustomed to sudden attacks, recovered his presence of mind. It did not take him very long. 'It might have been better for you if you had, cousin!' he said grimly.

'I don't think so,' said Sophy, quite unruffled. 'The little I have seen of brothers makes me glad that Sir Horace never burdened me with any.'

'Thank you! I know how I may take that, I suppose!'

'Well, I imagine you might, for although you have a great many antiquated notions I don't thank you *stupid*, precisely.'

'Much obliged! Have you any other criticisms you would care to make?'

'Yes, never fly into a niff when you are driving a high-couraged pair! You took that last corner much too fast.'

As Mr Rivenhall was accounted something of a Non-pareil, this thrust failed to pierce his armour. 'What an abominable girl you are!' he said, much more amiably. 'Come! We cannot quarrel all the way to Temple Bar! Let us cry a truce!'

'By all means,' she agreed cordially. 'Let us rather talk about my carriage. Do I go to Tattersall's for my horses?'

'Certainly not!'

'Dear cousin Charles, do you wish me to understand that I have the name wrong, or that there is a superior dealer?'

'Neither. What I wish you to understand is that females do not frequent Tattersall's!'

'Now, is this one of the things you would not like your sisters to do, or would it really be improper in me to go there?'

'Most improper!'

'If you escorted me?'

'I shall do no such thing.'

'Then how shall I manage?' she demanded. 'John Potton is an excellent groom, but I would not trust him to buy my horses for me. Indeed, I would not trust anyone, except, perhaps, Sir Horace, who knows exactly what I like.'

He perceived that she was in earnest, and not, as he had suspected, merely bent on roasting him. 'Cousin, if nothing will do for you but to drive yourself. I will put my tilbury at your disposal, and choose a suitable horse to go between the shafts.'

'One of your own?' enquired Sophy.

'None of my horses are at all suitable for you to drive,' he replied.

'Well, never mind!' said Sophy. 'I shall prefer to have my own phaeton-and-pair.'

'Have you the smallest notion what you would have to pay for a well-matched pair?' he demanded.

'No, tell me! I thought not above three or four hundred pounds?'

'A mere trifle! Your father, of course, would have not the least objection to your squandering three or four hundred pounds on a pair of horses!'

'Not the least, unless I allowed myself to be taken in like a goose, and bought some showy-looking animal for ever throwing out a splint, or a high-stepper found to be touched in the wind at the end of a mile.'

'I advise you to wait until he returns to England, then. He will no doubt choose you the very thing!' was all Mr Rivenhall would say.

Rather to his surprise, Sophy appeared to take this in perfectly good part, for she made no comment, and almost immediately desired him to tell her the name of the street they were driving down. She did not refer again to the phaeton-and-pair, and Mr Rivenhall, realizing that she was merely a little spoilt and in need of a set-down, palliated the severe snub he had dealt her by pointing out one or two places of interest which they passed, and asking her a few civil questions about the scenery of Portugal. Arrived at Temple Bar, he drew up before the narrow entrance to Hoare's Bank, and would have accompanied her inside had she not declined his escort, saying that he would do better to walk his horses, for she did not know how long she might be detained, and there was a sharp wind blowing. So he waited for her outside, reflecting that however unusual it might be for a young and unattached lady to do business in a bank she could not really come to any harm there. When she reappeared, in about twenty minutes' time, some senior official of the Bank came with her, and solicitously handed her up into the curricle. She seemed to be on terms of considerable friendship with this personage, but disclosed, in answer to a somewhat sardonic enquiry made by her cousin as they drove off, that this had been her first meeting with him.

'You surprise me!' said Mr Rivenhall. 'I had supposed he must have dandled you on his knee when you were a baby!'

'I don't think so,' she said. 'He didn't mention it, at all events. Where do we go now?'

He told her that he had some business to transact near St Paul's, adding that he should not keep her waiting above five minutes. If this was a shaft aimed at the length of time she had spent in the Bank he missed his aim, for Sophy said in the most amiable way that she did not mind waiting. This was a much more successful shaft: Mr Rivenhall began to think that in Miss Stanton-Lacy he had met an opponent to be reckoned with.

When he presently drew up in a street beside St Paul's, Sophy held out her hand, saying: 'I will take them.' He therefore put the reins into her hand, for although he did not trust her to control his spirited horses his groom was already at their heads, so that there was no likelihood of any mishap.

Sophy watched him walk into a tall building, and pulled off one of her lavender kid gloves. The east wind was blowing quite strongly: certainly strongly enough to whirl a lady's glove, tossed to it, into the gutter on the farther side of the road. 'Oh, my glove!' exclaimed Sophy. 'Please run quickly, or it will blow quite away! Don't fear for the horses: I can handle them!'

The groom found himself in a quandary. His master would certainly not expect him to leave the grays unattended; on the other hand, someone must rescue Miss Stanton-Lacy's glove, and the street was momentarily deserted. Judging by what he had been able to hear of the lady's conversation, she at least knew enough about driving to be able to hold the grays for a minute. They were standing quite quietly. The groom touched his hat, and strode across the road.

'Tell your master that it is too chilly to keep the horses standing!' Sophy called after him. 'I will tool the curricle round the streets for a few minutes, and come back to take him up when he is ready!'

The groom, who was stooping to pick up the glove, nearly fell over, so swiftly did he spin round. He had an excellent view of

Miss Stanton-Lacy driving at a smart pace up the street. He made a gallant but belated attempt to catch the curricle, but it swept round a corner just as the wind blew his hat off, and sent it bowling down the street.

It was nearly half an hour later when the curricle again came into sight. Mr Rivenhall, awaiting it with folded arms, had ample opportunity to observe with what precision his cousin rounded the corner, and how well she handled the reins and whip, but he did not appear to be much gratified, for he watched the approach of the vehicle with a scowl on his brow, and his lips tightly gripped together. Of his groom there was no sign.

Miss Stanton-Lacy, pulling up exactly abreast of Mr Rivenhall, said cheerfully: 'I beg pardon, I have kept you waiting! The thing is that I do not know my way about London, and became quite lost, and was obliged to enquire the directions no less than three times. But where is your groom?'

'I have sent him home!' replied Mr Rivenhall.

She looked down at him, her expressive eyes brimful of amusement. 'How very right of you!' she approved. 'I like a man to think of everything. You could never have quarrelled with me really *well* with that man standing up behind us, and overhearing every word you uttered.'

'How *dared* you drive my horses?' demanded Mr Rivenhall thunderously. He mounted into his seat, and snapped: 'Give me the reins at once!'

She relinquished them, and also the whip, but said disarmingly: 'To be sure, that was not very well-done of me, but you will own that there was no bearing your conduct in talking to me as though I were a silly chit scarcely able to drive a donkey.'

Mr Rivenhall's impatient mouth was once more set so rigidly that there seemed to be no likelihood of his owning anything at all.

'At least admit that I am able to handle your pair!' said Sophy.

'Well for you that I had taken the edge off them!' he retorted.

'How ungenerous of you!' said Sophy.

It was indeed ungenerous, and he knew it. He said furiously:

63

'Driving about the City, with not even a groom beside you! Very pretty behaviour, upon my word! It is a pity you have not a little more conduct, cousin! Or are these Portuguese manners?'

'Oh, no!' she replied. 'In Lisbon, where I am known, I could not indulge in such pranks, of course. Dreadful, was it not? I assure you, all the cits were staring at me! But do not put yourself into a pucker on that head! no one knows me in London!'

'No doubt,' he said sardonically, '*Sir Horace* would have applauded such behaviour!'

'No,' said Sophy. 'I think that Sir Horace would have rather expected you to have offered to let me drive your horses. Just so that you could have judged for yourself whether I was capable of handling a spirited pair,' she explained kindly.

'I let no one – *no one* – drive my horses but myself!'

'In general,' said Sophy, 'I think you are very right. It is amazing how swiftly a clumsy pair of hands will spoil the most tender mouth!'

Mr Rivenhall a most audibly ground his teeth.

Sophy laughed suddenly. 'Oh, don't be so out of reason cross, cousin!' she begged. 'You know very well your horses have taken no sort of hurt! Will you put me in the way of choosing a pair for my own use?'

'I will have nothing whatsoever to do with such a mad project!' he said harshly.

Sophy took this with equanimity. 'Very well,' she said. 'Perhaps it would suit you better to find an eligible husband for me. I am very willing, and I understand that you have some talent in that.'

'Have you no delicacy of mind?' demanded Mr Rivenhall.

'Yes, indeed! I daresay it would astonish you to know how much!'

'It would!'

'But with *you*, my dear cousin,' pursued Sophy, 'I know I need have no reserve. Do, pray, find me an eligible husband! I am not at all nice in my notions, and shall be satisfied with the barest modicum of virtues in my partner.'

'Nothing,' stated Mr Rivenhall, showing his cousin, as he swirled round the corner into the Haymarket, how to drive to an inch, 'would afford me greater satisfaction than to see you married to some man who would know how to control your extraordinary quirks!'

'Very creditably performed!' approved Sophy. 'But how would it have been if some dog had strayed into the road, or a poor soul have crossed the street at that moment?'

Mr Rivenhall's sense of humour betrayed him. He was obliged to bite back a laugh before replying: 'I find it a marvellous circumstance, cousin, that no one has yet strangled you!'

He found that he had lost his cousin's attention. Her head was turned away from him, and before he could discover what object of interest had caught her eye she had said quickly: 'Oh, if you please, would you stop? I have seen an old acquaintance!'

He complied with this request, and then saw, too late, who was walking down the street towards them. There could be no mistaking that graceful figure, or those guinea-gold locks, revealed by the doffing of a curly-brimmed beaver. Mr Augustus Fawnhope, perceiving that the lady in the curricle was waving a hand in his direction, halted, took off his hat, and stood with it in his hand, gazing enquiringly up at Sophy.

He was indeed a beautiful young man. His hair waved naturally from a brow of alabaster; his eyes were of a deep blue, a little dreamy, but so exquisitely set under arched brows, of such size and brilliance as to defy criticism; his mouth was moulded in curves to set a sculptor groping for the tools of his art. He was of moderate height, and exact proportions, and had no need to live upon a diet of potatoes steeped in vinegar to preserve his slender figure. Not that it would ever have entered his head to have done so; it was not the least of Mr Fawnhope's charms that he was utterly unconcerned with his appearance. It might have been supposed that he could not be unaware of the admiration this excited, but as he was preoccupied with his ambition to become a major poet, paying very little attention to what was said to him, and none at all to what was said about him, even his ill-wishers (such as Mr Rivenhall and Sir Charles Stuart) were forced to admit that it was very likely that this admiration had not as yet pierced the cloud of abstraction in which he wrapped himself.

But there was more than abstraction in the gaze turned upward to Miss Stanton-Lacy's face, and this circumstance was not lost on Mr Rivenhall, interpreting correctly the doubtful smile hovering on Mr Fawnhope's lips. Mr Fawnhope had not the faintest idea of the identity of the lady stretching down her hand to him in so friendly a fashion. However, he took it in his, and said How-do-you-do, in his soft, vague voice.

'Brussels,' said Sophy helpfully. 'We danced the quadrille at the Duchess of Richmond's ball, do you remember? Oh, are you acquainted with my cousin, Mr Rivenhall? You must know that I am staying with my aunt, in Berkeley Square, for the season. You must come to call upon us: I know she will be delighted!'

'Of course I remember!' said Mr Fawnhope, with less truth, than good manners. 'Enchanting to meet again, ma'am, – and so unexpectedly! I shall certainly do myself the pleasure of calling in Berkeley Square.'

He bowed, and stepped back. The grays, to whom Mr Rivenhall's impatience had communicated itself, bounded forward. Mr Rivenhall said: 'How charming for you to have met an old friend so soon after your arrival!'

'Yes, was it not?' agreed Sophy.

'I hope he will have contrived to recall your name before he avails himself of your invitation to visit you.'

Her lips twitched, but she replied with perfect comsure: 'Depend upon it, if he does not he will find someone to tell him what it is.'

'You are shameless!' he said angrily.

'Nonsense! You only say so because I drove your horses,' she answered. 'Never mind! I will engage not to do so again.'

'I'll take care of that!' he retorted. 'Let me tell you, my dear cousin, that I should be better pleased if you would refrain from meddling in the affairs of my family!'

'Now, that,' said Sophy, 'I am very glad to know, because if ever I should desire to please you I shall know just how to set about it. I daresay I shan't, but one likes to be prepared for any event, however unlikely.'

He turned his head to look at her, his eyes narrowed, and their expression by no means pleasant. 'Are you thinking of being so unwise as to cross swords with me?' he demanded. 'I shan't pretend to misunderstand you, cousin, and I will leave you in no doubt of my own meaning! If you imagine that I will ever permit that puppy to marry my sister, you have yet something to learn of me!'

'Pooh!' said Sophy. 'Mind your horses, Charles, and don't talk fustian to me!'

Five

'Pretty well, for one morning's work!' said Sophy.

Mr Rivenhall was less satisfied. His mother was dismayed to discover that so far from having taken a liking to his cousin he was appalled to think that they might be obliged to house her for months. 'I tell you frankly, ma'am, it will not do!' he said. 'God knows how long my uncle may be away! I only wish you may not live to regret the day when you consented to take charge of his daughter! The sooner you can fulfil the rest of his expectations, and marry her off to some poor wretch, the better it will be for the rest of us!'

'Good gracious, Charles!' said Lady Ombersley. 'What in the world has she done to put you out?'

He declined to answer this, merely saying that Sophy was pert, headstrong, and so badly brought up that he doubted whether any man would be fool enough to offer for her. His mother refrained from enquiring further into Sophy's iniquities, but instead seized the moment to suggest that as a prelude to finding a husband for her she should be allowed to give an evening party, with dancing. 'I do not mean a large affair,' she hastened to add. 'Perhaps ten couples, or so – in the drawing-room!'

'By all means!' he said. 'That will make it quite unnecessary for you to invite young Fawnhope!'

'Oh, quite!' she agreed.

'I should warn you, Mama,' he said, 'that we encountered him this morning! My cousin greeted him as an old and valued acquaintance, and begged him to call on her here!'

'Oh, dear!' sighed Lady Ombersley. 'How very unfortunate, to be sure! But I daresay she does know him, Charles, for she was with your uncle in Brussels last year.'

'She!' said Charles witheringly. 'He had no more notion who she was than the Emperor of China! But he will certainly call! I must leave you to deal with *that*, ma'am!'

With these very unfair words he strode out of his mother's room, leaving her to wonder in what way he supposed her to be able to deal with a morning-call paid by a young man of unexceptionable birth, who was the son of one of her oldest friends. She came to the conclusions that he had no more idea than she, and banished the matter from her mind, bending it instead to the far more pleasant problem of whom to invite to the first party she had held in two months.

She was presently interrupted by the entrance of her niece. Remembering Charles's dark words, she asked Sophy, with an assumption of severity, what she had done to vex him. Sophy laughed, and almost stunned her by replying that she had done nothing but steal his curricle, and tool it round the City for half an hour.

'Sophy!' gasped her ladyship. 'Charles's grays? You could never hold them!'

'To own the truth,' admitted Sophy, 'I had the devil's own work to do so! Oh, I beg your pardon! I did not mean to say that, dearest Aunt Lizzie! Don't scold! It comes of living with Sir Horace: I know I say the most shocking things, but I do try to mind my wretched tongue! No, and do not give Charles's pets another thought! He will come about presently. I daresay if he had not engaged himself to marry that tedious girl he would not be so stuffy!'

'Oh, Sophy!' said Lady Ombersley involuntarily. 'I own I cannot like Miss Wraxton, try as I will!'

'Like her! I should think not indeed!' exclaimed Sophy.

'Yes, but one should,' said Lady Ombersley unhappily. 'She is so very good, and I am sure she wishes to be a most dutiful daughter to me, and it is so ill-natured of me not to wish for a dutiful daughter! But when I think that in quite a short time now I shall have her living in the house – But I should not be talking in this style! It is most improper, and you must forget it, if you please, Sophy!'

Sophy paid no heed to this, but echoed: 'Living in the house! You are not serious, ma'am?'

Lady Ombersley nodded. 'There is nothing at all out of the way in such an arrangement, you know, my love. They will have their own apartments, of course, but . . .' She broke off, and sighed.

Sophy looked at her fixedly for a few moments, but, rather to her surprise, said nothing. Lady Ombersley tried to put these melancholy reflections out of her mind, and began to talk about the party she meant to give. Into these plans her niece entered with enthusiasm, and an efficiency that swept Lady Ombersley quite off her feet. By what stages she arrived at agreement with Sophy on all points she was never afterwards able to explain, either to Charles or to herself, but at the end of an interview which left her feeling bemused but convinced that no one could boast of having a sweeter-natured or more thoughtful niece than Sophy, she had certainly consented not only to allow Sophy and Cecilia to undertake all the necessary arrangements, but also to permit Sir Horace (through his daughter) to defray the cost of the entertainment.

'And now,' Sophy said buoyantly to Cecilia, 'you shall tell me where we must order the cards of invitation, and where you in general go for refreshments. I don't think we should leave that to my aunt's cook, for he would be busy for so many days he would have very little time for anything else, and that would make everything uncomfortable, which I don't at all wish.'

Cecilia regarded her in round-eyed astonishment. 'But Sophy, Mama said it should only be a quiet small party!'

'No, Cecy, it was your brother who said that,' replied Sophy. 'It is going to be a very large party.'

Selina, who was present at this conference, asked shrewdly: 'Does Mama know that?'

Sophy laughed. 'Not yet!' she admitted. 'Do you think she does not care for large parties?'

'Oh, no! Why, there were more than four hundred people invited to the ball she gave for Maria, were there not, Cecilia? Mama enjoyed it excessively, because it was such a capital success, and everyone complimented her on it. Cousin Mathilda told me so.'

'Yes, but the cost of it!' Cecilia said. 'She will not dare! Charles would be so angry!'

'Don't give him a thought!' recommended Sophy. 'It is Sir Horace who will bear the cost, not Charles. Make a list of all your acquaintances, Cecy, and I will make one of those of my friends who are in England, and then we will go out to order the cards. I imagine we shall not need more than five hundred.'

'Sophy,' said Cecilia, in a faint voice, 'are we going to send out *five hundred* invitations without even *asking* Mama?'

Imps of mischief danced in her cousin's eyes. 'Of course we are, dear goose! For once we have despatched them even your horrid brother cannot recall them!'

'Oh, famous, famous!' cried Selina, beginning to skip round the room. '*What* a rage he will be in!'

'*Dare* I?' breathed Cecilia, at once scared and dazzled.

Her sister begged her not to be poor-spirited, but it was Sophy who clinched the matter, by pointing out to her that she would not have to bear the responsibility, and was unlikely to incur much recrimination from her brother, who would have no hesitation in laying the blame at the right door.

Mr Rivenhall, meanwhile, had gone off to visit his betrothed. He arrived at the Brinklows' somewhat cheerless house in Brook Street still seething with indignation, but so thankless and perverse was his disposition that no sooner did he find his sentiments shared and his strictures on his cousin endorsed than he took an abrupt turn in quite another direction, and said much must be forgiven a girl who could handle his grays as Sophy had. From being a female sunk below reproach Sophy became rapidly an unconventional girl whose

71

unaffected manners were refreshing in an age of simpers and high flights.

This was not just to Miss Wraxton's taste. To be driving about the City unattended did not suit her sense of propriety, and she said so. Mr Rivenhall grinned. 'No, very true, but I suppose it was in some sort my fault: I *did* put up her back. There's no harm done: if she could control my grays, as fresh as they were, she's a capital whip. All the same, if I have anything to say to it she is not going to set up her own carriage while she remains in my mother's charge. Good God, we should never know from one moment to the next where she was, for, if I know anything of my abominable cousin Sophy, to drive decorously round the Park would not do for her at all!'

'You take it with a composure that does you the greatest credit, my dear Charles.'

'I didn't!' he interrupted, with a rueful laugh. 'She put me in a thundering rage!'

'I am sure that it is not wonderful that she should have. To drive a gentleman's horses without his leave shows a want of conduct that is above the line of being pleasing. Why, even *I* have never even requested you to let me take the reins!'

He looked amused. 'My dear Eugenia, I hope you never will, for I shall certainly refuse such a request! You could never hold my horses.'

If Miss Wraxton had not been so very well-bred she would at this tactless remark have returned a pretty hot rejoinder, for she prided herself a little on her handling of the ribbons; and, although she did not drive herself in London, owned an elegant phaeton which she used when staying at her home in Hampshire. As it was, she was obliged to pause for a moment before saying anything. During this brief period she swiftly formed the resolve of demonstrating to Charles, and his objectionable cousin, that a lady reared on the strictest principles of propriety could be quite as notable a horsewoman as any hoyden who had spent her girlhood junketing about the Continent. She had several times been complimented on her seat on a horse, and knew her style to be excellent. She said: 'If Miss Stanton-Lacy cares for such things, perhaps she would like to ride with me one afternoon in the park. That will give her thoughts another direction, diverting them from such foolish notions as setting up her own carriage. Let us make up a party, Charles! Dear Cecilia is not fond of the exercise, I know, or I should solicit her to join us. But Alfred will be pleased to go with me, and you may bring your cousin. Tomorrow? Pray beg her to go with us!'

Mr Rivenhall, an intolerant man, had no affection for his Eugenia's younger brother, and generally made it his business to avoid him, but he was struck by Miss Wraxton's nobility in promoting an engagement which (he guessed) would afford her little pleasure, and at once agreed to it, expressing at the same time his sense of obligation to her. She smiled at him, and said that it must be an object with her to exert herself in his interests. He was a man not much given to the making of graceful gestures, but at this he kissed her hand, and said that he knew well how utterly he could rely upon her in every predicament. Miss Wraxton then repeated the remark she had previously made to Lady Ombersley, that she was particularly sorry that, at this crisis in the Ombersley fortunes, circumstance had intervened to postpone her union with him. She rather thought that the indifferent state of dear Lady Ombersley's health made it impossible for her to manage her household just as Charles could wish. Her kind heart made her perhaps over-tolerant, and the languor induced by an ailing constitution rendered her blind to certain defects that could speedily be remedied by a helpful daughter-in-law. Miss Wraxton owned that she had been surprised to learn that Lady Ombersley had allowed herself to be persuaded by her brother – a very odd kind of man, her papa had told her – to assume the charge of his daughter for an unspecified length of time. She passed from this, in the smoothest fashion, to a gently worded criticism of Miss Adderbury, no doubt an excellent woman, but sadly lacking in accomplishments, or in control over her spirited charges. But this was a mistake: Mr Rivenhall would permit no criticism of Addy, who had guided his own first steps; and as for his uncle, Lord Brinklow's slighting comment made him instantly bristle in defence of his relative. Sir Horace, he informed Miss Wraxton, was a highly distinguished man, with a genius for diplomacy.

'But not, you will own, a genius for rearing a daughter!' said Miss Wraxton archly.

He laughed at that, but said: 'Oh, well! I don't know that there is any real harm in Sophy, after all!'

When Miss Wraxton's invitation was conveyed to Sophy she professed herself happy to accept it, and at once desired Miss Jane Storridge to press out her riding-dress. This garment, when she appeared in it on the following afternoon, filled Cecilia with envy, but slightly staggered her brother, who could not feel that a habit made of pale blue cloth, with epaulettes and frogs, à la Hussar, and sleeves braided half-way up the arm, would win approval from Miss Wraxton. Blue kid gloves and half-boots, a high-standing collar trimmed with lace, a muslin cravat, narrow lace ruffles at the wrists, and a tall-crowned hat, like a shako, with a peak over the eyes, and a plume of curled ostrich feathers completed this dashing toilette. The tightly fitting habit set off Sophy's magnificent figure to admiration; and from under the brim of her hat her brown locks curled quite charmingly; but Mr Rivenhall, appealed to by his sister to subscribe to her conviction that Sophy looked beautiful, merely bowed, and said that he was no judge of such matters.

However that might be, he was no mean judge of a horse, and when he set eyes on Salamanca, being walked up and down the road by John Potton, he did not withhold his praise, but said that he no longer wondered at Hubert's ecstasies. John Potton threw his mistress up into the saddle, and after allowing Salamanca to indulge his playfulness for a few moments Sophy brought him mincing up alongside Mr Rivenhall's bay hack, and they set off at a sedate pace in the direction of Hyde Park. Salamanca was inclined to resent the existence of sedan-chairs, dogs, crossing-sweepers, and took instant exception to a postman's horn, but

Mr Rivenhall, accustomed to be on the alert to prevent mis-adventure when riding with Cecilia through London streets, knew better than to offer advice or assistance to his cousin. She was very well able to control her mount for herself, which, reflected Mr Rivenhall, was just as well, since Salamanca could scarcely have been described as an ideal horse for a lady.

This comment was made by Miss Wraxton, whom they found awaiting them, with her brother, within the gates of the Park. Miss Wraxton, after one glance at Sophy's habit, transferred her gaze to Salamanca, and said: 'Oh, what a beautiful creature! But surely he is a little too strong for you, Miss Stanton-Lacy? You should commission Charles to find a well-mannered lady's horse for you to ride.'

'I daresay he would be only too delighted, but I have dis-covered that his notions and mine on *that* subject are widely separated,' replied Sophy. 'Moreover, though he is a trifle spirited, there is not an ounce of vice in Salamanca, and he has what the Duke calls excellent bottom – has carried me for league upon dreary league without a sign of flagging!' She leaned forward to pat Salamanca's gleaming black neck. 'To be sure, he has not yet lashed out at the end of a long day, which the Duke vows and declares Copenhagen did, when he dismounted from his back after Waterloo, but I hold that to be a virtue in him!'

'Indeed, yes!' said Miss Wraxton, ignoring the unbecoming pretension shown by this careless reference to England's Hero. 'You will let me introduce my brother to you, Miss Stanton-Lady. Alfred!'

Mr Wraxton, a pallid young gentleman with a receding chin, a loose, wet mouth, and a knowing look in his eyes, bowed, and said he was happy to make Miss Stanton-Lacy's acquaintance. He then asked her if she had been in Brussels at the time of the great battle, and added that he had some idea of joining as a Volunteer at the height of the scare. 'But from one cause and another nothing came of it,' he said. 'Do you know the Duke well? Quite the great man, ain't he? But perfectly affable, they tell me. I daresay you are on famous terms with him, for you knew him in Spain, didn't you?'

'My dear Alfred,' interposed his sister, 'Miss Stanton-Lacy will think you have less than common-sense if you talk such nonsense. She will tell you that the Duke has more important things to think of than all of us poor females who hold him in such admiration.'

Sophy looked rather amused. 'Well, no, I don't think I should say that,' she replied. 'But I was never one of his flirts, if that is what you mean, Mr Wraxton. I am not at all in his style, I assure you.'

'Shall we ride on?' suggested Miss Wraxton. 'You must tell me about your horse. Is he Spanish? Very handsome, but a little too nervous for my taste. But I am spoilt: my own dear Dorcas here is so very well-mannered.'

'Salamanca is not really nervous: he is merely funning,' said Sophy. 'As for manners, I hold him to be unequalled. Would you like to see me put him through his paces? Watch? He was Mameluke-trained, you know!'

'For heaven's sake, Sophy, not in the Park!' said Charles sharply.

She threw him one of her saucy smiles, and set Salamanca caracoling.

'Oh, pray be careful!' exclaimed Miss Wraxton. 'It is very dangerous! Charles, stop her! We shall have everyone staring at us!'

'You won't mind if I shake the fidgets out of his legs!' Sophy called. 'He is itching for a gallop!'

With that, she wheeled Salamanca about, and let him have his head down the stretch of tan that lay beside the carriage-road.

'Yoicks!' uttered Mr Wraxton, and set off in pursuit.

'My dear Charles, what is to be done with her?' said Miss Wraxton. 'Galloping in the Park, and in that habit, which I should blush to wear! I was never more shocked!'

'Yes,' he agreed, his eyes on the diminishing figure in the distance. 'But, by God, she can ride!'

'Of course, if you mean to encourage her in such pranks there is no more to be said.'

'I don't,' he replied briefly.

She was displeased, and said coldly: 'I must confess that I do not admire her style: I am reminded of nothing so much as the equestriennes at Astley's Amphitheatre. Shall we canter?'

In this sedate way they rode side by side down the tan until they saw Sophy galloping back to them, Mr Wraxton still in pursuit. Sophy reined in, wheeled, and fell in beside her cousin. 'How much I enjoyed that!' she said, her cheeks in a glow. 'I have not been on Salamanca's back for over a week. But tell me! Have I done wrong? So many prim persons stared as though they could not believe their eyes!'

'You should not ride in that neck-or-nothing fashion in the Park!' Charles replied. 'I should have warned you.'

'You should indeed! I was afraid it might be that. Never mind! I will be good now, and if anyone speaks of it to you you will say that it is only your poor little cousin from Portugal, who has been so badly brought-up that there is no doing anything about it.' She leaned forward to speak across him to Miss Wraxton. 'I appeal to you, Miss Wraxton! You are a horsewoman. Is it not insupportable to be held down to a canter when you long to gallop for miles?'

'Most irksome,' agreed Miss Wraxton.

At this moment Alfred Wraxton rejoined them, calling out: 'By jove, Miss Stanton-Lacy, you will take the shine out of them all! You are nothing to her, Eugenia!'

'We cannot go four abreast,' said Miss Wraxton, ignoring his remark. 'Charles, fall behind with Alfred! I cannot converse with Miss Stanton-Lacy across you.'

He complied with this request, and Miss Wraxton, bringing her mare alongside Salamanca, said with all the tact upon which she plumed herself: 'I am persuaded that you must find our London ways strange at first.'

'Why, I imagine they cannot differ greatly from those of Paris, or Vienna, or even Lisbon!' said Sophy.

'I have never visited those cities, but I believe – indeed I am sure! – that the tone of London is vastly superior,' said Miss Wraxton.

Her air of calm certainty struck Sophy as being so funny that she went into a peal of laughter. 'Oh, I beg your pardon!' she gasped. 'But it is so ridiculous, you know!'

'I expect it must seem so to you,' agreed Miss Wraxton, her calm quite unimpaired. 'I understated that a great deal of licence is permitted on the Continent to females. Here it is not so. Quite the reverse! To be thought bad *ton*, dear Miss Stanton-Lacy, would be very dreadful. I know that you will not take it amiss if I give you a hint. You will of course wish to attend the Assemblies at Almack's, for instance. I assure you, the veriest breath of criticism to reach the ears of the patronesses, and you may say farewell to any hope of obtaining a voucher from them. Tickets may not be purchased without a voucher, you know. It is most exclusive! The rules, too, are very strict, and must not be contravened by a hairsbreadth.'

'You terrify me,' said Sophy. 'Do you think I shall be blackballed?'

Miss Wraxton smiled. 'Hardly, since you will make your début under Lady Ombersley's aegis! She will no doubt tell you just how you should conduct yourself, if her health permits her to take you there. It is unfortunate that circumstances have prevented me from occupying that position which would have enabled me to have relieved her of such duties.'

'Forgive me!' interrupted Sophy, whose attention had been wandering, 'but I think Madam de Lieven is waving to me, and it would be very uncivil not to notice her!'

She rode off as she spoke, to where a smart barouche was drawn up beside the track, and leaned down from her saddle to shake the languid hand held up to her.

'Sophie!' pronounced the Countess. 'Sir Horace told me I should meet you here. You were galloping *ventre à terre*; never do so again! Ah, Mrs Burrell, permit me to present to you Miss Stanton-Lacy!'

The lady seated beside the Ambassador's wife bowed slightly, and allowed her lips to relax into an infinitesimal smile. This expanded a little when she observed Miss Wraxton, following in Sophy's wake, and she inclined her heard, a great mark of condescension.

Countess Lieven nodded to Miss Wraxton, but went on talking to Sophy. 'You are staying with Lady Ombersley. I am a little acquainted with her, and I shall call. She will spare you to me perhaps one evening. You have not seen Princess Esterhazy yet, or Lady Jersey? I shall tell them I have met you, and they will want to hear how Sir Horace does. What did I promise Sir Horace I would do? Ah, but of course! Almack's! I will send you a voucher, ma chère Sophie, but do not gallop in Hyde Park.' She then told her coachman to drive on, included the whole of Sophy's party in her light, valedictory smile, and turned to continue her interrupted conversation with Mrs Drummond Burrell.

'I was not aware that you were acquainted with the Countess Lieven,' said Miss Wraxton.

'Do you dislike her?' Sophy asked, aware of the coldness in Miss Wraxton's voice. 'Many people do, I know. Sir Horace calls her the great *intriguante*, but she is clever, and can be very amusing. She has a *tendre* for him, as I daresay you have guessed. I like Princess Esterhazy better myself, I own, and Lady Jersey better than either of them, because she is so much more sincere, in spite of that restless manner of hers.'

'Dreadful woman!' said Charles. 'She never stops talking! She is known as Silence, in London.'

'Is she? Well, I am sure, if she knows it, she does not care a bit, for she dearly loves a joke.'

'You are fortunate in knowing so many of the Patronesses of Almack's,' observed Miss Wraxton.

Sophy gave her irrepressible chuckle. 'To be honest, I think my good fortune lies in having such an accomplished flirt for a father!'

Mr Wraxton giggled at this, and his sister, dropping a little behind, brought her mare up on Mr Rivenhall's other side, and said in a low tone, under cover of some quizzing remark made to Sophy by Mr Wraxton: 'It is a pity that men will laugh when her liveliness betrays her into saying what cannot be thought becoming. It brings her too much into notice, and that, I fancy, is the root of the evil.'

He raised his brows. 'You are severe! Do you dislike her?'

'Oh, no, no!' she said quickly. 'It is merely that I have no great taste for that kind of sportive playfulness.'

He looked as though he would have liked to have said something more, but at this moment a very military-looking cavalcade came into sight, cantering easily towards them. It consisted of four gentlemen, whose dashing side-whiskers and soldierly bearing proclaimed their profession. They glanced idly at Mr Rivenhall's party. The next instant there was a shout, and a hurried reining-in, and one of the quartet exclaimed in ringing accents: 'By all that's wonderful, it's the Grand Sophy!'

Confusion and babel followed this, all four gentlemen pressing up to grasp Sophy's hand, and pelting her with questions. Where had she sprung from? how long had she been in England? why had they not been told of her arrival? how was Sir Horace?

'Oh, but, Sophy, you're a sight for sore eyes!' declared Major Quinton, who had first hailed her.

'You have Salamanca still! Lord, do you remember riding him through the Pyrenees when you nearly got snapped up by old Soult?'

'Sophy, what's your direction? Are you living in London now? Where's Sir Horace?'

She was laughing, trying to answer them all, while her horse sidled, and fidgeted, and tossed his head. 'Abroad. Never mind about me! What are you all doing in England? I thought you in France still! Don't tell me you have sold out!'

'Debenham has, lucky dog! I'm on furlough; Wolvey's stationed in England – what a thing it is to belong to the Gentleman's Sons! – and Talgarth has become a great man, almost a Tiger! Yes, I assure you! A.D.C. to the Duke of York.

You notice the air of consequence! But he is all condescension: not the least height in his manner – yet!'

'Silence, rattle!' said his victim. He was rather older than his companion, a handsome, dark man, with a decided air of fashion and a languid manner. 'Dear Sophy, I am tolerably certain that you cannot have been in London above many days. Not the smallest rumour of any volcanic disturbance has come to my ears, and you know how quick I am to get abreast of the news!'

She laughed. 'Oh, that is too bad of you, Sir Vincent! I don't create disturbances: you know I don't!'

'I know nothing of the kind, my child. When last I saw you, you were engaged in arranging in the most ruthless fashion the affairs of the most bewildered family of Belgians I have yet encountered. They had all my sympathy, but there was nothing I could do to help them: I know my limitations.'

'Those poor Le Bruns! Well, but *someone* had to help them out of such a tangle! I assure you, everything was settled *most* satisfactorily! But come! I forget my manners in all this excitement! Miss Wraxton, do pray forgive me, and allow me to present to you Colonel Sir Vincent Talgarth; and, beside him, Colonel Debenham. And this is Major Titus Quinton, and – oh, dear, ought I to have said your name first, Frances? it is one of the things I never know, but no matter! – Captain Lord Francis Wolvey! And this is my cousin, Mr Rivenhall. Oh, and Mr Wraxton, also!'

Miss Wraxton inclined her head politely; Mr Rivenhall, bowing slightly to the rest of the party, addressed himself to Lord Francis, saying: 'I don't think I ever met you, but your brother and I were up at Oxford together.'

Lord Francis at once leaned forward in his saddle to shake him by the hand. 'Now I know who you are!' he announced. 'You are Charles Rivenhall! Thought I couldn't be mistaken! How do you do? Do you still box? Freddy was used to say he never knew an amateur with a more punishing right!'

Mr Rivenhall laughed. 'Did he? He felt it often enough, but I take no credit for that: he was always glaringly abroad!'

Major Quinton, who had been regarding him intently, said: 'Then that is very likely where I have seen you. Jackson's Saloon! You are the fellow Jackson says he might have made into a champion if only you had not been a gentleman!'

This remark naturally beguiled all three men in a sporting conversation. Mr Wraxton hung on the outskirts of it, occasionally interpolating a few words which no one paid any heed to; Sophy smiled benignly to see her friends and her cousin so happily absorbed; and Colonel Debenham, who had excellent manners, and a kind heart, began to make painstaking conversation to Miss Wraxton. By tacit consent, the military gentlemen turned to accompany Mr Rivenhall's party up the track, and the entire cavalcade moved forward at a walking-pace.

Sophy found that Sir Vincent had brought his horse up to walk beside hers, and said suddenly: 'Sir Vincent, you are the very man I need! Let us draw a little ahead!'

'Nothing in this life, enchanting Juno, could afford me more pleasure!' he instantly responded. 'I have no fancy for the Fancy. On no account tell anyone that I said that! It is quite unworthy of me! Are you about to transport me by accepting a heart laid often at your feet, and as often spurned? Something informs me that I indulge my optimism too far, and that you are going to demand of me some service that will plunge me into a morass of trouble, and end in my being cashiered.'

'Nothing of the sort!' declared Sophy. 'But I never knew anyone, other than Sir Horace, whose judgement I would rather trust when it comes to buying a horse. Sir Vincent, I want to purchase a pair for my phaeton!'

They had by this time considerably outdistanced the rest of the party. Sir Vincent made his roan drop to a walk, and said brokenly: 'Allow me a moment in which to recover my manhood! So that is all the use you have for me!'

'Don't be so absurd!' said Sophy. 'What better use could I have for anyone?'

'Dear Juno, I have told you a great many times, and I shall tell you no more!'

'Sir Vincent,' said Sophy severely, 'you have dangled after every heiress who has come in your way from the day I first met you –'

'Shall I ever forget it? You had lost a front tooth, and torn your dress.'

'Very likely. Though I have not the least doubt that you don't recall the occasion at all, and have this instant made that up. You are a more hardened flirt even than Sir Horace, and you only offer for me because you know I shall not accept your suit. My fortune cannot be large enough to tempt you.'

'That,' acknowledged Sir Vincent, 'is true. But better men than I, my dear Sophy, have been known to cut their coats to suit their cloth.'

'Yes, but I am not your cloth, and you know very well that, indulgent though he may be, Sir Horace would never permit me to marry you, even if I wished to, which I do not.'

'Oh, very well!' sighed Sir Vincent. 'Let us talk of horse-flesh, then!'

'The thing is,' confided Sophy, 'that I was obliged to sell my carriage-horses when we left Lisbon, and Sir Horace had no time to attend to the matter before he sailed for Brazil. He said my cousin would advise me, but he was quite out! He will not.'

'Charles Rivenhall,' said Sir Vincent, looking at her from under drooping eyelids, 'is held to be no bad judge of a horse. What mischief are you brewing, Sophy?'

'None! He has said he will not stir in the matter, and also that it would be improper for me to visit Tattersall's. Is that true?'

'Well, it would certainly be unusual.'

'Then I won't do it: my aunt would be distressed, and she has enough to plague her already. Where else can I buy a pair that will suit me?'

He gazed meditatively ahead between his horse's ears. 'I wonder if you would care to buy two of Manningtree's break-downs before they come into the open market?' he said presently. 'Quite done-up, poor fellow, and is selling off all his cattle. What's your figure, Sophy?'

'Sir Horace told me not above four hundred, unless I saw a pair it would be a crime not to buy.'

'Manningtree would sell you his match bays for less than that. As handsome a pair as you could wish for: I should buy them myself if I had a feather to fly with.'

'Where may I see them?'

'Leave that to me: I'll arrange it. What's your direction?'

'At Lord Ombersley's house in Berkeley Square: that big one, at the corner!'

'Of course. So he is your uncle, is he?'

'No, but his wife is my aunt.'

'And Charles Rivenhall is therefore your cousin. Well, well! How do you contrive to amuse yourself, my Sophy?'

'I own, I did wonder how I should do so, but I find that the whole family is in a sad tangle, poor dears, and I do hope I may be able to make them more comfortable!'

'I have no particular liking for your uncle, who is one of my esteemed Chief's cronies; on the only occasion when I solicited your beautiful cousin Cecilia to dance with me at Almack's, her forbidding brother forestalled me in a fashion as swift as it was crude – someone ought to tell him that I am only interested in heiresses; and yet my withers are strangely wrung! Almost my heart goes out to the family. Do they tread blindly towards their doom, Sophy, or did they willingly receive a firebrand into their midst?'

She gave a chuckle. 'They tread blindly – but I am *not* a firebrand!'

'No, I used the wrong word. You are like poor Whinyates's rockets: no one knows what you will do next!'

Six

'Is the knocker never still?' demanded Charles of his mother, after the departure of the fourth morning-caller in one day.

'Never!' she replied proudly. 'Since that day when you took dear Sophy riding in the Park, I have received seven gentlemen – no, eight, counting Augustus Fawnhope. Princess Esterhazy, the Countess Lieven, Lady Jersey, and Lady Castlereagh have all left cards; and –'

'Was Talgarth amongst those who called, ma'am?'

She wrinkled her brow. 'Talgarth? Oh, yes! A most amiable man, with side-whiskers! To be sure he was!'

'Take care!' he warned her. '*That* connection will not do!'

She was startled. 'Charles, what can you mean? He seems to be on terms of great friendship with Sophy, and she told me Sir Horace had been acquainted with him for years!'

'I daresay, but if my uncle means to bestow Sophy upon him he is not the man I take him for! He is said to be a gazetted fortune-hunter; and is, besides, a gamester, with more debts than expectations, and such libertine propensities as scarcely render him a desirable catch in the marriage mart!'

'Oh, dear!' said Lady Ombersley, dismayed. She wondered whether she ought to tell her son that his cousin had gone out driving with Sir Vincent only a day earlier, and decided that no purpose could be served in dwelling on what was past. 'Perhaps I should drop a hint in Sophy's ear.'

'I doubt of its being well-received, ma'am. Eugenia has

already spoken with her on this subject. All that my cousin saw fit to reply was that she was quite up to snuff, and would engage not to allow herself to be seduced by Sir Vincent, or anyone else.'

'Oh, *dear!*' said Lady Ombersley again. 'She really should not say such things!'

'Just so, ma'am!'

'But, though I do not wish to offend you, Charles, I cannot help feeling that perhaps it was not quite wise of Eugenia to have spoken to her on such a subject. You know, my dear, she is not in any way related to Sophy!'

'Only Eugenia's strong sense of duty,' he said stiffly, 'and, I may add, Mama, her earnest desire to spare you anxiety, induced her to undertake a task which she felt to be excessively unpleasant.'

'It is very kind of her, I am sure,' said his mother, in a depressed voice.

'Where is my cousin?' he asked abruptly.

She brightened, for to this question she was able to return an unexceptionable answer. 'She has gone for a drive in the barouche with Cecilia and your brother.'

'Well, that should be harmless enough,' he said.

He would have been less satisfied on this point had he known that, having taken up Mr Fawnhope, whom they encountered in Bond Street, the occupants of the barouche were at that moment in Longacre, critically inspecting sporting vehicles. There were a great many of these, together with almost every variety of carriage, on view at the warehouse to which Hubert had conducted his cousin, and although Sophy remained firm in her preference for a phaeton, Cecilia was much taken with a caned whiskey, and Hubert, having fallen in love with a curricle, forcibly urged his cousin to buy it. Mr Fawnhope, appealed to for his opinion, was found to be missing, and was presently discovered seated in rapt contemplation of a state berlin, which looked rather like a very large breakfast-cup, poised upon elongated springs. It was covered with a domed roof, bore a great deal of gilding, and had a coachman's seat, perched over the front wheels which was covered in blue velvet with a gold fringe. 'Cinderella!' said Mr Fawnhope simply.

The manager of the warehouse said that he did not think the berlin – which he kept for show purposes – was quite what the lady was looking for.

'A coach for a princess,' said Mr Fawnhope, unheeding. 'This, Cecilia, is what you must drive in. You shall have six white horses to draw it, with plumes on their heads, and blue harness.'

Cecilia had no fault to find with this programme, but reminded him that they had come to help Sophy to choose a sporting carriage. He allowed himself to be dragged away from the berlin, but when asked to cast his vote between the curricle and the phaeton, would only murmur: *'What can little T.O. do? Why, drive a phaeton and two! Can little T.O. do no more? Yes, drive a phaeton and four!'*

'That's all very well,' said Hubert impatiently, 'but my cousin ain't Tommy Onslow, and for my part I think she will do better with this curricle!'

'You cannot scan the lines, yet they have a great deal of merit,' said Mr Fawnhope. 'How beautiful is the curricle! How swift! How splendid! Yet Apollo chose a phaeton. These carriages bewilder me: let us go away!'

'Who is Tommy Onslow? Does he indeed drive a phaeton and four?' asked Sophy, her eyes kindling. 'Now, that would be something indeed! What a bore that I have just bought a pair! I could never match them, I fear.'

'You could borrow Charles's grays,' suggested Hubert, grinning wickedly. 'By Jupiter, what a kick-up there would be!'

Sophy laughed, but shook her head. 'No, it would be an infamous thing to do! I shall purchase that phaeton: I have quite made up my mind.'

The manager looked startled, for the carriage she pointed at was not the phaeton he had supposed she would buy – an elegant vehicle, perfectly suited to a lady – but a high-perch model, with huge hind-wheels, and the body, which was hung directly over the front-axle, fully five feet from the ground. However, it was not his business to dissuade a customer from making an expensive purchase, so he bowed, and kept his inevitable reflections to himself.

Hubert, less tactful, said: 'I say, Sophy, it really ain't a lady's carriage! I only hope you may not overturn it round the first corner!'

'Not I!'

'Cecilia,' suddenly pronounced Mr Fawnhope, who had been studying the phaeton intently, 'must never ride in that vehicle!'

He spoke with such unaccustomed decision that everyone looked at him in surprise, and Cecilia turned quite pink with gratification at his solicitude.

'I assure you, I shan't overturn it,' said Sophy.

'Every feeling would be outraged by the sight of so exquisite a creature in such a turn-out as that!' pursued Mr Fawnhope. 'Its proportions are absurd! It was, moreover, built for excessive speed, and should be driven, if driven it must be, by some down-the-road man with fifteen capes and a spotted neck-cloth. It is not for Cecilia!'

'Well!' exclaimed Sophy. 'I thought you were afraid I might overturn her in it!'

'I am afraid of that,' replied Mr Fawnhope. 'The very thought of so ungraceful a happening must offend! It *does* offend! It intrudes its grossness upon the sensibilities; it blurs my vision of a porcelain nymph! Let us immediately leave this place!'

Cecilia, wavering between pleasure at hearing herself likened to a porcelain nymph, and affront at having her safety so little regarded, merely said that they could not leave until Sophy had concluded her purchase; but Sophy, a good deal amused, suggested that she should withdraw with her swain to await her in the barouche.

'Y'know,' Hubert said confidentially, when the pair had departed, 'I don't know that I blame Charles for not being able to stomach that fellow! He is quite paltry!'

Within three days of this transaction, Mr Rivenhall, exercising his grays in the Park, paused by the Riding House to take up his friend, Mr Wychbold, sauntering along in all the glory of pale yellow pantaloons, shining Hessians, and a coat of extravagant cut and delicate hue. 'Good God!' he ejaculated. 'What a devilish sight! Get up, Cyprian, and stop ogling all the females! Where have you been hiding yourself this age?'

Mr Wychbold mounted into the curricle, disposing his shapely limbs with rare grace, and replied, with a sigh: 'The call of duty, dear boy! Visiting the ancestral home! I do what I may with lavender-water, but the aroma of the stables and cow-byres is hard to overcome. Charles, much as I love you if I had *seen* that neckcloth before I consented to let you drive me round the Park – !'

'Don't waste that stuff on me!' recommended his friend. 'What's wrong with your chestnuts?'

Mr Wychbold, one of the shining lights of the Four-Horse Club, sighed mournfully. 'Dead lame! No, not both, but one, which is quite as bad. Would you believe it? I let my sister drive them! Take it as a maxim, Charles, that no woman is to be trusted to handle the ribbons!'

'You haven't yet met my cousin,' replied Mr Rivenhall, with a twisted smile.

'You are mistaken,' said Mr Wychbold calmly. 'I met her at the Gala night at Almack's, which, dear boy, you might have known, had you not absented yourself from that gathering.'

'Oh, you did, did you? I have no turn for that form of insipidity.'

'Wouldn't have done you any good if you had,' said Mr Wychbold. 'There was no getting near your cousin; at least, there wouldn't have been for you. *I* managed it, but I have a great deal of address. Danced the boulanger with her. Devilish fine girl!'

'Well, it's time you were thinking of getting married: offer for her! I shall be much obliged to you.'

'Almost anything else for your sake, dear boy, but I ain't a marrying man!' said Mr Wychbold firmly.

'I wasn't serious. To be honest with you, if you took such a notion into your head I should do my utmost to dissuade you. She is the most tiresome girl I ever hope to meet. The only thing I know to her credit is that she can drive to an inch. She had the damned impertinence to steal my curricle when my back was turned for five minutes.'

'She drove these grays?' demanded Mr Wychbold.

'She did. Well up to their bits, too. All to force me into buying a phaeton-and-pair for her to lionize in! I shan't do it, but I should rather like to see how she would handle such a turn-out.'

'No wish to raise false hopes,' said Mr Wychbold, who had been watching the approach of a dashing perch-phaeton, 'but can't help thinking that that's just what you're about to do, dear fellow! Though why your cousin should be driving Manningtree's bays beats me!'

'What?' ejaculated Mr Rivenhall sharply. His incredulous gaze fell upon the phaeton, coming towards him at a smart trot. Very much at home in the perilous vehicle, seated high above her horses, with her groom beside her, and holding her whip at exactly the correct angle, was Miss Stanton-Lacy, and if the sight afforded Mr Rivenhall pleasure he vouchsafed no sign whatever of this. He looked at first thunderstruck, and then more than usually grim. As the pace of the bays slackened, and dropped to a walk, he reined in his own pair. The two carriages came to a halt abreast of each other.

'Cousin Charles!' said Sophy. 'And Mr Wychbold! How do you do? Tell me, cousin, what do you think of them? I am persuaded I have a bargain in them.'

'Where,' demanded Mr Rivenhall, 'did you get those horses?'

'Now, Charles, for the lord's sake don't be bird-witted!' implied Mr Wychbold, preparing to descend from the curricle. 'You must see she has Manningtree's match-geldings there! Besides, I told you so, a minute ago. But how is this, Miss Stanton-Lacy? Is Manningtree selling up?'

'So I believe,' she smiled.

'By Jove, you have stolen a march on me, then, for I have had my eye on that pair ever since Manningtree sprang 'em on the town! How did you get wind of it, ma'am?'

'To own the truth, I knew nothing about the matter,' she confessed. 'It was Sir Vincent Talgarth who put me in the way of buying them.'

'That fellow!' interpolated Mr Rivenhall explosively. 'I might have known!'

'Yes, so you might,' she agreed. 'He is quite famous for knowing all the news before others have heard even a rumour. May I take you up, Mr Wychbold? If I have stolen a march on you, the least amends I can make is to offer to let you drive my pair.'

'Don't hesitate to tell me which of my mother's or my horses you would like me to remove from the stables to make room for these!' begged Mr Rivenhall, with savage civility. 'Unless, of course, you are setting up your own stables!'

'Dear Cousin Charles, I hope I know better than to put you to such shocking inconvenience! John Potton here has seen to all that. *You* are not to be troubled with my horses! Get down, John: you need not fear to let Mr Wychbold have your place, for if the horses should bolt with me he is better fitted to get them under control again then either of us.'

The middle-aged groom, having favoured Mr Wychbold with a long scrutiny, appeared to be satisfied, for he obeyed without making any comment. Mr Wychbold leaped up lightly into the phaeton; Sophy nodded farewell to her cousin; and the bays moved forward. Mr Rivenhall watched the phaeton smoulderingly for a moment to two, and then lowered his gaze to the groom's countenance. 'What the devil were you about to let your mistress buy a damned dangerous carriage like that?' he demanded.

'Don't you put yourself in a pucker over Miss Sophy, sir!' said John, in a fatherly way. 'Sir Horace himself couldn't stop her, not when she's got the bit between her teeth! Many's the time I've told Sir Horace he should have broke her to bridle, but he never done it, nor tried to.'

'Well, if I have much more –' Mr Rivenhall pulled himself up short, realizing how improper was this interchange. 'Damn your impudence!' he said, and set his grays in motion with a plunge that betrayed the state of his temper.

Mr Wychbold, meanwhile, was most gallantly refusing to take the reins from Miss Stanton-Lacy. 'Dashed if I ever thought I should say so, but it's a pleasure to be driven by a lady who handles 'em as well as you do, ma'am! Very sweet-goers, too: shouldn't be surprised if Charles had had his eye on 'em, which would account for him flying into one of his miffs.'

'No, no, I am sure you wrong him! He has flown into a miff because I bought them against his advice – indeed, in the face of his prohibition! Do you know my cousin well, sir?'

'Known him since we were at Eton.'

'Then tell me! Has he *always* wanted to rule the roast?'

Mr Wychbold considered this, but arrived at no very exact conclusion. 'Well, I don't know,' he said. 'Always one to take the lead, of course, but a man don't come the ruler over his friends, ma'am. At least . . .' He paused, recalling past incidents. 'Thing is, he's got an awkward temper, but he's a dashed good friend!' he produced. 'Told him times out of mind he ought to watch that devilish unpleasant tongue of his, but the fact is, ma'am, there's no one I'd liefer go to in a fix than Charles Rivenhall!'

'That is a tribute indeed,' she said thoughtfully.

Mr Wychbold coughed deprecatingly. 'Never mentioned the matter to me, of course, but the poor fellow's had a deal to bear, if the half of what one hears is true. Turned him sour. Often thought so! Though why the deuce he must needs get himself engaged to that –' he broke off in considerable confusion. 'Forgotten what I was going to say!' he added hastily.

'Then that settles it!' said Sophy, dropping her hands slightly, and allowing the bays to quicken their pace.

'Settles what?' asked Mr Wychbold.

'Why, Cecilia told me that you were his particular friend, and if *you* think it will not do I need have no scruples. Only fancy, Mr Wychbold, what misery for my dear aunt and those poor children to have that Friday-faced creature setting them all to rights! Living under the same roof, and, you may depend upon it, encouraging Charles to be as disagreeable as he can stare!'

'It don't bear thinking of!' said Mr Wychbold, much struck.

'It must be thought of!' replied Sophy resolutely.

'No use thinking of it,' said Mr Wychbold, shaking his head. 'Betrothal puffed in all the papers weeks ago! Would have been married by now if the girl hadn't had to put up a black ribbon. Very good match, of course: woman of quality, handsome dowry, I daresay, excellent connections!'

'Well,' said Sophy large-mindedly, 'if his *heart* is in the business, I suppose he must be permitted to have his way, but he shall *not* inflict her upon his family! But I do not think his heart has had anything to say in it, and as for her, she has none! There! That is cutting up a character indeed!'

Mr Wychbold, stirred to enthusiasm, said in a confidential tone: 'Know what, ma'am? Been on the Marriage Mart for two whole years! Fact! Set her cap at Maxstoke last year, but he sheered off. Odds shortened to evens, too, in the clubs, but he got clean away.' He sighed. 'Charles won't. In the Gazette, you know: poor fellow couldn't declare off now if he wanted to!'

'No,' agreed Sophy, her brow creased. '*She* could, however.'

'She *could*, but she won't,' said Mr Wychbold positively.

'We'll see!' said Sophy. 'At all events, I must and I will prevent her making those poor dears miserable! For that is what she does, I assure you! She is for ever coming to Berkeley Square, and casting everyone into the dumps! First it is my aunt, who goes to bed with the head-ache when she has had the creature with her for half an hour; then it is Miss Adderbury, to whom she says the horridest things in that odiously sweet voice she uses when she means to make mischief! She wonders that Miss Adderbury should not have taught the children to read Italian. She is surprised that she makes so little use of the backboard, and tells Charles that she fears little Amabel is growing to be round-shouldered! *Stuff!* She is trying even to persuade him to take their monkey away from the children. But what is worse than all is that she sets him against poor Hubert! That I cannot forgive! She does it in such a shabby way, too! I do not know how I kept my hands from her ears yesterday, for the silly boy had on a new waistcoat – quite dreadful, but he was so proud of it! – and what must she do but draw Charles's attention to it, pretending to chaff Hubert, you know, but contriving to make it appear that he was for ever buying new clothes, and squandering away his allowance on fripperies!'

'What a devilish woman!' exclaimed Mr Wychbold. 'Must say I shouldn't have expected Charles to take that kind of thing tamely! Never one to stand interference!'

'Oh, it is all done with such seeming solicitude that he doesn't see what lies at the root of it – yet!' said Sophy.

'Very bad business,' said Mr Wychbold. 'Nothing to be done, though.'

'That,' said Sophy severely, 'is what people always say when they are too lazy, or perhaps too timorous, to make a push to be helpful! I have a great many faults, but I am not lazy, and I am not timorous – though *that*, I know, is not a virtue, for I was born without any nerves at all, my father tells me, and almost no sensibility. I don't know that I shall, for I have not yet made up my mind just what I should do, but I *may* need your assistance in breaking this foolish engagement.' She perceived, in a quick glance at his face, that he was looking extremely scared, and added reassuringly: 'Very likely not, but one never knows, and it is always well to be prepared. Now I must put you down, for I see Cecilia awaiting me, and she has promised to let me drive her round the Park once she is assured I shan't overturn the phaeton.'

'No fear of that!' said Mr Wychbold, wondering what else this alarming young woman might overturn during her sojourn in Berkeley Square.

He shook hands, told her that if they would but allow females to belong to the Four-Horse Club he should certainly support her candidature, and sprang down from the phaeton, to exchange greetings with Cecilia, who, with Miss Adderbury and the children, were waiting beside the Drive. Gertrude, Amabel, and Theodore naturally asserted their claims to be taken up beside their cousin in preference to their elder sister, but after these had been firmly dealt with Mr Wychbold helped Cecilia to mount into the carriage, bowed, and strolled off.

It had struck Sophy immediately that Cecilia was looking pale, while the little governess was plainly labouring under a considerable degree of suppressed agitation; so, since she believed in getting to the root of any matter without wasting time on circumlocution, she at once demanded bluntly: 'Now, why are you looking as blue as megrim, Cecy?'

Tina, who during Mr Wychbold's occupation of the passenger's seat, had nestled inconspicuously behind her mistress's feet, now crawled out from beneath the drab rug, and jumped on to Cecilia's knee. Cecilia clasped her mechanically, and stroked her, but said in a tense voice: 'Eugenia!'

'Oh, the deuce take that creature!' exclaimed Sophy. 'Now what has she done?'

'She was walking here with Alfred,' said Cecilia, 'and she came upon us!'

'Well,' said Sophy reasonably, 'I own I do not like her, and Alfred is certainly the horridest little beast in nature, but I see nothing in that to put you so much out of countenance! He cannot have tried to put his arm round your waist if his sister was present!'

'Oh, Alfred – !' said Cecilia contemptuously. 'Not but what he *would* have me take his arm, and then squeezed it in the most odious way, and ogled, and said all the sort of things that make one itch to slap his face. But I care nothing for *him!* You see, Sophy, Augustus was with me!'

'Well?' said Sophy.

'It is true that we had fallen a little way behind Addy, for how can one have any rational conversation with the children chattering all the time? But she was *not* out of sight, and we had *not* stolen down a lonely path – at least, it wasn't one of the more frequented paths, but Addy was there all the time, so what could it signify? – and to say that I was meeting Augustus *cladestinely* is wickedly unjust! Anyone would suppose him to be some hateful adventurer, instead of someone I have known all my life, pretty well! Why shouldn't he walk in the Park? and if he does so, and we meet, pray, why should I not talk to him?'

'No reason at all. Did that repellent girl give you a scold?'

'Not me so much as poor Addy. She is in despair, for Eugenia seems to have said she was betraying mama's trust, and encouraging me in clandestine behaviour. She was quite odious to me, but she could not say anything very much, because Augustus was with me. She made him walk with her instead, and told Alfred to give me his arm, and I felt smirched, Sophy, *smirched*!'

'Anyone would, who was obliged to take Alfred's arm,' agreed Sophy.

'Not that! But Eugenia's manner! As though she had found me out in something disgraceful! And that is not the worst! Charles is driving here, and not a moment before you came up he went past us with Eugenia seated beside him. He gave the coldest look! She has told him all about it, depend upon it, and now he will be furious with me, and very likely work upon Mama as well, and everything will be so dreadful!'

'No, it won't,' said Sophy coolly. 'In fact, I shouldn't be at all surprised if this turned out to be a very good thing. I cannot explain all that to you now, but I do beg of you, Cecy, not to be so distressed! There is no need: I assure you there is none! Very likely Charles will not say a word to you about this.'

Cecilia turned incredulous eyes towards her. 'Charles not say a word! You don't know him! He was looking like a thunder-cloud!'

'I daresay he was; he very often does, and you are such a goose that you instantly quake like a blancmange,' replied Sophy. 'Presently, I shall set you down, and you will join poor little Addy, and continue your walk. I shall go home, where I am pretty sure to find your brother, for we have driven right round the Park now, and seen no sign of him and I know he will go back to Berkeley Square, for I heard him mention to my uncle that somebody called Eckington would be calling there at five o'clock.'

'Papa's agent,' said Cecilia listlessly. 'And I don't see, dearest Sophy, what it signifies, whether you find Charles at home or not, because he won't speak of this to you: why should he?'

'Oh, won't he just?' retorted Sophy. 'Depend upon it, by this time he will have persuaded himself that everything has been my fault from start to finish! Besides, he is furious with me for having bought this turn-out without his help; yes, and for having hired a stable of my own, too! He must be longing for me to come back to the house so that he can quarrel with me without fear of interruption. Poor man! I think I should put you down at once, Cecy.'

'How brave you are!' Cecilia said wonderingly. 'I do not know how you can bear it!'

'What, your brother's tantrums? I see nothing to be afraid of in them!'

Cecilia shuddered. 'It is not being afraid precisely, but I dread people being angry, and thundering at me! I cannot help it, Sophy, and I know it is poor-spirited of me, but my knees shake so, and I feel quite sick!'

'Well, they shan't be made to shake today,' said Sophy cheerfully. 'I am going to spike Charles's guns. Oh, see! There is Francis Wolvey! The very thing! He shall restore you to Addy for me.'

She drew up as she spoke, and Lord Francis, who had been chatting to two ladies in a landaulet, came up to the phaeton, exclaiming: 'Sophy, that's a capital turn-out! 'Servant, Miss Rivenhall! I wonder to see you trust yourself to such a madcap, I do indeed! She overturned me in a gig once. A *gig!*'

'What an unhandsome thing to say!' said Sophy indignantly. 'As though I could have helped it on such a road. Frenada! Oh, dear, what a long time ago it seems, to be sure! I came up with Sir Horace, and stayed with Mrs – Mrs –'

'Scovell,' supplied Lord Francis. 'She was the only lady living at Headquarters that winter, and used to hold loo-parties. Do you remember?'

'Of course I do! And more vividly still the fleas in that dreadful village! Francis, I must pick up John Potton, and be off: will you escort my cousin to meet her little brother and sisters? They are walking with their governess somewhere beside the Drive.'

Lord Francis, upon whom Cecilia's beauty had made a great impression, when he had met her on the occasion of his calling in Berkeley Square, promptly said that nothing could give him more pleasure, and reached up his hands to help her down from the phaeton. He said that he hoped that they would not too speedily encounter the schoolroom-party, and Cecilia, not impervious to his easy, friendly address, and evident admiration, began to look more cheerful. Sophy, well-satisfied, saw them walk off together, and drove on to where her groom awaited her, by the Stanhope Gate. He reported that he had watched Mr Rivenhall pass through it not many minutes earlier, and added, with a dry chuckle, that he looked to be on his high ropes still. 'Damned my impudence Miss Sophy, and fair jobbed at the grays' mouths!'

'Why, what had you said to enrage him?'

'All I said was you hadn't never been broke to bridle, missie, and what with him being in agreement with me, and not able to say so, there was nothing for it but to damn me and drive off. *I* don't blame him! Hot at hand, Miss Sophy, that's what you are!'

Upon her arrival in Berkeley Square, Sophy found that Mr Rivenhall had only just entered the house, having walked round from the mews. He was still wearing his caped driving-coat, and had paused by the table in the hall to pick up and read a note which had been sent by one of his friends. He looked up frowningly as Dassett admitted Sophy, but he did not speak. Tina, who had developed (her mistress considered) an ill-judged passion for his society, frisked gaily up to him, and employed every art known to her to attract his attention. He did indeed glance down at her, but so far from encouraging her advances, said curtly: 'Quiet!'

'Ah, so you are in before me!' remarked Sophy, pulling off her gloves. 'Now, give me your candid opinion of those bays! Mr Wychbold fancies you may have had an eye upon them yourself. Is that so?'

'Quite above my touch, cousin!' he replied.

'No, really? I gave four hundred guineas for them, and think I have a bargain.'

'Were you serious when you gave me to understand that you have set up your own stable?' he demanded.

'Certainly I was serious. A pretty thing it would be if my aunt were obliged to bear the charge of my horses! Besides, I may very likely purchase two more, if I can find a couple to match the bays. I am told that it is all the crack to drive a phaeton-and-four, though I suppose that would mean altering the shafts, which would be a bore.'

'I have no control over your actions, cousin,' he said coldly. 'No doubt if it seems good to you to make a spectacle of yourself in the Park, you will do so. But you will not, if you please, take any of my sisters up beside you!'

'But it doesn't please me,' she said. 'I have already taken Cecilia for a turn round the Drive. You have very antiquated notions, have you not? I saw several excessively smart sporting carriages being driven by ladies of the highest *ton*!'

'I have no particular objection to a phaeton and pair,' he said, still more coldly, 'though a perch model is quite unsuited to a lady. You will forgive me if I tell you that there is something more than a little fast in such a style of carriage.'

'Now, who in the world can have been spiteful enough to have put that idea into your head?' wondered Sophy.

He flushed, but did not answer.

'Did you see Cecilia?' asked Sophy. 'She was looking quite ravishing in that new hat your Mama was so clever as to choose for her!'

'I did see Cecilia,' he replied grimly. 'What is more, I, like you, cousin, know just how she had been spending her time! I am going to be extremely plain with you!'

'If you wish to be extremely plain with me,' she interrupted, 'come into the library! It is quite improper in you to be talking of family matters where you may be over-heard. Besides, I have something of a decidedly delicate nature to say to you.'

He strode at once to the door into the library, and flung it open. She went past him into the room, and he followed her, shutting the door behind him too soon for Tina, who was left on the other side. This made it necessary for him to open it again, Tina's orders to him to do so being at once shrill and imperative. This trifling anti-climax did nothing to improve his temper, and it was with a very unpleasant edge to his voice that he said: 'We will take the gloves off, Cousin Sophy! Whether or not it was you who arranged an assignation in the Park for my sister with young Fawnhope, I am well aware that you –'

'Isn't Cecilia dashing?' said Sophy approvingly. 'She walked with Fawnhope, and then with Alfred Wraxton, and I left her with Lord Francis! And that, dear Cousin Charles, is what I wanted to speak to you about! Far, *far* be it from me to interfere in the affairs of your family, but I think I ought perhaps to give you a hint. I know it is awkward for you, situated as you are, but you will know how to drop a word in Cecy's ear.'

He was thrown out of his stride by this unexpected gambit, and stared at her. 'What the devil are you talking about?'

'I don't entirely care to mention it,' said Sophy mendaciously, 'but you know how fond I am of Cecy! Then, too, I have been about the world, and have learnt to take care of myself. Cecy is such an innocent! There is not a particle of harm in Augustus Fawnhope, and Francis Wolvey is by far too great a gentleman to go beyond the line. But you should not encourage so lovely a girl as your sister to stroll about the park with the Dishonourable Alfred, Charles!'

He was so much taken aback that for a moment he did not say a word. Then he demanded an explanation.

'He is the kind of odious little toad who kisses the housemaids on the stairs,' replied Sophy frankly.

'My sister is not a housemaid!'

'No, and I do trust she will know how to keep him at arm's length.'

'May I know whether you have the slightest grounds for bringing this charge against Wraxton?'

'If you mean, have I seen him kiss a housemaid, no, dear Charles, I have not. If, on the other hand, you mean, has he tried to kiss me, yes, dear Charles, he has. In this very room, too.'

He looked angry and mortified. 'I am extremely sorry that you should have been annoyed in such a fashion under this roof,' he said, getting the words out with an effort.

'Oh, don't mind it! I told you I was able to take care of myself. But I doubt whether anyone could prevent his – his squeezing and stroking habits, or convince him that the style of his conversation is quite improper.'

She had been taking off her pelisse as she spoke, and she now laid it aside, and sat down on a winged chair beside the fireplace. After a moment he said, in a milder tone: 'I shall not pretend that I have any liking for Wraxton, for I have not. So far as it lies within my power I shall certainly discourage his visits to this house. My situation is, however, as you said yourself, awkward. I would not, upon any account, have this come to Miss Wraxton's ears.'

'No, indeed!' she said warmly. 'For you to be telling tales of her brother to Miss Wraxton would be the shabbiest thing!'

He was leaning his arm along the mantelpiece, and had been looking down into the fire, but at that he raised his head and shot a penetrating glance at Sophy. She thought there was a good deal of comprehension in his eyes, but he only said: 'Just so, cousin.'

'Do not refine too much upon it!' she advised him kindly. 'I do not meant to say that Cecy has a *tendre* for him, for she thinks him even more odious than I do.'

'I am well aware that she has no *tendre* for him, I thank you!' he retorted. 'She is infatuated with that puppy, Fawnhope!'

'Of course she is,' said Sophy.

'I am also aware that you have made it your business from the day you entered this house to encourage this folly by every means within your reach! You and Cecilia have been constantly seen in Fawnhope's company; you pretended he was a friend of yours so that he might have an excuse for calling here six days out of the seven; you –'

'In a word, Charles, I have thrown them continually together. I have, and if you had a grain of sense you would have done so weeks before I came to town!'

He was arrested for a moment, and then asked incredulously: 'Do you imagine by doing so you will cure Cecilia? Or that I am likely to believe you have any such intention in mind?'

'Well, I don't know,' she answered, giving the matter some thought. 'One of two things must happen, you know. Either she will grow weary of Augustus – and I must say I do think that very probable, because although he is so handsome, and can be very engaging when he chooses, he is shockingly tiresome, besides forgetting Cecilia's existence just when he should be most solicitous – or she will continue to love him, in spite of his faults. And if that happens, Charles, you will know that it is not an infatuation, and you will be obliged to consent to their marriage.'

'Never!' he said, with considerable violence.

'But you will,' she insisted. 'It would be wicked to try to force her into another marriage, and you would be cruel to attempt it.'

'I shall not force her into any marriage!' he flashed. 'It may interest you to know that I am extremely attached to Cecilia, and that it is for that reason, and not for any whim of my own, that I will not countenance her union with a man of Fawnhope's stamp! As for this glib notion you have that by throwing them together you will make Cecilia tire of him, you were never more mistaken! So far from tiring of his company, Cecilia seizes every opportunity to be alone with him! She is even so lost to all sense of propriety as to make Addy her dupe! Only this afternoon Miss Wraxton came upon her in a secluded path in the Park, alone with Fawnhope, having shaken off the restraint of Addy's presence. Clandestine meetings! Pretty behaviour in Miss Rivenhall of Ombersley, upon my word!'

'My dear Charles,' said Sophy, with unimpaired calm, 'you know very well that you are making that up.'

'I am doing no such thing! Do you imagine I would *make up* such a tale about my sister?'

'To own the truth, I think you would do anything when you are in one of your rages,' she said, smiling. 'There is no secret about her having walked with Fawnhope, but the rest of it springs from your disordered temper. Now, do not say that Miss Wraxton told you it was so, because I am sure she would never have told you such fibs about Cecilia! Shaken Addy off, indeed! She was never out of Addy's sight for a moment! Good gracious, don't you know Cecilia better than to be accusing her of clandestine behaviour? What a very vulgar expression to use, to be sure! Do stop making such a cake of yourself! Next you will be ranting at Cecy for having allowed a respectable young man whom she has known, I daresay, since they were both children, to walk a little way beside her, under the eye of her governess!'

Again she came under that hard scrutiny. 'Do you know this for a fact?' he asked, in an altered tone.

'Certainly I do, for Cecy told me just what had occurred. It seems that Miss Wraxton said something to Addy which distressed her very much – no doubt she misunderstood it! Miss Wraxton perhaps felt that Addy should have sent Augustus about his business, though how she could have done so I hardly know! But she has a great deal of sensibility, you know, and is readily upset.'

He looked annoyed, and said: 'Addy is not to be blamed; Cecilia is out of her control, and if she should have told my mother of these meetings – well, she was never one to carry tales of any of us!'

She said coaxingly: 'Do show her that you are not angry with her, Charles, and don't mean to turn her off after all these years!'

'Turn her off?' he echoed, astonished. 'What nonsense is this, pray?'

'Exactly what I said to her! Only she has taken it into her head that she is too old-fashioned in her ways to instruct the children, and seems to think she should be able to teach them the Italian tongue, and all sorts of refinements of the same nature.'

There was a slight pause. Mr Rivenhall sat down on the other side of the fireplace, and rather absently began to pull Tina's ears. He was frowning, and presently said, at his curtest: 'I have nothing whatsoever to say in the education of my sisters. It is my mother's business, and I cannot conceive how it could ever belong to anyone else.'

Sophy saw no need to labour this point, and merely agreed with him. He cast her a glance out of narrowed, searching eyes, but she preserved her countenance. He said: 'None of this has anything to do with what I have been saying to you. We did very well, cousin, before you began to turn this house upside-down! I shall be obliged to you if, in the future –'

'Why, what in the world have I done else?' she exclaimed.

He found himself quite unable to put into words the things that she had done, and was obliged to fall back upon her only tangible crime. 'You brought that monkey here, for one thing!' he said. 'No doubt with the kindest of intentions! But it is a most unsuitable animal to have bestowed on the children, and now, of course, they will think themselves ill-used when it is got rid of, as got rid of it must be!'

Her eyes began to dance. 'Charles, you are just trying to be disagreeable! You cannot feed Jacko on bits of apple, and teach him tricks, and warn the children to give him a blanket at night one day, and the next say he must be got rid of!'

He bit his lip, but the rueful grin would not be entirely suppressed. 'Who told you I had done so?'

'Theodore. And also that you carried him down on your shoulder when Miss Wraxton came to call, to show him off to her. I must say, I think that was foolish of you, for you know she does not like pets: she told us so. I am sure there is no reason why she should, and to plague her with them is not kind in you. I never let Tina tease her, you know.'

'You are mistaken!' he said quickly. 'She does not like monkeys, but it is only Lady Brinklow who dislikes dogs!'

'I expect she feels the same,' said Sophy, getting up, and giving her skirts a shake. 'One cannot help observing how often daughters resemble their mothers. Not in face, but in disposition. You must have remarked it!'

He seemed to be somewhat appalled by this. 'No, I have not. I do not think you can be right!'

'Oh, yes, only consider Cecy! She will be just like dear Aunt Lizzie when she is older.' She saw that the truth of this statement was having its effect upon him, and thought that she had given him enough to ponder for one day. She moved towards the door, saying: 'I must go and change my dress.'

He got up abruptly. 'No, wait!'

She looked over her shoulder. 'Yes?'

He did not seem to know what he wished to say. 'Nothing! It's no matter! Next time you insist on buying horses, you had better tell me what you want! To be employing strangers in the business is most undesirable!'

'But you assured me you would have no hand in it!' Sophy pointed out.

'Yes!' he said savagely. 'Nothing pleases you more than to put me in the wrong, does it?'

She laughed, and went away without answering him. Upstairs, she was pounced on by Cecilia, anxious to know what her fate was to be.

'If he speaks to you at all, it will be to warn you against Alfred Wraxton!' said Sophy, with a gurgle of amusement. 'I told him exactly how that toad conducts himself, and warned him to take care of you!'

'You did not!'

'I did! I have done an excellent day's work, in the most unprincipled way! Oh, tell Addy Charles does not blame her in the least! He won't say a word to my aunt about what happened, and I doubt whether he will say a word to you either. The only person he *may* say a word to is his precious Eugenia. I hope she will induce him to lose his temper.'

Seven

*C*ecilia was quite unable to believe that she was not to receive one of her brother's scolds, and, when she later came unexpectedly face to face with him on a bend in the stair she gave a gasp, and tried to stiffen her unruly knees. 'Hallo!' he said, running an eye over her exquisite ball-dress of gauze over satin. 'You are very smart! Where are you off to?'

'Lady Sefton is calling after dinner to take Sophy and me to Almack's,' she replied thankfully. 'Mama does not find herself equal to it this evening.'

'Taking the shine out of them all!' he said. 'You look very fine!'

'Why do you not accompany us?' she asked, plucking up courage.

'You would not spend the entire evening in Fawnhope's pocket if I did,' he observed dryly.

She lifted her chin. 'I should not under any circumstances spend the entire evening in any gentleman's pocket!'

'No, I believe you would not,' he agreed mildly. 'Not in my line, Cilly? Besides, I am engaged with a party of my own.'

His employment of her almost forgotten nursery-name made her retort with much less constraint: 'Daffy Club!'

He grinned: 'No: Cribb's Parlour!'

'How horrid you are! I suppose you are going to discuss the merits of a Bloomsbury Pet, or a Black Diamond, or – or –'

'A Mayfair Marvel,' he supplied. 'Nothing so interesting: I am going to blow a cloud with a few friends. And what do *you* know of Bloomsbury Pets, miss?'

She threw him a saucy look as she passed him on the way down the staircase. 'Only what I have learnt from my brothers, Charles!'

He laughed, and let her go, but before she had reached the bottom of the flight, leaned over the banisters, and said imperatively: 'Cecilia!' she looked up enquiringly. 'Does that fellow Wraxton annoy you?'

She was nearly betrayed into losing her gravity. She replied: 'Oh, well –! I daresay I could snub him easily enough, if – well, if I chose to do so!'

'You need not be deterred by any consideration that I know of. I need scarcely say that if Eugenia knew of it she would be the first to condemn his behaviour!'

'Of course,' she said.

Whether he spoke words of censure to Miss Wraxton no one was in a position to know. If he did, they must, Sophy thought, have been mild ones, for she did not appear to be in any way chastened. However, Sophy was granted one satisfaction. When next Miss Wraxton brought up the vexed question of Jacko, confiding to Lady Ombersley that she lived in dread of hearing that the monkey had bitten one of the children, Charles overheard her, and said impatiently: 'Nonsense!'

'I believe a monkey's bite is poisonous.'

'In that case I hope he may bite Theodore.'

Lady Ombersley uttered a protest, but Theodore, already soundly cuffed for hitting a cricket-ball from the Square-garden straight through one of the windows of a neighbouring house, merely grinned. Miss Wraxton, who did not feel that he had been adequately punished for such a piece of lawlessness, had already spoken her mind gravely on the subject. Charles had listened, but all he had said was: 'Very true, but it was a capital hit: I saw it.' This disregard for her opinion rankled with Miss Wraxton, and she now, with the archness which she too often employed when talking to children, read Theodore a playful lecture, telling him that he was fortunate in not being obliged to forfeit his new pet in retribution of his crime. Beyond casting her a glance of resentment, he paid no heed, but Gertrude blurted out: 'I believe you don't like Jacko because Sophy gave him to us!'

The truth of this embarrassingly forthright pronouncement struck most of those present with blinding effect. Miss Wraxton's cheeks flew two spots of colour; Lady Ombersley gave a gasp, and Cecilia stifled a giggle. Only Charles and Sophy remained unmoved, Sophy not raising her eyes from the sewing she was engaged on, and Charles saying blightingly: 'A stupid and an impertinent remark, Gertrude. You may return to the school-room, if you cannot conduct yourself more becomingly.'

Gertrude, who had arrived at the age when she cast herself into quite as much confusion as her elders, had already blushed hotly, and now fled in disorder from the room. Lady Ombersley began at once to talk of her projected expedition, with Sophy and Cecilia, to visit the Marquesa de Villacañas at Merton.

'One would not wish to be backward in any attention,' she said, 'so I shall make the effort, and we must hope it will not rain, for that would make it very disagreeable. I wish you will go with us, Charles. Your uncle's affianced wife, you know! I own, I do not care to drive out of town without a gentleman to go with me, though I am sure Radnor is perfectly to be trusted, and I should of course take my footmen.'

'My dear Mama, three able-bodied men should be enough to protect you on this hazardous journey!' he returned in some amusement.

'Don't tease Charles to go, Aunt Lizzie!' said Sophy, snipping off her thread. 'Sir Vincent vows he will ride there with us, for he has not met Sancia since Madrid days, when her husband was still alive, and they gave splendid parties for all the English officers.'

There was a slight pause before Charles said: 'If you wish it, Mama, I will certainly go with you. I can take my cousin in the curricle, and then you will not be crowded in your carriage.'

'Oh, I mean to go in my phaeton!' Sophy said unconcernedly.

'I thought it was your ambition to drive my grays?'

'Why, would you let me?'

'Perhaps.'

She laughed. 'Oh, no, no! I have no belief in *perhaps!* Take Cecilia!'

'Cecilia would by far rather go in my mother's landaulet. You may take the reins for part of the way.'

She said in a rallying tone: 'This is something indeed! I am overcome, Charles, and fear you cannot be feeling quite the thing!'

'It will be a delightful expedition,' said Miss Wraxton brightly. 'I am almost tempted, dear Lady Ombersley, to beg a place in your carriage!'

Lady Ombersley was too well-bred to betray consternation, but she said a little doubtfully: 'Well, my dear, of course – if Sophy does not think that there might be rather too many of us for the Marquesa! I should not wish to put her out in any way.'

'Not at all!' Sophy replied instantly. 'It is not in your power to put Sancia out, dearest Aunt Lizzie! She will not bestir herself in the least, but will leave everything to her major-domo. He is a Frenchman, and will be delighted to make arrangements for even so small a party as ours. I have only to write Sancia a letter, beg a frank from my uncle, and the thing is done – if she will rouse herself sufficiently to convey my message to Gaston!'

'How interesting it will be to meet a real Spanish lady!' remarked Miss Wraxton.

'For all the world as if Sancia had been a giraffe!' as Sophy afterwards said to Cecilia.

'I wish I had known you meant to accompany my mother!' Mr Rivenhall said, when he presently escorted Miss Wraxton to her carriage. 'I should have offered *you* a place in my curricle. I cannot cry off now, but it is a bore. I should not have said I would go had I not heard that Talgarth was to be of the party. God knows I don't care a jot whom my cousin marries, but I suppose, in the circumstances, we owe it to my uncle not to encourage *that* connection!'

'I am afraid her visit has brought extra cares upon you, my dear Charles. Much must be forgiven to a girl who has never known a mother's care, but I confess I had hoped that under your Mama's guidance she would have tried to conform to English standards of propriety.'

'Not she!' he said. 'It's my belief she delights in keeping us all upon tenterhooks! There is no guessing what she will be at next, while the terms she stands on with every rattle who ever wore a scarlet coat – not that I care for that! But to be encouraging Talgarth to dangle after her is the outside of enough. All very well to say she can look after herself: I daresay she can, but if she is seen too much in his company she will be talked about by every scandal-mongering busybody in town!'

Miss Wraxton, treasuring up these hasty words, was unwise enough to repeat the gist of them to Sophy not forty-eight hours later. During the hour of the fashionable Promenade, when walking in the Park with her maid, she came upon Sophy's phaeton, drawn up to allow Sophy to exchange a few words with the reprehensible Sir Vincent. He had one hand negligently on the step of the phaeton, and she was leaning a little down to say something that seemed to afford them both amusement. She saw Miss Wraxton, and nodded smilingly to her, but looked rather surprised when Eugenia came towards the phaeton, and addressed her. 'How do you do? So this is the carriage I hear so much of! At all events, you have a fine pair of horses, I see. You have driven them tandem! You are to be congratulated: I do not think I would trust myself to do so.'

'You are acquainted with Sir Vincent Talgarth, I believe,' Sophy said.

Sir Vincent received the coldest of bows, and the merest hint of a smile.

'Do you know,' said Miss Wraxton, looking up at Sophy, 'I really think I must ask you to take me up beside you for one turn! I am quite jealous of your prowess, I assure you!'

Sophy signed to John to alight, saying politely: 'Pray come with me, Miss Wraxton! I shall naturally be put on my mettle. Sir Vincent, we meet on Friday, then: you will call for us at Berkeley Square!'

Miss Wraxton, assisted by John Potton, mounted with credible grace into the awkwardly high carriage, and sat down beside Sophy, disposing her skirt neatly, and acknowledging Tina's presence by uttering: 'Dear little doggie!' a form of address which made the little greyhound shiver, and press closer to her mistress. 'I am so happy to have this opportunity of speaking with you, Miss Stanton-Lacy: I had come to think it impossible to find you when you should be alone! You are acquainted with so many people!'

'Yes, am I not fortunate?'

'Indeed, yes!' agreed Miss Wraxton, honey-sweet. 'Though sometimes, dear Miss Stanton-Lacy, when one has a multitude of friends, one is inclined not to be as careful as one should be, perhaps. I wonder if I might venture to put you a little on your guard! In Paris and Vienna I am sure you would be able to tell me how I should go on, but in London I must be more at home than you.'

'Oh, I should never be so impertinent as to tell you how to go on anywhere!' Sophy declared.

'Well, perhaps it would not be necessary,' acknowledged Miss Wraxton graciously. 'My Mama has always been a most careful parent, and very strict in her choice of governesses for her daughters. I have felt so much compassion for you, dear Miss Stanton-Lacy, situated as you are. You must so often have felt the want of a mother!'

'Not at all. Don't waste your compassion on me, I beg! I never wanted a mother while I had Sir Horace.'

'Gentlemen,' said Miss Wraxton, 'are not the same.'

'An unarguable statement. How do you like my bays?'

Miss Wraxton laid a hand on her knee. 'Allow me to speak without reserve!' she begged.

'Short of overturning you I can hardly prevent you,' Sophy

replied. 'But you had much better not, you know! I am very unbiddable, and if I were to lose my temper I might do what I should afterwards be sorry for.'

'But I must speak!' Miss Wraxton said earnestly. 'I owe it to your cousin!'

'Indeed! How is this?'

'You will understand that he does not like to mention the matter to you himself. He feels a certain delicacy –'

'I thought you were talking of Charles!' interrupted Sophy. 'Which cousin do you mean?'

'I am talking of Charles.'

'Nonsense! He has no delicate scruples.'

'Miss Stanton-Lacy, believe me, this air of levity is not becoming!' said Miss Wraxton, losing some of her sweetness. 'I do not think you can be aware of what is expected of a woman of quality! Or – forgive me! – how fatal it is to set up the backs of people, and to give rise to such gossip as must be as painful to the Rivenhalls as I am persuaded it would be to you!'

'Now, what in heaven's name comes next?' said Sophy, quite astonished. 'You cannot be so gothic as to suppose that because I drive a high-perch phaeton I give rise to gossip!'

'No, though one would have preferred to have seen you in some vehicle less sporting. But the habits of easy intercourse you are on with so many military gentlemen – rattles in scarlet coats, as Charles divertingly phrases it! – and in particular with that man I saw you conversing with a moment ago, make you appear a little *fast*, dear Miss Stanton-Lacy, which I know you would not wish! Sir Vincent's company cannot give you consequence, indeed, quite the reverse! A certain lady – of the first consideration! – commented to me only today upon his attaching himself to you so particularly.'

'I expect she has an interest there herself,' observed Sophy. 'He is a shocking flirt! And did my cousin Charles desire you to warn me against all these rattles?'

'He did not precisely desire me to do so,' answered Miss Wraxton scrupulously, 'but he has spoken to me on this head, and I know what his sentiments are. You must know that Society will look indulgently upon mere pranks, such as driving off in Charles's curricle, for Lady Ombersley's protection must give you countenance.'

'How fortunate I am!' said Sophy. 'But do you think you are wise to be seen in my company?'

'Now you are quizzing, Miss Stanton-Lacy!'

'No, I am only afraid that you may suffer for being seen in such a vehicle as this, and with so fast a female!'

'Hardly,' Miss Wraxton said gently. 'Perhaps it may be thought a little *odd* in me, for I do not drive myself in London, but I think my character is sufficiently well-established to make it possible for me to do – if I wished – what others might be imprudent to attempt.'

They were by this time within sight of the gate by Apsley House. 'Now let me understand you!' begged Sophy. 'If I were to do something outrageous while in your company, would your credit be good enough to carry me off?'

'Let us say my family's credit, Miss Stanton-Lacy. I may venture to reply, without hesitation, yes.'

'Capital!' said Sophy briskly, and turned her horses towards the gate.

Miss Wraxton, losing some of her assurance, said sharply: 'Pray, what are you about?'

'I am going to do what I have been wanting to do ever since I was told I must not, on any account!' replied Sophy. 'It is with me a kind of Bluebeard's chamber.'

The phaeton swung through the gateway, and turned sharply to the left, narrowly escaping collision with a ponderous lozenge-coach. Miss Wraxton uttered a stifled shriek, and clutched the side of the phaeton. 'Take care! Please pull up your horses at once! I do not wish to drive through the streets! Have you taken leave of your senses?'

'No, no, do not be afraid! I am quite sane. How glad I am that you chose to drive with me! Such an opportunity as this might never else have come in my way!'

'Miss Stanton-Lacy, I do not know what you mean, and again I must beg of you to pull up! I am not at all diverted by this prank, and I wish to alight from your phaeton instantly.'

'What, and walk along Piccadilly unattended? You cannot mean it!'

'*Stop!*' commanded Miss Wraxton, in almost shrill accents.

'On no account. Dear me, what a lot of traffic! Perhaps you had better not talk to me until I have weaved my way through all these carts and carriages.'

'For heaven's sake, at least slacken your pace!' Miss Wraxton besought her, in the liveliest alarm.

'I will, when we come to the turning,' promised Sophy, passing between a wagon and a mail-coach, with a matter of inches to spare. A moan from her companion caused her to add kindly: 'There is no need to be in a fright: Sir Horace made me drive through a gateway until I could be trusted not even to scrape the varnish.'

They were now ascending the rise in Piccadilly. With a strong effort at self-control, Miss Wraxton demanded: 'Tell me at once where you are taking me!'

'Down St James's Street,' replied Sophy coolly.

'What?' gasped Miss Wraxton, turning quite pale. 'You will do no such thing! No lady would be seen driving there! Amongst all the clubs – the object of every town saunterer! You cannot know what would be said of you! Stop this instant!'

'No, I want to see this Bow Window I hear so much of, and all the dandies who sit there. How wretched that Mr Brummell has been obliged to go abroad! Do you know, I never saw him in my life? Are you able to point out the various clubs to me? Shall we recognize White's, or are there other houses with bow windows?'

'This is your notion of raillery, Miss Stanton-Lacy! You are not serious!'

'Yes, I am. Of course, I should not have dared to do it without you sitting beside me, to lend me credit, but you have assured me that your position is unassailable, and I see that I need have no scruple in gratifying my ambition. I daresay your consequence is great enough to make it quite a fashionable drive for ladies. We shall see!'

No argument that Miss Wraxton could advance, and she advanced many, had the power to move her. She drove on inexorably. Wild ideas of springing from the phaeton crossed Miss Wraxton's mind, only to be rejected. It was too dangerous to be attempted. Had she been wearing a veil she might have pulled it over her face, and hoped to have escaped recognition, but her hat was a perfectly plain one, and bore only a modest bow of ribbon. She had not even a parasol, and was obliged to sit bolt upright, staring rigidly ahead of her the length of that disgraceful street. She did not utter a word until the horses swung round into Pall Mall, and then she said in a low voice, unsteady with rage and chagrin: 'I will never forgive you! never!'

'How uncharitable of you!' said Sophy lightly. 'Shall I set you down now?'

'If you dare to abandon me in this locality –'

'Very well, I will drive you to Berkeley Square. I do not know whether you will find my cousin at home at this hour, but at all events you may complain of me to my aunt, which I am sure you must be longing to do.'

'Do not speak to me!' said Miss Wraxton throbbingly.

Sophy laughed.

Outside Ombersley House she broke the silence. 'Can you get down without assistance? Having cast off my groom, together with your maid, I must drive the phaeton round to the stables myself.'

Miss Wraxton, vouchsafing no answer, climbed down, and walked up the steps to the front-door.

It was half an hour later before Dassett admitted Sophy into the house. She found Mr Rivenhall at that very moment coming down the stairs, and said at once. 'Ah, so you were at home! I am so glad!'

He was looking very stern, and replied in a level tone: 'Will you come into the library for a few minutes?'

She accompanied him there, and began to drag off her

driving-gloves with hands that were not quite steady. Her eyes were still sparkling, and a not unbecoming flush mantled her cheeks.

'Cousin, what, in God's name, possessed you?' demanded Mr Rivenhall.

'Oh, has not Miss Wraxton told you? I have realized an ambition!'

'You must be mad! Don't you know how improper it was of you to do such a thing?'

'Yes, indeed I knew, and should never have dared to do it without the protection of Miss Wraxton's presence! Do not look so dismayed! She assured me that even though I did something outrageous in her company her credit was good enough to carry me off! Surely you cannot doubt it!'

'Sophy, she cannot have said such a thing!'

She shrugged, and turned away. 'No? Have it as you will!'

'What had occurred? What reason had you for causing her such mortification?'

'I will leave Miss Wraxton to tell you what she chooses. I have said too much already: I do not like tale-bearers, and will not sink to that level! My actions are no concern of yours, Cousin Charles, and even less are they Miss Wraxton's.'

'What you have just done is very much her concern!'

'True. I stand corrected.'

'It is also my concern to see that you come to no harm while you are a guest in this house. Such conduct as you indulged in this afternoon might do you a great deal of harm, let me tell you!'

'My dear Charles, I am past praying for, as intimate as I am with rakes and rattles!' she flashed.

He stiffened. 'Who said that?'

'You, I understand, but you had too much delicacy to say it to my face. You should have known better than to think I should listen meekly to Miss Wraxton, however!'

'And you should know better than to imagine that I would deliver my strictures through Miss Wraxton, or anyone else!'

She lifted a hand to her cheek, and he saw that it was to dash away a tear-drop. 'Oh, be quiet! Cannot you see that I am too angry to talk with any moderation? My wretched tongue! But though you did not desire Miss Wraxton to scold me for you, you did discuss me with her, did you not?'

'Whatever I may have said I did not mean to be repeated. It was, however, extremely improper of me to have criticized you to Miss Wraxton. I beg your pardon!'

She pulled out her handkerchief from the sleeve of her habit, and blew her nose. Her flush died down; she said ruefully: 'Now I am disarmed. How provoking of you! Why could you not have flown into one of your rages? You are so disobliging! Was it so very bad to have driven down St James's Street?'

'You knew it was, for Miss Wraxton told you so. You have caused her a great deal of distress, Sophy.'

'Oh dear! I do such dreadful things when I lose my temper! Very well, it was wrong of me – very wrong! Must I beg her pardon?'

'You must see that you owe her an apology. If anything she may have said to you angered you, at least she had no such intention. She meant nothing but kindness, and is very much upset by the outcome. Mine is the blame, for having led her to suppose that I wished her to take you to task.'

She smiled. 'That's handsome of you, Charles! I am sorry: I have created an uncomfortable situation. Where is Miss Wraxton? In the drawing-room? Take me up to her, then, and I will do what I may to mend things!'

'Thank you,' he said, opening the door for her.

Miss Wraxton was found to have recovered from her agitation, and to be glancing through the pages of the Gentleman's Magazine. She glanced coldly at Sophy, and lowered her eyes again to the periodical. Sophy walked across the room, saying in her frank way: 'Will you forgive me? Indeed, I beg your pardon, and am very sorry! It was shocking conduct!'

'So shocking, Miss Stanton-Lacy, that I prefer not to speak of it.'

'If that means that you will try to forget it, I shall be very grateful to you.'

'Certainly I shall do so.'

'Thank you!' Sophy said. 'You are very kind!'

She turned and went quickly to the door. Mr Rivenhall was holding it, and detained her for a moment, saying in a much warmer voice than she had yet heard him use: 'If anyone should mention the affair to me, I shall say that having bought those bays of yours against my advice you were well served, for they got away with you!'

She smiled, but said: 'I wish you will do what you can to undo any harm I may have caused.'

'My dear girl, don't refine too much upon it! There is no need, I assure you.'

She cast him a look of gratitude, and left the room.

'You were not very generous, were you, Eugenia?' said Mr Rivenhall.

'I consider her behaviour unpardonable.'

'It is unnecessary to tell me so: you made it plain enough that you thought so.'

Her bosom swelled. 'I did not think to hear you take her part against me, Charles!'

'I have not done so, but the fault was not all hers. You had no right to take her to task, Eugenia, much less to repeat whatever ill-considered words I may have uttered! I am not surprised she was so angry: I have a temper myself!'

'You do not seem to consider the agony of mortification I have been obliged to suffer! What Mama would say if she knew –'

'Oh, enough, enough!' he said impatiently. 'You make too much of it! Let us, for heaven's sake, forget it!'

She was offended, but she saw that to persist would lower her in his eyes. It annoyed her to think that she had shown to less advantage than Sophy in the little scene that had been enacted. She forced herself to smile, and to say magniloquently: 'You are right: I have allowed myself to be too much moved. Please assure your cousin that I shall not think of the matter again!'

She had her reward, for he grasped her hand at once, saying: 'That is more like you! I knew I could not be mistaken in you!'

Eight

The two ladies did not meet again until the day of the expedition to Merton, Miss Wraxton, convinced that she had become notorious, having decided to pay a long deferred visit to her elder sister, who lived in Kent, and was famous for turning her guests to good account. Eugenia was not fond of running Lady Ealing's errands, or of playing with her numerous offpsring, but she was strongly of the opinion that she would be wise to absent herself from London until the inevitable whisperings had died down. The Rivenhalls thus enjoyed immunity from her punitive descents upon them for seven whole days, which was felt by almost all to be an advantage far outweighing the ills of Sophy's indiscretion. This did not reach the ears of Lady Ombersley, but was naturally known to the younger members of the household, some of whom were much shocked, while others, notably Hubert and Selina, considered that their cousin had taken a splendid lark. No apparent repercussions followed her exploit, and although she was obliged to endure much chaffing from her young relatives, even this very soon took a turn in another direction. A much more fruitful topic for jests presented itself in the shape of young Lord Bromford, who swam suddenly into the Rivenhall's ken, and was regarded by them as so much manna dropped from heaven.

Lord Bromford, who was almost unknown to the Polite World, had but lately, upon the death of his father, succeeded to a modest barony. He was the only surviving child of his parents, every one of his brothers and sisters (varying in number, according to popular report, from seven to seventeen) having died in infancy. It may have been for this reason that his mother had from the start deemed him unfit to be wrested from her care. No other reason was observable; although, as Sophy fair-mindedly pointed out to her cousins, a florid complexion and a full habit of body were not infallible signs of a robust constitution. He had been educated at home, and although there had been a project afoot to send him up to Oxford, a providential chill had intervened to save him from the perils of University life. It was well known to Lord Bromford that his heir's lungs were delicate, and it was only necessary for Lady Bromford to point out to him every day for several weeks the evils that would accrue from exposing Henry to the rigours of Oxford to induce him to give his consent to an alternative plan. Henry, accompanied by a clerical gentleman in whom Lady Bromford reposed the greatest confidence, was sent to Jamaica, on a visit to his uncle, the governor. The climate was said to be beneficial to persons with weak lungs, and it was not until Henry had been four days at sea that his Mama discovered that the island was periodically devastated by hurricanes. It was then too late to recall Henry, who proceeded on his voyage, being extremely sea-sick, but arriving at Port Royal without any trace of the cough which had cast his Mama into such a fever of anxiety. No hurricane occurred during his visit to sweep him away, and when he returned to England, a few months before attaining his majority, he was so stout that his Mama was able to congratulate herself on the success of her scheme. She did not immediately perceive that his eighteen-month sojourn apart from her had had the effect of making him occasionally disinclined to submit to her benevolent rule. On her advice, he changed his socks, wound mufflers round his neck, swathed his legs in warm rugs, and eschewed all harmful forms of sustenance; but when she advised him not to subject his person to the racket of London, he said, after due consideration, that he rather thought he should like to live in London; and when she proposed a very eligible match for him, he said he was much obliged to her, but had not yet made up his mind what sort of female he wished to marry. He did not argue: he merely turned his back on the eligible match, and took up his residence in London. His mother began to tell her friends that Henry could be led, but not driven; his valet, a plain-spoken man, said that his lordship was as obstinate as a pig.

He had been upon the town for some time before the Rivenhalls were more than vaguely aware of his existence. His intimates (whom Hubert stigmatized as a dull set of gudgeons) were not amongst their particular friends, and it was not until he met Sophy at Almack's, and stood up with her in a country dance, that the full glory of his personality burst upon them. For Lord Bromford, impervious alike to Cecilia's beauty, and to the eligibility of his Mama's choice, had made up his mind that Sophy would make him a suitable wife. He called in Berkeley Square, and at a moment when Hubert and Selina were with Lady Ombersley. He stayed for half an hour, imparting information to his hosts on such varied topics as the vegetation in Jamaica, and the effect of paregoric draughts upon the human system, and the Rivenhalls listened to him in stunned indignation until Sophy entered the room. Then the scales fell from before their eyes, and they perceived why his lordship had honoured them with a morning-call, and their boredom changed to unholy glee. Sophy's beau became in a trice the solid foundation upon which a lively set of young persons built the most preposterous of fabrications. No street-singer could lift his voice in the Square but what Hubert or Cecilia would declare it to be Lord Bromford, serenading Sophy; when he was confined to his house for three days with an internal disorder he was held to have fought a duel for the sake of her fine eyes; and the serial story of his adventures in the West Indies, conceived, added-to, and improved upon by three fertile brains, grew so outrageous as to draw protests from Lady Ombersley and Miss Adderbury. But Lady Ombersley, though she might deprecate such an excess of high spirits, could not help but be amused by the determination shown by Lord Bromford in his pursuit of her niece. He was for ever calling in Berkeley Square on the most slender of pretexts; he daily promenaded in the Park only to waylay Sophy, and be taken up into her phaeton; he even purchased a showy hack, and rod solemnly up and down the Row every morning in the hope that she might be exercising Salamanca there. More wonderful still, he prevailed upon his Mama to cultivate the acquaintance of Lady Ombersley, and to invite Sophy to go with her to one of the Concerts of Ancient Music. He was impervious to snubs, and when his Mama hinted to him that Sophy would scarcely make a suitable wife for a serious man, being wholly given over to frivolity, he said that he was confident that would be able to direct her thoughts into more sober channels.

The cream of the jest, thought the young Rivenhalls, was that Charles, in general so impatient of pretensions, was, for inscrutable reasons, encouraging his lordship. Charles said that there was a great deal of good in Lord Bromford. He said that Lord Bromford's conversation showed him to be a sensible man, and that his descriptions of Jamaica were extremely interesting. Only Selina (who was growing up, Charles said, to be disagreeably pert) ventured to observe that Lord Bromford's entrance into the house seemed to be the signal for Charles's departure for his club.

What with his lordship's courtship, the plans for the ball, the stream of visitors to the house, even Sophy's indiscretion, life in Berkeley Square had become all at once full of fun and excitement. Even Lord Ombersley was aware of it. 'By God, I don't know what's come over you all, for the place was used to be as lively as a tomb!' he declared. 'I'll tell you what, Lady Ombersley: I daresay I can prevail upon York to look in on your party. Nothing formal, y'know, but he's fixed in Stableyard for the present, and will very likely be pleased enough to drop in for half an hour.'

'Prevail upon the Duke of York to come to my party?' echoed Lady Ombersley, in the greatest astonishment. 'My dear Ombersley, you must be out of your senses! Ten, or perhaps twelve couples, getting up a dance in the drawing-room, and a couple of card-tables set out in the Crimson Saloon! I beg you will do no such thing!'

'Ten or twelve couples? No, no, Dassett would not be talking of red carpets and awnings for such a paltry affair as that!' said his lordship.

These ominous words struck a chill into his wife's soul. Beyond fixing the date for the party, and warning Cecilia not to forget to send a card to a very dull girl, who was her God-daughter, and must be invited, she had not as yet thought much about the engagement. She now nerved herself to ask her niece how many people were expected on the fatal night. The answer almost brought on one of her spasms. She was obliged to drink a little hartshorn and water, thoughtfully pressed into her hand by Cecilia, before she could recovered herself sufficiently to protest. She sat, alternately sipping the hartshorn, and sniffing her vinaigrette, and moaning that she shuddered to think what Charles would say. It took Sophy twenty minutes to convince her that since he was not to be asked to defray the expenses of the entertainment, it was no concern of his; and even then Lady Ombersley dreaded the inevitable moment of discovery, and could scarcely see him walk into the room without giving a nervous start.

Fortunately for the success of the expedition, the truth had not dawned upon Charles when the Ombersley party set out to visit the Marquesa de Villacañas at Merton. The omens seemed to be propitious: the Marquesa had written a very pretty letter to Lady Ombersley, expressing her pleasure in the proposed meeting, and begging her to bring with her as many of her interesting children as would care to come; the sun shone, and the day was warm, with no threat of April showers; and Miss Wraxton, who had returned to the metropolis in time to share in the treat, was in her most amiable humour, not even excluding Sophy from her good graces. At the last moment, Hubert suddenly announced his intention of accompanying the party, saying that he too wanted to see the giraffe. Sophy frowned him down, and as his mother had not caught what he said, but at once began to express her delight in having his company, the awkward moment passed unnoticed. Mr Rivenhall, having greeted Sir Vincent Talgarth with perfect civility, was standing exchanging conversation with him while the three ladies who were to drive in the landaulet arranged themselves in it, Miss Wraxton begging to be allowed to take the back seat, and Cecilia insisting that she should not. Everything seemed to be in train for a day of enjoyment, when Mr Fawnhope came round the corner of the Square, saw the cavalcade, and at once crossed the road towards it.

Mr Rivenhall's face hardened; he shot an accusing look at Sophy, but she shook her head. Mr Fawnhope, shaking hands with Lady Ombersley, asked whither she was bound. She told him, Merton, and he said elliptically: 'Statues, *Nolumus leges Angliae mutari.*'

'Very likely,' said Lady Ombersley almost tartly.

Miss Wraxton, who could never resist the temptation to display her superior education, smiled quite kindly at Mr Fawnhope, and said: 'Very true. King John, you know, is said to have slept at the Priory the night before he signed the Great Charter. It is a very historic spot, for we are told that it was the scene of the murder of Cenulph, King of Wessex. It has, of course, more recent historic associations,' she added, but repressively, for these more recent historic associations regrettably included a quite unmentionable female.

'Nelson!' said Mr Fawnhope. 'Romantic Merton! I will go with you.' He then climbed into the carriage, and took his place beside Cecilia, smiling seraphically at Lady Ombersley, and saying: 'Now I know what it is I wish to do. I had no notion when I got up this morning, but was filled with a vast discontent. I will go to Merton.'

'You cannot wish to go to Merton!' said Lady Ombersley, very much put-out, and hoping that Charles would not put her to the blush by saying something cutting to this tiresome young man.

'Yes,' said Mr Fawnhope. 'There will be verdure, and that, I think, is what my soul craves. *I, with my fair Cecilia, to Merton now will go, Where softly flows the Wandle, and daffodils that blow* – What an ugly word is Wandle! How displeasing to the ear! Why do you frown at me? May I not go with you?'

This sudden change from rapt poet into cajoling boy threw Lady Ombersley off her balance, and she replied in a mollified voice: 'I am sure we should be pleased to take you, Augustus, but we are going to visit the Marquesa de Villacañas, and she will not be expecting you.'

'Now there,' said Mr Fawnhope, 'is a beautiful name! Villa-cañas! It is most rich! A Spanish lady, with *"garments gay and rich as maybe, Decked with jewels had she on!"'*

'I'm sure I don't know,' replied Lady Ombersley crossly.

Sophy, much amused by Mr Fawnhope's utter impervious-ness to hints that he was not wanted, said laughingly: 'Yes, pearls worth a king's ransom. She even loves an English man: my father!'

'How splendid!' said Mr Fawnhope. 'I am so glad I came!'

Short of ordering him point-blank to get out of the carriage, there seemed to be no way of getting rid of him. Lady Ombersley cast her eldest son a despairing glance, and Cecilia an imploring one; and Miss Wraxton smiled in a reassuring way that was designed to show how perfect was her comprehension and how firm her resolve to keep an eye on Cecilia.

'Who is this Adonis?' Sir Vincent asked Mr Rivenhall. 'He and your sister, seated side by side, quite take one's breath away!'

'Augustus Fawnhope,' replied Mr Rivenhall curtly. 'Cousin, if you are ready, I will hand you up!'

Lady Ombersley, gathering that she had received a tacit consent to Mr Fawnhope's presence told her coachman to start, Sir Vincent and Hubert fell in behind the carriage, and Mr Rivenhall said to Sophy: 'If this is your doing – !'

'I promise you it is not. If I thought that he had the smallest notion of your hostility, I should say that he had rolled you up, Charles: horse, foot, and guns!'

He was obliged to laugh. 'I doubt if he would have the smallest notion of anything less violent than a blow from a cudgel. How you can tolerate the fellow – !'

'I told you that I was not at all nice in my ideas. Come, don't let us talk of him! I have sworn an oath to heaven not to quarrel with you today.'

'You amaze me! Why?'

'Don't be such an ape!' she begged. 'I want to drive your grays, of course!'

He took his place beside her in the curricle, and nodded to the groom to stand away from the gray's heads. 'Oh, that! When we are clear of the town, you shall do so.'

'That,' said Sophy, 'is a remark calculated, I daresay, to make me lose my temper at the outset. I shall not do it, however.'

'I don't doubt your skill,' he said.

'A handsome admission. It cost you an effort to make it, perhaps, and that makes it the more valuable. But the roads are so good in England that not much skill is required. You should see some of the tracks in Spain!'

'Deliberate provocation, Sophy!' said Mr Rivenhall.

She laughed, disclaimed, and began to ask him about hunting. Once beyond the narrow streets he let his horses lengthen their stride, and overtook, and passed, the landaulet. Miss Wraxton was seen to be conversing amicably with Mr Fawnhope, while Cecilia was looking bored. The reason was explained by Hubert, who rode beside the curricle for a little way, and disclosed that the subject under discussion was Dante's *Inferno*. 'And this I will say for Fawnhope!' he added handsomely, 'he knows that Italian stuff much better than your Eugenia, Charles, and can go on at it for hours, never at a loss! What's more, there's another fellow, called Uberti, or some such thing, and he knows him too. Sad stuff, if you ask me, but Talgarth – I say, he's a bang-up fellow, isn't he? – says he's devilish well-read. Cecilia don't like it above half. Jupiter, I should laugh if Eugenia were to cut her out with the poet!'

Receiving no encouragement from his brother to expatiate on this theme, he fell behind again to rejoin Sir Vincent. Mr

Rivenhall handed over the reins to Sophy, observing as he did so that he was glad not to be sitting in the landaulet.

She refrained from making any comment, and the rest of the drive passed very pleasantly, no controversial topics arising to mar the good relations between them.

The house procured for the Marquesa by Sir Horace was a spacious Palladian villa, prettily situated in charming gardens, and with a bluebell wood attached, which, though fenced off from the pleasure grounds, could be reached through some graceful iron gates, brought from Italy by a previous owner. A few shallow steps led up from the carriage-sweep to the front door, and this, upon the approach of the curricle, was flung open, and a thin man, dressed in black, came out of the house, and stood bowing on the top step. Sophy greeted him in her usual friendly fashion, and at once asked where Mr Rivenhall could stable his horses. The thin man snapped an imperative finger and thumb, rather in the manner of a conjuror, and a groom seemed to spring up out of nowhere, and ran to the grays' heads.

'I'll see them stabled, Sophy, and come in presently with my mother,' Mr Rivenhall said.

Sophy nodded, and walked up the steps, saying: 'There are two more in the party than you were expecting, Gaston. You won't mind that, I daresay.'

'It makes nothing, mademoiselle,' he replied grandly. 'Madam awaits you in the salon.'

The Marquesa was discovered reclining upon a sofa in a drawing-room facing the south lawn. The early spring sunshine was not overpowering, but the blinds had been drawn a little way across the windows to exclude it. As these were green, like the upholstery on the chairs, a subaqueous light dimly lit the apartment. Sophy immediately flung back the curtains, exclaiming as she did so: 'Sancia, you cannot go to sleep when your visitors are almost at the door!'

A faint moan came from the sofa. 'Sophie, my complexion! Nothing so injurious as sunshine! How often have I said it!'

Sophy walked over to her, and bent to kiss her. 'Yes, dearest Sancia, but my aunt will think you quite odd if you lie there in darkness while she gropes her way to you by guess. Do get up!'

'*Bien entendido* I get up when your aunt approaches,' said the Marquesa, with dignity. 'If she is at the door, it shall be now, I grudge no exertion.'

In proof of this statement, she disentangled a singularly beautiful embroidered shawl from about her feet, dropped it on the floor, and allowed Sophy to help her to rise.

She was an opulent brunette, dressed more in the French style than the English, and with her luxuriant black locks covered only by a mantilla, draped over a high comb. Her gown was of gauze over satin, drawn in tightly below her full breasts, and revealing a good deal more of her shape than Lady Ombersley was likely to think seemly. This, however, was slightly concealed by the various scarves and shawls which she draped round herself as protection against treacherous draughts. The mantilla was pinned to her low corsage by a large emerald brooch; more emeralds, set in massive gold, dangled from the lobes of her ears; and she wore her famous pearls, twisted twice round her throat, and hanging almost to her waist. She was extremely handsome, with large, sleepy brown eyes, and a creamy complexion, delicately tinted by the hand of an artist. She was little more than thirty-five, but her plumpness made her appear to be older. She did not look in the least like a widow, which was the first thought that occurred to Lady Ombersley when she presently entered the room, and took the languid hand held out to her.

'*Com' está?*' the Marquesa said, in her rich, lazy voice.

This terrified Hubert, who had been assured that she spoke excellent English. He cast a burning look of reproach at Sophy, who at once intervened, calling her future stepmother to order. The Marquesa smiled placidly, and said: '*De seguro!* I speak French and English, and both very well. Also German, but that not so well, yet better than most people. It is a profound happiness to meet the sister of Sir Horace, though you do not, I find, resemble him, *señora. Valgamé!* are these then all your sons and daughters!'

Lady Ombersley made haste to reassure her, and to perform the necessary introductions. The Marquesa lost interest in these before very long, but smiled in a general way upon her guests, and begged them all to sit down. Sophy told her that in Sir Vincent she beheld an old acquaintance, so she gave him her hand, and said that she remembered him perfectly. No one believed her, least of all Sir Vincent; but when she had been reminded of a certain evening on the Prado, she began to laugh, and said yes, now indeed she did remember him, *pechero* that he was! She then, having had time to assimilate the perfection of Cecilia's features, complimented Lady Ombersley on her beauty, which, she said, was in the best English style, and much admired upon the Continent. Apparently feeling that something was due to Miss Wraxton, she smiled kindly at her, and said that she also was very English. Miss Wraxton, who did not grudge Cecilia her beauty (for she had been brought up to think beauty only skin-deep), replied that she feared that she was not above the ordinary, and that in England the fashion was for dark women.

This subject having been pretty well thrashed out, silence fell, the Marquesa lying back against the cushions in one corner of the sofa, and Lady Ombersley wondering what topic of conversation would interest this lethargic lady. Mr Fawnhope, who had retired to the brocade-covered window-seat, sat gazing out upon the verdure his soul craved; Hubert regarded his hostess with a fascinated eye; and Mr Rivenhall, adapting himself to his company, picked up a periodical from the table at his elbow, and casually flicked over the pages. It was left to Miss Wraxton, with her fine social sense, to fill the breach, which she did by telling the Marquesa that she was a great admirer of *Don Quixote.*

'All the English are,' responded the Marquesa. 'And they will none of them say the name correctly. In Madrid, when the English army was there, every officer told me that he so much admired Cervantes, though mostly it was not true. But we have also Quevedo, and Espinel, and Montelban, to name only a few. In poetry, too –'

'*El Fenix de España*,' interpolated Mr Fawnhope, suddenly entering into the conversation.

The Marquesa looked approvingly at him. 'That is so. You are familiar with the works of Lope de Vega? Sophie,' she said, breaking into her own tongue, 'this young man with the face of an angel reads Spanish!'

'Very indifferently,' said Mr Fawnhope, quite unmoved by this embarrassing description of his face.

'We will talk together,' said the Marquesa.

'Certainly not,' said Sophy firmly. 'At least, not if you mean to do so in Spanish.'

Fortunately for the success of the party, Gaston came in at this moment to announce that refreshments were laid out in the dining-room. It was soon discovered that however indolent a hostess the Marquesa might be her maître d'hôtel left nothing to chance. A profusion of succulent foreign dishes awaited the guests, garnished with aspic, or spread with subtle sauces, and served with various light wines. Jellies, trifles, syllabubs, puptons of fruit, and coffee creams in cups of almond paste rounded off what the Marquesa called a light *marienda*. From the sparing way in which Miss Wraxton partook of a few of the delicacies it was not difficult to see that she considered such lavish hospitality vulgar; but Hubert, making a hearty meal, began to think the Marquesa a very good sort of woman after all. When he saw how many coffee creams, Italian rusks, and brandy-cherries she herself consumed, in the most negligent fashion, his manner towards her became tinged with respect bordering on awe.

The repast at an end, Gaston bent to his mistress's ear, and reminded her that the gate into the wood had been unlocked. She said: 'Ah, yes! The bluebell wood! So pretty! These young people would like to wander through it, *señora*, while you and I repose ourselves a little.'

It would never have occurred to Lady Ombersley to suggest a siesta to a visitor; but since she invariably dozed during the afternoon she had no real fault to find with this programme, and accompanied the Marquesa into the drawing-room. Here she at first endeavoured to engage the Marquesa in talk of her brother, but without much success. The Marquesa said: 'It is not amusing to be a widow, and, besides, I prefer England to Spain, since it is now very impoverished there. But to be *madrusta* to Sophie – ! No, and a thousand times no!'

'We are all very fond of my dear niece,' said Lady Ombersley, bristling.

'I also, but she is too fatiguing. One does not know what next she will do, or, which is worse by far, what she will make one do that one does not wish at all.'

Lady Ombersley found herself quite unable to resist the temptation of indulging in a little gentle malice. 'My dear ma'am, I am sure my niece could never persuade you to exert yourself in any way disagreeable to you!'

'But yes!' said the Marquesa simply. 'It is plain that you do not know Sophie. To withstand her is much, much more fatiguing still!'

Meanwhile, the subject of this exchange was arranging a flower in Hubert's button-hole, in the formal garden. Mr Rivenhall had gone off in the direction of the stables, and the four others were wending their way, through the shrubbery, towards the bluebell wood, Mr Fawnhope having been visited by inspiration which only the sight of Cecilia in the wood could, he said, bring to fruition. So far, he had only achieved one line of his poem, but he felt it to be promising. '*When amidst bluebells my Cecilia treads,*' he murmured.

'Quite Carolinian!' remarked Miss Wraxton.

Mr Fawnhope's verse was at all times derivative, but he liked being told so no better than any other poet, so he took his Cecilia's hand and would have led her away had not Miss Wraxton been on the alert to prevent just such a happening. With determination she stayed beside the lovers, and presently, by a happy reference to Cowper, succeeded in diverting Mr Fawnhope's attention from Cecilia to herself. Sir Vincent, finding solace for boredom in amusement at this situation, bided his time, and was presently rewarded. Cecilia, unable to bear a part in the elevated discussion in progress (for she was no great reader), began to drop behind. Sir Vincent fell in beside her, and in a very short space of time coaxed her out of her crossness, and, indeed, out of the wood as well. He said that profound as was his admiration for Miss Wraxton's intellect he found her conversation oppressive. Woods and blue-stockings, he said, exercised a lowering effect upon his spirits. He thought the ground was damp: certainly unfit walking for a delicately nurtured lady. He took Cecilia instead to inspect the dovecot, and since he was skilled in the art of flirtation, and she was lovely enough to make a little dalliance a pleasant way of whiling away a dull afternoon, they contrived to pass an agreeable hour together.

While all this was going on, Sophy was walking in the shrubbery with Hubert. She had not failed to notice that during the past few days he had swung between exaggeratedly high spirits, and fits of black depression. She had mentioned the matter to Cecilia, but Cecilia had merely said that Hubert had always been moody, and had not seemed to be inclined to think any more about it. But Sophy could not see anyone in the grip of care without instantly wishing to discover the cause, and, if possible, to rectify it. She thought she was now on good enough terms with him to venture to broach the matter to him, and so, it seemed, she was, although he could not be said to confide in her, he did not, as she had been afraid he might, mount upon a high horse. Yes, he confessed, he was a trifle worried, but it was no great matter, and he expected to have put it all behind him in a very few days' time.

Sophy, who had led the way to a rustic seat, now obliged him to sit down beside her on it. Tracing a pattern on the gravel path with the point of her parasol, she said: 'If it is money – and it nearly always is: it is the most odious thing! – and you do not care to ask your papa for it, I expect I could help you.'

'Much good it would be to ask my father!' said Hubert. 'He hasn't a feather to fly with, and what is so dashed unjust, when you consider, the only time I ever applied to him he went into a worse rage than Charles does!'

'Does Charles go into a rage?'

'Oh, well – ! Not, not precisely, but I don't know but what I'd liefer he did!' replied Hubert bitterly.

She nodded. 'Then you don't wish to approach him. Do pray, tell me!'

'Certainly not!' said Hubert, on his dignity. 'Devilish good of you, Sophy, but I haven't come to *that* yet!'

'Come to what?' she demanded.

'Borrowing money from females, of course! Besides, there's no need. I shall come about, and before I go up to Oxford again, thank the lord!'

'How?'

'Never mind, but it can't fail! If it does – but it will not! I may have a father who – well, no sense in talking of *him!* And I may have a dashed disagreeable brother, holding so tightly to the purse-strings that you'd think he was a Jew, but fortunately for me I've a couple of good friends – whatever Charles may say!'

'Oh!' said Sophy, digesting this information. Disagreeable Charles might be, but she was shrewd enough to suspect that if he condemned any of Hubert's friends there might be much to be said in his defence. 'Does he dislike your friends?'

Hubert gave a short laugh. 'Lord, yes! Just because they are knowing 'uns, and kick up a lark every now and then, he proses like a Methodist, and – Here, Sophy, you won't start talking to Charles, will you?'

'Of course I shall do no such thing!' she said indignantly. 'Why, what a creature you must think me!'

'No, I don't, only – Oh, well, it don't signify! I shall be as merry as a grig in a week's time, and I don't mean to get into a fix again, I can tell you!'

She was obliged to be satisfied with this assurance, for he would say no more. After taking another turn round the shrubbery, she left him, and went back to the house.

She found Mr Rivenhall seated under the elm tree on the

south lawn, with Tina, who was sleeping off a large repast, at his feet. 'If you want to see a rare picture, Sophy,' he said, 'peep in at the drawing-room window! My mother is sound asleep on one sofa, and the Marquesa on another.'

'Well, if that is their notion of enjoyment I don't think we should disturb them,' she replied. 'It would not be mine, but I do *try* to remember that some people like to spend half their days doing nothing at all.'

He made room for her to sit down beside him. 'No, I fancy idleness is not your besetting sin,' he agreed. 'Sometimes I wonder whether it would not be better for the rest of us if it were, but we have agreed not to quarrel today, so I shall not pursue that thought. But, Sophy, what is my uncle about to be marrying that woman?'

She wrinkled her brow. 'She is very good-natured, you know, and Sir Horace says he likes reposeful females.'

'I am astonished that you have sanctioned so unsuitable a match.'

'Nonsense! I have nothing to say to it.'

'I imagine you have everything to say to it,' he retorted. 'Don't play off the airs of an innocent to me, cousin! I know you well enough to be tolerably certain that you rule my uncle with a rod of iron, and have probably guarded him from dozens of Marquesas in your time!'

She laughed. 'Well, yes,' she admitted. 'But, then, they would none of them have made the poor angel at all comfortable, and I do think perhaps Sancia may. I have long made up my mind to it that he should marry again, you know.'

'Next you will say that this match is of your making!'

'Oh, no! There is never the least need to make matches for Sir Horace!' she said frankly. 'He is the most susceptible creature imaginable, and, which is so dangerous, if a pretty woman will but weep on his shoulder he will do anything she wants!'

He did not reply, and she saw that his attention was fixed on Cecilia and Sir Vincent, who had that instant come round a corner of the clipped yew hedge. A slight frown descended on to his brow, which made Sophy say severely: 'Now, don't take one of your pets because Cecy flirts a little with Sir Vincent! You should be thankful to see her taking interest in some other man than Mr Fawnhope. But there is no pleasing you!'

'I am certainly not pleased with *that* connection!'

'Oh, you have no cause to feel alarm! Sir Vincent is only interested in heiresses, and has no intention of offering for Cecy.'

'Thank you, it is not on that score that I feel alarm,' he answered.

She could say no more, for by this time the other couple had come up to them. Cecilia, who was looking prettier than ever, described how Sir Vincent had been so obliging as to find a servant who gave him some maize for the pigeons. She had fed them, and her cousin thought she had taken far more delight in encouraging them to take maize from between her lips than in listening to Sir Vincent's practised compliments.

They were soon joined by Hubert. He shot Sophy a glance so pregnant with mischief that in spite of his high shirt-points, his elaborate neckcloth, and his fashionable waistcoat he looked very much more like a schoolboy than the town-beau he fancied himself. She could not imagine what mischief he could have found to perform in the little time since she had left him, but before she could speculate very seriously on this problem her attention was diverted by the Marquesa, who appeared at the drawing-room window, and made signs indicative of her desire that they should all come into the house. Civility obliged even Mr Rivenhall to obey the summons. They found the Marquesa so much refreshed by her nap as to have become quite animated. Lady Ombersley had awakened from slumber, uttering the mystic words: *Lotion of the Ladies of Denmark*, which had operated so powerfully upon her hostess as to make her sit bolt upright upon her sofa, exclaiming: 'But no! Better distilled water of green pineapples, I assure you!' By the time the party on the south lawn entered the house the two elder ladies had thoroughly explored every path known to them that led to the preservation of the complexion, and if they differed on such points as the value of raw veal laid on the face at night to remove wrinkles, they found themselves at one over the beneficial effects of chervil water, and crushed strawberries.

It now being at least two hours since the light *marienda* had been consumed, the Marquesa stood in urgent need of further sustenance, and warmly invited her guests to partake of tea and angel cakes. It was then that Lady Ombersley became aware of the absence of Miss Wraxton and Mr Fawnhope from the gathering, and demanded to know where they were. Cecilia replied, with a shrug, that they were no doubt quoting poetry to each other in the wood; but when twenty minutes passed without their putting in an appearance not only Lady Ombersley, but her elder son also, became a trifle restive. Then it was that Sophy remembered Hubert's look of mischief. She glanced across at him, and saw his expression was so unconcerned as to be wholly incredible. In deep foreboding she made an excuse to change her seat to one beside his, and whispered, under cover of the general conversation: 'You dreadful creature, what have you done?'

'Locked them into the wood!' he whispered in return. 'That will teach her to play propriety!'

She had to bite back a laugh, but managed to say, with suitable severity: 'It will not do! If you have the key, give it to me so that no one will observe you!'

He said: 'What a spoil-sport you are!' but soon found an opportunity to drop it into her lap, for although it had seemed, at the time, a splendid idea to lock the gate into the wood, he had been realizing for some minutes that to release the imprisoned couple without scandal might prove to be rather more difficult.

'It is so unlike dear Eugenia!' said Lady Ombersley. 'I cannot think what they can be about!'

'*En verdad*, it is not difficult to imagine!' remarked the Marquesa, rather amused. 'So beautiful a young man and so romantic a scene!'

'I will go and look for them,' said Mr Rivenhall, getting up, and walking out of the room.

Hubert began to look a little alarmed, but Sophy exclaimed

suddenly: 'I wonder if one of the gardeners can have locked the gate again, thinking that we had all left the wood? Excuse me, Sancia!'

She overtook Mr Rivenhall in the shrubbery, and called out: 'So stupid! Sancia, you know, lives in dread of robbers and has trained all her servants never to leave a gate or a door unlocked! One of the gardeners, supposing us all to have gone back to the house, locked the gate into the wood. Gaston had the key: here it is!'

A bend in the gravel walk brought the gates into the wood within view. Miss Wraxton was standing by them, and it was plain to the meanest intelligence that she was in no very amiable humour. Behind her, seated upon a bank, and absorbed in metrical composition, was Mr Fawnhope, to all appearances divorced from the world.

As Mr Rivenhall fitted the key into the lock, Sophy said: 'I am so sorry! It is all the fault of Sancia's absurd terrors! Are you very bored and chilled, Miss Wraxton?'

Miss Wraxton had endured a trying half-hour. Upon finding herself shut into the wood, she had first asked Mr Fawnhope if he could not climb over the fence, and when he had replied, quite simply, that he could not, she had requested him to shout. But the ode that was burgeoning in his head had by this time taken possession of him, and he had said that the sylvan setting was just the inspiration he needed. After that, he sat down on the bank, and drew out his notebook and a pencil, and whenever she begged him to bestir himself to procure her release, all he said, and that in a voice that showed how far away were his thoughts, was 'Hush!' Consequently she was in a mood ripe for murder when the rescue party at last arrived on the scene, and was betrayed into an unwise accusation, 'You did this!' she flung at Sophy, quite white with anger.

Sophy, who felt sorry for her being discovered in so ridiculous a situation, replied soothingly: 'No, it was a foolish servant, who thought we had all gone back to the house. Never mind! Come and drink some of Sancia's excellent tea!'

'I don't believe you. You are unprincipled, and vulgar, and –'

'Eugenia!' said Mr Rivenhall sharply.

She gave an angry sob, but said no more. Sophy went into the wood to rouse Mr Fawnhope from his abstraction, and Mr Rivenhall said: 'It was nothing but an accident, and there is no need to be so put-out.'

'I am persuaded your cousin did it to make me a laughing-stock,' she said in a low voice.

'Nonsense!' he replied coldly.

She saw that he was by no means in sympathy with her, and said: 'I need hardly tell you that my aim was to prevent your sister spending the whole afternoon in that odious young man's company.'

'With the result that she spent it in Talgarth's company,' he retorted. 'There was no reason for you to be so busy, Eugenia. My mother's presence, not to mention my own, made your action – I shall say *unnecesssary!*'

It might have been supposed that these words of censure filled Miss Wraxton's cup to the brim, but upon entering the drawing-room she found that she had still to endure the Marquesa's comments. The Marquesa favoured the company with a disquisition on the licence allowed to young English ladies, contrasting it with the strict chaperonage of Spanish damsels; and everyone, with the exception of Mr Rivenhall, who was markedly silent, felt for Miss Wraxton in her chagrin, and made great efforts to placate her, Sophy going so far as to give up her place in the curricle to her on the homeward journey. She was insensibly mollified, but when, later, she tried to justify her actions to her betrothed, he cut her short, saying too much noise had been made already over a trivial occurrence.

'I cannot believe that any of the servants were responsible,' she insisted.

'You would do better to pretend to believe it, however.'

'Then you do not think so either!' she exclaimed.

'No, I think Hubert did it,' he replied coldly. 'And if I am right, you have my cousin to thank for speedily releasing you.'

'Hubert!' she cried. 'Why should he do such an ungentlemanly thing, pray?'

He shrugged. 'Possibly for a jest, possibly because he resented your interference in Cecilia's affairs, my dear Eugenia. He is much attached to his sister.'

She said in a deeply mortified tone: 'If that is so, I hope you mean to take him to task!'

'I shall do nothing so ill-judged,' responded Mr Rivenhall, at his most blighting.

Nine

hortly after this not entirely successful day in the country Mr Rivenhall announced his intention of going down to Ombersley for a spell. His mother had no objection to advance, but realizing that the dread moment of disclosure had now come, said, with an assumption of calm she was far from feeling, that she hoped he would come back to London in time to attend Sophy's party.

'Is it so important?' he asked. 'I have no turn for dancing, Mama, and such an evening as you will no doubt pass is of all things most insipid!'

'Well, it is rather important?,' she confessed. 'It would be thought rather strange if you were absent, dear Charles!'

'Good heavens, Mama, I have been absent from all such affairs in this house!'

'As a matter of fact, this party is to be a little larger than we first thought it would be!' she said desperately.

He bent one of his disconcerting stares upon her. 'Indeed! I had collected that some twenty persons were to be invited?'

'There – there will be a few more than that!' she said.

'How many more?'

She became intent on disentangling the fringe of her shawl from the arm of her chair. 'Well, we thought perhaps it would be best – since it is our first party for your cousin, and your uncle particularly desired me to launch her upon society – to give a set ball, Charles! And your father promises to bring the Duke of York to it, if only for half an hour! It seems he is well-acquainted with Horace: I am sure it is most gratifying!'

'How many persons, ma'am, have you invited to this precious ball?' demanded Mr Rivenhall, ungratified.

'Not – not above four hundred!' faltered his guilty parent. 'And they will not all of them come, dear Charles!'

'Four hundred!' he exclaimed. 'I need not ask whose doing this is! And who, ma'am, is to foot the bill for this entertainment?'

'Sophy – that is to say, your uncle, of course! I assure you the cost it not to come upon you!'

He was not in the least soothed by this, but, on the contrary, rapped out: 'Do you imagine I will permit that wretched girl to pay for parties in this house? If you have been mad enough, ma'am, to consent to this scheme –'

Lady Ombersley prudently sought refuge in tears, and began to grope for her smelling-salts. Her son eyed her in a baffled way, and said with painstaking restraint: 'Pray do not cry, Mama! I am well aware whom I have to thank for this.'

An interruption, welcome to Lady Ombersley, occurred in the shape of Selina, who bounced into the room, exclaiming: 'Oh, Mama! When we gave the ball for Cecilia, did we –' She then perceived her eldest brother, and broke off short, looking extremely conscious.

'Go on!' said Mr Rivenhall grimly.

Selina gave her head a slight toss. 'I suppose you know all about Sophy's ball: well, I am sure I don't care, for you cannot stop it now that all the cards of invitation have gone out, and three hundred and eighty seven persons have accepted! Mama, Sophy says that when she and Sir Horace held a great reception in Vienna, Sir Horace warned the police-officers of it, so that they were able to keep the street clear, and tell the coachmen where to go, and so-on. Did we not do the same for Cecilia's ball?'

'Yes, and the link-boys as well,' replied Lady Ombersley, emerging briefly from her handkerchief, but retiring into its protection again immediately.

'Yes, Mama, and the champagne!' said Selina, determined to discharge the whole of her errand. 'Should it be ordered from Gunters, with all the rest? Or –'

'You may inform your cousin,' interrupted Mr Rivenhall, 'that the champagne will be provided from our own cellars!' He then turned his shoulder on his young sister, and demanded of his parent: 'How does it come about that Eugenia has not mentioned this affair to me? Has she not been invited to your ball?'

One desperately enquiring eye emerged from the handkerchief, wildly seeking enlightenment of Selina.

'Good gracious, Charles!' said that damsel, shocked. 'Can you have forgotten the bereavement in Miss Wraxton's family? I am sure if she has told us once she has told us a dozen times that propriety forbids her to attend any but the most quiet parties!'

'This, too, is my cousin's work, I collect!' he said, his lips tightening. 'I must say, ma'am, I might have expected, if you were bent on this folly, that you would have sent a card to my promised wife!'

'Of course, Charles, of course!' said Lady Ombersley. 'If it has not been done, it is a foolish oversight! Though it is perfectly true that Eugenia has told us that while she is in black gloves –'

'Oh, Mama, don't!' cried Selina impetuously. 'You know she will cast a damper over everything, with that long face of hers, just like a horse –'

'How dare you?' interrupted Mr Rivenhall furiously.

Selina looked a little frightened, but muttered: 'Well, she *does*, whatever you may choose to think, Charles!'

'More of my cousin's work, no doubt!'

Selina flushed, and cast down her eyes. Mr Rivenhall turned to his mother. 'Be so good as to tell me, ma'am, in what manner this affair is arranged between you and Sophy! Does she give you a draft on my uncle's bank, or what?'

'I – I don't precisely know!' said Lady Ombersley. 'I mean, it has not been discussed yet! Indeed, Charles, I did not know myself until the just the other day that so many people had been invited!'

'Well, *I* know, Mama!' said Selina. 'The bills are all sent to Sophy, and you will not be troubled with them at all!'

'I thank you!' Charles said, and walked abruptly out of the room.

He found his cousin in the small saloon at the back of the house which was generally known as the Young Ladies' Room. She was engaged in compiling some kind of a list, but she looked up at the opening of the door, and smiled at Charles. 'Are you looking for Cecilia? She has gone out to do some shopping in Bond Street, with Miss Adderbury.'

'No, I am not looking for Cecilia!' he answered. 'My business is with you, cousin, and will not take me long. I am informed that my mother is giving a ball in your honour on Tuesday, and by some extraordinary piece of mismanagement the bills for this have been sent to you. Will you be so obliging as to find them, and give them to me?'

'On your high ropes again, Charles?' she said, lifting her brows. 'This is Sir Horace's ball, not my aunt's: there is no mismanagement.'

'Sir Horace may be master in his own house – though that I doubt! – but he is not master in this one! If my mother chooses to hold a ball, she may do so, but in no circumstances will the charge fall upon my uncle. It is intolerable that you should have persuaded my mother to consent to such a scheme! Give me what bills you have, if you please!'

'But I do not please,' replied Sophy. 'Neither Sir Horace nor you, dear cousin, is the master in this house. I have my Uncle Ombersley's consent to what I have done.' She saw with satisfaction that she had utterly taken him aback, and added: 'If I were you, Charles, I would go for a nice walk in the Park. I have always found that there is nothing so beneficial to the temper as exercise in the fresh air.'

He controlled himself with a strong effort. 'Cousin, I am in earnest! I cannot and I will not tolerate such a situation as this!'

'But no one has asked you to tolerate anything at all,' she pointed out. 'If my uncle and aunt are satisfied with my arrangements, pray what have you to say to them?'

He said through shut teeth: 'I think I told you once before, cousin, that we did very well here before you came to upset all our comfort!'

'Yes, you did, and what you meant, Charles, was that until I came no one dared to flout you. You should be grateful to me – or at any rate, Miss Wraxton should, for I am sure you would have made an odious husband before I came to stay with your Mama.'

This put him in mind of a complaint he could with justice make. He said stiffly: 'Since you have brought up Miss Wraxton's name, I shall be much obliged to you, cousin, if you will refrain from telling my sisters that she has a face like a horse!'

'But, Charles, no blame attaches to Miss Wraxton! She cannot help it, and that, I *assure* you, I have always pointed out to your sisters!'

'I consider Miss Wraxton's countenance particularly well-bred!'

'Yes, indeed, but you have quite misunderstood the matter! I *meant* a particularly well-bred horse!'

'You meant, as I am perfectly aware, to belittle Miss Wraxton!'

'No, no! I am very fond of horses!' Sophy said earnestly.

Before he could stop himself he found that he was replying to this. 'Selina, who repeated this remark to me, is *not* fond of horses, however, and she –' He broke off, seeing how absurd it was to argue on such a head.

'I expect she will be, when she has lived in the same house with Miss Wraxton for a month or two,' said Sophy encouragingly.

Mr Rivenhall, restraining an impulse to box his cousin's ears, flung out of the room, slamming the door behind him. At the foot of the stairs he encountered Lord Bromford, who was handing his hat and overcoat to a footman. Mr Rivenhall, seeing how he

145

might, in some measure, be revenged on Sophy, greeted him with a great affability, asked him if he meant to attend Tuesday's ball, and, upon hearing that his lordship was much looking forward to the engagement, said: 'Have you come to bespeak my cousin's hand to the cotillion? You are wise! She will certainly be besieged with solicitations! Dassett, you will find Miss Stanton-Lacy in the Yellow Saloon! Take his lordship up to her!'

'Do you think I should?' said Lord Bromford anxiously. 'It was not danced in Jamaica, you know, but I have been taking lessons, and two of the steps I know tolerably well. Will there be waltzing? I do not waltz. I do not think it seemly. I hope Miss Stanton-Lacy does not waltz. I do not like to see a lady doing so.'

'Everyone waltzes nowadays,' said Mr Rivenhall bent on his fell intent. 'You should take lessons in that too, Bromford, or you will be quite cut out!'

'I do not think,' said Lord Bromford, having considered the matter gravely, 'that one should sacrifice one's principles to gratify a female's whim. I do not think the quadrille objectionable, although I am aware that there are many who do not permit it to be danced in their houses. In the country dance I am prepared to take my part. There is authority for the exercise of dancing, by which I mean to signify the round, or country-dance, in the works of the Ancients. Plato, you know, recommended that children should be taught to dance; and several classic writers deemed it an excellent recreation after serious study.'

But at this point Mr Rivenhall bethought him of a pressing engagement, and fled the house. Lord Bromford followed the butler upstairs to the drawing-room, Dasset having his own views on the impropriety of ushering single gentlemen into the Young Ladies' Room. When Sophy, duly chaperoned by Selina, joined him there, he lost no time in begging her to dance the cotillion with him. Sophy, trusting that one of her Peninsula friends would come to her rescue, said how sorry she was to be obliged to refuse him. She was, she said, already engaged. His face fell, and he looked even a little offended, exclaiming. 'How can this be, when your cousin told me to make haste to be first with you?'

'My cousin Charles? Did he indeed?' said Sophy appreciatively. 'Well, no doubt he did not know that my hand has been claimed these past three days. Perhaps we may stand up together for one of the country-dances.'

He bowed, and said: 'I have been telling your cousin that we have good authority for indulging in country-dances. They cannot, I believe, be considered harmful. The waltz, on the other hand, I cannot approve of.'

'Oh, you do not waltz? I am so glad – I mean, one does not think of your indulging in anything so frivolous, Lord Bromford!'

He appeared to be pleased by this; he settled himself deeper in his chair, and said: 'You raise an interesting thesis, ma'am. One is familiar with the phrase. *A man may be known by the company he keeps*: can it be that he may also be known by the dances he permits himself to indulge in?'

Since neither lady had any views to advance on this subject, it was fortunate that his question was purely rhetorical. He began to expand the topic, and was only interrupted by the arrival of Mr Wychbold, who came first to offer to escort Sophy and her cousins to witness a wild beast show, and second to beg the honour of partnering her in the cotillion. She was obliged to deny him, but with regret, for Mr Wychbold was a notable dancer, performing every stop in the cotillion with grace and elegance.

However, when Tuesday dawned she had acquired a far from contemptible partner in Lord Francis Wolvey. The fact that he had first applied for Miss Rivenhall's hand she bore with great fortitude, saying that in Christian charity to all other young females Cecilia should lose no time in disposing of herself in wedlock.

It was plain from the outset that the ball was to be one of the season's successes. Even the weather favoured it. From dawn till dinner-time Ombersley House was the scene of restless activity, and the road outside noisy with the wheels of tradesmen's carts, and the whistling of innumerable errand-boys. Mr Rivenhall arrived from the country just as two men in shirtsleeves and leather breeches were erecting an awning across the flag-way to the road; and another, wearing a baize apron, laying a red carpet down the steps, under Dassett's lofty supervision. Inside the house, Mr Rivenhall almost collided with a footman, staggering in the direction of the ballroom with a gigantic potted palm clasped to his bosom, and avoided him only to be faintly screamed at by the housekeeper, who was carrying a pile of the best table-damask to the dining-room. Dassett, who had followed Mr Rivenhall into the house, informed him, with satisfaction, that they would sit down thirty to dinner at eight o'clock. He added that her ladyship was laid down upon her bed in preparation for the revels, and that his lordship had personally selected the wines to be served at dinner. Mr Rivenhall, who seemed to be resigned rather than delighted, nodded, and asked whether any letters awaited him.

'No, sir,' replied Dassett. 'I should mention that the band of Scots Greys will play during supper, Miss Sophy being acquainted with the Colonel, who will be amongst the dinner-guests. A vast improvement, if I may say so, sir, on the Pandean pipes, which have become quite common since we had them for Miss Cecilia's ball last year. Miss Sophy, I venture to say, is a lady as knows precisely how things should be done. A great pleasure, if I may be pardoned the liberty, to work for Miss Sophy, for she thinks of everything, and I fancy there will be no hitch to mar the festivities.'

Mr Rivenhall grunted, and went off to his own apartments. When he next appeared, it was to join the rest of his family in the drawing-room a few minutes only before eight o'clock. His two young sisters, who were deriving much entertainment from hanging over the banisters of the staircase leading to the school-room floor, informed him in penetrating whispers that he looked so smart they could not believe that there would be any other gentleman to rival him. He looked up, laughing, for although he had a good figure, and was dressed with propriety in black satin knee-breeches, a white waistcoat, striped stockings, and a waisted coat with very long tails, he knew that he would be sartorially outshone by half the male guests. But his little sisters' wholehearted admiration certainly softened his mood, and after promising faithfully to send a servant up to the schoolroom with ices later on, he went on to the drawing-room and was even able to bring himself to compliment his sister and cousin on their gowns.

Sophy had chosen a dress of her favourite pomona-green crape, which she wore over a slip of white satin. It had tiny puff-sleeves of lace and seed-pearls, and was lavishly trimmed with lace. Particularly fine diamond drops hung from her ears; her pearl necklace was clasped round her throat; and an opera-comb was set behind the elaborate knot of hair on the crown of her head. Jane Storridge had brushed and pomaded her side-curls until they glowed richly chestnut in the candlelight. Green-striped satin slippers, long gloves, and a fan of frosted crape on ivory sticks completed her toilet. Lady Ombersley, while approving of this striking ensemble, could not forbear gazing at Cecilia with eyes misty with maternal pride. All the youth and beauty of the Upper Ten Thousand would be present at her ball tonight, she reflected, in a large-minded spirit, but there was not a girl amongst them who would not be cast into the shade by Cecilia, a dream-princess in white spider-gauze, glinting a little when she moved, and the light caught the silver acorns embroidered on the delicate material. Cecilia's curls, with only a silver ribbon threaded through them, were like spun gold; her eyes a clear, translucent blue; her mouth a perfect bow. Beside Sophy she seemed ethereal; her father, surveying her with easy affection, said she made him think of a fairy: Queen Mab, or Titania, was it? He needed Eugenia Wraxton to set him right.

He was to have her. Miss Wraxton, after prolonged con-sideration, had decided to attend Sophy's ball, gaining her Mama's consent by assuring her that she should certainly not take part in any dancing. She was the first of the dinner-guests to arrive, and was attended by her brother Alfred, who ogled

Cecilia and Sophy through his quizzing-glass, paying them such extravagant compliments as to bring a faint flush to Cecilia's cheeks, and a sparkling look into Sophy's eyes. Miss Wraxton, who was attired in discreet lavender crape, and had come determined to please, and to be pleased, also complimented the cousins on their appearance. Her remarks, however, were in far better taste, and won a warm look from Charles. At the first opportunity, he engaged her attention, going over to put a chair for her, and saying: 'I had not dared to hope that you would be present tonight. Thank you!'

She smiled, and pressed his hand slightly. 'Mama did not quite like it, but she agreed that it would be proper for me to come, in the circumstances. I shall not dance, I need hardly say.'

'I am delighted to hear it: you present me with a capital excuse for following your example!'

She looked gratified, but said: 'No, no, you are to do your duty, Charles! I insist upon it!'

'The Marquesa de Villacañas!' announced Dassett.

'Good God!' ejaculated Charles, under his breath.

The Marquesa came into the room, magnificent, and decidedly exotic, in gold satin, casually adorned with ruby or emerald brooches, chains, and necklaces. An immensely high Spanish comb was in her hair, with a mantilla draped over it; an aroma of heavy perfume hung about her; and a very long train swept the floor behind her. Lord Ombersley drew a deep breath, and moved forward to greet with real enthusiasm a guest so worthy of his notice.

Mr Rivenhall forgot that he was not on speaking-terms with his abominable cousin, and said in her ear: 'How in the world did you rouse her to so much effort?'

She laughed. 'Oh, she wished in any event to spend a few days in London, so all I had to do was to engage a suite of rooms for her at the Pulteney Hotel, and to charge Pepita, her maid, most straitly, to send her to us tonight.'

'I am astonished that she could be brought even to contemplate so much exertion!'

'Ah, she knew I would go myself to fetch her if she failed!'

More guests were arriving; Mr Rivenhall moved away to assist his parents in receiving them; the big double drawing-room began to fill up; and at only a few minutes past eight o'clock Dasset was able to announce dinner.

The guests assembled for dinner were of a quality to fill any hostess's bosom with pride, including as they did a great many members of the diplomatic set, and two Cabinet Ministers, with their wives. Lady Ombersley could cram her rooms with as many members of the nobility as she cared to invite, but since her husband took little interest in politics, Government circles were rather beyond her reach. But Sophy, barely acquainted with the very well-born but equally undistinguished people who made up the larger part of the Polite World, had been bred up in Government circles, and, from the day when she first did up her hair and let down her skirts, had been entertaining celebrated persons, and was on the friendliest of terms with them. Her, or perhaps Sir Horace's, acquaintances preponderated at her aunt's board, but not even Miss Wraxton, on the watch for signs of presumption in her, could find any fault with her demeanour. It might have been expected, since all the arrangements for the party had been hers, that she would have put herself forward more than was becoming, but so far from doing so she seemed to be in a retiring mood, bearing no part in greeting guests upstairs, and confining her conversation at table, most correctly, to the gentlemen on her either side. Miss Wraxton, who had labelled her a hoyden, was obliged to own that her company manners at least were above reproach.

The ball, which began at ten o'clock, was held in the huge room built for the purpose at the back of the house. It was lit by hundreds of candles in a great crystal chandelier hanging from the ceiling, and since this had been unswathed from its holland covering three days before so that both footmen and the pantry-boy could wash and polish its lustres, it sparkled like a collection of mammoth diamonds. Masses of flowers were arranged in set pieces at either end of the room, and an excellent orchestra had been engaged, quite regardless (Mr Rivenhall bitterly reflected) of expense.

The room, large as it was, soon became so crowded with elegant persons that it seemed certain that the function would receive the final accolade, in being voted a sad crush. No hostess could desire more.

The ball opened with a country-dance, in which Mr Rivenhall, in honour bound, stood up with his cousin. He performed his part with propriety, she hers with grace; and Miss Wraxton, watching from a route-chair at one side of the room, smiled graciously upon them both. Mr Fawnhope, a most beautiful dancer, had led Cecilia into the same set, a circumstance that considerably annoyed Mr Rivenhall. He thought that Cecilia should have reserved the opening dance for some more important guest, and he derived no satisfaction from overhearing more than one tribute to the grace and beauty of such an arresting couple. Nowhere did Mr Fawnhope shine to more advantage than in a ballroom, and happy was the lady who stood up with him. Envious eyes followed Cecilia, and more than one dark beauty wished that, since Mr Fawnhope, himself so angelically fair, unaccountably preferred gold hair to black, she could change her colouring to suit his fancy.

Lord Bromford, one of the earliest arrivals, failed, owing to Mr Rivenhall's sense of duty, to secure Sophy's hand for the first dance, and as a waltz followed the country-dance it was some time before he was able to stand up with her. While waltzing was in progress he stood watching the performers, and in due course gravitated to Miss Wraxton's side, and entertained her with an exposition of his views on the waltz. With these she was to some extent in sympathy, but she expressed herself more moderately, saying that while she herself would not care to waltz, the dance could not be altogether frowned on now that it had been sanctioned at Almack's.

'I did not see it danced at Government House,' said Lord Bromford.

Miss Wraxton, who was fond of reading books of travels, said:

'Jamaica! How much I envy you, sir, your sojourn in that interesting island! I am sure it must be one of the most romantic places imaginable.'

Lord Bromford, whose youth had never been charmed by tales of the Spanish Main, replied that it had much to recommend it, and went on to describe the properties of its medicinal springs, and the great variety of marbles to be found in the mountains, all of which Miss Wraxton listened to with interest, telling Mr Rivenhall later that she thought his lordship had a well-informed mind.

It was half-way through the evening when Sophy, breathless from an energetic waltz with Mr Wychbold, was standing at the side of the room, fanning herself, and watching the couple still circling round the floor while her partner went to procure a glass of iced lemonade for her, was suddenly accosted by a pleasant-looking gentleman, who came up to her, and said with a smile: 'My friend, Major Quinton, promised that he would present me to the Grand Sophy, but the wretched fellow goes from one set to the next, and never spares me a thought! How do you do, Miss Stanton-Lacy? You will forgive my informality, won't you? It is true that I have no business here, for I was not invited, but Charles assures me that had I not been believed to be still laid upon a bed of sickness I must have received a card.'

She looked at him in that frank way of hers, summing him up. She liked what she saw. He was a man in the early thirties, not precisely handsome, but with a pleasing countenance redeemed from the commonplace by a pair of humorous gray eyes. He was above the medium height, and a good pair of shoulders, and an excellent leg for a riding-boot.

'It is certainly too bad of Major Quinton,' Sophy said smilingly. 'But you know what a rattle-pate he is! Ought we to have sent you a card? You must forgive us! I hope your illness was not of a serious nature?'

'Alas, merely painful and humiliating!' he replied. 'Would you believe that a man of my age could fall a victim to so childish a complaint, ma'am? – Mumps!'

Sophy dropped her fan, exclaiming: 'What did you say? *Mumps?*'

'Mumps,' he repeated, picking up the fan, and giving it back to her. 'I do not wonder at your astonishment!'

'Then you,' said Sophy, 'are Lord Charlbury!'

He bowed. 'I am, and I perceive that my fame has gone before me. I own, I should not have chosen to figure in your mind as the man with mumps, but so, I see, it is!'

'Let us sit down,' said Sophy.

He looked amused, but accompanied her at once to a sofa against the wall. 'By all means! But may I not get you a glass of lemonade?'

'Mr Wychbold – I expect you are acquainted with him – has already gone to do so. I should like to talk to you for a little while, for I have heard a great deal about you, you know.'

'Nothing could please me more, for *I* have heard a great deal about you, ma'am, and it has inspired me with the liveliest desire to meet you!'

'Major Quinton,' said Sophy, 'is a shocking quiz, and I daresay has given you quite a false notion of me!'

'I must point out to you, ma'am,' he retaliated, 'that we are both in the same case, for you know *me* only as a man with mumps, and at the risk of sounding like a coxcomb I must assure you that *that* must have given *you* an equally false notion of *me!*'

'You are perfectly right,' said Sophy seriously. 'It did give me a false notion of you!' Her eyes followed Cecilia and Mr Fawnhope round the room; she drew a breath, and said: 'Things may be a trifle difficult.'

'That,' said Lord Charlbury, his eyes following hers, 'I had already realized.'

'I cannot conceive,' said Sophy, with strong feeling, 'what can have possessed you, sir, to contract mumps at such a moment!'

'It was not done by design,' said his lordship meekly.

'Nothing could have been more ill-judged!' said Sophy.

'Not ill-judged!' he pleaded. 'Unfortunate!'

Mr Wychbold came up just then with Sophy's lemonade. 'Hallo, Everard!' he said. 'I didn't know you were fit to be seen yet! How are you, dear boy?'

'Bruised in spirit, Cyprian, bruised in spirit! My sufferings under the complaint that struck me down were as nothing to what I now undergo. Shall I ever live it down?'

'Oh, I don't know!' replied Mr Wychbold consolingly. 'Dashed paltry thing to happen to one, of course, but the town's memory ain't long. Why, do you remember poor Bolton taking a toss into the Serpentine, clean over his horse's head? No one talked of anything else for almost a week. Poor fellow had to rusticate for a while, but it blew over, y'know!'

'Must it be rustication?' Lord Charlbury asked.

'Oh no account!' said Sophy decidedly. She waited until Mr Wychbold's attention was claimed by a lady in puce satin, and then turned towards her companion, and said forthrightly: 'Are you a very good dancer, sir?'

'Not, I fancy, above the average, ma'am. Certainly not to compare with the exquisite young man we are both watching.'

'In that case,' said Sophy, 'I would not, if I were you, solicit Cecilia to waltz!'

'I have already done so, but your warning is unnecessary: she is engaged for every waltz, and also the quadrille. The most I can hope for is to stand up with her in a country-dance.'

'Don't do it!' Sophy advised him. 'To be trying to talk to anyone when you should be attending to the figure is always fatal, believe me!'

He turned his head, and gave her back a look as frank as her own. 'Miss Stanton-Lacy, you are plainly aware of my circumstances. Will you tell me in what case I stand, and who is the Adonis monopolizing Miss Rivenhall?'

'He is Augustus Fawnhope, and he is a poet.'

'That has an ominous ring,' he said lightly. 'I know the family, of course, but I think I have not previously encountered this sprig.'

'Very likely you might not, for he was used to be with Sir

Charles Stuart, in Brussels. Lord Charlbury, you look to me like a sensible man!'

'I had rather I had a head like a Greek coin,' he remarked ruefully.

'You must understand,' said Sophy, disregarding this frivolity, 'that half of the young ladies in London are in love with Mr Fawnhope.'

'I can readily believe it, and I grudge him only one of his conquests.'

She would have replied, but they were interrupted. Lord Ombersley, who had gone away after dinner, now reappeared, accompanied by an elderly and immensely corpulent man in whom no one had the least difficulty in recognizing a member of the Royal Family. He was, in fact, the Duke of York, that one of Farmer George's sons who most nearly resembled him. He had the same protuberant blue eye, and beaky nose, the same puffy cheeks, and pouting mouth, but he was a much larger man than his father. He appeared to be in imminent danger of bursting out of his tightly stretched pantaloons, he wheezed, when he spoke, but he was plainly a genial prince, ready to be pleased, standing on very little ceremony, and chatting affably to anyone who was presented to him. Both Cecilia and Sophy had this honour. His Royal Highness's appreciation of Cecilia's beauty was quite as broadly expressed as Mr Wraxton's had been, and no one could doubt that had he met her in some less public spot it would not have been many minutes before the ducal arm would have been round her waist. Sophy aroused no such amorous tendency in him, but he talked very jovially to her, asked her how her father did, and opined, with a loud laugh, that by this time Sir Horace was enjoying himself amongst all the Brazilian beauties, the dog that he was! After that, he exchanged greetings with several friends, circulated about the room for a while, and finally withdrew to the library with his host and two other of his intimates for rubber of whist.

Cecilia, escaping from the Royal presence with burning cheeks (for she hated to be the target of fulsome compliments), was intercepted by Mr Fawnhope, who said with great simplicity: 'You are more beautiful tonight than I had thought possible!'

'Oh, do not!' she exclaimed involuntarily. 'How insufferably hot it is in this room!'

'You are flushed, but it becomes you. I will take you on to the balcony.'

She made no demur, though this large term merely described the veriest foothold built outside each one of the twelve long windows of the ballroom, and fenced in with low iron railings. Mr Fawnhope parted the heavy curtains that veiled the window at the far end of the room, and she passed through them into a shallow embrasure. After a slight struggle with the bolt, Mr Fawnhope succeeded in opening the double window, and she was able to step out on to the narrow ledge. A chill breeze fanned her cheeks; she said: 'Ah, what a night! The stars!'

'*The evening star, love's harbinger!*' quoted Mr Fawnhope, somewhat vaguely scanning the heavens.

This idyll was rudely interrupted. Mr Rivenhall, having observed the retreat of the young couple, had followed them, and now stepped through the brocade curtains, saying harshly: 'Cecilia, are you lost to *all* sense of propriety? Come back into the ballroom at once!'

Startled, Cecilia turned quickly. Already agitated by the unexpected encounter with Lord Charlbury, her nerves betrayed her into a hasty rejoinder. 'How dare you, Charles?' she said, in a trembling voice. 'Pray, what impropriety am I guilty of in seeking the fresh air in the company of my affianced husband?'

She took Mr Fawnhope's hand as she spoke, and confronted her brother with her chin up, and her cheeks very much flushed. Lord Charlbury, who had drawn back the curtain with one hand, stood perfectly still, as pale as she was red, steadfastly regarding her.

'Oh!' cried Cecilia faintly, snatching her hand from Mr Fawnhope's to press it to her cheek.

'May I know, Cecilia, if what you have just announced is the truth?' asked his lordship, not a trace of emotion in his well-bred voice.

'Yes!' she uttered.

'The devil it is not!' said Mr Rivenhall.

'You must permit me to offer you my felicitations,' said Lord Charlbury, bowing. He then let the curtain fall, and walked away the length of the ballroom in the direction of the doors.

Sophy, about to take her place with Major Quinton in the set which was forming, deserted her partner with a word of excuse, and overtook his lordship in the anteroom. 'Lord Charlbury!'

He turned. 'Miss Stanton-Lacy! Will you tender my apologies to Lady Ombersley for my not taking formal leave of her? She is not at present in the ballroom.'

'Yes, never mind that! What has occurred to make you leave so early?'

'I came, ma'am, with one purpose only in mind. It has been rendered useless for me to stay by your cousin's announcement a moment since that she is betrothed to young Fawnhope.'

'What a goose she is!' remarked Sophy cheerfully. 'I saw her go apart with Augustus, and I saw Charles follow her. Depend upon it, this is all his doing! I could box his ears! Do you ever ride in the Park?'

'Do I *what?*' he asked, bewildered.

'Ride in the Park!'

'Certainly I do, but –'

'Then do so tomorrow morning! Not too early, for I daresay I shall not be in bed until four o'clock! At ten, then; don't fail!'

She waited for no answer, but went back into the ballroom, leaving him to stare after her in considerable surprise. At any other time he would have smiled at her odd, abrupt ways, but he was a man in love, labouring under a crushing blow, and although he could maintain his calm manner it was at present beyond his power to feel any amusement.

Ten

It was with no real expectation of meeting Sophy that Lord Charlbury had a horse saddled next morning, and betook himself to Hyde Park, for it seemed to him that a young lady who had danced the night through would not be very likely to be found riding in the Park by ten o'clock next day. But he had not cantered once round the Row when he saw a magnificent black horse coming towards him, and recognized Sophy on its back. He reined in, and pulled off his hat, exclaiming: 'I made sure you would still be abed, and fast asleep! Are you made of iron, Miss Stanton-Lacy?'

She pulled Salamanca up, sidling and prancing. 'Pooh!' she said, laughing at him. 'Did you think me such a poor creature as to be prostrated by one ball, sir?'

He turned his horse, and fell in beside her. John Potton followed at a discreet distance. Lord Charlbury complimented Sophy on Salamanca, but was cut short.

'Very true, he is a superb horse, but we have not met to talk of horses. *Such* a kick-up as there has been in Berkeley Square! Charles, of course – all Charles!' The most diverting thing of all – do be diverted! indeed, there is no need for that grave face! – is that Augustus Fawnhope was quite as much taken aback as you or Charles!'

'Are you telling me that he does not *wish* to marry Cecilia!' demanded Charlbury.

'Oh – ! In some misty future! Certainly not immediately! I

expect, you know, being a poet, he would much prefer to be the victim of a hopeless passion!' said Sophy merrily.

'Coxcomb!'

'If you like. I danced one waltz with him last night, when you had left us, and I do think I was very helpful, for I suggested to him a number of genteel occupations of a gainful nature, and promised to look about me for some great man in need of a secretary.'

'I hope he was grateful to you,' said Charlbury heavily.

'Not in the least! Augustus does not want to be any man's secretary, for he has a soul quite above such mundane matters as acquiring a respectable competence. I showed him what his future would be, in the prettiest way imaginable! Love in a cottage, you know, and a dozen hopeful children prattling at his knee.'

'You are a most unaccountable girl!' he exclaimed, looking at her in a good deal of amusement. 'Did this picture appal him?'

'Of course it did, but he is very chivalrous, and has now made up his mind to an early marriage. For anything I know he may be planning a flight to the Border.'

'What!' ejaculated his lordship.

'Oh, have no fear! Cecilia is by far too well brought-up to consent to such a scandalous thing! Let us have just one gallop! I know it is wrong, but there seem to be only nursemaids in the Park this morning. Good God, I am quite at fault! There is Lord Bromford, on that fat cob of his! I must tell you that he left the ball at midnight, because late hours are injurious to his health. Now we *must* gallop, or he will join us, and tell us about Jamaica!'

They flew down the track, Salamanca always just ahead of Charlbury's rat-tailed gray, and so rousing Lord Charlbury to enthusiasm. 'By God, that's a capital horse!' he said. 'I do not know how you contrive to hold him, ma'am! Surely he is too strong for you?'

'I daresay, but he has charming manners, you see. Now we will proceed more soberly! Should you object very much to telling me whether you still desire to marry my cousin? You may snub me, if you choose!'

He replied rather ruefully: 'Will you think me contemptible if I tell you, yes?'

'Not at all. You would be foolish to refine too much upon what happened last night. Only consider! Instead of first fixing your interest with Cecilia, you applied to my uncle for leave to address her —'

'It is usual to do so!' he pointed out.

'It may be punctilious, but it is the greatest folly imaginable, particularly if you mean to contract mumps before you have even had time to offer for her!'

'It would, I collect, be useless to assure you that I did *not* mean to contract mumps! I had reason to believe that my suit would not be distasteful to her.'

'I expect she was very well-disposed towards you,' agreed Sophy cordially. 'But she had not then seen Augustus Fawnhope. At least, she had, but it seems that he was covered in spots at that time, so no one could expect her to fall in love with him.'

'I don't find the reflection precisely comforting, Miss Stanton-Lacy.'

'Call me Sophy! Everyone does, and we are going to become excessively friendly.'

'Are — are we?' he said. 'I mean, I am delighted to hear you say so, of course!'

She laughed. 'Oh pray don't be alarmed! If you still wish to marry Cecilia — and I must tell you that although I thought otherwise before I had met you, I have now made up my mind to it that you would suit capitally — I will show you just how you must go on.'

He could not help smiling. 'I am much obliged to you! But if she loves young Fawnhope —'

'You must, if you please, consider for a moment!' said Sophy earnestly. 'Only think how it was! No sooner had you declared yourself to my uncle than you contracted a ridiculous complaint. *She* was informed that she was to become your wife — quite gothic, and most ill-judged! – and along came Augustus Fawnhope, looking, you will own, like a prince out of a fairy-tale, and what must he do but turn his back on all the poor females who were setting their caps at him, and fall in love with Cecilia's beauty! My dear sir, he wrote poems in her praise! He calls her a nymph, and says that her eyes put the stars to shame, and such stuff as that!'

'Good God!' said his lordship.

'Exactly so! You cannot wonder that she was swept off her feet. I daresay you had never so much as thought of calling her a nymph!'

'Miss Stanton – Sophy! Even to win Cecilia, I cannot write poetry, and if I could I'll be dashed if I would write such – Well, in any event I have no turn in that direction!'

'Oh, no, you must not attempt to outshine Augustus in *that* line!' said Sophy. 'Your strength lies in being precisely the kind of man who can procure one a chair when it has come on to rain.'

'I beg your pardon?'

'Can you not?' she asked, turning her head to look at him with raised brows.

'I expect I could, but –'

'Believe me, it is by far more important than being able to turn a verse!' she told him. 'Augustus is quite unable to do so. I know, because he failed miserably at the Chelsea Gardens. I thought he would, which is why I made him escort Cecilia and me there on a day when you could see it would come on to pour. Our muslins were soaked, and I daresay we should have died of an inflammation of the lung had not one of my old friends procured a hackney to convey us home. Poor Cecy! she became almost cross with Augustus!'

He burst out laughing. 'Major Quinton spoke nothing but the truth about you!' he declared. 'I am already terrified of you!'

She smiled, but said: 'Well, you need not be, for I mean to help you.'

'That is what terrifies me.'

'Nonsense! You are trying to quiz me. We have established that you can procure chairs in a rainstorm; I am also of the opinion that when you invite a party to supper at the Piazza the waiters do not fob you off with a table in a draught.'

'No,' he agreed, regarding her with a fascinated eye.

'Augustus, of course, is not in a position to invite us to supper at the Piazza, because my aunt would certainly not permit us to accept, but he did once entertain us to tea here, in the Park, and I could not but see that he is just the kind of man whom the waiters serve last. I feel sure I can rely upon you to see to it that everything goes without the least hitch when you invite us to the theatre, and to supper afterwards. You will be obliged, of course, to invite my aunt as well, but –'

'For heaven's sake!' he interrupted. 'You cannot suppose that in the situation in which we now stand Cecilia would consent to make one of a party of my making!'

'Certainly I do,' she replied coolly. 'What is more, you will invite Augustus.'

'No, that I will not!' he declared.

'Then you will be a great gaby. You must understand that Cecilia has been driven into announcing that she means to marry Augustus! You were not there to engage her affections; Augustus was sighing verses to her left eyebrow; and to clinch the matter my cousin Charles behaved in the most tyrannical fashion, forbidding her to think of Augustus, and fairly ordering her to marry you! I assure you, it would have been wonderful indeed if she had not made up her mind to do not such thing!'

He rode in silence beside her for some moments, frowning between his horse's ears. 'I see,' he said at last. 'At least – Well, at all events, you don't advise me to despair!'

'I don't suppose,' said Sophy honestly, 'that I should ever advise anyone to despair, for I can't bear such poor-spirited conduct!'

'What *do* you advise me to do?' he asked. 'I seem to be wholly in your hands!'

'Withdraw your suit!' said Sophy.

He looked sharply at her. 'No! I mean to make a push –'

'You will call in Berkeley Square this afternoon,' said Sophy, with an utmost patience, 'and you will request the favour of a few minutes alone with Cecilia. When you see her –'

'I shall not see her. She will deny herself!' he said bitterly.

'She will see you, because I shall tell her she owes it to you to do so. I wish you will not keep on interrupting me!' He begged pardon meekly, and she continued: 'When you see her, you will assure her that you have no desire to distress her, that you will never mention the matter again to her. You will be excessively noble, and she will feel that you sympathize with her, and if you can convey to her also the sense of your heart being broken, however well you contrive to conceal it, so much the better!'

'I am strongly of the opinion that Major Quinton grossly understated the case!' said his lordship, with feeling.

'Very likely. Gentlemen can never see when a little duplicity is needed. You, I have no doubt, if I left you to your own devices, would storm and rant at Cecilia, so that all would end in a quarrel, and you would find it quite impossible to visit the house, even! But if she knows that you will not enact her tragedies she will be perfectly pleased to see you as often as you care to come to Berkeley Square.'

'How can I visit in Berkeley Square when she is betrothed to another man? If you imagine that I'll play the love-lorn suitor in the hope of arousing pity in Cecilia's breast you were never more at fault! As well be a lap-dog!'

'Much better,' said Sophy. 'You will visit in Berkeley Square to see me. You cannot too suddenly seem to transfer your interest in my direction, of course, but it would be an excellent start if you were to find an opportunity of telling Cecilia today how droll and entertaining you think me.'

'Do you know,' he said seriously, 'you are the most startling female it has ever been my fortune to meet? You will observe that I do not say good or ill fortune, for I haven't the smallest notion which it will prove to be!'

She laughed. 'But will you do what I tell you?'

'Yes,' he replied. 'To the best of my poor ability. But I wish I knew the extent of the dark scheme you are revolving in your head.'

She turned her head to look at him, her expressive eyes questioning, and at the same time acknowledging a hit. 'But I have told you!'

'I have a notion there is more to it than what you have told me.'

She looked mischievous, but would only shake her head. They had reached the Stanhope Gate again, and she reined in, holding out her hand. 'I must go now. Pray don't be afraid of me! I never do people any harm – indeed I don't! Goodbye! At about four o'clock, mind!'

She reached Berkeley Square to find the house in a state of considerable uneasiness, Lord Ombersley, informed by his wife of Cecilia's overnight announcement, having flown into a passion of exasperation at the folly, ingratitude, and selfishness of daughters; and Hubert and Theodore between them having chosen this singularly inappropriate moment to allow Jacko to escape from the schoolroom. Sophy was met on her arrival by various distracted persons, who lost no time in pouring their woes or grievances into her ears. Cecilia, shaken by the interview with her father, wanted to carry her off instantly to the seclusion of her bedchamber; Miss Adderbury wished to explain that she had repeatedly warned Mr Hubert not to excite the monkey; Theodore desired to impress upon everyone that it had all been Hubert's fault; Hubert demanded that she should help him to recover the monkey before its escape came to Charles's ears; and Dassett, having observed with disfavour the enthusiasm with which both footmen entered into the chase, delivered himself of an icily civil monologue, the gist of which seemed to be that Wild Animals roaming at large in a Nobleman's Residence were not what he had been accustomed to, or what he could bring himself to tolerate. As this speech contained a dark threat to Inform His Lordship instantly, it appeared to Sophy that her most pressing duty was to soothe Dassett's feelings, half a dozen persons having informed her that Lord Ombersley was in a dreadful temper. So she told Cecilia that she would come to her room presently, and considerably mollified the butler by rejecting the services of the footmen. Cecilia, who besides her interview with Lord Ombersley, had endured a few moments with her elder brother, and half an hour with Lady Ombersley, was in no mood for monkeys, and said, rather hysterically, that she supposed she might have expected that Jacko would be thought of more importance than herself. Selina, who was thoroughly enjoying the atmosphere of drama and impending doom that hung over the house, hissed: 'H'sh! Charles is in the library!' Cecilia retorted that she did not care where he was, and rushed upstairs to her bedroom.

'What a commotion!' exclaimed Sophy, amused.

Her voice, penetrating the shut library door, reached the sharp ears of Tina, who, during her absence from the house, had attached herself to Mr Rivenhall. She at once demanded to be allowed to rejoin her mistress, and her insistence brought Mr Rivenhall upon the scene, for he was obliged to open the door for her. Perceiving that a large part of his family appeared to be assembled in the hall, he somewhat coldly enquired the reason. Before anyone could answer him, Amabel, in the basement, gave a warning shriek, Jacko suddenly erupted into the hall from the nether regions, gibbered at the sight of Tina, and swarmed up the window curtains to a place of safety well out of anyone's reach. Amabel then came storming up the basement-stairs, closely followed by the housekeeper, who at once lodged an impassioned protest with Mr Rivenhall. The dratted monkey, she said, had wantonly destroyed two of the best dish-clothes, and had scattered a bowl of raisins all over the kitchen-floor.

'If that damned monkey cannot be controlled,' said Mr Rivenhall, making no apology for the violence of his language, 'it must be got rid of!'

Theodore, Gertrude, and Amabel at once burst into a spirited accusation against Hubert, who, they averred, had wantonly teased Jacko. Hubert, conscious of a rent coat-pocket, retired into the background, and Mr Rivenhall, eyeing his juniors with revulsion, walked forward to the window, and held up his hand, saying calmly: 'Come along!'

Jacko's reply to this, though voluble, was incomprehensible. His general attitude, however, was contumacious, so that everyone was surprised when, upon Mr Rivenhall's repeating his command, he began to descend the curtain. Tina, in whole-hearted agreement with Dassett and the housekeeper on the undesirability of monkeys in noblemen's residences, caused a slight set-back by barking, but Sophy snatched her up and muffled her before Jacko had had time to retreat again to the top of the window. Mr Rivenhall, acidly requesting his audience to refrain from making any noise or sudden move-ment, again commanded Jacko to come down. Jacko, satisfied that Tina was under strong guard, reluctantly descended, allowed himself to be seized, and clasped both skinny arms round Mr Rivenhall's neck. Unimpressed by this mark of affection, Mr Rivenhall detached him, handed him over to Gertrude, and warned her not to permit him to escape again. The schoolroom party then withdrew circumspectly, scarcely able to believe that their pet was not to be wrested from them; and Sophy, smiling warmly upon Mr Rivenhall, said: 'Thank you! There is some magic in you which makes all animals trust you, I think. When I am most vexed with you I cannot but remember it!'

'The only magic, cousin, lay in not alarming an already frightened animal,' he replied dampingly, and went back into the library, and shut the door.

'Phew!' uttered Hubert, emerging from the embrasure at the head of the basement-stairs. 'Sophy, only look what that dashed brute has done to my new coat!'

'Give it to me! I'll mend it for you – and for heaven's sake, you wretched creature, don't kick up any more larks today!' said Sophy.

He grinned at her, stripped off the coat, and handed it to her.

'What *did* happen last night?' he asked. 'Don't know when I've seen my father in such a taking! Is Cecilia going to marry Fawnhope?'

'Ask her!' Sophy advised him. 'I will have your coat ready for you in twenty minutes: come to my room then, and you shall have it!'

She ran up the stairs and, without waiting to change her riding-habit, sat down by the window to repair the rent caused by Jacko's fury. She was a deft needlewoman, and had mended half the tear with her tiny stitches when Cecilia came to her room. Cecilia was strongly of the opinion that Hubert might have found someone else to do his mending, and begged her to put it aside. This, however, Sophy refused to do, merely saying: 'I can listen to you while I work, you know. What a goose you were last night, Cecy!'

This brought Cecilia's chin up. She enunciated with great clarity; 'I am betrothed to Augustus, and if I may not marry him I will marry no one!'

'I daresay, but to make such an announcement in the middle of a ball!'

'Sophy, I thought *you* would feel for me!'

It occurred to Sophy suddenly that the fewer people to sympathize with Cecilia the better it would be, so she kept her head bent over her work, and said lightly: 'Well, and so I do, but I still think it was a ridiculous moment to choose for making such an announcement!'

Cecilia began to tell her again what provocation had been supplied by Charles; she agreed, but absently, and appeared to be more exercised with the set of Hubert's coat than with Cecilia's wrongs. She shook it out, smoothed the darn she had made, and, when Hubert came knocking at the door, cut Cecilia short to jump up and restore the garment to him. The end of all this was that when, at four o'clock, Lord Charlbury sent up his card, with a request to see Miss Rivenhall, Cecilia, almost forced to accede to his wishes, found in him her only sympathizer. One glance at her pale face, and tragic mouth, banished from his mind all notion of duplicity. He stepped quickly forward, took the hand so shrinkingly held out to him, and said in a deeply concerned voice. 'Do not look so unhappy! Indeed, I have not come to distress you!'

Her eyes filled with tears; her hand slightly returned the pressure of his before it was withdrawn; and she managed to say something in a suffocated voice, about his kindness, and her own regret. He obliged her to be seated, himself took a chair near to hers, and said: 'My sentiments have undergone no change: indeed, I believe it to be impossible that they should! But I have been told – I have understood – that yours were never engaged. Believe me, if you cannot return my regard, I honour you for having the courage to say so! That you should be constrained to accept my suit, when your heart is given to another, is a thought wholly repugnant to me! Forgive me! I think you have had to bear a great deal on *this* head which I never intended, or indeed, dreamed – But I have said enough! Only let me assure you that I will do all that lies in my power to put an end to such intolerable promptings!'

'You are all consideration – all goodness!' Cecilia uttered. 'I am so sorry that – that expectations which it is not in my power to fulfil should have been raised! If my gratitude for a sensibility which permits you to feel for me in my present predicament, for a chivalry which –' Her voice became wholly suspended by tears; she could only turn away her face, and make a gesture imploring his understanding.

He took her hand, and kissed it. 'Say no more! I always thought the prize beyond my reach. Though you deny me that nearer relationship which I so ardently desire, we may continue friends? If there is any way in which I can serve you, will you tell me of it? That would be a happiness indeed!'

'Oh, do not say so! You are too good!'

The door opened. Mr Rivenhall came into the room, checked an instant on the threshold, when he saw Charlbury, and looked as though he would have retired again. Charlbury rose, however, and said: 'I am glad you are at home, Charles, for I believe I can settle this business better with you than with anyone. Your sister and I have agreed that we shall not suit.'

'I see,' said Mr Rivenhall, dryly. 'There seems to be nothing I can profitably say, except that I am sorry. I conclude that you wish me to inform my father that there is to be no engagement?'

'Lord Charlbury has been everything that is most kind – most magnanimous!' whispered Cecilia.

'That I can believe,' responded Mr Rivenhall.

'Nonsense!' Charlbury said, taking her hand. 'I shall leave you now, but I hope I may still visit this house, on terms of friendship. Your friendship I must always value, you know. Perhaps I may not dance at your wedding, but I shall wish you very happy, upon my honour!'

He pressed her hand, released it, and went out of the room, followed by Mr Rivenhall, who escorted him downstairs to the hall, saying: 'This is a damnable business, Everard. She is out of her senses! But as for marrying that puppy – no, by God!'

'Your cousin tells me it is all my fault for having wilfully contracted mumps!' Charlbury said ruefully.

'Sophy!' Mr Rivenhall ejaculated, in anything but loving accents. 'I do not think we have a day's peace since that girl entered the house!'

'I shouldn't think you would,' said his lordship, reflectively. 'She is the oddest female I ever met, but I own I like her! Do you not?'

'No, I do not!' said Mr Rivenhall.

He saw Charlbury off the premises, and turned back into the house just as Hubert came down the stairs, in long bounds. 'Hallo, where are you off to in such haste?' he enquired.

'Oh, nowhere!' Hubert answered. 'Just out!'

'When do you go up to Oxford again?'

'Next week. Why?'

'Do you care to go with me to Thorpe Grange tomorrow? I must go down, and shall stay a night, I daresay.'

Hubert shook his head. 'No, I can't. I'm off to stay with Harpenden for a couple of nights, you know.'

'I didn't. Newmarket?'

Hubert flushed. 'Dash it, why should I not go to Newmarket, if I choose?'

'There is no reason why you should not, but I could wish that you would choose your company more wisely. Are you set on it? We could ride over from Thorpe, if you liked.'

'Very good of you, Charles, but I'm promised to Harpenden, and can't fail now!' Hubert said gruffly.

'Very well. Don't draw the bustle too much!'

Hubert hunched his shoulder. 'I knew you would say that!'

'I'll say something else, and you may believe it! I can't and I won't be saddled with your racing debts, so don't bet beyond your means!'

He waited for no answer, but went upstairs again to the drawing-room, where he found his sister still seated where he had left her, weeping softly into a shred of a handkerchief. He tossed his own into her lap. 'If you must be a watering-pot, take mine!' he recommended. 'Are you satisfied? You should be! It is not every girl who can boast of having rejected a man like Charlbury!'

'I do not boast of it!' she retorted, firing up. 'But I care nothing for wealth and position! Where my affections are not engaged –'

'You might care for worth of character, however! You could search England without finding a better fellow, Cecilia. Don't flatter yourself you have found one in your poet! I wish you may not live to regret this day's work.'

'I am aware that Lord Charlbury has every amiable quality,' she said, in a subdued voice, and mopping her wet cheeks with his handkerchief. 'Indeed, I believe him to be the finest gentleman of my acquaintance, and if I am crying it is from sorrow at having been obliged to wound him!'

He walked over to the window, and stood looking out into the square. 'It is useless now to remonstrate with you. After your announcement last night it is not very likely that Charlbury would desire to marry you. What do you mean to do? I may tell you now that my father will not consent to your marriage with Fawnhope.'

'Because you will not let him consent! Can you not be content, Charles, with making a marriage of convenience yourself, without wishing me to do the same?' she cried hotly.

He stiffened. 'It is not difficult to perceive my cousin's influence at work!' he said. 'Before her arrival in London, you would not have spoken so to me! My regard for Eugenia –'

'If you *loved*, Charles, you would not talk of your *regard* for Eugenia!'

It was at this inappropriate moment that Dassett ushered Miss Wraxton into the room. Cecilia whisked her brother's handkerchief out of sight, a tide of crimson flooding her cheeks; Mr Rivenhall turned away from the window, and said with a palpable effort: 'Eugenia! We did not expect this pleasure! How do you do?'

She gave him her hand, but turned her gaze upon Cecilia saying: 'Tell me it is not so! I was never more shocked in my life than when Alfred told me what had occurred last night!'

Almost insensibly the brother and sister drew closer together. 'Alfred!' repeated Mr Rivenhall.

'He told me, when he drove home after the ball, that he could not choose but overhear what Cecilia had said to you, Charles. And Lord Charlbury! I could not believe it to have been possible!'

Loyalty, as much as the ties of affection, kept Mr Rivenhall ranged on the side of his sister, for he looked to be very much annoyed, which indeed he was, for he thought it inexcusable of Cecilia to have placed him in such a situation. He said repressively: 'If you mean that Cecilia and Lord Charlbury have made up their minds to it they would not suit, you are quite correct. I do not know what business it is of Alfred's, or why he must run to you with what he – overhears!'

'My dear Charles, he knows that what concerns your family must be also my concern!'

'I am much obliged to you, but I have no wish to discuss the matter.'

'Excuse me! I must go to my mother!' Cecilia said.

She escaped from the room; Miss Wraxton looked significantly at Mr Rivenhall, and said: 'I do not wonder you are vexed. It has been a sadly mismanaged business, and I fancy we have not far to seek for the influence that prompted dear Cecilia to behave in a way so unlike herself!'

'I have not the smallest conjecture as to you meaning.'

His tone, which was forbidding, warned her that she would be wise to turn the subject, but her dislike of Sophy had become such an obsession with her that she was impelled to continue.

'You must have noticed, dear Charles, that our sweet sister has fallen quite under the sway of her cousin. I cannot think it will lead to anything but disaster. Miss Stanton-Lacy doubtless has many excellent qualities, but I have always thought that you were right in saying she had too little delicacy of mind.'

Mr Rivenhall, who had decided that Sophy was to blame for his sister's conduct, said without an instant's hesitation: 'You are mistaken: I never made any such remark!'

'Did you not? Something of that nature I think you once said to me, but it hardly signifies! It is a thousand pities that dear Lady Ombersley was forced to receive her as a guest at this precise time. Every time I enter the house I am conscious of a change in it! Even the children –'

'It is certainly by far more lively,' he interrupted.

She gave vent to rather an artificial laugh. 'It is certainly less *peaceful*!' She began to smooth the wrinkles from her gloves. 'Do you know, Charles, I have always so much admired the *tone* of this house? Your doing, I know well! I cannot but feel a little melancholy when I see that ordered calm – a certain dignity, I should say – shattered by wild spirits. Poor little Amabel, I thought the other day, is growing quite out of hand! Of course, Miss Stanton-Lacy encourages her unthinkingly. One must remember that she herself has had a strangely irregular upbringing!'

'My cousin,' said Mr Rivenhall, with finality, 'has been extremely kind to the children, and is a great favourite with my mother. I must add that it is a pleasure to see my mother's spirits so much improved by Sophy's presence. Have you any errands in this part of the town? May I escort you? I must be in Bond Street in twenty minutes' time.'

In face of so comprehensive a snub as this it was impossible for Miss Wraxton to say more. Her colour rose, and her lips tightened, but she managed to suppress an acid retort, and to say with the appearance at least of complaisance: 'Thank you, I have to call at the library for Mama. I came in the barouche, and shall be glad to take you up as far as your destination.'

Since this was Jackson's Boxing Saloon, she could hardly have been expected to have been pleased, for she did not care for sport of any kind, and considered boxing a peculiarly low form of it. But apart from quizzing Mr Rivenhall archly for his obvious preference for a horrid prizefighter's society than for her own she made no comment.

Cecilia, meanwhile, had fled, not to Lady Ombersley, but to her cousin, whom she discovered seated before her dressing-table, scanning a slip of paper. Jane Storridge was putting away her habit, but when Cecilia came into the room she seemed to feel that she was not wanted, for she gave an audible sniff, picked up Sophy's riding-boots, and went away with them under her arm.

'What do you suppose this can be, Cecy?' asked Sophy, still studying with knit brows the paper in her hand. 'Jane says she found it by the window, and thought it must be mine. What a funny name! *Goldhanger, Bear Alley, Fleet Lane.* I do not know the writing, and cannot conceive how – Oh, how stupid! It must have fallen out of the pocket of Hubert's coat!'

'Sophy!' said Cecilia, 'I have had the most dreadful interview with Charlbury!'

Sophy laid the paper down. 'Good gracious, how is this!'

'I find my spirits utterly overborne!' declared Cecilia, sinking into a chair. 'No one – *no one!* – could have behaved with more exquisite sensibility! I wish you had not persuaded me to see him! Nothing could have been more painful!'

'Oh, do not give him a thought!' said Sophy bracingly. 'Let us rather think what is to be done about fixing Augustus in some genteel occupation!'

'How can you be so heartless?' demanded Cecilia. 'When he was so kind, and I could not but see how much I had grieved him!'

'I daresay he will recover speedily enough,' Sophy replied, in a careless way. 'Ten to one he will fall in love with another female before the month is out!'

Cecilia did not look as though she found this prophecy consoling, but after a moment she said: 'I am sure I wish he may, for to be ruining a man's life is no very pleasant thing, I can tell you!'

'Do you think it will rain? Dare I wear my new straw hat? I have a mind to flirt with Charlbury myself: I liked him.'

'I wish you may succeed,' said Cecilia, a trifle stiffly. 'I do not think him a man at all given to flirting, however. The tone of his mind is too nice for such a pastime as that!'

Sophy laughed. 'We'll see! Do tell me which hat I should wear! The straw is so ravishing, but if it were to come on to mizzle —'

'I don't care which hat you wear!' snapped Cecilia.

Eleven

The rest of the day passed uneventfully, Sophy driving Cecilia in Hyde Park in her phaeton, setting her down to enjoy a stroll with Mr Fawnhope, encountered by previous arrangement by the Riding House, and taking up in her stead Sir Vincent Talgarth, who only deserted her when he perceived the Marquesa de Villacañas's barouche drawn up beside the rails that separated Rotten Row from the carriageway. The Marquesa, who was attracting no little attention by the number and height of the curled ostrich plumes in her hat, welcomed him with her lazy smile, and told Sophy that she found the shops in London wholly inferior to those in Paris. Nothing she had seen in Bond Street that day had tempted her to undo her purse-strings. But Sir Vincent knew of a *modiste* in Bruton Street who might be trusted to recognize at a glance the style and quality of such a customer, and he offered to escort the Marquesa to her establishment.

Sophy knit her brows a little over this, but before she had time to think much on the subject her attention was claimed by Lord Bromford. Civility obliged her to invite him to take a turn about the Park in her phaeton. He got up beside her, and after telling her how much enjoyment he had derived from the Ombersley ball, made her a formal offer of marriage. Sophy declined this, without hesitation and without embarrassment. Lord Bromford, disconcerted only for a minute, said that his ardour had made him too precipitate, but that he did not despair of a happy issue. 'When your parent returns to these shores,' he pronounced, 'I shall formally apply to him for leave to address you. You are very right to insist upon so much propriety, and I must beg your pardon for having contravened the laws of etiquette. Only the strong passion under which I labour – and I must tell you that not the most forceful representations of my mother, a Being to whom I, in filial duty, tender the most profound respect, have had the power to alter my decision – only, as I have said, this passion could have induced me to forget –'

'I think,' said Sophy, 'that you should take your seat in the House of Lords. Have you done so?'

'It is strange,' responded his lordship, swelling slightly, 'that you should ask me that question, for I am upon the point of doing so. I shall be presented by a sponsor no less distinguished for his high lineage than for his forensic attainments, and I trust –'

'I have no doubt at all that you are destined to become a great man,' said Sophy. 'No matter how lengthy, or how involved your periods, you *never* lose yourself in them! How charming the foliage is on those beech trees! Do you know any tree to rival the beech? I am sure I do not!'

'Certainly a graceful tree,' conceded Lord Bromford, patronizing the beech. 'Hardly, however, to rank in majesty with the mahogany, which grows in the West Indies; or in usefulness with the lancewood. I wonder, Miss Stanton-Lacy, how may persons are aware that the lancewood supplies the shafts for their carriages?'

'In the southern provinces of Spain,' countered Sophy, 'the cork oak grows in great profusion.'

'Another interesting tree to be found in Jamaica,' said his lordship, 'is the ballata. We have also the rosewood, the ebony, the lignum vitae –'

'The northern parts of Spain,' said Sophy defiantly, 'are more remarkable for the many varieties of shrubs which grow there, including what we call the jarales, and the ladanum bush, and – and – Oh, there is Lord Francis! I shall have to put you down, Lord Bromford!'

He was reluctant, but since Lord Francis was waving to Sophy, and showed every desire to speak to her, he was unable to demur. When the phaeton drew up, he climbed ponderously down from it, and Lord Francis leaped equally nimbly up into it, saying: 'Sophy, that was a capital ball last night! What a lovely creature your cousin is, to be sure!'

Sophy set her horses in motion again. 'Francis, *does* the cork oak grow in the southern provinces in Spain?'

'Lord, Sophy, how should I know? You were in Cadiz! Can't you recall? Who cares for cork oaks, in any event?'

'I hope,' said Sophy warmly, 'that when you have done with being the worst flirt in Europe, Francis, you will win a *very* beautiful wife, for you deserve one! Do you know anything about the ballata?'

'Never heard of it in my life! What is it? A new dance?'

'No, it's a tree, and it grows in Jamaica. I hope she will be as good-natured as she is beautiful.'

'Trust me for that! But, y'know, Sophy, it ain't like you to be boring on and on about trees! What's come over you?'

'Lord Bromford,' sighed Sophy.

'What, that prosy fellow you had up beside you just now? He told Sally Jersey last night how valuable guinea-grass was for horses and cattle: heard him! Never saw poor Silence so silenced!'

'I wish she had given him one of her set-downs. I must put you down when we reach the Riding House, for Cecilia will be waiting for me.'

Cecilia and her swain were found at the appointed spot. Lord Francis sprang down from the phaeton, and it was he who handed Cecilia up into it, Mr Fawnhope having become rapt in contemplation of a clump of daffodils, which caused him to throw out a hand, murmuring: '"*Daffodils that come before the swallow dares!*"'

Cecilia's spirits did not appear to have derived much benefit from her meeting with her lover. His plans for their future maintenance seemed to be a trifle vague, but he had an epic poem in his head, which might win him fame in a night, he thought. While this was in preparation, he would not object, he said, to accepting a post as a librarian. But as Cecilia was unable to imagine that her father or her brother would feel any marked degree of satisfaction in giving her in marriage to a librarian, this very handsome concession on Mr Fawnhope's part merely added to her despondency. She had gone so far as to suggest to him that he should embrace the profession of Politics, but he had only said: 'How sordid!' which did not augur well for this excellent scheme. When he had added that since the death of Mr Fox, ten years earlier, there was no leader a man of sensibility could attach himself to, this remark had only served to show her how very improbable it was that his politics would find more favour with her family than his poetic aspirations.

Sophy, gathering the gist of all this from Cecilia's somewhat elliptical remarks, took up a buoyant attitude, saying: 'Oh, well! We must find a great man who is willing to become his patron!' which gave Cecilia a poor notion of her understanding.

Sophy was able to restore to Hubert the scrap of paper which had fallen from his pocket before going down to dinner that evening. Until this moment she had not thought much about it, but his manner of receiving it from her was so strange that it set up in her head various speculations which he was far from desiring. He almost snatched it from her hand, exclaiming: 'Where did you find this?' and when she explained, in the most temperate manner, that she thought it must have fallen out of the pocket of the coat she had mended for him, he said: 'Yes, it is mine, but I did not know I had put it there! I cannot tell you what it signifies, but pray do not mention it to anyone!'

She could only assure him that she had no intention of doing so, but he appeared to be so much discomposed that some inevitable reflections were set up in her brain. These did not come to fruition until she saw him upon his return from his visit to his friend Mr Harpenden, when his demeanour was so much that of a man who had received some stunning blow that she seized the earliest opportunity that offered of asking him if anything were amiss. Mr Rivenhall, who had left London twenty-four hours earlier for Thorpe Grange, the estate in Leicestershire which he had inherited from his great-uncle, had not yet returned to London; but Hubert made it plain to his cousin that even had his elder brother been in London, not the direst necessity would have induced him to apply to him.

'He has not minced matters! He told me in round terms that he would not – Oh well! no matter for that!'

'I daresay,' said Sophy, in her calm way, 'that Charles might very likely say more than he meant. I wish you will tell me what has gone awry, Hubert! My conjecture is that you have lost perhaps a large sum at Newmarket?'

'If that were all!' he exclaimed unguardedly.

'Well, if it is not all, I wish you will tell the full sum of it, Hubert!' she said, with one of her friendly smiles. 'I assure you, you are quite safe in my hands, for Sir Horace brought me up to think there was nothing more odious than to be the kind of person who blabbed secrets abroad. But I know that you are in trouble of some sort, and I do think I ought, if you will tell me nothing, to drop a hint in your brother's ear, for ten to one you will make bad much worse if you go on in this way, with no one to advise you!'

He turned pale. 'Sophy, you would not – !'

Her eyes twinkled. 'No, of course I would not!' she admitted. 'You are so *very* loth to tell me anything that I am quite forced to ask you. Is it anything to do with a woman? What Sir Horace would call a bit of muslin, perhaps?'

'*Sophy!* Upon my word – ! No! Nothing of that sort!'

'Money, then?'

He did not answer, and after a moment she patted the sofa on which she sat invitingly, and said: 'Do, pray, come and sit down! I don't suppose it is by half as bad as you fear.'

He gave a short laugh, but after a little more persuasion sat down beside her, and sank his head in between his clenched fists. 'I shall come about. If the worst comes to the worst, a man may always enlist!'

'True,' she agreed. 'But I know something of the Army, and I do not think that life in the ranks would suit you at all. Besides, it would very much distress my aunt, you know!'

It was not to be supposed that a young gentleman of Hubert's order would readily confide his difficulties into the ears of a female, and that female not quite as old as he was himself; but after a good deal of coaxing Sophy managed to extract his story from him. It was not a very coherent tale, and she was obliged to prompt him several times during its recital, but in the end she gathered that he had fallen into the clutches of a moneylender. There had been some trouble over debts contracted during the previous year at Oxford, the full sum of which he had not dared to disclose to his brother, hoping, in the immemorial way of youth, to be able to discharge them himself. He had knowing friends who knew all the gaming-houses in London; quite a brief run of luck at French hazard, or roulette, would have set all to rights; but when, during the Christmas vacation, he had sought this method of recuperating his fortunes only the most unprecedented bad luck had attended his efforts. He still shuddered whenever he recalled those ruinous, and, indeed, terrifying evenings, a circumstance which led his sapient cousin to infer that gaming held little attraction for him. Faced with large debts of honour, already in hot water with his formidable brother for far smaller debts, what could he do but jump into the river, or go to the Jews? And even so, he assured Sophy, he would never have gone near a curst money-lender had he not felt certain of being able to pay the shark off within six months.

'You mean, when you come of age next month?' Sophy asked.

'Well, no,' he admitted, colouring. 'Though I fancy that was what old Goldhanger thought, when he agreed to lend me the money. I never told him so, mind! All I said was that I was certain of coming into possession of a large sum and I *was*, Sophy! I did not think it could possibly fail! Bob Gilmorton – he is a particular friend of mine! – knows the owner well, and he swore to me the horse could not lose!'

Sophy, who had an excellent memory, instantly recognized

the name of Goldhanger as being the one she had read on the scrap of paper discovered in her bedroom, but she made no comment on this, merely enquiring whether the perfidious horse had lost his race.

'Unplaced!' said Hubert, with a groan.

She nodded wisely. 'Sir Horace says that if ever you trust to a horse to set your fortune to rights he always *is* unplaced,' she observed. 'He says also that if you game when your pockets are to let you will lose. It is only when you are very *well-breeched* that you may expect to win. Sir Horace is *always* right!'

Declining to argue this point, Hubert spoke for several embittered minutes on the running of his horse, casting such grave aspersions upon the owner, the trainer, and the jockey as must have rendered him liable to prosecution for slander had they been uttered to anyone less discreet than his cousin. She let him run on, listening sympathetically, and only when he had talked himself to a standstill did she bring him back to what she thought a far more important point.

'Hubert, you are not of age,' she said. 'And I know that it is quite illegal to lend money to minors, because when young Mr – well, never mind the name, but we knew him well! – when a young man of my acquaintance got into just such a fix, he came to Sir Horace for advice, and that is what Sir Horace said. I believe there are excessively heavy penalties for doing such a thing.'

'Well, I know that,' Hubert answered. 'Most of 'em won't do it, but – well, the thing is that a friend of mine knew of this fellow, Goldhanger, and gave me his direction, and – and told me what I should say, and the sort of interest I should have to pay – not that that seemed to matter *then*, because I thought –'

'Is it very heavy?' Sophy interrupted.

He nodded. 'Yes, because, though I lied about my age he knew, of course, that I'm not yet twenty-one, and – and he had me pretty well at his mercy. And I thought I should have been able to have paid it all off after that race.'

'How much did you borrow, Hubert?'

'Five hundred,' he muttered.

'Good gracious, did you lose all that at cards?' she exclaimed.

'No, but I wanted a hundred to lay on that curst screw, you see,' he explained. 'It was of no use only to borrow enough to pay my debts, because how was I to pay back Goldhanger?'

Sophy could not help laughing at this ingenious method of finance, but as Hubert looked rather hurt she begged pardon, and said: 'It is evident to me that your Mr Goldhanger is an infamous rascal!'

'Yes,' Hubert said, looking a little haggard. 'He's an old devil, and I was a fool ever to go near him. I didn't know as much about him then as I do now, of course, but still, as soon as I saw him – But it's too late to be repining over that!'

'Yes, much too late, besides there is no need to be in despair! I am certain that you have nothing to fear, because he must know he cannot recover his money from a minor, and would never dare to sue you for it.'

'Dash it, Sophy, I must pay the fellow back what I owe him! Besides, there's worse. He insisted on my giving him a pledge, and – and I did!'

He sounded so guilty that several hair-raising possibilities flashed through Sophy's mind. 'Hubert, you did not pledge a family heirloom, or – or something of that nature, did you?'

'Good God, no! I'm not as bad as *that!*' he cried indignantly. 'It was mine, and I shouldn't call it an heirloom, precisely, though if ever it was discovered that I had lost it I daresay there would be the deuce of a kick-up, and I should be abused as though I were a pickpocket! Grandfather Stanton-Lacy left it to me: stupid sort of thing, *I* think, because men don't wear 'em nowadays. He did, of course, and my mother says the sight of it brings him back to her as nothing else could, because she never saw him without it on his hand – so you may judge what would happen if she knew I had pledged it! It's a ring, you know: a great, square emerald, with diamonds all round it. Fancy wearing such a thing as that! Why, one would look like Romeo Coates, or some wealthy cit trying to lionize! Mama always kept it, and I never knew it had been left to me until I went to a masquerade last year, and she gave it to me to wear, and told me it was mine. And when Goldhanger demanded I should give him a pledge, I – I couldn't think of anything else, and – well, I knew where Mama kept it, and I took it! And don't tell me I stole it from her, because it was no such thing, and she only kept it because I had no use for it!'

'No, no, of course I know you would not steal anything!' Sophy said hastily.

He studied his knuckles with rapt interest. 'No. Mind, I don't say I ought to have taken it for my mother's case, but – it *was* my own!'

'Well, naturally you ought not!' said Sophy. 'I daresay she would be vexed with you, so we must recover it at once.'

'I wish I might, but there's no chance of that now! I don't know what to do! When that horse failed, I was ready to blow my brains out! I shan't do so, because I don't suppose it would mend matters, besides creating a dashed scandal.'

'What a good thing you told me the whole! I know exactly what you should do. Make a clean breast of the business to your brother! He will very likely give you a tremendous scold, but you may depend upon his helping you out of this fix.'

'You don't know him! Scold, indeed! Depend upon it, he would make me come down from Oxford, and thrust me into the Army, or some such thing! I'll try everything before I apply to him!'

'Very well, I will lend you five hundred pounds,' said Sophy.

He flushed. 'You're a great gun, Sophy – no, but I don't mean that! – a capital girl! I'm devilish grateful, but of course I could not borrow money from you! No, no, pray don't say any more! It is out of the question! Besides, you don't understand! The old bloodsucker made me sign a bond to pay him fifteen per cent interest a month!'

'Good God, you never agreed to such an iniquitous thing!'

'What else could I do! I had to have the money to pay my gaming debts, and I knew it was useless to go to Howard and

Gibbs, or any of those fellows, for they would have shown me the door.'

'Hubert, I am persuaded there is nothing he can do to extort one penny of interest from you! Why, in law he could not even recover the principal! Only let me lend you five hundred pounds, and take it to him, and insist upon his restoring to you the bond you signed, and your ring! Tell him that if he does not choose to accept the principal he may do his worst!'

'And have him inform at Oxford against me! I tell you, Sophy, he is an out-and-out villain! He would do me all the harm that lay in his power! He is not a regular money-lender: in fact, I'm pretty certain he's what they call a lock, or a fence: a receiver, you know. What's more, he would refuse to give me back the ring, and even if I brought him to book he would have sold it, I expect.'

Nothing that Sophy could urge had the power to move him. He was plainly in considerable dread of Mr Goldhanger, and since she found this incomprehensible she could only suppose that some darker threat than had been disclosed to her was being held over his head. She made no attempt to discover what this might be, for she felt reasonably certain that it would not have impressed her. Instead, she asked him what he intended to do to extricate himself from his difficulties, if he would neither apply to his brother nor accept a loan from her. The answer was not very definite, Hubert being young enough still to cherish youth's ineradicable belief in timely miracles. He said several times that he had a month left to him before he need do anything desperate, and while agreeing reluctantly that he might in the end be forced to go to his brother evidently felt that something would happen to make this unnecessary. With an attempt at lightheartedness, he begged Sophy not to trouble her head over it, and as she perceived that it would be useless to continue arguing with him she said no more.

But when he had left her she sat for some time with her chin in her hand, pondering the matter. Her first impulse, which was to place the whole affair in the hands of Sir Horace's lawyer, she regretfully discarded. She was well-enough acquainted with Mr Meriden to know that he would most strenuously resist her determination to pay five hundred pounds into a moneylender's hands. Any advice he might be expected to give her could only lead to the disclosure of Hubert's folly, which was naturally unthinkable. Her mind flitted through the ranks of her friends, but they too had to be discarded, for the same reason. But since she was not one to abandon any project she had once decided on she did not for as much as an instant entertain the idea of leaving her young cousin to settle his difficulties for himself. There seemed to be no other course open to her but to confront the villainous Mr Goldhanger herself. This decision was not reached without careful consideration, for although she was not in the least afraid of Mr Goldhanger she was perfectly well-aware that young ladies did not visit usurers, and that such conduct would be thought outrageous by any person of breeding. However, since she could perceive no reason why anyone, except perhaps, Hubert, should ever know anything at all about it, she came to the conclusion, that to hang back from missish scruples would be stupid and spiritless: not the sort of behaviour to be expected of Sir Horace Stanton-Lacy's daughter.

Having made up her mind to intervene in Hubert's affairs, it was characteristic of her that she wasted no time in further heart-burnings. It was also characteristic of her that she made no attempt to persuade herself that she might with propriety draw upon Sir Horace's funds to defray Hubert's debt. In her view, which he would undoubtedly have shared, it was one thing to spend five hundred pounds on a ball to launch herself into London society, and quite another to force him into an act of generosity towards a nephew of whose very existence he was in all probability oblivious. Instead, she unlocked her jewel-case, and, after turning over its contents, abstracted from it the diamond ear-rings Sir Horace had bought for her at Rundell and Bridge only a year earlier. They were singularly fine stones, and it cost her a slight pang to part with them; but the rest of her more valuable jewelry had been left to her by her mother, and although she had not the smallest recollection of this lady her scruples forbade her to part with her trinkets.

Upon the following day, she contrived to excuse herself from accompanying Lady Ombersley and Cecilia to a silk warehouse in the Strand, and instead, sallied forth quite unaccompanied to those noted jewellers, Rundell and Bridge. The shop was empty of customers when she arrived, but the sight of a young lady of commanding height and presence, and dressed, moreover, in the first style of elegance, brought the head salesman hurrying forward, all eagerness to oblige. He was an excellent man of business who prided himself on never forgetting the face of a valued customer. He recognized Miss Stanton-Lacy at a glance, set a chair for her with his own august hands, and begged to be told what he might have the honour of showing her. When he discovered the true nature of her business he looked thunderstruck, but swiftly concealed his amazement, and, by a flicker of the eyelids, conveyed to an intelligent underling an order to summon on to the scene Mr Bridge himself. Mr Bridge, gliding into the shop, and bowing politely to the daughter of a patron who had bought many expensive trinkets of him (though mostly for quite a different class of female), begged Sophy to go with him into his private office at the back of the show-room. Whatever he may have thought of her wish to dispose of ear-rings carefully chosen by herself only a year before he kept to himself. A civil enquiry for Sir Horace having elicited the information that he was at present in Brazil, Mr Bridges, putting two and two together, instantly resolved to buy the ear-rings back at a handsome figure, instead of resorting, as had been his first intention, to the time-honoured custom of explaining to his client just why the price of diamonds had fallen so low. He had no intention of selling the ear-rings again; he would put them by until the return of Sir Horace from Brazil. Sir Horace, he shrewdly suspected, would repurchase them; and his gratification at being able to do so reasonably would no doubt find expression, in the future, in buying a great many more expensive trifles from the jewellers who had behaved in so gentlemanly a way towards his only daughter. The transaction, therefore, between Miss Stanton-Lacy and Mr Bridges was conducted on the most genteel lines possible, each party being perfectly satisfied with the bargain, Mr Bridges, the soul of discretion, kept Miss Stanton-Lacy in his private office until two other customers had left the shop. He fancied that Sir Horace might not wish it to be known that his daughter had been reduced to selling her jewelry. Without a blink he agreed to pay Sophy five hundred pounds in bills; without a blink he counted them out on the table before her; and without the least diminution in respect did he presently bow her out of the shop.

The bills stuffed into her muff, Sophy next hailed a hackney, and desired the coachman to driver her to Bear Alley. The vehicle she selected was by no means the first or the smartest which lumbered past her, but it was driven by the most prepossessing jarvey. He was a burly, middle-aged man, with a rubicund and jovial countenance, in whom Sophy felt that she might repose a certain degree of confidence, this belief being strengthened by the manner in which he received her order. After eyeing her shrewdly, and stroking his chin with one mittened hand, he gave it as his opinion that she had mistaken the direction, Bear Alley not being, to his way of thinking, the sort of locality to which a lady of her quality would wish to be taken.

'No, is it a back-slum?' asked Sophy.

'It ain't the place for a young lady,' repeated the jarvey, declining to commit himself on this point. He added that he had daughters of his own, begging her pardon.

'Well, back-slum or not, that is where I wish to go,' said Sophy. 'I have business with a Mr Goldhanger there, who, I daresay, is a great rogue; and you look to me just the sort of man I may trust not to drive off, and leave me there.'

She got up into the hackney; the jarvey shut the door upon her; climbed back on to the box, and, after expressing to the ambient air his desire to be floored if ever he should be so betwattled again, besought his horse to get up.

Bear Alley, which led eastward from the Fleet Market, was a narrow and malodorous lane, where filth of every description lay mouldering between the uneven cobbles. The shadow of the great prison seemed to brood over the whole district, and even the people who trod the streets, or lounged on doorsteps, had a depressed look not entirely attributable to their circumstances. The coachman enquired of a man in a greasy muffler whether he knew Mr Goldhanger's abode, and was directed to a house half-way up the alley, his informant hesitating palpably before answering, and seemingly disinclined to enter into any sort of conversation.

A dingy hackney, once a gentleman's coach, attracted little notice, but when it drew up, and a tall, well-dressed young woman alighted, holding up her flounced skirts to avoid soiling them against a pile of garbage, several loafers and two small, ragged boys drew near to stare at her. Various comments were made, but these were happily phrased in such cant terms as were quite incomprehensible to Sophy. She had been stared out of countenance in too many Spanish and Portuguese villages to be in any way discomposed by the attention she was attracting, and after running a critical eye over her audience beckoned to one of the small boys, and said with a smile: 'Tell me, does a man called Goldhanger live here?'

The urchin gaped at her, but when she held out a shilling to him, caught his breath sharply, and, stretching out a claw of a hand, uttered: 'Fust floor!' He then grabbed the coin and took to his heels before any of his seniors could relieve him of it.

The glimpse of largesse made the crowd converge on Sophy, but the jarvey climbed down from the box, his whip in his hand, and genially invited anyone who had a fancy for a little of the home-brewed to come on. No one accepted the invitation, and Sophy said: 'Thank you, but pray do not start a brawl! I wish you will wait for me here, if you please.'

'If I were you, missie,' said the jarvey earnestly, 'I'd keep out of a ken like this here, that's what I'd do! You don't know what might happen to you!'

'Well, if anything happens to me,' responded Sophy cheerfully, 'I shall give a loud scream, and you may come in and rescue me. I shall not, I think, keep you waiting for very long.'

She then picked her way through the kennel, and entered the house which had been pointed out to her. The door stood open, and a flight of uncarpeted stairs lay at the end of a short passage. She went up them, and found herself on a small landing. Two doors gave on to this, so she knocked on them both, in an imperative way. There was a pause, and she had an unpleasant feeling that she was being watched. She looked round, but there was no one in sight, and it was only when she turned her head again that she saw that an unmistakable eye was regarding her through a small hole in one of the panels of the door at the back of house. It disappeared instantly, there was the sound of a key turning in a lock, and the door was slowly opened to reveal a thin, swarthy individual, with long greasy curls, a semitic nose, and an ingratiating leer. He was dressed in a suit of rusty black, and nothing about him suggested sufficient affluence to lend as much as five hundred pence to anyone. His hooded eyes rapidly took in every detail of Sophy's appearance, from the curled feathers in her high-crowned hat to the neat kid boots upon her feet.

'Good-morning!' said Sophy. 'Are you Mr Goldhanger?'

He stood, a little bent, before her, wiping his hands together. 'And what would you be wanting with Mr Goldhanger, my lady?' he asked.

'I have business with him,' replied Sophy. 'So if you are he please do not keep me standing in this dirty passage any longer! I cannot conceive why you do not at least sweep the floor!'

Mr Goldhanger was considerably taken aback, a thing that had not happened to him for a very long time. He was accustomed to receiving all sorts and conditions of visitors, from furtive persons who stole into the house under cover of darkness and spilled strange wares upon the desk under the light of one oil lamp, to haggard-eyed young men of fashion seeking relief from their immediate obligations, but never before had he opened his door to a self-possessed young lady who took him to task for not sweeping the floors.

'I wish you will stop staring at me in that foolish way!' said Sophy. 'You have already peered at me through that hole in the door, and you must by now have convinced yourself that I am not a law-officer in disguise.'

Mr Goldhanger protested. The insinuation that he would not welcome a visit from a law-officer seemed to wound him. However, he stood back to allow Sophy to enter the room, and invited her to take a chair on one side of the large desk which occupied the centre of the floor.

'Yes, but I shall be obliged to you if you will first dust it,' she said.

Mr Goldhanger performed this office with one of his long coat-tails. He heard the key grate behind him, and turned sharply to see his visitor removing it from the lock.

'You won't object to my locking the door, I daresay,' said Sophy. 'I don't in the least desire to be interrupted by any of your acquaintances, you see. And since I should much dislike to be spied on you will permit me to stuff my handkerchief into that Judas of yours.' She removed one hand from her large swansdown muff as she spoke, and poked a corner of her handkerchief into the hole.

Mr Goldhanger had the oddest feeling that the world had begun to revolve in reverse. For years he had taken care never to get into any situation he was unable to command, and his visitors were more in the habit of pleading with him than of locking the door, and ordering him to dust the furniture. He could see no particular harm in allowing Sophy to retain the key, for although she was a large young woman he had no doubt of being able to wrest it from her, should such a need arise. The instinct of his race made him prefer, whenever possible, to maintain a manner of the utmost urbanity, so he now smiled, and bowed, and said that my lady was welcome to do what she pleased in his humble abode. He then betook himself to the chair on the other side of the desk, and asked what he might have the honour of doing for her.

'I have come on a very simple matter,' responded Sophy. 'It is merely to recover from you Mr Hubert Rivenhall's bond, and the emerald ring given you as a pledge.'

'That,' said Mr Goldhanger, smiling more ingratiatingly than ever, 'is indeed a simple matter. I shall be delighted to oblige you, my lady. I need not ask whether you have brought with you the funds, for I am sure such a business-like young lady –'

'Now, that is excellent!' interrupted Sophy cordially. 'I find that so many persons imagine that if one is a female one has no head for business, and that, of course, leads to a sad waste of time. I must tell you at once that when you lent five hundred pounds to Mr Rivenhall you lent money to a minor. I expect I need not explain to you what *that* means.'

She smiled in the most friendly way as she spoke these words, and Mr Goldhanger smiled back at her, and said softly: 'What a well-informed young lady, to be sure! If I sued Mr Rivenhall for my money I could not recover it. But I do not think Mr Rivenhall would like me to sue him for it.'

'Of course he would not,' Sophy agreed. 'Moreover, although it was extremely wrong of you to have lent him any money, it seems unjust that you should not at least recover the principal.'

'Most unjust,' said Mr Goldhanger. 'There is also a little matter of the interest, my lady.'

Sophy shook her head. 'No, I shan't pay you a penny in interest, which may perhaps teach you a lesson to be more careful in future. I have with me five hundred pounds in bills, and when you have handed me the bond and the ring I will give them to you.'

Mr Goldhanger could not help laughing a little at this, for although he had not very much sense of humour he could not but be tickled at the thought that he would forgo his interest at the command of a young lady. 'I think I prefer to keep the bond and the ring,' he said.

'I expect you would prefer it,' said Sophy.

'You should consider, my lady, that I could do Mr Rivenhall a great deal of harm,' Mr Goldhanger pointed out. 'He is up at Oxford, isn't he? Yes, I don't think they would be pleased there if they knew of his little transaction with me. Or –'

'They would not be at all pleased,' said Sophy. 'It would be a trifle awkward for you, though, would it not? But perhaps you could persuade them that you had no notion that Mr Rivenhall was under age.'

'Such a clever young lady!' smiled Mr Goldhanger.

'No, but I have a great deal of common-sense, which tells me that if you refuse to give up the bond and the ring the best course for me to pursue would be to drive at once to Bow Street and lay the whole matter before the magistrate there.'

The smile faded: Mr Goldhanger watched her through narrowed eyelids. 'I don't think you would be wise to do that,' he said.

'Don't you? Well, I think it is the wisest thing I could possibly do, and I have a strong feeling that they would like to have news of you in Bow Street.'

Mr Goldhanger shared this feeling. But he did not believe that Sophy meant what she said, his clients having the most providential dislike to publicity. He said: 'I think my Lord Ombersley would prefer to pay me my money.'

'I daresay he would, and that is why I have told him nothing about it, for I think it nonsensical to be blackmailed by such a creature as you, all for the want of a little courage!'

This unprecedented point of view began to engender in Mr Goldhanger a dislike for his guest. Women, he knew, were unpredictable. He leaned forward in his chair, and tried to explain to her some of the more disagreeable consequences that would befall Mr Rivenhall if he repudiated any part of his debt. He spoke well, and it was a sinister little speech that seldom failed to impress his hearers. It failed today.

'All this,' said Sophy, cutting him short, 'is nonsense and you must know that as well as I do. All that would happen to Mr Rivenhall would be that he would get a great scold, and be in disgrace with his father for a while, and as for being sent down from Oxford, no such thing! They will never know anything about it there, because it is my belief that you do worse things than lending money at extortionate rates to young men, and once I have been to Bow Street, ten to one they will contrive to put you in prison on quite another charge! What is more, the instant it becomes known to the law-officers that you lent money to a minor you will be unable to recover a penny of it. So pray do not talk any more to me in that absurd way! I am not in the least afraid of you, or of anything you can do.'

'You are very courageous,' said Mr Goldhanger gently. 'Also you have much common-sense, as you told me. But I too have common-sense, my lady, and I do not think that you came to see me with the consent, or even the knowledge of your parents, or your maid, or even of Mr Hubert Rivenhall. Perhaps you would indeed inform against me at Bow Street: I do not know, but perhaps you may never be granted the opportunity. Now I should not like to be harsh to such a beautiful young lady, so shall we agree to a little compromise? You will give me the five hundred pounds you have brought with you, and those pretty pearls you wear in your ears, and I will hand you Mr Rivenhall's bond, and we shall both of us be satisfied.'

Sophy laughed. 'I imagine you would be more than satisfied!' she said. 'I will give you five hundred pounds for the bond and the ring, and nothing more.'

'But perhaps you have loving parents who would be willing to give me much, much more to have you restored to them, alive, my lady, and unhurt?'

He rose from his chair as he spoke, but his objectionable guest, instead of displaying decent alarm, merely withdrew her right hand from her muff. In it she held a small but eminently serviceable pistol. 'Pray sit down again, Mr Goldhanger!' she said.

Mr Goldhanger sat down. He believed that no female could stand loud reports, much less pull triggers, but he had seen quite enough of Sophy to be reluctant to put this belief to the test. He begged her not to be foolish.

'You must not be afraid that I don't know how to handle guns,' Sophy told him reassuringly. 'Indeed, I am a very fair shot. Perhaps I ought to tell you that I have lived for some time in Spain, where of course they have a great many unpleasant people, such as bandits. My father taught me to shoot. I am not such a fine shot as he is, but at this range I would engage to put a bullet through any part of you I chose.'

'You are trying to frighten me,' said Mr Goldhanger querulously, 'but I am not frightened of guns in women's hands, and I know very well it is unloaded!'

'Well, if you move out of that chair you will discover that it is loaded,' said Sophy. 'At least, you will be dead, but I expect you will know how it happened.'

Mr Goldhanger gave an uneasy laugh. 'And what would happen to *you*, my lady?' he asked.

'I don't suppose that anything very much would happen to me,' she replied. 'And I cannot conceive how that should interest you when you were dead. However, if it does, I will tell you just what I should say to the law-officers.'

Mr Goldhanger, forgetting his urbanity, said testily that he did not desire to hear it.

'You know,' said Sophy, frowning slightly, 'I cannot help thinking that it might be a very good thing if I were to shoot you in any event. I did not mean to when I first came because naturally I cannot approve of murder, but I see that you are a very evil man, and I cannot help wondering if a really courageous person would not shoot now, and so rid the world of someone who has done a great deal of harm in it.'

'Put that silly gun away, and we will talk business!' Mr Goldhanger besought her.

'There is nothing more to talk about, and I feel much more comfortable with the gun in my hand. Are you going to give me what I came for, or shall I go to Bow Street, and inform them there that you tried to kidnap me?'

'My lady,' said Mr Goldhanger, on a whining note, 'I am only a poor man! You –'

195

'You will be much richer when I have paid you back your five hundred pounds,' Sophy pointed out.

He brightened, for it had really seemed for a few minutes as though he might be forced to forgo even this sum. 'Very well,' he said. 'I do not wish any unpleasantness, so I will give back the bond. The ring I cannot give back, for it was stolen from me.'

'In that event,' said Sophy. 'I shall certainly go to Bow Street, because I am persuaded they will not believe there, any more than I do, that it was stolen. If you have not got it, you must have sold it, and *that* means you may be prosecuted. I enquired of a most respectable jeweller only this morning what the law is with regard to pledged articles.'

Mr Goldhanger, revolted by this unwomanly knowledge of the law, cast her a glance of loathing, and said: 'I have not sold it!'

'No, and it was not stolen from you either. I expect it is in one of the drawers of this desk, together with the bond, for I can't imagine why you should have bought such a handsome piece of furniture, unless it was to lock valuables away in it. And it may even be that you keep a gun of your own in it, so perhaps I should warn you that if you pulled the trigger quicker than I did, I left a letter at my home to inform my – parents precisely where I had gone to, and what my purpose was.'

'If I had a daughter like you, I would be ashamed to own her!' said Mr Goldhanger, with real feeling.

'Nonsense!' said Sophy. 'You would probably be very proud of me, and would have taught me how to pick pockets. And if you had a daughter like me she would have scrubbed your floors for you, and washed your shirt, so you would have been a deal better off then you are now. Pray do not keep me waiting any longer, for I am quite tired of talking to you, and, indeed, have found you a dead bore from the outset!'

Mr Goldhanger had been called a villain, a bloodsucker, a cheat, a devil, a ghoul and innumerable other hard names, but never had anyone told him that he was a dead bore, and never had any of his victims looked at him with such amused contempt.

He would have like to have closed his long, bony fingers round Sophy's throat, and choked the life slowly out of her. But Sophy held a gun, so instead he unlocked the drawer in his desk, and sought in it with a trembling hand for what he wanted. He thrust a ring and a scrap of paper across the desk, and said: 'The money! Give me my money!'

Sophy picked the bond up, and read it; then she put it, with the ring, into her muff, and withdrew from this convenient receptacle a wad of bills, and laid it on the desk. 'There it is,' she said.

Mechanically, he began to count the bills, Sophy rose. 'And now, if you please, will you be so obliging as to turn your chair round with its back to the door?'

Mr Goldhanger almost snarled at her, but he complied with this request, saying over his shoulder: 'You need not be afraid! I am very glad to see you go!' he added, quivering with fury: 'Doxy!'

Sophy chuckled. Fitting the key into the lock, and turning it, she said: 'Well, I really believe I would rather be a doxy than a turnip dressed up in a sheet to frighten silly boys!'

'Turnip?' repeated Mr Goldhanger, stupefied. '*Turnip – ?*'

But his unwelcome guest had gone.

Twelve

*H*ubert was on his way upstairs to his room that evening when he met his cousin, coming down from the schoolroom. She said: 'Hubert! The very person I wanted! Wait, I have something for you!' She then went into her own room, and came back in a minute or two, looking mischievous, and said: 'Shut your eyes, and stretch out your hand!'

'Now, Sophy, is this something horrid?' he demanded suspiciously.

'Of course it is not!'

'Well, you look as though you meant to hoax me,' he said, but he obediently shut his eyes, and held out one hand. Sophy placed his ring, and his bond in it, and told him he might now open his eyes. He did so, and suffered so severe a shock that he dropped the ring. '*Sophy!*'

'What a careless creature you are!' she remarked. 'Don't neglect to burn that silly piece of paper! I very nearly did it myself, for I am sure it would be just like you to leave it in your pocket, but then I thought you would like to see for yourself that it really had been recovered.'

He bent to pick the ring up. 'B – but, Sophy, how – who – how came this into your hands?'

'I had it from Mr Goldhanger, of course.'

He gave a gasp. 'Had it from – You did not go to that old devil's house! You *could* not have done so!'

'Yes, I did. What should stop me?'

'Good God!' he ejaculated. He grasped her wrist, and said sharply. 'Why did he give it up to you? Do you tell me you paid the money I owed him?'

'Oh, don't give that a thought! I happened to have five hundred pounds by me, and you will pay me back sometime, I expect. There is no need to look so shocked, you silly boy!'

'Sophy, I cannot *bear* it!' he said, in a strangled voice. 'Besides he lent it to me at fifteen per cent per month, and I know well he would never have parted with my bond for a penny less than was his due! Sophy, tell me the truth!'

'I have done so. Of course, he did not like it very much, but he was obliged to do what I wanted, because I told him I should go to Bow Street if he refused. I think you were very right about him, Hubert! He is probably in league with every thief in London, for the instant I made that threat I could see how uneasy I had made him, so very likely he does not at all wish to be brought under the notice of the magistrates.'

'Goldhanger allowed himself to be frightened into giving up these things? *Goldhanger?*' he said incredulously.

'Well, what else could he do? I told him it was nonsensical to suppose that anything very dreadful would happen to you, if the whole matter *was* laid bare; and he knew that if I did go to Bow Street he would never be able to recover a penny of his money.'

'*You* with that slimy villain! Were you afraid, Sophy?' he asked wonderingly.

'No, not a bit.' She added apologetically: 'You know, I haven't the least sensibility! Sir Horace says it is quite shocking, and *most* unfeminine. But, to own the truth, I thought Goldhanger a ridiculous person. I was by far more afraid of El Moro! He was one of the guerrilleros, and a dreadful rogue! He and his men broke into the house one night when Sir Horace was away – but never mind that! People who are for ever recounting their adventures are the most tedious persons imaginable!'

'Sophy, he might have done you some mischief –'

'Yes, but I had my pistol with me, so he very soon thought better of that notion!' she explained.

'Sophy, Sophy, what am I to do?' he exclaimed.

'Nothing: there is nothing left to be done. I must go, or I shall be late for dinner. Don't forget to burn that paper!'

She vanished into her room, cutting short his stammered thanks and protestations, and since he did not see her alone again that night he was unable to repeat them. He was engaged with a party of his own, but his friends found him in an unconvivial mood. His thoughts were, indeed, in a sad turmoil, and although his relief at being rid of his debt to Goldhanger had been at first overwhelming, it was succeeded, as soon as he had had time to think the matter over, by a most uncomfortable feeling of guilt. That Sophy, a mere female (and younger than himself), should not only have paid off his debt, but should also have visited on his behalf such a person as Goldhanger, made him squirm in his chair. Blue Ruin did little to clear his intellect, and when he sought Berkeley Square in the early hours of the morning he was no nearer a solution of this new difficulty than he had been at the start of the evening, the only coherent thought in his head being that in some undiscovered way he must instantly pay his cousin five hundred pounds.

Mr Rivenhall returned from Leicestershire on the following day, arriving in Berkeley Square at a somewhat infelicitous moment. Jane Storridge, whose vigilance Sophy had not sufficiently taken into account, had not only discovered that the diamond drops were missing from her mistress's jewel-case, but had raised such a hue and cry in the servant's quarters that Mrs Ludstock, the housekeeper, felt herself called upon to inform Lady Ombersley that while she was sure she did not know what servants were coming to these days she would take her dying oath that none of the maids under her control had touched Miss Sophy's ear-rings; and, further, that anybody might be pardoned for thinking that a lady's maid worthy of the name would take better care of her mistress's valuables than Miss Storridge seemed to suppose was necessary. With the gist of these remarks Dassett also wished to be identified, and so pregnant with unuttered offence was his manner that Lady Ombersley became quite flustered, realizing that she stood upon the brink of a domestic disaster. She sent for Jane Storridge, and Mr Rivenhall arrived in time to hear the end of a dialogue between the three servants so icily civil, so bristling with veiled innuendo as to terrify poor Lady Ombersley. Before he had the opportunity of demanding an explanation, Sophy herself came in, in her walking-dress, saying that she and Cecilia were going out to do some shopping, and had her aunt any commissions for her? Lady Ombersley greeted her with relief, and at once asked her why she had not disclosed the loss of her ear-rings.

Sophy did not start, but a very slight flush rose to her cheeks. She replied with perfect composure: 'I have not lost any ear-rings, dear ma'am. What is this?'

'Oh, my love, your maid says that your diamond drops are gone from your case, and I would not have had such a thing happen for the world!'

Sophy bent to kiss her cheek. 'Aunt Lizzie, I am so sorry! It is quite my fault for having been so stupid as to forget to tell Jane! They are not lost: I took them to the jeweller to be cleaned, and reset. One of the hooks was a little loose. How foolish of you to have worried her ladyship, Jane, before first asking me if I knew where the ear-rings were!'

'Cleaned?' cried Miss Storridge. 'Why, Miss Sophy, as though I did not take all your jewels to Rundell and Bridge to be cleaned when we first came to London!'

'Yes, but I thought on the night of our ball that those drops looked quite dull,' responded Sophy. 'Go away now, Jane: her ladyship has been plagued enough!'

She was aware of her cousin's eyes upon her face, and a swift glance in his direction had informed her that there was an uncomfortably searching expression in them. However, he said nothing, so she got rid of her maid, ascertained that her aunt had no commissions for her to execute, and went off, devoutly trusting that neither she nor Mr Rivenhall would notice the continued absence of her diamond ear-rings.

But on the following day, just as she had sat down to a light luncheon with Lady Ombersley, Cecilia, Selina, and Hubert, Mr Rivenhall walked into the room, and handed her a small package. 'Your ear-rings, cousin,' he said briefly. 'I think you will find that they have now been cleaned to your satisfaction.'

For once in her life, Sophy was bereft of all power of speech. Fortunately, he did not seem to expect her to say anything, for he turned away to carve himself a slice of ham, and began to talk to his mother, desiring to know whether she wished to spend any part of the summer in Brighton that year. Lady Ombersley referred this question to Sophy. Brighton did not agree with her constitution, but the Regent had made the resort so fashionable that any number of distinguished persons would flock there in June, and if Sophy wished it she would certainly hire a house there for some part of the season.

Cecilia, who had her own reasons for wanting to remain in town, said: 'Oh, Mama, you know you are never well in Brighton! Pray do not let us go! I am sure there is nothing more stupid than those parties at the Pavilion, and the excessive heat in the rooms quite knocks you up!'

Sophy at once disclaimed any wish to visit the place; and the rest of the meal was spent in discussing the rival attractions of Ombersley, Thorpe Grange, and Scarborough, with some reminiscences from Lady Ombersley on a summer she had spent at Ramsgate before the Regent's patronage of Brighton had quite cast this resort into the shade.

When they rose from the table, Hubert, who had been trying unavailingly for some time to get his cousin alone, blurted out: 'Are you busy, Sophy? Would you care to stroll in the garden for a while?'

'Thank you! By and by, perhaps! Charles, may I have a word with you at your convenience?'

He met her direct gaze unsmilingly. 'By all means! Now, if you wish.'

Lady Ombersley looked vaguely surprised; Selina exclaimed: 'Secrets! Are you hatching a plot, I wonder? Shall we like it?'

'Nothing so exciting,' replied Sophy lightly. 'Merely, Charles executed a commission for me.'

She accompanied him across the hall to the library. She was never one to beat about the bush, and no sooner had he shut the door than she said, without preamble: 'Now, if you please, tell me what this means! How did you know that I had sold my earrings, and why have you – as I suppose – bought them back for me?'

'I bought them back because I can think of only two reasons why you should have disposed of them.'

'Indeed! And what may they be, Cousin Charles?'

'I have never been permitted to see the bills for your ball, but I have some experience in these matters, and I can possibly guess at a rough total. If that is your explanation, you can want none from me. The arrangement was repugnant to me from the outset, as well you know.'

'My dear Charles, I have a great many expenses of which you know nothing at all! You are being absurd, you know!'

'I do not think that you have any expenses which your father would be unprepared to meet.'

She was silent for a moment. Then she said: 'You have not yet told me what is the second of the reasons that occurred to you.'

He looked at her under frowning brows. 'My fear is that you have lent the money to Hubert.'

'Good gracious! Banish it!' she exclaimed, laughing. 'Pray, why should I do such a thing?'

'I hope you have not. The young fool was at Newmarket with a set of fellows I could wish at Jericho. Did he lose a large sum there?'

'Surely he would tell you if he had, rather than me!'

He walked over to his desk, and rather absently tidied some paper that lay on it. 'It may have been that he was afraid to,' he said. He looked up. 'Was that it?'

'I needed the money for reasons into which I will not take you,' she replied. 'I must point out to you, Charles, that you have not yet answered my other question. How did you guess that I had sold the ear-rings?'

'It was not a conjecture: I knew.'

'How is this possible? You were not hidden in the shop, I assume!'

'No, I was not. But I called in Brook Street on my way home yesterday, and saw Miss Wraxton.' He hesitated, and again looked across at his cousin. 'You must understand that Miss Wraxton felt it to be her duty to tell me that she feared you might be in some difficulty! She was in Rundell and Bridge's with Lady Brinklow when you were transacting this sale. It appears that Bridge had not properly closed the door into his office; Miss Wraxton recognized your voice, and could not help but overhear something you said to Bridge.'

Her hand, which was lying on the back of a chair, closed tightly on the polished wood, but relaxed again after a moment. She said, in a voice from which all emotion had been banished: 'There is no end to Miss Wraxton's solicitude. How very obliging of her to have interested herself in my affairs! I expect it was delicacy that forbade her to speak to me rather than to you.'

He flushed. 'You must remember that I am betrothed to Miss Wraxton. In the circumstances, she thought it her duty to mention the matter to me. She felt that she did not stand upon such terms with you as could make it possible for her to ask you for an explanation.'

'Well, that is certainly true,' said Sophy. 'Neither of you, my dear cousin, stands upon such terms with me! And if you have any notion of asking me for an explanation of anything I choose to do, let me tell you that you may go to the devil!'

He smiled. 'Then perhaps it is as well that Eugenia did not venture to address you on this head, for she would have been much shocked at being told to go to the devil! Do you always talk like your father when you lose your temper, Sophy?'

'No, not invariably. I beg your pardon! But it was quite intolerable!'

'I daresay, but I should not have asked you for an explanation had you not sought this interview.'

'You should have paid no heed to Miss Wraxton! As for repurchasing my ear-rings, good God, what a fix you have placed me in!'

As she spoke, the door opened behind her, and Hubert came into the room. He was looking extremely white, but perfectly determined, and he said jerkily: 'I beg pardon, but I have been wanting to speak to you all day, Sophy, and – and to Charles! So I have come!'

Mr Rivenhall said nothing, nor did he cast him more than one of his penetrating glances, but Sophy turned, and held out her hand. 'Yes, pray come in, Hubert!' she said, smiling at him.

He took her hand, and pressed it a little convulsively. 'Cecilia told me about your ear-rings, and all the kick-up – Sophy, was it *that?* For if it was, and, indeed, in any event! I can't and I won't stand it! I had rather by far tell Charles the whole!'

Her hand returned the pressure of his before releasing it. She said in her calm way: 'Well, you know, Hubert, I always thought you made a mistake not to tell Charles, for Mr Wychbold told me once that there was no one he would liefer go to in a fix. And if *he* could trust him, how much more reason must *you* have to do so! I am persuaded you will do much better without me, so I will leave you.'

She did not look at Mr Rivenhall to see what effect her words might have had on him, but walked immediately out of the room.

There had been an effect; Mr Rivenhall said quietly: 'I think I know what it is, but tell me! Newmarket?'

'It is worse than that! Oh, yes, I lost at Newmarket, but that's the least part of it!' Hubert said.

Mr Rivenhall nodded to a chair. 'Sit down. What's the worst part of it?'

Hubert did not avail himself of this invitation. Apprehension made him assume a belligerent tone that in no way expressed his feelings. 'You may as well know that I didn't tell you the whole of my debts, last year!'

'Young fool!' commented his brother, without heat.

'I know that, but you said – Oh, well, it doesn't signify talking of that now!'

'You should know I don't mean all I say when I am angry. However, if my tongue's to blame, I'm sorry for it. Go on!'

'I know I ought to have told you,' Hubert muttered. 'And I wish to God I had, instead of –' He broke off, drew a breath, and started again. 'I thought I might be able to come about. I – you won't like this! You need not tell me it was wrong, for I know that! But other fellows –'

'Well, I won't tell you it was wrong, then. But let me know what it was, for I am quite in the dark as yet!'

'I went with – a man I know – to a – place in Pall Mall. And another in St James's Place. Roulette, and French Hazard! And I lost the devil of a sum of money!'

'Oh, my God!' Mr Rivenhall exclaimed sharply. 'Have we not had enough of that in this family?'

The bitterness is his voice, grown suddenly harsh, made Hubert wince, and retire behind a barrier of sullenness. 'Well, I knew you would be in a rage, but I don't see that it was so very bad! I wish I had not had such infamous luck, but everyone plays, after all!'

It seemed for a moment as though his brother would have returned a stinging answer, but he checked himself, and walked over to the window instead, and stood frowning out. After a pause, he said abruptly: 'Do you know the sum of my father's gaming debts?'

Hubert was surprised, for the subject had never before been mentioned between them. He replied: 'No. That is, I do know that they must have been rather heavy, of course, but I never heard the exact sum.'

Mr Rivenhall told him.

There was a stunned silence. Hubert broke it at last. 'But – but – My *God*, Charles! You're – you're not bamming me, are you?'

Mr Rivenhall gave a short laugh.

'But – Charles, *you* did not pay all that?'

'Hardly. I settled some part, but the estate is still grossly encumbered. I need not take you into all that. Now that my father has given the management into my hands I have a reasonable hope of being able to tow the family out of the river Tick. But compounding with creditors, spending my life contriving ways and means with our man of business is the very devil!'

'Good God, I should rather think it would be! Listen, Charles, I'm damned sorry I should have added to it all!'

Mr Rivenhall came back to the desk. 'Yes, I know. Your debt is no great matter, but if gaming is in your blood as well –'

'Well, it ain't! You needn't fear for that, for I don't care for cards above half, and I can assure you I had no pleasure in going to those damned hells!' He took a turn about the room, a frown slowly gathering on his brow. He stopped suddenly, and exclaimed: 'Why didn't you tell me? Dash it, I'm not a child! You should have told me.'

Mr Rivenhall looked at him, half smiling. 'Yes, perhaps I should,' he said mildly. 'But the fewer people to know the better. Even my mother does not know the whole.'

'Mama! No, indeed! I should think not! But I had a right to be told, instead of being allowed to go on as though – It is just like you, Charles, to shoulder everything, and to suppose no one can do the least thing but yourself! I daresay there might be a dozen ways in which I could help you! It seems to me that I ought to come down from Oxford at once, and find an eligible post somewhere, or join the army – no, that won't do, because you would have to buy me a commission, and even if I didn't join a cavalry regiment, or the Guards –'

'It certainly will not do!' interrupted his brother, amused, and rather touched. 'You'll oblige me by staying where you are! We are not on our last legs yet. Why, you bacon-brained young idiot, what do you suppose my object is but to see that you, and Theodore, and the girls don't suffer through my father's curst folly? If you choose to help me to run the estate, you may do so, and I shall be grateful, for Eckington is growing past it. I can't be rid of him, for he has been with us so long that I daresay he would break his heart, but he is of very little use, and I've no great degree of confidence in young Badsey yet. Have you a head for business?'

'I don't know, but I'll precious soon learn!' replied Hubert, with determination. 'When I come down for the Long Vacation, you may teach me. And mind, Charles! No keeping me in the dark!'

'No, very well. But you are still keeping *me* a little in the dark, you know. When did you lose all this money? Not lately, surely?'

'At Christmas. Well, I had better make a clean breast of the whole! I went to a rascally moneylender, and I borrowed five hundred from him, for six months. I thought I should have won every penny back, and more beside, at Newmarket. But the damnable screw was unplaced!' He saw his brother's expression, and said: 'You need not look like that! I swear I shall never do so again as long as I live! Of course I ought to have come rather to you, but –'

'You should have come to me, and that you did not must have been far more my fault than yours!'

'Oh, well, I don't know that!' Hubert said uncomfortably. 'I expect if I had been rather better acquainted with you I should have done so. Sophy said I should do so from the start, and, lord, if I'd had the least notion of what she meant to do I would have run to you straight away!'

'Then you did not apply to her for that money?'

'Good God, no! Charles, you *can't* think I would borrow money from Sophy?'

'I didn't think it. But neither did I think we were so ill-acquainted that – Well, never mind that! How did Sophy know of this, and if you did not borrow the money from her, why did she sell her ear-rings?'

'She guessed I was all to pieces. She made me tell her, and when I said I had rather not say a word to you, she offered to lend me the money. Of course I refused! But she knew where Goldhanger lived, and, without telling me what she meant to do, she went to see him herself, and got back my note of hand, and my ring. I had to pledge Grandfather Stanton-Lacy's emerald, you see. I don't know how she did it, for she swears she did not pay the old devil a penny of the interest. She is the most redoubtable girl! But I couldn't stand *that*, as you may suppose!'

'Sophy went to a moneylender?' repeated Mr Rivenhall incredulously. 'Nonsense! She cannot have done such a thing!'

'Well, she ain't one to tell fibs, and that's what she said!' declared Hubert.

Not many minutes later, Sophy, reading in the Yellow Parlour, was interrupted by the entrance of Mr Rivenhall, who came in, and closed the door behind him, saying bluntly: 'I seem to be very much in your debt, cousin. Yes, Hubert has told me the whole. I hardly know what I can say to you.'

'You are not at all in my debt,' replied Sophy. 'You have given me back my ear-rings! There is nothing to be said, in fact! You know that Miss Wraxton is in the drawing-room, with your mother? Lord Bromford, too, which is why I have sought refuge here.'

'There is a great deal to be said,' he replied, disregarding. 'I wish to God you had told me!'

'I am persuaded you could not seriously expect me to betray Hubert's confidence to you. You must not think, however, that I encouraged him to keep you in the dark. I advised him most earnestly to tell you the fix he was in, but he seemed to be in such dread of doing so that I might not persist.' She saw a slightly rigid look on his face, and added: 'I believe it is often so, between brothers, where there is a considerable disparity of age. And you are very formidable, upon occasion, are you not?'

'It seems so, indeed. Don't imagine I am not grateful to you, Sophy! I don't know by what means you discovered the coil he had tangled himself in —'

'Oh, it was not so difficult! The poor boy has been looking quite hagridden ever since I came to London! After his return from Newmarket, it was plain to be seen that something of a disastrous nature must have befallen him. He did not wish to confide in me, but a threat to tell you of my suspicions brought the whole stupid story out.'

He looked at her, his eyes hard and bright. 'I know well it is I who should have noticed there was something preying on Hubert's mind!'

He was evidently deeply mortified; she said: 'You have many other things to think about, perhaps. Men do not notice as quickly as women do. I am very glad that he has told you all. Don't refine too much upon it! I am quite sure that he has had a lesson he will be in no danger of forgetting.'

'I believe you are right. I used to think him as volatile as – well, I was used to think him volatile, but he has given me reason to indulge the hope that I was mistaken! But, Sophy, I don't yet know the whole of this deplorable business! Whom did you employ in it?'

'No one, upon my honour!' she assured him at once. 'I considered the matter from every aspect, and although I was much inclined, at first, to consult my father's lawyer, I soon saw that it would not do. There was no one I could apply to without divulging Hubert's part in the business. So I set about it myself.'

'Sophy, you cannot have gone to this creature yourself!'

'Yes, I did. Oh, I know it was dreadfully fast and bold of me, but I thought nobody would ever know! And then, too, I could not but reflect how much you must dislike Hubert's affairs becoming known outside our immediate circle.'

She saw that he was looking at her in patent disbelief, and raised her brows enquiringly.

'Hubert has told me enough about Goldhanger to make it perfectly plain to me what sort of a man he is!' he said. 'Do not tell me he willingly relinquished a note of hand and a valuable pledge to you for no more than the bare principal!'

She smiled. 'Most unwillingly! But only consider at what a disadvantage he stood! He had lent his money to a minor and he could not recover a penny of it, at law. I fancy he was glad to see

back his principal. The instant I said I would go to Bow Street –
a shot drawn at a venture, too! – I could see that I had discomposed him. My dear Charles, what Hubert found to alarm
him in such a creature I cannot imagine. A bogey to frighten
children!'

He was watching her closely, his brows knit. 'This sounds to
me pure fantasy, Sophy! From what I collect, this was no
accredited moneylender, but an out-and-out villain! Do you tell
me he made no effort to extort his interest from you?'

'No, he tried to frighten me into paying him, or giving him my
pearl ear-rings. But Hubert had warned me with what manner
of person I should have to deal, and I took the precaution of
carrying my pistol with me.'

'*What?*'

She was surprised, and again raised her brows. 'My pistol,' she
repeated.

His mortification found expression in disbelief. 'This must be
nonsense! I wish you will tell me the truth! You do not ask me to
believe that you carry a pistol about your person! I tell you now
that I do not believe it!'

She got up quickly, a sparkle in her eye. 'Indeed? Wait! I shall
not be gone above a minute or two!'

She whisked herself out of the room, only to reappear very
soon afterwards with her silver-mounted gun in her hand. 'Do
you not believe it, Charles? Do you not?' she demanded.

He stared at the weapon. 'Good God! *You?*' He held out his
hand, as though he would have taken it from her, but she
withheld it.

'Take care! It is loaded!'

He replied impatiently: 'Let me see it!'

'Sir Horace,' said Sophy provocatively, 'told me always to be
careful, and never to give it into the hands of anyone I was not
perfectly satisfied could be trusted to handle it.'

For an astounded moment, Mr Rivenhall, who was no mean
shot, stared at her. The pent-up emotions in his breast got the
better of him. He flung over to the fireplace, and ripped down

from the overmantel an invitation-card which had been stuck into a corner of a large, gilded mirror. 'Hold that up, stand there, and give me that gun!' he commanded.

Sophy laughed, and obeyed, standing quite fearlessly with her back to one wall, and holding the card out by one corner. 'I warn, it throws a trifle left!' she said coolly.

He was white with anger, an anger that had very little to do with her slighting reference to his ability to handle a pistol, but even as he levelled the gun, he seemed in some measure to recollect himself, for he lowered his arm again, and said: 'I cannot! Not with a pistol I don't know!'

'Faintheart!' mocked Sophy.

He cast her a glance of dislike, stepped forward to twitch the card out of her hand, and stuck it against the wall under the corner of a picture. In great interest, Sophy watched him walk away to the other end of the room, turn, jerk up his arm, and fire. An explosion, deafening in the confined space of the room, shattered the stillness, and the bullet, nicking one edge of the card, buried itself in the wall.

'I told you that it threw left,' Sophy reminded him, critically surveying his handiwork. 'Shall we reload it so that I can show you what *I* can do?'

They looked at one another. The enormity of this conduct suddenly dawned on Mr Rivenhall, and he began to laugh. 'Sophy, you – you *devil!*'

That made Sophy laugh too, so when a startled crowd of persons burst into the room a minute to two later, they found only a scene of unbridled mirth. Lady Ombersley, Cecilia, Miss Wraxton, Lord Bromford, Hubert, one of the footmen, and two housemaids all clustered in the doorway, evidently in the expectation of beholding the results of a shocking accident. 'I could murder you, Sophy!' said Mr Rivenhall.

'Unjust! Did *I* tell you to do it?' she countered. 'Dear Aunt Lizzie, do not look so alarmed! Charles was – was merely satisfying himself that my pistol was in order!'

By this time the eyes of most of the company had discovered

the rent in the wall. Lady Ombersley, clutching Hubert's arm for support, faintly enunciated: 'Are you *mad*, Charles?'

He looked a little guiltily at the havoc he had wrought. 'I must be, I suppose. The damage can soon be made good, however. It *does* throw left, Sophy. I would give much to see you fire it! What a pity I cannot take you to Manton's!'

'Is that Sophy's pistol?' asked Hubert, much interested. 'By Jupiter, you are an out-and-outer, Sophy! But what possessed you to fire it here, Charles? You *must* be mad!'

'It was naturally, an accident,' pronounced Lord Bromford. 'A man in his senses, which we cannot doubt Lord Rivenhall to be, does not, of intent, fire a pistol in the presence of ladies. My dear Miss Stanton-Lacy, you have sustained a severe shock to the nerves! It could not be otherwise. Let me beg you to repose yourself for a while!'

'I am not such a poor creature!' Sophy replied, her eyes still brimming with laughter. 'Charles will bear me out, if there is any truth in him, that I neither squeaked nor jumped! Sir Horace nipped such bad habit in the bud by soundly boxing my ears!'

'I am sure you are always an example to us all!' said Miss Wraxton acidly. 'One can only envy you your iron composure! I, alas, am made of weaker stuff, and must confess to have been very much startled by such an unprecedented noise in the house. I do not know what you can have been about, Charles. Or is it indeed Miss Stanton-Lacy's pistol, and was she exhibiting her skill to you?'

'On the contrary, it was I who shot disgracefully wide of my mark. May I clean this for you, Sophy?'

She shook her head, and held out her hand for the gun. 'Thank you, but I like to clean and load it myself.'

'Load it?' gasped Lady Ombersley. 'Sophy, you do not mean to load that horrid thing again, *surely?*'

Hubert laughed. 'I said she was a redoubtable girl, Charles! I say, Sophy, do you always keep it loaded?'

'Yes, for how can one tell when one may need it, and what is the use of an empty pistol! You know, what a delicate business it is, too! I daresay Charles can do it in a trice, but I cannot!'

He gave the gun into her hand. 'If we go down to Ombersley this summer, we must have a match, you and I,' he said. As their hands met, and she took the gun, he grasped her wrist, and held it for a moment. 'An infamous thing to have done!' he said, in a slightly lowered tone. 'I beg your pardon – and I thank you!'

Thirteen

*I*t was not to be supposed that this incident would be
pleasing to Miss Wraxton. A degree of understanding
seemed to be existent between Mr Rivenhall and his
cousin which was not at all to her taste, for although she was not
in love with him, and, indeed, would have considered such an
emotion very far beneath her station, she had made up her mind
to marry him, and was feminine enough to resent his paying the
least attention to any other female.

Fortune had not smiled upon Miss Wraxton. She had been
contracted, in schoolroom days, to a nobleman of impeccable
lineage, and respectable fortune, who had been carried off by an
attack of small-pox before she was of an age to be formally
affianced to him. Several eligible gentlemen had shown faint
tendencies to dangle after her during her first two seasons upon
the Marriage Mart, for she was a handsome girl with a
handsome portion; but for unaccountable reasons none of them
had come up to scratch, as her elder brother rather vulgarly
phrased it. Mr Rivenhall's offer had been made at a moment
when she had begun to fear that she might be left upon the shelf,
and had been thankfully received. Miss Wraxton, reared in the
strictest propriety, had never taken any undesirably romantic
notions into her head, and had had no hesitation informing her
Papa that she was willing to receive Mr Rivenhall's addresses.
Lord Brinklow, who held Lord Ombersley in the greatest
aversion, would certainly not have entertained Mr Rivenhall's
offer for as much as a minute had it not been for the providential

death of Matthew Rivenhall. But the old Nabob's fortune was something not to be despised even by the most sanctimonious of peers. Lord Brinklow had informed his daughter that Charles Rivenhall's suit carried his blessing with it; and Lady Brinklow, a sterner moralist even than her spouse, had clearly indicated to Eugenia where her duty lay, and by what means she might hope to detach Charles from his unregenerate family. An apt pupil, Miss Wraxton had thereafter lost no opportunity of pointing out to Charles, in the most tactful way, the delinquencies and general undesirability of his father, and his brothers and sisters. She was actuated by the purest of motives; she considered that the volatility of Lord Ombersley and Hubert was prejudicial to Charles's interest; she heartily despised Lady Ombersley; and as heartily deprecated the excessive sentiment which made Cecilia contemplate marriage with a penniless younger son. It seemed to her that to detach Charles from his family must be her first object, but sometimes she was seduced into playing with the notion of reclaiming the Ombersley household from the abyss of impropriety into which it had fallen. Becoming engaged to Mr Rivenhall at a moment when he was exacerbated by his father's excesses, her gentle words had fallen on fruitful soil. A naturally joyless nature, reared on bleak principles, could perceive only the most deplorable tendencies in a lively family's desire for enjoyment. Charles, wrestling with mountainous piles of bills, was much inclined to think that she was right. It was only since Sophy's arrival that his sentiments seemed to have undergone a change. Miss Wraxton could not deceive herself into under-rating Sophy's ruinous influence upon Charles's character; and since she was not, in spite of her learning, very wise, she tried to counteract it in a variety of ways that served merely to set up his back. When she enquired whether Sophy had offered him an explanation of her visit to Rundell and Bridge, and, in justice to his cousin, he felt himself obliged to tell her some part of the truth, her evil genius had inspired her to point out to him the total unreliability of Hubert's character, his resemblance to his father, and the ill-judged nature of Sophy's admittedly good-natured conduct in the affair. But Mr Rivenhall was already writhing under the lash of his own conscience, and since, with all his faults, he was not one to burk a clear issue, these remarks found no favour with him. He said: 'I blame myself. That any hasty words of mine should have made Hubert feel that anything would be preferable to confiding his difficulties to me must be an everlasting reproach to me! I have to thank my cousin for showing me how much I have erred! I hope I may do better in the future. I had no intention – but I see now how unsympathetic I must have appeared to him! I'll take good care poor little Theodore does not grow up in the belief that he must at all costs conceal his peccadilloes from me!'

'My dear Charles, I assure you this is an excess of sensibility!' Miss Wraxton said soothingly. '*You* are not to be held accountable for the behaviour of your brothers!'

'You are wrong, Eugenia: I am six years older than Hubert, and since I know – none better! – that my father would never concern himself with any one of us, it was my duty to take care of the younger ones! I do not scruple to say this to you, for you know how we are circumstanced!'

She replied without hesitation: 'I am persuaded you have always done your duty! I have seen how you have tried to introduce into your father's household more exact standards of conduct, a greater notion of discipline, and of management. Hubert can have been in no doubt of your sentiments upon this occasion, and to *condone* his behaviour – which I must think quite shocking! – would be most improper. Miss Stanton-Lacy's intervention, which was, of course, meant in the kindest way, sprang from impulse, and cannot have been dictated by her conscience. Painful though it might have been to her, there can be no doubt that it was her duty to have told you the whole, and immediately! To have paid off Hubert's debts in that fashion was merely to encourage him in his gaming propensities. I fancy that a moment's reflection must have convinced her of this, but, alas, with all her good qualities I fear that Miss Stanton-Lacy is not much given to the indulgence of rational thought!'

He stared at her, an odd expression in his eyes which she was at a loss to interpret. 'If Hubert had confided in you, Eugenia, would you have come to me with his story?' he asked.

'Undoubtedly,' she replied. 'I should not have known an instant's hesitation.'

'Not an instant's hesitation!' he repeated. 'Although it was a confidence made in the belief that you would not betray it?'

She smiled at him. 'That, my dear Charles, is a great piece of nonsense. To be boggling at such a thing as that when one's duty is so plain is what I have no patience with! My concern for your brother's future career must have convinced me that I had no other course open to me than to divulge his wrong-doing to you. Such ruinous tendencies must be checked, and since your father, as you have said, does not concern himself with –'

He interrupted her without apology. 'These sentiments may do honour to your reason, but not to your heart, Eugenia! You are a female: perhaps you do not understand that a confidence reposed in you must – *must!* – be held sacred! I said that I wished she had told me, but it was untrue! I could not wish anyone to betray a confidence! Good God, would I do so myself?'

These rapidly uttered words brought a flush to her cheek; she said sharply: 'I collect that Miss Stanton-Lacy – I presume she is also a female! – does understand this?'

'Yes,' he replied. 'She does. Perhaps that is one of the results of her upbringing! It is an excellent one! Perhaps she knew what must be the result of her action; perhaps she only went to Hubert's rescue from motives of generosity: I don't know that; I have not enquired of her! The outcome has been happy – far happier than would have been the case had she divulged all to me! Hubert is too much of a man to shelter behind his cousin: he confessed the whole to me!'

She smiled. 'I am afraid your partiality makes you a trifle blind, Charles! Once you had discovered that Miss Stanton-Lacy had sold her jewelry you were bound to discover the rest! Had I not been in a position to apprise you of this circumstance, I wonder if Hubert would have confessed?'

He said sternly: 'Such a speech does you no credit! I do not know why you should be so unjust to Hubert, or why you should so continually wish me to think ill of him! I *did* think ill of him, and I have been proved wrong! Mine has been the fault: I treated him as though he were still a child, and I his mentor. I should have done better to have taken him into my counsels. None of this would have happened had he and I been better friends. He said to me, *Had we been better acquainted – !* You may judge of my feelings upon hearing *that* from my brother!' He gave a short laugh. 'A leveller indeed! Jackson himself could not have floored me more completely!'

'I fear,' said Miss Wraxton, at her sweetest, 'that if you mean to use boxing-cant I can never hope to understand you, Charles. No doubt your cousin, with her superior knowledge, would appreciate such language!'

'I should not be at all surprised!' he retorted, nettled.

Not all her training could prevent her saying: 'You seem to cherish an extraordinary regard for Miss Stanton-Lacy!'

'I'! he ejaculated, thunderstruck. 'For Sophy? Good God! I thought my sentiments towards her were sufficiently well-known! I wish to heaven we were rid of her, but I suppose I need not be so prejudiced as to be blind to her good qualities!'

She was mollified. 'No, indeed, and I hope I am not either! What a pity it is that she will not entertain Lord Bromford's suit! He is an excellent man, with a good understanding, and such sobriety of judgment as must, I fancy, exercise a beneficial effect upon any female.' She saw that he was looking at her with a good deal of amusement, and added: 'I had thought that you were inclined to encourage his suit?'

'It is nothing to me whom Sophy marries!' he said. 'She would never take Bromford, though! Well for him!'

'I am afraid Lady Bromford feels as you do,' Miss Wraxton said. 'She and Mama are acquainted, you know, and I have had some conversation with her on this subject. She is a most excellent woman! She has been telling me of the delicacy of Lord Bromford's constitution, and of her fear for him. I could not but feel for her! One cannot but agree with her that your cousin would never make him a good wife!'

'The very worst!' he said, laughing. 'God knows why such a fellow should have taken it into his head to fall in love with Sophy! You may imagine how Cecilia and Hubert roast her over it! As for the tales they make up of his adventures in the West Indies, even my mother has been thrown into whoops! He is the most absurd oddity!'

'I cannot agree with you,' she said. 'And even though I did, I could not listen with anything but pain to a man's sensibility being made a mock of.'

This reproof had the effect of making Mr Rivenhall recollect an engagement in the neighbourhood which necessitated his instant departure. He had never before found himself so little in accord with his betrothed.

On the other hand, never before had he been in such charity with his cousin, a happy state of affairs which lasted for very nearly a week. It inspired him to gratify an expressed wish of hers to see Kemble act. While making no secret of the fact that he found the great player's affections insupportable, his odd mispronunciations ruining his most brilliant histrionic flights, he took a box at Convent Garden, and escorted Sophy there, with Cecilia and Mr Wychbold. Sophy was a trifle disappointed in an actor of whom she had heard so much praise, but the evening passed very agreeably, ending at the fashionable hotel in Henrietta Street, known as the Star. Here, Mr Rivenhall, proving himself to be an excellent host, had ordered a private dining-room, and a most elegant supper. His mood was so amiable as even to preclude his making a slighting remark about Kemble's acting. Mr Wychbold was chatty and obliging; Cecilia in her best looks; and Sophy lively enough to set the ball of conversation rolling gaily at the outset. In fact, Cecilia said, when she later bade her brother good-night, that she had not been so much diverted for months.

'Nor I,' he responded. 'I cannot think why we do not go out more often together, Cilly. Do you suppose our cousin would care to see Karen? I believe he is appearing in a new play at the Lane.'

Cecilia could feel no doubts on this head, but before Mr Rivenhall had had time to put a half-formulated plan into execution he had been forestalled, and the better understanding set up between him and Sophy had begun noticeably to wane. Lord Charlbury, obedient to the commands of his instructress, begged Lady Ombersley to honour him by bringing her daughter and her niece to a little theatre-party of his making. Mr Rivenhall bore up perfectly well under this, but when it leaked out, later, that Mr Fawnhope had made one of the party, his equanimity suffered a severe set-back. Nothing, it seemed, could have excelled the evening's delights! Even Lady Ombersley, who had been decidedly disturbed by the unexpected presence of Mr Fawnhope, succumbed to the combined attentions of her host, and of her old friend, General Retford, who had certainly been invited to entertain her. The play, *Bertram*, was pronounced to have been most affecting; Kean's acting was beyond praise; and quite the most delightful supper-party at the Piazza had wound up the evening. Much of this Mr Rivenhall gathered from his mother, but some of it he had from Cecilia, who was at immense pains to tell him how much she had enjoyed herself. She said that Sophy had been in high spirits, but failed to mention that Sophy's spirits had taken the form of flirtation with her host. Cecilia was naturally glad to find that her rejected suitor was not nursing a broken heart, and almost equally glad to think that she herself had no turn for a form of amusement that showed her otherwise charming cousin in a very poor light. As for Lord Charlbury's volunteering to show Sophy how his father, a sad rake, had been used to take snuff from a lady's wrist, and Sophy's instantly holding out her hand, that, thought Cecilia, was the outside of enough! She was happy to reflect that Augustus would never behave in such an audacious fashion. He had certainly no notion of doing so that evening. The tragedy he had witnessed had fired him with an ambition to write a lyrical drama, and although it would have been impossible to have found fault with his manners as a guest, Cecilia had a strong suspicion that his thoughts were otherwhere.

Bad as this evening had been, there was worse, in Mr Rivenhall's estimation, to follow. Until Lord Charlbury's emergence from a sick-room, Sophy's most frequent cavalier (or, as Mr Rivenhall preferred savagely to dub him, her *cicisbeo*) had been Sir Vincent Talgarth. But Lord Charlbury was soon seen to have supplanted Sir Vincent. He met her on horseback in the Park in the mornings; he was to be observed seated in her phaeton at the hour of the promenade; he stood up with her for two dances at Almack's; took her in his own curricle to a military review; and even acted as her escort on a visit to Merton. His lordship made no secret of the fact that he had enjoyed his expedition enormously, his sense of humour being much tickled by the Marquesa's rich and languorous personality. He told Sophy that he would have been happy to have remained for twice as long in her company. Any lady, he declared, who, overcome by the fatigue of entertaining morning-callers, closed her eyes, and went to sleep under their startled gaze, was something quite out of the ordinary, and worthy of being cultivated. She smiled, and agreed to it, but she was secretly a little dismayed. It had been a shock to her to find Sir Vincent seated with the Marquesa. He had not been her only visitor: the Marquesa's brief sojourn at the Pulteney had drawn to her several gentlemen who had enjoyed her hospitality in Madrid: but he was all too plainly her most assiduous visitor. Major Quinton had been there too, as well as Lord Francis Wolvey, and Mr Fawnhope. Mr Fawnhope's presence was easily explained: he rather thought of writing a tragedy about Don John of Austria, whose brief but glorious career seemed to him eminently suited to lyric drama. He had already composed some moving lines for his hero to utter upon his fevered deathbed, and he thought that the Marquesa might reasonably be expected to be in a position to divulge to him many details of Spanish life and customs that would prove invaluable to him in the writing of his masterpiece. In the event, the Marquesa's knowledge of the customs obtaining in her country in the sixteenth century was considerably less than his own, but she was not to discourage a handsome young man from visiting her, so she smiled sleepily upon him, and invited him to come again, when she had no other company to engage her attention.

Sophy, who had never connected Mr Fawnhope with any manly attribute, was quite surprised to discover that he had ridden out to visit the Marquesa on a pure-bred mare she would not herself have disdained to possess. He rode back to London, behind her phaeton, and handled the pretty, playful creature well, she noticed. She confided to Lord Charlbury that she thought it would be to his advantage if Cecilia were never to see her poet upon a horse.

He sighed. 'Do not think, dear Sophy, that I have not a great deal of pleasure in your society, but where is all this leading me? Do you know, for I do not?'

'I depend upon its leading you just where you would wish to be,' she replied seriously. 'Pray trust me! Cecilia by no means likes to see you dancing attendance on me, I can assure you!'

Cecilia was not the only one to derive no pleasure from this spectacle. Mr Rivenhall, possibly because he still cherished hopes that a match might be made up between Charlbury and his sister, regarded it with the greatest dislike; and Lord Bromford, finding himself quite cut out, developed such a degree of hostility towards his rival as made it almost impossible for him to meet him even with the appearance of complaisance.

'It seems to me a very extraordinary circumstance,' he told his chief sympathizer, 'that a man who has been dangling after one female – as the common phrase runs! – for more weeks than I care to enumerate should be so fickle as to transfer his attentions to another in so short a time! I confess, I have no comprehension of such conduct. Had I, dear Miss Wraxton, not been about the world a little, and learnt something of the frailty of mankind, I must have been totally at a loss! But I do not scruple to tell *you* that I never liked Charlbury about half. *His* conduct does not astonish me. I am only grieved, and I may add, surprised, to see Miss Stanton-Lacy so taken-in!'

'No doubt,' said Miss Wraxton pleasantly, 'a lady who had been used to live upon the Continent must be expected to regard these matters in rather a different light from that in which such poor stay-at-homes as myself must look upon them. I believe that *flirting* is quite a pastime amongst foreign ladies.'

'My dear ma'am,' said his lordship, 'I must tell you that I am by no means an advocate of travel for ladies. It does not seem to me to be a necessary thing for the education of the weaker sex, although for a man I think it to be indispensable. I should not be astonished to learn that Charlbury had never set foot outside this island, which is a circumstance that makes me wonder more than ever at Miss Stanton-Lacy's partiality for his society.'

Lord Bromford's hostility was perfectly well known to its object. Charlbury, cantering along the Row with Sophy, said to her once: 'If I come out of this masquerade with a whole skin I may think myself fortunate! Are you determined I shall be slain, Sophy, you wretch?'

She laughed. 'Bromford?'

'He or Charles. Of the two, I hope it may be he who calls me out. I daresay he cannot hit a haystack at twelve yards, but Rivenhall I know to be a capital shot.'

She turned her head to look at him. 'Do you think so indeed? Charles?'

He returned her look, his own eyes quizzing her. 'Yes, Madam Innocence! Doubtless because of the slight upon his sister! Tell me – you are always frank! – do you make a practice of setting everyone to partners wherever you go?'

'No,' she replied. 'Not unless I am persuaded it would be better for them!'

He laughed and laughed, and was still laughing when they encountered Mr and Miss Rivenhall, riding side by side towards them.

Sophy greeted her cousins with unaffected pleasure, altogether refraining from expressing her surprise at seeing Cecilia indulging in a form of exercise she was not much addicted to. She and Charlbury turned their horses to ride with the Rivenhalls, and she made no objection when, after a little way, Mr Rivenhall obliged her to fall behind the other two, and proceed at a sedate pace down the track. She said: 'I like that bay of yours, Charles.'

'You may like him,' returned Mr Rivenhall disagreeably, 'but you are not going to ride him!'

She cast him a sidelong look, brimful of mischief. 'No, dear Charles?'

'Sophy,' said Mr Rivenhall, descending rapidly from the autocratic to the merely threatening, 'if you dare to have your saddle put upon my Thunderer, I will strangle you, and throw your body into the Serpentine!'

She gave the gurgle of laughter that never failed to bring his twisted grin into being. 'Oh, no, Charles, would you indeed? Well, I do not blame you! If ever I find you astride Salamanca, I shall certainly shoot you – and *I* can make allowance for a gun that throws a little left!'

'Yes?' said Mr Rivenhall. 'Well, my dear cousin, when we go down to Ombersley I shall derive much satisfaction from watching your marksmanship! You shall show me what you can do with my duelling pistols. They do not throw left, or even right: I am rather nice in the choice of my weapons!'

'Duelling pistols!' said Sophy, much impressed. 'I had not thought it of you, Charles! How many times have you been *out*? Do you always kill your man?'

'Rarely!' he retorted. 'Duelling has gone sadly out of fashion, dear Sophy! I am so sorry to be obliged to disappoint you!'

'No,' she said, shaking her head. 'I had no *real* expection of hearing that you had done anything so dashing!'

That made him laugh. He flung up a hand, in the gesture of a swordsman acknowledging a hit. 'Very well, Sophy! *Touché!*'

'Do you fence?'

'Indifferently. Why?'

'Oh, merely that it is something I have never learnt!'

'Good God, how is this! I had thought Sir Horace *must* have taught you how to handle a small-sword!'

'No,' said Sophy, making her mouth prim. 'And he has not taught me how to box either, so there are two things, Charles, which you must be able to do better than I can!'

'You quite outstrip me,' he agreed suavely. 'Particularly in the art of dalliance!'

She instantly disconcerted him by making an attack direct. 'Dalliance, Charles? You do not, I hope, accuse me of *flirting*?'

'Do I not?' he said grimly. 'Enlighten me, I beg, on the nature of your dealings with Charlbury!'

She showed him an innocent face. 'But, Charles, how is this? Surely I could not be mistaken! All is at an end between him and Cecilia! You cannot suppose it possible that I would encourage his advances if that were not so!'

The bay horse broke into a canter, and was checked. Mr Rivenhall said furiously: 'Foolery! Don't try to humbug me, Sophy! Charlbury and you – ! Why, what a gull you must think me!'

'Oh, no!' Sophy assured him soulfully. 'But there is nothing I would not do to oblige Sir Horace, and I would far rather marry Charlbury than Bromford!'

'It sometimes seems to me,' said Mr Rivenhall, 'that *delicacy* is a virtue utterly unknown to you!'

'Yes, tell me about it!' she said, with immense cordiality.

He did not avail himself of this invitation, but said in a biting tone: 'I should warn you, perhaps, that Charlbury's determined pursuit is fast making you the talk of the town. Whether you care a button for that I know not, but since my mother is responsible for you I must own that I should be grateful to you if you would behave with a little more discretion!'

'You told me once before of something else I could do if ever I should wish to please you,' remarked Sophy thoughtfully. 'I must say, I hope I never shall wish to, for, try as I may, I *cannot* recall what it was!'

'You have been determined, have you not, to make me dislike you, from the very day we met?' he shot at her.

'Not at all: you did so without the least encouragement!'

He rode beside her in silence for moments, saying at last, in a stiff voice: 'You are mistaken. I do not dislike you. That is to say, there have been many times when I have liked you very well. Nor need you imagine that I forget how much I stand in your debt.'

She interrupted him. 'You do not! Let me hear no more of that, if you please! Tell me about Hubert! I heard you tell my aunt that you had received a letter from him. Is he well?'

'Perfectly, I imagine. He only wrote to desire me to send him a book he had left behind.' He grinned suddenly. 'And to tell me of his determination to attend all his lectures! If I did not think that *that* resolution must fail, I would post up to Oxford immediately! Such virtue could only end in his seeking relief in the most shocking excesses. Let me say one thing to you, Sophy! I have never said it: we were interrupted before I could do so, and I have never found the opportunity since! I must always be grateful to you for showing me, as you did, how much at fault I had been in my dealings with Hubert.'

'That is nonsense, but I could show you, if you would permit me, how much at fault you are in your dealings with Cecilia!' she said.

His face hardened. 'Thank God! On that subject we are not likely to agree!'

She said no more, but allowed Salamanca to break into a canter, and to overtake Lord Charlbury and Cecilia.

She found them conversing comfortably, the constraint Cecilia had felt upon finding herself obliged to ride alone in his company having been speedily banished by the friendly ease of his manners. Neither by word nor by look did he remind her of what lay between them, but began to talk to her at once on some unexceptionable subject that he knew would interest her. This made a pleasant change for her, Mr Fawnhope's conversation being, at present, almost wholly confined to the scope and structure of his great tragedy. To listen to a poet arguing with himself – for she could scarcely have been said to have borne any part in the discussion – on the merits of blank verse as a dramatic medium was naturally a privilege of which any young lady must be proud, but there could be no denying that to talk for half an hour to a man who listened with interest to anything she said was, if not precisely a relief, certainly a welcome variation in her life. Not for nothing had his lordship endured the world for ten more years than his youthful rival. Mr Fawnhope's handsome face and engaging smile might dazzle the female eye, but Mr Fawnhope had not yet learnt the art of conveying to a lady the gratifying impression that he considered her a fragile creature, to be cherished, and in every way considered. Lord Charlbury might be constitutionally incapable of addressing her as Nymph, or of comparing bluebells unfavourably with her eyes, but Lord Charlbury would infallibly provide a cloak for her if the weather were inclement, lift her over obstacles she could well climb without assistance, and in every way convince her that in his eyes she was a precious being whom it was impossible to guard too carefully.

It would have been too much to have said that Cecilia was regretting her rejection of his lordship's suit, but when Sophy and Charles joined her she was certainly conscious of a faint feeling of dissatisfaction at having her tête-à-tête interrupted.

She tried to discuss the matter in a dispassionate way with Sophy, later, but found it curiously hard to utter any of the sentiments she had persuaded herself she felt. Finally, she bent her head over a piece of embroidery, and asked her cousin whether Lord Charlbury had yet offered for her.

Sophy laughed at this. 'Good God, no, you goose! Charlbury has no serious intentions towards me.'

Cecilia kept her eyes lowered. 'Indeed? I should have said that he showed the most decided partiality for you.'

'My dear Cecy, I would not tease you by adverting to this subject, but I am persuaded that what Charlbury wears on his sleeve is not his heart. I should not wonder at it if he were to end his days a bachelor.'

'I do not think it,' said Cecilia, snipping her silk. 'And nor, I fancy, do you, Sophy. He will offer for you, and – and I hope you will accept him, because if one were not in love with another I cannot imagine any gentleman one would prefer to him.'

'Well, we shall see!' was all Sophy would say.

Fourteen

The notion of writing a tragedy having taken strong possession of Mr Fawnhope's mind, he appeared to banish from it any immediate plan for seeking remunerative employment. On several occasions he arrived in Berkeley Square, quite impervious to Mr Rivenhall's brutal snubs, carrying in his pocket the latest instalment of his play, which he read to Cecilia and to Sophy, and once even to Lady Ombersley, who complained afterwards that she had not understood a word of it. He seemed to spend a good many afternoons at Merton as well, but when Sophy questioned him about Sancia's other guests he could never remember with any clarity who had been present. But Sir Vincent, when he came to call in Berkeley Square, made no secret of the fact that he was very often at Merton. Sophy a blunt creature, told him roundly that she mistrusted him, and would thank him to remember that Sancia was betrothed to Sir Horace.

Sir Vincent laughed gently, and pinched her chin, holding it an instant too long, and tilting up her face. 'Will you, Sophy?' he said, quizzing her. 'But when I offered to run in your harness you would have none of me! Be reasonable, Juno! If you reject me, you cannot expect me to respond docilely to your hand on my rein!'

She put up her hand to grasp his wrist. 'Sir Vincent, you shall not serve Sir Horace a backhanded turn!' she said.

'Why not?' he asked coolly. 'Do you think he would not do the same to me? You are such a splendid innocent, adorable Juno?!'

Since Mr Rivenhall chose this inauspicious moment to walk

into the drawing-room Sophy was unable to say more. Without embarrassment, Sir Vincent released her, and moved forward to greet his host. His reception was frosty; he was given no encouragement to prolong his visit; and no sooner had he taken leave, and parted, than Mr Rivenhall gave his cousin, without reserve, the benefit of his opinion of her behaviour in encouraging a notorious rake to practise familiarities with her. Sophy listened to him with an air of great interest, but if he had hoped to abash her he was disappointed, for all she said in reply was: 'I think your scolds are capital, Charles, for you are never at a loss for a word! But would you call me an *incorrigible* flirt!'

'Yes, I would! You encourage every scarlet coat you have ever met to haunt the house! You set the town talking with your shameless conduct in keeping Charlbury dangling after you, and not content with that you allow a fellow like Talgarth to behave to you as though you had been an inn-servant!'

She opened her eyes at him. '*Charles!* is that what you do? pinch their chins? Well, I was never more astonished1 I don't think you should!'

'Don't try my temper too far, Sophy!' he said dangerously. 'If you knew how my hands itch to box your ears, you would take care!'

'Oh, I am sure you never would!' she said, smiling. 'You know Sir Horace did not teach me how to box, and how unfair it would be! Besides, why should you care a button what I do? I am not one of your sisters!'

'Thank God for it!'

'Yes, indeed, for you are the horridest brother, you know! Do stop making a cake of yourself! Sir Vincent is a sad case, but he would never do me any harm, I assure you. *That* would be quite against his code, for he knew me when I was a little girl, and he is a friend of Sir Horace's. I must say, he is the oddest creature! Sancia, it is perfectly plain, he does not hold to be in the least sacred.' Her brow creased. 'I am much afraid of what he may do in that direction. I wonder if I ought to say I will marry him after all?'

'What!' exclaimed Mr Rivenhall. 'Marry that fellow? Not while you are under this roof!'

'Yes, but I cannot help thinking that perhaps I owe it to Sir Horace,' she explained. 'I own, it would be a sacrifice, but I am sure he trusts me to take care of Sancia while he is away, and I don't at all perceive how I am to prevent Sir Vincent from stealing her affections, unless I marry him myself. He has so much address, you know!'

'You appear to me,' said Mr Rivenhall scathingly, 'to have taken leave of your senses! You will scarcely expect me to believe that you would entertain the thought of marriage with that man!'

'But, Charles, I find you most unreasonable!' she pointed out. 'Not a week ago you said that the sooner I was married and out of this house the better pleased you would be, but when I said perhaps I might marry Charlbury you flew into a passion, and now you will not hear of poor Sir Vincent either!'

Mr Rivenhall made no attempt to answer this. He merely cast a darkling glance at his cousin, and said: 'Only one thing could surprise me, and that would be to learn that Talgarth had offered for you!'

'Well, you must be surprised,' said Sophy placidly, 'because he has done so a score of times. It is become a habit with him, I think. But I know what you mean, and you are right: he would be very much disconcerted if I took him at his word. I might, of course, become engaged to him, and cry off when Sir Horace returns, but it seems rather a shabby thing to do, don't you think?'

'Extremely so!'

She sighed. 'Yes, and he is so clever that I daresay he would guess what I was about. I might, I suppose, remove to Merton, and that would certainly make it awkward for Sir Vincent. But Sancia would not like that at all, I fear.'

'She has my sympathy!'

Sophy looked at him. Under his amazed and horrified gaze, large tears slowly welled over her eyelids, and rolled down her cheeks. She did not sniff, or gulp, or even sob: merely allowed her tears to gather and fall.

'*Sophy!*' ejaculated Mr Rivenhall, visibly shaken. He took an involuntary step towards her, checked himself, and said, rather disjointedly: 'Pray do not! I did not mean – I had no intention – You know how it is with me! I say more than I mean, when – Sophy, for God's sake do not cry!'

'Oh, do not stop me!' begged Sophy. 'Sir Horace says it is my *only* accomplishment!'

Mr Rivenhall glared at her. '*What!*'

Very few persons are able to do it!' Sophy assured him. 'I discovered it by the veriest accident when I was only seven years old. Sir Horace said I should cultivate it, for I should find it most useful.'

'You – you –' Words failed Mr Rivenhall. 'Stop at once!'

'Oh, I have stopped!' said Sophy, carefully wiping the drops away. 'I cannot continue if I don't keep sad thoughts in my mind, such as you saying unkind things to me, or –'

'I do not believe you felt the slightest inclination to cry!' declared Mr Rivenhall roundly. 'You did it only to set me at a disadvantage! You are, without exception, the most abominable, shameless – Don't start again!'

She laughed. 'Very well, but if I am so horrid, perhaps it would be better for me to go to stay with Sancia.'

'Understand this! said Mr Rivenhall. 'My uncle left you expressly to my mother's care, and in this you will remain until such time as he returns to England! As for these nonsensical notions about the Marquesa, *you* are not to be held responsible for anything she may choose to do!'

'Where the well-being of the persons to whom one is attached is concerned, one cannot say that one is not responsible,' said Sophy simply. 'One should make a push to be of service. Yet I do not perceive what I should do in this event. I wish it had been possible for Sancia to have stayed in Sir Horace's own house!'

'At Ashtead? How should that serve?'

'It is not so near to town,' she pointed out.

'Sixteen or seventeen miles only, I daresay!'

'More than twice as far away as Merton, however. But it is useless to repine over that. Sir Horace says the place is in disrepair, quite unfit to live in. He means to set it all to rights when he comes back to England. I only wish it may not be too late!'

'Why should it be too late?' asked Mr Rivenhall, wilfully misunderstanding her. 'I assume Lacy Manor does not stand entirely empty! Does not my uncle leave some servants in charge?'

'Only the Claverings, and, I suppose, a man to look after the gardens, and the farm. But that, you know very well, is not what I meant!'

'If you take my advice,' said Mr Rivenhall, 'you will not meddle in the Marquesa's affairs!' He added caustically: 'Or in anyone else's! – And spare yourself the trouble of telling me that you do not mean to take my advice, for that I know already!'

Sophy folded her hands in her lap, and began to twiddle her thumbs, so absurd an expression of docility on her face that he was obliged to smile.

But as the season advanced he smiled less and less frequently. Since she had not yet been presented at Court, Sophy was not invited to the Regent's grand fête at Carlton House, but there was scarcely another society event which she did not grace. In honour bound, Mr Rivenhall accompanied his mother and her two charges to many of these functions, but as he was obliged to spend a considerable part of his time watching his sister dancing with Mr Fawnhope, and his cousin flirting outrageously with Charlbury, it was scarcely surprising that he should have been goaded into saying that he would be thankful when July saw the Ombersley household safely bestowed at Ombersley Court. He also expressed the wish that Sophy would choose between her various suitors, so that he might one day return to a house empty of visitors. Miss Wraxton said hopefully that perhaps Sir Horace would not be much longer absent from England, but as the one letter so far received from this erratic gentleman had not mentioned any prospect of a speedy return from Brazil, he was unable to set much store by this.

'If,' said Miss Wraxton, casting down her eyes in pretty bashfulness, 'she should still be with dear Lady Ombersley in September, Charles, I think I must beg her to be one of my bridesmaids. It would be only civil!'

He agreed to it, but only after a moment's pause. 'I trust that by then my uncle may have returned. God knows what mischief she will find to plague me – us – with at Ombersley, but no doubt she will discover something!'

But when July came there was no question of Ombersley. Mr Rivenhall, fulfilling an old promise, took his three younger sisters to Astley's Amphitheatre to celebrate Gertrude's birthday, and within a week of this dissipation Dr Baillie had been called in to prescribe for Amabel.

She had begun to show signs of ill-health almost at once, and although the doctor repeatedly assured Mr Rivenhall later, that there was no saying where she might have contracted fever, he continued obstinately to blame himself. It was evident, that the little girl was very ill, her head aching continually, her feverishness increasing alarmingly at night. The dread spectre of typhus raised its head, and not all Dr Baillie's assurances that Amabel's complaint was a milder form of this scourge, neither so infectious nor so dangerous, could allay Lady Ombersley's fears. Miss Adderbury, with Selina and Gertrude, was sent off incontinent to Ombersley; and Hubert, staying for the first few weeks of the Long Vacation with relatives in Yorkshire, warned by express not to venture near Berkeley Square until all danger should be past. Lady Ombersley would have banished Cecilia and Sophy too could she have prevailed upon either of them to have listened to her prayers, but they were adamant. Sophy said that she had had much experience of far deadlier fevers than Amabel's, and had never caught any worse infection than the measles; and Cecilia, hanging affectionately over her mother, told her that nothing short of force would detach her from her side. Poor Lady Ombersley could only cling to her, and weep. Her constitution was not strong enough to enable her to support with fortitude the illnesses of her children. With all the wish in the world to tend Amabel with her own hands, she could not bear the sight of the child's discomfort. Her sensibility overcame her resolution; the very sight of the hectic flush on Amabel's cheeks brought on one of her worst spasms, so that Cecilia had to help her from the sickroom to her own bed, and to send her maid to beg Dr Baillie to visit her before he should leave the house. Lady Ombersley could not forget the tragic death under similar circumstances, of the little daughter who had followed Maria into the world, and from the start of Amabel's illness abandoned hope of her recovery.

It was felt to be unfortunate that Mr Rivenhall should also have gone to stay with his aunt in Yorkshire, for his presence always exercised a calming effect upon his mother in times of stress; and Amabel, as the fever waxed, often cried for Charles to come to her. It was hoped that a man's voice might soothe her, so her father was introduced into her room, and tried clumsily to coax her into rationality. He was not afraid of infection, the doctor having told him that it was rare for an adult person to contract the disease, but although he was much affected by the sight of his little daughter's condition, he had never paid much attention to his children, and now failed to quiet her. Indeed, his tears flowed so freely that he was obliged to leave the room.

Dr Baillie, dubiously eyeing old Nurse, shook his head and sent Mrs Pebworth to Berkeley Square. Mrs Pebworth, a voluminous female, with a watery eye, and mountainous bonnet, smiled fondly upon the two young ladies who received her, and bade them, in a husky voice, to have no fears, since the little dear would be safe in her charge. Within twelve hours of her arrival, she was addressing vituperative remarks to the closed door of the mansion, having been, at the orders of Miss Stanton-Lacy, shown off the premises by the redoubtable Jane Storridge. A nurse, Sophy bluntly informed Dr Baillie, who refreshed herself continually from a square bottle, and slept the night through in a chair by the fire while her patient tossed and moaned, they could well dispense with. So, when Mr Rivenhall, posting south immediately on receipt of the tidings from London, arrived in Berkeley Square, it was to find his mother suffering from nervous palpitations, his father seeking relief at White's or Wattier's, his sister snatching an hour's sleep on her bed, and his cousin in command of the sickroom.

When trouble descended upon the household, Lady Ombersley forgot all Charles's disagreeable ways, and was much inclined to think him her only support. Her joy at seeing him walk into her dressing-room was only alloyed by her fear that he might catch the typhoid. She was reclining on the sofa, but heaved herself up to cast her arms about his neck, exclaiming: 'Charles! Oh, my dear son, thank God you are come! It is so terrible, and I know she will be taken from me, like my poor little Clara!'

A burst of tears ended this speech, and for some minutes he was fully occupied in soothing the agitation of her spirits. When she was calmer, he ventured to question her on the nature of Amabel's complaint. Her replies were disjointed, but she said enough to convince him that the case was desperate, and the illness contracted perhaps at Astley's amphitheatre. He was so much appalled that he could say nothing for several moments, but got up abruptly from the chair by the sofa, and strode over to stare out of the window. His mother, wiping her eyes, said: 'If only I were not so wretchedly weak! You know, Charles, how I must long to be beside my child! But the sight of her, so wasted, so flushed, brings on my worst palpitations, and if she recognizes me at all she cannot help but be distressed! They will scarcely allow me to enter the room!'

'It is not fit for you,' he said mechanically. 'Who nurses her? Is Addy here?'

'No, no, Dr Baillie thought it wiser to send the other children off to Ombersley! He sent us a dreadful creature – at least, I never saw her, but Cecilia said she was a drunken wretch! – and Sophy sent her packing. Old Nurse is in charge, and you know how she is to be trusted! And the girls help her, so that Dr Baillie assures me I need feel no uneasiness on that head. He says that dearest Sophy is a capital sick-nurse, and that the disease is running its proper course, but oh, Charles, I cannot persuade myself that she will be spared!'

He came back to her side at once, and devoted himself to the task of comforting her alarms with more patience than might have been expected in one of his hasty temper. When he could escape, he did so, and went upstairs to find his sister. She had just got up from her bed, and was coming out of her room as he reached the landing. She was looking pale, and tired, but her face lit up at sight of him, and she exclaimed in a hushed voice: 'Charles! I knew we might depend upon your coming! Have you been to my mother? She has felt the need of your presence so much!'

'I have this instant come from her dressing-room. Cilly, Cilly, she tells me Amabel began to ail within a few days of that accursed evening at Astley's!'

'Hush! Come into my room! Amabel is in the Blue Spare-room, and you must not talk so loud just here! We thought that too, but Dr Baillie says it could hardly be so. Recollect that the other two are well! Addy sent up word only yesterday.' She softly closed the door of her bedroom. 'I must not stay above a minute: Mama will be needing me.'

'My poor girl, you look fagged to death!'

'No, no, I am not! Why, there is hardly anything that I do, so that it chafes me dreadfully sometimes, when I see Sophy and that good, kind maid of hers carrying all the burden on their shoulders! For Nurse is growing too old to be able to manage, you know, and it affects her sadly to see poor little Amabel so uncomfortable. But if one of us is not continually with Mama she frets herself into one of her spasms – you know her way! But now you are here you will relieve me of that duty!' She smiled, and pressed his hand. 'I never thought to be so glad to see anyone! Amabel too! She so often calls for you, and wonders where you can be! If I had not known that you would come, I must have sent for you! You are not afraid of infection?' He made an impatient gesture. 'No, I was sure you would not think of that. Sophy is out walking – Dr Baillie impresses on us the need for exercise in the fresh air, and we are very obedient, I assure you! Nurse sits with Amabel during the afternoon.'

'May I see her! It would not agitate her?'

'No, indeed! It must soothe her, I believe. If she is awake, and – and herself, would you care to come to her room now? You will find her wretchedly altered, poor little thing!'

She led him to the sickroom, and went softly in. Amabel was restless, and very hot, fretfully rejecting any suggestions for her relief, but when she saw her favourite brother her heavy eyes brightened perceptibly, and a faint smile came into her little flushed face. She held out her hand, and he took it, and spoke gently and cheerfully to her, in a way that seemed to do her good. She did not wish to let him go, but at a sign from Cecilia he disengaged his hand from the feeble clutch on it, promising to come back again presently if Amabel would be a good girl, and swallow the medicine Nurse had ready for her.

He was a good deal shocked by her appearance, and found it difficult to believe Cecilia's assurance that when the fever had passed the patient would speedily recover her lost weight. Nor could he feel that old Nurse was competent to have the command of a sickroom. Cecilia agreed to this, but comforted him by saying that it was Sophy who was in command.

'Dr Baillie says that no one could manage better, and, indeed, Charles, you would not doubt it could you but see how good Amabel is with her! She has such resolution, such firmness! Poor Nurse does not like to force the little dear to do what she does not wish to, and then, too, she had old-fashioned notions that will not do for Dr Baillie. But our cousin, he says, may be trusted to obey his directions implicitly. Oh, you could not wrest her away from Amabel! It would be fatal, for she frets if Sophy is too long absent from her room.'

'We are very much obliged to Sophy,' he said. 'But it is not right that she should be doing such work! Setting aside the risk of infection, she did not come to us to act as sick-nurse!'

'No,' Cecilia said. 'She did not, of course, but – but – I don't know how it is, but she seems to be so much a part of our family that one does not consider such things as that!'

He was silent, and she left him, saying that she must go to their mother. When, later, he saw Sophy, and attempted to remonstrate with her, she cut him very short.

'I am delighted you are come home, my dear Charles, for nothing could do Amabel more good. Your poor Mama, too, needs the support of your presence. But if you mean to talk in that nonsensical style I shall soon be wishing you a thousand miles off!'

'You have your own engagements,' he persisted. 'I daresay I must have seen as many as a dozen cards of invitation on the mantelpiece in the Yellow Saloon! I cannot think it right that you should forgo all your amusements for the sake of my little sister!'

Her eyes laughed at him. 'No, indeed! What a shocking thing that I should be obliged to forgo a few balls! How shall I survive it, I wonder? How delightful it would be in me to be demanding my aunt's chaperonage at parties with the house in this upset! Now, pray do not let me hear any more on this head, but instead of vexing yourself with such absurdities, try what you may do to divert my aunt's mind! You know her nervous disposition, and how the least thing upsets her constitution! The charge of keeping her soothed and calm falls upon poor Cecy, for your Papa, if you will not be offended with me for saying so, is not of the smallest use in such a crisis at this!'

'I know it,' he responded. 'I will do what I may: I can well imagine how arduous a task Cecilia finds it. Indeed, I was shocked to see her looking so fagged!' He hesitated, and then said, a little stiffly: 'Miss Wraxton, perhaps, might be of service there. I would not suggest her entertaining Amabel's room, but I am sure, if she would sit with my mother sometimes it must be of benefit! The tone of her mind is such that –' He broke off, perceiving a change in his cousin's expression and said with some asperity: 'I am aware that you dislike Miss Wraxton, but even you will allow that her calm good sense must be of value in this predicament!'

'My dear Charles, do not eat me! I have no doubt it is just as you say!' Sophy replied. 'Try if she will come to this house!'

More she would not say, but it was not long before Mr Rivenhall had discovered that his betrothed, while sympathizing most sincerely with his family on their affliction, had no intention of exposing her person to the dangers of infection. She told him, clasping his hand fondly, that her Mama had most expressly forbidden her to enter the house until all danger should be past. It was true: Lady Brinklow herself told Mr Rivenhall so. Upon learning that he had had the imprudence to visit Amabel, she became visibly alarmed, and begged him not to repeat the visit. Miss Wraxton added the weight of her own counsel. 'Indeed, Charles, it is not wise! There can be no need for you to run such a risk, moreover. Gentlemen in sickrooms are quite out of place!'

'Are you afraid that I may take the disease, and convey it to you?' he asked, in his blunt way. 'I beg your pardon! I should not have come to call upon you! I will not do so again until Amabel is well.'

Lady Brinklow hailed this decision with obvious relief, but it was going too far for her daughter, who at once assured Mr Rivenhall that he was talking nonsense, and must always be a welcome caller in Brook Street. He thanked her, but took his leave of her almost immediately.

His opinion of her was not improved by finding, upon his return to Berkeley Square, that Lord Charlbury was sitting with his mother. It soon transpired that he was a regular visitor to the house, and, whatever his motive might be, Mr Rivenhall could not but honour him for his indifference to the danger of infection.

Another regular called was Mr Fawnhope, but since his only object in coming was to see Cecilia, Mr Rivenhall was easily able to refrain from succumbing to any feelings of gratitude towards him for his intrepid visits. But Cecilia was looking so worn and anxious that, with rare restraint, he curbed his bitter tongue, and made no reference whatsoever to her lover's frequent presence in the house.

Had he but known it, Mr Fawnhope's visits were affording Cecilia quite as little pleasure as he could have desired. It was midway through the second week of Amabel's illness, and that she was very seriously unwell Dr Baillie did not waste his time denying to her nurses. Cecilia had no inclination towards any form of dalliance, and no interest in poetic drama. She carried up to the sickroom a remarkably fine bunch of grapes, saying in a low tone to Sophy that Lord Charlbury had brought them for Amabel, having sent all the way to his country seat for them. He was said to possess some of the finest succession-houses in the country, besides a pinery which, he promised, should yield the best of its fruits to Amabel, as soon as they should become ripe enough to be eaten.

'How very kind! said Sophy, setting the dish upon a table. 'I did not know Charlbury had called: I had thought it was Augustus.'

'They were both here,' Cecilia replied. 'Augustus wished to give me a poem he has written, on a sick child.'

Her tone was non-committal. Sophy said: 'Dear me! I mean, how charming! Was it pretty?'

'I daresay it may have been. I find I do not care for poems on such a subject,' Cecilia said quietly.

Sophy said nothing. After a moment, Cecilia added: 'Although it was impossible for me to return Lord Charlbury's regard, I must always be sensible of the delicacy of his behaviour, and the extreme kindness he has shown us in our trouble. I – I wish you may be brought to reward him, Sophy! You are in general above-stairs, and so cannot know the many hours he has spent with my mother, talking to her, and playing at backgammon with her, only, I am persuaded, to relieve us a little of that duty.'

Sophy could not help smiling at this. 'Not to relieve me, Cecy, for he must know that the care of my aunt does not fall upon me!

If a compliment is intended, you must certainly take it to yourself.'

'No, no, it is mere goodness of heart! That he has an ulterior motive I will not credit.' She smiled, and added quizzingly: 'I could wish that your *other* beau would do half as much!'

'Bromford? Do not tell me he has ventured within a hundred paces of the house! I should certainly not believe you!'

'No, indeed! And I have it from Charles that he avoids him as though he too were infected. Charles makes a jest of it, but Eugenia's conduct he does not mention.'

'It would be too much to expect of him.'

A movement from the bed put an end to the conversation, nor was the subject again referred to by the cousins. Amabel's illness, reaching its climax, banished all other thoughts from their heads. For several days, the gravest fears possessed the minds of all those who continually saw the invalid; and old Nurse, obstinately refusing to believe in new-fangled diseases, brought on one of Lady Ombersley's worst attacks of nervous spasms by confiding in her that she had recognized the complaint from the start as being typhus. It took the combined exertions of Lady Ombersley's son, daughter, and physician to disabuse her mind of this hideous conviction; while his lordship, to whom she had communicated it, sought relief in the only way that seemed to him possible, and, in consequence, not only had to be escorted home from his club, but suffered so severe a recrudescence of his gout that he was unable to leave his room for several days afterwards.

But Amabel survived the crisis. The fever began to abate; and although its ravages left her listless and emaciated, Dr Baillie was able to assure her mother that, provided that there was no relapse, he now entertained reasonable hopes of her complete recovery. He handsomely gave Sophy much of the credit for the improvement in the little girl's condition; and Lady Ombersley, shedding tears, said that she shuddered to think where they would any of them have been without her dearest niece.

'Well, well, she is a very capable young lady, and so too is Miss

Rivenhall,' said the doctor. 'While *they* are with Miss Amabel you may be easy, ma'am!'

Mr Fawnhope, ushered into the room five minutes later, was the first recipient of the glad tidings, and instantly dashed off a little lyric in commemoration of Amabel's emergence from danger. Lady Ombersley thought it particularly touching, and begged to be given a copy; but since it dealt more with the pretty picture of Cecilia bending over the sickbed than with Amabel's sufferings it quite failed to please the person for whom it was intended. With far more gratitude did Cecilia receive an exquisite bouquet of flowers brought by Lord Charlbury for her small sister. She saw him only to thank him. He did not importune her to remain in his company, but said, upon her excusing herself immediately: 'Indeed I understand! I had not hoped to have been granted even a minute of your time. It was like you to have come downstairs. If only I could be sure that I have not interrupted your too hard-earned rest!'

'No, no!' she said, scarcely able to command her voice. 'I was sitting with my sister, and when your flowers were brought up to her room I could not help but run down to tell you of her delight in them. Too good, too kind! Forgive me! I must not stay!'

It had been hoped that when the invalid began to mend the constant attendance on her of her sister or her cousin might become less necessary, but it was soon found that she was too weak to be patient, and became fretful if left for too long in the care of Nurse or Jane Storridge. Mr Rivenhall, softly entering the sickroom one evening shortly after midnight, was shocked to discover not Nurse but Sophy seated by the small fire that was kept burning in the grate. She was sewing by the light of a branch of candles, but she looked up when the door opened, and smiled, and laid a finger to her lips. A screen was drawn between the candles and the bed, so that Mr Rivenhall could only dimly perceive his sister. She seemed to be sleeping. He closed the door soundlessly, and trod over to the fire, whispering: 'I understood Nurse was to sit up with her at night. How is this? It is not fit for you, Sophy!'

She glanced at the clock on the mantelpiece, and began to fold up her work. Nodding towards the door that stood ajar into the dressing-room, she replied in a low tone: 'Nurse is laid down upon the sofa there. Poor soul, she is knocked-up! Amabel is very restless tonight – has been so all day. Don't be alarmed! It is an excellent sign when a patient becomes peevish, and hard to manage. But she has been so much in the habit of getting her own way with Nurse that she will not mind her as she should. Sit down: I am going to heat some milk for her to drink, and, if you will, you may coax her to do so when she wakes.'

'You must be tired to death!' he said.

'No, not at all: I was asleep all the afternoon,' she returned, setting a small saucepan on the hob. 'Like the Duke, I can sleep at any hour! Poor Cecy can never get a wink during the day, so we have decided that she must not attempt to sit up at night.'

'You mean that you have decided it,' he said.

She only smiled and shook her head. He said no more, but sat watching her as she knelt by the fire, her attention on the milk slowly heating on the hob. After a few minutes, Amabel began to stir. Almost before her feeble, plaintive cry of 'Sophy!' had been uttered, Sophy had risen to her feet, and moved to the bedside. Amabel was hot, thirsty, uncomfortable, and disinclined to believe that anything could do her good. To be raised, so that her pillows could be shaken and turned, made her cry; she wanted Sophy to bathe her forehead, but complained that the lavender-water stung her eyes when she did so.

'Hush, you will shock your visitor if you cry!' Sophy said, smoothing her tangled curls. 'Do you know there is a gentleman come to see you?'

'Charles?' Amabel asked, forgetting her woes for a moment.

'Yes, Charles, so you must let me tidy you a little, and straighten the sheets. There! Now, Charles, Miss Rivenhall will be pleased to receive you!'

She removed the screen, so that the candlelight fell on the bed, and nodded to Charles to sit down beside his sister. He did so, holding the claw-like little hand in his, and talking to the child in a cheerful way that succeeded in diverting her until Sophy brought a cup of milk to the bedside. The sight of this at once made her peevish. She wanted nothing; it would make her sick to swallow any milk; why would not Sophy leave her in peace?

'I hope you don't mean to be so unkind as to refuse it, when I have come especially to hold the cup for you,' Charles said, taking it from his cousin. 'A cup with roses on it, too! Now, where had you this! I am sure I do not recognize it!'

'Cecilia gave it to me for my very own,' Amabel replied. 'But I don't wish for any milk. It is the middle of the night, not the proper time for drinking milk!'

'I hope Charles has admired your real roses,' said Sophy, sitting down on the edge of the bed, and raising Amabel to rest against her shoulder. 'We are so jealous, Charles, Cecy and I! Amabel has such a fine beau that we are cast quite into the shade. Only look at the bouquet he brought her!'

'Charlbury!' he said, smiling.

'Yes, but I like your posy best,' Amabel said.

'Of course you do,' said Sophy. 'So take a sip of the milk he is offering you! I must tell you that a gentleman's feelings are very easily wounded, my dear, and *that*, you know, would never do!'

'Very true,' Charles corroborated. 'I shall be thinking that you have a greater regard for Charlbury than for me, and that will very likely make me fall into a melancholy.'

That made her laugh weakly, and so, between nonsense and coaxing, she was persuaded to drink nearly all the milk. Sophy laid her gently down again, but nothing would do but that both Charles and Sophy should stay beside her.

'Yes, but no more talking,' Sophy said. 'I am going to tell you about another of my adventures, and if your interrupt me I shall lose the thread.'

'Oh, yes, tell about the time you were lost in the Pyrenees!' begged Amabel drowsily.

Sophy did so, her voice sinking as the little girl's eyelids began to droop. Mr Rivenhall sat still and silent on the other side of the bed, watching his sister. Presently Amabel's deeper breathing

246

betrayed that she slept. Sophy's voice ceased; she looked up, and met Mr Rivenhall's eyes. He was staring at her, as though a thought, blinding in its novelty, had occurred to him. Her gaze remained steady, a little questioning. He rose abruptly, half-stretched out his hand, but let it fall again, and, turning, went quickly out of the room.

Fifteen

pon the following day, Sophy did not encounter her cousin. He visited Amabel at an hour when he knew Sophy to be resting, and was not at home to dinner. Lady Ombersley feared that something had occurred to vex him, for although his manner towards her was unfailingly patient, and he abated none of his solicitude for her comfort, his brow was clouded, and he replied to many of her remarks quite at random. He submitted, however, to the penance of a hand at cribbage with her; and when the game was interrupted by the arrival of Mr Fawnhope, with a copy of his poem for Lady Ombersley, and a posy of moss-roses for Cecilia, he was sufficiently master of himself to greet the visitor, if not with enthusiasm, at least with civility.

Mr Fawnhope, having written some thirty lines of his tragedy the previous day, with which he was not dissatisfied, was in a complaisant humour, neither chasing an elusive epithet, nor brooding over an infelicitous line. He said everything that was proper, and, when all enquiries into the invalid's condition were exhausted, conversed on various topics so much like a sensible man that Mr Rivenhall found himself quite in charity with him, and was only driven from the room by Lady Ombersley's request to the poet to read aloud to her his lyric on Amabels' deliverance from danger. Even this abominable affectation could not wholly dissipate the kindlier feelings with which he regarded Mr Fawnhope, whose continued visits to the house gave him a better opinion of the poet than was at all deserved. Cecilia could have told him that Mr Fawnhope's intrepidity sprang more from a sublime unconsciousness of the risk of infection than from any deliberate heroism; but since she was not in the habit of discussing her lover with her brother he continued in a happy state of ignorance, himself too practical a man to comprehend the density of the veil in which a poet could wrap himself.

He never again visited the sickroom at a moment when he might expect to find his cousin there, and when they met at the dinner-table his manner towards her was so curt as to border on the brusque. Cecilia, knowing how very much obliged to Sophy he thought himself, was astonished, and more than once pressed her cousin to tell her whether they had quarrelled. But Sophy would only shake her head, and look mischievous.

Amabel continued to mend, although slowly, and with many set-backs, and all the irrational fidgets of a convalescent. For twelve hours nothing would do for her but to have Jacko brought to her room. Only Sophy's forcible representations prevented Mr Rivenhall from posting down to Ombersley Court to bring back the indispensable monkey, so anxious was he that nothing should be allowed to retard his little sister's recovery. But Tina, hitherto excluded, to her great indignation, from attendance on her mistress in the sickroom, made an excellent substitute for Jacko, and was only too content to curl up on the quilt under Amabel's caressing hand.

At the beginning of the fourth week of the illness, Dr Baillie began to talk of the propriety of removing his patient into the country. But here he encountered an unexpected and obstinate opposition from Lady Ombersley. He had once mentioned to her the possibility of a relapse, and this had taken such strong possession of her mind that no inducement could serve to make her consent to Amabel's going out of reach of his expert care. She represented to him the unwisdom of restoring Amabel to the society of her sisters and her noisy brother, soon to be enjoying his summer holiday at Ombersley. The little girl was still languid, disinclined for any exertion, and wincing at sudden sounds: she would do better in London, under his eye, and in the fond care of her Mama. Now that all danger was past, Lady Ombersley's maternal instinct could assert itself. She, and she alone, should bear the charge of her youngest daughter's convalescence. In the event, to lie upon the sofa in Mama's dressing-room, to drive sedately out with her in the barouche, just suited Amabel's present humour, and so it was settled, both Cecilia and Sophy disclaiming any desire to leave London for the country.

Town was very thin of company, but the weather was not so sultry as to make the streets disagreeable. The month was showery, and few were the days when even the most modish young lady cared to venture forth without a pelisse, or a shawl.

Others beside the Ombersley family had chosen to remain in town until August. Lord Charlbury was still to be found in Mount Street; Mr Fawnhope in his rooms off St James's; Lord Bromford, deaf to the entreaties of his mother, refused to retire into Kent; and the Brinklows found several excellent excuses for remaining in Brook Street. As soon as all danger of infection was over, Miss Wraxton was once more to be seen in Berkeley Square, gracious to everyone, even caressing towards Lady Ombersley and Amabel, and very full of wedding-schemes. Mr Rivenhall found pressing business to attend to on his estates; and if Miss Wraxton chose to assume that his frequent absences from town were accounted for by his desire to set his house in order for her reception, she was quite at liberty to do so.

Cecilia, less robust than her cousin, did not recover so quickly from the anxiety and exertion of her four weeks' incarceration. She was a good deal pulled-down, and had lost a little of her bloom. She was rather silent, too, a fact that did not escape her brother's eye. He taxed her with it; and, when she returned an evasive answer, and would have left the room, detained her, saying: 'Don't go, Cilly!'

She waited, looking enquiringly at him. After a moment, he asked abruptly: 'Are you unhappy?'

Her colour rose, and her lips trembled in spite of herself. She made a protesting gesture, turning away her face, for it was impossible to explain to him the turmoil raging in her own heart.

To her surprise, he took her hand, and pressed it, saying awkwardly, but in a softened tone: 'I never meant you to be unhappy. I did not think – You are such a good girl, Cilly! I suppose, if your poet will but engage on some respectable profession, I must withdraw my opposition, and let you have your way.'

Amazement held her motionless, only her startled eyes flying to his face. She allowed her hand to lie in his, until he released it, and turned away, as though he did not choose to meet her wide gaze.

'You thought me cruel – unfeeling! No doubt I must have seemed so, but I have never desired anything but your happiness! I cannot be glad of your choice, but if your mind is made up, God forbid I should have any hand in parting you from one whom you sincerely love, or in promoting your marriage to a man you cannot care for!'

'Charles!' she uttered faintly.

He said over his shoulder, and with some difficulty: 'I have come to see that nothing but misery could result from such a union. You at least shall not be subjected to a lifetime of regret! I will speak to my father. You have resented my influence with him: *this* time it shall be exerted in your favour.'

At any other moment his words must have prompted her to have enquired into their unexpressed significance, but shock seemed to suspend her every faculty. She found not a word to say, and experienced the greatest difficulty in preventing herself from bursting into tears. He turned his head, and said, with a smile: 'What an ogre I must appear to you, to have so taken your breath away, Cilly! Don't stare at me so unbelievingly! You shall marry your poet: my hand on it!'

She put out her own mechanically, managed to speak two words: 'Thank you!' and ran out of the room, unable to say more, or to control her emotion.

She sought the seclusion of her own bedchamber, her thoughts in such disorder that it was long before her agitation had at all subsided.

Never had opposition been withdrawn at so inopportune a moment; never had a victory seemed more empty! Almost without her knowledge, her sentiments, during the past weeks, had been undergoing a change. Now that her brother had accorded her his permission to marry the man of her choice she discovered that her feeling for Augustus had been no more than the infatuation Charles had always thought it. Opposition had fostered it, leading her into the fatal error of almost publicly announcing her unalterable determination to marry Augustus or no one. Lord Charlbury, so superior to Augustus in every way, had accepted her rejection of his suit, and had turned his attention elsewhere; and whatever unacknowledged hope she might have cherished of seeing his affections reanimate towards her must now be quite at an end. To confess to Charles that he had been right from the start, and she most miserably mistaken, was impossible. She had gone too far; nothing now remained to her but to accept the fate she had insisted on bringing on herself; and, for pride's sake, to show a smiling face to the world.

She showed it first to Sophy, resolutely begging her to felicitate her upon her happiness. Sophy was thunderstruck. 'Good God! She exclaimed, stupefied. 'Charles will *promote* this match?'

'He does not wish me to be unhappy. He never wished it. Now that he is convinced that I am in earnest he will place no bar in my way. Indeed, he was so good as to promise that he would speak to Papa for me! That must decide it: Papa always does what Charles desires him to.' She saw that her cousin was regarding her fixedly, and continued quickly: 'I have never known Charles kinder! He spoke of the misery of being forced into a marriage against one's inclination. He said *I* should not spend a lifetime of regret. Oh, Sophy, can it be that he no longer cares for Eugenia? The suspicion cannot but obtrude!'

'Good gracious, he never did care for her!' replied Sophy scornfully. 'And if he has but just discovered it, *that* is no reason for –' She broke off, darting a swift glance at Cecilia, and perceiving much more than her cousin would have wished. 'Well!

This is a day of miracles indeed!' she said. 'Of course I felicitate you with all my heart, dearest Cecy! When is your betrothal to be announced?'

'Oh, not until Augustus is settled in – in some respectable occupation!' Cecilia answered. 'But *that* will not be long, I am persuaded! Or his tragedy may take, you know.'

Sophy agreed to this without a blink, and listened with an assumption of interest to Cecilia's various schemes for the future. That these were couched in somewhat melancholy terms she allowed to pass without comment, merely repeating her congratulations, and wishing her cousin every happiness. But behind these mendacities her brain was working swiftly. She perfectly understood the fix Cecilia was in, and never for an instant thought of wasting her breath in expostulation. Something far more drastic than expostulation was needed in this case, for no lady who had entered into an engagement in the teeth of parental opposition could be expected to cry off from it the instant she had gained the sanction she had so insistently demanded. Willingly could Sophy have boxed Mr Rivenhall's ears. To remain adamant when opposition could only strengthen his sister's resolve had been bad enough; to withdraw his opposition at a moment when Charlbury was in a fair way to ousting the poet from her affections was an act of such insanity that it put Sophy out of all patience with him. Thanks to Alfred Wraxton's predilection for gossip, Cecilia's secret engagement to Mr Fawnhope was widely known. She had, moreover, been at some pains to display to Society her determination to wed him. It would need something very drastic indeed to induce so gently-bred a girl to fly in the face of all convention. If Mr Rivenhall had agreed to the match Sophy could not suppose that the official announcement would be long delayed; once this had appeared in the Gazette nothing, she thought, would prevail upon Cecilia to brand herself a jilt. It was even doubtful if she could be induced to cry off before the announcement had been made, for she presumably had a greater dependence on the strength of Mr Fawnhope's attachment than her shrewder cousin could share;

and her tender heart would shrink from giving such pain to one who had been so faithful a lover.

As for Mr Rivenhall's extraordinary change of face, this was not perhaps so inexplicable to Sophy as to his sister; but although the sentiments which had prompted it could not but gratify her she was unable to deceive herself into thinking that he had any intention of terminating his engagement to Miss Wraxton. It was not to be expected of him: careless of appearances he might be, but no man of his breeding could offer such an affront to a lady. Nor could Sophy suppose that Miss Wraxton, surely aware of the tepid nature of his regard for her, would herself put an end to an alliance that held so little prospect of future happiness for either of the contracting parties. Miss Wraxton's talk was all of her approaching nuptials, and it was quite evident that marriage to a man with whom she scarcely shared a thought was preferable to her than a continued existence as a spinster.

Sophy, cupping her chin in her hands, sat weaving her toils undismayed by a situation which would certainly have daunted a less ruthless female than herself. Those who knew her best would have taken instant alarm, knowing that, her determination once taken, no consideration of propriety would deter her from embarking on schemes which might well prove to be as outrageous as they were original.

'Surprise is the essence of attack.'

The phrase, once uttered by a General in her presence, came into her head. She pondered it, and found it good. Nothing short of surprise would wrench Charles or Cecilia from the paths of convention, so surprise they should have in full measure.

The immediate outcome of all this cogitation was an interview with Lord Ombersley, caught on his return to Berkeley Square from a day at the races. His lordship, firmly led into his own sanctum, scented danger, and made hast to inform his niece that he was pressed for time, having a dinner-engagement that must be kept within the hour.

'Never mind that!' said Sophy. 'Have you seen Charles this day, sir?'

'Of course I have seen Charles!' replied his lordship testily. 'I saw him this morning!'

'But not since then? He has not spoken to you of Cecilia's affairs?'

'No, he has not! And I'll tell you this, Sophy! I want to hear no more of Cecilia's affairs! My mind's made up: I won't have her marrying this poet-fellow!'

'My dear sir,' said Sophy, warmly clasping his hand, 'do not budge from that stand! I must tell you that Charles is about to counsel you to sanction the engagement, and you must not!'

'What?' ejaculated his lordship. 'You're certainly out there, Sophy! Charles won't hear of it, and for once he's right! What should get into the silly chit to make her reject as good as man as you may find – I was never more incensed! To whistle Charlbury, with all his fortune, down the wind – !'

His niece firmly drew him to the sofa, and obliged him to sit down on it beside her. 'Dear Uncle Bernard, if you will only do precisely as I bid you she will marry Charlbury!' she assured him. 'But you must promise me most faithfully not to permit Charles to overbear your judgement!'

'But, Sophy, I keep telling you –'

'Charles has told Cecilia that he will no longer withhold his consent.'

'Good God, has he taken leave of his senses too? You must be mistaken, girl!'

'Upon my honour, I am not! It is the stupidest thing, and will very likely wreck everything, unless you can be trusted to remain firm. Now, my dear uncle, never mind why Charles has taken this start! Only attend to me! When Charles speaks to you about this, you must refuse to entertain the notion of Cecy's marrying Augustus Fawnhope. In fact, it would be an excellent stratagem if you were to say that you are of the same mind as ever, and mean her to marry Charlbury!'

Lord Ombersley, slightly bewildered, entered on a feeble expostulation. 'Much good that would do, when Charlbury has withdrawn his offer!'

'It is of no consequence at all. Charlbury is still extremely desirous of marrying Cecilia, and, if you choose, you may tell her so. She will say that she means to marry her tiresome Augustus, because she is in honour bound to do so. You may rave at her as much as you please – as much as you did when she first made her resolve known to you! But the important thing, dear sir, is that you should remain adamant! I will do the rest.'

He looked suspiciously at her. 'Now, Sophy, this won't do! It was you who helped her to live in that damned poet's pocket, for Charles told me so!'

'Yes, and only see with what splendid results! She no longer has any real desire to wed him, and has come to see how superior Charlbury is! If Charles had not meddled, all would have gone just as you would have wished!'

'I don't understand a word of this!' complained his lordship.

'Very likely not: it has in great measure been due to poor little Amabel's illness.'

'But,' persisted her uncle, painstakingly attempting to follow the thread of her argument, 'if she is now willing to listen to Charlbury, why the devil don't he renew his suit?'

'I daresay he would, if I would let him. It would be useless. Only consider it, sir, in what a fix poor Cecy finds herself! She has kept Augustus dangling after her for months, has sworn she will wed him or none! You have only to consent to the alliance and she must feel herself bound to marry him! At all costs any formal announcement must be stopped! You may do this, and I beg you will! Do not listen to anything Charles may say to you!' Her expressive eyes laughed at him. 'Be as disagreeable to Cecilia as you were before! Nothing could serve the purpose better!'

He pinched her cheek, 'You rogue! But if Charles has changed his mind – You know, Sophy, I am no hand at argument!'

'Then do not argue with him! You have only to fly into a towering passion, and *that*, I know, you are well able to do!'

He chuckled, seeing in this pronouncement a compliment. 'Yes, but if they give me no peace –'

'My dear sir, you may seek refuge at White's! Leave the rest to me! If you will but do your part, I fancy I cannot fail to do mine. I have only this to add! – On no account must you divulge that I have been speaking to you on this matter! Promise!'

'Oh, very well!' said his lordship. 'But I'll tell you what, Sophy! I'd as lief take young Fawnhope into my family as that sour creature Charles must needs bring into it!'

'Oh, certainly!' she responded coolly. '*That* could never answer! I have known it since first I came to London, and I now entertain a reasonable hope of terminating that entanglement. Only do your part, and we may all come about!'

'Sophy!' exclaimed her uncle explosively. 'What the devil do you mean to be about now?'

But she would only laugh, and whisk herself out of the room.

The upshot of this interview staggered the household. For once Mr Rivenhall failed to bend his parent to his will. His representations to Lord Ombersley of the enduring nature of Cecilia's passion fell quite wide of the mark, and were only productive of an outburst of rage that surprised him. Knowing that his heir would speedily out-argue him, and dreading nothing so much as a struggle against a will far stronger than his own, Lord Ombersley scarcely allowed him an opportunity to open his mouth. He said that however high-handed Charles might be in the management of the estates, he was still not his sisters' guardian. He added that he had always considered Cecilia more than half-promised to Charlbury, and would not consent to her marriage with another.

'Unfortunately, sir,' said Charles dryly, 'Charlbury no longer affects my sister. His eyes are turned in quite another direction.'

'Pooh! Nonsense! The fellow haunts the place!'

'Exactly so, sir! Encouraged by my cousin!'

'Don't believe a word of it!' said his lordship. 'Sophy wouldn't have him.' Charles gave a short laugh. 'And if he did offer for her, I still wouldn't permit Cecilia to marry that nincompoop of hers, and so you may tell her!'

Mr Rivenhall did tell her, but as he added consolingly that he had little doubt of being able to talk his father round to his way of thinking, he was not surprised at her calm manner of receiving the news. Not even a tirade from Lord Ombersley, delivered over the dinner-table, quite shattered her composure, although she had the greatest dislike of angry voices, and could not help wincing a little, and changing colour.

The person to be least affected by the parental dictate was Mr Fawnhope. When informed that it would not be possible immediately to send the notice of the betrothal to the society journals, he blinked, and said vaguely: 'Were we about to do so? Did you tell me? I might not have been attending. I am in a great worry about Lepanto, you know. It is useless to deny that battle-scenes upon the stage are never felicitous, yet how to avoid it? I have been pacing the floor the better part of the night, and am no nearer to solving the problem.'

'I must tell you, Augustus, that it is unlikely that we shall be married this year,' said Cecilia.

'Oh, yes, very unlikely!' he agreed. 'I don't think I should think of marriage until the play is off my hands.'

'No, and we must remember that Charles stipulates that you should find some respectable employment before the engagement is announced.'

'That quite settles it, then,' said Mr Fawnhope. 'The question is how far one might, with propriety, employ the methods of the Greek dramatists to overcome the difficulty.'

'Augustus!' said Cecilia, in a despairing voice. 'Is your play more to you than I am?'

He looked at her in surprise, perceived that she was in earnest, and at once took her hand, and kissed it, and said, smiling at her: 'How absurd you are, my beautiful angel! How could anything or anyone be more to me than my Saint Cecilia? It is for your sake that I am writing the play. Should you dislike the notion of a chorus, in the Greek style?'

Lord Charlbury, finding that his rival continued, even without the excuse of enquiring after Amabel's condition, to visit in Berkeley Square, took fright and demanded an explanation of his preceptress. He was driving her down to Merton in his curricle at the time, and when she told him frankly what had occurred, he kept his eyes fixed on the road ahead, and for several moments said nothing. At last, with a palpable effort, he produced: 'I see. When may I expect to see the announcement?'

'Never,' replied Sophy. 'Don't look so hagged, my dear Charlbury! I assure you, there is no need. Poor Cecy has discovered these many weeks that she mistook her own heart!'

At that he turned his head quickly to look at her. 'Is this so indeed? Sophy, don't trifle with me! I own, I had thought – I had hoped – Then I shall try my fortune once more, before it is too late!'

'Charlbury, for a sensible man you say the stupidest things!' Sophy told him. 'Pray, what do you imagine must be her answer in this predicament?'

'But if she no longer loves Fawnhope – if she perhaps regrets turning me off – ?'

'She does, of course, but it is one of those things which appear to be so easy until one considers a little more deeply. Do so! If your situations were reversed – you the impoverished poet, Augustus, the man of fortune – perhaps she might be brought to listen to you. But it is not so! Here is her poet, whom she has declared she will marry in despite of all her family – and you will allow that he has been uncommonly faithful to her!'

'He – ! If he has a thought to spare for anything beyond his trumpery verses I will only myself astonished!'

'He has not, of course, but you will scarcely expect my cousin to believe that! He has attached himself to her to the exclusion of every other female since before I came to England, and that, you know, must rank in the eyes of the world as devotion of no common order! You, my poor Charlbury, labour under all the disadvantages of rank and fortune! How heartless Cecilia must be to cast off her poet to wed you! You may depend upon it that this circumstance weighs with her! Her disposition is tender: she will not, without good reason, inflict pain upon one whom she believes loves her with all his heart. There is only one thing to be done: we must give her good reason for doing so.'

He knew her well enough to feel a considerable degree of uneasiness. 'For God's sake, Sophy, what now do you mean to do?'

'Why, make her feel that it is you who are to be pitied, to be sure!'

Uneasiness changed to the deepest foreboding. 'Good God! How?'

She laughed. 'I daresay it will suit you better not to know, Charlbury!'

'Now, Sophy, listen to me!'

'No, why should I? You say nothing to the point, and, besides, here we are already, and there is no time to enter upon a discussion! You must continue to trust me, if you please!'

The curricle was already bowling up the sweep to the Marquesa's door. 'The lord knows I don't, and never have!' he retorted.

They found the Marquesa alone, and suprisingly wide-awake. She welcomed Sophy affectionately, yet with a little constraint, and soon disclosed that she had only returned two days since from Brighton, where she had been sojourning for a fortnight.

'Brighton!' exclaimed Sophy. 'You told me nothing of this, Sancia! Pray, what took you there so suddenly?'

'But, Sophie, how should I tell you anything when you shut yourself up in a sickroom, and do not visit me any more?' complained the Marquesa. 'To remain always in one place – *majadero!*'

'Very true, but you had the intention of living retired until Sir Horace's return. I daresay you may have had tidings of him –'

'No, I assure you! Not one word!'

'Oh!' said Sophy, slightly disconcerted. 'Well, he had a prosperous voyage, and I daresay he will be with us again at any time now. For it is not likely that at this time of year they will encounter any very unfavourable weather, you know. Has the Duke of York been staying with his brother?'

The Marquesa opened her sleepy eyes wide. 'But, Sophie, how should I know? They are alike, the royal princes: gross and – what is it? – *embotado!* I do not know one from the other.'

Sophy was obliged to be satisfied. Her escort, when they drove away, asked curiously: 'Why were you put out, Sophy? Must not the Marquesa follow the rest of the world to Brighton?'

She sighed. 'Not if Sir Vincent Talgarth was there also, which is what I fear. I never saw her so animated!'

'Disappointing! She won my heart originally by falling asleep under my eyes!'

She laughed, and said no more, a slight abstraction possessing her until she was set down in Berkeley Square, and found Mr Rivenhall awaiting her return in considerable ill-humour. This instantly revived her, and she had no hesitation in informing him, upon demand, where she had been.

'You did not go alone!'

'By no means: Charlbury drove me there.'

'I see? First you must set the town talking with Talgarth, and now with Charlbury! Famous!'

'I do not perfectly understand you,' said Sophy, as one innocently seeking enlightenment. 'I thought your objection to Sir Vincent was that he has the name for being a great rake. Surely you do not suspect Charlbury of this! Why, you were even desirous at one time of wedding your sister to him.'

'I am even more desirous that my cousin should not earn for herself the reputation of being *fast!*'

'Why?' asked Sophy, looking him in the eye. He made her no answer, and, after a moment, she said: 'What right have you, Charles, to take exception to what I may choose to do?'

'If your own good taste –'

'What right, Charles?'

'None!' he said. 'Do as you please! It can be of no consequence to me! You have an easy conquest in Everard! I had not thought him so fickle. Take care you do not lose your other suitor through encouraging this flirtation – for that is all I believe it to be!'

'Bromford? Now, what a shocking thing that would be! You do right to put me on my guard! Charlbury lives in dread of being called out by him.'

'I might have known I should meet with nothing but levity in you!'

'If you will scold me so absurdly. I am not always so.'

'Sophy – !' He took a hasty step towards her, his hand going out, but almost immediately dropping to his side again. 'I wish you had never come amongst us!' he said, and turned away, to lean his arm along the mantelpiece, and stare down at the empty grate.

'That is not kind, Charles.'

He was silent.

'Well, you will be rid of me soon, I daresay. I depend upon seeing Sir Horace at any time now. You will be glad!'

'I must be glad.' The words were uttered almost inaudibly, and he did not raise his head, or make any movement to prevent her leaving the room.

The exchange had taken place in the library. She stepped out into the hall just as Dassett opened the front door to admit Mr Wychbold, very natty in a driving-coat of innumerable capes, shining Hessians, and an enormous nosegay stuck into his buttonhole. He was in the act of laying his tall beaver-hat down upon a marble-topped table, but at the sight of Sophy he used it to lend flourish to his bow. 'Miss Stanton-Lacy! Very obedient servant, ma'am!'

She was surprised to see him, for he had been out of town for some weeks. As she shook hands, she said: 'How delightful this is! I did not know you were in London! How do you do?'

'Only reached town today, ma'am. Heard of your troubles from Charlbury: never more shocked in my life! Came at once to enquire!'

'That is like you! Thank you, she is almost well now, although dreadfully thin, poor little dear, and languid still! You are the very person I wished to see! Are you driving yourself? Must you instantly see my cousin, or will you take me for a turn round the Park?'

He was driving his phaeton, and there could be only one answer to her request. With the greatest gallantry he bowed her out of the house, warning her, however, that she would encounter none but cits in the Park at this season.

'And what, sir, would you have me say to Mr Rivenhall?' asked Dassett, fixing his disapproving eye on a point above Mr Wychbold's left shoulder.

'Oh, tell him I called, and was sorry to find him from home!' replied Mr Wychbold, with an insouciance the butler found offensive.

'Have you been out in your own phaeton, ma'am?' Mr Wychbold asked, as he handed Sophy in the carriage. 'How do your bays go on?'

'Very well. I have not been driving them today, however, but have been to Merton with Charlbury.'

'Oh – ah!' he said, with a slight cough and a sidelong look.

'Yes, making myself the talk of the town!' Sophy said merrily. 'Who told you so? The arch-enemy?'

He set his pair in motion, nodding gloomily. 'Came smash up to her in Bond Street on my way here. Felt obliged to stop. She has put off her black ribands!'

'And means to marry Charles next month!' said Sophy, who, having reached habits of easy intercourse with Mr Wychbold, never stood upon ceremony with him.

'Told you so,' he pointed out, with a certain melancholy satisfaction.

'So you did, and I replied that I might need your good offices. Do you make a prolonged stay in town, or are you off again immediately?'

'Next week. But, y'know, ma'am, there ain't anything to be done! Pity, but there it is.'

'We shall see. What do you think would happen if you were to tell Charles one day that you had seen me driving off in a post-chaise and four with Charlbury?'

'He would plant me a facer,' responded Mr Wychbold, without hesitation. 'What's more: shouldn't blame him!'

'Oh!' said Sophy, disconcerted. 'Well, I am sure I don't wish him to do that. But if it were true?'

'Wouldn't believe me. No need for you to go off with Charlbury. Not the kind of fellow to engage in such freaks, either.'

'I know that, but it might be contrived. He would not plant you a facer if you only asked him *why* I was leaving town with Charlbury for my escort, would he?'

After giving this his consideration, Mr Wychbold admitted that he might be spared the facer on these terms.

'Will you do it?' Sophy asked him. 'If I were to send you word to your lodgings, would you make certain that Charles knows of it? Is he not always at White's in the afternoon?'

'Well, you may generally find him there, but I would not say always,' replied Mr Wychbold cautiously. 'Besides, I shan't see you driving off!'

'You may, if you choose to give yourself the trouble of walking round to Berkeley Square!' she retorted. 'If you have word from me, you will know it to be true, and may tell Charles with a clear conscience. I'll take care he knows of it when he comes home, but sometimes he does not come in to dinner. And that would ruin everything! Well, no! not everything, perhaps, but I have always found it to be an excellent scheme to kill two birds with one stone whenever it may be possible!'

Mr Wychbold gave this his profound consideration. Having turned all the implications of Sophy's words over in his brain, he said suddenly: 'Know what I think?'

'No, tell me!'

'No wish to throw a rub in the way, mind!' Mr Wychbold said. 'Not a particular friend of mine, Charlbury. Very good sort of a fellow, I believe, but he don't happen to have come much in my way.'

'But what do you think?' demanded Sophy, impatient of this divagation.

'Think Charles may very likely call him out,' said Mr Wychbold, 'Come to think of it, bound to! Devilish fine shot, Charles! Just thought I would mention it!' he added apologetically.

'You are right, and I am very much obliged to you for putting me in mind of such a possibility!' said Sophy warmly. 'I would not for the world place Charlbury in jeopardy! But there will not be the least need for such a measure, you know.'

'Ah, well!' said Mr Wychbold comfortably. 'Daresay he won't do more than drop him a few times, then! Draw his claret, I mean!'

'Fisticuffs? Oh no! surely he would not!'

'Well, he will,' said Mr Wychbold, without hesitation. 'Last time I saw Charles, don't scruple to tell you he was in such a miff with Charlbury he said it would be wonderful if he did not plant him a flush hit one of these days! Devil of a fellow with his fives, is Charles! Don't know how Charlbury displays: shouldn't think he would be a match for Charles, though.' Waxing enthusiastic, he added: 'Prettiest fighter, for an amateur, I ever saw in my life! Excellent science and bottom, never any trifling or shifting! No mere flourishing, and very rarely abroad!' he recollected himself suddenly, and broke off in some confusion, and begged pardon.

'Yes, never mind that!' said Sophy, her brow creased. 'I must think of this, for it won't do at all. If I make Charles angry, which, I own, I wish to do –'

'No difficulty in that,' interpolated Mr Wychbold encouragingly. 'Very quick temper! Always has had!'

She nodded. 'And would be only too glad of an excuse to hit someone, I have no doubt. Of course, I see how I could prevent him doing Charlbury a mischief.' She drew a breath. 'Resolution is all that is needed!' she said. 'One should never shrink from the performance of unpleasant tasks to obtain a laudable object, after all! Mr Wychbold, I am very much obliged to you! I now see just what I must do, and I should not be at all surprised if it answered *both* purposes to admiration!'

Sixteen

$\mathcal{M}$iss Wraxton, learning of Mr Rivenhall's consent to his sister's marriage to Mr Fawnhope, was so genuinely shocked that she could not forbear remonstrating with him. With her customary good sense, she pointed out the evil consequences of such a match, begging him to consider well before he abetted Cecilia in her folly. He heard her in silence, but when she had talked herself out of arguments he said bluntly: 'I have given my word. I cannot but agree with much of what you have said. I do not like the match, but I will have no hand in forcing my sister into a marriage she does not desire. I believed that she must soon recover from what seemed to me a mere infatuation. She has not done so. I am forced to acknowledge that her heart is engaged: not her fancy only.'

She raised her brows, her expression one of faint distaste. 'My dear Charles! This is not like you! I daresay I have not far to seek for the influence which prompts you to utter such a speech, but I own that I scarcely expected you to repeat sentiments so much at variance with your disposition, and (I must add) your breeding.'

'Indeed! You will have to explain your meaning more fully, if I am to understand you, Eugenia, for I am quite abroad!'

She said gently: 'Surely not! We have so often conversed on this head! Are we not agreed that there is something very unbecoming in a daughter's setting up her will in opposition to her parents?'

'In general, yes.'

'And in *particular*, Charles, when it comes to be a question of her marriage. Her parents must be the best judges of what will be most proper for her. There is something very forward and disagreeable in a girl's *falling in love*, as the common phrase is. No doubt underbred persons make quite a practice of it, but I fancy a man of birth and upbringing would prefer to see rather more restraint in the lady he marries. The language you have adopted – forgive me, dear Charles! – surely belongs more to the stage than to your mother's drawing-room!'

'Does it?' he said. 'Tell me, Eugenia! Had I offered for your hand without the consent of your father, would you have entertained my suit?'

She smiled. 'We need not consider absurdities! You, of all men, would not have done so!'

'But if I had?'

'Certainly not,' she replied, with composure.

'I am obliged to you!' he said satirically.

'You should be,' she said. 'You could scarcely have wished the future Lady Ombersley to have been a female without reserve or filial obedience!'

His eyes were very hard and keen. 'I begin to understand you,' he said.

'I knew you would, for you are a man of sense. I am no advocate, I need scarcely say, for a marriage where there is no mutual esteem. That could hardly prosper! Certainly, if Cecilia holds Charlbury in distaste, it would have been wrong to have compelled her to marry him.'

'Generous!'

'I hope so,' she said gravely. 'I should not wish to be other than generous towards your sisters – towards all your family! It must be one of my chief objects to promote their welfare, and I assure you I mean to do so!'

'Thank you,' he said, in a colourless tone.

She turned a bracelet upon her arm. 'You are inclined to regard Miss Stanton-Lacy with indulgence, I know, but I think you will allow that her influence in this house has not been a happy one, in many respects. Without her encouragement, I venture to think that Cecilia would not have behaved as she has.'

'I don't know that. You would not say that her influence was not a happy one had you seen her nursing Amabel, supporting both my mother and Cecilia in their anxiety! That is something I can never forget.'

'I am sure no one could wish you to. One is glad to be able to praise her conduct in that emergency without reserve.'

'I owe it to her also that I stand now upon such easy terms with Hubert. *There* she has done nothing but good.'

'Well, on that point we have always differed, have we not?' she said pleasantly. 'But I have no wish to argue with you on such a subject! I only hope that Hubert continues to go on well.'

'Very well. I might almost say *too* well, for what must the ridiculous fellow do but think himself in honour bound to make up some lost study during this vacation! He is gone off on a reading-party!' He laughed suddenly. 'If he does not fall into a melancholy through all this virtue, I must surely expect to hear that he is in some shocking scrape soon!'

'I'm afraid you are right,' she agreed seriously. 'There is an instability of purpose that must continuously distress you.'

He stared at her incredulously, but before he could speak, Dassett had ushered Lord Bromford into the room. He at once went forward to shake hands, greeting this new guest with more amiability than was usual, but saying: 'I fear you are out of luck: my cousin has gone out driving.'

'I was informed of it at the door – How do you do, ma'am? – but I considered it proper to step upstairs to felicitate you upon your sister's happy recovery,' replied his lordship. 'I have had occasion to call in our good Baillie – excellent man! – and he swore upon his honour there was not the least lingering danger of infection.'

Judging from the curl of Mr Rivenhall's lip that he was about to make a sardonic rejoinder, Miss Wraxton intervened rather hastily. 'Have you been indisposed, dear Lord Bromford? This is sad hearing! No serious disorder, I must hope?'

'Baillie does not consider it so. He thinks the season has been uncommonly sickly: such inclement weather, you know, and very likely to produce affections of the throat, to which I am peculiarly susceptible. My mother has been, you may imagine, quite in a worry, for my constitution is delicate – it would be idle to deny that it is delicate! I was obliged to keep to my room above a week.'

Mr Rivenhall, leaning his broad shoulders against the mantelpiece, drove his hands into the pockets of his breeches, and presented all the appearance of a man willing to be amused. Lord Bromford did not recognize the signs, but Miss Wraxton did, and was cast into an agony of apprehension. She once more hurried into speech. 'Sore throats have been very prevalent, I believe. I do not wonder that Lady Bromford was anxious. You were well-nursed, I know!'

'Yes,' he concurred. 'Not that my complaint was of such a nature as to – In short, even Mama owns herself to have been moved by the devotion of Miss Stanton-Lacy to her little cousin!' He bowed to Mr Rivenhall, who graciously inclined his head in acknowledgement of the courtesy, only spoiling the effect by a peculiarly saturnine grin. 'I have been put in mind of certain lines from *Marmian*, in this connection.'

Miss Wraxton, who had heard enough of Sophy's perfections in a sickroom, could only be grateful to Mr Rivenhall for interpolating: 'Yes, we know them well!'

Lord Bromford, who had started to repeat *O woman, in our hours of ease!* was thrown a little out of his stride by this, but recovered directly, and pronounced: 'Any doubts that might have been nourished of the true womanliness of Miss Stanton-Lacy's character, must, I venture to say, have been lulled to rest.'

At this moment, Dassett reappeared to announce that Lady Brinklow's carriage was at the door. Miss Wraxton, who had only been set down in Berkeley Square while her parent executed a commission in Bond Street, was obliged to take her leave. Lord Bromford said that since neither Lady Ombersley nor her niece was at home he would not trespass longer upon the premises, and within a very few minutes Mr Rivenhall was able to have his laugh out in comfort. Lord Bromford, who was a favourite with Lady Brinklow, was offered a seat in the landaulet, and beguiled the short drive to Brooke Street with an exact account of the symptoms of his late indisposition.

Mr Rivenhall, for all his resolve to hold his cousin at arm's length, could not resist the temptation of recounting this passage to her. She enjoyed the joke just as he had known she would, but put an abrupt end to his amusement by exclaiming involuntarily: 'How well he and Miss Wraxton would suit! Now, why did I never think of that before?'

'Possibly,' said Mr Rivenhall frostily, 'you may have recalled that Miss Wraxton is betrothed to me!'

'I don't think *that* was the reason,' said Sophy, considering it. She lifted an eyebrow at him. 'Offended, Charles?'

'Yes!' said Mr Rivenhall.

'Oh, Charles, I wonder at you!' she said, with her irrepressible gurgle of mirth. 'So *untruthful!*'

As she beat a strategic retreat upon the words, he was left to glare at the unresponsive door.

He told his mother roundly that Sophy's conduct went from bad to worse, but the full measure of her iniquity did not burst upon him until two days later, when, upon ordering his groom to harness his latest acquisition to his tilbury, he was staggered to learn that Miss Stanton-Lacy had driven out in this equipage not half an hour earlier.

'Taken my tilbury out?' he repeated. His voice sharpened. 'Which horse?' he demanded.

The groom shook visibly. 'The – the young horse, sir!'

'You – harnessed – the young horse for Miss Stanton-Lacy to drive?' said Mr Rivenhall, giving his words such awful weight as almost to deprive his henchman of all power of speech.

'Miss said – miss was sure – you would have no objection, sir!'

stammered this unfortunate. 'And seeing as how she has twice driven the grays, sir, and me not having no orders contrary – and her saying as all was right – I thought she had your permission, sir!'

Mr Rivenhall, in a few pungent words, swept this illusion from his mind, adding a rider which summarily disposed of any pretensions his groom might have cherished of being able to think at all. The groom, not daring to venture on an explanation of the circumstances, waited in miserable silence for his dismissal. It did not come. Mr Rivenhall was a stern master, but also a just one, and even in his wrath he had a very fair notion of the means his unprincipled cousin must have employed to gain her ends. He checked himself suddenly, and rapped out: 'Where has she gone? To Richmond? Answer!'

Seeing the culprit quite unable to collect his wits, Lord Ombersley's own groom intervened, saying obsequiously: 'Oh no, sir! No, indeed! My lady and Miss Cecilia set out in the barouche an hour ago for Richmond! And Miss Amabel with them, sir!'

Mr Rivenhall, who knew that a visit had been arranged to a cousin who lived at Richmond, stared at him with knit brows. It had certainly been agreed that Sophy was to have accompanied her aunt and cousins, and he was at a loss to imagine what could have caused her to change her mind. But this was a minor problem. The young chestnut she had had the temerity to drive out was a headstrong animal, quite unaccustomed to town-traffic, and certainly unfit for a lady to handle. Mr Rivenhall could control him, but even so notable a whip as Mr Wychbold had handsomely acknowledged that the brute was a rare handful. Mr Rivenhall, thinking of some of the chestnut's least engaging tricks, felt himself growing cold with apprehension. It was this fear that lent the edge to his anger. A certain degree of anger he must always have felt at having his horse taken out without his permission, but nothing to compare with the murderous rage that now consumed him. Sophy had behaved unpardonably – and that her conduct was strangely unlike her he was in no mood to consider – and might even now be lying upon the cobbles with a broken neck.

'Saddle Thunderer, and the brown hack!' he commanded suddenly. 'Quick!'

Both grooms flew to carry out this order, exchanging glances that spoke volumes. No ostlers, trained to change coach-horses in fifty seconds, could have worked faster; and while a couple of stable-hands still stood gaping at such unaccustomed doings, Mr Rivenhall, followed at a discreet distance by his groom, was riding swiftly in the direction of Hyde Park.

He had judged correctly, but it was perhaps unfortunate that he should have come up with his cousin just as the young chestnut, first trying to rear up between the shafts at the sight of a small boy flying a kite, made a spirited attempt to kick the floor-boards out of the carriage. Mr Rivenhall, who had almost believed that he could forgive all if only he should find his cousin unharmed, found that he had been mistaken. Pale with fury, he dismounted, dragged the bridle over Thunderer's head, thrust it into the groom's hand, with a brief order to him to lead the horse home, swung himself into the tilbury, and possessed himself of the reins. For several moments he was fully occupied with his horse, and Sophy had leisure to admire his skill. She did not think she had managed so very badly herself, for, with the best will in the world to do so, the chestnut had not bolted with her, but she did not pretend to Mr Rivenhall's mastery over a high-couraged, half-broke animal. Assuaging Mr Rivenhall's wrath formed no part of her schemes, but in spite of herself she exclaimed: 'Ah, you are a capital whip! I never knew how good until today!'

'I don't need you to tell me so!' he flashed, face and voice at curious variance with his steady hands. 'How dared you do this? How dared you? If you had broken your neck you would have come by your deserts! That you have not broken my horse's knees I must think a miracle!'

'Pooh!' said Sophy, atoning for her previous error by laying this promising faggot upon the smouldering fire.

The result was all that she had hoped it might be. The drive back to Berkeley Square did not occupy very many minutes, but Mr Rivenhall crammed into them every pent-up exasperation of the past fortnight. He tore his cousin's character to shreds; condemned her manners, her morals, and her upbringing; expressed his strong desire to have the schooling of her, and, in the same breath, pitied the man who should be fool enough to marry her; and fervently looked forward to the day when he should be relieved of her unwelcome presence in his home.

It was doubtful whether Sophy could have stemmed the tide of this eloquence. In the event, she made no attempt to do so, but sat with folded hands, and downcast eyes, beside her accuser. That his rage had been fanned, quite irrationally, to white heat by finding her unhurt she had no doubt at all. There had been moments during her escapade when she had doubted her ability to bring either herself or the horse off safely. She had never been more glad to see her cousin; and one glance at his face had been enough to assure her that he had suffered a degree of anxiety out of all proportion to the concern even the keenest whip might be expected to feel for his horse. He might say what he pleased; she was not deceived.

He set her down in Berkeley Square, telling her roughly that she might alight without his assistance. She obeyed him, and without so much as waiting to see her admitted into the house he drove off towards the mews.

That was shortly after noon. Mr Rivenhall did not return to the house, and, as soon as she was satisfied that there was no fear of his walking in on her, his wholly unchastened cousin first summoned the under-footman to her, and sent him on an errand to the nearest livery-stables; and then sat down to write several careful notes. By two o'clock, John Potton, puzzled but unsuspicious, was trotting down to Merton with one of these in his pocket. Had he been privileged to know its contents he might not have ridden so cheerfully out of London.

'*Dearest Sancia,*' Sophy wrote. '*I find myself in the most dreadful predicament, and most earnestly beg of you to join me at Lacy Manor immediately. Do not fail me, or I shall be utterly ruined! Ashtead lies only ten miles from Merton, so you need not fear to be fatigued. I leave London within the hour, and wholly depend upon you. Ever your devoted Sophy.'*

Upon the footman's return from his errand, he was gratified to receive half-a-guinea for his pains; and set forth again with alacrity to deliver two sealed letters. One of these he left at Mr Wychbold's lodging; the other he carried from Lord Charlbury's house to Manton's Shooting Gallery, and thence to Brooks's Club, where he finally ran his quarry to earth. Lord Charlbury, summoned to the hall to receive the billet in person, read it in considerable astonishment, but handsomely rewarded the bearer, and charged him to inform Miss Stanton-Lacy that he was entirely at her disposal.

Meanwhile, Miss Stanton-Lacy, who had thoughtfully given her too zealous a maid a holiday, instructed a startled housemaid to pack her night-gear in a portmanteau, and sat down to write two more letters. She was still engaged on this task when Lord Charlbury was shown into the saloon. She looked up, smiling, and said: 'I knew I might depend on you! Thank you! Only let me finish this note!'

He waited until the door had closed behind Dassett before demanding: 'What in heaven's name is amiss, Sophy? Why must you go to Ashtead?'

'It is my home: Sir Horace's house!'

'Indeed! I was not aware – But so suddenly! You aunt – your cousin – ?'

'Don't tease me!' she begged. 'I will explain it to you on the way, if you will be so good as to give me your escort! It is not far – may be accomplished in one stage, you know!'

'Of course I will escort you!' he replied at once. 'Is Rivenhall away from home?'

'It is impossible for me to ask him to go with me. Pray let me finish this note for Cecilia!'

He begged pardon, and moved away to a chair by the window. Good manners forbade him to press her for an explanation she was plainly reluctant to offer, but he was very much puzzled. The mischievous look had quite vanished from her eyes; she seemed to be in an unusually grave mood: a circumstance that threw him off his guard, and made him only anxious to be of service to her.

The note to Cecilia was soon finished, and closed with a wafer. Sophy rose from the writing-table, and Charlbury ventured to ask whether she desired him to drive her to Ashtead in his curricle.

'No, no, I have hired a post-chaise! I daresay it will be here directly. You did not come in your curricle?'

'No, I walked from Brooks's. You are making a stay in the country?'

'I hardly know. Will you wait while I put on my hat and cloak?'

He assented, and she went away, returning presently with Tina frisking about her in the expectation of being taken for a walk. The hack-chaise was already at the door, and Dassett, quite as mystified as Lord Charlbury, had directed a footman to strap Miss Stanton-Lacy's portmanteau on to the back. Sophy gave her two last notes into his hand, directing him to be sure that Mr and Miss Rivenhall received them immediately upon their return to the house. Five minutes later she was seated in the chaise beside Charlbury, and expressing the hope that the threatened rain-storm would hold off until they reached Lacy Manor. Tina jumped up into her lap, and she then told his lordship that she had encountered in the Green Park just such another Italian greyhound, who had made no secret of his admiration of Tina. Tina's coquetry had to be described; this led to an amusing account of the jealousy of Mr Rivenhall's spaniel, brought up by him from the country for a couple of nights; and in this way, by easy gradations, Lord Charlbury found himself discussing pheasant-shooting, fox-hunting, and various other sporting pursuits. These topics lasted until the Kennington turnpike had been passed, by which time his lordship's faculties, at first bewildered, were very much on the alert. He fancied that the mischief was back in Sophy's eye. At Lower Tooting, he politely allowed his gaze to be directed to the curious churchtower, with its circular form surmounted by a square wooden frame, with a low spire of shingles above it; but when Sophy leaned back again in her corner of the chaise, he said, watching her face: 'Sophy, are we by chance eloping together?'

Her rich chuckle broke from her. 'No, no, it is not as bad as that! Must I tell you?'

'I know very well you have some abominable scheme afoot! Tell me at once!'

She threw him a sidelong look, and he had now no doubt that the mischief was back in her eye. 'Well, the truth is, Charlbury, that I have kidnapped you.'

After a stunned moment, he began to laugh. In this she readily joined him, but when he had recovered from the first absurdity of the notion, he said: 'I might have known there was devilry afoot when I saw that your faithful Potton was absent! But what is this, Sophy? Why am I kidnapped? To what end?'

'So that I may be so compromised that you will be obliged to marry me, of course,' replied Sophy matter-of-factly.

This cheerful explanation had the effect of making him start bolt upright, exclaiming: '*Sophy!*'

She smiled. 'Oh, don't be alarmed! I have sent John Potton with a letter to Sancia begging her to come to Lacy Manor at once.'

'Good God, do you place any dependence upon her doing so?'

'Oh, yes, certainly! She has a very kind heart, you know, and would never fail me when I particularly desired her help.'

He relaxed against the squabs again, but said: 'I don't know what you deserve! I am still quite in a puzzle: why have you done it?'

'Why, don't you see? I have left behind me a letter for Cecilia, telling her that I am about to sacrifice myself –'

'Thank you!' interjected his lordship.

'– *and* you,' continued Sophy serenely, 'so that my uncle may be silenced at last. You know, for I told you so, that I persuaded

276

im to announce to poor Cecy his unalterable decision that she was to wed you! If I know Cecy, the shock will bring her post-haste to Ashtead, to rescue the pair of us. If, my dear Charlbury, you cannot help yourself in that eventuality, I wash my hands of you!'

'I can find it in me to wish you had done so long since!' was his ungrateful response. 'Outrageous, Sophy, *outrageous!* And what if neither she nor the Marquesa comes to Lacy Manor? Let me tell you that nothing will serve to induce me to compromise you!'

'No, indeed! I should dislike it excessively. If *that* happened, I fear you will be obliged to spend the night at Leatherhead. It is not very far from Lacy Manor, and I believe you may be tolerably comfortable at the Swan. Or you might hire a chaise to carry you back to London. But Sancia at least will not fail.'

'Have you told Cecilia that you have *kidnapped* me?' he demanded. She nodded, and he exclaimed: 'I could murder you! What a trick to play! And what a figure I must cut!'

'She won't think of that. Do you recall that I told you only the other day that she must be made to pity you instead of Augustus? Besides that, I am persuaded she will suffer perfect torments of jealousy. Only fancy! I was quite at a stand until I remembered what I had once heard pronounced by a most distinguished soldier! "Surprise is the essence of attack!" The most fortunate circumstance!'

'Was it not?' he said sarcastically. 'I have a very good mind to get down at the next pike!'

'You will ruin all if you do.'

'It is *abominable*, Sophy!'

'Yes, if the motive were not pure!'

He said nothing, and she too remained silent for several minutes. At last, having turned it over in his mind, he said: 'You had better tell me the whole. That I have only heard half I have no doubt at all! Where does Charles Rivenhall stand in all this?'

She folded her hands on Tina's back. 'Alas! I have quarrelled so dreadfully with Charles that I am obliged to seek refuge at Lacy Manor!' she said mournfully.

277

'And have doubtless left a note behind you to inform him of this!'

'Of course!'

'I foresee a happy meeting!' he commented bitterly.

'That,' she acknowledged, 'was the difficulty! But I think I can overcome it. I promise you, Charlbury, you shall come out of this with a whole skin – well, no, perhaps not quite that, but very nearly!'

'You do not know how much you relieve my mind! I daresay I may not be a match for Rivenhall, either with pistols or with my fists, but give me credit for not being quite so great a poltroon as to fear a meeting with him!'

'I do,' she assured him. 'But it can serve no good purpose for Charles to *mill you down* – have I that correctly?'

'Quite correctly!'

'– or to put a bullet through you,' she ended, her serenity unshaken.

He was obliged to laugh. 'I see that Rivenhall is more to be pitied than I am! Why did you quarrel with him?'

'I had to make an excuse for flying from Berkeley Square! You must perceive that! I could not think of nothing else to do but to take out that young chestnut he has bought lately. A beautiful creature! Such grand, sloping shoulders! Such an action! But quite unbroke to London traffic, and by far too strong for any female to hold!'

'I have seen the horse. Do you tell me seriously, Sophy, that you took him out?'

'I did – shocking, was not it? I assure you, I suffered a real qualm in my conscience! No harm, however! He did not bolt with me, and Charles came to the rescue before I found myself in real difficulty. The things he said to me – ! I have never seen him in such a fury! If only I could remember the half of the insults he flung at my head! It is no matter, however: they gave me all the cause I needed to fly from his vicinity.'

He closed his eyes for an anguished moment. 'Informing him, no doubt, that you had sought *my* protection?'

278

'No, there was no need: Cecy will tell him that!'

'What a fortunate circumstance, to be sure! I hope you mean to contribute a handsome wreath to my obsequies?'

'Certainly! In the nature of things, it is likely that you will predecease me.'

'If I survive this adventure there can be no question of that. Your fate is writ clear: you will be murdered. I cannot conceive how it comes about that you were not murdered long since!'

'How odd! Charles himself once said that to me, or something like it!'

'There is nothing odd in it: any sensible man must say it!'

She laughed, but said: 'No, you are unjust! I have never yet done the least harm to anyone! It may be that with regard to Charles my stratagems may not succeed: in your case I am convinced they must! That may well content us. Poor Cecy! Only conceive how dreadful to be obliged to marry Augustus, and to spend the rest of one's life listening to his poems!'

This aspect of the situation struck Lord Charlbury so forcibly that he was smitten to silence. He said nothing of deserting Sophy when they stopped at the next pike, but appeared to be resigned to his fate.

Lacy Manor, which lay a little way off the turnpike road, was an Elizabethan house, considerably added to in succeeding generations, but still retaining much of its original beauty. It was reached by an avenue of noble trees, and had once been set amongst well-tended formal gardens. These, through the circumstance of Sir Horace's being not only an absentee but also a careless landlord, had become overgrown of late years, so that the shrubbery was indistinguishable from the wilderness, and unpruned rose bushes rioted at will in unweeded flower-beds. The sky had become overcast all day, but a fitful ray of sunlight, penetrating the lowering clouds, showed the mullioned windows of the house much in need of cleaning. A trail of smoke issued from one chimney, the only observable sign that the house was still inhabited. Sophy, alighting from the chaise, looked about her critically, while Charlbury tugged at the iron bell-pull beside the front-door.

'Everything seems to be in shocking disorder!' she observed. 'I must tell Sir Horace that it will not do! He should not neglect the house in this way. There is work here for an army of gardeners! He never liked the place, you know. I have sometimes wondered if it was because my mother died here.' Lord Charlbury made a sympathetic sound in his throat, but Sophy continued cheerfully: 'But I daresay it is only because he is shockingly indolent! Ring the bell again, Charlbury!'

After a prolonged interval, they heard the sound of footsteps within the house, to be followed immediately by the scrape of bolts being drawn back, and the clank of a chain removed from the door.

'I am reconciled, Sophy!' announced Charlbury. 'Never did I hope to find myself existing between the covers of a library novel! Will there be cobwebs, and a skeleton under the stairs?'

'I fear not, but only think how delightful if there should be!' she retorted. She added, as the door was opened, and a surprised face appeared in the aperture: 'Good-day, Clavering! Yes, it is I indeed, and I have come home to see how you and Mathilda go on!'

The retainer, a spare man with grizzled locks and a bent back, peered at her for a moment before gasping: 'Miss Sophy! Lor', miss, if we'd thought you was coming – ! Such a turn as it give me, to hear the bell a-pealing! Here, Matty! Matty, I say! It's Miss Sophy!'

A female form, as stout as he was lean, appeared in the background, uttering distressful sounds, and trying to untie the strings of a grimy apron. Much flustered, Mrs Clavering begged her young mistress to step into the house, and to excuse the disorder everywhere. They had had no warning of her advent: the master had said he would take order when he returned from foreign parts: she doubted whether there was as much as a pinch of tea in the house: if she had but known of Miss Sophy's intention to visit them she would have had the chimneys swept, and the best parlour cleaned and taken out of Holland covers.

Sophy soothed her agitation with the assurance that she had come prepared to find the house in disarray, and stepped into the hall. This was a large apartment, panelled and low-pitched, from which, at one end, a handsome staircase of oak rose in easy flights to the upper floors of the house. The chairs were all shrouded in Holland covers, and a film of dust lay over the gate-legged table in the centre of the room. The air struck unpleasantly dank, and a large patch of damp on one wall made this circumstance easily understandable.

'We must open all the windows, and light fires!' Sophy said briskly. 'Has the Marquesa – has a Spanish lady arrived yet?'

She was assured that no Spanish lady had been seen at the Manor, a circumstance in which the Claverings seemed to think they deserved to be congratulated.

'Good!' said Sophy. 'She will be here presently, and we must strive to make things a little more comfortable before we admit her. Bring some wood, and kindling for this fire, Clavering, and do you, Matty, pull off these covers! If there is no tea in the house, I am sure there is some ale! Bring some for Lord Charlbury, if you please! Charlbury, I beg your pardon for inviting you to so derelict a house! Wait, Clavering! Are the stables in decent order? I don't wish the chaise to drive away, and the horses must be baited, and rubbed down, and the post-boys refreshed!'

Lord Charlbury, abandoning his scruples to enjoyment of this situation, said: 'Will you permit me to attend to that matter for you? If Clavering will show me the way to your stables – ?'

'Yes, pray do so!' said Sophy gratefully. 'I must see which rooms are most fit to be used, and until we have a fire lit here it will be most uncomfortable for you.'

His lordship, correctly interpreting this to mean that he would be very much in the way if he stayed in the house, went off with Clavering to lead the post-boys to the stables – happily still water-tight, and under the charge of an aged pensioner, whose rheumy eye perceptibly brightened at the sight of even such cattle as job-horses. A stout cob, and a couple of farm-horses, were the only occupants of the commodious stables, but the pensioner assured him that there was both bedding and fodder enough, and further undertook to regale the post-boys in his own cottage, which adjoined the stables.

Lord Charlbury then strolled about the gardens until some heavy drops of rain drove him back to the house. There he found that the covers had been taken off the chairs in the hall. A duster employed, and a fire lit in the gigantic hearth.

'It is not really cold,' said Sophy, 'but it will make everything appear more cheerful!'

His lordship, dubiously eyeing the puffs of smoke issuing from the fireplace into the room, agreed to this meekly enough, and even made a show of warming his hands at the small blue flame showing amidst the coals. A more violent gust of smoke caused him to retreat, seized by a fit of coughing. Sophy knelt to thrust a poker under the black mass, raising it to let the draught through. 'It's my belief there may be a starling's nest in the chimney,' she observed dispassionately. 'Mathilda, however, says fires always smoke for a while when the chimneys are cold. We shall see! I found some tea in one of the cupboards in the pantry, and Mathilda is bringing it to us directly. She had no notion it was there: I wonder how long it has lain hidden in the cupboard?'

'I wonder?' echoed his lordship, fascinated by the thought of this relic of forgotten days, at Lacy Manor.

'Fortunately, tea does not turn bad with keeping,' said Sophy. 'At least – does it?'

'I have no idea, but that we shall also see,' returned Charlbury. He began to walk about the hall, inspecting the pictures and the ornaments. 'What a shame it is that this place should be left to go to ruin!' he remarked. 'That is a charming Dresden group, and I have quite lost my heart to that Harlequin over there. I wonder your father would not rather prefer to hire his house to some respectable people while he is employed abroad than let it rot!'

'Well, for a great many years he allowed my aunt Clara to live here,' exclaimed Sophy. 'She was most eccentric, and kept cats, and died two years ago.'

'I don't think she took very good care of the house,' said Charlbury, putting up his glass to inspect a landscape in a heavy gilded frame.

'No, I fear she cannot have. Never mind! Sir Horace will soon put it to rights. Meanwhile, Mathilda is to set the breakfast parlour in order, and we may sit there, and be cosy presently.' She frowned slightly. 'The only thing that troubles me a little is dinner,' she confided. 'It does not appear to me that Mathilda has the least notion of cookery, and I must confess that I have not either. You may say that this is a trifling circumstance, but –'

'No,' interrupted his lordship, with great firmness. 'I shall say nothing of the sort! Are we dining here? Must we?'

'Oh, yes, I am sure we must make up our minds to that!' she replied. 'I am not quite certain when we may expect to see Cecilia, but I hardly think she will reach us before seven o'clock, for she was gone to Richmond with my aunt, you know, and they will very likely spend the afternoon there. Are you interested in pictures? Shall I take you to show you the Long Gallery? The best ones are hung there, I think.'

'Thank you, I should like to see them. Are you expecting Rivenhall to accompany his sister?'

'Well, I *imagine* he will. After all, she will hardly set forth alone, and he must surely be the person she would turn to in such a predicament. There is no saying, of course, but you may depend upon it that if Charles does not come with Cecy he will follow her swiftly. Let us go up to the Gallery until tea is ready for us!'

She led the way to the staircase, pausing by a chair to pick up from it her large travelling-reticule. The Gallery, which ran along the north side of the house, was in sepulchral darkness, heavy curtains having been drawn across its several tall windows. Sophy began to fling these back, saying: 'There are two Vandykes, and something that is *said* to be a Holbein, though Sir Horace doubts it, and *that* is my mother's portrait, done by Hoppner. I don't remember her myself, but Sir Horace never cared for this likeness: he says it makes her simper, which she never did.'

'You are not very like her,' Charlbury remarked, looking up at the portrait.

'Oh, no! She was thought a great beauty!' Sophy said.

He smiled, but made no comment. They passed on to the next picture, and so the length of the Gallery, when Sophy supposed that Mathilda would have set the tea-tray for them. She thought the curtains should be drawn again, so Charlbury went to the windows to perform this duty for her. He had shut the light out from two of them, and had stretched out his hand to grasp one of the curtains of the third when Sophy, from behind him, said: 'Stay just as you are for an instant, Charlbury. Can you see the summer-house from where you stand?'

He stood still, his arm across the window, and had just begun to say: 'I can see something through the trees which might be –' when there was a loud report, and he sprang aside, clutching his forearm, which felt as though a red-hot wire had seared it. For a moment, his senses were entirely bewildered by the shock; then he became aware that his sleeve was singed and rent, that blood we welling up between his fingers, and that Sophy was laying down an elegant little pistol.

She was looking a trifle pale, but she smiled reassuringly at him, and said, as she came towards him: 'I *do* beg your pardon! An infamous thing to have done, but I thought it would very likely make it worse for you if I warned you!'

'Sophy, have you run mad?' he demanded furiously, beginning to twist his handkerchief round his arm. 'What the devil do you mean by it?'

'Come into one of the bedchambers, and let me bind it up! I have everything ready. I was afraid you might be a little cross, for I am sure it must have hurt you abominably. It took the greatest resolution to make me do it,' she said, gently propelling him towards the door.

'But *why*? In God's name, what have I done that you must needs put a bullet through me?'

'Oh, nothing in the world! That door, if you please, and take off your coat. My dread was that my aim might falter, and I should break your arm, but I am sure I have not, have I?'

'No, of course you have not! It is hardly more than a graze, but I still don't perceive why –'

She helped him to take off his coat, and to roll up his sleeve. 'No, it is only a slight flesh wound: I am so thankful!'

'So am I!' said his lordship grimly. 'I may think myself fortunate not to be dead, I suppose!'

She laughed. 'What nonsense! At that range? However, I do think Sir Horace would have been proud of me, for my aim was as steady as though I were shooting at a wafer, and it would not have been wonderful, you know, if my hand had trembled. Sit down, so that I may bathe it!'

He obeyed, holding his arm over the bowl of water she had so thoughtfully provided. He had a very lively sense of humour, and now that the first shock was over, he could not prevent his lip quivering. 'Yes, indeed!' he retorted. 'One can readily imagine a parent's pleasure at such an exploit! Resolution is scarcely the word for it, Sophy! Don't you even mean to fall into a swoon at the sight of the blood?'

She looked quickly up from her task of sponging the wound. 'Good God, no! I am not *missish*, you know!'

At that he flung back his head and broke into a shout of laughter. 'No, no, Sophy! You're not missish!' he gasped, when he could speak at all. 'The Grand Sophy!'

'I wish you will keep still!' she said severely, patting his arm with a soft cloth. 'See, it is scarcely bleeding now! I will dust it with basilicum powder, and bind it up for you, and you may be comfortable again.'

'I am not in the least comfortable, and shall very likely be in a high fever presently. Why did you do it, Sophy?'

'Well,' she said, quite seriously, 'Mr Wychbold said that Charles would either call you out for this escapade, or knock you down, and I don't at all wish anything of that nature to befall you.'

This effectually put a period to his amusement. Grasping her wrist with his sound hand, he exclaimed. 'Is this true? By God, I have a very good mind to box your ears! Do you imagine that I am afraid of Charles Rivenhall?'

'No, I daresay you are not, but only conceive how shocking it would be if Charles perhaps killed you, all through my fault!'

'Nonsense!' he said angrily. 'And if either of us were crazy enough to let it come to that, which, I assure you, we are not – !'

'No, I feel you are right, but also I think Mr Wychbold was right in thinking that Charles would – what does he call it? – *plant you a facer?*'

'Very likely, but although I may be no match for Rivenhall, I might still give quite a tolerable account of myself!'

She began to wind a length of lint round his forearm. 'It could not answer,' she said. 'If you were to floor Charles, Cecy would not like it above half; and if you imagine, my dear Charlbury, that a back eye and a bleeding nose will help your cause with her, you must be a great gaby!'

'I thought,' he said sarcastically, 'that she was to be made to pity me?'

'Exactly so! And that is the circumstance which decided me to shoot you!' said Sophy triumphantly.

Again, he was quite unable to help laughing. But the next moment he was testily pointing out to her that she had made so thick a bandage round his arm as to prevent his being able to drag the sleeve of his coat over it.

'Well, the sleeve is quite spoilt, so it is of no consequence,' said Sophy. 'You may button the coat across your chest, and I will fashion you a sling for your arm. To be sure, it is only a flesh wound, but it will very likely start to bleed again, if you do not hold your arm up. Let us go downstairs, and see whether Mathilda has yet made tea for us!'

Not only had the harassed Mrs Clavering done so, but she had sent the gardener's boy running off the village to summon to her assistance a stout, red-cheeked damsel, whom she proudly presented to Sophy as her sister's eldest. The damsel, bobbing a

286

curtsy, disclosed that her name was Clementina. Sophy, feeling that Lacy Manor might be required to house several persons that night, directed her to collect blankets and sheets, and to set them to air before the kitchen fire. Mrs Clavering, still toiling to make the breakfast-parlour habitable, had set the tea-tray in the hall, where the fire had begun to burn more steadily. Puffs of smoke still from time to time gushed into the room, but Lord Charlbury, pressed into a deep chair, and given a cushion for the support of his injured arm, felt that it would have been churlish to have animadverted upon this circumstance. The tea, which seemed to have lost a little of its fragrance through its long sojourn in the panty cupboard, was accompanied by some slices of bread-and-butter and a large, and rather heavy plum-cake, of which Sophy partook heartily. Outside, the rain fell heavily, and the sky became so leaden that very little light penetrated into the low-pitched rooms of the Manor. A stringent search failed to discover any other candles than tallow ones, but Mrs Clavering soon brought a lamp into the hall, which, as soon as she had drawn the curtains across the windows, made the apartment seem excessively cosy, Sophy informed Lord Charlbury.

It was not long before their ears were assailed by the sound of an arrival. Sophy jumped up at once. 'Sancia!' she said, and cast her guest a saucy smile. 'Now you may be easy!' She picked up the lamp from the table, and carried it to the door, which she set wide, standing on the threshold, with the lamp held high to cast its light as far as possible. Through the driving rain she perceived the Marquesa's barouche-landau drawn up by the porch, and, as she watched, Sir Vincent Talgarth sprang out of the carriage, and turned to hand down the Marquesa. In another instant, Mr Fawnhope had also alighted, and stood transfixed, gazing at the figure in the doorway, while the rain beat unheeded upon his uncovered head.

'Oh, *Sophie*, why?' wailed the Marquesa, gaining the shelter of the porch. 'This rain – ! My dinner! It is too bad of you!'

Sophy, paying no heed to her plaints, addressed herself fiercely to Sir Vincent. 'Now, what the deuce does this mean?

Why have you accompanied Sancia, and why the *devil* have you brought Augustus Fawnhope?'

He was shaken by gentle laughter. 'My dear Juno, do let me come in out of the wet! Surely your own experience of Fawnhope must have taught you that one does not *bring* him: he comes! He was reading the first two acts of his tragedy to Sancia when your messenger arrived. Until the light failed, he continued to do so during the drive.' He raised his voice, calling: 'Come into the house, rapt poet! You will be soaked if you stand there any longer!'

Mr Fawnhope started, and moved forward.

'Oh, well!' said Sophy, making the best of things. 'I suppose he must come in, but it is the greatest mischance!'

'It is you!' announced Mr Fawnhope, staring at her. 'For a moment, as you stood there, the lamp held above your head. I thought I beheld a goddess! A goddess, or a vestal virgin!'

'Well, if I were you,' interposed Sir Vincent practically, 'I would come in out of the rain while you make up your mind.'

Seventeen

*L*ady Ombersley, and her daughters, driving soberly home from Richmond, in the late afternoon, reached Berkeley Square to find Miss Wraxton awaiting their return. After affectionately embracing Lady Ombersley, she explained that she had ventured to sit down to wait for her, since she was the bearer of a message from her Mama. Lady Ombersley, feeling a little anxious about Amabel, who was looking tired and had complained of a slight head-ache on the way home, answered absently: 'Thank your Mama so much, my dear. Amabel, come up to my dressing-room, and I will bathe your forehead with vinegar! You will be better directly, my love!'

'Poor little dear!' said Miss Wraxton. 'She looks sadly peaked still! You know, ma'am, that we have put off our black gloves. Mama is desirous of holding a dress-party in honour of the approaching Event – quite a small affair, for so many people of consequence are out of town! – but she would not for the world fix upon a day that will not suit your arrangements. You behold in me her envoy!'

'So kind of her!' murmured her ladyship. 'We shall be most happy – any day that your mother likes to appoint: we have very few engagements at present! Excuse me, I must not stay! Amabel is not quite well yet, you know! Cecilia will arrange it with you. Say everything from me to your Mama which is proper! Come, dearest!'

She led her youngest daughter to the stairs as she spoke, quite failing to perceive that Cecilia, to whom Dassett had silently handed Sophy's note, was not attending to a word she said. Under the butler's interested gaze, Cecilia, reading the letter in the blankest amazement, had turned alarmingly pale. She looked up, as she reached the end, and started forward, her lips parted, as though she would have recalled her mother. She recollected herself in a moment, and tried to be calm. But the hands with which she folded Sophy's letter shook perceptibly, and her whole appearance was that of one who had sustained a severe shock. Miss Wraxton observed it, and moved towards her, saying solicitously: 'You are not quite well, I am afraid! You have not received bad news?'

Dassett, whose fingers had itched to break open the wafer that sealed Sophy's letter, coughed, and said disinterestedly: 'Will Miss Stanton-Lacy be returning to town this evening, miss? Her abigail is in quite a taking, not having had any notion that Miss was going into the country.'

Cecilia looked at him in rather a dazed way, but pulled herself together sufficiently to reply with tolerable composure: 'Yes, I think so. Oh, yes, certainly she will come back tonight!'

If this answer failed to gratify Dassett's thirst for knowledge, it at least made Miss Wraxton prick up her ears. Taking Cecilia's arm, she led her towards the library, saying in her well-modulated voice: 'The drive has fatigued you. Be so good, Dassett, as to bring a glass of water to the library, and some smelling-salts! Miss Rivenhall is feeling a trifle faint.'

Cecilia, whose constitution was not strong, was indeed feeling faint, and could only be grateful when obliged to lie down upon the sofa in the library. Miss Wraxton deftly removed her pretty bonnet, and began to chafe her hands, abstracting from one of them the note which Cecilia was feebly clutching. Dassett soon came in with the desired requirements, which Miss Wraxton took from him, with a calm word of thanks and of dismissal. The faintness, which had only been momentary, was already passing off, and Cecilia was able to sit up, to sip the water, and to refresh herself with a few sniffs at the smelling-bottle. Miss Wraxton, meanwhile, in the most assured manner possible, had picked up Sophy's letter, and was making herself mistress of its contents.

'*You wondered, dearest Cecy, why, at the last, I would not accompany you to Richmond. Let this note be my explanation! I have thought long over the unfortunate situation in which you are placed, and I see only one way to put an end to the distress you have been made to suffer through my uncle's implacable determination to see you married to C. I believe him to have been strengthened in this resolve by C. himself, but I will not pain you by writing more on this subject. Were C. removed, I cannot but believe that my uncle must soon relent towards F.*

'*Charles will tell you that we have quarrelled. While the original fault I must own to have been mine, his manner to me, the language he held – so violent, so uncontrolled! – makes it impossible for me to remain any longer under this roof. I am removing immediately to Lacy Manor, and have prevailed upon C. to be my escort. Trust me to make it impossible for him to leave Lacy Manor tonight! He is a gentleman, and although his heart can never be mine, his hand I am persuaded he must offer me, and you may be easy at last.*

'*Do not fear for me! You are aware of my wish to establish myself, and although my affections are no more engaged than C.'s and I must shrink from the means his indifference forces me to employ, I daresay we shall contrive to rub along tolerably together. If I can be of assistance to you in this way, my dearest cousin, I shall have my reward. Ever your devoted Sophy.*'

'Good God!' exclaimed Miss Wraxton, startled out of her calm. 'Is this possible? Bad though I have thought her conduct, I would not have believed that she could have gone to such lengths as this! Unhappy girl! There is not a word of contrition! No breath of shame! My poor Cecilia, I do not wonder that you should find yourself overcome! You have been wretchedly deceived!'

'Oh, what are you about?' Cecilia cried, starting up. 'Eugenia, you had no right to read my letter! Give it to me at once, if you please, and never dare to mention its contents to a living soul!'

Miss Wraxton handed it to her, but said: 'Rather than have me summon Lady Ombersley to you, I thought you would prefer that I should discover what had so much upset you. As for not mentioning the contents, I imagine this news must be all over London by tomorrow! I do not know when I have been so much shocked!'

'All over London! No, that it shall not be!' Cecilia said vehemently. 'Sophy – Charlbury! It cannot, *must* not be! I shall set out for Ashtead immediately. How could she do such a thing? How *could* she? It is all her goodness – her wish to help me, but how dare she go off with Charlbury?' She tried to read the letter again, but crumpled it in her hand, shuddering. 'A quarrel with Charles! Oh, but she must know he does not mean the things he says when he is in a rage! She *does* know it! He shall go with me to fetch her home! Where is he? Someone must go at once to White's!'

Miss Wraxton, who had been thinking, laid a detaining hand on her arm. 'Pray calm yourself, Cecilia! Consider a little! If your unfortunate cousin has quarrelled so bitterly with Charles, very likely his going could only do more harm than good. I believe you are right in this, however, that it will not do to let matters take their course. The scandal that must result would be such as none of us could contemplate without revulsion. I dread the effect it may have upon dear Lady Ombersley above everything. The wretched girl must be rescued from herself.'

'And Charlbury!' Cecilia interjected, wringing her hands 'It is all my folly! I must set out at once!'

'You shall do so, and I will go with you,' said Miss Wraxton nobly. 'Only permit me sufficient time, while you order your Papa's chaise to be got ready, to write a note for my mother. I daresay one of the servants would carry it round to Brook Street for me. I shall inform her merely that I have been persuaded to pass the evening with you here, and she will not find it remarkable.'

'You!' exclaimed Cecilia, staring at her. 'Oh, no, no! I mean, it is excessively kind in you, dear Eugenia, but I had rather you did not come!'

'You will scarcely go alone,' Miss Wraxton reminded her.

'Sophy's maid shall accompany me. I beg of you, do not let a word of this pass your lips!'

'My dear Cecilia, surely you will not permit a servant into your confidence? As well tell the town-crier! If you will not accept my company, I must think myself obliged to divulge the whole to Lady Ombersley. I consider it my duty to go with you, and I am persuaded it is what Charles would desire me to do. *My* being at Lacy Manor must lend propriety to the whole; for an engaged woman, you know, stands upon a different footing from an unattached girl.'

'Oh, I do not know what to say! I wish to heaven you had never set eyes on Sophy's letter!'

'I think it may be as well for all of us that I did set eyes on it,' replied Miss Wraxton, with a smile. 'You are scarcely in a fit state, dear Cecilia, to conduct this delicate affair with any degree of composure, let me tell you. Which is it to be! Shall I go with you, or do you prefer me to lay the whole before your Mama?'

'Very well, come then!' Cecilia said, almost pettishly. 'Though why you should wish to, when I know very well that you dislike Sophy amazingly, I am at a loss to understand!'

'Whatever my sentiments towards your cousin may be,' pronounced Miss Wraxton, looking quite saintly, 'I trust that I may never forget my duty as a Christian.'

The ready colour flooded Cecilia's cheeks. She was a gentle girl, but this speech made her so cross that she said waspishly: 'Well, I daresay Sophy will contrive to make you look foolish, because she always does, and it will serve you right, Eugenia, for meddling in what does not concern you!'

But Miss Wraxton, knowing that her hour of triumph had arrived, merely smiled in an irritating way, and recommended her to think what would be best to say to her Mama.

Cecilia replied with dignity that she knew just what she should say, and moved towards the door. Before she had reached it, it was opened, and Dassett came in again, this time to inform her that Lord Bromford had called, and desired the favour of a word with her.

'You should have denied me!' Cecilia said. 'I cannot see Lord Bromford now!'

'No, miss,' said Dassett. 'But his lordship seems quite set on seeing either you, or her ladyship, miss, and her ladyship is with Miss Amabel and does not wish to be disturbed.' He gave his deprecating cough. 'I should perhaps mention that his lordship, knowing that Miss Sophy has gone out of town, is extremely wishful to learn of her direction.'

'Who told him that Miss Sophy is gone out of town?' Cecilia said sharply.

'That I could not take it upon myself to say, miss. Not having received any orders to the contrary, I did not consider it my place to deny the fact, when his lordship condescended to enquire of me if it was true.'

Cecilia cast rather a helpless glance at Miss Wraxton, who at once took the conduct of affairs into her capable hands.

'Pray desire his lordship to step into this room!' she said.

Dassett bowed, and withdrew.

'Eugenia! Take care what you are about! What do you mean to say to him!'

Miss Wraxton replied gravely: 'That must depend upon circumstances. We do not know how much he is aware of, and we ought not to forget that *he* has as much interest in your cousin as any of us.'

'No such thing!' Cecilia said. 'Sophy would never marry him!'

'She has certainly shown herself unworthy of his devotion. I hope she may not have cause to be thankful to marry *any* respectable man who offers for her.'

Since Lord Bromford was ushered into the room at that moment, Cecilia was spared the necessity of answering her.

His lordship was looking extremely anxious, but no anxiety could suffice to make him abate the formality of his greetings. These were performed with great punctilio, nor did he forget to make civil enquiry after the state of Amabel's health. He then begged pardon for importuning Miss Rivenhall to grant him an audience, and, after only a little circumlocution, came to the point of his visit. He had seen Miss Stanton-lacy driving along Piccadilly in a hack-chaise and four, Lord Charlbury beside her, and baggage tied on behind the chaise.

'My cousin has been called suddenly out of town,' said Cecilia, in a cool tone that might have been expected to have damped pretension.

'With only that fellow for her companion!' he exclaimed, very much shocked. 'Besides – and this is a circumstance which makes it appear the more extraordinary – I was engaged to drive out with her this afternoon!'

'She had forgotten,' Cecilia said. 'She will be so sorry! You must forgive her.'

He regarded her intently for a moment, and what he saw in her face caused him to turn towards her companion, and to say earnestly: 'Miss Wraxton, I appeal to you! It is useless to tell me that Miss Stanton-Lacy has not left London clandestinely! How should Rivenhall have permitted her to go off in such a fashion? Pardon me, but Charlbury's attentions – marked, you will agree, beyond the bounds of propriety! – have given rise to the most dreadful suspicions in my mind. It cannot be unknown to you that I have an interest there myself! I had flattered myself that upon Sir Horace Stanton-Lacy's return to England – But this sudden departure – baggage strapped on behind, too!' he stopped, apparently overcome.

Miss Wraxton said smoothly: 'Miss Stanton-Lacy is at all times impatient of convention. She has driven down to her home at Ashtead, but I am confident that the persuasions of Miss Rivenhall and myself must weigh with her, and she will return to London with us tonight. We are about to set forth for Ashtead immediately.'

He seemed to be much struck, and said at once: 'This is like you! I understand you, I believe! I have known that fellow for a libertine these many weeks! Depend upon it, he has quite taken her in! Does Rivenhall accompany you?'

'We go alone,' Miss Wraxton said. 'You have guessed the truth, and will readily appreciate that our endeavours now must be fixed on keeping this unhappy event from the ears of the world.'

'Yes, indeed!' he said eagerly. 'But it is not to be thought of that two delicately nurtured females should undertake such a mission, unsupported by the firmness of a man! I think I should escort you. I think it is what I should do. I shall call Charlbury to book. His conduct in this affair has shown me what he is. He has grossly deceived Miss Stanton-Lacy, and shall answer for it!'

An indignant protest rose to Cecilia's lips, but Miss Wraxton intervened swiftly, to say: 'Your sentiments do you honour, and, for my own part, I must say that I shall be grateful to you for the protection of your escort. Only the most stringent necessity could prevail upon me to undertake such a mission without the support of a responsible gentleman!'

'I will have my horse saddled at once!' he announced, in a voice of stern resolution. 'I can tell you, it will be wonderful if I do not call Charlbury out! I am not, in general, an advocate of the barbarous custom of duelling, but circumstances, you know, alter cases, and such conduct must not go unpunished! I will be off home on the instant, and shall be with you again in the least time possible!'

He barely stayed to grasp both their hands before hurrying from the room. Cecilia, fairly weeping with annoyance, began to upbraid Miss Wraxton, but this lady, losing not a jot of her self-possession, replied: 'It was unfortunate that he should have been aware of Miss Stanton-Lacy's elopement, perhaps, but it could do no good to leave *that* suspicion in his mind. I own, the presence of a man of sense will be a comfort to me, and if, my dear Cecilia, his chivalrous nature should prompt him to renew his offer for your cousin's hand, it would be a solution to all our difficulties, and, I must add, a great deal more than she deserves!'

'That prosy bore!' Cecilia exclaimed.

'I am aware that Lord Bromford's merits have consistently been undervalued in this house. For my part, I have found him a sensible man, feeling just as he ought upon serious subjects, and having a great deal of interesting information to impart to those who are not too frivolous to attend to him.'

Unable to control her swelling emotions, Cecilia ran out of the room, more than half inclined to take her mother fully into her confidence.

But Lady Ombersley, finding that Amabel's pulse was too rapid, was so wholly absorbed in the sufferer as to have little attention to spare for anyone else. Knowing the delicate state of her parent's nerves, Cecilia forbore to add to her anxieties. She told her merely that a message from Lacy Manor had taken Sophy post-haste into Surrey, but that since she felt it to be unfitting for her cousin to remain in a deserted house alone, she was setting out, either to bear her company or to persuade her to return to London. Upon Lady Ombersley's showing some astonishment, she divulged that Sophy had quarrelled with Charles. This distressed Lady Ombersley, but scarcely surprised her. Too well did she know her son's bitter tongue! She would not have had such a thing happen for the world, and must, she said, have gone after Sophy herself had not Amabel seemed so unwell. She did not like to think of her daughter's travelling alone, but upon hearing of Miss Wraxton's resolve to go with her was able to be tranquil again, and to give her permission for the journey.

Meanwhile, Miss Wraxton, busily writing in the library, was unable to resist the temptation of inscribing a note to her betrothed, as well as to her Mama. Now, at last, Charles should be brought to acknowledge the moral turpitude of his cousin, and her own magnanimity! She gave both notes to Dassett, with instructions for their immediate delivery; and was presently able to climb into the Ombersley travelling-chaise in the happy consciousness of having punctiliously performed her duty. Not even Cecilia's pettishness had the power to allay her self-satisfaction. Never had Cecilia shown herself so out of temper! She replied to her companion's moralizings with the briefest of monosyllables, and was even so unfeeling, when the rain began to fall, as to refuse point-blank to have the third seat in the chaise pulled out to accommodate Lord Bromford, riding unhappily behind the vehicle, with his coat collar turned up, and an expression on his face of the most acute misery. Miss Wraxton represented to her the propriety of desiring one of the out-riders to lead his lordship's horse, while his lordship travelled in comfort within the chaise; but all Cecilia could find to say was that she hoped the odious man would contract an inflammation of the lungs, and die of it.

Scarcely an hour later, Dassett was as nearly put out of countenance as it was possible for a person of his dignity and experience to be by the arrival in Berkeley Square of a second post-chaise. This, also a hack-vehicle, was drawn by four sweating horses, and was caked in mud up to the axles. A number of trunks and portmanteaux were piled on the back, and on the roof. A soberly-dressed individual first jumped down, and ran up the steps of the Ombersley mansion to set the bell pealing. By the time the door had been opened by a footman, and Dassett stood ready to receive guests upon the threshold, a much larger figure had descended in a leisurely way from the chaise, and, after tossing a couple of guineas to the postilions, and exchanging a jovial word with them, trod unhurriedly up the steps to the door.

Dassett, who afterwards described his condition to the house-keeper, as fairly flummoxed, found himself unable to do more than stammer: 'Go-good-evening, sir! We – we were not expecting you, sir!'

'Wasn't expecting myself,' said Sir Horace stripping off his gloves. 'Devilish good voyage! Not a day above two months at sea! Tell your people to see all that lumber of mine carried into the house! Her ladyship well?'

Dassett, helping him to struggle out of his caped great-coat, said that her ladyship was as well as could be looked for.

'That's good,' said Sir Horace, walking over to a large mirror, and bestowing an expert touch or two upon his cravat. 'How's my daughter?'

'I – I believe Miss Sophy to be enjoying excellent health, sir!'

'Ay, she always does. Where is she?'

'I regret to inform you, sir, that Miss Sophy has gone out of town,' replied Dassett, who would have been pleased to have discussed the mystery of Sophy's disappearance with almost anyone else.

'Oh? Well, I'll see her ladyship,' said Sir Horace, displaying, in the butler's opinion, an unnatural want of interest in his only child's whereabouts.

Dassett took him up to the drawing-room, and left him there while he went in search of her ladyship's maid. Amabel having just dropped off to sleep, it was not many minutes before Lady Ombersley came hurrying into the drawing-room, and almost cast herself upon her brother's manly bosom. 'Oh, my dear Horace!' she exclaimed. 'How glad I am to see you! How sorry to think – But you are safely home!'

'Well, there's no need for you to ruin my necktie, just because of that, Lizzie!' said her undemonstrative relative, disengaging himself from her embrace. 'Never been in any danger that I knew of! You don't look very stout! In fact, you look quite knocked-up! What's amiss? If it's stomach trouble, I knew a fellow once, ten times worse than ever you were, who got himself cured by magnetism and warm ale. Fact!'

Lady Ombersley made haste to assure him that if she looked knocked-up it was only through anxiety; and began at once to tell him about Amabel's illness, dwelling fondly on Sophy's goodness through this trying period.

'Oh, Sophy's a capital nurse!' he said. 'How do you go on with her? Where is the girl?'

This question flustered Lady Ombersley quite as much as it had flustered Dassett. She faltered that Sophy would be so sorry! If only she had guessed that her Papa was on his way to London she would surely not have gone.

'Yes, Dassett said she was gone out of town,' responded Sir Horace, disposing his large limbs in an easy chair, and crossing one shapely leg over the other. 'Never expected to find any of you here at this season, but, of course, if one of the children is ill, that explains it. Where's Sophy gone to!'

'I think – I was busy with Amabel when Cecilia told me, but think she said that dearest Sophy had gone down to Lacy Manor!

He looked surprised. 'What the deuce should take her there The place ain't fit to live in! Don't tell me Sophy's putting it to rights, because I'm by no means sure – However, never mind that!'

'No, no, I don't think she had any such idea! At least – Oh Horace, I don't know what you will say to me, but I very much fear that Sophy has run away from us because of something that happened today!'

'Shouldn't think so at all,' said Sir Horace coolly. 'Not like my little Sophy to enact you a Cheltenham tragedy. What did happen?'

'I do not properly understand it: I was not here! But Cecilia seemed to think that – that Sophy and Charles had fallen out! Of course, I know he has a dreadful temper, but I am persuaded he cannot have meant – And Sophy has never before taken the least notion when he – Because it is not the first time they have quarrelled!'

'Well, don't put yourself in a taking, Lizzie,' recommended Sir Horace, maintaining his placidity without effort. 'Fallen out with Charles, eh? Well, I thought she would. Daresay it will do him good. How's Ombersley?'

'Really, Horace!' said his sister indignantly. 'One would suppose you not to have a scrap of affection for dear Sophy!'

'You're out there, old lady, for I'm devilish fond of her,' he returned. 'That don't mean I'm going to make a cake of myself over her tricks, though. Daresay she wouldn't thank me. You may depend upon it she's up to some mischief!'

As Dassett came in at this moment, with suitable refreshment for the traveller, the conversation had to be suspended. When he had withdrawn, Lady Ombersley resumed it, saying: 'At least I am able to assure you that you will see Sophy tonight, for Cecilia has gone with Miss Wraxton to bring her back!'

'Who's Miss Wraxton?' enquired Sir Horace, pouring himself out a glass of Madeira.

'If you ever listened to a word anyone says to you, Horace, you would know that Miss Wraxton is the lady Charles is about to marry!'

'Well, why didn't you say so?' said Sir Horace, sipping his wine. 'Can't expect me to carry a lot of names in my head! I remember now, though: girl you said was a dead bore.'

'I never said any such thing!' retorted Lady Ombersley. 'To be sure, I cannot quite like – But it was you who said she sounded to you like a dead bore!'

'If I said it, you may depend upon it I was right. Quite a tolerable wine, this. Now I come to think of it, you told me Cecilia was in a way to be married too: Charlbury, ain't it?'

Lady Ombersley sighed. 'Alas, it went off! Cecilia could not be brought to accept him. And now Charles has ceased to object so very much to Augustus Fawnhope, and although Ombersley says he will never countenance it, I daresay he will. You may as well know Horace, that Lord Charlbury has been showing Sophy a great deal of most distinguishing attention.'

'Has he, by Jupiter?'

They were interrupted by the sound of an impatient step on the stair, to be following an instant later by the hasty entrance into the room of Mr Rivenhall, who held an open sheet of letter-paper in one hand, and had not stayed even to divest himself of his driving-coat before dashing upstairs in search of his mother.

Mr Rivenhall was looking extremely forbidding, and also a little pale. After stabling the chestnut that afternoon, he had first gone off to Bond Street, to work off some of his fury in a sparring-bout with Gentleman Jackson, and had then repaired to White's, where he had spent an hour playing billiards, and fighting an impulse to go back to Berkeley Square, to tell his provoking cousin that he had not meant a word of it. It was when he left the billiard-room that he encountered his friend Mr Wychbold. Mr Wychbold, obedient to his orders, asked him whither Miss Stanton-Lacy was bound; and upon his replying curtly: 'Nowhere, to my knowledge,' said, not without an inward qualm: 'Yes, she is, dear boy! Saw her driving off in a post-chaise and four. What's more, she had Charlbury with her.'

Mr Rivenhall stared at him. 'Driving off in a post-chaise and four? You are certainly mistaken!'

'Couldn't have been!' said Mr Wychbold, sustaining his rôle manfully.

'Foxed, then. My cousin is at home!' he added, as his friend seemed inclined to argue the matter: 'What's more, Cyprian, I'll thank you not to spread such a tale about the town!'

'No, no, shouldn't dream of doing so!' Mr Wychbold made haste to assure him.

Mr Rivenhall then went off to the subscription-room, with the intention of playing a rubber or two of whist. The tables were all made up, and it was while he stood watching the play of a hand his eyes on the cars, and his mind dwelling obstinately and uneasily on Mr Wychbold's ridiculous delusion, that Miss Wraxton's note was brought to him. The perusal of it had the effect of instantly killing any desire to play whist, and of sending him off to Berkeley Square without one word of excuse to those who had invited him to take part in the next rubber. He let himself into the house, found Sophy's letter to him laid upon the table in the hall, read it, and straightway went up the stairs two at a time in search of Lady Ombersley.

'Perhaps, Mama, you may be able to explain to me –' he began to say, in a furious voice, and then broke off short, perceiving that she was not alone. 'I beg your pardon! I did not know –' Again he broke off, as Sir Horace raised his quizzing-glass, the better to observe him. 'Oh!' he said, a wealth of sinister meaning in his voice. 'So it's you, is it, sir? Famous! You could not have come at a better moment!'

Shocked at the most unrespectful tone he had adopted, Lady Ombersley ventured on a feeble protest. 'Charles! Pray –!'

He paid no heed to her, but strode forward into the room. 'You will no doubt like to know, sir, that your precious daughter has gone off with Everard Charlbury!' he announced.

'Has she?' said Sir Horace. 'What has she done that for, I

302

wonder? *I've* no objection to her marrying Charlbury! Good family; handsome property!'

'She did it,' said Mr Rivenhall, 'to infuriate me! And as for her marrying Charlbury she will do no such thing!'

'Oh, won't she?' said Sir Horace, keeping his glass levelled on his nephew's face. 'Who says so?'

'*I* say so!' snapped Mr Rivenhall. 'What is more, she has not the smallest intention of such a thing! If you do not know your daughter, I do!'

Lady Ombersley, who had listened in speechless dismay to this interchange, now found enough voice to say faintly: 'No, no, she would not run away with Charlbury! You must be mistaken! Alas, Charles, I fear this is your doing! You must have been dreadfully unkind to poor Sophy!'

'Oh, dreadfully unkind, ma'am! I actually had the brutality to take exception to her stealing the young chestnut from my stables, and, without one word to me, driving him in the Park! That she is not lying with a broken neck at this moment is no fault of hers!'

'Now, that,' said Sir Horace fairmindedly, 'was wrong of her! In fact, I'm surprised to hear of her behaving so improperly, for it is not at all like her. What should have got into her to make her do such a thing?'

'Merely her damnable desire to pick a quarrel with me!' said Mr Rivenhall bitterly. 'I see it all now, clearly enough, and if she is not careful she will find she has succeeded better than she bargained for!'

'I am afraid, my boy,' said his uncle, an irrepressible twinkle in his eyes, 'that you do not like my little Sophy!'

'Your *little* Sophy, sir, has not allowed me – us! – one moment's peace or comfort since she descended upon this house!' said Mr Rivenhall roundly.

'Charles, you shall not say so!' cried his mother, flushing. 'It is unjust! How can you – how *can* you, when you recall her goodness, her devotion – !' Her voice failed; she groped blindly for her handkerchief.

The colour rose also to Mr Rivenhall's cheeks. 'I do not forget that, ma'am. But this exploit – !'

'I cannot think where you can have had such a notion! It is untrue! Sophy went away because of the intemperate language you used towards her, and as for imagining that Charlbury was with her –'

'I know he was with her!' he interrupted. 'If I needed proof, I have it in this note she was so obliging as to leave for me! She makes no secret of it!'

'In that case,' said Sir Horace, refilling his glass, 'she is certainly up to some mischief. Try this Madeira, my boy: I'll say this for your father, he's a capital judge of a wine!'

'But, Charles, this is terrible!' gasped Lady Ombersley. 'Thank heaven I did not forbid Cecilia to go after her! Only think what a scandal! Oh, Horace pray believe I had no suspicion!'

'Lord, *I'm* not blaming you, Elizabeth! I told you not to let Sophy worry you! Well able to take care of herself: always was!'

'I declare, Horace, you pass all bounds! Is it *nothing* to you that your daughter is in a fair way to ruining herself?'

'Ruining herself!' said Mr Rivenhall contemptuously. 'Do you indeed believe in such a fairy-tale, ma'am? Have you lived with my cousin for six months without getting her measure? If that Spanish woman is not also at Lacy Manor at this moment I give you leave to call me a blockhead!'

'Oh, Charles, I pray you may be right!'

Sir Horace began to polish his eyeglass with considerable assiduity. 'Sancia, eh? I was meaning to speak to you about her, Lizzie. Is she still at Merton?'

'Pray, where else should she be, Horace?'

'I just wondered,' he said, studying the result of his labours. 'I daresay Sophy may have told you of my intentions in that direction.'

'Of course she did, and I paid her a visit, as I suppose you must have wished me to do! But I must say, my dear Horace, that I cannot conceive what should possess you to offer for her!'

'That's the trouble,' he replied. 'One gets carried away, Lizzie! And there's no denying she's a devilish fine woman. In fact, it wouldn't have surprised me to have heard she had someone else dangling after her. Pity I settled her out at Merton! But there it is! One does these things on the spur of the moment, and it is not until one has had leisure to reflect – However, I don't mean to complain!'

'Plenty of beauties in Brazil, sir?' enquired his nephew sardonically.

'I don't want any of your impudence, my boy!' said Sir Horace genially. 'Fact of the matter is, I doubt if I'm a marrying man!'

'Well, if it's any consolation to you,' said Mr Rivenhall, 'you may know that my cousin has being doing her possible to hold Talgarth off from the Marquesa!'

'Now, why the devil,' demanded Sir Horace, roused to irritability, 'must Sophy meddle? Talgarth, eh? Didn't know he was in England! Well, well! He has a great deal of address, has Vincent, and, what's more, I'll wager he has an eye to Sancia's fortune!'

Lady Ombersley, quite affronted, broke in on this, exclaiming: 'I think you are quite shameless! And what has all this to do with poor Sophy's escapade? You sit there, as though you had no concern in her affairs, while all the time she is trying to ruin herself! And you may say what you choose, Charles, but if it is true that she has gone off with Charlbury, it is the most shocking thing imaginable, and she must be brought back at once!'

'She will be!' said Mr Rivenhall. 'Can you doubt it, when you have sent off Cecilia and Eugenia, in the highest style of romance, to rescue her, ma'am?'

'I did no such thing! I knew nothing of this, but naturally I would not let your sister go alone, so when she told me that Eugenia had been kind enough to offer to accompany her, what could I do but be grateful?' She paused, struck by an unexplained circumstance. 'But how do you know that they went to rescue her, Charles? If Dassett is so lost to all sense of his position as to gossip to you –'

'No such thing! I am indebted to Eugenia herself for my information! And I must take leave to say, ma'am, that if you and my sister had been so obliging as to have kept this news to yourselves, I might have been spared a damned impertinent letter from Eugenia! What can have possessed you to have confided such a tale to her is something I can never cease to marvel at! Good God, don't you know that she will spread it all over town that my cousin has behaved outrageously?'

'But I did not!' almost wailed his mother. 'Charles, I did *not!*'

'One of you must have done so!' he said impatiently. He turned to his uncle. 'Well, sir, do you mean to remain there, commending my father's taste in wine, or do you mean to accompany me to Ashtead?'

'Set out for Ashtead at this hour, when I have been travelling for two days?' said Sir Horace. 'Now, do, my boy, have a little common-sense! Why should I?'

'I imagine that your parental feeling, sir, must provide you with the answer! If it does not, so be it! *I* am leaving immediately!'

'What do you mean to do when you reach Lacy Manor?' asked Sir Horace, regarding him in some amusement.

'Wring Sophy's neck!' said Mr Rivenhall savagely.

'Well, you don't need my help for that, my dear boy!' said Sir Horace, settling himself more comfortably in his chair.

Eighteen

The first few minutes following the arrival of the Marquesa's party from Merton were taken up with that lady's freely expressed complaints of the situation in which she found herself. The draught occasioned by the opening of the front door, had caused the fire to belch forth clouds of acrid smoke into the hall, and not all Mrs Clavering's distracted efforts had sufficed to make this apartment look other than neglected. Mrs Clavering, much impressed by the richness of the Marquesa's attire, stood bobbing curtsies to her; and the Marquesa, quite unimpressed by Mrs Clavering, said: *Madre de Dios!* If I had brought Gaston it might then have been supportable, and if my cook as well, better still! Why must I come to you in this house, Sophie? Why do you send for me so suddenly, and when it is raining, moreover? *Su conducta es perversa!'*

Sophy at once told her that she had been summoned to play a duenna's part, an explanation which made an instant appeal to one in whose veins ran the purest Castilian blood. So well-satisfied was the Marquesa that she forgot to enquire why Sophy had placed herself in a situation that required the attendance of any other duenna than her aunt, but said approvingly that Sophy had conducted herself with great propriety, and she grudged no fatigue in such a cause. After that, she became aware of Charlbury's presence, and with an effort of memory even recalled his name.

'Hallo, are you hurt?' Sir Vincent asked, nodding at his lordship's arm-sling. 'How came that about?'

'Never mind that!' said Sophy, relieving Charlbury of the necessity of answering. 'Why are *you* here, Sir Vincent?'

'That, my dear Juno,' he replied, his eyes glinting at her, 'is a long and delicate story. I might, you know, ask the same question. I shan't, of course, because explanations are apt to be tedious, and what is teasing me more at this present is the far more important subject of dinner. I fear you may not have been expecting so large a party?'

'No, I was not, and heaven knows what we shall find to eat!' Sophy admitted. 'I think, perhaps, I should go into the kitchen, and discover what there may be in the larder. For it is very likely, I must tell you, that my cousin Cecilia will arrive to dine here. And more than probably Charles also!'

'Oh, Miss Sophy, if only you'd have given us warning!' exclaimed Mrs Clavering distressfully. 'I'm sure I don't know how to contrive dinner, not for the likes of you, miss, for I am not accustomed, and there's nothing ready but a pig's cheek, which Clavering fancied for his supper!'

'It is evident,' said the Marquesa, removing the plumed hat from her luxuriant curls, and laying it down on a chair, 'that this *moza de cocina* knows nothing, so that I must exert myself a little. That is bad, but worse, *infinitamente*, that we should starve. And you will remember it, Sophie, and be grateful to me, so that you do not quarrel with me! For I must tell you, *de una vez*, that I think it will not suit me to be married to Sir Horace after all, for he is very restless, and Brazil I should not like, but, on the contrary I will remain in England, but an English cook I will not have! So I have married Sir Vincent, and I am now not the Marquesa de Villacañas, but Lady Talgarth, which is a name I cannot pronounce *convenientemente*, but no matter! One must accustom oneself.'

This speech not unnaturally stunned her audience into silence for several moments. Sir Vincent drew out his snuff-box, and delicately inhaled a pinch of his favourite mixture. It was he who broke the silence. 'So the murder is out!' he remarked. 'Do not look so aghast, Sophy! Remember that our dear Sancia is to cook the dinner!'

'This,' suddenly announced Mr Fawnhope, who had not been attending to a word of the conversation, 'is a singularly beautiful house! I shall go all over it.'

He then picked up the lamp from the table, and bore it off towards one of the doors that opened on to the hall. Sir Vincent took it from him, and restored it to its place, saying kindly: 'You shall do so, my dear young friend, but take this candle, if you please!'

'Sir Vincent,' said Sophy, a martial light in her eye, 'if I were a man, you would suffer from this *treachery!*'

'Dear Sophy, you shoot better than nine out of ten men of my acquaintance, so if any one of us had the forethought to bring with him a pair of duelling-pistols – ?'

'No one,' said the Marquesa, with decision, 'shall shoot a pistol, because it is of all things what I most detest, and, besides, it is more important that we should prepare dinner!'

'I suppose,' said Sophy regretfully, 'that that is true. One must eat! But I now perceive how right my cousin Charles was to warn me to have nothing to do with you, Sir Vincent! I did not think you would have served Sir Horace such a back-handed turn!'

'All is fair, dear Sophy, in love and war!' he said sententiously.

She was obliged to bite back the retort that sprang to her lips. He smiled understandingly, and moved towards her, taking her hand, and saying in a lowered voice: 'Consider, Juno! *My* need is far greater than Sir Horace's! How could I resist?'

' "*Amor ch'a null'amato amar perdona,*" ' dreamily remarked Mr Fawnhope, whose peregrinations about the hall had brought within earshot.

'Exactly so, my poet!' said Sir Vincent cordially.

'I need Miss Wraxton to translate that for me,' said Sophy, 'but if it means what I think it does it is no such thing! However, there is nothing more foolish than to be making a great noise over what cannot be helped, so I shall say no more. Besides, I have more important things to think of!'

'Certainly that is so,' agreed the Marquesa. 'There is a way of preparing fresh-killed chickens, so Vincent shall at once kill me two chickens, for chickens this woman tells me there are in abundance, and I shall contrive.'

She then withdrew with Mrs Clavering to the kitchen-premises, her demi-train of mull-muslin sweeping regally behind her over the floor, and picking up a great deal of dust on the way. Sophy and Sir Vincent followed her; and as Mr Fawnhope had by this time discovered the library, and had gone in to inspect the books by the light of his tallow candle, Lord Charlbury was left alone. He was soon rejoined by Sir Vincent, who came back into the hall bearing a crusted bottle, and some glasses. 'Sherry,' he said, setting down the glasses. 'If the slaughter of chickens is my fate, I must be fortified. But I trust I shall prevail upon the retainer to commit the actual deed. How *did* you hurt your arm?'

'Sophy put a bullet through it,' replied his lordship.

'Did she indeed? What a redoubtable female she is, to be sure! I suppose she had her reasons?'

'They were not what you might be pardoned for imagining!' retorted Charlbury.

'I never indulge commonplace thoughts,' said Sir Vincent, carefully wiping the neck of the bottle, and beginning to pour out the wine. 'Not, at all events, in relation to the Grand Sophy. Here, try this! God knows how long it has lain in the cellar! I collect I don't drink to your elopement?'

'Good God, no!' said Charlbury, almost blenching at the thought. 'I am devoted to Sophy – quite and unalterably devoted to her! – but heaven preserve me from marriage with her!'

'If heaven did not, I fancy Rivenhall would,' observed Sir Vincent. 'This wine is perfectly tolerable. Don't finish the bottle before I come back, and don't waste it on the poet!'

He strolled off again, presumably to oversee the execution in the hen-roost, and Lord Charlbury, rendering up silent thanks for his wounded arm, poured himself out a second glass of sherry. After a short interval, Mr Fawnhope emerged from the library, bearing a worm-eaten volume in his hand. This he reverently displayed to his lordship, saying simply: '*La Hermosura de Angélica!* One never knows where one may light upon a treasure. I must show it to the Marquesa. Whose is this enchanting house?'

'Sir Horace Stanton-Lacy's,' replied Charlbury, in some amusement.

'Providence must have led me to it. I could not imagine what brought me here, but it doesn't signify. When I saw Sophy standing in the open doorway, holding aloft the lamp, the scales fell from my eyes, and all doubts were resolved. I am engaged to dine somewhere or other, but I shan't regard it.'

'You don't feel that you should perhaps ride back to town to keep your engagement?' suggested his lordship.

'No,' replied Mr Fawnhope simply. 'I prefer to be here. There is also a *Galatea*, but not an original copy.' He then sat down at the table, and opened the book, poring over it until interrupted by Sophy, who came in with a bundle of candles tucked under one arm, and a shallow wooden box held carefully between her hands. Beside her, a mixture of curiosity and jealousy, pranced her little greyhound, from time to time springing up to reach the box.

Mr Fawnhope leaped to his feet, and held out his hands to take the box from her. 'Give it to me! An urn you might bear, but not a sordid box!'

She relinquished it, saying practically: 'Mrs Clavering will bring that presently, but it is not yet time for the tea-tray, you know. We have not dined! Careful! Poor little things, they have no mother!'

'Sophy, what in the *world* – ? Exclaimed Charlbury, perceiving that the box contained a brood of yellow ducklings. 'You do not mean to cook these for dinner, I do trust?'

'Good gracious, no! Only Mr Clavering has been rearing them in the warmth of the kitchen, and Sancia complains that they will run under her feet. Set the box down in this corner, Augustus: Tina will not harm them!'

He obeyed her, and the ducklings, all vigorously cheeping, at once struggled out of the box, one of them, more venturesome than the rest, setting forth on an exploratory expedition. Sophy caught it, and held it cupped in her hands, while Tina, quite disgusted, jumped on to a chair, and lay down with her head pointedly averted. Mr Fawnhope's smile swept across his face and he quoted: '"*Lo, as a careful housewife runs to catch One of her feather'd creatures broke away!*"'

'Yes, but I think that if we were to spread something over the top of the box they will not break away,' said Sophy. 'Charlbury's driving-coat will answer famously! You do not object, Charlbury?'

'Yes, Sophy, I do object!' he said firmly, removing the garment from her hands.

'Very well, then –' She stopped, for Tina had lifted her head, her ears on the prick, and had uttered a sharp bark. The sound of horses and of carriage-wheels was heard. Sophy turned to Mr Fawnhope, saying quickly: 'Augustus, pray will you step into the kitchen – you will find it at the end of the passage at the back there! – and desire Mrs Clavering to give you a cloth, or a blanket, or some such thing? You need not make haste to return, for I daresay Sancia would like you to pluck a chicken.'

'Is the Marquesa in the kitchen?' said Mr Fawnhope. 'What is she doing there? I wish her to see this book I have found in the library!'

Sophy picked it up from the table, and gave it to him. 'Yes, pray show it to her! She will like it excessively! Pay no heed if you should chance to hear the door-bell: I will open the door!'

She fairly thrust him towards the door at the back of the hall, and, having seen him safely through it shut it, and said in a conspiratorial voice: 'Cecilia! Take care of the ducklings!'

She was still holding the one she had picked up, when she set the front-door wide. The rain had stopped, and the moonlight showed through a break in the clouds. Hardly had Sophy opened the door than her cousin almost fell upon her neck. 'Sophy! Oh, my dearest Sophy – No, it was too shocking of you!

You must have known I could not wish – Sophy, Sophy, how *could* you do such a thing?'

'Cecy, pray take care! This poor little duckling! Oh, good God! Miss Wraxton!'

'Yes, Miss Stanton-Lacy, *I!*' said Miss Wraxton, joining the group in the porch. 'You did not, I fancy, expect to see me!'

'No, and you will be very much in the way!' replied Sophy frankly. 'Go in, Cecy!'

She gave her cousin a gentle push across the threshold as she spoke. Cecilia stood transfixed, as Charlbury, rising from his chair by the fire, stepped forward, his left arm interestingly reposing in its sling. Cecilia was carrying a reticule and a feather-muff, but she let both fall to the ground in her consternation. 'Oh!' she exclaimed faintly. 'You are hurt! Oh, Charlbury!'

She moved towards him with both hands held out, and his lordship, acting with great presence of mind, hurriedly disengaged his arm from the sling, and received her in a comprehensive embrace. 'No, no, dearest Cecilia! The merest scratch!' he assured her.

Such heroism caused Cecilia to shed tears. 'It is all my fault! My wretched folly! I can never cease to blame myself! Charlbury, only tell me you forgive me!'

'Never, for wearing a hat which prevents my kissing you!' he said, with a shaken laugh.

She raised her head at that, smiling through her tears, and he contrived to kiss her in spite of the hat. Sophy, effectually blocking the entrance, observed this passage with all the air of one well-satisfied with her labours.

'Will you be good enough to allow us to enter?' said Miss Wraxton, in frozen accents.

'Us?' said Sophy, quickly looking round. She perceived a stout figure behind Miss Wraxton, in a soaked coat, and a sodden beaver, and, after peering incredulously for a moment, exclaimed: 'Good God! Lord Bromford? Now, what the deuce does this mean?'

Cecilia, who had cast off her hat to join her muff on the floor, raised her head from the broad shoulder that was supporting it to say huskily: 'Oh Sophy, pray do not be cross with me! Indeed it was not my doing! Charlbury, what happened? How do you come to be hurt?'

His lordship, still clasping her to his bosom, rolled an anguished eye at Sophy. She came promptly to this rescue. 'Only a flesh wound, dearest Cecy! Footpads – or do I mean highwaymen? – yes, highwaymen! Just a flurry of shots, you know, and poor Charlbury had the misfortune to be hit! But they were driven off, and we took no other hurt. Charlbury behaved with the greatest presence of mind imaginable – perfectly cool, and *more* than a match for such rascals!'

'Oh, *Charlbury!*' sighed Cecilia, overcome by the thought of such intrepid conduct.

His lordship, soothingly patting her shoulder, could not resist asking: 'How many of the desperate ruffians did I vanquish, Sophy?'

'That,' said Sophy, quelling him with a frown, 'we shall never know!'

Miss Wraxton's cool voice broke in on this. However glad she might be to see Cecilia's difference with Charlbury made up, her sense of propriety was really lacerated by the spectacle of Cecilia nestling within his lordship's arm. 'My dear Cecilia, pray recollect yourself!' she said, blushing, and averting her gaze.

'I do not know what I should do!' suddenly announced Lord Bromford, in lamentable accents. 'I came with the purpose of calling this fellow to book, but I have caught a cold!'

'If that is to my address,' said Charlbury, 'a cold may well be the least of the ills that will shortly befall you! Don't tread on the ducklings!'

'No, indeed!' said Sophy, swooping on one that had narrowly escaped death under Bromford's foot. 'What a clumsy creature you are! Do, pray, take heed where you are stepping!'

'I should not be amazed if already I have a fever,' said Bromford, uneasily eyeing the ducklings. 'Miss Wraxton, these birds! One does not keep birds in the house! I do not understand why they are running all over the floor. There is another! I do not like it. It is not what I have been used to.'

'I hope, dear Lord Bromford, that nothing that has occurred this day is what either you or I has been used to,' responded Miss Wraxton. 'Do let me beg of you to take off that greatcoat! Believe that it was no wish of mine that you were compelled to ride through such a downpour! If you have done your constitution any lasting injury I can never forgive myself for having accepted your escort! Your boots are wet through! Nothing can be more fatal than chilled feet! Miss Stanton-Lacy, *is* it too much to request that a servant – I presume there is a servant here? – should be sent for to remove Lord Bromford's boots?'

'Yes, because he has gone out to kill chickens,' replied Sophy. 'Cecy, help me to collect the ducklings, and put them back into the box! If we were to place your muff on top of them they will very likely believe it to be their mother, and settle down!'

Cecilia having no fault to find with this scheme, it was at once put into execution. Miss Wraxton, who had coaxed Lord Bromford into a deep chair by the fire, said: 'This levity will not serve, Miss Stanton-Lacy! Even you will allow that your conduct demands some explanation! Are you aware of the terrible consequences which must have followed on this – this escapade, had your cousin and I not come to rescue you from the disgrace your appear to regard so lightly!'

Lord Bromford sneezed.

'Oh, hush, Eugenia!' begged Cecilia. 'How can you talk so? All's well that ends well!'

'You must be lost to every scruple of female delicacy, Cecilia, if you can think it *well* for your cousin to show such a brazen face, when she has lost both character and reputation!'

The door at the back of the hall opened to admit the Marquesa, a sacking-apron tied round her waist, and a large ladle in her hand. 'Eggs I must instantly have!' she announced. 'And Lope de Vega I will not have, though in general a fine poet, but not in the kitchen! Someone must go to the chicken-house, and tell Vincent to bring me eggs. Who are these people?'

315

It might have been supposed that the appearance on the scene of the Marquesa would have filled Miss Wraxton's Christian soul with relief, but no such emotion was visible in her countenance, which, on the contrary, froze into an expression of such chagrin as to be almost ludicrous. She could find not a word to say, and was unable to command herself enough even to shake hands with the Marquesa.

Lord Bromford, always punctilious, rose from his chair and bowed. Sophy presented him, and he begged pardon for having contracted what he feared would prove to be a dangerous cold. The Marquesa held him off with the ladle, saying: 'If you have a cold, do not approach me! Now I see that it is Miss Rivenhall, whose beauty is entirely English; and that other one, also in the English *estilo*, but less beautiful. I do not think two chickens will be enough, so that man with the cold must eat the pig's cheek. But eggs I must have!'

Having delivered herself of this ultimatum, she withdrew, paying not the smallest heed to Lord Bromford's agitated protest that all forms of pork were poison to him, and that a bowl of thin gruel was all that he felt himself able to swallow. He seemed to feel that Miss Wraxton was the only person amongst those present who was likely to sympathize with him, for he looked piteously at her. She responded at once, assuring him that he should not be asked to eat the pig's cheek. 'If it were possible to remove you from this draughty hall!' she said, casting an angry glance at Sophy. 'Had I known that I was coming to an establishment which appears to be something between a fowl-yard and Bedlam, I would never have set forth from town!'

'Well, I must say I wish you had known it, then,' said Sophy candidly. 'We could have been comfortable enough, if only you and Lord Bromford had minded you own business, and now I suppose we must make gruel, and mustard foot-baths!'

'A mustard foot-bath,' said Lord Bromford eagerly, 'would be the very thing! I do not say that it will entirely arrest the chill: we must not raise our hopes too high! but if we can prevent its descending upon the lungs it will be a great thing! Thank you! I am very much obliged to you!'

'Good gracious, you absurd creature, I did not mean it!' Sophy cried, breaking into laughter.

'No!' said Miss Wraxton. 'We may readily believe you have not a grain of womanly compassion, Miss Stanton-Lacy! Do not be uneasy, Lord Bromford! If any efforts of *mine* can save you from illness they shall not be spared!'

He pressed her hand in a speaking way, and allowed her to press him gently down again into his chair.

'Meanwhile,' said Charlbury, 'let us not forget that eggs the Marquesa must have! I had better try to find Talgarth and the hen-house.'

Sophy, who was looking thoughtful, said slowly: 'Yes. And I *think* – Charlbury, bring a candle into the breakfast-parlour, and let us see if it is warm enough yet for Lord Bromford to sit in!'

He went with her into this apartment, and had no sooner passed the doorway than she clasped his wrist, and said in an urgent undervoice: 'Never mind the eggs! Go to the stables, and direct the Ombersley servants to pole up the horses again! You may change them at the inn in the village, or, if not there, at Epsom! Take Cecilia back to London! Only think how embarrassing for her to be obliged to meet Augustus now! She would dislike it excessively! Besides, it is quite ridiculous for so many people to be crowded into the house, and not at all what I bargained for!'

He grimaced, but said: 'If I do it, will you go with us?'

'What, to sit bodkin between you? No, I thank you!'

'But I cannot leave you here!'

'Nonsense! It would not suit me at all to be going to London yet!'

He set the candlestick down, and took her hands in his, and held them firmly. 'Sophy, I owe you a debt of gratitude: thank you, my dear! You may command me in anything: shall I remove Miss Wraxton?'

'No, for I have had a capital notion about her. She shall stay to nurse Bromford, and very likely they will make a match of it!'

His shoulders shook. 'Oh, Sophy, Sophy!'

'No, do not laugh! I do feel I ought to make some provision for her, poor girl! I cannot permit her to marry Charles, and make them all unhappy at Ombersley House, but I am persuaded she and Bromford would deal extremely. Do not make me any more pretty speeches, but go down to the stables at once! I'll tell Cecy!'

She then thrust him back into the hall, and, while he let himself out of the house, went back to the group about the fire, and said: 'It is tolerably cosy in the parlour, and if you choose to sit there for a little while, Lord Bromford, one of the bedchambers shall be prepared for you, and I will send Clavering to pull off your boots. Do you take him in, Miss Wraxton, and see him comfortably bestowed!'

'I trust the chimney may not smoke as badly as this one!' said Miss Wraxton acidly. 'Nothing could be worse! Lord Bromford has coughed twice already!'

'How shocking! You should take him away at once.'

His lordship, who was sitting in a miserable huddle, shivering and sneezing, thanked her in a feeble voice, and rose from his chair with Miss Wraxton's kindly help. Hardly had they gone into the parlour, than Mr Fawnhope came into the hall, saying severely: 'The drawing of hens is revolting! No one should be called upon to witness such an operation! The Marquesa must have eggs.'

Cecilia, who had given a violent start, and perceptibly changed colour, exclaimed: 'Augustus!'

'Cecilia!' said Mr Fawnhope, staring at her in astonishment. 'You were not here before, were you?'

'No,' she said, blushing furiously. 'Oh, no! I – I came with Miss Wraxton!'

'Oh, was that how it was?' he said, rather relieved. 'I did not think I had seen you.'

She said resolutely, but in some little agitation: 'Augustus, I will not trifle with you! I must tell you I find I have made a great mistake. I cannot marry you!'

'Noble, noble girl!' Mr Fawnhope said, much moved. 'I honour you for this frankness, and must ever deem myself fortunate to have been permitted to adore you. The experience has purified and strengthened me: you have inspired me with a poetic fervour for which the world may yet thank you, as I do! But marriage is not for such as I am. I must put aside the thought. I *do* put it aside! You should marry Charlbury, but my play you must allow me to dedicate to you!'

'Th-thank you!' faltered Cecilia, a good deal taken aback.

'Well, she is going to marry Charlbury,' said Sophy bracingly. 'And now that that is settled, Augustus, pray will you go and find the eggs for Sancia?'

'I know nothing of eggs,' he said. 'I fetched Talgarth from the cellar, and he has gone in search of them. I am going to write a poem that has been taking shape in my brain this past hour. Should you object if I entitled it *To Sophia, Holding a Lamp*?'

'Not in the least,' said Sophy affably. 'Take this candle, and go into the library! Shall I tell Clavering to light a fire there for you?'

'It is of no consequences, thank you,' he replied absently, receiving the candlestick from her, and wandering off in the direction of the library.

No sooner had the door closed behind him than Cecilia said, in some confusion: 'Has he understood me? Why did you not tell me that he was here, Sophy? I do not know how to look him in the face!'

'No, and you shall not be called upon to do so, dearest Cecy! Charlbury has gone to order the chaise: you must go back to Berkeley Square immediately! Only conceive of my aunt's anxiety!'

Cecilia, who had been about to demur, wavered perceptibly at this. She was still wavering when Lord Charlbury came back to the house, cheerfully announcing that the chaise would be at the door in five minutes' time. Sophy at once picked up her cousin's hat, and fitted it becomingly over her sunny locks. Between her efforts, and those of Lord Charlbury, she was presently escorted, resistless, out of the house, and handed up into the chaise. His lordship, pausing only to bestow upon his benefactress a hearty embrace, jumped up after her; the steps were let up, the door slammed upon the happy couple, and the equipage was driven away. Sophy, having waved a last farewell from the porch, turned back into the house, where she found Miss Wraxton awaiting her in an alarming state of frigidity. Miss Wraxton apprehending (she said) that no assistance from the Marquesa need be expected, desired to be conducted to the kitchen, where she proposed to brew a posset, used in her family for generations as a cure for colds. Not only did Sophy lead her to the kitchen, but she also quelled the Marquesa's protests, and commanded that the Claverings set water on to boil for a mustard foot-bath. The unfortunate Claverings, labouring up the back-stairs with coals, blankets, and cans of hot water, were kept fully occupied for nearly half an hour, at the end of which time, Lord Bromford was tenderly escorted upstairs to the best spare-bedroom, divested of his boots, and his coat, coaxed into the dressing-gown Sir Vincent had had the forethought to pack into his valise, and installed in a winged chair by the fire. Sir Vincent's protests at having not only his dressing-gown, but also his nightshirt and cap wrested from him were silenced by Sophy's representations that she herself was relinquishing to Miss Wraxton her portmanteau, with all the night-gear which it contained. 'And considering how unhandsome your behaviour has been, Sir Vincent, I must say that I shall think it excessively shabby of you if you demur at rendering me this small service!' she declared roundly.

He cocked an eyebrow at her. 'And you, Sophy? Will you not be remaining here for the night?' he laughed, seeing her at a loss for an answer, and said: 'In a previous age you would have been burnt at the stake, and rightly so, Juno! Very well: I will play your game!'

Within half an hour of this passage, Sophy, seated at the table in the hall, which she had drawn into the ingle-nook by the fire, heard the sound for which she had been waiting. She was engaged in building card-houses, having found an aged and grimy pack in the breakfast-parlour, and she made no attempt to answer the imperative summons of the bell. Clavering came into the hall from the back premises, looking harassed, and opened the door. Mr Rivenhall's decisive accents pleasurably assailed Sophy's ears. 'Lacy Manor? Very well! Be good enough to direct my groom to the stables! I'll announce myself!'

Mr Rivenhall then shut the aged servitor out of the house, and stepped into the hall, shaking the raindrops from his curly-brimmed beaver. His eye alighted on Sophy, absorbed in architecture, and he said with the greatest amiability imaginable: 'Good evening, Sophy! I am afraid you must have quite given me up, but it has been raining, you know, the moonlight quite obscured by clouds!'

At this point, Tina, who had been leaping up at him in an ecstasy of delight, began to bark, so he was obliged to acknowledged her welcome before he could again make himself heard. Sophy, laying a card delicately upon her structure, said; 'Charles, this is too kind in you! Have you come to rescue me from the consequences of my indiscretion?'

'No, to wring your neck!'

She opened her eyes at him. 'Charles! Don't you know that I have ruined my reputation?'

He took off his driving-coat, shook it, and cast it over a chair-back. 'Indeed? In that event, I am quite out: I was ready to swear I should find the Marquesa with you!'

The ready laughter sprang to her eyes. 'How odious you are! How came you to guess that?'

'I know you too well. Where's my sister?'

Sophy resumed her house-building. 'Oh, she has driven back to London with Charlbury! I daresay their chaise may have met you on your way.'

'Very likely. I was in no case to be studying the panels of chance vehicles. Did Miss Wraxton accompany them?'

She looked up. 'Now, how do you know that Miss Wraxton came with Cecilia?' she asked.

'She was so obliging as to send a note round to White' informing me of her intention,' he replied grimly. 'Is she here still?'

'Well, she is, but I fancy she is very much occupied,' said Sophy. She bent to pick up one of the ducklings, which awakening from a refreshing slumber under Cecilia's muff, had climbed out of the box again, and was trying to establish itself in the flounces of her gown. 'Take this, dear Charles, while I pour you out a glass of sherry!'

Mr Rivenhall, automatically extended his hand, found himself in possession of a ball of yellow down. It did not seem to be worth while to enquire why he was given a duckling to hold, so he sat down on the table's edge, stroking the creature with one finger, and watching his cousin.

'That, of course,' said Sophy serenely, 'explains why you have come.'

'It explains nothing of the sort, and well you know it!' said Mr Rivenhall.

'How wet your coat is!' remarked Sophy, spreading it out before the fire. 'I do trust you may not have caught a chill!'

'Of course I have not caught a chill!' he said impatiently 'Besides, it has not been raining this last half hour!'

She handed him a glass of sherry. 'I am so much relieved! Poor Lord Bromford contracted the most shocking cold! He had meant to have called Charlbury out, you know, but when he reached us he could only sneeze.'

'*Bromford?*' he exclaimed. 'You do not mean to tell me he is here?'

'Yes, indeed: Miss Wraxton brought him. I *think* she hoped he might have offered for me, and so saved my reputation, but the poor man was quite prostrated by this horrid chill, which he fears may descend upon his lungs. It puts all else out of his mind, and one cannot be surprised at it.'

'Sophy, are you trying to humbug me?' demanded Mr Rivenhall suspiciously. 'Even Eugenia would not bring that blockhead down upon you!'

'Miss Wraxton does not consider him a blockhead. She says he is a man of sense, and one who –'

'Thank you! I have heard enough!' he interrupted. 'Here, take this creature! Where is Eugenia?'

She received the duckling from him, and restored it to its brethren in the box. 'Well, if she is not still brewing possets in the kitchen, I expect you may find her with Bromford in the best spare-bedroom,' she replied.

'*What?*'

'Persuading him to swallow a little thin gruel,' explained Sophy, looking the picture of innocence. 'The second door at the top of the stairs, dear Charles!'

Mr Rivenhall tossed off the glass of sherry, set it down, informed his cousin ominously that he would deal with her presently, and strode towards the stairs, accompanied by Tina, who frisked gaily at his heels, apparently convinced that he was about to provide sport for her of no common order. Sophy went down the passage to inform the harassed Marquesa that although two of the dinner-guests had departed, another had appeared in their stead.

Mr Rivenhall, meanwhile, had mounted the stairs, and had, without ceremony, flung open the door of the best spare-bedroom. A domestic scene met his affronted gaze. In a chair drawn up beside a clear fire sat Lord Bromford, a screen drawn to protect his person from the draught from the window; both his feet in a steaming bath of mustard-and-water; a blanket reinforcing Sir Vincent's dressing-gown over his shoulders; and in his hands a bowl of gruel and a spoon. Hovering solicitously about him was Miss Wraxton, ready either to add more hot water to the bath from the kettle on the hob, or to replace the bowl of gruel with the posset of her making.

'Upon my word!' said Mr Rivenhall explosively.

'The draught!' protested his lordship. 'Miss Wraxton! I can feel the air blowing about my head!'

'Pray close the door, Charles!' said Miss Wraxton sharply. 'Have you no consideration? Lord Bromford is extremely unwell!'

'So I perceive!' he retorted, advancing into the room. 'Perhaps, my dear Eugenia, you would like to explain to me what the devil you mean by this?'

She replied instantly, her colour heightened: 'Thanks to your sister's inhumanity – I can call it nothing else! – in refusing to permit me to offer a seat to Lord Bromford in the chaise, he has taken a shocking chill, which I only pray may not have a lasting effect upon his constitution!'

'I never credited Cecilia with so much good sense! If she had had enough to prevent her, and you, from setting forth upon an expedition which was as needless as it was meddlesome, I should be even more grateful! You have for once in your life been thoroughly at fault, Eugenia! Let it be a lesson to you to be a little less busy in future!'

Those best acquainted with Mr Rivenhall's powers of self expression would have considered this speech a very mild reproof. Miss Wraxton, in whose presence he had hitherto most meticulously guarded his tongue, could scarcely believe her ears. 'Charles!' she uttered, outraged.

'Did you imagine that you would make me believe ill of Sophy with your foolish and spiteful letter!' he demanded. 'You have tried to set me against her from the outset, but you over-reached yourself today, my girl! How dared you write in such terms to me! How could you have been so crassly stupid as to suppose that Sophy could ever need *your* countenance to set her right in the eyes of the world, or that I would believe one word of slander against her?'

'Sir!' said Lord Bromford, with as much dignity as could be expected of a man with both feet in a mustard-bath. 'You shall answer to me for those words!'

'Certainly! When and where you please!' replied Mr Rivenhall, with alarming promptitude.

'I beg you will not heed him, Lord Bromford!' cried Miss Wraxton, much agitated. 'He is beside himself! If a meeting were to take place between you on *my* account I could never hold up my head again! Pray be calm! I am sure your pulse is umultuous, and how shall I ever face dear Lady Bromford?'

He clasped her restraining hand, and held it, saying a moved oice: 'Too good, too excellent creature! With all your attain-nents, your scholarship, still to retain those attributes peculiar to our womanhood – ! I cannot but think of the poet's lines –'

'Take care,' interpolated Mr Rivenhall disagreeably. 'You hought of them in connection with my cousin, and it won't do o repeat yourself!'

'Sir!' said Lord Bromford, glaring at him. 'I was about to say hat Miss Wraxton has shown herself in very sooth –'

'A ministering angel! So I knew! Try for another poet!'

'I must request you, sir,' said Miss Wraxton icily, 'to leave this oom immediately – and to take that horrid little dog of Miss tanton-Lacy's with you! I can only be thankful that my eyes ave been opened to your true character before it was too late! ou will oblige me by sending an announcement to the Gazette hat our engagement is at an end!'

'It shall be done at once,' said Mr Rivenhall, bowing. 'Pray accept my profound regrets, and my earnest wishes for your uture happiness, ma'am!'

'Thank you! If I cannot felicitate you upon the contract you re no doubt about to enter into, at least I can pray that you may ot be too sadly disappointed in the character of the lady you nean to marry!' said Miss Wraxton, a spot of colour burning in either cheek.

'No, I don't think I shall be disappointed,' said Mr Rivenhall, with a sudden and rueful grin. 'Shocked, maddened, and tunned perhaps, but not disappointed! Come, Tina!'

Descending again to the hall, he found Sophy seated on the floor beside the ducklings' box, preventing their attempts to escape. Without looking up, she said: 'Sir Vincent has found several bottles of excellent burgundy in the cellar, and Sancia says we shall not be obliged to eat the pig's cheek after all.' 'Talgarth?' exclaimed Mr Rivenhall, bristling with hostility. 'What the devil brings him here?'

'He came with Sancia. It is the most shocking thing, Charles,

and how I am to face Sir Horace I don't know! He has *marri*
Sancia! I cannot think what is to be done!'

'Nothing at all: your father will be delighted! I forgot to infor
you, my dear cousin, that he arrived in town sometime before
left, and is even now in Berkeley Square, awaiting your retur
He appeared to feel no small degree of annoyance at learning
your efforts to save the Marquesa from Talgarth.'

'Sir Horace in London?' Sophy exclaimed, her face lightin
up. 'Oh, Charles, and I not there to welcome him! Why did yo
not tell me at once?'

'I had other things to think of. Get up!'

She allowed him to pull her to her feet, but said: 'Charles, ar
you freed from your engagement?'

'I am,' he replied. 'Miss Wraxton has terminated ou
engagement.'

'And Cecy has terminated hers to Augustus, so now I can –'

'Sophy, I don't pretend to know why she should have done so
any more than I understand why you keep a brood of ducklin
in the house, but neither of these problems interests me ver
particularly at this present! I have something more important t
say to you!'

'Of course!' said Sophy. 'Your horse! Well, indeed, Charles,
am very sorry to have displeased you so much!'

'*No!*' said Mr Rivenhall, grasping her shoulders, and givin
her a shake. 'You know – Sophy, you *know* I could not mean –
You did not run away from London because of *that*?'

'But, Charles, naturally I did! I had to have some excuse! You
must perceive that I had to!'

'Devil!' said Mr Rivenhall, and caught her into so crushing a
embrace that she protested, and Tina danced round them
barking excitedly. 'Quiet!' commanded Mr Rivenhall. He too
Sophy's throat between his hands, pushing up her chin. 'Will you
marry me, vile and abominable girl that you are?'

'Yes, but, mind, it is only to save my neck from being wrung!
Sophy replied.

The opening of the library-door made him release her, anc

look quickly over his shoulder. Mr Fawnhope, wearing an expression of almost complete abstraction, came into the hall with a paper in his hand. 'There is no ink in there,' he complained, 'and I have broken the point of my pencil. I have abandoned the notion of hailing you as Vestal virgin: there is something awkward in those syllables. My opening line now reads, *Goddess, whose steady hands upheld* – but I must have ink!'

With these words, and without paying the least heed to Mr Rivenhall, he walked across to the door leading to the back-premises, and disappeared through it.

Mr Rivenhall turned a face of undisguised horror upon Sophy. 'Good God!' he said. 'You might have warned me that *he* was here! And what the deuce did he mean by that stuff?'

'Well, I *think*,' said Sophy confidentially, 'that he now means to be in love with me, Charles. He likes the way I hold a lamp, and he says he would like to see me with an urn.'

'Well, he is not going to see you with an urn!' said Mr Rivenhall, revolted. He cast a glance round the hall, saw a pelisse lying on one chair, and snatched it up. 'Put this on! Where is your hat?'

'But, Charles, we *cannot* leave poor Sancia with all these dreadful people in the house! It is too base!'

'Yes, we can! You don't imagine I am going to sit down to dinner with Eugenia and that damned poet, do you? Is this your muff? *Must* we take these ducklings?'

'No, it is Cecilia's, and now they will be all over the floor again! Charles, how provoking of you!'

Sir Vincent, who had come into the hall with a couple of bottles, set them down in the hearth, saying: 'How do you do, Rivenhall? Sophy, is there any ink in the house? The poet is searching for some in the larder, and driving my poor Sancia distracted.'

'Talgarth,' said Mr Rivenhall, firmly grasping Sophy by one wrist, 'I beg you will take care of these infernal ducklings, and I wish you a very pleasant evening! Sir Horace has arrived in town, and I must instantly restore his daughter to him!'

'Rivenhall,' said Sir Vincent gravely, 'I perfectly understand you, and I applaud your presence of mind. Allow me to offer you my felicitations! I will convey your apologies to my wife. Let me advice you to lose no time in taking your departure! The poet will all too shortly return!'

'Sir Vincent!' cried Sophy, dragged irresistibly to the door. 'Give my portmanteau to Miss Wraxton, and beg her to make what use she pleases of the contents! Charles, this is crazy! Did you come in your curricle? What if it should begin to rain again? I shall be drenched!'

'Then you will be well-served!' retorted her unchivalrous cousin.

'Charles!' uttered Sophy, shocked. 'You cannot love me!'

Mr Rivenhall pulled the door to behind them, and in a very rough fashion jerked her into his arms, and kissed her. 'I don't: I dislike you excessively!' he said savagely.

Entranced by these lover-like words, Miss Stanton-Lacy returned his embrace with fervour, and meekly allowed herself to be led off to the stables.

Also by Georgette Heyer in Arrow

Black Sheep
Bath society-belle Abigail Wendover has tried hard to detach her spirited niece Fanny from a plausible fortune-hunter. Her efforts become vastly more complicated with the arrival of Miles Calverleigh. The black sheep of his family – why, that would be a connection more shocking even than Fanny's unwise liaison with his nephew!

Friday's Child
Rejected by Miss Milborne for his unsteadiness of character, wild Lord Sheringham flies back to London in a rage, vowing to marry the first woman to cross his way. And who should he see but Hero Wantage, the young and charmingly unsophisticated girl, who has loved him since childhood . . . ?

Faro's Daughter
Renowned gamester and entirely void of a romantic disposition, Max Ravenscar regards all eligible females with indifference. But when he meets the beautiful Deborah Grantham, mistress of her aunt's gaming house, he finds himself ill-prepared for such a worthy opponent.

Frederica
Rich and handsome, the Marquis of Alverstoke sees no reason to put himself out for anyone. Until a distant connection applies to him for help. Plunged headlong into one drama after another by the large Merriville family, which includes the beautiful Frederica, Alverstoke is surprised to find himself far from bored . . .

arrow books

Venetia

In all her twenty-five years, lovely Venetia Lanyon has never been further than Harrogate, nor enjoyed the attentions of any but her two wearisomely persistent suitors. Then, in one extraordinary encounter, she finds herself involved with her neighbour, a libertine whose way of life has scandalised the North Riding for years.

Regency Buck

It is in regrettable circumstances that beautiful Judith Taverner and her brother Peregrine first encounter Julian St John Audley. The man, they both agree, is an insufferably arrogant dandy. But unfortunately for them, he is also the Fifth Earl of Worth, a friend of the Regent and, quite by chance, their legal guardian.

An Infamous Army

In 1815, beneath the aegis of the Army of Occupation, Brussels is the gayest town in Europe. And the widow Lady Barbara Childe, as outrageous as she is beautiful, is at the centre of all that is fashionable and light-hearted. When she meets Charles Audley, handsome aide-de-camp to the great Duke of Wellington himself, her *joie de vivre* knows no bounds – until the eve of the fateful Battle of Waterloo . . .

Sylvester

Endowed with rank, wealth and elegance, the Duke of Salford posts into Wiltshire to discover if the Hon Phoebe Marlow will meet his exacting requirements for a bride. Intriguingly, his visit causes Phoebe to flee her home and when they meet again on the road to London, Phoebe, already caught in one *imbroglio*, now knows she soon could be well deep in another . . .

arrow books